Supermen

ALSO BY GARDNER DOZOIS

ANTHOLOGIES

A Day in the Life
Another World
Best Science Fiction Stories of the Year
    #6–10
The Best of Isaac Asimov's Science
    Fiction Magazine
Time Travellers from Isaac Asimov's
    Science Fiction Magazine
Transcendental Tales from Isaac
    Asimov's Science Fiction Magazine
Isaac Asimov's Aliens
Isaac Asimov's Mars
Isaac Asimov's SF Lite
Isaac Asimov's War
Isaac Asimov's Planet Earth
    (with Sheila Williams)
Isaac Asimov's Robots
    (with Sheila Williams)
Isaac Asimov's Cyberdreams
    (with Sheila Williams)
Isaac Asimov's Skin Deep
    (with Sheila Williams)
Isaac Asimov's Ghosts
    (with Sheila Williams)
Isaac Asimov's Vampires
    (with Sheila Williams)
Isaac Asimov's Moons
    (with Sheila Williams)
Isaac Asimov's Christmas
    (with Sheila Williams)
Isaac Asimov's Detectives
    (with Sheila Williams)
The Year's Best Science Fiction, #1–18
Future Earths: Under African Skies
    (with Mike Resnick)
Future Earths: Under South American
    Skies (with Mike Resnick) (anthology)
Future Power
    (with Jack Dann) (anthology)

FICTION

Strangers
The Visible Man (collection)
Nightmare Blue
    (with George Alec Effinger)
The Peacemaker
Geodesic Dreams (collection)
Slow Dancing Through Time
    (with Jack Dann, Michael Swanwick,
    Susan Casper, and Jack C.
    Haldeman II)

NONFICTION

The Fiction of James Tiptree, Jr.
Aliens! (with Jack Dann)
Unicorns! (with Jack Dann)
Magicats! (with Jack Dann)
Magicats 2 (with Jack Dann)
Bestiary! (with Jack Dann)
Mermaids! (with Jack Dann)
Sorcerers! (with Jack Dann)
Demons! (with Jack Dann)
Dogtales! (with Jack Dann)
Ripper! (with Susan Casper)
Seaserpents! (with Jack Dann)
Dinosaurs! (with Jack Dann)
Little People! (with Jack Dann)
Dragons! (with Jack Dann)
Horses! (with Jack Dann)
Unicorns 2 (with Jack Dann)
Invaders! (with Jack Dann)
Angels! (with Jack Dann)
Dinosaurs II (with Jack Dann)
Hackers (with Jack Dann)
Timegates (with Jack Dann)
Clones (with Jack Dann)
Armageddon (with Jack Dann)
Modern Classics of Science Fiction
Modern Classic Short Novels of
    Science Fiction
Modern Classics of Fantasy
Killing Me Softly
Dying for It
Immortals (with Jack Dann)
Roads Not Taken (with Stanley
    Schmidt)
The Good Old Stuff
The Good New Stuff
Explorers
Isaac Asimov's Werewolves
    (with Sheila Williams)
The Furthest Horizon

Supermen

TALES OF THE POSTHUMAN FUTURE

Gardner Dozois

St. Martin's Griffin

New York

www.stmartins.com

ISBN 0-312-27569-2

First Edition: January 2002

10 9 8 7 6 5 4 3 2 1

Contents

Preface

The fact that the other planets of our solar system were not likely abodes for life was becoming obvious even by the early middle of the twentieth century to anyone who kept up with science—which usually includes science-fiction writers. As the century progressed and space probes actually began to *visit* other planets to collect hard data, it became harder and harder for SF writers (those who respected what was "known to be known" about the physical universe by scientists, anyway) to get away with stories set on a fictional Mars or Venus with Earth-like conditions, unlike previous generations of writers who could fill the Solar System with oxygen-breathing, English-speaking humanoid natives for their heroes to have sword fights with and/or fall in love with. Who knew any better? Certainly not the general public, probably not even the science-fiction-reading general public.

By the late sixties and early seventies though, space probes had "proved" that the solar system was nothing but an "uninteresting" collection of balls of rock and ice, or hellholes of deadly heat and pressure with atmospheres of poisonous gas. No available abodes for life, or at least for anything resembling Terran life. No sword-swinging, six-armed green warriors. No beautiful egg-laying princesses in flowing diaphanous gowns. Little room, in fact, for any story line that didn't feature the characters lumbering around in space suits for the entire arc of the plot.

So where were the SF writers going to *set* the "realistic" tales of space exploration and colonization that had become increasingly popular since the fifties, ushered in by "new" generations of SF writers such as Arthur C. Clarke, Robert A. Heinlein, Poul Anderson, Hal Clement, and a dozen others?

Although some writers immediately whisked themselves and their stories away to other solar systems or even to other Galaxies, far outside the writ of embarrassing and hampering Fact where they could set up whatever worlds they chose, to many writers (especially those with a "hard-science" bent, who were the very types to want to write a "realistic space story" in the first place), this was cheating—as the now more-widely-understood limitations of Einsteinian relativity seemed to say that Faster Than Light travel was impossible, and that therefore interstellar travel itself (let alone far-flung interstellar empires) would be difficult-to-impossible, to achieve.

If humans couldn't live on the available worlds in the Solar System, and you couldn't *leave* the Solar System to find more salubrious real estate elsewhere, then what were you going to do if you were a writer who wanted to write about the exploration and colonization of alien worlds?

Increasingly, as the last decades of the century unwound, SF writers (those who didn't ignore the whole problem and create a magic Faster Than Light drive, anyway) turned to one of two strategies.

Science-fiction writer James Blish described those two strategies rather succinctly: You can change the planet to accommodate the colonists, or the colonists to accommodate the planet.

The first of these methods, changing the planet to provide more Earthlike conditions for the colonists, creating new, inhabitable worlds out of old, uninhabitable worlds by science and technology, has become known in the genre as "terraforming," and it was the territory explored in the previous anthology in this sequence, *Worldmakers: SF Adventures in Terraforming*, previously released by St. Martin's Griffin.

The *second* method, redesigning humans so that they are able to survive on alien planets under alien conditions, has become known as "pantropy" (a word coined by Blish himself), and it is the territory explored (along with other deliberate, engineered changes to the human form and nature) in the anthology that you hold in your hands, *Supermen: Tales of the Posthuman Future*.

One of the characteristics of genre is that ideas about a given topic *evolve* as the years progress, and one writer builds upon the work that another has done. "Consensus futures" form, as writers come to de facto agreements as to what a certain aspect of the future will be like, if only by having their own thinking on the subject influenced by the ideas set forth in other work; especially attractive or persuasive "memes" can race across the genre in only a couple of years, transforming everything in their path, like Kurt Vonnegut's "Ice-Nine," so that suddenly everyone is writing about O'Neill colonies, or nanotech, or Virtual Reality . . . only to erode again as the old paradigms and the old assumptions are questioned by *new* ideas that make *new* alternatives possible . . . so that a new consensus future forms. And so on, ad infinitum. This kind of literary evolution can happen with dazzling speed, with sometimes two or three paradigm-shifts in ideas about the future jostling each other in the span of a single decade.

The "pantropy" story has evolved as well, in the more than forty years that have passed since Blish coined the term. At first, in most stories, only relatively minor changes in the basic human form were made, just enough, say, to enable humans to survive in the thin-air and low-oxygen (as it was perceived then) environment of Mars (the culmination of this kind of "pantropy" story is probably Fred Pohl's *Man Plus*). Gradually, the changes became more radical, with the technicians in something like A. E. Van Vogt's *The Silkie* creating whole space-living races who shared almost nothing in common with the basic human stock from which they were conjured from. At some point, the concept began to broaden-out from the idea of creating new forms of humans for a specific practical purpose, adapting them to survive in a specific alien environment, to stories wherein new forms of humans were created just because we *could* create them. Where the reins of evolution are taken over by humans, who then consciously direct it, using science and technology to radically alter the basic form and function of the human animal, deliberately creating "supermen"—or, at least, our evolutionary successors.

At first, these changes were brought about by surgery or other brute-force technological methods, but, as the century progressed, and speculation about the oncoming Biological Revolution proliferated, this sort of story increasingly merged with the "genetic engineering" story (almost all of Cordwainer Smith's "Instrumentality" stories could be fit into this category, for instance), and, later, even began to employ nanotechnology as well as an enabling device in the creation of its superhumans: cyberpunk attitudes—brought into the field in the eighties by writers such as Bruce Sterling, William Gibson, Pat Cadigan, Rudy Rucker, and others—about the weakness of the ties between human identity and the human body itself, especially the idea of "downloading" the intelligence and personality of a human into a computer or an artificial-body-environment of some sort, would also have a major influence on the superman story . . . by this time already beginning to be referred to here and there as the "Posthuman" story.

This kind of story kicked into high gear in the mid nineties as writers such as Greg Egan, Brian Stableford, Michael Swanwick, Robert Reed, Paul J. McAuley, and a number of others began to devote a large part of their considerable output to it, and it has continued to proliferate—and perhaps even to pick up speed—as we continue on into the new century ahead. To date, in the short-fiction arena, *Interzone* and *Asimov's Science Fiction* are the markets that have devoted the most attention to explorations of what we might call (we'd *better*, actually, since it's the subtitle!) the Posthuman Future—but it spreads farther all the time, and I strongly suspect that examination of the idea of posthumanity, with all its complex and sometimes contradictory implications for both good *and* ill, is going to be (in fact, already *is*) one of the major thematic concerns of science fiction in the first part of the twenty-first century. Other than the authors included in this anthology, and those already mentioned, the posthuman future has also been explored (or is being explored), to one degree or another, by writers as various as Greg Bear, Iain Banks, Vernor Vinge, Stephen Baxter, Gwyneth Jones, Colin Greenland, Richard Wadholm, Ian McDonald, Nancy Kress, Walter Jon Williams, A. A. Attanasio, Peter F. Hamilton, Ursula K. Le Guin, Alastair Reynolds, Geoff Ryman, Kage Baker, John Varley, Brian W. Aldiss, Kate Wilhelm, Stephen Dedman, Phillip C. Jennings, R. Garcia y Robertson . . . and in the multidimensional, infinitely expandable version of this anthology, I'd use stories by all of these authors, and a dozen more besides.

Back here in the real world, however, the space available was sharply limited. Of course, as always, some stories I would have liked to use had to be omitted because the reprint rights were encumbered in some way, or because they'd been reprinted too many times recently (like Nancy Kress's "Beggars in Spain") or because they were just too long (like Walter Jon Williams's "Elegy for Angels and Dogs") to fit into even a long book like this one with all the *other* long stories I wanted to use—but even with all those stories out of the running (and even discarding all those stories that *suck*—or, at least, that I didn't like), there were still a *lot* of stories left to consider. The superman theme is one of the most popular in genre history, and has generated hundreds of stories over the last fifty years, ranging from the rawest of juvenile power-fantasies to profound and sophisticated work such as Theodore Sturgeon's "Baby Is Three." More winnowing-screens were clearly called for.

The most obvious winnowing-screen, and the most useful, was to eliminate stories wherein the posthumans were produced by accident, as part of the aftermath of atomic war, or by the blind, random forces of evolution; I wanted stories where the creation of posthumnans was *deliberate*, a willed act, something accomplished through the use of science and technology. Although it cost me good stories from everybody from Kuttner to Van Vogt to Sturgeon, this winnowing-screen *also* eliminated at a blow hundreds (if not thousands—there must be hundreds from the fifties alone, when such stories were one of the most common tropes in the genre) of stories about "mutants"—usually mutants produced by the effect of radiation on human DNA—as well as stories about people who spontaneously develop psi talents (telepathy, precognition, telekinesis, and a host of other "wild talents"), either because of the effects of radiation (or some other contaminant) in the environment, or just because they represent "the next step" in the process of human evolution, whose day has come (it also eliminated the more comic-bookish sort of story where someone is given superhuman powers by being bitten by a radioactive spider, or falling into a vat of toxic waste—although they were never really serious contenders in the first place).

The next winnowing-screen was that I didn't want any stories where the superman turned out to be *really* an alien in hiding among us, or an android, or a robot. (Or an angel, or a demon, or a wizard, or a witch—I didn't want any fantasy stories about people with magical powers; this was going to be a science-fiction anthology, by God! . . . and any superhuman powers exhibited would have to have some kind of reasonably plausible scientific rationale.)

I also decided that stories about people who have themselves "downloaded" into computers or remote-controlled artificial "bodies" of some sort, or who are "copied" in a discorporate state into Virtual Reality worlds—although such stories could reasonably be said to be about people living a posthuman existence, and so potentially includable—were not really what I was after here: being off at a slight tangent to what I *was* looking for; stories of individuals living into the posthuman future in their own flesh—or what remained of it, anyway—after the incomprehensibly advanced science and technology of that future was done with them.

Even with all these winnowing-screens in place, there were still too many stories I would have liked to use to use them all, forcing me into some of the toughest choices I can recall in my entire career as an anthologist. There's a *lot* of good material of similar sorts out there to be found, once you're through with *this* book.

Would we ordinary, garden-variety human beings *like* the Posthuman Future if we were somehow suddenly catapulted into it? Or would we find it a terrifying, hostile, and incomprehensible place, a place we were no more equipped to understand and deal with successfully than an Australopithecus would be equipped to deal with Times Square? Are human beings, as we understand the term, as the term *has been* understood for thousands upon thousands of years, on the way out? Doomed to extinction, or at least to enforced obsolescence in some future equivalent of a game reserve or a zoo? Certainly the prospect for "normal" humans sometimes seems bleak in these stories, with author after author postulating the inevitability of a constantly widening gap between the human and the posthuman condition . . . with the humans left ever farther behind, unable to cope.

Of course, today's authors can't *really* give us the view from a posthuman intelligence, any more than an Australopithecus could have written a story seen through the eyes of a contemporary twenty-first-century human. The stories, after all, are being written by people on *this* side of the posthuman gulf—and no matter how ingenious the speculations they contain, no matter how lavish and radical the imaginations of the authors, they remain of necessity limited by being the *human* perspective of what posthumanity might be like. To those individuals who actually *live* through the Vingean Singularity and on into the world of posthumanity, let alone to those produced in generations to come, it may all seem quite different. Already there are stories by writers such as Stableford, Sterling, Ryman, Marusek, and others that hint that the Posthuman Future won't be such a bad place after all—or won't *seem* so to us after we get there, anyway . . . which may not be nearly as far away as you think.

Maybe someday, in the unknown and unknowable future, a *real* Posthuman Entity will come across this book, and riffle through it, and laugh, or at least smile with wistful nostalgia, at how naive and limited and constrained our ideas were of what posthumanity would be like, all of us stuck back here in the murk of the benighted and backward twenty-first century, of how far off the mark our speculations were, muse about how we could never have come even *close* to predicting what *really* happened. . . .

And, with luck, and if things move fast enough, maybe that Posthuman Entity will even be *you*, transformed past all recognition.

The Chapter Ends

POUL ANDERSON

One of the best-known writers in science fiction, Poul Anderson made his first sale in 1947, while he was still in college, and in the course of his subsequent career has published almost a hundred books (in several different fields: as Anderson has written historical novels, fantasies, and mysteries, in addition to SF), sold hundreds of short pieces to every conceivable market, and won seven Hugo Awards, three Nebula Awards, and the Tolkein Memorial Award for Life Achievement.

Anderson had trained to be a scientist, taking a degree in physics from the University of Minnesota, but the writing life proved to be more seductive, and he never did get around to working in his original field of choice. Instead, the sales mounted steadily, until by the late fifties and early sixties, he may have been one of the most prolific writers in the genre.

In spite of his high output of fiction, he somehow managed to maintain an amazingly high standard of literary quality as well, and by the early mid-sixties was also on his way to becoming one of the most honored and respected writers in the SF genre. At one point during this period—in addition to nonrelated work and lesser series such as the "Hoka" stories he was writing in collaboration with Gordon R. Dickson—Anderson was running three of the most popular and prestigious series in science fiction all at the same time: the "Technic History" series detailing the exploits of the wily trader Nicholas Van Rijn (which includes novels such as The Man Who Counts, The Trouble Twisters, Satan's World, Mirkheim, The People of the Wind, and collections such as Trader to the Stars and The Earth Book of Stormgate); the extremely popular series relating the adventures of interstellar secret agent Dominic Flandry, probably the most successful attempt to cross SF with the spy thriller, next to Jack Vance's "Demon Princes" novels (the Flandry series includes novels such as A Circus of Hells, The Rebel Worlds, The Day of Their Return, Flandry of Terra, A Knight of Ghosts and Shadows, A Stone in Heaven, and The Game of Empire, and collections such as Agent of the Terran Empire); and, my own personal favorite, a series that took us along on assignment with the agents of the Time Patrol (including the collections The Guardians of Time, Time Patrolman, The Shield of Time, and The Time Patrol).

When you add to this amazing collection of memorable titles the impact of the best of Anderson's non-series novels—works such as Brain Wave, Three Hearts and Three lions, The Night Face, The Enemy Stars, and The High Crusade, all of which were being published in addition to the series books—it becomes clear that Anderson dominated the late fifties and the pre-New Wave sixties in a way that only Robert A. Heinlein, Isaac Asimov, and Arthur C. Clarke could rival. And, like them, he remained an active and dominant figure right through the seventies, eighties, and nineties.

Here's a compelling look into the far future, at a moment when the race is *beginning to split into human and posthuman camps. Even in this early story—published in 1953—it's clear that the gulf can only* widen . . . *often with tragic results.*

Anderson's other books (among many *others) include:* The Broken Sword, Tau Zero, A Midsummer Tempest, Orion Shall Rise, The Boat of a Million Years, Harvest of Stars, The Fleet of Stars, Starfarers, *and* Operation Luna. *His short work has been collected in* The Queen of Air and Darkness and Other Stories, Fantasy, The Unicorn Trade *(with Karen Anderson),* Past Times, The Best of Poul Anderson, Explorations, *and, most recently, the retrospective collection* All One Universe. *His most recent book is a new novel,* Genesis—*on bestseller lists at the beginning of the oughts as well. Until his death on July 31, 2001, Anderson lived in Orinda, California, with his wife (and fellow writer), Karen.*

I

"No," said the old man.

"But you don't realize what it means," said Jorun. "You don't know what you're saying."

The old man, Kormt of Huerdar, Gerlaug's son, and Speaker for Soils Township, shook his head till the long, grizzled locks swirled around his wide shoulders. "I have thought it through," he said. His voice was deep and slow and implacable. "You gave me five years to think about it. And my answer is no."

Jorun felt a weariness rise within him. It had been like this for days now, weeks, and it was like trying to knock down a mountain. You beat on its rocky flanks till your hands were bloody, and still the mountain stood there, sunlight on its high snow fields and in the forests that rustled up its slopes, and it did not really notice you. You were a brief thin buzz between two long nights, but the mountain was forever.

"You haven't thought at all," he said with a rudeness born of exhaustion. "You've only reacted unthinkingly to a dead symbol. It's not a human reaction, even, it's a verbal reflex."

Kormt's eyes, meshed in crow's-feet, were serene and steady under the thick gray brows. He smiled a little in his long beard, but made no other reply. Had he simply let the insult glide off him, or had he not understood it at all? There was no real talking to these peasants; too many millennia lay between, and you couldn't shout across that gulf.

"Well," said Jorun, "the ships will be here tomorrow or the next day, and it'll take another day or so to get all your people aboard. You have that long to decide, but after that it'll be too late. Think about it, I beg of you. As for me, I'll be too busy to argue further."

"You are a good man," said Kormt, "and a wise one in your fashion. But you are blind. There is something dead inside you."

He waved one huge gnarled hand. "Look around you, Jorun of Fulkhis. This is *Earth.* This is the old home of all humankind. You cannot go off and forget it. Man cannot do so. It is in him, in his blood and bones and soul; he will carry Earth within him forever."

Jorun's eyes traveled along the arc of the hand. He stood on the edge of the town. Behind him were its houses—low, white, half-timbered, roofed with thatch or red tile, smoke rising from the chimneys; carved galleries overhung the narrow, cobbled, crazily twisting streets; he heard the noise of wheels and wooden clogs, the shouts of children at play. Beyond that were trees and the incredible ruined walls of Sol City. In front of him, the wooded hills were cleared and a gentle landscape of neat fields and orchards rolled down toward the distant glitter of the sea; scattered farm buildings, drowsy cattle, winding gravel roads, fence walls of ancient marble and granite, all dreaming under the sun.

He drew a deep breath. It was pungent in his nostrils. It smelled of leaf mold, plowed earth baking in the warmth, summery trees and gardens, a remote ocean odor of salt and kelp and fish. He thought that no two planets ever had quite the same smell, and that none was as rich as Terra's.

"This is a fair world," he said slowly.

"It is the only one," said Kormt. "Man came from here; and to this, in the end, he must return."

"I wonder—" Jorun sighed. "Take me; not one atom of my body was from this soil before I landed. My people lived on Fulkhis for ages, and changed to meet its conditions. They would not be happy on Terra."

"The atoms are nothing," said Kormt. "It is the form which matters, and that was given to you by Earth."

Jorun studied him for a moment. Kormt was like most of this planet's ten million or so people—a dark, stocky folk, though there were more blond and red-haired throwbacks here than in the rest of the Galaxy. He was old for a primitive untreated by medical science—he must be almost two hundred years old—but his back was straight, and his stride firm. The coarse, jut-nosed face held an odd strength. Jorun was nearing his thousandth birthday, but couldn't help feeling like a child in Kormt's presence.

That didn't make sense. These few dwellers on Terra were a backward and impoverished race of peasants and handicraftsmen; they were ignorant and unadventurous; they had been static for more thousands of years than anyone knew. What could they have to say to the ancient and mighty civilization which had almost forgotten their little planet?

Kormt looked at the declining sun. "I must go now," he said. "There are the evening chores to do. I will be in town tonight if you should wish to see me."

"I probably will," said Jorun. "There's a lot to do, readying the evacuation, and you're a big help."

The old man bowed with grave courtesy, turned, and walked off down the road. He wore the common costume of Terran men, as archaic in style as in its woven-fabric material: hat, jacket, loose trousers, a long staff in his hand. Contrasting the drab blue of Kormt's dress, Jorun's vivid tunic of shifting rainbow hues was like a flame.

The psychotechnician sighed again, watching him go. He liked the old fellow. It would be criminal to leave him here alone, but the law forbade force—physical or mental—and the Integrator on Corazuno wasn't going to care whether or not one aged man stayed behind. The job was to get the *race* off Terra.

A *lovely world*. Jorun's thin mobile features, pale-skinned and large-eyed, turned around the horizon. A *fair world we came from*.

There were more beautiful planets in the Galaxy's swarming myriads—the indigo world-ocean of Loa, jeweled with islands; the heaven-defying mountains of Sharang; the sky of Jareb, that seemed to drip light—oh, many and many, but there was only one Earth.

Jorun remembered his first sight of this world, hanging free in space to watch it after the grueling ten-day run, thirty thousand light-years, from Corazuno. It was blue as it turned before his eyes, a burnished turquoise shield blazoned with the living green and brown of its lands, and the poles were crowned with a glimmering haze of aurora. The belts that streaked its face and blurred the continents were cloud, wind and water and the gray rush of rain, like a benediction from heaven. Beyond the planet hung its moon, a scarred golden crescent, and he had wondered how many generations of men had looked up to it, or watched its light like a broken bridge across moving waters. Against the enormous cold of the sky—utter black out to the distant coils of the nebulae, thronging with a million frosty points of diamond-hard blaze that were the stars—Earth had stood as a sign of haven. To Jorun, who came from Galactic center and its uncountable hosts of suns, heaven was bare, this was the outer fringe where the stars thinned away toward hideous immensity. He had shivered a little, drawn the envelope of air and warmth closer about him, with a convulsive movement. The silence drummed in his head. Then he streaked for the north-pole rendezvous of his group.

Well, he thought now, *we have a pretty routine job. The first expedition here, five years ago, prepared the natives for the fact they'd have to go. Our party simply has to organize these docile peasants in time for the ships*. But it had meant a lot of hard work, and he was tired. It would be good to finish the job and get back home.

Or would it?

He thought of flying with Zarek, his teammate, from the rendezvous to this area assigned as theirs. Plains like oceans of grass, wind-rippled, darkened with the herds of wild cattle whose hoofbeats were a thunder in the earth; forests, hundreds of kilometers of old and mighty trees, rivers piercing them in a long steel gleam; lakes where fish leaped; spilling sunshine like warm rain, radiance so bright it hurt his eyes, cloud-shadows swift across the land. It had all been empty of man, but still there was a vitality here which was almost frightening to Jorun. His own grim world of moors and crags and spindrift seas was a niggard beside this; here life covered the earth, filled the oceans, and made the heavens clangorous around him. He wondered if the driving energy within man, the force which had raised him to the stars, made him half-god and half-demon, if that was a legacy of Terra.

Well—man had changed; over the thousands of years, natural and controlled adaptation had fitted him to the worlds he had colonized, and most of his many races could not now feel at home here. Jorun thought of his own party: round, amber-skinned Chuli from a tropic world, complaining bitterly about the cold and dryness; gay young Cluthe, gangling and bulge-chested; sophisticated Taliuvenna of the flowing dark hair and the lustrous eyes—no, to them Earth was only one more planet, out of thousands they had seen in their long lives.

And I'm a sentimental fool.

II

He could have willed the vague regret out of his trained nervous system, but he didn't want to. This was the last time human eyes would ever look on Earth, and somehow Jorun felt that it should be more to him than just another psychotechnic job.

"Hello, good sir."

He turned at the voice and forced his tired lips into a friendly smile. "Hello, Julith," he said. It was a wise policy to learn the names of the townspeople, at least, and she was a great-great-granddaughter of the Speaker.

She was some thirteen or fourteen years old, a freckle-faced child with a shy smile, and steady green eyes. There was a certain awkward grace about her, and she seemed more imaginative than most of her stolid race. She curtsied quaintly for him, her bare foot reaching out under the long smock which was daily female dress here.

"Are you busy, good sir?" she asked.

"Well, not too much," said Jorun. He was glad of a chance to talk; it silenced his thoughts. "What can I do for you?"

"I wondered—" She hesitated, then, breathlessly: "I wonder if you could give me a lift down to the beach? Only for an hour or two. It's too far to walk there before I have to be home, and I can't borrow a car, or even a horse. If it won't be any trouble, sir."

"Mmmmm—shouldn't you be at home now? Isn't there milking and so on to do?"

"Oh, I don't live on a farm, good sir. My father is a baker."

"Yes, yes, so he is. I should have remembered." Jorun considered for an instant. There was enough to do in town, and it wasn't fair for him to play hooky while Zarek worked alone. "Why do you want to go to the beach, Julith?"

"We'll be busy packing up," she said. "Starting tomorrow, I guess. This is my last chance to see it."

Jorun's mouth twisted a little. "All right," he said; "I'll take you."

"You are very kind, good sir," she said gravely.

He didn't reply, but held out his arm, and she clasped it with one hand while her other arm gripped his waist. The generator inside his skull responded to his will, reaching out and clawing itself to the fabric of forces and energies which was physical space. They rose quietly, and went so slowly seaward that he didn't have to raise a windscreen.

"Will we be able to fly like this when we get to the stars?" she asked.

"I'm afraid not, Julith," he said. "You see, the people of my civilization are born this way. Thousands of years ago, men learned how to control the great basic forces of the cosmos with only a small bit of energy. Finally they used artificial mutation—that is, they changed themselves, slowly, over many generations, until their brains grew a new part that could generate this controlling force. We can now, even, fly between the stars, by this power. But your people don't have that brain, so we had to build space ships to take you away."

"I see," she said.

"Your great-great-grandchildren can be like us, if your people want to be changed thus,"

"They didn't want to change before," she answered. "I don't think they'll do it now, even in their new home." Her voice held no bitterness; it was an acceptance.

Privately, Jorun doubted it. The psychic shock of this uprooting would be bound to destroy the old traditions of the Terrans; it would not take many centuries before they were culturally assimilated by Galactic Civilization.

Assimilated—nice euphemism. Why not just say—eaten?

They landed on the beach. It was broad and white, running in dunes from the thin, harsh, salt-streaked grass to the roar and tumble of surf. The sun was low over the watery horizon, filling the damp, blowing air with gold. Jorun could almost look directly at its huge disc.

He sat down. The sand gritted tinily under him, and the wind rumpled this hair and filled his nostrils with its sharp wet smell. He picked up a conch and turned it over in his fingers, wondering at the intricate architecture of it.

"If you hold it to your ear," said Julith, "you can hear the sea." Her childish voice was curiously tender around the rough syllables of Earth's language.

He nodded and obeyed her hint. It was only the small pulse of blood within him—you heard the same thing out in the great hollow silence of space—but it did sing of restless immensities, wind and foam, and the long waves marching under the moon.

"I have two of them myself," said Julith. "I want them so I can always remember this beach. And my children and their children will hold them, too, and hear our sea talking." She folded his fingers around the shell. "You keep this one for yourself."

"Thank you," he said. "I will."

The combers rolled in, booming and spouting against the land. The Terrans called them the horses of God. A thin cloud in the west was turning rose and gold.

"Are there oceans on our new planet?" asked Julith.

"Yes," he said. "It's the most Earthlike world we could find that wasn't already inhabited. You'll be happy there."

But the trees and grasses, the soil and the fruits thereof, the beasts of the field and the birds of the air and the fish of the waters beneath, form and color, smell and sound, taste and texture, everything is different. Is alien. The difference is small, subtle, but it is the abyss of two billion years of separate evolution, and no other world can ever quite be Earth.

Julith looked straight at him with solemn eyes. "Are you folk afraid of Hulduvians?" she asked.

"Why, no," he said. "Of course not."

"Then why are you giving Earth to them?" It was a soft question, but it trembled just a little.

"I thought all your people understood the reason by now," said Jorun. "Civilization—the civilization of man and his non-human allies—has moved inward, toward the great star-clusters of Galactic center. This part of space means nothing to us any more; it's almost a desert. You haven't seen starlight till you've been by Sagittarius. Now the Hulduvians are another civilization. They are not the least bit like us; they live on big, poisonous worlds like Jupiter and Saturn. I think they would seem like pretty nice monsters if they weren't so alien to us that neither side can really understand the other. They use the cosmic energies too, but in a different way—and their way interferes with ours just as ours interferes with theirs. Different brains, you see.

"Anyway, it was decided that the two civilizations would get along best by just staying away from each other. If they divided up the Galaxy between them, there would be no interference; it would be too far from one civilization to the other. The Hulduvians were, really, very nice about it. They're willing to take the outer rim, even if there are fewer stars, and let us have the center.

"So by the agreement, we've got to have all men and manlike beings out of their territory before they come to settle it, just as they'll move out of ours. Their colonists won't be coming to Jupiter and Saturn for centuries yet; but even so, we have to clear the Sirius Sector now, because there'll be a lot of work to do elsewhere. Fortunately, there are only a few people living in this whole part of space. The Sirius Sector has been an isolated, primi—ah— quiet region since the First Empire fell, fifty thousand years ago."

Julith's voice rose a little. "But those people are *us*!"

"And the folk of Alpha Centauri and Procyon and Sirius and—oh, hundreds of other stars. Yet all of you together are only one tiny drop in the quadrillions of the Galaxy. Don't you see, Julith, you have to move for the good of all of us?"

"Yes," she said. "Yes, I know all that."

She got up, shaking herself. "Let's go swimming."

Jorun smiled and shook his head. "No, I'll wait for you if you want to go."

She nodded and ran off down the beach, sheltering behind a dune to put on a bathing-suit. The Terrans had a nudity taboo, in spite of the mild interglacial climate; typical primitive irrationality. Jorun lay back, folding his arms behind his head, and looked up at the darkening sky. The evening star twinkled forth, low and white on the dusk-blue horizon. Venus—or was it Mercury? He wasn't sure. He wished he knew more about the early history of the Solar System, the first men to ride their thunderous rockets out to die on unknown hell-worlds—the first clumsy steps toward the stars. He could look it up in the archives of Corazuno, but he knew he never would. Too much else to do, too much to remember. Probably less than one per cent of mankind's throngs even knew where Earth was, today—though, for a while, it had been quite a tourist center. But that was perhaps thirty thousand years ago.

Because this world, out of all the billions, has certain physical characteristics, he thought, *my race has made them into standards. Our basic units of length and time and acceleration, our comparisons by which we classify the swarming planets of the Galaxy, they all go back ultimately to Earth. We bear that unspoken memorial to our birthplace within our whole civilization, and will bear it forever. But has she given us more than that? Are our own selves, bodies and minds and dreams, are they also the children of Earth?*

Now he was thinking like Kormt, stubborn old Kormt who clung with such a blind strength to this land simply because it was his. When you considered all the races of this wander-footed species—how many of them there were, how many kinds of man between the stars! And yet they all walked upright; they all had two eyes and a nose between and a mouth below; they were all cells of that great and ancient culture which had begun here, eons past, with the first hairy half-man who kindled a fire against night. If Earth had not had darkness and cold and prowling beasts, oxygen and cellulose and flint, that culture might never have gestated.

I'm getting illogical. Too tired, nerves worn too thin, psychosomatic control slipping. Now Earth is becoming some obscure mother-symbol for me.

Or has she always been one, for the whole race of us?

A seagull cried harshly overhead and soared from view.

The sunset was smoldering away and dusk rose like fog out of the ground. Julith came running back to him, her face indistinct in the gloom. She was breathing hard, and he couldn't tell if the catch in her voice was laughter or weeping.

"I'd better be getting home," she said.

III

They flew slowly back. The town was a yellow twinkle of lights, warmth gleaming from windows across many empty kilometers. Jorun set the girl down outside her home.

"Thank you, good sir," she said, curtseying. "Won't you come in to dinner?"

"Well—"

The door opened, etching the girl black against the ruddiness inside. Jorun's luminous tunic made him like a torch in the dark. "Why, it's the starman," said a woman's voice.

"I took your daughter for a swim," he explained. "I hope you don't mind."

"And if we did, what would it matter?" grumbled a bass tone. Jorun recognized Kormt; the old man must have come as a guest from his farm on the outskirts. "What could we do about it?"

"Now, Granther, that's no way to talk to the gentleman," said the woman. "He's been very kind. Won't you come eat with us, good sir?"

Jorun refused twice, in case they were only being polite, then accepted gladly enough. He was tired of cookery at the inn where he and Zarek boarded. "Thank you."

He entered, ducking under the low door. A single long, smoky-raftered room was kitchen, dining room, and parlor; doors led off to the sleeping quarters. It was furnished with a clumsy elegance, skin rugs, oak wainscoting, carved pillars, glowing ornaments of hammered copper. A radium clock, which must be incredibly old, stood on the stone mantel, above a snapping fire; a chemical-powdered gun, obviously of local manufacture, hung over it. Julith's parents, a plain, quiet peasant couple, conducted him to the end of the wooden table, while half a dozen children watched him with large eyes. The younger children were the only Terrans who seemed to find this removal an adventure.

The meal was good and plentiful: meat, vegetables, bread, beer, milk, ice cream, coffee, all of it from the farms hereabouts. There wasn't much trade between the few thousand communities of Earth; they were practically self-sufficient. The company ate in silence, as was the custom here. When they were finished, Jorun wanted to go, but it would have been rude to leave immediately. He went over to a chair by the fireplace, across from one in which Kormt sprawled.

The old man took out a big-bowled pipe and began stuffing it. Shadows wove across his seamed brown face, his eyes were a gleam out of darkness. "I'll go down to City Hall with you soon," he said. "I imagine that's where the work is going on."

"Yes," said Jorun. "I can relieve Zarek at it. I'd appreciate it if you did come, good sir. Your influence is very steadying on these people."

"It should be," said Kormt. "I've been their Speaker for almost a hundred years. And my father Gerlaug was before me, and his father Kormt was before him." He took a brand from the fire and held it over his pipe, puffing hard, looking up at Jorun through tangled brows. "Who was your great-grandfather?"

"Why—I don't know. I imagine he's still alive somewhere, but—"

"I thought so. No marriage. No family. No home. No tradition." Kormt shook his massive head, slowly. "I pity you Galactics!"

"Now please, good sir—" Damn it all, the old clodhopper could get as irritating as a faulty computer. "We have records that go back to before man left this planet. Records of everything. It is you who have forgotten."

Kormt smiled and puffed blue clouds at him. "That's not what I meant."

"Do you mean you think it is good for men to live a life that is unchanging, that is just the same from century to century—no new dreams, no new triumphs, always the same grubbing rounds of days? I cannot agree."

Jorun's mind flickered over history, trying to evaluate the basic motivations of his opponent. Partly cultural, partly biological, that must be it. Once Terra had been the center of the civilized universe. But the long migration starward, especially after the fall of the First Empire, drained off the most venturesome elements of the population. That drain went on for thousands of years.

You couldn't call them stagnant. Their life was too healthy, their civilization too rich in its own way—folk art, folk music, ceremony, religion, the intimacy of family life which the Galactics had lost—for that term. But to one who flew between the streaming suns, it was a small existence.

Kormt's voice broke in on his reverie. "Dreams, triumphs, work, deeds, love and life and finally death and the long sleep in the earth," he said. "Why should we want to change them? They never grow old; they are new for each child that is born."

"Well," said Jorun, and stopped. You couldn't really answer that kind of logic. It wasn't logic at all, but something deeper.

"Well," he started over, after a while, "as you know, this evacuation was forced on us, too. We don't want to move you, but we must."

"Oh, yes," said Kormt. "You have been very nice about it. It would have been easier, in a way, if you'd come with fire and gun and chains for us, like the barbarians did long ago. We could have understood you better then."

"At best, it will be hard for your people," said Jorun. "It will be a shock, and they'll need leaders to guide them through it. You have a duty to help them out there, good sir."

"Maybe." Kormt blew a series of smoke rings at his youngest descendant, three years old, who crowed with laughter and climbed up on his knee. "But they'll manage."

"You can't seem to realize," said Jorun, "that you are the *last man on Earth* who refuses to go. You will be *alone*. For the rest of your life! We couldn't come back for you later under any circumstances, because there'll be Hulduvian colonies between Sol and Sagittarius which we would disturb in passage. You'll be alone, I say!"

Kormt shrugged. "I'm too old to change my ways; there can't be many years left me, anyway. I can live well, just off the food-stores that'll be left here." He ruffled the child's hair, but his face drew into a scowl. "Now, no more of that, good sir, if you please; I'm tired of this argument."

Jorun nodded and fell into the silence that held the rest. Terrans would sometimes sit for hours without talking, content to be in each other's nearness. He thought of Kormt, Gerlaug's son, last man on Earth, altogether alone, living alone and dying alone; and yet, he reflected, was that solitude any greater than the one in which all men dwelt all their days?

Presently the Speaker set the child down, knocked out his pipe and rose. "Come, good sir," he said, reaching for his staff. "Let us go."

They walked side by side down the street, under the dim lamps and past the yellow windows. The cobbles gave back their footfalls in a dull clatter. Once in a while they passed someone else, a vague figure which bowed to Kormt. Only one did not notice them, an old woman who walked crying between the high walls.

"They say it is never night on your worlds," said Kormt.

Jorun threw him a sidelong glance. His face was a strong jutting of highlights from sliding shadow. "Some planets have been given luminous skies," said the technician, "and a few still have cities, too, where it is always light. But when every man can control the cosmic energies, there is no real reason for us to live together; most of us dwell far apart. There are very dark nights on my own world, and I cannot see any other home from my own—just the moors."

"It must be a strange life," said Kormt. "Belonging to no one."

They came out on the market-square, a broad paved space walled in by houses. There was a fountain in its middle, and a statue dug out of the ruins had been placed there. It was broken, one arm gone—but still the white slim figure of the dancing girl stood with youth and laughter, forever under the sky of Earth. Jorun knew that lovers were wont to meet here, and briefly, irrationally, he wondered how lonely the girl would be in all the millions of years to come.

The City Hall lay at the farther end of the square, big and dark, its eaves carved with dragons, and the gables topped with wing-spreading birds. It was an old building; nobody knew how many generations of men had gathered here. A long, patient line of folk stood outside it, shuffling in one by one to the registry desk; emerging, they went off quietly into the darkness, toward the temporary shelters erected for them.

Walking by the line, Jorun picked faces out of the shadows. There was a young mother holding a crying child, her head bent over it in a timeless pose, murmuring to soothe it. There was a mechanic, still sooty from his work, smiling wearily at some tired joke of the man behind him. There was a scowling, black-browed peasant who muttered a curse as Jorun went by; the rest seemed to accept their fate meekly enough. There was a priest, his head bowed, alone with his God. There was a younger man, his hands clenching and unclenching, big helpless hands, and Jorun heard him saying to someone else: "—if they could have waited till after harvest. I hate to let good grain stand in the field."

Jorun went into the main room, toward the desk at the head of the line. Hulking hairless Zarek was patiently questioning each of the hundreds who came, hat in hand, before him: name, age, sex, occupation, dependents, special needs or desires. He punched the answers out on the recorder machine, half a million lives were held in its electronic memory.

"Oh, there you are," his bass rumbled. "Where've you been?"

"I had to do some concy work," said Jorun. That was a private code term, among others: concy, conciliation, anything to make the evacuation go smoothly. "Sorry to be so late. I'll take over now."

"All right. I think we can wind the whole thing up by midnight." Zarek smiled and clapped him on the back to go out for supper and sleep. Jorun beckoned to the next Terran and settled down to the long, almost mindless routine of registration. He was interrupted once by Kormt, who yawned mightily and bade him good night; otherwise it was a steady, half-conscious interval in which one anonymous face after another passed by. He was dimly surprised when the last one came up. This was a plump, cheerful, middle-aged fellow with small shrewd eyes, a little more colorfully dressed than the others. He gave his occupation as merchant—a minor tradesman, he explained, dealing in the little things it was more convenient for the peasants to buy than to manufacture themselves.

"I hope you haven't been waiting too long," said Jorun. Concy statement.

"Oh, no." The merchant grinned. "I knew those dumb farmers would be here for hours, so I just went to bed and got up half an hour ago, when it was about over."

"Clever," Jorun rose, sighed, and stretched. The big room was cavernously empty, its lights a harsh glare. It was very quiet here.

"Well, sir, I'm a middling smart chap, if I say it as shouldn't. And you know, I'd like to express my appreciation of all you're doing for us."

"Can't say we're doing much." Jorun locked the machine.

"Oh, the apple-knockers may not like it, but really, good sir, this hasn't been any place for a man of enterprise. It's dead. I'd have got out long ago if there'd been any transportation. Now, when we're getting back into civilization, there'll be some real opportunities. I'll make my pile inside of five years, you bet."

Jorun smiled, but there was a bleakness in him. What chance would this barbarian have even to get near the gigantic work of civilization—let alone comprehend it or take part in it. He hoped the little fellow wouldn't break his heart trying.

"Well," he said "good night, and good luck to you."

"Good night, sir. We'll meet again, I trust."

Jorun switched off the lights and went out into the square. It was completely deserted. The moon was up now, almost full, and its cold radiance dimmed the lamps. He heard a dog howling far off. The dogs of Earth—such as weren't taken along—would be lonely, too.

Well, he thought, *the job's over. Tomorrow, or the next day, the ships come.*

<h1 style="text-align:center">IV</h1>

He felt very tired, but didn't want to sleep, and willed himself back to alertness. There hadn't been much chance to inspect the ruins, and he felt it would be appropriate to see them by moonlight.

Rising into the air, he ghosted above roofs and trees until he came to the dead city. For a while he hovered in a sky like dark velvet, a faint breeze murmured around him, and he heard the remote noise of crickets and the sea. But stillness enveloped it all, there was no real sound.

Sol City, capital of the legendary First Empire, had been enormous. It must have sprawled over forty or fifty thousand square kilometers when it was in its prime, when it was the gay and wicked heart of human civilization and swollen with the lifeblood of the stars. And yet those who built it had been men of taste, they had sought out genius to create for them. The city was not a collection of buildings; it was a balanced whole, radiating from the mighty peaks of the central palace, through colonnades and parks and leaping skyways, out to the temple-like villas of the rulers. For all its monstrous size, it had been a fairy sight, a woven lace of polished metal and white, black, red stone, colored plastic, music and light—everywhere light.

Bombarded from space; sacked again and again by the barbarian hordes who swarmed maggot-like through the bones of the slain Empire; weathered, shaken by the slow sliding of Earth's crust; pried apart by patient, delicate roots; dug over by hundreds of generations of archaeologists, treasure-seekers, the idly curious; made a quarry of metal and stone for the ignorant peasants who finally huddled about it—still its empty walls and blind windows, crumbling arches and toppled pillars held a ghost of beauty and magnificence which was like a half-remembered dream. A dream the whole race had once had.

And now we're waking up.

Jorun moved silently over the ruins. Trees growing between tumbled blocks dappled them with moonlight and shadow; the marble was very white and fair against darkness. He hovered by a broken caryatid, marveling at its exquisite leaping litheness; that girl had borne tons of stone like a flower in her hair. Further on, across a street that was a lane of woods, beyond a park that was thick with forest, lay the nearly complete outline of a house. Only its rain-blurred walls stood. But he could trace the separate rooms; here a noble had entertained his friends, robes that were fluid rainbows, jewels dripping fire, swift cynical interplay of wits like sharpened swords rising above music and the clear sweet laughter of dancing girls; here people whose flesh was now dust had slept and made love and lain side-by-side in darkness to watch the moving pageant of the city; here the slaves had lived and worked and sometimes wept; here the children had played their ageless games under willows, between banks of roses. Oh, it had been a hard and cruel time; it was well gone but it had lived. It had embodied man, all that was noble and splendid and evil and merely wistful in the race, and now its late children had forgotten.

A cat sprang up on one of the walls and flowed noiselessly along it, hunting. Jorun shook himself and flew toward the center of the city, the imperial palace. An owl hooted somewhere, and a bat fluttered out of his way like a small damned soul blackened by hellfire. He didn't raise a wind-screen, but let the air blow around him, the air of Earth.

The palace was almost completely wrecked, a mountain of heaped rocks, bare bones of "eternal" metal gnawed thin by steady ages of wind and rain and frost, but once it must have been gigantic. Men rarely built that big nowadays, they didn't need to; and the whole human spirit had changed, become ever more abstract, finding its treasures within itself. But there had been an elemental magnificence about early man and the works he raised to challenge the sky.

One tower still stood—a gutted shell, white under the stars, rising in a filigree of columns and arches which seemed impossibly airy, as if it were built of moonlight. Jorun settled on its broken upper balcony, dizzily high above the black-and-white fantasy of the ruins. A hawk flew shrieking from its nest, then there was silence.

No—wait—another yell, ringing down the star ways, a dark streak across the moon's face. "Hai-ah!" Jorun recognized the joyful shout of young Cluthe, rushing through heaven like a demon on a broomstick, and scowled in annoyance. He didn't want to be bothered now. Jorun was little older than Cluthe—a few centuries at most—but he came of a melancholy folk; he had been born old.

.

Another form pursued the first. As they neared, Jorun recognized Taliu-venna's supple outline. Those two had been teamed up for one of the African districts, but—

They sensed him and came wildly out of the sky to perch on the balcony railing and swing their legs above the heights. "How're you?" asked Cluthe. His lean face laughed in the moonlight. "Whoo-oo, what a flight!"

"I'm all right," said Jorun. "You through in your sector?"

"Uh-huh. So we thought we'd just duck over and look in here. Last chance anyone'll ever have to do some sightseeing on Earth."

Taliuvenna's full lips drooped a bit as she looked over the ruins. She came from Yunith, one of the few planets where they still kept cities, and was as much a child of their soaring arrogance as Jorun of his hills and tundras and great empty seas. "I thought it would be bigger," she said.

"Well, they were building this fifty or sixty thousand years ago," said Cluthe. "Can't expect too much."

"There is good art left here," said Jorun. "Pieces which for one reason or another weren't carried off. But you have to look around for it."

"I've seen a lot of it already, in museums," said Taliuvenna. "Not bad."

"C'mon, Tally," cried Cluthe. He touched her shoulder and sprang into the air. "Tag! You're it!"

She screamed with laughter and shot off after him. They rushed across the wilderness, weaving in and out of empty windows, and broken colonnades, and their shouts woke a clamor of echoes.

Jorun sighed. *I'd better go to bed*, he thought. *It's late.*

The spaceship was a steely pillar against a low gray sky. Now and then a fine rain would drizzle down, blurring it from sight; then that would end, and the ship's flanks would glisten as if they were polished. Clouds scudded overhead like flying smoke, and the wind was loud in the trees.

The line of Terrans moving slowly into the vessel seemed to go on forever. A couple of the ship's crew flew above them, throwing out a shield against the rain. They shuffled without much talk or expression, pushing carts filled with their little possessions. Jorun stood to one side, watching them go by, one face after another—scored and darkened by the sun of Earth, the winds of Earth, hands still grimy with the soil of Earth.

Well, he thought, *there they go. They aren't being as emotional about it as I thought they would. I wonder if they really do care.*

Julith went past with her parents. She saw him and darted from the line and curtsied before him.

"Good-by, good sir," she said. Looking up, she showed him a small and serious face. "Will I ever see you again?"

"Well," he lied, "I might look in on you sometime."

"Please do! In a few years, maybe, when you can."

It takes many generations to raise a people like this to our standard. In a few years—to me—she'll be in her grave.

"I'm sure you'll be very happy," he said.

She gulped. "Yes," she said, so low he could hardly hear her. "Yes, I know

I will." She turned and ran back to her mother. The raindrops glistened in her hair.

Zarek came up behind Jorun. "I made a last-minute sweep of the whole area," he said. "Detected no sign of human life. So it's all taken care of, except your old man."

"Good," said Jorun tonelessly.

"I wish you could do something about him."

"So do I."

Zarek strolled off again.

A young man and woman, walking hand in hand, turned out of the line not far away and stood for a little while. A spaceman zoomed over to them. "Better get back," he warned. "You'll get rained on."

"That's what we wanted," said the young man.

The spaceman shrugged and resumed his hovering. Presently the couple re-entered the line.

The tail of the procession went by Jorun and the ship swallowed it fast. The rain fell harder, bouncing off his force-shield like silver spears. Lightning winked in the west, and he heard the distant exuberance of thunder.

Kormt came walking slowly toward him. Rain streamed off his clothes and matted his long gray hair and beard. His wooden shoes made a wet sound in the mud. Jorun extended the force-shield to cover him. "I hope you've changed your mind," said the Fulkhisian.

"No, I haven't," said Kormt. "I just stayed away till everybody was aboard. Don't like good-bys."

"You don't know what you're doing," said Jorun for the—thousandth?—time. "It's plain madness to stay here alone."

"I told you I don't like good-bys," said Kormt harshly.

"I have to go advise the captain of the ship," said Jorun. "You have maybe half an hour before she lifts. Nobody will laugh at you for changing your mind."

"I won't." Kormt smiled without warmth. "You people are the future, I guess. Why can't you leave the past alone? I'm the past." He looked toward the far hills, hidden by the noisy rain. "I like it here, Galactic. That should be enough for you."

"Well, then—" Jorun held out his hand in the archaic gesture of Earth. "Good-by."

"Good-by." Kormt took the hand with a brief, indifferent clasp. Then he turned and walked off toward the village. Jorun watched him till he was out of sight.

The technician paused in the air-lock door, looking over the gray landscape and the village from whose chimneys no smoke rose. *Farewell, my mother*, he thought. And then, surprising himself: *Maybe Kormt is doing the right thing after all.*

He entered the ship and the door closed behind him.

Toward evening, the clouds lifted and the sky showed a clear pale blue—as if it had been washed clean—and the grass and leaves glistened. Kormt came out of the house to watch the sunset. It was a good one, all flame and gold. A pity little Julith wasn't here to see it; she'd always liked sunsets. But Julith was so far away now that if she sent a call to him, calling with the speed of light, it would not come before he was dead.

Nothing would come to him. Not ever again.

He tamped his pipe with a horny thumb and lit it and drew a deep cloud into his lungs. Hands in pockets, he strolled down the wet streets. The sound of his clogs was unexpectedly loud.

Well, son, he thought, *now you've got a whole world all to yourself, to do with just as you like. You're the richest man who ever lived.*

There was no problem in keeping alive. Enough food of all kinds was stored in the town's freeze-vault to support a hundred men for the ten or twenty years remaining to him. But he'd want to stay busy. He could maybe keep three farms from going to seed—watch over fields and orchards and livestock, repair the buildings, dust and wash and light up in the evening. A man ought to keep busy.

He came to the end of the street, where it turned into a graveled road winding up toward a high hill, and followed that: Dusk was creeping over the fields, the sea was a metal streak very far away and a few early stars blinked forth. A wind was springing up, a soft murmurous wind that talked in the trees. But how quiet things were!

On top of the hill stood the chapel, a small steepled building of ancient stone. He let himself in the gate and walked around to the graveyard behind. There were many of the demure white tombstones—thousands of years of Solis Township, men and women who had lived and worked and begotten, laughed and wept and died. Someone had put a wreath on one grave only this morning; it brushed against his leg as he went by. Tomorrow it would be withered, and weeds would start to grow. He'd have to tend the chapel yard, too. Only fitting.

He found his family plot and stood with feet spread apart fists on hips, smoking and looking down at the markers, Gerlaug Kormt's son, Tarna Huwan's daughter; these hundred years had they lain in the earth. Hello, Dad, hello, Mother. His fingers reached out and stroked the headstone of his wife. And so many of his children were here, too; sometimes he found it hard to believe that tall Gerlaug and laughing Stamm and shy, gentle Huwan were gone. He'd outlived too many people.

I had to stay, he thought. *This is my land, I am of it and I couldn't go. Someone had to stay and keep the land, if only for a little while. I can give it ten more years before the forest comes and takes it.*

Darkness grew around him. The woods beyond the hill loomed like a wall. Once he started violently; he thought he heard a child crying. No, only a bird. He cursed himself for the senseless pounding of his heart.

Gloomy place here, he thought. *Better get back to the house.*

He groped slowly out of the yard, toward the road. The stars were out now. Kormt looked up and thought he had never seen them so bright. Too bright; he didn't like it.

Go away, stars, he thought. *You took my people, but I'm staying here. This is my land.* He reached down to touch it, but the grass was cold and wet under his palm.

The gravel scrunched loudly as he walked, and the wind mumbled in the hedges, but there was no other sound. Not a voice called; not an engine turned; not a dog barked. No, he hadn't thought it would be so quiet.

And dark. No lights. Have to tend the street lamps himself—it was no fun, not being able to see the town from here, not being able to see anything except the stars. Should have remembered to bring a flashlight, but he was old and absentminded, and there was no one to remind him. When he died, there would be no one to hold his hands; no one to close his eyes and lay him in the earth—and the forests would grow in over the land and wild beasts would nuzzle his bones.

But I knew what. What of it? I'm tough enough to take it.

The stars flashed and flashed above him. Looking up, against his own will, Kormt saw how bright they were, how bright and quiet. And how very far away! He was seeing light that had left its home before he was born.

He stopped, sucking in his breath between his teeth. "No," he whispered.

This was his land. This was Earth, the home of man; it was his and he was its. This was the *land*, and not a single dust mote, crazily reeling and spinning through an endlessness of dark and silence, cold and immensity. Earth could not be so alone!

The last man alive. The last man in all the world!

He screamed, then, and began to run. His feet clattered loud on the road; the small sound was quickly swallowed by silence, and he covered his face against the relentless blaze of the stars. But there was no place to run to, no place at all.

JAMES BLISH

The late James Blish was one of the most prominent science-fiction writers of the fifties and sixties, and one of the first to concentrate on the use of biological science and technology in SF (he was himself a microbiologist). His "pantropy" (a word coined by Blish himself) stories, including his most famous one, "Surface Tension," and the other stories (including this one) later collected in The Seedling Stars, *are among the first science-fiction stories to investigate the idea that humans could be redesigned and reengineered so that they would be able to survive on alien planets under alien conditions . . . thus opening the door for later investigations of posthumanity, and thus ancestral to all such stories. And even right here, near the beginning of SF's examination of the theme, we can see that Blish was well aware that crossing the threshold into posthumanity was a one-way journey. Once you went through that doorway, you could not go back again. Nor would you necessarily want to . . .*

Blish's best-known novel was probably A Case of Conscience, *still one of SF's most subtle and profound explorations of the theme of religious faith, for which he won a well-deserved Hugo Award in 1959. Also well known at the time—and quite probably an influence on the work of Robert Reed, Ian McDonald, Alastair Reynolds, and other modern practitioners of the vast-scope-and-scale Space Opera—was his "Okie" series, wide-screen adventure novels that featured whole Terran cities taking off for the stars, powered by antigravity devices, and which culminates with the death and rebirth of the entire universe; the individual Okie novels—*Earthman, Come Home; They Shall Have Stars; The Triumph of Time; *and* A Life for the Stars—*were collected in the omnibus volume* Cities in Flight. *Blish's other novels include* Black Easter, The Day After Judgement, Doctor Mirabilis, The Night Shapes, The Frozen Years, *and* Jack of Eagles. *The best of Blish's short fiction—stories such as "A Work of Art," "Common Time," "The Box," and "Midsummer Century"—holds up well even today, and has been gathered in collections such as* Galactic Cluster, Anywhen, Midsummer Century, *and* The Best Science Fiction Stories of James Blish. *Under the name of William Atheling, Blish was also one of the most important early SF critics, rivaled only by his friend and sometime-collaborator, Damon Knight; "Atheling's" reviews were gathered in* The Issue At Hand *and* More Issues At Hand. *Blish died in 1975.*

The murmurs of discontent—Captain Gorbel, being a military man, thought of it as "disaffection"—among the crew of the R.S.S. *Indefeasible* had reached the point where they could no longer be ignored, well before the ship had come within fifty light-years of its objective.

Sooner or later, Gorbel thought, sooner or later this idiotic seal-creature is going to notice them.

Captain Gorbel wasn't sure whether he would be sorry or glad when the Adapted Man caught on. In a way, it would make things easier. But it would be an uncomfortable moment, not only for Hoqqueah and the rest of the pantrope team, but for Gorbel himself. Maybe it would be better to keep sitting on the safety valve until Hoqqueah and the other Altarians were put off on—what was its name again? Oh yes, Earth.

But the crew plainly wasn't going to let Gorbel put it off that long.

As for Hoqqueah, he didn't appear to have a noticing center anywhere in his brain. He was as little discommoded by the emotional undertow as he was by the thin and frigid air the Rigellian crew maintained inside the battlecraft. Secure in his coat of warm blubber, his eyes brown, liquid and merry, he sat in the forward greenhouse for most of each ship's day, watching the growth of the star Sol in the black skies ahead.

And he talked. Gods of all stars, how he talked! Captain Gorbel already knew more about the ancient—the *very* ancient—history of the seeding program than he had had any desire to know, but there was still more coming. Nor was the seeding program Hoqqueah's sole subject. The Colonization Council delegate had had a vertical education, one which cut in a narrow shaft through many different fields of specialization—in contrast to Gorbel's own training, which had been spread horizontally over the whole subject of spaceflight without more than touching anything else.

Hoqqueah seemed to be making a project of enlarging the captain's horizons, whether he wanted them enlarged or not.

"Take agriculture," he was saying at the moment. "This planet we're to seed provides an excellent argument for taking the long view of farm policy. There used to be jungles there; it was very fertile. But the people began their lives as farmers with the use of fire, and they killed themselves off in the same way."

"How?" Gorbel said automatically. Had he remained silent, Hoqqueah would have gone on anyhow; and it didn't pay to be impolite to the Colonization Council, even by proxy.

"In their own prehistory, fifteen thousand years before their official zero date, they cleared farmland by burning it off. Then they would plant a crop, harvest it, and let the jungle return. Then they burned the jungle off and went through the cycle again. At the beginning, they wiped out the greatest abundance of game animals Earth was ever to see, just by farming that way. Furthermore the method was totally destructive to the topsoil.

"But did they learn? No. Even after they achieved spaceflight, that method of farming was standard in most of the remaining jungle areas—even though the bare rock was showing through everywhere by that time."

Hoqqueah sighed. "Now, of course, there are no jungles. There are no seas, either. There's nothing but desert, naked rock, bitter cold, and thin, oxygen-poor air—or so the people would view it, if there were any of them left. *Tapa* farming wasn't solely responsible, but it helped."

Gorbel shot a quick glance at the hunched back of Lieutenant Averdor, his adjutant and navigator. Averdor had managed to avoid saying so much as one word to Hoqqueah or any of the other pantropists from the beginning of the trip. Of course he wasn't required to assume the diplomatic burdens involved—those were Gorbel's crosses—but the strain of dodging even normal intercourse with the seal-men was beginning to tell on him.

Sooner or later, Averdor was going to explode. He would have nobody to blame for it but himself, but that wouldn't prevent everybody on board from suffering from it.

Including Gorbel, who would lose a first-class navigator and adjutant.

Yet it was certainly beyond Gorbel's authority to order Averdor to speak to an Adapted Man. He could only suggest that Averdor run through a few mechanical courtesies, for the good of the ship. The only response had been one of the stoniest stares Gorbel had ever seen, even from Averdor, with whom the captain had been shipping for over thirty Galactic years.

And the worst of it was that Gorbel was, as a human being, wholly on Averdor's side.

"After a certain number of years, conditions change on any planet," Hoqqueah babbled solemnly, waving a flipperlike arm to include all the points of light outside the greenhouse. He was working back to his primary obsession: the seeding program. "It's only logical to insist that man be able to change with them—or, if he can't do that, he must establish himself somewhere else. Suppose he had colonized only the Earthlike planets? Not even those planets remain Earthlike forever, not in the biological sense."

"Why would we have limited ourselves to Earthlike planets in the first place?" Gorbel said. "Not that I know much about the place, but the specs don't make it sound like an optimum world."

"To be sure," Hoqqueah said, though as usual Gorbel didn't know which part of his own comment Hoqqueah was agreeing to. "There's no survival value in pinning one's race forever to one set of specs. It's only sensible to go on evolving with the universe, so as to stay independent of such things as the aging of worlds, or the explosions of their stars. And look at the results! Man exists now in so many forms that there's always a refuge somewhere for any threatened people. That's a great achievement—compared to it, what price the old arguments about sovereignty of form?"

"What, indeed?" Gorbel said, but inside his skull his other self was saying: Ah-ha, he smells the hostility after all. Once an Adapted Man, always an Adapted Man—and always fighting for equality with the basic human form. But it's no good, you seal-snouted bureaucrat. You can argue for the rest of your life, but your whiskers will always wiggle when you talk.

And obviously you'll never stop talking.

"And as a military man yourself, you'd be the first to appreciate the military advantages, Captain," Hoqqueah added earnestly. "Using pantropy, man has seized thousands of worlds that would have been inaccessible to him otherwise. It's enormously increased our chances to become masters of the galaxy, to take most of it under occupation without stealing anyone else's planet in the process. An occupation without dispossession—let alone without bloodshed. Yet if some race other than man should develop imperial ambitions, and try to annex our planets, it will find itself enormously outnumbered."

"That's true," Captain Gorbel said, interested in spite of himself. "It's probably just as well that we worked fast, way back there in the beginning. Before somebody else thought up the method, I mean. But, how come it *was* us? Seems to me that the first race to invent it should've been a race that already had it—if you follow me."

"Not quite, Captain. If you will give me an example—?"

"Well, we scouted a system once where there was a race that occupied two different planets, not both at the same time, but back and forth," Gorbel said. "They had a life-cycle that had three different forms. In the first form they'd winter over on the outermost of the two worlds. Then they'd change to another form that could cross space, mother-naked, without ships, and spend the rest of the year on the inner planet in the third form. Then they'd change back into the second form and cross back to the colder planet.

"It's a hard thing to describe. But the point is, this wasn't anything they'd worked out; it was natural to them. They'd evolved that way." He looked at Averdor again. "The navigation was tricky around there during the swarming season."

Averdor failed to rise to the bait.

"I see; the point is well taken," Hoqqueah said, nodding with grotesque thoughtfulness. "But let me point out to you, Captain, that being already able to do a thing doesn't aid you in thinking of it as something that needs to be perfected. Oh, I've seen races like the one you describe, too—races with polymorphism, sexual alteration of generation, metamorphosis of the insect life-history type, and so on. There's a planet named Lithia, about forty light-years from here, where the dominant race undergoes complete evolutionary recapitulation *after* birth—not before it, as men do. But why should any of them think of form-changing as something extraordinary, and to be striven for? It's one of the commonplaces of their lives, after all."

A small bell chimed in the greenhouse. Hoqqueah got up at once his movements precise and almost graceful despite his tubbiness. "Thus endeth the day," he said cheerfully. "Thank you for your courtesy, Captain."

He waddled out. He would, of course, be back tomorrow.

And the day after that.

And the next day—unless the crewmen hadn't tarred and feathered the whole bunch by then.

If only, Gorbel thought distractedly, if only the damned Adapts weren't so quick to abuse their privileges! As a delegate of the Colonization Council, Hoqqueah was a person of some importance, and could not be barred from entering the greenhouse except in an emergency. But didn't the man know that he shouldn't use the privilege each and every day, on a ship manned by basic-form human beings most of whom could not enter the greenhouse at all without a direct order?

And the rest of the pantropists were just as bad. As passengers with the technical status of human beings, they could go almost anywhere in the ship that the crew could go—and they did, persistently and unapologetically, as though moving among equals. Legally, that was what they were—but didn't they know by this time that there was such a thing as prejudice? And that among common spacemen the prejudice against their kind—and against any Adapted Man—always hovered near the borderline of bigotry?

There was a slight hum as Averdor's power chair swung around to face the captain. Like most Rigellian men, the lieutenant's face was lean and harsh, almost like that of an ancient religious fanatic, and the starlight in the greenhouse hid nothing to soften it; but to Captain Gorbel, to whom it was familiar down to its last line, it looked especially forbidding now.

"Well?" he said.

"I'd think you'd be fed to the teeth with that freak by this time," Averdor said without preamble. "Something's got to be done, Captain, before the crew gets so surly that we have to start handing out brig sentences."

"I don't like know-it-alls any better than you do," Gorbel said grimly. "Especially when they talk nonsense—and half of what this one says about spaceflight is nonsense, that much I'm sure of. But the man's a delegate of the Council. He's got a right to be up here if he wants to."

"You can bar anybody from the greenhouse in an emergency—even the ship's officers."

"I fail to see any emergency," Gorbel said stiffly.

"This is a hazardous part of the galaxy—potentially, anyhow. It hasn't been visited for millennia. That star up ahead has nine planets besides the one we're supposed to land on, and I don't know how many satellites of planetary size. Suppose somebody on one of them lost his head and took a crack at us as we went by?"

Gorbel frowned. "That's reaching for trouble. Besides, the area's been surveyed recently at least once—otherwise we wouldn't be here."

"A sketch job. It's still sensible to take precautions. If there should be any trouble, there's many a Board of Review that would call it risky to have unreliable, second-class human types in the greenhouse when it breaks out."

"You're talking nonsense."

"Dammit, Captain, read between the lines a minute," Averdor said harshly. "I know as well as you do that there's going to be no trouble that we can't handle. And that no reviewing board would pull a complaint like that on you if there were. I'm just trying to give you an excuse to use on the seals."

"I'm listening."

"Good. The Indefeasible is the tightest ship in the Rigellian navy, her record's clean, and the crew's morale is almost a legend. We can't afford to start gigging the men for their personal prejudices—which is what it will amount to, if those seals drive them to breaking discipline. Besides, they've got a right to do their work without a lot of seal snouts poking continually over their shoulders."

"I can hear myself explaining that to Hoqqueah."

"You don't need to," Averdor said doggedly. "You can tell him, instead, that you're going to have to declare the ship on emergency status until we land. That means that the pantrope team, as passengers, will have to stick to their quarters. It's simple enough."

It was simple enough, all right. And decidedly tempting.

"I don't like it," Gorbel said. "Besides, Hoqqueah may be a know-it-all, but he's not entirely a fool. He'll see through it easily enough."

Averdor shrugged. "It's your command," he said. "But I don't see what he could do about it even if he did see through it. It'd be all on the log and according to regs. All he could report to the Council would be a suspicion—and they'd probably discount it. Everybody knows that these second-class types are quick to think they're being persecuted. It's my theory that that's why they *are* persecuted, a lot of the time at least."

"I don't follow you."

"The man I shipped under before I came on board the *Indefeasible*," Averdor said, "was one of those people who don't even trust themselves. They expect everybody they meet to slip a knife into them when their backs are turned. And there are always other people who make it almost a point of honor to knife a man like that, just because he seems to be asking for it. He didn't hold that command long."

"I see what you mean," Gorbel said. "Well, I'll think about it."

But by the next ship's day, when Hoqqueah returned to the greenhouse, Gorbel still had not made up his mind. The very fact that his own feelings, were on the side of Averdor and the crew made him suspicious of Averdor's "easy" solution. The plan was tempting enough to blind a tempted man to flaws that might otherwise be obvious.

The Adapted Man settled himself comfortably and looked out through the transparent metal. "Ah," he said. "Our target is sensibly bigger now, eh, Captain? Think of it: in just a few days now, we will be—in the historical sense—home again."

And now it was riddles! "What do you mean?" Gorbel said.

"I'm sorry; I thought you knew. Earth is the home planet of the human race, Captain. There is where the basic form evolved."

Gorbel considered this unexpected bit of information cautiously. Even assuming that it was true—and it probably was; that would be the kind of thing Hoqqueah would know about a planet to which he was assigned—it didn't seem to make any special difference in the situation. But Hoqqueah had obviously brought it out for a reason. Well, he'd be trotting out the reason, too, soon enough; nobody would ever accuse the Altarian of being taciturn.

Nevertheless, he considered turning on the screen for a close look at the planet. Up to now he had felt not the slightest interest in it.

"Yes, there's where it all began," Hoqqueah said. "Of course at first it never occurred to those people that they might produce pre-adapted children. They went to all kinds of extremes to adapt their environment instead, or to carry it along with them. But they finally realized that with the planets, that won't work. You can't spend your life in a space suit, or under a dome, either.

"Besides, they had had form trouble in their society from their earliest days. For centuries, they were absurdly touchy over minute differences in coloring and shape, and even in thinking. They had regime after regime that tried to impose its own concept of the standard citizen on everybody, and enslaved those who didn't fit the specs."

Abruptly, Hoqqueah's chatter began to make Gorbel uncomfortable. It was becoming easier and easier to sympathize with Averdor's determination to ignore the Adapted Man's existence entirely.

"It was only after they'd painfully taught themselves that such differences really don't matter that they could go on to pantropy," Hoqqueah said. "It was the logical conclusion. Of course, a certain continuity of form had to be maintained, and has been maintained to this day. You cannot totally change the form without totally changing the thought processes. If you give a man the form of a cockroach, as one ancient writer foresaw, he will wind up thinking like a cockroach, not like a human being. We recognized that. On worlds where only extreme modifications of the human form would make it suitable—for instance, a planet of the gas giant type—no seeding is attempted. The Council maintains that such worlds are the potential property of other races than the human, races whose psychotypes would not have to undergo radical change in order to survive there."

Dimly, Captain Gorbel saw where Hoqqueah was leading him, and he did not like what he saw. The seal-man, in his own maddeningly indirect way, was arguing his right to be considered an equal in fact as well as in law. He was arguing it, however, in a universe of discourse totally unfamiliar to Captain Gorbel, with facts whose validity he alone knew and whose relevance he alone could judge. He was, in short, loading the dice, and the last residues of Gorbel's tolerance were evaporating rapidly.

"Of course there was resistance back there at the beginning," Hoqqueah said. "The kind of mind that had only recently been persuaded that colored men are human beings was quick to take the attitude that an Adapted Man— any Adapted Man—was the social inferior of the 'primary' or basic human type, the type that lived on Earth. But it was also a very old idea on the Earth that basic humanity inheres in the mind, not in the form.

"You see, Captain, all this might still have been prevented, had it been possible to maintain the attitude that changing the form even in part makes a man less of a man than he was in the 'primary' state. But the day has come when that attitude is no longer tenable—a day that is the greatest of all moral watersheds for our race, the day that is to unite all our divergent currents of attitudes toward each other into one common reservoir of brotherhood and purpose. You and I are very fortunate to be on the scene to see it."

"Very interesting," Gorbel said coldly. "But all those things happened a long time ago, and we know very little about this part of the galaxy these days. Under the circumstances—which you'll find clearly written out in the log, together with the appropriate regulations—I'm forced to place the ship on emergency alert beginning tomorrow, and continuing until your team disembarks. I'm afraid that means that henceforth all passengers will be required to stay in quarters."

Hoqqueah turned and arose. His eyes were still warm and liquid, but there was no longer any trace of merriment in them.

"I know very well what it means," he said. "And to some extent, I understand the need—though I had been hoping to see the planet of our birth first from space. But I don't think *you* quite understand *me*, Captain. The moral watershed of which I spoke is not in the past. It is now. It began the day that the Earth itself became no longer habitable for the so-called basic human type. The flowing of the streams toward the common reservoir will become bigger and bigger as word spreads through the galaxy that Earth itself has been seeded with Adapted Men. With that news will go a shock of recognition—the shock of realizing that the 'basic' types are now, and have been for a long time, a very small minority, despite their pretensions."

Was Hoqqueah being absurd enough to threaten—an unarmed, comical seal-man shaking a fist at the captain of the *Indefeasible?* Or—

"Before I go, let me ask you this one question, Captain. Down there is your home planet, and my team and I will be going out on its surface before long. Do you dare to follow us out of the ship?"

"And why should I?" Gorbel said.

"Why, to show the superiority of the basic type, Captain," Hoqqueah said softly. "Surely you cannot admit that a pack of seal-men are your betters, on your own ancestral ground!"

He bowed and went to the door. Just before he reached it, he turned and looked speculatively at Gorbel and at Lieutenant Averdor, who was staring at him with an expression of rigid fury.

"Or can you?" he said. "It will be interesting to see how you manage to comport yourselves as a minority. I think you lack practice."

He went out. Both Gorbel and Averdor turned jerkily to the screen, and Gorbel turned it on. The image grew, steadied, settled down.

When the next trick came on duty, both men were still staring at the vast and tumbled desert of the Earth.

Slow Tuesday Night

R. A. LAFFERTY

R. A. Lafferty started writing in 1960, at the relatively advanced age (for a new writer, anyway) of forty-six, and in the years before his retirement in 1987, he published some of the freshest and funniest short stories ever written, almost all of them dancing on the borderlines between fantasy, science fiction, and the tall tale in its most boisterous and quintessentially American of forms.

Lafferty has published memorable novels that stand up quite well today—among the best of them are Past Master, The Devil Is Dead, The Reefs of Earth, *the historical novel* Okla Hannali, *and the totally unclassifiable* The Fall of Rome—*but it is stories like "Narrow Valley," "Thus We Frustrate Charlemagne," "Hog-Belly Honey," "The Hole on the Corner," "All Pieces of a River Shore," "Among the Hairy Earthmen," "Seven Day Terror," "Continued on Next Rock," "All But the Words," and many others, that would establish his reputation, all clearly demonstrating his characteristic virtues: folksy exuberance, a singing lyricism of surprising depth and power, outlandish imagination, a store of offbeat erudition matched only by Avram Davidson, and a strong, shaggy sense of humor unrivaled by anyone.*

His short work has been gathered in the landmark collection Nine Hundred Grandmothers, *as well as in* Strange Doings, Does Anyone Else Have Something Further to Add?, Golden Gate and Other Stories, *and* Ringing the Changes. *Lafferty retired from writing in 1987, at age seventy-three. His other books include the novels* Archipelago, My Heart Leaps Up, Fourth Mansions, Arrive At Easterwine, Space Chantey, *and* The Flame Is Green. *Lafferty won the Hugo Award in 1973 for his story "Eurema's Dam," and in 1990 received the World Fantasy Award, the prestigious Life Achievement Award. His most recent books are the collections* Lafferty in Orbit *and* Iron Star. *He lives in Oklahoma.*

Here, with characteristic brio and elan, he shows us that if you're worried about the accelerating rate of Future Shock, just hang on a moment—you ain't see nothing yet!

A panhandler intercepted the young couple as they strolled down the night street.

"Preserve us this night," he said as he touched his hat to them, "and could you good people advance me a thousand dollars to be about the recouping of my fortunes?"

"I gave you a thousand last Friday," said the young man.

"Indeed you did," the panhandler replied, "and I paid you back tenfold by messenger before midnight."

"That's right, George, he did," said the young woman. "Give it to him, dear. I believe he's a good sort."

So the young man gave the panhandler a thousand dollars, and the panhandler touched his hat to them in thanks and went on to the recouping of his fortunes.

As he went into Money Market, the panhandler passed Ildefonsa Impala, the most beautiful woman in the city.

"Will you marry me this night, Ildy?" he asked cheerfully.

"Oh, I don't believe so, Basil," she said. "I marry you pretty often, but tonight I don't seem to have any plans at all. You may make me a gift on your first or second, however. I always like that."

But when they had parted she asked herself: "But whom will I marry tonight?"

The panhandler was Basil Bagelbaker, who would be the richest man in the world within an hour and a half. He would make and lose four fortunes within eight hours; and these not the little fortunes that ordinary men acquire, but titanic things.

When the Abebaios block had been removed from human minds, people began to make decisions faster, and often better. It had been the mental stutter. When it was understood what it was, and that it had no useful function, it was removed by simple childhood metasurgery.

Transportation and manufacturing had then become practically instantaneous. Things that had once taken months and years now took only minutes and hours. A person could have one or several pretty intricate careers within an eight-hour period.

Freddy Fixico had just invented a manus module. Freddy was a Nyctalops, and the modules were characteristic of these people. The people had then divided themselves—according to their natures and inclinations—into the Auroreans, the Hemerobians, and the Nyctalops—or the Dawners, who had their most active hours from four A.M. till noon; the Day-Flies, who obtained from noon to eight P.M.; and the Night-Seers, whose civilization thrived from eight P.M. to four A.M. The cultures, inventions, markets and activities of these three folk were a little different. As a Nyctalops, Freddy had just begun his working day at eight P.M. on a slow Tuesday night.

Freddy rented an office and had it furnished. This took one minute, negotiation, selection and installation being almost instantaneous. Then he invented the manus module; that took another minute. He then had it manufactured and marketed; in three minutes it was in the hands of key buyers.

It caught on. It was an attractive module. The flow of orders began within thirty seconds. By ten minutes after eight every important person had one of the new manus modules, and the trend had been set. The module began to sell in the millions. It was one of the most interesting fads of the night, or at least the early part of the night.

Manus modules had no practical function, no more than had Sameki verses. They were attractive, of a psychologically satisfying size and shape, and could be held in the hands, set on a table, or installed in a module niche of any wall.

Naturally Freddy became very rich. Ildefonsa Impala, the most beautiful woman in the city, was always interested in newly rich men. She came to see Freddy about eight-thirty. People made up their minds fast, and Ildefonsa had

hers made up when she came. Freddy made his own up quickly and divorced
Judy Fixico in Small Claims Court. Freddy and Ildefonsa went honeymooning
to Paraiso Dorado, a resort.

It was wonderful. All of Ildy's marriages were. There was the wonderful
floodlighted scenery. The recirculated water of the famous falls was tinted
gold; the immediate rocks had been done by Rambles; and the hills had been
contoured by Spall. The beach was a perfect copy of that at Merevale, and
the popular drink that first part of the night was blue absinthe.

But scenery—whether seen for the first time or revisited after an interval—is striking for the sudden intense view of it. It is not meant to be
lingered over. Food, selected and prepared instantly, is eaten with swift en-
joyment; and blue absinthe lasts no longer than its own novelty. Loving, for
Ildefonsa and her paramours, was quick and consuming; and repetition would
have been pointless to her. Besides, Ildefonsa and Freddy had taken only the
one-hour luxury honeymoon.

Freddy wished to continue the relationship, but Ildefonsa glanced at a
trend indicator. The manus module would hold its popularity for only the
first third of the night. Already it had been discarded by people who mattered.
And Freddy Fixico was not one of the regular successes. He enjoyed a full
career only about one night a week.

They were back in the city and divorced in Small Claims Court by nine
thirty-five. The stock of manus modules was remandered, and the last of it
would be disposed to bargain hunters among the Dawners, who will buy
anything.

"Whom shall I marry next?" Ildefonsa asked herself. "It looks like a slow
night."

"Bagelbaker is buying," ran the word through Money Market, but Bagelbaker was selling again before the word had made its rounds. Basil Bagelbaker
enjoyed making money, and it was a pleasure to watch him work as he dominated the floor of the Market and assembled runners and a competent staff
out of the corner of his mouth. Helpers stripped the panhandler rags off him
and wrapped him in a tycoon toga. He sent one runner to pay back twentyfold
the young couple who had advanced him a thousand dollars. He sent another
with a more substantial gift to Ildefonsa Impala, for Basil cherished their
relationship. Basil acquired title to the Trend Indication Complex and had
certain falsifications set into it. He caused to collapse certain industrial empires that had grown up within the last two hours, and made a good thing
of recombining their wreckage. He had been the richest man in the world
for some minutes now. He became so money-heavy that he could not maneuver with the agility he had shown an hour before. He became a great fat
buck, and the pack of expert wolves circled him to bring him down.

Very soon he would lose that first fortune of the evening. The secret of
Basil Bagelbaker is that he enjoyed losing money spectacularly after he was
full of it to the bursting point.

A thoughtful man named Maxwell Mouser had just produced a work of
actinic philosophy. It took him seven minutes to write it. To write works of
philosophy one used the flexible outlines and the idea indexes; one set the

activator for such a wordage in each subsection; an adept would use the paradox feed-in, and the striking-analogy blender; one calibrated the particular-slant and the personality-signature. It had to come out a good work, for excellence had become the automatic minimum for such productions.

"I will scatter a few nuts on the frosting," said Maxwell, and he pushed the lever for that. This sifted handfuls of words like chthonic and heuristic and prozymeides through the thing so that nobody could doubt it was a work of philosophy.

Maxwell Mouser sent the work out to publishers, and received it back each time in about three minutes. An analysis of it and reason for rejection was always given—mostly that the thing had been done before and better. Maxwell received it back ten times in thirty minutes, and was discouraged. Then there was a break.

Ladion's work had become a hit within the last ten minutes, and it was now recognized that Mouser's monograph was both an answer and a supplement to it. It was accepted and published in less than a minute after this break. The reviews of the first five minutes were cautious ones; then real enthusiasm was shown. This was truly one of the greatest works of philosophy to appear during the early and medium hours of the night. There were those who said it might be one of the enduring works and even have a holdover appeal to the Dawners the next morning.

Naturally Maxwell became very rich, and naturally Ildefonsa came to see him about midnight. Being a revolutionary philosopher, Maxwell thought that they might make some free arrangement, but Ildefonsa insisted it must be marriage. So Maxwell divorced Judy Mouser in Small Claims Court and went off with Ildefonsa.

This Judy herself, though not so beautiful as Ildefonsa, was the fastest taker in the city. She only wanted the men of the moment for a moment, and she was always there before even Ildefonsa. Ildefonsa believed that she took the men away from Judy; Judy said that Ildy had her leavings and nothing else.

"I had him first," Judy would always mock as she raced through Small Claims Court.

"Oh that damned urchin!" Ildefonsa would moan. "She wears my very hair before I do."

Maxwell Mouser and Ildefonsa Impala went honeymooning to Musicbox Mountain, a resort. It was wonderful. The peaks were done with green snow by Dunbar and Fittle. (Back at Money Market, Basil Bagelbaker was putting together his third and greatest fortune of the night, which might surpass in magnitude even his fourth fortune of the Thursday before.) The chalets were Switzier than the real Swiss and had live goats in every room. (And Stanley Skuldugger was emerging as the top Actor-Imago of the middle hours of the night.) The popular drink for that middle part of the night was Glotzenglubber, Eve Cheese and Rhine wine over pink ice. (And back in the city the leading Nyctalops were taking their midnight break at the Toppers' Club.)

Of course it was wonderful, as were all of Ildefonsa's. But she had never been really up on philosophy, so she had scheduled only the special thirty-five-minute honeymoon. She looked at the trend indicator to be sure. She found that her current husband had been obsoleted, and his opus was now referred to sneeringly as Mouser's Mouse. They went back to the city and were divorced in Small Claims Court.

The membership of the Toppers' Club varied. Success was the requisite of membership. Basil Bagelbaker might be accepted as a member, elevated to the presidency, and expelled from it as a dirty pauper from three to six times a night. But only important persons could belong to it, or those enjoying brief moments of importance.

"I believe I will sleep during the Dawner period in the morning," Overcall said. "I may go up to this new place, Koimopolis, for an hour of it. They're said to be good. Where will you sleep, Basil?"

"Flop house."

"I believe I will sleep an hour by the Midian Method," said Burnbanner. "They have a fine new clinic. And perhaps I'll sleep an hour by the Prasenka Process, and an hour by the Dormidio."

"Crackle has been sleeping an hour every period by the natural method," said Overcall.

"I did that for half an hour not long since," said Burnbanner. "I believe an hour is too long to give it. Have you tried the natural method, Basil?"

"Always. Natural method and a bottle of red-eye."

Stanley Skuldugger had become the most meteoric actor-imago for a week. Naturally he became very rich, and Ildefonsa Impala went to see him about three A.M.

"I had him first!" rang the mocking voice of Judy Skuldugger as she skipped through her divorce in Small Claims Court. And Ildefonsa and Stanley-boy went off honeymooning. It is always fun to finish up a period with an actor-imago who is the hottest property in the business. There is something so adolescent and boorish about them.

Besides, there was the publicity, and Ildefonsa liked that. The rumor-mills ground. Would it last ten minutes? Thirty? An hour? Would it be one of those rare Nyctalops marriages that lasted through the rest of the night and into the daylight off-hours? Would it even last into the next night as some had been known to do?

Actually it lasted nearly forty minutes, which was almost to the end of the period.

It had been a slow Tuesday night. A few hundred new products had run their course on the markets. There had been a score of dramatic hits, three-minute and five-minute capsule dramas, and several of the six-minute long-play affairs. *Night Street Nine*—a solidly sordid offering—seemed to be in as the drama of the night unless there should be a late hit.

Hundred-storied buildings had been erected, occupied, obsoleted, and de-molished again to make room for more contemporary structures. Only the mediocre would use a building that had been left over from the Day Fliers or the Dawners, or even the Nyctalops of the night before. The city was rebuilt pretty completely at least three times during an eight-hour period.

The period drew near its end. Basil Bagelbaker, the richest man in the world, the reigning president of the Toppers' Club, was enjoying himself with his cronies. His fourth fortune of the night was a paper pyramid that had risen to incredible heights; but Basil laughed to himself as he savored the manipulation it was founded on.

Three ushers of the Toppers' Club came in with firm step.

"Get out of here, you dirty bum!" they told Basil savagely. They tore the tycoon's toga off him and then tossed him his seedy panhandler's rags with a three-man sneer.

"All gone?" Basil asked. "I gave it another five minutes."

"All gone," said a messenger from Money Market. "Nine billion gone in five minutes, and it really pulled some others down with it."

"Pitch the busted bum out!" howled Overcall and Burnbanner and the other cronies.

"Wait, Basil," said Overcall. "Turn in the President's Crosier before we kick you downstairs. After all, you'll have it several times again tomorrow night."

The period was over. The Nyctalops drifted off to sleep clinics or leisure-hour hideouts to pass their ebb time. The Auroreans, the Dawners, took over the vital stuff.

Now you would see some action! Those Dawners really made fast decisions. You wouldn't catch them wasting a full minute setting up a business.

A sleepy panhandler met Ildefonsa Impala on the way.

"Preserve us this morning, Ildy," he said, "and will you marry me the coming night?"

"Likely I will, Basil," she told him. "Did you marry Judy during the night past?"

"I'm not sure. Could you let me have two dollars, Ildy?"

"Out of the question. I believe a Judy Bagelbaker was named one of the ten best-dressed women during the frou-frou fashion period about two o'clock. Why do you need two dollars?"

"A dollar for a bed and a dollar for red-eye. After all, I sent you two million out of my second."

"I keep my two sorts of accounts separate. Here's a dollar, Basil. Now be off! I can't be seen talking to a dirty panhandler."

"Thank you, Ildy. I'll get the red-eye and sleep in an alley. Preserve us this morning."

Bagelbaker shuffled off whistling "Slow Tuesday Night."

And already the Dawners had set Wednesday morning to jumping.

Aye, and Gomorrah

SAMUEL R. DELANY

Samuel R. Delany was widely acknowledged during the sixties as one of the two most important and influential American SF writers of that decade (the other being Roger Zelazny). He won the Nebula Award in 1966 for Babel 17, *won two more Nebulas in 1967 for* The Einstein Intersection *and for his first short story, "Aye, and Gomorrah," and his 1968 novella "Time Considered as a Helix of Semi-Precious Stones," won both the Nebula and Hugo awards. By 1969, critic Algis Budrys was hailing him as "the best science-fiction writer in the world"—an opinion it would have been possible to find a great deal of support for, at least on the American side of the Atlantic; he is still regarded by many critics as one of our greatest living authors. His monumental novel* Nova *was, in my opinion, one of the very best SF novels of the sixties, and its influence on everything from the Shaper/Mechanist stories of Bruce Sterling, on through William Gibson and Michael Swanwick, and on to the work of nineties' authors such as Paul J. McAuley and Alastair Reynolds, is impossible to overestimate.*

Delany only ever wrote a handful of short stories—unlike Zelazny, he made his biggest impact on the field with his novels—but they deserve to be numbered among the best short work of the sixties. Aside from the stories already named, they include the marvelous novella "The Star Pit," the ornately titled "We, In Some Strange Power's Employ, Move On A Rigorous Line," "Corona," and "Dog in a Fisherman's Net." Almost all of his short fiction was assembled in the landmark collection Driftglass. *Which contains the elegant, tight, and poetically intense story that follows, an early look at the posthuman condition, as science makes the boundary lines of race, class, and even sex, obsolete, in favor of sharply drawn new boundaries. . . .*

After Nova, *Delany fell silent for seven years, and when he did return, it was with work that no longer had as broad an appeal within the genre, like the immense, surreal* Dhalgren—*which did, however, become a best-seller outside of the usual genre boundaries, and help to gain him wide, new audiences. Although he did publish two more science-fiction novels,* Triton *and* Stars in My Pocket Like Grains of Sand, *most of his work throughout the decades that followed took him beyond the boundaries of the genre as they are usually drawn, first with a series of ornate and somewhat abstract intellectual fantasy works such as* Flight from Neveryon, The Bridge of Lost Desire, *and* Tales of Neveryon, *and then on into mainstream works such as* Atlantis: Three Tales *and* The Mad Men; *he has also created a large body of criticism and nonfiction writing, including* Times Square Red, Times Square Blue, 1984, The Jewel-Hinged Jaw, Starboard Wine, The Straits of Messina, The American Shore, The Motion of Light in Water, Heavenly Breakfast, *and* Silent Interviews: on Languages, Race, Sex, Science Fiction, and Some Comics. *Delany's other books include the novels* The Jewels of Aptor, The Fall of the Towers, The Ballad of Beta-2, *and* Empire Star.

And came down in Paris:

Where we raced along the Rue de Médicis with Bo and Lou and Muse inside the fence, Kelly and me outside, making faces through the bars, making noise, making the Luxembourg Gardens roar at two in the morning. Then climbed out, and down to the square in front of St. Sulpice where Bo tried to knock me into the fountain.

At which point Kelly noticed what was going on around us, got an ashcan cover, and ran into the pissoir, banging the walls. Five guys scooted out; even a big pissoir only holds four.

A very blond young man put his hand on my arm and smiled. "Don't you think, Spacer, that you . . . people should leave?"

I looked at his hand on my blue uniform. "*Est-ce que tu es un frelk?*"

His eyebrows rose, then he shook his head. "Une *frelk*," he corrected. "No. I am not. Sadly for me. You look as though you may once have been a man. But now . . ." He smiled. "You have nothing for me now. The police." He nodded across the street where I noticed the gendarmerie for the first time. "They don't bother us. You are strangers, though . . ."

But Muse was already yelling, "Hey, come on! Let's get out of here, huh?" And left. And went up again.

And came down in Houston:

"God damn!" Muse said. "Gemini Flight Control—you mean this is where it all started? Let's get *out* of here, *please!*"

So took a bus out through Pasadena, then the monoline to Galveston, and were going to take it down the Gulf, but Lou found a couple with a pickup truck—

"Glad to give you a ride, Spacers. You people up there on them planets and things, doing all that good work for the government."

—who were going south, them and the baby, so we rode in the back for two hundred and fifty miles of sun and wind.

"You think they're frelks?" Lou asked, elbowing me. "I bet they're frelks. They're just waiting for us to give 'em the come-on."

"Cut it out. They're a nice, stupid pair of country kids."

"That don't mean they ain't frelks!"

"You don't trust anybody, do you?"

"No."

And finally a bus again that rattled us through Brownsville and across the border into Matamoros where we staggered down the steps into the dust and the scorched evening with a lot of Mexicans and chickens and Texas Gulf shrimp fishermen—who smelled worst—and *we* shouted the loudest. Forty-three whores—I counted—had turned out for the shrimp fishermen, and by the time we had broken two of the windows in the bus station, they were all laughing. The shrimp fishermen said they wouldn't buy us no food but would get us drunk if we wanted, 'cause that was the custom with shrimp fishermen. But we yelled, broke another window; then, while I was lying on my back on the telegraph-office steps, singing, a woman with dark lips bent over and put her hands on my cheeks. "You are very sweet." Her rough hair fell forward. "But the men, they are standing around and watching *you*. And that is taking up *time*. Sadly, their time is our money. Spacer, do you not think you . . . people should leave?"

I grabbed her wrist. *"Usted!"* I whispered. *"Usted es una frelka?"*

"Frelko in español." She smiled and patted the sunburst that hung from my belt buckle. "Sorry. But you have nothing that . . . would be useful to me. It is too bad, for you look like you were once a woman, no? And I like women, too . . ."

I rolled off the porch.

"Is this a drag, or is this a drag!" Muse was shouting. "Come *on*! Let's *go*!"

We managed to get back to Houston before dawn, somehow. And went up. And came down in Istanbul:

That morning it rained in Istanbul.

At the commissary we drank our tea from pear-shaped glasses, looking out across the Bosphorus. The Princes Islands lay like trash heaps before the prickly city.

"Who knows their way in this town?" Kelly asked.

"Aren't we going around together?" Muse demanded. "I thought we were going around together."

"They held up my check at the purser's office," Kelly explained. "I'm flat broke. I think the purser's got it in for me," and shrugged. "Don't want to, but I'm going to have to hunt up a rich frelk and come on friendly," went back to the tea; *then* noticed how heavy the silence had become. "Aw, come *on*, now! You gape at me like that and I'll bust every bone in that carefully-conditioned-from-puberty body of yours. Hey you!" meaning me. "Don't give me that holier-than-thou gawk like you never went with no frelk!"

It was starting.

"I'm not gawking," I said and got quietly mad.

The longing, the old longing.

Bo laughed to break tensions. "Say, last time I was in Istanbul—about a year before I joined up with this platoon—I remember we were coming out of Taksim Square down Istiqlal. Just past all the cheap movies, we found a little passage lined with flowers. Ahead of us were two other spacers. It's a market in there, and farther down they got fish, and then a courtyard with oranges and candy and sea urchins and cabbage. But flowers in front. Anyway, we noticed something funny about the spacers. It wasn't their uniforms; they were perfect. The haircuts: fine. It wasn't till we heard them talking—they were a man and woman dressed up like spacers, trying *to pick up frelks*! Imagine, queer for frelks!"

"Yeah," Lou said. "I seen that before. There were a lot of them in Rio."

"We beat hell out of them two," Bo concluded. "We got them in a side street and went to *town*!"

Muse's tea glass clicked on the counter. "From Taksim down Istiqlal till you get to the flowers? Now why didn't you say that's where the frelks were, huh?" A smile on Kelly's face would have made that okay. There was no smile.

"Hell," Lou said, "nobody ever had to tell me where to look. I go out in the street and frelks smell me coming. I can spot 'em halfway along Piccadilly. Don't they have nothing but tea in this place? Where can you get a drink?"

Bo grinned. "Moslem country, remember? But down at the end of the Flower Passage there're a lot of little bars with green doors and marble counters where you can get a liter of beer for about fifteen cents in lira. And they're all these stands selling deep-fat-fried bugs and pig's-gut sandwiches—"

"You ever notice how frelks can put it away? I mean liquor, not . . . pig's guts."

And launched off into a lot of appeasing stories. We ended with the one about the frelk some spacer tried to roll who announced: "There are two things I go for. One is spacers; the other is a good fight . . ."

But they only allay. They cure nothing. Even Muse knew we would spend the day apart, now.

The rain had stopped, so we took the ferry up the Golden Horn. Kelly straight off asked for Taksim Square and Istiqlal and was directed to a dolmush, which we discovered was a taxicab, only it just goes one place and picks up lots and lots of people on the way. And it's cheap.

Lou headed off over Ataturk Bridge to see the sights of New City. Bo decided to find out what the Dolma Boche really was; and when Muse discovered you could go to Asia for fifteen cents—one lira and fifty krush— well, Muse decided to go to Asia.

I turned through the confusion of traffic at the head of the bridge and up past the gray, dripping walls of Old City, beneath the trolley wires. There are times when yelling and helling won't fill the lack. There are times when you must walk by yourself because it hurts so much to be alone.

I walked up a lot of little streets with wet donkeys and wet camels and women in veils; and down a lot of big streets with buses and trash baskets and men in business suits.

Some people stare at spacers; some people don't. Some people stare or don't stare in a way a spacer gets to recognize within a week after coming out of training school at sixteen. I was walking in the park when I caught her watching. She saw me see and looked away.

I ambled down the wet asphalt. She was standing under the arch of a small, empty mosque shell. As I passed she walked out into the courtyard among the cannons.

"Excuse me."

I stopped.

"Do you know whether or not this is the shrine of St. Irene?" Her English was charmingly accented. "I've left my guidebook home."

"Sorry. I'm a tourist too."

"Oh." She smiled. "I am Greek. I thought you might be Turkish because you are so dark."

"American red Indian." I nodded. Her turn to curtsy.

"I see. I have just started at the university here in Istanbul. Your uniform, it tells me that you are—" and in the pause, all speculations resolved "—a spacer."

I was uncomfortable. "Yeah." I put my hands in my pockets, moved my feet around on the soles of my boots, licked my third from the rear left molar—did all the things you do when you're uncomfortable. *You're so exciting when you look like that*, a frelk told me once. "Yeah, I am." I said it too sharply, too loudly, and she jumped a little.

So now she knew I knew she knew I knew, and I wondered how we would play out the Proust bit.

"I'm Turkish," she said. "I'm not Greek. I'm not just starting. I'm a graduate in art history here at the university. These little lies one makes for strangers to protect one's ego . . . why? Sometimes I think my ego is very small."

That's one strategy.

"How far away do you live?" I asked. "And what's the going rate in Turkish lira?" That's another.

"I can't pay you." She pulled her raincoat around her hips. She was very pretty. "I would like to." She shrugged and smiled. "But I am . . . a poor student. Not a rich one. If you want to turn around and walk away, there will be no hard feelings. I shall be sad, though."

I stayed on the path. I thought she'd suggest a price after a little while. She didn't.

And *that's* another.

I was asking myself, *What do you want the damn money for anyway?* when a breeze upset water from one of the park's great cypresses.

"I think the whole business is sad." She wiped drops from her face. There had been a break in her voice and for a moment I looked too closely at the water streaks. "I think it's sad that they have to alter you to make you a spacer. If they hadn't, then *we* . . . If spacers had never been, then we could not be . . . the way we are. Did you start out male or female?"

Another shower. I was looking at the ground and droplets went down my collar.

"Male," I said. "It doesn't matter."

"How old are you? Twenty-three, twenty-four?"

"Twenty-three," I lied. It's reflex. I'm twenty-five, but the younger they think you are, the more they pay you. But I didn't *want* her *damn* money—

"I guessed right then." She nodded. "Most of us are experts on spacers. Do you find that? I suppose we have to be." She looked at me with wide black eyes. At the end of the stare, she blinked rapidly. "You would have been a fine man. But now you are a spacer, building water-conservation units on Mars, programming mining computers on Ganymede, servicing communication relay towers on the moon. The alteration . . ." Frelks are the only people I've ever heard say "the alteration" with so much fascination and regret. "You'd think they'd have found some other solution. They could have found another way than neutering you, turning you into creatures not even androgynous; things that are—"

I put my hand on her shoulder, and she stopped like I'd hit her. She looked to see if anyone was near. Lightly, so lightly then, she raised her hand to mine.

I pulled my hand away. "That are what?"

"They could have found another way." Both hands in her pockets now.

"They could have. Yes. Up beyond the ionosphere, baby, there's too much radiation for those precious gonads to work right anywhere you might want to do something that would keep you there over twenty-four hours, like the moon, or Mars, or the satellites of Jupiter—"

"They could have made protective shields. They could have done more research into biological adjustment—"

"Population Explosion time," I said. "No, they were hunting for any excuse to cut down kids back then—especially deformed ones."

"Ah, yes." She nodded. "We're still fighting our way up from the neo-puritan reaction to the sex freedom of the twentieth century."

"It was a fine solution." I grinned and hung my hand over my crotch. "I'm happy with it." I've never known why that's so much more obscene when a spacer does it.

"Stop it," she snapped, moving away.

"What's the matter?"

"Stop it," she repeated. "Don't do that! You're a child."

"But they choose us from children whose sexual responses are hopelessly retarded at puberty."

"And your childish, violent substitutes for love? I suppose that's one of the things that's attractive. Yes, I know you're a child."

"Yeah? What about frelks?"

She thought a while. "I think they are the sexually retarded ones they miss. Perhaps it was the right solution. You really don't regret you have no sex?"

"We've got you," I said.

"Yes." She looked down. I glanced to see the expression she was hiding. It was a smile. "You have your glorious, soaring life, *and* you have us." Her face came up. She glowed. "You spin in the sky, the world spins under you, and you step from land to land, while we . . ." She turned her head right, left, and her black hair curled and uncurled on the shoulder of her coat. "We have our dull, circled lives, bound in gravity, *worshiping* you!"

She looked back at me. "Perverted, yes? In love with a bunch of corpses in free fall!" She suddenly hunched her shoulders. "I don't like having a free-fall-sexual-displacement complex."

"That always sounded like too much to say."

She looked away. "I don't like being a frelk. Better?"

"I wouldn't like it either. Be something else."

"You don't choose your perversions. *You* have no perversions at all. You're free of the whole business. I love you for that, Spacer. My love starts with the fear of love. Isn't that beautiful? A pervert substitutes something unattainable for 'normal' love: the homosexual, a mirror, the fetishist, a shoe or a watch or a girdle. Those with free-fall-sexual-dis—"

"Frelks."

"Frelks substitute—" she looked at me sharply again "—loose, swinging meat."

"That doesn't offend me."

"I wanted it to."

"Why?"

"You don't have desires. You wouldn't understand."

"Go on."

"I want you because you can't want me. That's the pleasure. If someone really had a sexual reaction to . . . us, we'd be scared away. I wonder how many people there were before there were you, waiting for your creation. We're necrophiles. I'm sure grave-robbing has fallen off since you started going up. But you don't understand . . ." She paused. "If you did, then I wouldn't be scuffing leaves now and trying to think from whom I could borrow sixty lira." She stepped over the knuckles of a root that had cracked the pavement. "And that, incidentally, is the going rate in Istanbul."

I calculated. "Things still get cheaper as you go east."

"You know," and she let her raincoat fall open, "you're different from the others. You at least *want* to know—"

I said, "If I spat on you for every time you'd said that to a spacer, you'd drown."

"Go back to the moon, loose meat." She closed her eyes. "Swing on up to Mars. There are satellites around Jupiter where you might do some good. Go up and come down in some other city."

"Where do you live?"

"You want to come with me?"

"Give me something," I said. "Give me something—it doesn't have to be worth sixty lira. Give me something you like, anything of yours that means something to you."

"No!"

"Why not?"

"Because I—"

"—don't want to give up part of that small ego. None of you frelks do!"

"You really don't understand I just don't want to buy you?"

"You have nothing to buy me with."

"You are a child," she said. "I love you."

We reached the gate of the park. She stopped, and we stood time enough for a breeze to rise and die in the grass.

"I . . ." she offered tentatively, pointing without taking her hand from her coat pocket. "I live right down there."

"All right," I said. "Let's go."

A gas main had once exploded along this street, she explained to me, a gushing road of fire as far as the docks, overhot and overquick. It had been put out within minutes, no building had fallen, but the charred fascias glittered. "This is sort of an artist and student quarter." We crossed the cobbles. "Yuri Pasha, number fourteen. In case you're ever in Istanbul again." Her door was covered with black scales, the gutter was thick with garbage.

"A lot of artists and professional people are frelks," I said, trying to be inane.

"So are lots of other people." She walked inside and held the door. "We're just more flamboyant about it."

On the landing there was a portrait of Ataturk. Her room was on the second floor. "Just a moment while I get my key—"

Marsscapes! Moonscapes! On her easel was a six-foot canvas showing the sunrise flaring on a crater's rim! There were copies of the original Observer pictures of the moon pinned to the wall, and pictures of every smooth-faced general in the International Spacer Corps.

On one corner of her desk was a pile of those photo magazines about spacers that you can find in most kiosks all over the world: I've seriously heard people say they were printed for adventurous-minded high-school children. They've never seen the Danish ones. She had a few of those, too. There was a shelf of art books, art history texts. Above them were six feet of cheap paper-covered space operas: *Sin on Space Station #12*, *Rocket Rake*, *Savage Orbit*.

"Arrack?" she asked. "Ouzo or pernod? You've got your choice. But I may pour them all from the same bottle." She set out glasses on the desk, then opened a waist-high cabinet that turned out to be an icebox. She stood up with a tray of lovelies: fruit puddings, Turkish delight, braised meats.

"What's this?"

"Dolmades. Grape leaves filled with rice and pignoli."

"Say it again?"

"Dolmades. Comes from the same Turkish word as 'dolmush.' They both mean 'stuffed.' " She put the tray beside the glasses. "Sit down."

I sat on the studio-couch-that-becomes-bed. Under the brocade I felt the deep, fluid resilience of a glycogel mattress. They've got the idea that it approximates the feeling of free fall. "Comfortable? Would you excuse me for a moment? I have some friends down the hall. I want to see them for a moment." She winked. "They like spacers."

"Are you going to take up a collection for me?" I asked. "Or do you want them to line up outside the door and wait their turn?"

She sucked a breath. "Actually, I was going to suggest both." Suddenly she shook her head. "Oh, what do you want!"

"What will you give me? I want something," I said. "That's why I came. I'm lonely. Maybe I want to find out how far it goes. I don't know yet."

"It goes as far as you will. Me? I study, I read, paint, talk with my friends—" she came over to the bed, sat down on the floor "—go to the theater, look at spacers who pass me on the street, till one looks back; I am lonely, too." She put her head on my knee. "I want something. But," and after a minute neither of us had moved, "you are not the one who will give it to me."

"You're not going to pay me for it," I countered. "You're not, are you?"

On my knee her head shook. After a while she said, all breath and no voice, "Don't you think you . . . should leave?"

"Okay," I said, and stood up.

She sat back on the hem of her coat. She hadn't taken it off yet.

I went to the door.

"Incidentally." She folded her hands in her lap. "There is a place in New City you might find what you're looking for, called the Flower Passage—"

I turned toward her, angry. "The frelk hangout? Look, I don't *need* money? I said *anything* would do! I don't want—"

She had begun to shake her head, laughing quietly. Now she lay her cheek on the wrinkled place where I had sat. "Do you persist in misunderstanding? It is a spacer hangout. When you leave, I am going to visit my friends and talk about . . . ah, yes, the beautiful one that got away. I thought you might find . . . perhaps someone you know."

With anger, it ended.

"Oh," I said. "Oh, it's a spacer hangout. Yeah. Well, thanks."

And went out. And found the Flower Passage, and Kelly and Lou and Bo and Muse. Kelly was buying beer, so we all got drunk, and ate fried fish and fried clams and fried sausage, and Kelly was waving the money around, saying, "You should have seen him! The changes I put that frelk through, you should have *seen* him! Eighty lira is the going rate here, and he gave me a hundred and fifty!" and drank more beer.

And went up.

Nobody's Home

JOANNA RUSS

Joanna Russ would begin selling in the late fifties but did not become widely known until the late sixties. Even Russ's early work—stories such as "My Dear Emily," "There is Another Shore, You Know, Upon the Other Side," and "The New Men"—would display the same kind of wit, sophistication, and elegance of style that characterized her later work, and she might have established her reputation years earlier than she did if she had continued to steadily produce work like this, but her output was sparse throughout the first half of the decade, and mostly overlooked.

By 1967, Russ would be attracting attention with her "Alyx" stories, which at first seemed to be merely better-than-usually written sword & sorcery stories, featuring a tough-minded and wily female cutpurse rather than the usual male hero, sort of the Gray Mouser in drag (this may seem an obvious enough reversal now, when the fantasy genre is flooded with sword-swinging Amazons and swashbuckling women adventurers, but it was radical stuff at the time). The Alyx stories would veer suddenly into science fiction with "The Barbarian" in Orbit 3, *in which Alyx outwits a degenerate time-traveller; and then Alyx herself would be snatched out of the past and thrown into a decadent and fascinating future for Russ's first novel, 1968's* Picnic on Paradise, *the work with which she would make her first significant impact on the field, a work that even now strikes me as one of the best novels of the late sixties.*

By the early seventies, Russ would have published her complex second novel And Chaos Died, *won a Nebula Award for her controversial feminist story "When It Changed," and was producing work like the story that follows, "Nobody's Home," a sleek, sly, and blackly witty story that was years ahead of its time, especially in its brilliant depiction of what the society of the future was going to be like, and, more importantly, what the people who lived in it were going to be like—and how inferior we ourselves would appear by comparison, if we could somehow be measured against them. The rest of the genre wouldn't catch up to the kind of thing Russ was doing here, with unruffled ease and elegance, until the late eighties.*

By the early seventies, Russ was also, in some circles at least, one of the most hated writers in the business. I'm not quite sure why, since there were other writers around who were producing work that ostensibly seemed much farther from the aesthetic center of the field. Perhaps it was her large body of critical work—she was the regular reviewer for F&SF at one point—in which she would express a lot of unpopular opinions, although her often-incisive criticism can be shown to have had a demonstrable effect on other writers, such as Le Guin. Maybe it was just that she was an uppity woman who wouldn't stay in her place. Later, when she published her fierce and passionate feminist novel The Female Man *in 1975, she became a bête noire of unparalleled blackness, practically the Antichrist. Perhaps all this furor, added to the general malaise of the late seventies, contributed to her slow drift out of the field. She published two more books in the next three years—including her weakest novel, 1977's* We Who Are About To—*and then fell silent for several years.*

She returned to SF in 1982 with her Nebula- and Hugo-winning novella "Souls," and with the other stories that would go into making up Extra(ordinary) People, *and this time, ironically, instead of the conservative wing, it was the young, leftist, radical new writers who fiercely attacked her as part of the sellout Hugo-winning establishment. Almost nothing has been heard from Russ in SF since then, perhaps not surprisingly, although I hope that one day she'll decide to take another tour of duty on the barricades.*

Russ's other books include the novel The Two of Them, *the collections* The Zanzibar Cat, Extra(ordinary) People, The Adventures of Alyx, *and* The Hidden Side of the Moon, *and the critical works* Magic Mommas, Trembling Sisters, Puritans, and Perverts *and* How to Suppress Women's Writing.

After she had finished her work at the North Pole, Jannina came down to the Red Sea refineries, where she had family business, jumped to New Delhi for dinner, took a nap in a public bed in Queensland, walked from the hotel to the station, bypassed the Leeward Islands (where she thought she might go, but all the stations were busy), and met Charley to watch the dawn over the Carolinas.

"Where've you been, dear C?"

"Tanzania. And you're married."

"No."

"I heard you were married," he said. "The Lees told the Smiths who told the Kerguelens who told the Utsumbés and we get around, we Utsumbés. A new wife, they said. I didn't know you were especially fond of women."

"I'm not. She's my husbands' wife. And we're not married yet, Charley. She's had hard luck: a first family started in '35, two husbands burned out by an overload while arranging transportation for a concert—of all things, pushing papers, you know!—and the second divorced her, I think, and she drifted away from the third (a big one), and there was some awful quarrel with the fourth, people chasing people around tables, I don't know."

"Poor woman."

In the manner of people joking and talking lightly, they had drawn together, back to back, sitting on the ground and rubbing together their shoulders and the backs of their heads. Jannina said sorrowfully, "What lovely hair you have, Charley Utsumbé, like metal mesh."

"All we Utsumbés are exceedingly handsome." They linked arms. The sun, which anyone could chase around the world now, see it rise or set twenty times a day, fifty times a day—if you wanted to spend your life like that—rose dripping out of the cypress swamp. There was nobody around for miles. Mist drifted up from the pools and low places.

"My God," he said, "it's summer! I have to be at Tanga now."

"What?" said Jannina.

"One loses track," he said apologetically. "I'm sorry, love, but I have unavoidable business at home. Tax labor."

"But why summer, why did its being summer—"

"Train of thought! Too complicated" (and already they were out of key, already the mild affair was over, there having come between them the one obligation that can't be put off to the time you like, or the place you like; off he'd go to plug himself into a road-mender or a doctor, though it's of some advantage to mend all the roads of a continent at one time).

She sat cross-legged on the station platform, watching him enter the booth and set the dial. He stuck his head out the glass door.

"Come with me to Africa, lovely lady!"

She thumbed her nose at him. "You're only a passing fancy, Charley U!" He blew a kiss, enclosed himself in the booth, and disappeared. (The trans-matter field is larger than the booth, for obvious reasons; the booth flicks on and off several million times a second and so does not get transported itself, but it protects the machinery from the weather and it keeps people from losing elbows or knees or slicing the ends off a package or a child. The booths at the cryogenics center at the North Pole have exchanged air so often with those of warmer regions that each has its own micro-climate; leaves and seeds, plants and earth, are piled about them. Don't Step on the Grass!—say the notes pinned to the door—Wish to Trade Pawlownia Sapling for Sub-arctic Canadian Moss; Watch Your Goddamn Bare Six-Toed Feet!; Wish Amateur Cellist for Quartet, Six Months' Rehearsal Late Uhl with Reciter; I Lost a Squirrel Here Yesterday, Can You Find It Before It Dies? Eight Children Will be Heartbroken—Cecilia Ching, Buenos Aires.)

Jannina sighed and slipped on her glass woolly; nasty to get back into clothes, but home was cold. You never knew where you might go, so you carried them. Years ago (she thought) I came here with someone in the dead of winter, either an unmatched man or someone's starting spouse—only two of us, at any rate—and we waded through the freezing water and danced as hard as we could and then proved we could sing and drink beer in a swamp at the same time, good Lord! And then went to the public resort on the Ile de la Cité to watch professional plays, opera, games—you have to be good to get in there!—and got into some clothes because it was chilly after sundown in September—no, wait, it was Venezuela—and watched the lights come out and smoked like mad at a café table and tickled the robot waiter and pretended we were old, really old, perhaps a hundred and fifty. . . . Years ago!

But *was* it the same place? she thought, and dismissing the incident forever, she stepped into the booth, shut the door, and dialed home: the Himalayas. The trunk line was clear. The branch stop was clear. The family's transceiver (located in the anteroom behind two doors, to keep the task of heating the house within reasonable limits) had damn well better be clear, or somebody would be blown right into the vestibule. Momentum- and heat-compensators kept Jannina from arriving home at seventy degrees Fahrenheit internal temperature (seven degrees lost for every mile you teleport upward) or too many feet above herself (rise to the east, drop going west, to the north or south you are apt to be thrown right through the wall of the booth). Someday (thought Jannina) everybody will decide to let everybody live in decent climates. But not yet. Not this everybody.

She arrived home singing "The World's My Back Yard, Yes, the World Is My Oyster," a song that had been popular in her first youth, some seventy years before.

The Komarovs' house was hardened foam with an automatic inside line to the school near Naples. It was good to be brought up on your own feet. Jannina passed through; the seven-year-olds lay with their heads together and their bodies radiating in a six-personed asterisk. In this position (which was supposed to promote mystical thought) they played Barufaldi, guessing the identity of famous dead personages through anagrammatic sentences, the first letters of the words of which (unscrambled into aphorisms or proverbs) simultaneously spelled out a moral and a series of Goedel numbers (in a previously agreed-upon code) which—

"Oh, my darling, how felicitous is the advent of your appearance!" cried a boy (hard to take, the polysyllabic stage). "Embrace me, dearest maternal parent! Unite your valuable upper limbs about my eager person!"

"Vulgar!" said Jannina, laughing.

"Non sum filius tuus?" said the child.

"No, you're not my body-child; you're my god-child. Your mother bequeathed me to you when she died. What are you learning?"

"The eternal parental question," he said, frowning. "How to run a helicopter. How to prepare food from its actual, revolting, raw constituents. Can I go now?"

"*Can* you?" she said. "Nasty imp!"

"Good," he said, "I've made you feel guilty. Don't *do* that," and as she tried to embrace him, he ticklishly slid away. "The robin walks quietly up the branch of the tree," he said breathlessly, flopping back on the floor.

"That's not an aphorism." (Another Barufaldi player.)

"It is."

"It isn't."

"It is."

"It isn't."

"It is."

"It—"

The school vanished; the antechamber appeared. In the kitchen Chi Komarov was rubbing the naked back of his sixteen-year-old son. Parents always kissed each other; children always kissed each other. She touched foreheads with the two men and hung her woolly on the hook by the ham radio rig. Someone was always around. Jannina flipped the cover off her wrist chronometer: standard regional time, date, latitude-longitude, family computer hookup clear. "At my age I ought to remember these things," she said. She pressed the computer hookup: Ann at tax labor in the schools, bit-a-month plan, regular Ann; Lee with three months to go, five years off, heroic Lee; Phuong in Paris, still rehearsing; C.E. gone, won't say where, spontaneous C.E.; Ilse making some repairs in the basement, not a true basement, really, but the room farthest down the hillside. Jannina went up the stairs and then came down and put her head round at the living-and-swimming room.

Through the glass wall one could see the mountains. Old Al, who had joined them late in life, did a bit of gardening in the brief summers, and generally stuck around the place. Jannina beamed. "Hullo, Old Al!" Big and shaggy, a rare delight, his white body hair. She sat on his lap. "Has she come?"

"The new one? No," he said.

"Shall we go swimming?"

He made an expressive face. "No, dear," he said. "I'd rather go to Naples and watch the children fly helicopters. I'd rather go to Nevada and fly them myself. I've been in the water all day, watching a very dull person restructure coral reefs and experiment with polyploid polyps."

"You mean *you* were doing it."

"One gets into the habit of working."

"But you didn't have to!"

"It was a private project. Most interesting things are."

She whispered in his ear.

With happily flushed faces, they went into Old Al's inner garden and locked the door.

Jannina, temporary family representative, threw the computer helmet over her head and, thus plugged in, she cleaned house, checked food supplies, did a little of the legal business entailed by a family of eighteen adults (two triplet marriages, a quad, and a group of eight). She felt very smug. She put herself through by radio to Himalayan HQ (above two thousand meters) and hooking computer to computer—a very odd feeling, like an urge to sneeze that never comes off—extended a formal invitation to one Leslie Smith ("Come stay, why don't you?"), notifying every free Komarov to hop it back and fast. Six hikers might come for the night—back-packers. More food. First thunderstorm of the year in Albany, New York (North America). Need an extra two rooms by Thursday. Hear the Palnatoki are moving. Can't use a room. Can't use a kitten. Need the geraniums back, Mrs. Adam, Chile. The best maker of hand-blown glass in the world has killed in a duel the second-best maker of hand-blown glass for joining the movement toward ceramics. A bitter struggle is foreseen in the global economy. Need a lighting designer. Need fifteen singers and electric pansensicon. Standby tax labor xxxxxpj through xxxyq to Cambaluc, great tectogenic—

With the guilty feeling that one always gets gossiping with a computer, for it's really not reciprocal, Jannina flipped off the helmet. She went to get Ilse. Climbing back through the white foam room, the purple foam room, the green foam room, everything littered with plots and projects of the clever Komarovs or the even cleverer Komarov children, stopping at the baby room for Ilse to nurse her baby. Jannina danced staidly around studious Ilse. They turned on the nursery robot and the television screen. Ilse drank beer in the swimming room, for her milk. She worried her way through the day's record of events—faults in the foundation, some people who came from Chichester and couldn't find C.E. so one of them burst into tears, a new experiment in genetics coming round the gossip circuit, an execrable set of equations from some imposter in Bucharest.

"A duel!" said Jannina.

They both agreed it was shocking. And what fun. A new fashion. You had to be a little mad to do it. Awful.

The light went on over the door to the tunnel that linked the house to the antechamber, and very quickly, one after another, as if the branch line had just come free, eight Komarovs came into the room. The light flashed again; one could see three people debouch one after the other, persons in boots, with coats, packs, and face masks over their woollies. They were covered with snow, either from the mountain terraces above the house or from some other place, Jannina didn't know. They stamped the snow off in the antechamber and hung their clothes outside; "Good heavens, you're not circumcised!" cried someone. There was as much handshaking and embracing all around as at a wedding party. Velet Komarov (the short, dark one) recognized Fung Pao-yu and swung her off her feet. People began to joke, tentatively stroking one another's arms. "Did you have a good hike? Are you a good hiker, Pao-yu?" said Velet. The light over the antechamber went on again, though nobody could see a thing since the glass was steamed over from the collision of hot with cold air. Old Al stopped, halfway into the kitchen. The baggage receipt chimed, recognized only by family ears—upstairs a bundle of somebody's things, ornaments, probably, for the missing Komarovs were still young and the young are interested in clothing, were appearing in the baggage receptacle. "Ann or Phuong?" said Jannina; "five to three, anybody? Match me!" but someone strange opened the door of the booth and peered out. Oh, a dizzying sensation. She was painted in a few places, which was awfully odd because really it was old-fashioned; and why do it for a family evening? It was a stocky young woman. It was an awful mistake (thought Jannina). Then the visitor made her second mistake. She said:

"I'm Leslie Smith." But it was more through clumsiness than being rude. Chi Komarov (the tall, blond one) saw this instantly, and snatching off his old-fashioned spectacles, he ran to her side and patted her, saying teasingly:

"Now, haven't we met? Now, aren't you married to someone I know?"

"No, no," said Leslie Smith, flushing with pleasure.

He touched her neck. "Ah, you're a tightrope dancer!"

"Oh, no!" exclaimed Leslie Smith.

"*I'm* a tightrope dancer," said Chi. "Would you believe it?"

"But you're too—too *spiritual*," said Leslie Smith hesitantly.

"Spiritual, how do you like that, family, spiritual?" he cried, delighted (a little more delighted, thought Jannina, than the situation really called for) and he began to stroke her neck.

"What a lovely neck you have," he said.

This steadied Leslie Smith. She said, "I like tall men," and allowed herself to look at the rest of the family. "Who are these people?" she said, though one was afraid she might really mean it.

Fung Pao-yu to the rescue: "Who are these people? Who are they, indeed! I doubt if they are anybody. One might say, 'I have met these people,' but has one? What existential meaning would such a statement convey? I myself, now, I have met them. I have been introduced to them. But they are like the Sahara; it is all wrapped in mystery; I doubt if they even have names," etc. etc. Then lanky Chi Komarov disputed possession of Leslie Smith with Fung Pao-yu, and Fung Pao-yu grabbed one arm and Chi the other; and she jumped up and down fiercely; so that by the time the lights dimmed and the food came, people were feeling better—or so Jannina judged. So embarrassing and delightful to be eating fifteen to a room! "We Komarovs are famous for eating whatever we can get whenever we can get it," said Velet proudly. Various Komarovs in various places, with the three hikers on cushions and Ilse at full length on the rug. Jannina pushed a button with her toe and the fairy lights came on all over the ceiling. "The children did that," said Old Al. He had somehow settled at Leslie Smith's side and was feeding her so-chi from his own bowl. She smiled up at him. "We once," said a hiking companion of Fung Pao-yu's, "arranged a dinner in an amphitheater where half of us played servants to the other half, with forfeits for those who didn't show. It was the result of a bet. Like the bad old days. Did you know there were once *five billion people* in this world?"

"The gulls," said Ilse, "are mating on the Isle of Skye." There were murmurs of appreciative interest. Chi began to develop an erection and everyone laughed. Old Al wanted music and Velet didn't; what might have been a quarrel was ended by Ilse's furiously boxing their ears. She stalked off to the nursery.

"Leslie Smith and I are both old-fashioned," said Old Al, "because neither of us believes in gabbing. Chi—your theater?"

"We're turning people away." He leaned forward, earnestly, tapping his fingers on his crossed knees. "I swear, some of them are threatening to commit suicide."

"It's a choice," said Velet reasonably.

Leslie Smith had dropped her bowl. They retrieved it for her.

"Aiy, I remember—" said Pao-yu. "What I remember! We've been eating dried mush for three days, tax-issue. Did you know one of my dads killed himself?"

"No!" said Velet, surprised.

"Years ago," said Pao-yu. "He said he refused to live to see the time when chairs were reintroduced. He also wanted further genetic engineering, I believe, for even more intelligence. He did it out of spite, I'm sure. I think he wrestled a shark. Jannina, is this tax-issue food? Is it this year's style tax-issue sauce?"

"No, next year's," said Jannina snappishly. Really, some people! She slipped into Finnish, to show up Pao-yu's pronunciation. "Isn't that so?" she asked Leslie Smith.

Leslie Smith stared at her.

More charitably Jannina informed them all, in Finnish, that the Komarovs had withdrawn their membership in a food group, except for Ann, who had taken out an individual, because what the dickens, who had the time? And tax-issue won't kill you. As they finished, they dropped their dishes into the garbage field and Velet stripped a layer off the rug. In that went, too. Indulgently Old Al began a round:

"Red."

"Sun," said Pao-yu.

"The Red Sun Is," said one of the triplet Komarovs.

"The Red Sun Is—High," said Chi.

"The Red Sun Is High, The," Velet said.

"The Red Sun Is High, The Blue—" Jannina finished. They had come to Leslie Smith, who could either complete it or keep it going. She chose to declare for complete, not shyly (as before) but simply by pointing to Old Al.

"The red sun is high, the blue," he said. "Subtle! Another: Ching."

"Nü."

"Ching nü ch'i."

"Ching nü ch'i ch'u."

"Ssu."

"Wo."

"Ssu wo yü." It had got back to Leslie Smith again. She said, "I can't do that." Jannina got up and began to dance—I'm nice in my nasty way, she thought. The others wandered toward the pool and Ilse reappeared on the nursery monitor screen, saying, "I'm coming down." Somebody said, "What time is it in the Argentine?"

"Five A.M."

"I think I want to go."

"Go then."

"I go."

"Go well."

The red light over the antechamber door flashed and went out.

"Say, why'd you leave your other family?" said Ilse, settling near Old Al where the wall curved out. Ann, for whom it was evening, would be home soon; Chi, who had just got up a few hours back in western America, would stay somewhat longer; nobody ever knew Old Al's schedule and Jannina herself had lost track of the time. She would stay up until she felt sleepy. She followed a rough twenty-eight-hour day, Phuong (what a nuisance that must be at rehearsals!) a twenty-two-hour one, Ilse six hours up, six hours dozing. Jannina nodded, heard the question, and shook herself awake.

"I didn't leave them. They left me."

There was a murmur of sympathy around the pool.

"They left me because I was stupid," said Leslie Smith. Her hands were clasped passively in her lap. She looked very genteel in her blue body paint, a stocky young woman with small breasts. One of the triplet Komarovs, flirting in the pool with the other two, choked. The non-aquatic members of the family crowded around Leslie Smith, touching her with little, soft touches; they kissed her and exposed to her all their unguarded surfaces, their bellies, their soft skins. Old Al kissed her hands. She sat there, oddly unmoved. "But I *am* stupid," she said. "You'll find out." Jannina put her hands over her ears: "A masochist!" Leslie Smith looked at Jannina with a curious, stolid look. Then she looked down and absently began to rub one blue-painted knee. "Luggage!" shouted Chi, clapping his hands together, and the triplets dashed for the stairs. "No, I'm going to bed," said Leslie Smith; "I'm tired," and quite simply, she got up and let Old Al lead her through the pink room, the blue room, the turtle-and-pet room (temporarily empty), the trash room, and all the other rooms, to the guest room with the view that looked out over the cold hillside to the terraced plantings below.

"The best maker of hand-blown glass in the world," said Chi, "has killed in a duel the second-best maker of hand-blown glass in the world."

"For joining the movement to ceramics," said Ilse, awed. Jannina felt a thrill: this was the bitter stuff under the surface of life, the fury that boiled up. A bitter struggle is foreseen in the global economy. Good old tax-issue stuff goes toddling along, year after year. She was, thought Jannina, extraordinarily grateful to be living now, to be in such an extraordinary world, to have so long to go before her death. So much to do!

Old Al came back into the living room. "She's in bed."

"Well, which of us—?" said the triplet-who-had-choked, looking mischievously round from one to the other. Chi was about to volunteer, out of his usual conscientiousness, thought Jannina, but then she found herself suddenly standing up, and then just as suddenly sitting down again. "I just don't have the nerve," she said. Velet Komarov walked on his hands toward the stairs, then somersaulted, and vanished, climbing. Old Al got off the hand-carved chest he had been sitting on and fetched a can of ale from it. He levered off the top and drank. Then he said, "She really is stupid, you know." Jannina's skin crawled.

"Oooh," said Pao-yu. Chi betook himself to the kitchen and returned with a paper folder. It was coated with frost. He shook it, then impatiently dropped it in the pool. The redheaded triplet swam over and took it. "Smith, Leslie," he said. "Adam Two, Leslie. Yee, Leslie. Schwarzen, Leslie."

"What on earth does the woman *do* with herself besides get married?" exclaimed Pao-yu.

"She drove a hovercraft," said Chi, "in some out-of-the-way places around the Pacific until the last underground stations were completed. Says when she was a child she wanted to drive a truck."

"Well, you can," said the redheaded triplet, "can't you? Go to Arizona or the Rockies and drive on the roads. The sixty-mile-an-hour road. The thirty-mile-an-hour road. Great artistic recreation."

"That's not work," said Old Al.

"Couldn't she take care of children?" said the redheaded triplet. Ilse sniffed.

"Stupidity's not much of a recommendation for that," Chi said. "Let's see—no children. No, of course not. Overfulfilled her tax work on quite a few routine matters here. Kim, Leslie. Went to Moscow and contracted a double with some fellow, didn't last. Registered as a singleton, but that didn't last, either. She said she was lonely and they were exploiting her."

Old Al nodded.

"Came back and lived informally with a theater group. Left them. Went into psychotherapy. Volunteered for several experimental, intelligence-enhancing programs, was turned down—hm!—sixty-five come the winter solstice, muscular coordination average, muscular development above average, no overt mental pathology, empathy average, prognosis: poor. No, wait a minute, it says, 'More of the same.' Well, that's the same thing."

"What I want to know," added Chi, raising his head, "is who met Miss Smith and decided we needed the lady in this Ice Palace of ours?"

Nobody answered. Jannina was about to say, "Ann, perhaps?" but as she felt the urge to do so—surely it wasn't right to turn somebody off like that, *just* for that!—Chi (who had been flipping through the dossier) came to the last page, with the tax-issue stamp absolutely unmistakable, woven right into the paper.

"The computer did," said Pao-yu and she giggled idiotically.

"Well," said Jannina, jumping to her feet, "tear it up, my dear, or give it to me and I'll tear it up for you. I think Miss Leslie Smith deserves from us the same as we'd give to anybody else, and I—for one—intend to go *right up there*—"

"After Velet," said Old Al dryly.

"*With* Velet, if I must," said Jannina, raising her eyebrows, "and if you don't know what's due a guest, Old Daddy, I do, and I intend to provide it. Lucky I'm keeping house this month, or you'd probably feed the poor woman nothing but seaweed."

"You won't like her, Jannina," said Old Al.

"I'll find that out for myself," said Jannina with some asperity, "and I'd advise you to do the same. Let her garden with you, Daddy. Let her squirt the foam for the new rooms. And now"—she glared round at them—"I'm going to clean *this* room, so you'd better hop it, the lot of you," and dashing into the kitchen, she had the computer helmet on her head and the hoses going before they had even quite cleared the area of the pool. Then she took the helmet off and hung it on the wall. She flipped the cover off her wrist chronometer and satisfied herself as to the date. By the time she got back to the living room there was nobody there, only Leslie Smith's dossier lying on the carved chest. There was Leslie Smith; there was all of Leslie Smith. Jannina knocked on the wall cupboard and it revolved, presenting its openable side; she took out chewing gum. She started chewing and read about Leslie Smith.

Q: What have you seen in the last twenty years that you particularly liked?

A: I don't . . . the museum, I guess. At Oslo. I mean the . . . the mermaid and the children's museum, I don't care if it's a children's museum.

Q: Do you like children?

A: Oh no.

(No disgrace in *that*, certainly, thought Jannina.)

Q: But you liked the children's museum.

A: Yes, sir. . . . Yes. . . . I liked those little animals, the fake ones, in the—the—

Q: The crèche?

A: Yes. And I liked the old things from the past, the murals with the flowers on them, they looked so real.

(Dear God!)

Q: You said you were associated with a theater group in Tokyo. Did you like it?

A: No . . . yes. I don't know.

Q: Were they nice people?

A: Oh yes. They were awfully nice. But they got mad at me, I suppose. . . . You see . . . well, I don't seem to get things quite right, I suppose. It's not so much the work, because I do that all right, but the other . . . the little things. It's always like that.

Q: What do you think is the matter?

A: You . . . I think you know.

Jannina flipped through the rest of it: normal, normal, normal. Miss Smith was as normal as could be. Miss Smith was stupid. Not even very stupid. It was too damned bad. They'd probably have enough of Leslie Smith in a week, the Komarovs; yes, we'll have enough of her (Jannina thought), never able to catch a joke or a tone of voice, always clumsy, however willing, but never happy, never at ease. You can get a job for her, but what else can you get for her? Jannina glanced down at the dossier, already bored.

Q: You say you would have liked to live in the old days. Why is that? Do you think it would have been more adventurous or would you like to have had lots of children?

A: I . . . you have no right . . . You're condescending.

Q: I'm sorry. I suppose you mean to say that then you would have been of above-average intelligence. You would, you know.

A: I know. I looked it up. Don't condescend to me.

Well, it *was* too damned bad! Jannina felt tears rise in her eyes. What had the poor woman done? It was just an accident, that was the horror of it, not even a tragedy, as if everyone's forehead had been stamped with the word "Choose" except for Leslie Smith's. She needs money, thought Jannina, thinking of the bad old days when people did things for money. Nobody could take to Leslie Smith. She wasn't insane enough to stand for being hurt or exploited. She wasn't clever enough to interest anybody. She certainly wasn't feeble-minded; they couldn't very well put her into a hospital for the feeble-minded or the brain-injured; in fact (Jannina was looking at the dossier again), they had tried to get her to work there and she had taken a good, fast swing at the supervisor. She had said the people there were "hideous" and "revolting." She had no particular mechanical aptitudes. She had no particular interests. There was not even anything for her to read or watch; how could there be? She seemed (back at the dossier) to spend most of her time either working or going on public tours of exotic places, coral reefs and places like that. She enjoyed aqualung diving, but didn't do it often because that got boring. And that was that. There was, all in all, very little one could do for Leslie Smith. You might even say that in her own person she represented all the defects of the bad old days. Just imagine a world made up of such creatures! Jannina yawned. She slung the folder away and padded into the kitchen. Pity Miss Smith wasn't good-looking, also a pity that she was too well balanced (the folder said) to think that cosmetic surgery would make that much difference. Good for you, Leslie, you've got some sense; anyhow.

Jannina, half asleep, met Ann in the kitchen, beautiful, slender Ann reclining on a cushion with her so-chi and melon. Dear old Ann. Jannina nuzzled her brown shoulder. Ann poked her.

"Look," said Ann, and she pulled from the purse she wore at her waist a tiny fragment of cloth, stained rusty brown.

"What's that?"

"The second-best maker of hand-blown glass—oh, you know about it— well, this is his blood. When the best maker of hand-blown glass in the world had stabbed to the heart the second-best maker of hand-blown glass in the world, and cut his throat, too, some small children steeped handkerchiefs in his blood and they're sending pieces all over the world."

"Good God!" cried Jannina.

"Don't worry, my dear," said lovely Ann; "it happens every decade or so. The children say they want to bring back cruelty, dirt, disease, glory, and hell. Then they forget about it. Every teacher knows that." She sounded amused. "I'm afraid I lost my temper today, though, and walloped your god-child. It's in the family, after all."

Jannina remembered when she herself had been much younger and Annie, barely a girl, had come to live with them. Ann had played at being a child and had put her head on Jannina's shoulder, saying, "Jannie, tell me a story." So Jannina now laid her head on Ann's breast and said, "Annie, tell me a story."

Ann said: "I told my children a story today, a creation myth. Every creation myth has to explain how death and suffering came into the world, so that's what this one is about. In the beginning, the first man and the first woman lived very contentedly on an island until one day they began to feel hungry. So they called to the turtle who holds up the world to send them something to eat. The turtle sent them a mango and they ate it and were satisfied, but the next day they were hungry again.

" 'Turtle,' they said, 'send us something to eat.' So the turtle sent them a coffee berry. They thought it was pretty small, but they ate it anyway and were satisfied. The third day they called on the turtle again and this time the turtle sent them two things: a banana and a stone. The man and woman did not know which to choose, so they asked the turtle which thing it was they should eat. 'Choose,' said the turtle. So they chose the banana and ate that, but they used the stone for a game of catch. Then the turtle said, 'You should have chosen the stone. If you had chosen the stone, you would have lived forever, but now that you have chosen the banana, Death and Pain have entered the world, and it is not I who can stop them.' "

Jannina was crying. Lying in the arms of her old friend, she wept bitterly, with a burning sensation in her chest and the taste of death and ashes in her mouth. It was awful. It was horrible. She remembered the embryo shark she had seen when she was three, in the Auckland Cetacean Research Center, and how she had cried then. She didn't know what she was crying about. "Don't, don't!" she sobbed.

"Don't what?" said Ann affectionately. "Silly Jannina!"

"Don't, don't," cried Jannina, "don't, it's true, it's true!" and she went on in this way for several more minutes. Death had entered the world. Nobody could stop it. It was ghastly. She did not mind for herself but for others, for her godchild, for instance. He was going to die. He was going to suffer. Nothing could help him. Duel, suicide, or old age, it was all the same. "This life!" gasped Jannina. "This awful life!" The thought of death became entwined somehow with Leslie Smith, in bed upstairs, and Jannina began to cry afresh, but eventually the thought of Leslie Smith calmed her. It brought her back to herself. She wiped her eyes with her hand. She sat up. "Do you want a smoke?" said beautiful Ann, but Jannina shook her head. She began to laugh. Really, the whole thing was quite ridiculous.

"There's this Leslie Smith," she said, dry-eyed. "We'll have to find a tactful way to get rid of her. It's idiotic, in this day and age."

And she told lovely Annie all about it.

The Hero as Werwolf

GENE WOLFE

Gene Wolfe is perceived by many critics to be one of the best—perhaps the best—SF and fantasy writers working today. His most acclaimed work is the tetralogy The Book of the New Sun, *individual volumes of which have won the Nebula Award, the World Fantasy Award, and the John W. Campbell Memorial Award. He followed this up with a popular new series that included* Nightside the Long Sun, The Lake of the Long Sun, Calde of the Long Sun, *and* Exodus from the Long Sun, *and has recently launched another new series with the novels* On Blue's Waters *and* In Green's Jungles. *His other books include the classic novels* Peace *and* The Devil in a Forest, *both recently re-released, as well as* Soldier in the Mist, Free Live Free, Soldier of Arate, There Are Doors, Castleview, Pandora by Holly Hollander, *and* The Urth of the New Sun. *His short fiction has been collected in* The Island of Doctor Death and Other Stories and other Stories, Gene Wolfe's Book of Days, The Wolfe Archipelago, *the World Fantasy Award–winning collection* Storeys From the Old Hotel, *and* Endangered Species.

In the evocative story that follows, he shows us what the Posthuman Future looks like from the other *perspective—the perspective of those who don't make the cut, and who must watch that glittering future world recede into the distance day by day, leaving them behind. . . .*

> Feet in the jungle that leave no mark!
> Eyes that can see in the dark—the dark!
> Tongue—give tongue to it! Hark! O Hark!
> Once, twice and again!
> —Rudyard Kipling
> "Hunting Song of the Seeonee Pack"

An owl shrieked, and Paul flinched. Fear, pavement, flesh, death, stone, dark, loneliness and blood made up Paul's world; the blood was all much the same, but the fear took several forms, and he had hardly seen another human being in the four years since his mother's death. At a night meeting in the park he was the red-cheeked young man at the end of the last row, with his knees together and his scrupulously clean hands (Paul was particularly careful about his nails) in his lap.

The speaker was fluent and amusing; he was clearly conversant with his subject—whatever it was—and he pleased his audience. Paul, the listener and watcher, knew many of the words he used; yet he had understood nothing in the past hour and a half, and sat wrapped in his stolen cloak and his own thoughts, seeming to listen, watching the crowd and the park—this, at least, was no ghost-house, no trap; the moon was up, nightblooming flowers scented the park air, and the trees lining the paths glowed with self-generated blue light; in the city, beyond the last hedge, the great buildings new and old were mountains lit from within.

Neither human nor master, a policeman strolled about the fringes of the audience, his eyes bright with stupidity. Paul could have killed him in less than a second, and was enjoying a dream of the policeman's death in some remote corner of his mind even while he concentrated on seeming to be one of *them*. A passenger rocket passed just under the stars, trailing luminous banners.

The meeting was over and he wondered if the rocket had in some way been the signal to end it. The masters did not use time, at least not as he did, as he had been taught by the thin woman who had been his mother in the little home she had made for them in the turret of a house that was once (she said) the Gorous'—now only a house too old to be destroyed. Neither did they use money, of which he like other old-style *Homo sapiens* still retained some racial memory, as of a forgotten god—a magic once potent that had lost all force.

The masters were rising, and there were tears and laughter and that third emotional tone that was neither amusement nor sorrow—the silken sound humans did not possess, but that Paul thought might express content, as the purring of a cat does, or community, like the cooing of doves. The policeman bobbed his hairy head, grinning, basking in the recognition, the approval, of those who had raised him from animality. *See* (said the motions of his hands, the writhings of his body) *the clothing you have given me. How nice! I take good care of my things because they are yours. See my weapon. I perform a useful function—if you did not have me, you would have to do it yourselves.*

If the policeman saw Paul, it would be over. He was too stupid, too silly, to be deceived by appearances as his masters were. He would never dare, thinking him a master, to meet Paul's eye, but he would look into his face seeking approval, and would see not what he was supposed to see but what was there. Paul ducked into the crowd, avoiding a beautiful woman with eyes the color of pearls, preferring to walk in the shadow of her fat escort where the policeman would not see him. The fat man took dust from a box shaped like the moon and rubbed it between his hands, releasing the smell of raspberries. It froze, and he sifted the tiny crystals of crimson ice over his shirt-front, grunting with satisfaction; then offered the box to the woman, who refused at first, only (three steps later) to accept when he pressed it on her.

They were past the policeman now. Paul dropped a few paces behind the couple, wondering if they were the ones tonight—if there would be meat tonight at all. For some, vehicles would be waiting. If the pair he had selected were among these, he would have to find others quickly.

They were not. They had entered the canyons between the buildings; he dropped farther behind, then turned aside.

Three minutes later he was in an alley a hundred meters ahead of them, waiting for them to pass the mouth. (The old trick was to cry like an infant, and he could do it well; but he had a new trick—a better trick, because too many had learned not to come down an alley when an infant cried. The new trick was a silver bell he had found in the house, small and very old. He took it from his pocket and removed the rag he had packed around the clapper. His dark cloak concealed him now, its hood pulled up to hide the pale gleam of his skin. He stood in a narrow doorway only a few meters away from the alley's mouth.)

They came. He heard the man's thick laughter, the woman's silken sound. She was a trifle silly from the dust the man had given her, and would be holding his arm as they walked, rubbing his thigh with hers. The man's black-shod foot and big belly thrust past the stonework of the building—there was a muffled moan.

The fat man turned, looking down the alley. Paul could see fear growing in the woman's face, cutting, too slowly, through the odor of raspberries. Another moan, and the man strode forward, fumbling in his pocket for an illuminator. The woman followed hesitantly (her skirt was of flowering vines the color of love, and white skin flashed in the interstices; a serpent of gold supported her breasts).

Someone was behind him. Pressed back against the metal door, he watched the couple as they passed. The fat man had gotten his illuminator out and held it over his head as he walked, looking into corners and doorways.

They came at them from both sides, a girl and an old, gray-bearded man. The fat man, the master, his genetic heritage revised for intellection and peace, had hardly time to turn before his mouth gushed blood. The woman whirled and ran, the vines of her skirt withering at her thought to give her leg-room, the serpent dropping from her breasts to strike with fangless jaws at the flying-haired girl who pursued her, then winding itself about the girl's ankles. The girl fell; but as the pearl-eyed woman passed, Paul broke her neck. For a moment he was too startled at the sight of other human beings to speak. Then he said, "These are mine."

The old man, still bent over the fat man's body, snapped: "Ours. We've been here an hour and more." His voice was the creaking of steel hinges, and Paul thought of ghost-houses again.

"I followed them from the park." The girl, black-haired, gray-eyed when the light from the alley-mouth struck her face, was taking the serpent from around her legs—it was once more a lifeless thing of soft metal mesh. Paul picked up the woman's corpse and wrapped it in his cloak. "You gave me no warning," he said. "You must have seen me when I passed you."

The girl looked toward the old man. Her eyes said she would back him if he fought, and Paul decided he would throw the woman's body at her.

"Somebody'll come soon," the old man said. "And I'll need Janie's help to carry this one. We each take what we got ourselves—that's fair. Or we whip you. My girl's worth a man in a fight, and you'll find I'm still worth a man myself, old as I be."

"Give me the picking of his body. This one has nothing."

The girl's bright lips drew back from strong white teeth. From somewhere under the tattered shirt she wore, she had produced a long knife, and sudden light from a window high above the alley ran along the edge of the stained blade; the girl might be a dangerous opponent, as the old man claimed, but Paul could sense the femaleness, the woman-rut from where he stood. "No," her father said. "You got good clothes. I need these." He looked up at the window fearfully, fumbling with buttons.

"His cloak will hang on you like a blanket."

"We'll fight. Take the woman and go away, or we'll fight."

He could not carry both, and the fat man's meat would be tainted by the testicles. When Paul was young and there had been no one but his mother to do the killing, they had sometimes eaten old males; he never did so now. He slung the pearl-eyed woman across his shoulders and trotted away.

Outside the alley the streets were well lit, and a few passers-by stared at him and the dark burden he carried. Fewer still, he knew, would suspect him of being what he was—he had learned the trick of dressing as the masters did, even of wearing their expressions. He wondered how the black-haired girl and the old man would fare in their ragged clothes. *They must live very near.*

His own place was that in which his mother had borne him, a place high in a house built when humans were the masters. Every door was nailed tight and boarded up; but on one side a small garden lay between two wings, and in a corner of this garden, behind a bush where the shadows were thick even at noon, the bricks had fallen away. The lower floors were full of rotting furniture and the smell of rats and mold, but high in his wooden turret the walls were still dry and the sun came in by day at eight windows. He carried his burden there and dropped her in a corner. It was important that his clothes be kept as clean as the masters kept theirs, though he lacked their facilities. He pulled his cloak from the body and brushed it vigorously.

"What are you going to do with me?" the dead woman said behind him.

"Eat," he told her. "What did you think I was going to do?"

"I didn't know." And then: "I've read of you creatures, but I didn't think you really existed."

"We were the masters once," he said. He was not sure he still believed it, but it was what his mother had taught him. "This house was built in those days—that's why you won't wreck it: you're afraid." He had finished with the cloak; he hung it up and turned to face her, sitting on the bed. "You're afraid of waking the old times," he said. She lay slumped in the corner, and though her mouth moved, her eyes were only half open, looking at nothing.

"We tore a lot of them down," she said.

"If you're going to talk, you might as well sit up straight." He lifted her by the shoulders and propped her in the corner. A nail protruded from the wall there; he twisted a lock of her hair on it so her head would not loll; her hair was the rose shade of a little girl's dress, and soft but slightly sticky.

"I'm dead, you know."

"No, you're not." They always said this (except, sometimes, for the children) and his mother had always denied it. He felt that he was keeping up a family tradition.

"Dead," the pearl-eyed woman said. "Never, never, never. Another year, and everything would have been all right. I want to cry, but I can't breathe to."

"Your kind lives a long time with a broken neck," he told her. "But you'll die eventually."

"I am dead now."

He was not listening. There were other humans in the city; he had always known that, but only now, with the sight of the old man and the girl, had their existence seemed real to him.

"I thought you were all gone," the pearl-eyed dead woman said thinly. "All gone long ago, like a bad dream."

Happy with his new discovery, he said: "Why do you set traps for us, then? Maybe there are more of us than you think."

"There can't be many of you. How many people do you kill in a year?" Her mind was lifting the sheet from his bed, hoping to smother him with it; but he had seen that trick many times.

"Twenty or thirty." (He was boasting.)

"So many."

"When you don't get much besides meat, you need a lot of it. And then I only eat the best parts—why not? I kill twice a month or more except when it's cold, and I could kill enough for two or three if I had to." (*The girl had had a knife.* Knives were bad, except for cutting up afterward. But knives left blood behind. He would kill for her—she could stay here and take care of his clothes, prepare their food. He thought of himself walking home under a new moon, and seeing her face in the window of the turret.) To the dead woman he said: "You saw that girl? With the black hair? She and the old man killed your husband, and I'm going to being her here to live." He stood and began to walk up and down the small room, soothing himself with the sound of his own footsteps.

"He wasn't my husband." The sheet dropped limply now that he was no longer on the bed. "Why didn't you change? When the rest changed their genes?"

"I wasn't alive then."

"You must have received some tradition."

"We didn't want to. We are the human beings."

"Everyone wanted to. Your old breed had worn out the planet; even with much better technology, we're still starved for energy and raw materials because of what you did."

"There hadn't been enough to eat before," he said, "but when so many changed, there was a lot. So why should more change?"

It was a long time before she answered, and he knew the body was stiffening. That was bad, because as long as she lived in it the flesh would stay sweet; when the life was gone, he would have to cut it up quickly before the stuff in her lower intestine tainted the rest.

"Strange evolution," she said at last. "Man become food for men."

"I don't understand the second word. Talk so I know what you're saying." He kicked her in the chest to emphasize his point, and knocked her over; he heard a rib snap. . . . She did not reply, and he lay down on the bed. His mother had told him there was a meeting place in the city where men gathered on certain special nights—but he had forgotten (if he had ever known) what those nights were.

"That isn't even metalanguage," the dead woman said, "only children's talk."

"Shut up."

After a moment he said: "I'm going out. If you can make your body stand, and get out of here, and get down to the ground floor, and find the way out, then you may be able to tell someone about me and have the police waiting when I come back." He went out and closed the door, then stood patiently outside for five minutes.

When he opened it again, the corpse stood erect with her hands on his table, her tremors upsetting the painted metal circus-figures he had had since he was a child—the girl acrobat, the clown with his hoop and trained pig. One of her legs would not straighten. "Listen," he said, "you're not going to do it. I told you all that because I knew you'd think of it yourself. They always do, and they never make it. The farthest I've ever had anyone get was out the door and to the top of the steps. She fell down them, and I found her at the bottom when I came back. You're dead. Go to sleep."

The blind eyes had turned toward him when he began to speak, but they no longer watched him now. The face, which had been beautiful, was now entirely the face of a corpse. The cramped leg crept toward the floor as he watched, halted, began to creep downward again. Sighing, he lifted the dead woman off her feet, replaced her in the corner, and went down the creaking stairs to find the black-haired girl.

"There has been quite a few to come after her," her father said, "since we come into town. Quite a few." He sat in the back of the bus, on the rearmost seat that went completely across the back like a sofa. "But you're the first ever to find us here. The others, they hear about her, and leave a sign at the meetin'."

Paul wanted to ask where it was such signs were left, but held his peace.

"You know there ain't many folks at *all* anymore," her father went on. "And not many of *them* is women. And *damn few* is young girls like my Janie. I had a fella here that wanted her two weeks back—he said he hadn't had no real woman in two years; well, I didn't like the way he said *real*, so I said what did he do, and he said he fooled around with what he killed, sometimes, before they got cold. You never did like that, did you?"

Paul said he had not.

"How'd you find this dump here?"

"Just looked around." He had searched the area in ever-widening circles, starting at the alley in which he had seen the girl and her father. They had one of the masters' cold boxes to keep their ripe kills in (as he did himself), but there was the stink of clotted blood about the dump nonetheless. It was behind a high fence, closer to the park than he would have thought possible.

"When we come, there was a fella living here. Nice fella, a German. Name was Curtain—something like that. He went sweet on my Janie right off. Well,

I wasn't too taken with having a foreigner in the family, but he took us in and let us settle in the big station wagon. Told me he wanted to wed Janie, but I said no, she's too young. Wait a year, I says, and take her with my blessing. She wasn't but fourteen then. Well, one night the German fella went out and I guess they got him, because he never come back. We moved into this here bus then for the extra room."

His daughter was sitting at his feet, and he reached a crooked-fingered hand down and buried it in her midnight hair. She looked up at him and smiled. "Got a pretty face, ain't she?" he said.

Paul nodded.

"She's a mite thin, you was going to say. Well, that's true. I do my best to provide, but I'm feared, and not shamed to admit to it."

"The ghost-houses," Paul said.

"What's that?"

"That's what I've always called them. I don't get to talk to many other people."

"Where the doors shut on you—lock you in."

"Yes."

"That ain't ghosts—now don't you think I'm one of them fools don't believe in them. I know better. But that ain't ghosts. They're always looking, don't you see, for people they think ain't right. That's us. It's electricity does it. You ever been caught like that?"

Paul nodded. He was watching the delicate swelling Janie's breasts made in the fabric of her filthy shirt, and only half-listening to her father; but the memory penetrated the young desire that half embarrassed him, bringing back fear. The windows of the bus had been set to black, and the light inside was dim—still it was possible some glimmer showed outside. *There should be no lights in the dump.* He listened, but heard only katydids singing in the rubbish.

"They thought I was a master—I dress like one," he said. "That's something you should do. They were going to test me. I turned the machine over and broke it, and jumped through a window." He had been on the sixth floor, and had been saved by landing in the branches of a tree whose bruised twigs and torn leaves exuded an acrid incense that to him was the very breath of panic still; but it had not been the masters, or the instrument-filled examination room, or the jump from the window that had terrified him, but waiting in the ghost-room while the walls talked to one another in words he could sometimes, for a few seconds, nearly understand.

"It wouldn't work for me—got too many things wrong with me. Lines in my face; even got a wart—they never do."

"Janie could."

The old man cleared his throat; it was a thick sound, like water in a downspout in a hard rain. "I been meaning to talk to you about her; about why those other fellas I told you about never took her—not that I'd of let some of them: Janie's the only family I got left. But I ain't so particular I don't want to see her married at all—not a bit of it. Why, we wouldn't of come here if it weren't for Janie. When her monthly come, I said to myself, she'll be wantin' a man, and what're you goin' to do way out here? Though the country was gettin' bad anyway, I must say. If they'd of had real dogs, I believe they would have got us several times."

He paused, perhaps thinking of those times, the lights in the woods at night and the running, perhaps only trying to order his thoughts. Paul waited, scratching an ankle, and after a few seconds the old man said: "We didn't want to do this, you know, us Pendeltons. That's mine and Janie's name— Pendelton. Janie's Augusta Jane, and I'm Emmitt J."

"Paul Gorou," Paul said.

"Pleased to meet you, Mr. Gorou. When the time come, they took one whole side of the family. They was the Worthmore Pendeltons; that's what we always called them, because most of them lived thereabouts. Cousins of mine they was, and second cousins. We was the Evershaw Pendeltons, and they didn't take none of us. Bad blood, they said—too much wrong to be worth fixing, or too much that mightn't get fixed right, and then show up again. My ma—she's alive then—she always swore it was her sister Lillian's boy that did it to us. The whole side of his head was pushed in. You know what I mean? They used to say a cow'd kicked him when he was small, but it wasn't so—he's just born like that. He could talk some—there's those that set a high value on that—but the slobber'd run out of his mouth. My ma said if it wasn't for him we'd have got in sure. The only other thing was my sister Clara that was born with a bad eye—blind, you know, and something wrong with the lid of it, too. But she was just as sensible as anybody. Smart as a whip. So I would say it's likely Ma was right. Same thing with your family, I suppose?"

"I think so. I don't really know."

"A lot of it was die-beetees. They could fix it, but if there was other things too they just kept them out. Of course when it was over there wasn't no medicine for them no more, and they died off pretty quick. When I was young, I used to think that was what it meant: die-beetees—you died away. It's really sweetening of the blood. You heard of it?"

Paul nodded.

"I'd like to taste some sometime, but I never come to think of that while there was still some of them around."

"If they weren't masters—"

"Didn't mean I'd of killed them," the old man said quickly. "Just got one to gash his arm a trifle so I could taste of it. Back then—that would be twenty aught nine, close to fifty years gone it is now—there was several I knowed that was just my age. . . . What I was meaning to say at the beginning was that us Pendeltons never figured on anythin' like this. We'd farmed, and we meant to keep on, grow our own truck and breed our own stock. Well, that did for a time, but it wouldn't keep."

Paul, who had never considered living off the land, or even realized that it was possible to do so, could only stare at him.

"You take chickens, now. Everybody always said there wasn't nothing easier than chickens, but that was when there was medicine you could put in the water to keep off the sickness. Well, the time come when you couldn't get it no more than you could get a can of beans in those stores of theirs that don't use money or cards or anything a man can understand. My dad had two hundred in the flock when the sickness struck, and it took every hen inside of four days. You wasn't supposed to eat them that had died sick, but we did it. Plucked 'em and canned 'em—by that time our old locker that plugged in the wall wouldn't work. When the chickens was all canned, Dad saddled a horse we had then and rode twenty-five miles to a place where the new folks grew chickens to eat themselves. I guess you know what happened to him, though—they wouldn't sell, and they wouldn't trade. Finally he begged them. He was a Pendelton, and used to cry when he told of it. He said the harder he begged them, the scareder they got. Well, finally he reached out and grabbed one by the leg—he was on his knees to them—and he hit him alongside the face with a book he was carryin'."

The old man rocked backward and forward in his seat as he spoke, his eyes half closed. "There wasn't no more seed but what was saved from last year then, and the corn went so bad the ears wasn't no longer than a soft dick. No bullets for Dad's old gun, nowhere to buy new traps when what we had was lost. Then one day just afore Christmas these here machines just started tearing up our fields. They had forgot about us, you see. We threw rocks but it didn't do no good, and about midnight one come right through the house. There wasn't no one living then but Ma and Dad and brother Tom and me and Janie. Janie wasn't but just a little bit of a thing. The machine got Tom in the leg with a piece of two-by-four—rammed the splintery end into him, you see. The rot got to the wound and he died a week after; it was winter then, and we was living in a place me and Dad built up on the hill out of branches and saplings."

"About Janie," Paul said. "I can understand how you might not want to let her go—"

"Are you sayin' you don't want her?" The old man shifted in his seat, and Paul saw that his right hand had moved close to the crevice where the horizontal surface joined the vertical. The crevice was a trifle too wide, and he thought he knew what was hidden there. He was not afraid of the old man, and it had crossed his mind more than once that if he killed him there would be nothing to prevent his taking Janie.

"I want her," he said. "I'm not going away without her." He stood up without knowing why.

"There's been others said the same thing. I would go, you know, to the meetin' in the regular way; come back next month, and the fella'd be waitin'."

The old man was drawing himself to his feet, his jaw outthrust belligerently. "They'd see her," he said, "and they'd talk a lot, just like you, about how good they'd take care of her, though there wasn't a one brought a lick to eat when he come to call. Me and Janie, sometimes we ain't et for three, four days—they never take account of that. Now here, you look at her."

Bending swiftly, he took his daughter by the arm; she rose gracefully, and he spun her around. "Her ma was a pretty woman," he said, "but not as pretty as what she is, even if she is so thin. And she's got sense too—I don't keer what they say."

Janie looked at Paul with frightened, animal eyes. He gestured, he hoped gently, for her to come to him, but she only pressed herself against her father.

"You can talk to her. She understands."

Paul started to speak, then had to stop to clear his throat. At last he said: "Come here, Janie. You're going to live with me. We'll come back and see your father sometimes."

Her hand slipped into her shirt; came out holding a knife. She looked at the old man, who caught her wrist and took the knife from her and dropped it on the seat behind him, saying, "You're going to have to be a mite careful around her for a bit, but if you don't hurt her none she'll take to you pretty quick. She wants to take to you now—I can see it in the way she looks."

Paul nodded, accepting the girl from him almost as he might have accepted a package, holding her by her narrow waist.

"And when you get a mess of grub she likes to cut them up, sometimes, while they're still movin' around. Mostly I don't allow it, but if you do—anyway, once in a while—she'll like you better for it."

Paul nodded again. His hand, as if of its own volition, had strayed to the girl's smoothly rounded hip, and he felt such desire as he had never known before.

"Wait," the old man said. His breath was foul in the close air. "You listen to me now. You're just a young fella and I know how you feel, but you don't know how I do. I want you to understand before you go. I love my girl. You take good care of her or I'll see to you. And if you change your mind about wanting her, don't you just turn her out. I'll take her back, you hear?"

Paul said, "All right."

"Even a bad man can love his child. You remember that, because it's true."

Her husband took Janie by the hand and led her out of the wrecked bus. She was looking over her shoulder, and he knew that she expected her father to drive a knife into his back.

They had seen the boy—a brown-haired, slightly freckled boy of nine or ten with an armload of books—on a corner where a small, columniated building concealed the entrance to the monorail, and the streets were wide and empty. The children of the masters were seldom out so late. Paul waved to him, not daring to speak, but attempting to convey by his posture that he wanted to ask directions; he wore the black cloak and scarlet-slashed shirt, the gold sandals and wide-legged black film trousers proper to an evening of pleasure. On his arm Janie was all in red, her face covered by a veil dotted with tiny synthetic bloodstones. Gem-studded veils were a fashion now nearly extinct among the women of the masters, but one that served to conceal the blankness of eye that betrayed Janie, as Paul had discovered, almost instantly. She gave a soft moan of hunger as she saw the boy, and clasped Paul's arm more tightly. Paul waved again.

The boy halted as though waiting for them, but when they were within five meters, he turned and dashed away. Janie was after him before Paul could stop her. The boy dodged between two buildings and raced through to the next street; Paul was just in time to see Janie follow him into a doorway in the center of the block.

He found her clear-soled platform shoes in the vestibule, under a four-dimensional picture of Hugo de Vries. De Vries was in the closing years of his life, and in the few seconds it took Paul to pick up the shoes and conceal them behind an aquarium of phosphorescent cephalopods, had died, rotted to dust, and undergone rebirth as a fissioning cell in his mother's womb with all the labyrinth of genetics still before him.

The lower floors, Paul knew, were apartments. He had entered them sometimes when he could find no prey on the streets. There would be a school at the top.

A confused, frightened-looking woman stood in an otherwise empty corridor, a disheveled library book lying open at her feet. As Paul pushed past her, he could imagine Janie knocking her out of the way, and the woman's horror at the savage, exultant face glimpsed beneath her veil.

There were elevators, a liftshaft, and a downshaft, all clustered in an alcove. *The boy would not have waited for an elevator with Janie close behind him. . . .*

The liftshaft floated Paul as spring water floats a cork. Thickened by conditioning agents, the air remained a gas; enriched with added oxygen; it stimulated his whole being, though it was as viscous as corn syrup when he drew it into his lungs. Far above, suspended (as it seemed) in crystal and surrounded by the books the boy had thrown down at her, he saw Janie with her red gown billowing around her and her white legs flashing. She was going to the top, apparently to the uppermost floor, and he reasoned that the boy, having led her there, would jump into the downshaft to escape her. He got off at the eighty-fifth floor, opened the hatch to the downshaft, and was rewarded by seeing the boy only a hundred meters above him. It was a simple matter then to wait on the landing and pluck him out of the sighing column of thickened air.

The boy's pointed, narrow face, white with fear under a tan, turned up toward him. "Don't," the boy said. "Please, sir, good master—" but Paul clamped him under his left arm, and with a quick wrench of his right broke his neck.

Janie was swimming head down with the downshaft current, her mouth open and full of eagerness, and her black hair like a cloud about her head. She had lost her veil. Paul showed her the boy and stepped into the shaft with her. The hatch slammed behind him, and the motion of the air ceased.

He looked at Janie. She had stopped swimming and was staring hungrily into the dead boy's face. He said, "Something's wrong," and she seemed to understand, though it was possible that she only caught the fear in his voice. The hatch would not open, and slowly the current in the shaft was reversing, lifting them; he tried to swim against it but the effort was hopeless. When they were at the top, the dead boy began to talk; Janie put her hand over his mouth to muffle the sound. The hatch at the landing opened, and they stepped out onto the hundred-and-first floor. A voice from a loudspeaker in the wall said: *"I am sorry to detain you, but there is reason to think you have undergone a recent deviation from the optimal development pattern. In a few minutes I will arrive in person to provide counseling; while you are waiting, it may be useful for us to review what is meant by 'optimal development.' Look at the projection.*

"In infancy the child first feels affection for its mother, the provider of warmth and food. . . ." There was a door at the other end of the room, and Paul swung a heavy chair against it, making a din that almost drowned out the droning speaker.

"Later one's peer group becomes, for a time, all-important—or nearly so. The boys and girls you see are attending a model school in Armstrong. Notice that no tint is used to mask the black of space above their air-tent."

The lock burst from the doorframe, but a remotely actuated hydraulic cylinder snapped it shut each time a blow from the chair drove it open. Paul slammed his shoulder against it, and before it could close again put his knee where the shattered bolt-socket had been. A chrome-plated steel rod as thick as a finger had dropped from the chair when his blows had smashed the wood and plastic holding it; after a moment of incomprehension, Janie dropped the dead boy, wedged the rod between the door and the jamb, and slipped through. He was following her when the rod lifted, and the door swung shut on his foot.

He screamed and screamed again, and then, in the echoing silence that followed, heard the loudspeaker mumbling about education, and Janie's sobbing, indrawn breath. Through the crack between the door and the frame, the two-centimeter space held in existence by what remained of his right foot, he could see the livid face and blind, malevolent eyes of the dead boy, whose will still held the steel rod suspended in air. "Die," Paul shouted at him. "Die! You're dead!" The rod came crashing down.

"This young woman," the loudspeaker said, *"has chosen the profession of medicine. She will be a physician, and she says now that she was born for that. She will spend the remainder of her life in relieving the agonies of disease."*

Several minutes passed before he could make Janie understand what it was she had to do.

"After her five years' training in basic medical techniques, she will specialize in surgery for another three years before—"

It took Janie a long time to bite through his Achilles' tendon; when it was over, she began to tear at the ligaments that held the bones of the tarsus to the leg. Over the pain he could feel the hot tears washing the blood from his foot.

Halfjack

ROGER ZELAZNY

Like a number of other writers, the late Roger Zelazny began publishing in 1962 in the pages of Cele Goldsmith's Amazing. *This was the so-called "Class of '62," whose membership also included Thomas M. Disch, Keith Laumer, and Ursula K. Le Guin. Everyone in that "class" would eventually achieve prominence, but some of them achieved it faster than others, and Zelazny's subsequent career would be one of the most meteoric in the history of SF. The first Zelazny story to attract wide notice was "A Rose for Ecclesiastics," published in 1963 (it was later selected by vote of the SFWA membership to have been one of the best SF stories of all time). By the end of that decade, he had won two Nebula Awards and two Hugo Awards and was widely regarded as one of the two most important American SF writers of the sixties (the other was Samuel R. Delany). By the end of the seventies, although his critical acceptance as an important science-fiction writer had dimmed, his long series of novels about the enchanted land of Amber—beginning with* Nine Princes in Amber—*had made him one of the most popular and best-selling fantasy writers of our time, and inspired the founding of worldwide fan clubs and fanzines.*

*Zelazny's early novels were, on the whole, well-received (*This Immortal *won a Hugo, as did his most famous novel* Lord of Light), *but it was the strong and stylish short work he published in magazines like* F&SF *and* Amazing *and* Worlds of If *throughout the middle years of the decade that electrified the genre, and it was these early stories—stories such as "This Moment of the Storm," "The Doors of His Face, The Lamps of His Mouth," "The Graveyard Heart," "He Who Shapes," "For a Breath I Tarry," "The Keys to December," and "This Mortal Mountain"—that established Zelazny as a giant of the field, and that many still consider to be his best work. These stories are still amazing for their invention and elegance and verve, for their good-natured effrontery and easy ostentation, for the risks Zelazny took in pursuit of eloquence without ruffling a hair, the grace and nerve he displayed as he switched from high-flown pseudo-Spenserian to wisecracking Chandlerian slang to vivid prose-poetry to Hemingwayesque starkness in the course of only a few lines— and for the way he made it all look easy and effortless, the same kind of illusion Fred Astaire used to generate when he danced.*

Here's a vivid and lyrical look into the life of a posthuman, accomplishing in a few short pages what many another writer would have taken a five-hundred-page novel to spell out.

Zelazny won another Nebula and Hugo Award in 1976 for his novella "Home Is the Hangman," another Hugo in 1986 for his novella "24 Views of Mt. Fuji, by Hosiki," and a final Hugo in 1987 for his story "Permafrost." His other books include, in addition to the multivolume Amber *series, the novels* This Immortal, The Dream Master, Isle of the Dead, Jack of Shadows, Eye of Cat, Doorways in the Sand, Today We Choose Faces, Bridge of Ashes, To Die in Italbar, *and* Roadmarks, *and the collections* Four For Tomorrow, The Doors of His Face, the Lamps of His Mouth and Other Stories, The Last Defender of Camelot, *and* Frost and Fire. *Among his last books are two collaborative novels,* A Farce to Be Reckoned With, *with Robert Sheckley, and* Wilderness *with Gerald Hausman, and as editor, two anthologies,* Wheel of Fortune *and* Warriors of Blood and Dream. *Zelazny died in 1995. Since his death, several posthumous collaborative novels have been published, including* Psychoshop, *with the late Alfred Bester, and* Donnerjack *and* Lord Demon, *both with Jane LIndskold. A tribute anthology to Zelazny, featuring stories by authors who had been inspired by his work,* Lord of the Fantastic, *was published in 1998.*

He walked barefoot along the beach. Above the city several of the brighter stars held for a few final moments against the wash of light from the east. He fingered a stone, then hurled it in the direction from which the sun would come. He watched for a long while until it had vanished from sight. Eventually it would begin skipping. Before then, he had turned and was headed back, to the city, the apartment, the girl.

Somewhere beyond the skyline a vehicle lifted, burning its way into the heavens. It took the remainder of the night with it as it faded. Walking on, he smelled the countryside as well as the ocean. It was a pleasant world, and this a pleasant city—spaceport as well as seaport—here in this backwater limb of the galaxy. A good place in which to rest and immerse the neglected portion of himself in the flow of humanity, the colors and sounds of the city, the constant tugging of gravity. But it had been three months now. He fingered the scar on his brow. He had let two offers pass him by to linger. There was another pending his consideration.

As he walked up Kathi's street, he saw that her apartment was still dark. Good, she would not even have missed him, again. He pushed past the big front door, still not repaired since he had kicked it open the evening of the fire, two—no, three—nights ago. He used the stairs. He let himself in quietly.

He was in the kitchen preparing breakfast when he heard her stirring.

"Jack?"

"Yes. Good morning."

"Come back."

"All right."

He moved to the bedroom door and entered the room. She was lying there, smiling. She raised her arms slightly.

"I've thought of a wonderful way to begin the day."

He seated himself on the edge of the bed and embraced her. For a moment she was sleep-warm and sleep-soft against him, but only for a moment.

"You've got too much on," she said, unfastening his shirt.

He peeled it off and dropped it. He removed his trousers. Then he held her again.

"More," she said, tracing the long fine scar that ran down his forehead, alongside his nose, traversing his chin, his neck, the right side of his chest and abdomen, passing to one side of his groin, where it stopped.

"Come on."

"You didn't even know about it until a few nights ago."

She kissed him, brushing his cheeks with her lips.

"It really does something for me."

"For almost three months—"

"Take it off. Please."

He sighed and gave a half-smile. He rose to his feet.

"All right."

He reached up and put a hand to his long, black hair. He took hold of it. He raised his other hand and spread his fingers along his scalp at the hairline. He pushed his fingers toward the back of his head and the entire hairpiece came free with a soft, crackling sound. He dropped the hairpiece atop his shirt on the floor.

The right side of his head was completely bald; the left had a beginning growth of dark hair. The two areas were precisely divided by a continuation of the faint scar on his forehead.

He placed his fingertips together on the crown of his head, then drew his right hand to the side and down. His face opened vertically, splitting apart along the scar, padded synthetic flesh tearing free from electrostatic bonds. He drew it down over his right shoulder and biceps, rolling it as far as his wrist. He played with the flesh of his hand as with a tight glove, finally withdrawing the hand with a soft, sucking sound. He drew it away from his side, hip, and buttock, and separated it at his groin. Then, again seating himself on the edge of the bed, he rolled it down his leg, over the thigh, knee, calf, heel. He treated his foot as he had his hand, pinching each toe free separately before pulling off the body glove. He shook it out and placed it with his clothing.

Standing, he turned toward Kathi, whose eyes had not left him during all this time. Again, the half-smile. The uncovered portions of his face and body were dark metal and plastic, precision-machined, with various openings and protuberances, some gleaming, some dusky.

"Halfjack," she said as he came to her. "Now I know what that man in the café meant when he called you that."

"He was lucky you were with me. There are places where that's an unfriendly term."

"You're beautiful," she said.

"I once knew a girl whose body was almost entirely prosthetic. She wanted me to keep the glove on—at all times. It was the flesh and the semblance of flesh that she found attractive."

"What do you call that kind of operation?"

"Lateral hemicorporectomy."

After a time she said. "Could you be repaired? Can you replace it some way?"

He laughed.

"Either way," he said. "My genes could be fractioned, and the proper replacement parts could be grown. I could be made whole with grafts of my own flesh. Or I could have much of the rest removed and replaced with biomechanical analogues. But I need a stomach and balls and lungs, because I have to eat and screw and breathe to feel human."

She ran her hands down his back, one on metal, one on flesh.

"I don't understand," she said when they finally drew apart. "What sort of accident was it?"

"Accident? There was no accident," he said. "I paid a lot of money for this work, so that I could pilot a special sort of ship. I am a cyborg. I hook myself directly into each of the ship's systems."

He rose from the bed, went to the closet, drew out a duffel bag, pulled down an armful of garments, and stuffed them into it. He crossed to the dresser, opened a drawer, and emptied its contents into the bag.

"You're leaving?"

"Yes."

He entered the bathroom, emerged with two fistfuls of personal items, and dropped them into the bag.

"Why?"

He rounded the bed, picked up his bodyglove and hairpiece, rolled them into a parcel, and put them inside the bag.

"It's not what you may think," he said then, "or even what I thought just a few moments ago."

She sat up.

"You think less of me," she said, "because I seem to like you more now that I know your secret. You think there's something pathological about it—"

"No," he said, pulling on his shirt, "that's not it at all. Yesterday I would have said so and used that for an excuse to storm out of here and leave you feeling bad. But I want to be honest with myself this time, and fair to you. That's not it."

He drew on his trousers.

"What then?" she asked.

"It's just the wanderlust, or whatever you call it. I've stayed too long at the bottom of a gravity well. I'm restless. I've got to get going again. It's my nature, that's all. I realized this when I saw that I was looking to your feelings for an excuse to break us up and move on."

"You can wear the bodyglove. It's not that important. It's really you that I like."

"I believe you, I like you, too. Whether you believe me or not, your reactions to my better half don't matter. It's what I said, though. Nothing else. And now I've got this feeling I won't be much fun anymore. If you really like me, you'll let me go without a lot of fuss."

He finished dressing. She got out of the bed and faced him.

"If that's the way it has to be," she said. "Okay."

"I'd better just go, then. Now."

"Yes."

He turned and walked out of the room, left the apartment, used the stairs again, and departed from the building. Some passersby gave him more than a casual look, cyborg pilots not being all that common in this sector. This did not bother him. His step lightened. He stopped in a pay-booth and called the shipping company to tell them that he would haul the load they had in orbit: the sooner it was connected with the vessel, the better, he said.

Loading, the controller told him, would begin shortly and he could ship up that same afternoon from the local field. Jack said that he would be there and then broke the connection. He gave the world half a smile as he put the sea to his back and swung on through the city, westward.

Blue-and-pink world below him, black sky above, the stars a snapshot snowfall all about, he bade the shuttle pilot good-bye and keyed his airlock. Entering the *Morgana*, he sighed and set about stowing his gear. His cargo was already in place and the ground computers had transferred course information to the ship's brain. He hung his clothing in a locker and placed his body glove and hairpiece in compartments.

He hurried forward then and settled into the control web, which adjusted itself about him. A long, dark unit swung down from overhead and dropped into position at his right. It moved slowly, making contact with various points on that half of his body.

—*Good to have you back. How was your vacation, Jack?*

—*Oh. Fine. Real fine.*

—*Meet any nice girls?*

—*A few.*

—*And here you are again. Did you miss things?*

—*You know it. How does this haul look to you?*

—*Easy, for us. I've already reviewed the course programs.*

—*Let's run over the systems.*

—*Check. Care for some coffee?*

—*That'd be nice.*

A small unit descended on his left, stopping within easy reach of his mortal hand. He opened its door. A bulb of dark liquid rested in a rack.

—*Timed your arrival. Had it ready.*

—*Just the way I like it, too. I almost forgot. Thanks.*

Several hours later, when they left orbit, he had already switched off a number of his left-side systems. He was merged even more closely with the vessel, absorbing data at a frantic rate. Their expanded perceptions took in the near-ship vicinity and moved out to encompass the extrasolar panorama with greater-than-human clarity and precision. They reacted almost instantaneously to decisions great and small.

—*It is good to be back together again, Jack.*

—*I'd say.*

Morgana held him tightly. Their velocity built.

Dancers in the Time-Flux

ROBERT SILVERBERG

Here's a visit to the very far future, a literary territory that has always fascinated Robert Silverberg, and a vivid demonstration that even when thousands or tens of thousands of years of evolution and technological advances separate the human from the posthuman, they may find that they still have a few things in common—depending on what dreams they share.

Robert Silverberg is one of the most famous SF writers of modern times, with dozens of novels, anthologies, and collections to his credit. As both writer and editor, Silverberg was one of the most influential figures of the Post New Wave era of the seventies, and continues to be at the forefront of the field to this very day, having won a total of five Nebula Awards and four Hugo Awards.

Born in Brooklyn, New York, in 1935, Silverberg, like Poul Anderson before him, started a successful career as an SF writer while he was still in college; his first novel was sold in 1954, while he was a junior at Columbia University; by 1955, still prior to graduation, he was earning "quite a good living" by writing, and by 1956, he had won his first Hugo Award. He spent a period of some years in the late fifties and early sixties away from the field, writing a long string of well-received nonfiction books, but by the late sixties he'd returned to the genre, and during the first half of the seventies, the so-called "New Silverberg" would produce a large and remarkable body of work: the brilliant Dying Inside, *easily one of the best books of the seventies,* Downward to the Earth, The Book of Skulls, Tower of Glass, The World Inside, The Second Trip, A Time of Changes, The Stochastic Man, *and* Shadrack In The Furnace, *as well as high-quality short work such as "Born With the Dead," "Sundance," "In Entropy's Jaws," "Breckenridge and the Continuum," "Push No More" "In the Group," "Capricorn Games," "Trips," "Swartz Between the Galaxies," and many more. Seldom has SF witnessed such a concentrated outpouring of high-level talent, work that would be highly influential on writers such as Barry N. Malzberg and the later Gregory Benford, to name just two, and which I strongly suspect was influential on writers of subsequent generations—such as Alexander Jablokov—as well. When you add in the influence that Silverberg would exert on the field through his editorship of the* New Dimensions *original anthology series, the most important anthology series of its day, you can see that the strength of Silverberg's impact on the SF world of the seventies can hardly be overestimated.*

In 1976, depressed by the general malaise that had settled over the field at the time, and perhaps exhausted from his efforts over the previous years, Silverberg publicly announced his "retirement" . . . and, indeed, would not write another word until 1980, when he suddenly came out of retirement to write his huge science-fantasy novel (also set in the far future), Lord Valentine's Castle. *His output of new fiction was relatively low in the early years of the decade, but when a new surge of creative energy revitalized the field in the mid-eighties, Silverberg shifted into high gear once again, and as what might perhaps be referred to—a bit facetiously—as the "New New Silverberg," poured out another torrent of high-quality work such as "The Pope of the Chimps," "Multiples," "The Palace at Midnight," "We Are for the Dark," "In Another Country," "Basileus," "The Secret Sharer," "Enter a Soldier." Later: "Enter Another," "Sailing to Byzantium," "Beauty in the Night," "Death Do Us Part," "The Colonel in Autumn," and dozens of others, as well as a score of best-selling novels—a torrent that shows no signs of running dry even here at the beginning of a new century.*

Silverberg's other books include the novels Son of Man, Thorns, Up the Line, The Man in the Maze, Tom O'Bedlam, Star of Gypsies, At Winter's End, The Face of the Waters, Kingdoms of the Wall, Hot Sky at Morning, *and two novel-length expansions of famous Isaac Asimov stories,* Nightfall *and* The Ugly Little Boy. *His collections include* Unfamiliar Territory, Capricorn Games, Majipoor Chronicles, The Best of Robert Silverberg, At The Conglomeroid Cocktail Party, Beyond the Safe Zone, *and a massive retrospective collection,* The Collected Stories of Robert Silverberg, Volume One: Secret Sharers. *His reprint anthologies are far too numerous to list here, but they include* The Science Fiction Hall of Fame, Volume One *and the distinguished* Alpha *series, among dozens of others. His most recent books are the novels* The Alien Years, Lord Prestimion, *and* Mountains of Majipoor. *He lives with his wife, writer Karen Haber, in Oakland, California.*

Under a warm golden wind from the west, Bhengarn the Traveler moves steadily onward toward distant Crystal Pond, his appointed place of metamorphosis. The season is late. The swollen scarlet sun clings close to the southern hills. Bhengarn's body—a compact silvery tube supported by a dozen pairs of sturdy three-jointed legs—throbs with the need for transformation. And yet the Traveler is unhurried. He has been bound on this journey for many hundreds of years. He has traced across the face of the world a glistening trail that zigzags from zone to zone, from continent to continent, and even now still glimmers behind him with a cold brilliance like a thread of bright metal stitching the planet's haunches. For the past decade he has patiently circled Crystal Pond at the outer end of a radical arm one-tenth the diameter of the Earth in length; now, at the prompting of some interior signal, he has begun to spiral inward upon it.

The path immediately before him is bleak. To his left is a district covered by furry green fog; to his right is a region of pale crimson grass sharp as spikes and sputtering with a sinister hostile hiss; straight ahead a roadbed of black clinkers and ashen crusts leads down a shallow slope to the Plain of Teeth, where menacing porcelaneous outcroppings make the wayfarer's task a taxing one. But such obstacles mean little to Bhengarn. He is a Traveler, after all. His body is superbly designed to carry him through all difficulties. And in his journeys he has been in places far worse than this.

Elegantly he descends the pathway of slag and cinders. His many feet are tough as annealed metal, sensitive as the most alert antennae. He tests each point in the road for stability and support, and scans the thick layer of ashes for concealed enemies. In this way he moves easily and swiftly toward the plain, holding his long abdomen safely above the cutting edges of the cold volcanic matter over which he walks.

As he enters the Plain of Teeth he sees a new annoyance: an Eater commands the gateway to the plain. Of all the forms of human life—and the Traveler has encountered virtually all of them in his wanderings, Eaters, Destroyers, Skimmers, Interceders, and the others—Eaters seem to him the most tiresome, mere noisy monsters. Whatever philosophical underpinnings form the rationale of their bizarre way of life are of no interest to him. He is wearied by their bluster and offended by their gross appetites.

All the same, he must get past this one to reach his destination. The huge creature stands straddling the path with one great meaty leg at each edge and the thick fleshy tail propping it from behind. Its steely claws are exposed, its fangs gleam, driblets of blood from recent victims stain its hard reptilian hide. Its chilly inquisitive eyes, glowing with demonic intelligence, track Bhengarn as the traveler draws near.

The Eater emits a boastful roar and brandishes its many teeth.

"You block my way," Bhengarn declares.

"You state the obvious," the Eater replies.

"I have no desire for an encounter with you. But my destiny draws me toward Crystal Pond, which lies beyond you."

"For you," says the Eater, "nothing lies beyond me. Your destiny has brought you to a termination today. We will collaborate, you and I, in the transformation of your component molecules."

From the spiracles along his sides the Traveler releases a thick blue sigh of boredom. "The only transformation that waits for me is the one I will undertake at Crystal Pond. You and I have no transaction. Stand aside."

The Eater roars again. He rocks slightly on his gigantic claws and swishes his vast saurian tail from side to side. These are the preliminaries to an attack, but in a kind of ponderous courtesy, he seems to be offering Bhengarn the opportunity to scuttle back up the ash-strewn slope.

Bhengarn says, "Will you yield place?"

"I am an instrument of destiny."

"You are a disagreeable, boastful ignoramus," says Bhengarn calmly, and consumes half a week's energy driving the scimitars of his spirit to the roots of the world. It is not a wasted expense of soul, for the ground trembles, the sky grows dark, the hill behind him creaks and groans, the wind turns purplish and frosty. There is a dull droning sound that the Traveler knows is the song of the time-flux, an unpredictable force that often is liberated at such moments. Despite that, Bhengarn will not relent. Beneath the Eater's splayed claws the fabric of the road ripples. Sour smells rise from sudden crevasses. The enormous beast utters a yipping cry of rage and lashes his tail vehemently against the ground. He sways; he nearly topples; he calls out to Bhengarn to cease his onslaught, but the Traveler knows better than to settle for a half-measure. Even more fiercely he presses against the Eater's bulky form.

"This is unfair," the Eater wheezes. "My goal is the same as yours: to serve the forces of necessity."

"Serve them by eating someone else today," answers Bhengarn curtly, and with a final expenditure of force shoves the Eater to an awkward untenable position that causes it to crash down onto its side. The downed beast, moaning, rakes the air with his claws but does not arise, and as Bhengarn moves briskly past the Eater, he observes that fine transparent threads, implacable as stone, have shot forth from a patch of swamp beside the road and are rapidly binding the fallen Eater in an unbreakable net. The Eater howls. Glancing back, Bhengarn notices the threads already cutting their way through the Eater's thick scales like tiny streams of acid. "So, then," Bhengarn says, without malice, "the forces of necessity will be gratified today after all, but not by me. The Eater is to be eaten. It seems that this day I prove to be the instrument of destiny." And without another backward look, he passes quickly onward into the plain. The sky regains its ruddy color, the wind becomes mild once more, the Earth is still. But a release of the time-flux is never without consequences, and as the Traveler trundles forward, he perceives some new creature of unfamiliar form staggering through the mists ahead, confused and lost, lurching between the shining lethal formations of the Plain of Teeth in seeming ignorance of the perils they hold. The creature is upright, two-legged, hairy, of archaic appearance. Bhengarn, approaching it, recognizes it finally as a primordial human, swept millions of years past its own true moment.

"Have some care," Bhengarn calls. "Those teeth can bite!"

"Who spoke?" the archaic creature demands, whirling about in alarm.

"I am Bhengarn the Traveler. I suspect I am responsible for your presence here."

"Where are you? I see no one! Are you a devil?"

"I am a Traveler, and I am right in front of your nose."

The ancient human notices Bhengarn, apparently for the first time, and leaps back, gasping. "Serpent!" he cries. "Serpent with legs! Worm! Devil!" Wildly he seizes rocks and hurls them at the Traveler, who deflects them easily enough, turning each into a rhythmic juncture of gold and green that hovers, twanging softly, along an arc between the other and himself. The archaic one lifts an immense boulder, but as he hoists it to drop it on Bhengarn, he overbalances and his arm flies backward, grazing one of the sleek teeth behind him. At once the tooth releases a turquoise flare and the man's arm vanishes to the elbow. He sinks to his knees, whimpering, staring bewilderedly at the stump and at the Traveler before him.

Bhengarn says, "You are in the Plain of Teeth, and any contact with these mineral formations is likely to be unfortunate, as I attempted to warn you."

He slides himself into the other's soul for an instant, pushing his way past thick encrusted stalagmites and stalactites of anger, fear, outraged pride, pain, disorientation, and arrogance, and discovers himself to be in the presence of one Olivier van Noort of Utrecht, former tavernkeeper at Rotterdam, commander of the voyage of circumnavigation that set forth from Holland on the second day of July 1598 and traveled the entire belly of the world, a man of exceedingly strong stomach and bold temperament, who has experienced much, having gorged on the meat of penguins at Cape Virgines and the isle called Pantagorns, having hunted beasts not unlike stags and buffaloes and ostriches in the cold lands by Magellan's Strait, having encountered whales and parrots and trees whose bark had the bite of pepper, having had strife with the noisome Portugals in Guinea and Brazil, having entered into the South Sea on a day of diverse storms, thunders, and lightnings, having taken ships of the Spaniards in Valparaiso and slain many Indians, having voyaged thence to the Isles of Ladrones or Thieves, where the natives bartered bananas, coconuts, and roots for old pieces of iron, overturning their canoes in their greed for metal, having suffered a bloody flux in Manila of eating palmitos, having captured vessels of China laden with rice and lead, having traded with folk on a ship of the Japans, whose men make themselves bald except a tuft left in the hinder part of the head, and wield swords that would, with one stroke, cut through three men, having traded also with the barebreasted women of Borneo, bold and impudent and shrewd, who carry ironpointed javelins and sharp darts, and having after great privation and the loss of three of his four ships and all but forty-five of his 248 men, many of them executed by him or marooned on remote islands for their mutinies but a good number murdered by the treacheries of savage enemies, come again to Rotterdam on the twenty-sixth of August in 1601, bearing little in the way of salable goods to show for his hardships and calamities. None of this has any meaning to Bhengarn the Traveler except in the broadest, which is to say that he recognizes in Olivier van Noort a stubborn and difficult man who has conceived and executed a journey of mingled heroism and foolishness that spanned vast distances, and so they are brothers, of a sort, however millions of years apart. As a fraternal gesture, Bhengarn restores the newcomer's arm. That appears to be as bewildering to the other as was its sudden loss. He squeezes it, moves it cautiously back and forth, scoops up a handful of pebbles with it. "This is Hell, then," he mutters, "and you are a demon of Satan."

"I am Bhengarn the Traveler, bound toward Crystal Pond, and I think that I conjured you by accident out of your proper place in time while seeking to thwart that monster." Bhengarn indicates the fallen Eater, now half dissolved. The other, who evidently had not looked that way before, makes a harsh choking sound at the sight of the giant creature, which still struggles sluggishly. Bhengarn says, "The time-flux has seized you and taken you far from home, and there will be no going back for you. I offer regrets."

"You offer regrets? A worm with legs offers regrets! Do I dream this, or am I truly dead and gone to Hell?"

"Neither one."

"In all my sailing round the world I never saw a place so strange as this, or the likes of you, or of that creature over yonder. Am I to be tortured, demon?"

"You are not where you think you are."

"Is this not Hell?"

"This is the world of reality."

"How far are we, then, from Holland?"

"I am unable to calculate it," Bhengarn answers. "A long way, that's certain. Will you accompany me toward Crystal Pond, or shall we part here?"

Noort is silent a moment. Then he says, "Better the company of demons than none at all, in such a place. Tell me straight, demon: am I to be punished here? I see hellfire on the horizon. I will find the rivers of fire, snow, toads, and black water, will I not? And the place where sinners are pronged on hooks jutting from blazing wheels? The ladders of red-hot iron, eh? The wicked broiling on coals? And the Arch-Traitor himself, sunk in ice to his chest—he must be near, is he not?" Noort shivers. "The fountains of poison. The wild boars of Lucifer. The aloes biting bare flesh, the dry winds of the abyss—when will I see them?"

"Look there," says Bhengarn. Beyond the Plain of Teeth a column of black flame rises into the heavens, and in it dance creatures of a hundred sorts, melting, swirling, coupling, fading. A chain of staring lidless eyes spans the sky. Looping whorls of green light writhe on the mountaintops. "Is that what you expect? You will find whatever you expect here."

"And yet you say this is not Hell?"

"I tell you again, it is the true world, the same into which you were born long ago."

"And is this Brazil, or the Indies, or some part of Africa?"

"Those names mean little to me."

"Then we are in the Terra Australis," says Noort. "It must be. A land where worms have legs and speak good Dutch, and rocks can bite, and arms once lost can sprout anew—yes, it must surely be the Terra Australis, or else the land of Prester John. Eh? Is Prester John your king?" Noort laughs. He seems to be emerging from his bewilderment. "Tell me the name of this land, creature, so I may claim it for the United Provinces, if ever I see Holland again."

"It has no name."

"No name! No name! What foolishness! I never found a place whose folk had no name for it, not even in the endless South Sea. But I will name it, then. Let this province be called New Utrecht, eh? And all this land, from here to the shores of the South Sea, I annex hereby to the United Provinces in the name of the States-General. You be my witness, creature. Later I will draw up documents. You say I am not dead?"

"Not dead, not dead at all. But far from home. Come, walk beside me, and touch nothing. This is troublesome territory."

"This is strange and ghostly territory," says Noort. "I would paint it, if I could, and then let Mynheer Brueghel look to his fame, and old Bosch as well. Such sights! Were you a prince before you were transformed?"

"I have not yet been transformed," says Bhengarn. "That awaits me at Crystal Pond." The road through the plain now trends slightly uphill; they are advancing into the farther side of the basin. A pale-yellow tint comes into the sky. The path here is prickly with little many-faceted insects whose hard sharp bodies assail the Dutchman's bare tender feet. Cursing, he hops in wild leaps, bringing him dangerously close to outcroppings of teeth, and

Bhengarn, in sympathy, fashions stout gray boots for him. Noort grins. He gestures toward his bare middle, and Bhengarn clothes him in a shapeless gray robe.

"Like a monk, is how I look!" Noort cries. "Well, well, a monk in Hell! But you say this is not Hell. And what kind of creature are you, creature?"

"A human being," says Bhengarn, "of the Traveler sort."

"A human being!" Noort booms. He leaps across a brook of sparkling bubbling violet-hued water and waits on the far side as Bhengarn trudges through it. "A human under an enchantment, I would venture."

"This is my natural form. Humankind has not worn your guise since long before the falling of the Moon. The Eater you saw was human. Do you see, on yonder eastern hill, a company of Destroyers turning the forest to rubble? They are human."

"The wolves on two legs up there?"

"Those, yes. And there are others you will see. Awaiters, Breathers, Skimmers—"

"These are mere noises to me, creature. What is human? A Dutchman is human! A Portugal is human! Even a Chinese, a black, a Japonder with a shaven head. But those beasts on yon hill? Or a creature with more legs than I have whiskers. No, Traveler, no! You flatter yourself. Do you happen to know, Traveler, how it is that I am here? I was in Amsterdam, to speak before the Lords Seventeen and the Company in general, to ask for ships to bring pepper from the Moluccas, but they said they would choose Joris van Spilbergen in my place—do you know Spilbergen? I think him much overpraised—and then all went dizzy, as though I had taken too much beer with my gin—and then—then—ah, this is a dream, is it not, Traveler? At this moment I sleep in Amsterdam. I am too old for such drinking. Yet never have I had a dream so real as this, and so strange. Tell me: when you walk, do you move the legs on the right side first, or the left?" Noort does not wait for a reply. "If you are human, Traveler, are you also a Christian, then?"

Bhengarn searches in Noort's mind for the meaning of that, finds something approximate, and says, "I make no such claim."

"Good. Good. There are limits to my credulity. How far is this Crystal Pond?"

"We have covered most of the distance. If I proceed at a steady pace, I will come shortly to the land of smoking holes, and not far beyond that is the approach to the Wall of Ice, which will demand a difficult but not impossible ascent, and just on the far side of that I will find the vale that contains Crystal Pond, where the beginning of the next phase of my life will occur." They are walking now through a zone of sparkling rubbery cones of a bright vermilion color, from which small green Stangarones emerge in quick succession to chant their one-note melodies. The flavor of a heavy musk hangs in the air. Night is beginning to fall. Bhengarn says, "Are you tired?"

"Just a little."

"It is not my custom to travel by night. Does this campsite suit you?" Bhengarn indicates a broad circular depression bordered by tiny volcanic fumaroles. The ground here is warm and spongy, moist, bare of vegetation.

Bhengarn extends an excavator claw and pulls free a strip of it, which he hands to Noort, indicating that he should eat. Noort tentatively nibbles. Bhengarn helps himself to some also. Noort, kneeling, presses his knuckles against the ground, makes it yield, mutters to himself, shakes his head, rips off another strip and chews it in wonder. Bhengarn says, "You find the world much changed, do you not?"

"Beyond all understanding, in fact."

"Our finest artists have worked on it since time immemorial, making it more lively, more diverting. We think it is a great success. Do you agree?"

Noort does not answer. He is staring bleakly at the sky, suddenly dark and jeweled with blazing stars. Bhengarn realizes that he is searching for patterns, navigators' signs. Noort frowns, turns round and round to take in the full circuit of the heavens, bites his lip, finally lets out a low groaning sigh and says, "I recognize nothing. Nothing. This is not the northern sky, this is not the southern sky, this is not any sky I can understand." Quietly he begins to weep. After a time he says somberly, "I was not the most adept of navigators, but I knew something, at least. And I look at this sky and I feel like a helpless babe. All the stars have changed places. Now I see how lost I am, how far from anything I ever knew, and once it gave me great pleasure to sail under strange skies, but not now, not here, because these skies frighten me and this land of demons offers me no peace. I have never wept, do you know that, creature, never, not once in my life! But Holland—my house, my tavern, my church, my sons, my pipe—where is Holland? Where is everything I knew? The skies above Magellan's Strait were not the thousandth part so strange as this." A harsh heavy sob escapes him, and he turns away, huddling into himself.

Compassion floods Bhengarn for this miserable wanderer. To ease Noort's pain, he summons fantasies for him, dredging images from the reservoirs of the ancient man's spirit and hurling them against the sky, building a cathedral of fire in the heavens, and a royal palace, and a great armada of ships with bellying sails and the Dutch flag fluttering, and the watery boulevards of busy Amsterdam and the quiet streets of little Haarlem, and more. He paints for Noort the stars in their former courses, the Centaur, the Swan, the Bear, the Twins. He restores the fallen Moon to its place and by its cold light creates a landscape of time lost and gone, with avenues of heavy-boughed oaks and maples, and drifts of brilliant red and yellow tulips blazing beneath them, and golden roses arching in great bowers over the thick, newly mowed lawn. He creates fields of ripe wheat, and haystacks high as barns, and harvesters toiling in the hot sultry afternoon. He gives Noort the aroma of the Sunday feast and the scent of good Dutch gin and the sweet dense fumes of his long clay pipe. Noort nods and murmurs and clasps his hands, and gradually his sorrow ebbs and his weeping ceases, and he drifts off into a deep and easy slumber. The images fade. Bhengarn, who rarely sleeps, keeps watch until first light comes and a flock of fingerwinged birds passes overhead, shouting shrilly, jesting and swooping.

Noort is calm and quiet in the morning. He feeds again on the spongy soil and drinks from a clear emerald rivulet and they move onward toward

Crystal Pond. Bhengarn is pleased to have his company. There is something crude and coarse about the Dutchman, perhaps even more so than another of his era might be, but Bhengarn finds that unimportant. He has always preferred companions of any sort to the solitary march, in his centuries of going to and fro upon the Earth. He has traveled with Skimmers and Destroyers, and once a ponderous Ruminant, and even on several occasions visitors from other worlds who have come to sample the wonders of Earth. At least twice Bhengarn has had as his traveling companion a castaway of the time-flux from some prehistoric era, though not so prehistoric as Noort's. And now it has befallen him that he will go to the end of his journey with this rough hairy being from the dawn of humanity's day. So be it. So be it.

Noort says, breaking a long silence as they cross a plateau of quivering gelatinous stuff, "Were you a man or a woman before the sorcery gave you this present shape?"

"I have always had this form."

"No. Impossible. You say you are human, you speak my language—"

"Actually, you speak *my* language," says Bhengarn.

"As you wish. If you are human, you must once have looked like me. Can it be otherwise? Were you born a thing of silvery scales and many legs? I will not believe that."

"Born?" says Bhengarn, puzzled.

"Is this word unknown to you?"

"Born," the Traveler repeats. "I think I see the concept. To *begin*, to *enter*, to *acquire one's shape*—"

"Born," says Noort in exasperation. "To come from the womb. To hatch, to sprout, to drop. Everything alive has to be born!"

"No," Bhengarn says mildly. "Not any longer."

"You talk nonsense," Noort snaps, and scours his throat angrily and spits. His spittle strikes a node of assonance and blossoms into a dazzling mound of green and scarlet jewels. "Rubies," he murmurs. "Emeralds. I could puke pearls, I suppose." He kicks at the pile of gems and scatters them; they dissolve into spurts of moist pink air. The Dutchman gives himself over to a sullen brooding. Bhengarn does not transgress on the other's taciturnity; he is content to march forward in his steady plodding way, saying nothing.

Three Skimmers appear, prancing, leaping. They are heading to the south. The slender golden-green creatures salute the wayfarers with pulsations of their great red eyes. Noort, halting, glares at them and says hoarsely to Bhengarn, "These are human beings, too?"

"Indeed."

"Natives of this realm?"

"Natives of this era," says Bhengarn. "The latest form, the newest thing, graceful, supple, purposeless." The Skimmers laugh and transform themselves into shining streaks of light and soar aloft like a trio of auroral rays. Bhengarn says, "Do they seem beautiful to you?"

"They seem like minions of Satan," says the Dutchman sourly. He scowls. "When I awaken, I pray I remember none of this. For if I do, I will tell the tale to Willem and Jan and Piet, and they will think I have lost my senses, and mock me. Tell me I dream, creature. Tell me I lie drunk in an inn in Amsterdam."

"It is not so," Bhengarn says gently.

"Very well. Very well. I have come to a land where every living thing is a demon or a monster. That is no worse, I suppose, than a land where everyone speaks Japanese and worships stones. It is a world of wonders, and I have seen more than my share. Tell me, creature, do you have cities in this land?"

"Not for millions of years."

"Then where do the people live?"

"Why, they live where they find themselves! Last night we lived where the ground was food. Tonight we will settle by the Wall of Ice. And tomorrow—"

"Tomorrow," Noort says, "we will have dinner with the Grand Diabolus and dance in the Witches' Sabbath. I am prepared, just as I was prepared to sup with the penguin-eating folk of the Cape, that stood six cubits high. I will be surprised by nothing." He laughs. "I am hungry, creature. Shall I tear up the earth again and stuff it down?"

"Not here. Try those fruits."

Luminous spheres dangle from a tree of golden limbs. Noort plucks one, tries it unhesitatingly, claps his hands, takes three more. Then he pulls a whole cluster free, and offers one to Bhengarn, who refuses.

"Not hungry?" the Dutchman asks.

"I take my food in other ways."

"Yes, you breathe it in from flowers as you crawl along, eh? Tell me, Traveler: to what end is your journey? To discover new lands? To fulfill some pledge? To confound your enemies? I doubt it is any of these."

"I travel out of simple necessity, because it is what my kind does, and for no special purpose."

"A humble wanderer, then, like the mendicant monks who serve the Lord by taking to the highways?"

"Something like that."

"Do you ever cease your wanderings?"

"Never yet. But cessation is coming. At Crystal Pond I will become my utter opposite, and enter the Awaiter tribe, and be made immobile and contemplative. I will root myself like a vegetable, after my metamorphosis."

Noort offers no comment on that. After a time he says, "I knew a man of your kind once. Jan Huyghen van Linschoten of Haarlem, who roamed the world because the world was there to roam, and spent his years in the India of the Portugals and wrote it all down in a great vast book, and when he had done that went off to Novaya Zemlya with Barents to find the chilly way to the Indies, and I think would have sailed to the Moon if he could find the pilot to guide him. I spoke with him once. My own travels took me farther than Linschoten, do you know? I saw Borneo and Java and the world's hinder side, and the thick Sargasso Sea. But I went with a purpose other than my own amusement or the gathering of strange lore, which was to buy pepper and cloves, and gather Spanish gold, and win my fame and comfort. Was that so wrong, Traveler? Was I so unworthy?" Noort chuckles. "Perhaps I was, for I brought home neither spices nor gold nor most of my men, but only the fame of having sailed around the world. I think I understand you, Traveler. The spices go into a cask of meat and are eaten and gone; the gold is only yellow metal; but so long as there are Dutchmen, no one will forget that Olivier van Noort, the tavernkeeper of Rotterdam, strung a line around the middle of the world. So long as there are Dutchmen." He laughs. "It is folly to travel for profit. I will travel for wisdom from now on. What do you say, Traveler? Do you applaud me?"

"I think you are already on the proper path," says Bhengarn. "But look, look there: the Wall of Ice."

Noort gasps. They have come around a low headland and are confronted abruptly by a barrier of pure white light, as radiant as a mirror at noon, that spans the horizon from east to west and rises skyward like an enormous palisade filling half the heavens. Bhengarn studies it with respect and admiration. He has known for hundreds of years that he must ascend this wall if he is to reach Crystal Pond, and that the wall is formidable; but he has seen no need before now to contemplate the actualities of the problem, and now he sees that they are significant.

"Are we to ascend that?" Noort asks.

"I must. But here, I think, we shall have to part company."

"The throne of Lucifer must lie beyond that icy rampart."

"I know nothing of that," says Bhengarn, "but certainly Crystal Pond is on the farther side, and there is no other way to reach it but to climb the wall. We will camp tonight at its base, and in the morning I will begin my climb."

"Is such a climb possible?"

"It will have to be," Bhengarn replies.

"Ah. You will turn yourself to a puff of light like those others we met, and shoot over the top like some meteor. Eh?"

"I must climb," says Bhengarn, "using one limb after another, and taking care not to lose my grip. There is no magical way of making this ascent." He sweeps aside fallen branches of a glowing blue-limbed shrub to make a campsite for them. To Noort he says, "Before I begin the ascent tomorrow, I will instruct you in the perils of the world, for your protection on your future wanderings. I hold myself responsible for your presence here, and I would not have you harmed once you have left my side."

Noort says, "I am not yet planning to leave your side. I mean to climb that wall alongside you, Traveler."

"It will not be possible for you."

"I will make it possible. That wall excites my spirit. I will conquer it as I conquered the storms of the Strait and the fevers of the Sargasso. I feel I should go with you to Crystal Pond, and pay my farewells to you there, for it will bring me luck to mark the beginning of my solitary journey by witnessing the end of yours. What do you say?"

"I say wait until the morning," Bhengarn answers, "and see the wall at close range, before you commit yourself to such mighty resolutions."

During the night a silent lightstorm plays overhead; twisting turbulent spears of blue and green and violet radiance clash in the throbbing sky, and an undulation of the atmosphere sends alternating waves of hot and cool air racing down from the Wall of Ice. The time-flux blows, and frantic figures out of forgotten eras are swept by now far aloft, limbs churning desperately, eyes rigid with astonishment. Noort sleeps through it all, though from time to time he stirs and mutters and clenches his fists. Bhengarn ponders his obligations to the Dutchman, and by the coming of the sharp blood-hued dawn, he has arrived at an idea. Together they advance to the edge of the Wall; together they stare upward at that vast vertical field of shining white-ness, smooth as stone. Hesitantly Noort touches it with his fingertip, and hisses at the coldness of it. He turns his back to it, paces, folds and unfolds his arms.

He says finally, "No man or woman born could achieve the summit of that wall. But is there not some magic you could work, Traveler, that would enable me to make the ascent?"

"There is one. But I think you would not like it."

"Speak."

"I could transform you—for a short time, only a short time, no longer than the time it takes to climb the wall—into a being of the Traveler form. Thus we could ascend together."

Noort's eyes travel quickly over Bhengarn's body—the long tubular ser-pentine thorax, the tapering tail, the multitude of powerful little legs—and a look of shock and dismay and loathing comes over his face for an instant, but just an instant. He frowns. He tugs at his heavy lower lip.

Bhengarn says, "I will take no offense if you refuse."

"Do it."

"You may be displeased."

"Do it! The morning is growing old. We have much climbing to do. Change me, Traveler. Change me quickly." A shadow of doubt crosses Noort's features. "You will change me back, once we reach the top?"

"It will happen of its own accord. I have no power to make a permanent transformation."

"Then do what you can, and do it now!"

"Very well," says Bhengarn, and the Traveler, summoning his fullest force, drains metamorphic energies from the planets and the stars and a passing comet, and focuses them and hurls them at the Dutchman, and there is a buzzing and a droning and a shimmering and when it is done, a second Traveler stands at the foot of the Wall of Ice.

Noort seems thunderstruck. He says nothing; he does not move; only after a long time does he carefully lift his frontmost left limb and swing it forward a short way and put it down. Then the one opposite it; then several of the middle limbs; then, growing more adept, he manages to move his entire body, adopting a curious wriggling style, and in another moment he appears to be in control. "This is passing strange," he remarks at length. "And yet it is almost like being in my own body, except that everything has been changed. You are a mighty wizard, Traveler. Can you show me now how to make the ascent?"

"Are you ready so soon?"

"I am ready," Noort says.

So Bhengarn demonstrates, approaching the wall, bringing his penetrator claws into play, driving them like pitons into the ice, hauling himself up a short distance, extending the claws, driving them in, pulling upward. He has never climbed ice before, though he has faced all other difficulties the world has to offer, but the climb, though strenuous, seems manageable enough. He halts after a few minutes and watches as Noort, clumsy but determined in his altered body, imitates him, scratching and scraping at the ice as he pulls himself up the face until they are side by side. "It is easy," Noort says.

And so it is, for a time, and then it is less easy, for now they hang high above the valley and the midday sun has melted the surface of the wall just enough to make it slick and slippery, and a terrible cold from within the mass of ice seeps outward into the climbers, and even though a Traveler's body is a wondrous machine fit to endure anything, this is close to the limit. Once Bhengarn loses his purchase, but Noort deftly claps a claw to the middle of his spine to hold him firmly until he has dug in again; and not much later the same happens to Noort, and Bhengarn grasps him. As the day wanes they are so far above the ground that they can barely make out the treetops below, and yet the top of the wall is too high to see. Together they excavate a ledge, burrowing inward to rest in a chilly nook, and at dawn they begin again, Bhengarn's sinuous body winding upward over the rim of their little cave and Noort following with less agility. Upward and upward they climb, never pausing and saying little, through a day of warmth and soft perfumed breezes and through a night of storms and falling stars, and then through a day of turquoise rain, and through another day and a night and a day and then they are at the top, looking out across the broad unending field of ferns and bright blossoms that covers the summit's flat surface, and as they move inward from the rim, Noort lets out a cry and stumbles forward, for he has resumed his ancient form. He drops to his knees and sits there panting, stunned, looking in confusion at his fingernails, at his knuckles, at the hair on the backs of his hands, as though he has never seen such things before. "Passing strange," he says softly.

"You are a born Traveler," Bhengarn tells him.

They rest a time, feeding on the sparkling four-winged fruits that sprout in that garden above the ice. Bhengarn feels an immense calmness now that the climax of his peregrination is upon him. Never had he questioned the purpose of being a Traveler, nor has he had regret that destiny gave him that form, but now he is quite willing to yield it up.

"How far to Crystal Pond?" Noort asks.

"It is just over there," says Bhengarn.

"Shall we go to it now?"

"Approach it with great care," the Traveler warns. "It is a place of extraordinary power."

They go forward; a path opens for them in the swaying grasses and low fleshy-leaved plants; within minutes they stand at the edge of a perfectly circular body of water of unfathomable depth and of a clarity so complete that the reflections of the sun can plainly be seen on the white sands of its infinitely distant bed. Bhengarn moves to the edge and peers in, and is pervaded by a sense of fulfillment and finality.

Noort says, "What will become of you here?"

"Observe," says Bhengarn.

He enters Crystal Pond and swims serenely toward the farther shore, an enterprise quickly enough accomplished. But before he has reached the midpoint of the pond, a tolling sound is heard in the air, as of bells of the most pure quality, striking notes without harmonic overtones. Sudden ecstasy engulfs him as he becomes aware of the beginning of his transformation: his body flows and streams in the flux of life, his limbs fuse, his soul expands. By the time he comes forth on the edge of the pond, he has become something else, a great cone of passive flesh, which is able to drag itself no more than five or six times its own length from the water, and then sinks down on the sandy surface of the ground and begins the process of digging itself in. Here the Awaiter Bhengarn will settle, and here he will live for centuries of centuries, motionless, all but timeless, considering the primary truths of being. Already he is gliding into the Earth.

Noort gapes at him from the other side of the pond.

"Is this what you sought?" the Dutchman asks.

"Yes. Absolutely."

"I wish you farewell and Godspeed, then!" Noort cries.

"And you—what will become of you?"

Noort laughs. "Have no fears for me! I see my destiny unfolding!"

Bhengarn, nestled now deep in the ground, enwombed by the earth, immobile, established already in his new life, watches as Noort strides boldly to the water's edge. Only slowly, for an Awaiter's mind is less agile than a Traveler's, does Bhengarn comprehend what is to happen.

Noort says, "I've found my vocation again. But if I'm to travel, I must be equipped for traveling!"

He enters the pond, swimming in broad awkward splashing strokes, and once again the pure tolling sound is evoked, a delicate carillon of crystalline transparent tone, and there is sudden brilliance in the pond as Noort sprouts the shining scales of a Traveler, and the jointed limbs, and the strong thick tail. He scuttles out on the far side wholly transformed.

"Farewell!" Noort cries joyously.

"Farewell," murmurs Bhengarn the Awaiter, peering out from the place of his long repose as Olivier van Noort, all his legs ablaze with new energy, strides away vigorously to begin his second circumnavigation of the globe.

Spook

BRUCE STERLING

One of the most powerful and innovative new talents to enter SF in the past few decades, Bruce Sterling sold his first story in 1976. By the end of the eighties, he had established himself—with a series of stories set in his exotic "Shape/Mechanist" future, with novels such as the complex and Stapeldonian Schismatrix, *and with the well-received* Islands in the Net *as well as with his editing of the influential anthology* Mirrorshades: The Cyberpunk Anthology *and the infamous critical magazine* Cheap Truth, *as perhaps the prime driving force behind the revolutionary "Cyberpunk" movement in science fiction, and also as one of the best new "hard science" writers to enter the field in some time. His other books include a critically acclaimed nonfiction study of First Amendment issues in the world of computer networking,* The Hacker Crackdown: Law and Disorder on the Electronic Frontier, *the novels* The Artificial Kid, Involution Ocean, Heavy Weather, Holy Fire, *and* Distraction; *a novel in collaboration with William Gibson,* The Difference Engine; *and the landmark collections* Crystal Express *and* Globalhead. *His most recent books include the omnibus collection (it contains the novel* Schismatrix *as well as most of his Shaper/Mechanist stories)* Schismatrix Plus; *a new collection,* A Good Old-Fashioned Future, *and a new novel,* Zeitgeist. *His story "Bicycle Repairman" earned him a long-overdue Hugo in 1997, and he won another Hugo in 1997 for his story "Taklamakan." He lives with his family in Austin, Texas.*

Sterling has long been one of the writers in the genre most concerned with figuring out what a "posthuman" would really be like, a subject that continues to involve him to this very day. Here's a fast-paced and hard-edged early take on the theme, one with some disconcerting surprises in store.

For Rudy Rucker

The spook was peeling off from orbit, headed for Washington, D.C., and it felt just great. The spook twisted convulsively in his seat, grinning out the Plexiglas at the cheery red-hot glow of the shuttle's wind edges.

Far below, the unnatural green of genetically altered forests showed the faint scars of old-time roads and fence lines. The spook ran long, narrow, agile fingers through the roots of his short-cropped blue hair. He hadn't made groundfall in ten months. Already the cooped-up feeling of the orbiting zaibatseries was peeling off cold and crisp like a snake's skin.

The shuttle decelerated through Mach 4 with a faint, delicious shiver. The spook twisted in his seat and turned a long, slanted, green glance past the sleeping plutocrat in the seat beside him and at a woman across the aisle. She had that cool, starved zaibatsery look and those hollow veinwebby eyes. . . .

Looked like the gravity was giving her trouble already, she'd spent too much time floating along those low-grav zaibatsery axes of rotation. She'd pay for it when they made groundfall, when she'd have to shuffle all cute from waterbed to waterbed, like helpless prey. . . . The spook looked down; his hands were making unconscious twitchy, clawing motions in his lap. He picked them up and shook the tension out of them. Silly little hands. . . .

The forests of the Maryland Piedmont skinned by like green video. Washington and the DNA recombo labs of Rockville, Maryland, were 1,080 clean-ticking seconds away. He couldn't remember when he'd ever had so much fun. Inside his right ear, the computer whispered, whispered. . . .

The shuttle albatrossed down on the reinforced runway, and airport groundcraft foamed it cool. The spook decamped, clutching his valise.

A chopper was waiting for him from the private security apparat of the Replicon corporation. While it flew him to Replicon's Rockville HQ, he had a drink, shuddering a little at the intuitive impact of the unspoken paradigms of the chopper's interior. The techniques he had learned in the zaibatsery espionage camp oozed up his hindbrain like psychotic flashbacks. Under the impact of gravity, fresh air, and plush upholstery, whole sections of his personality were decaying at once.

He was as sweet and fluid as the heart of a rotting melon. This was fluidity, slick as grease, all right. . . . Acting on intuition, he opened his valise, took a mechanical comb from a grooming case, and flicked it on with the iridescent nail of his right thumb. Black dye from the comb's vibrating teeth soothed and darkened his blue zaibatsery coif.

He unplugged the tiny jack that was coupled to the auditory nerve of his right ear and unclipped his computer earring. Humming to himself to cover the gaps in its whispering, he opened a flat case clipped inside the valise and restored the minicomp earring to its own padded socket. Inside the case were seven others, little jeweled globes packed with microminiature circuitry, soaked tight with advanced software. He plugged in a new one and hung it from his pale, pierced lobe. It whispered to him about his capabilities, in case he had forgotten. He listened with half an ear.

The chopper landed on the Replicon emblem on the rooftop pad of the four-story apparat headquarters. The spook walked to the elevator. He nibbled a bit of skin from the corner of his nail and flicked it into the recessed slot of a biopsy analyzer, then rocked back and forth on his clean new heels, grinning, as he was weighed and scanned and measured by cameras and sonar.

The elevator door slid open. He stepped inside, staring ahead easily, happy as a shadow. It opened again, and he walked down a richly paneled hall and into the office suite of the head of Replicon security.

He gave his credentials to the secretary and stood rocking on his heels while the young man fed them through his desk-top computer. The spook blinked his narrow green eyes; the corporate Muzak was soaking into him like a hot bath.

Inside, the security chief was all iron-gray hair and tanned wrinkles and big ceramic teeth. The spook took a seat and went limp as wax as the man's vibrations poured over him. The man bubbled over with ambition and corruption like a rusting barrel full of chemical waste. "Welcome to Rockville, Eugene."

"Thank you, sir," the spook said. He sat up straighter, taking on the man's predatory coloration. "It's a pleasure."

The security chief looked idly into a hooded data screen. "You come highly recommended, Eugene. I have data here on two of your operations for other members of the Synthesis. In the Amsterdam Gill Piracy case, you stood up under pressure that would have broken a normal operative."

"I was at the head of my class," said the spook, smiling guilelessly. He didn't remember anything about the Amsterdam case. It had all slicked aside, erased by the Veil. The spook looked placidly at a Japanese kakemono wall hanging.

"We here at Replicon don't often enlist the help of your zaibatsery apparat," the chief said. "But our cartel has been allotted a very special operation by the Synthesis coordinating board. Although you're not a member of the Synthesis, your advanced zaibatsery training is crucial to the mission's success."

The spook smiled blandly, waving the toe of his decorated shoe. Talk of loyalties and ideologies bored him. He cared very little about the Synthesis and its ambitious efforts to unite the planet under one cybernetic-economic web.

Even his feelings about his native zaibatseries were not so much "patriotism" as the sort of warm regard that a worm feels for the core of an apple. He waited for the man to come to the point, knowing that his earring computer could replay the conversation if he missed anything.

The chief toyed with an electronic stylus, leaning back in his chair. "It hasn't been easy for us," he said, "facing the ferment of the postindustrial years, watching a relentless brain drain into the orbital factories, while overpopulation and pollution wrecked the planet. Now we find we can't even put the pieces back together without help from your orbiters. You can appreciate our position, I hope."

"Perfectly," said the spook. Using his zaibatsery training and the advantages of the Veil, it wasn't hard at all to put on the man's skin and see through his eyes. He didn't like it much, but it wasn't difficult.

"Things are settling down now, since most of the craziest groups have killed themselves off or emigrated into space. The Earth cannot afford the cultural variety you have in your orbiting city-states. Earth must unite its remaining resources under the Synthesis aegis. The conventional wars are over for good and all. What we face now is a war of states of mind."

The chief began doodling absently with the light pen on a convenient videoscreen. "It's one thing to deal with criminal groups, like the Gill Pirates, and another entirely to confront those, ah, cults and sects who refuse outright to join the Synthesis. Since the population diebacks of the 2000s, large sections of the undeveloped world have gone to seed. . . . This is especially true of Central America, south of the People's Republic of Mexico. . . . It's there that we face a dissident cult calling itself the Maya Resurgence. We Synthetics are confronting a cultural mind-set, what your apparat, Eugene, would call a paradigm, that is directly opposed to everything that unites the Synthesis. If we can stop this group before it can solidify, all will be well. But if their influence continues to spread, it may provoke militancy among the Synthesis. And if we are forced to resort to arms, our own fragile concordance will come apart at the seams. We can't afford to remilitarize, Eugene. We can't afford those suspicions. We need everything we have left to continue to fight eco-logical disaster. The seas are still rising."

The spook nodded. "You want me to destabilize them. Make their para-digm untenable. Provoke the kind of cognitive dissonance that will cause them to crumble from within."

"Yes," the chief said. "You are a proven agent. Tear them apart."

The spook said delicately, "If I find it necessary to use interdicted weapons . . . ?"

The chief paled, but set his teeth and said bravely, "Replicon must not be implicated."

It took four days for the small solar-powered zeppelin to float and whir its way from the dikes of Washington, D.C., to the bloated Gulf of Honduras. The spook rode alone, on a sealed flight. He spent most of the trip in a semiparalyzed state, with the constant whisper of his computer taking the place of conscious thought.

At last the zep's programming brought it to a grayish waterlogged section of wave-lapped tropical forest near the dock of New Belize. The spook had himself lowered by cable to a firm patch by the churned-up earth of the docks. He waved cheerily to the crew of a three-masted schooner, who had been disturbed from their afternoon siesta by his almost silent arrival.

It was good to see people again. Four days with only his fragmentary self for company had left the spook antsy and hungry for companionship.

It was suffocatingly hot. Wooden crates of bananas were ripening odorif-erously on the dock.

New Belize was a sad little town. Its progenitor, Old Belize, was underwater somewhere miles out in the Caribbean, and New Belize had been hastily cobbled together from leftovers. The center of the town was one of the pre-fabricated geodomes the Synthesis used for headquarters in its corporate con-cessions. The rest of the town, even the church, clung to the dome's rim like the huts of villagers around a medieval fortress. When and if the seas rose farther, the dome would move easily, and the native structures would drown with the rest.

Except for its dogs and flies, the town slept. The spook picked his way through the mud to a bumpy street of corduroyed driftwood. An Amerindian woman in a filthy shawl watched him from her butcher's stall beside one of the dome's airlocks. She brushed flies from a suspended pig's carcass with a palm-leaf fan, and as his eyes locked with hers he felt a paradigmatic flash of her numb misery and ignorance, like stepping on an electric eel. It was weird and intense and new, and her stupefied pain meant absolutely nothing to him except for its novelty; in fact, he could barely stop himself from leaping over her dirty counter and embracing her. He wanted to slide his hands up under her long cotton blouse and slip his tongue into her wrinkled mouth; he wanted to *get right under her skin* and peel it off like a snake's. . . . Wow! He shook himself and went in through the airlock.

Inside, if smelled of the Synthesis, compressed and tangy like the air in a diving bell. It was not a large dome, but not a lot of room was needed for the modern management of information. The dome's lower floor was loosely divided into working offices with the usual keyboards, voice decoders, translators, videoscreens, and com channels for satellites and electric mail. The personnel ate and slept upstairs. In this particular station, most of them were Japanese.

The spook mopped sweat from his forehead and asked a secretary in Japanese where he might find Dr. Emilio Flores.

Flores ran a semi-independent health clinic that had slipped suspiciously from Synthetic control. The spook was forced to take a seat in the doctor's waiting room, where he played antique videogames on a battered old display screen.

Flores had an endless clientele of the lame, halt, diseased, and rotting. These Belizeans seemed bewildered by the dome and moved tentatively, as if afraid that they might break the walls or floor. The spook found them intensely interesting. He studied their infirmities—mostly skin disease, fevers, and parasitic infestations, with a sprinkling of septic wounds and fractures—with an analytic eye. He had never before seen people so sick. He tried to charm them with his expertise on the videogames, but they preferred to murmur to one another in English patois or sit huddled and shivering in the air conditioning.

At last the spook was allowed to see the doctor. Flores was a short, balding Hispanic, wearing a physician's traditional white business suit. He looked the spook up and down. "Oh," he said. "Now your illness, young man, is one I have seen before. You want to travel. Into the interior."

"Yes," the spook said. "To Tikal."

"Have a seat." They sat down. Behind Flores's chair a nuclear magnetic resonator sat ticking and blinking to itself. "Let me guess," the doctor said, steepling his fingers. "The world seems like a dead end to you, young man. You couldn't make the grade or get the training to migrate to the zaibatseries. And you can't bear wasting your life cleaning up a world your ancestors ruined. You dread a life under the thumb of huge cartels and corporations that starve your soul to fill their pockets. You long for a simpler life. A life of the spirit."

"Yes, sir."

"I have the facilities here to change your hair and skin color. I can even arrange the supplies that will give you a decent chance of making it through the jungle. You have the money?"

"Yes, sir. Bank of Zurich." The spook produced an electronic charge card.

Flores fitted the card into a desktop slot, studied the read-out, and nodded. "I won't deceive you, young man. Life among the Maya is harsh, especially at first. They will break you and remold you exactly as they want. This is a bitter land. Last century this area fell into the hands of the Predator Saints. Some of the diseases the Predators unleashed are still active here. The Resurgence is heir to Predator fanaticism. They, too, are killers."

The spook shrugged. "I'm not afraid."

"I hate killing," the doctor said. "Still, at least the Maya are honest about it, while the cost-benefit policies of the Synthetics have made the entire local population into prey. The Synthetics will not grant me funds of any kind to prolong the lives of so-called nonsurvival types. So I compromise my honor by accepting the money of Synthetic defectors, and finance my charities with treason. I am a Mexican national, but I learned my profession at a Replicon university."

The spook was surprised. He hadn't known there was still a Mexican "nation." He wondered who owned its government.

The preparations took eight days. The clinic's machines, under Flores's token direction, tinted the spook's skin and irises and reworked the folds around his eyes. He was inoculated against the local and the artificially introduced strains of malaria, yellow jack, typhus, and dengue fever. New strains of bacteria were introduced into his gut to avoid dysentery, and he was given vaccines to prevent allergic reactions to the inevitable bites of ticks, fleas, chiggers, and, worst of all, burrowing screwworms.

When the time came for him to bid farewell to the doctor, the spook was reduced to tears. As he mopped his eyes, he pressed hard against his left cheekbone. There was a clicking sound inside his head and his left sinus cavity began to drain. He carefully but unobtrusively caught the draining fluid in his handkerchief. When he shook hands in farewell, he pressed the wet cloth against the bare skin of the doctor's wrist. He left the handkerchief on Flores's desk.

By the time the spook and his mules had passed the cornfields and entered the jungle, the schizophrenic toxins had taken effect and the doctor's mind had shattered like a dropped vase.

The jungle of lowland Guatemala was not a happy place for an orbiter. It was a vast canny morass of weeds run wild that had known man for a long time. In the twelfth century, it had been cauterized for the irrigated cornfields of the original Maya. In the twentieth and twenty-first it had been introduced to the sinister logic of bulldozers, flamethrowers, defoliants, and pesticides. Each time, with the death of its oppressors, it had sprung back, nastier and more desperate than before.

The jungle had once been threaded by the trails of loggers and chicleros, seeking mahogany and chicle trees for the international market. Now there were no such trails, because there were no such trees left.

This was not the forest primeval. It was a human artifact, like the genetically altered carbon-dioxide gobblers that stood in industrial ranks across the Synthetic forests of Europe and North America. These trees were the carpetbaggers of an ecological society smashed and in disarray: thorn, mesquite, cabbage palm, winding lianas. They had swallowed whole towns; even, in places, whole oil refineries. Swollen populations of parrots and monkeys, deprived of their natural predators, made nights miserable.

The spook took constant satellite checks of his position and was in no danger of losing his way. He was not having any fun. Disposing of the rogue humanitarian had been too easy to enjoy. His destination was the sinister hacienda of the twentieth-century American millionaire, John Augustus Owens, now the headquarters of the Mayan brain trust.

The stuccoed roof-combs of the Tikal pyramids were visible from treetops thirty miles away. The spook recognized the layout of the Resurgent city from satellite photographs. He traveled till dark and spent the night in the decaying church of an overgrown village. In the morning he killed his two mules and set out on foot.

The jungle outside Tikal was full of hunters' trails. A mile outside the city the spook was captured by two sentries armed with obsidian-studded clubs and late-twentieth-century automatic rifles.

His guards looked too tall to be actual Mayans. They were probably outside recruits rather than the indigenous Guatemalan Indians who made up the core of the city's population. They spoke only Maya, mixed with distorted Spanish. With the help of his computer, the spook began eagerly sucking in the language, meanwhile complaining plaintively in English. The Veil gave him a talent for languages. He had already learned and forgotten over a dozen.

His arms were bound behind him and he was searched for weapons, but not otherwise harmed. His captors marched through a suburban complex of thatched houses, cornfields, and small gardens. Turkeys scratched and gobbled underfoot. He was turned over to the theocrats in an elaborate wooden office at the foot of one of the secondary pyramids.

There he was interrogated by a priest, who put aside a headdress and jade lip plug to assume the careful colorlessness of a bureaucrat. The priest's English was excellent, and his manner had that ingrained remoteness and casual assumption of total power that only a long acquaintance with industrial-scale power structures could breed. The spook slipped easily into the expected responses. With immediate success, he posed as a defector from the Synthesis, in search of the so-called "human values" that the Synthesis and the zaibat-series had dismissed as obsolete.

He was escorted up the pyramid's limestone stairs and imprisoned near the apex in a small but airy stone cell. His integration into Mayan society, he was told, would come only when he had emptied himself of old falsehoods and was cleansed and reborn. In the meantime, he would be taught the language. He was instructed to watch the daily life of the city and to expect a vision.

The cell's barred windows provided a splendid view of Tikal. Ceremonies were carried out every day on the largest temple pyramid; priests climbed like sleepwalkers up its steep stairs, and stone caldrons sent black threads of smoke rising into the pitiless Guatemalan sky. Tikal held almost fifty thousand people, a tremendous number for a preindustrial city.

At dawn, water glittered from a hand-dug limestone reservoir east of the city. At dusk the sun set in the jungle beyond a sacred cenote, or sacrificial well. About a hundred yards from the cenote was a small but elaborate stone pyramid, closely guarded by men with rifles, which had been erected over the bombproof shelter of the American millionaire, Owens. When the spook craned his neck and peered through the stone bars, he could see the entrances and exits there of the city's highest-ranking priests.

The cell went to work on him the first day. The combination of his spook training, the Veil, and his computer protected him, but he observed the techniques with interest. During the day, he was hit with occasional blasts of subsonics, which bypassed the ear and dug right into the nervous system, provoking disorientation and fear. At night hidden speakers used hypnagogic indoctrination techniques, peaking around three A.M. when biorhythmic resistance was lowest. Mornings and evenings, priests chanted aloud at the temple's summit, using a mantralike repetition as old as humanity itself. Combined with the mild sensory deprivation of the chamber, its effect was powerful. After two weeks of this treatment, the spook found himself chanting his language lessons aloud with an ease that seemed magical.

In the third week they began drugging his food. When things began to trail and pattern about two hours after lunch, the spook realized he was not facing the usual vibratory thrill of subsonics but a powerful dose of psilocybin. Psychedelics were not the spook's drugs of choice, but he rode out the dose without much difficulty. The peyote next day was considerably harder—he could taste its bitter alkaloids in his tortillas and black beans—but he ate it all anyway, suspecting that his intake and output were monitored. The day crawled by, with spasms of nausea alternating with elation-states that made him feel his pores were bleeding spines. He peaked sometime after sunset, when the city gathered by torchlight to watch two young women in white robes plummet fearlessly from a stone catafalque into the cold green depths of the sacred well. He could almost taste the chill green limestone water in his own mouth as the drugged girls quietly drowned.

In the fourth and fifth weeks, his diet of native psychedelics was cut back. He was acculturated by being escorted around the city by two young priestesses of his own apparent age. They rounded out the subliminal language lessons and began to introduce him to the Resurgence's carefully crafted theology. By now a normal man would have been sufficiently pulverized to cling to them like a child. It had been a severe ordeal even for the spook, and he sometimes had to struggle against the urge to rip both priestesses to pieces like a pair of tangerines.

Halfway through his second month he was put to work on probation in the cornfields, and allowed to sleep in a hammock in a thatched house. Two other recruits shared the hut, where they struggled to reintegrate their shattered psyches along approved cultural lines. The spook didn't like being cooped up with them; they were so broken up that there was nothing left for him to pick up on.

He was tempted to creep out at night, ambush a couple of priests, and break them up, just to get a healthy flow of disintegrative paranoia going, but he bided his time. It was a tough assignment. The power elite's consumption of drugs had accustomed them to psychotomimetic states, and if he used his implanted schizophrenic weaponry prematurely he might actually reinforce the local paradigm. Instead he began to plan an assault on the millionaire's bunker. Presumably, most of the arsenal of the Predator Saint was still intact: cultured plague germs, chemical agents, possibly even a privately owned warhead or two. The more he thought about it, the more tempted he was to simply murder the entire colony. It would save him a lot of grief.

On the night of the next full moon he was allowed to attend a sacrifice. The rainy season was due, and it was necessary to coax the rain gods with the death of four children. The children were drugged with mushrooms and adorned with flint and jade and thickly embroidered robes. Pepper was blown into their eyes to evoke the rain tears of sympathetic magic, and they were escorted to the edge of the catafalque. Drums and flutes and a chanted litany combined with the moonlight and torchlight to throw an intensely hypnotic ambience over the worshipers. The air reeked of copal incense, and to the spook's empathic senses it seemed as thick as cheese. He let himself soak into the crowd, and it felt wonderful. It was the first time he'd had any fun in ages.

A high-ranking priestess weighted down with armlets and a towering feathered headdress paced slowly along the front lines of the crowd, distributing ladles of fermented balche from a jug. The spook shuffled forward for his share.

There was something very odd about the priestess. At first he thought she was just blasted on psychedelics, but her eyes were clear. She held out the ladle for him to sip, and when his fingers touched hers, she looked into his face and screamed.

Suddenly he knew what was wrong. "Eugenia!" he gasped. She was another spook.

She went for him. There was nothing elegant about the hand-to-hand combat techniques of spooks. The martial arts, with their emphasis on calmness and control, didn't work for operatives only partly conscious to begin with. Instead, ingrained conditioning simply stripped them down into screaming, clawing, adrenaline-crazed maniacs, impervious to pain.

The spook felt murderous hysteria rising up within him. To stand and fight was certain death; his only hope was to escape into the crowd. But as he fended off the woman's rush, strong hands were already seizing him. Snarling, he broke free, spinning toward the lip of the broad edge of the sacred well, then turned, looked: torches, ugly fear, a crazed face, the plumes of warriors nearing, the clack of automatic rifles, no time for a rational decision. Pure intuition, then. He turned and threw himself headfirst into the wide, dank, empty gloom of the sacred well.

The water was a hard shock. He floated on his back, rubbing the sting of impact from his face. The water was thready with filaments of algae. A fish nibbled his bare leg beneath his cotton shirt. He knew all too well what it ate. He looked at the cenote walls. No hope there—they were as smooth as glass, as smooth as if they had been fused with lasers, or fireball-blasted.

Time passed. A white form came plummeting downward, belly-flopping into the water with a lethal smack. They were sacrificing the children.

Something grabbed his foot and pulled him under.

Water filled his nose. He was too busy choking to fight his way free. He was pulled down into the blackness. Water seared his lungs and he passed out. The spook awoke in a straitjacket and looked up at a ceiling of creamy antiseptic white. He was in a hospital bed. He moved his head on the pillow and realized that his scalp had been shaved.

To his left an antique monitor registered his pulse and breathing. He felt awful. He waited for his computer to whisper something, and realized that it was gone. Rather than feeling its loss, however, he felt, somehow, repulsively *whole*. His brain ached like an overstuffed stomach.

From his right, he heard faint, harsh breathing. He twisted his head to look. Sprawled on a waterbed was a withered, naked old man, cyborged into a medusa complex of life-support machinery. A few locks of colorless hair clung to the old man's age-spotted scalp, and his sunken sharp-nosed face had the look of long-forgotten cruelty. . . . An EEG registered a few flickers of comatose delta waves from the hindbrain. It was John Augustus Owens.

The sound of sandals on stone. It was the female spook. "Welcome to the Hacienda Maya, Eugene."

He stirred feebly in his straitjacket, trying to pick up her vibrations. It was like trying to swim in air. With growing panic, he realized that his paradigmatic empathy was gone. "What in hell . . ."

"You're whole again, Eugene. It feels strange, doesn't it? After all those years of being a junkyard of other people's feelings? Can you remember your real name yet? That's an important first step. Try."

"You're a traitor." His head weighed ten tons. He sank back into the pillow, feeling too stupid even to regret his indiscretion. Tattered remnants of his spook training said he ought to flatter her. . . .

"My real name," she said precisely, "was Anatolya Zhukova, and I was sentenced to corrective education by the Brezhnevograd People's Zaibatsery. . . . You were a dissident or so-called criminal of some kind also, before the Veil robbed you of your personality. Most of our top people here are from orbit, Eugene. We're not the stupid Terran cultists you were led to believe. Who hired you, anyway? Yamato Corporation? Fleisher S. A.?"

"Don't waste your time."

She smiled. "You'll come around. You're human now, and the Resurgence is humanity's brightest hope. Look."

She held up a glass flask. Inside it, something like a threaded cloudy film floated slowly in a yellowish plasma. It seemed to squirm. "We took this out of your head, Eugene."

He gasped. "The Veil."

"Yes, the Veil. It's been riding on the top of your cortex for God knows how long now, breaking you up, keeping you fluid. Robbing you of your personality. You were nothing better than a psychopath in harness."

He closed his eyes, stunned. She said, "We understand Veil technology here, Eugene. We use it ourselves, sometimes, on sacrificial victims. They can emerge from the well, touched by the Gods. Troublemakers turned divinely into saints. It fits in well with the old Mayan traditions of trepanation; a triumph of social engineering, really. They're very competent here. They managed to capture me without knowing anything about the spook apparat but rumors."

"You tried to take them out?"

"Yes. They caught me alive and won me over. And even without the Veil I have enough perception left to tell a spook when I see one." Again, she smiled. "I was faking mania when I attacked you. I only knew you had to be stopped at any cost."

"I could have ripped you apart."

"Then, yes. But now you've lost your maniac phase, and we've killed your implanted weapons. Cloned bacteria producing schizophrenic toxins in your sinuses. Altered sweat glands oozing emotional hormones. Nasty! But you're safe now. You're nothing more or less than a normal human being."

He consulted his interior state. His brain felt like a dinosaur's. "Do people really feel like this?"

She touched his cheek. "You haven't begun to feel. Wait until you've lived with us awhile, seen the plans we've made, in the finest traditions of the Predator Saints. . . ." She looked reverently at the machine-pumped corpse across the room. "Overpopulation, Eugene—that's what ruined us. The Saints took the moral effort of genocide upon themselves. Now the Resurgents have taken up the challenge of building a stable society—without the dehumanizing technology that has always, inevitably, been turned against us. The Mayans had the right idea—a civilization of social stability, ecstatic communion with the Godhead, and a firm appreciation of the cheapness of human life. They simply didn't go far enough. They didn't kill enough people to keep their population in check. With a few small changes in the Mayan theology we have brought the whole system into balance. It's a balance that will outlast the Synthesis by centuries."

"You think primitives armed with stone knives can triumph over the industrialized world?"

She looked at him pityingly. "Don't be naive. Industry really belongs in space, where there's room and raw materials, not in a biosphere. Already the zaibatseries are years ahead of Earth in every major field. The Earth's industrial cartels are so drained of energy and resources trying to clean up the mess they inherited that they can't even handle their own industrial espionage. And the Resurgent elite is armed to the teeth with the weaponry, and the spiritual inheritance, of the Predator Saints. John Augustus Owens dug the cenote of Tikal with a low-yield neutron bomb. And we own stores of twentieth-century binary nerve gas that we could smuggle, if we wanted, into Washington, or Kyoto, or Kiev. . . . No, as long as the elite exists, the Synthetics can't dare to attack us head-on—and we intend to go on protecting this society until its rivals are driven into space, where they belong. And now you and I, together, can avert the threat of paradigmatic attack."

"There'll be others," he said.

"We've co-opted every attack made upon us. People want to live real lives, Eugene—to feel and breathe and love and be of simple human worth. They want to be something more than flies in a cybernetic web. They want something realer than empty pleasures in the luxury of a zaibatsu can-world. Listen, Eugene. I'm the only person who has ever put on the spook's Veil and then returned to humanity, to a thinking, feeling, genuine life. We can understand each other."

The spook considered this. It was frightening and bizarre to be rationally thinking on his own, without a computer helping to manage his stream of consciousness. He hadn't realized how stiff and painful thinking was. The weight of consciousness had crushed the intuitive powers that the Veil had once set free. He said incredulously, "You think we could *understand* each other? By ourselves?"

"Yes!" she said. "You don't know how much I've needed it!"

The spook twitched in his straitjacket. There was a roaring in his head. Half-smothered segments of his mind were flaming, like blown coals, back into blazing life. "Wait!" he shouted. "Wait!" He had remembered his name and, with it, what he was.

Outside Replicon's Washington headquarters, snow was sifting over the altered evergreens. The head of security leaned back in his chair, fiddling with his light pen. "You've changed, Eugene."

The spook shrugged. "You mean the skin? The zaibatsery apparat can deal with that. I'm dead tired of this bodyform, anyway."

"No, it's something else."

"Of course, I was robbed of the Veil." He smiled flatly. "To continue. Once the traitress and I had become lovers, I was able to discover the location and guard codes of the nerve-gas armaments. Immediately thereafter I faked an emergency, and released the chemical agents within the sealed bunker. They had all sought safety there, so their own ventilation system destroyed all but two of them. Those two I hunted down and shot later the same night. Whether the cyborg Owens 'died' or not is a matter of definition."

"You won the woman's trust?"

"No. That would have taken too long. I simply tortured her until she broke." Again, he smiled. "Now the Synthesis can move in and dominate the Mayan population, as you would any other preindustrial culture. A few transistor radios will knock the whole flimsy structure over like a deck of cards."

"You have our thanks," said the chief. "And my personal congratulations."

"Save it," said the spook. "Once I've faded back into the shadows under the Veil, I'll forget all this anyway. I'll forget that my name is Simpson. I'll forget that I am the mass murderer responsible for the explosion of the Leyland Zaibatsery and the death of eight thousand orbiters. By any standards I am a deadly hazard to society who fully deserves to be psychically destroyed." He fixed the man with a cold, controlled, and feral grin. "And I face my own destruction happily. Because now I've seen life from both sides of the Veil. Because now I know for sure what I've always suspected. Being human just isn't enough fun."

Understand

TED CHIANG

In the clever and ingenious chiller that follows, we learn that no matter how smart you are, even if you're a super-genius of superhuman capability, you always have to worry that there might be someone out there who's smarter still. . . .

Ted Chiang has made a big impact on the field with only a handful of stories, five stories all told, published in places such as Omni, Asimov's Science Fiction, Full Spectrum 3, Starlight 2, *and* Vanishing Acts. *He won the 1990 Nebula Award with his first published story, "Tower of Babylon," and won the 1991* Asimov's *Reader's Award with his third, "Understand," as well as winning the John W. Campbell Award for Best New Writer in that same year. After 1991, he fell silent for several years before making a triumphant return in 1998 with his novella "Story of Your Life," which won him another Nebula Award in 1999. Since then, he's returned in 2000 with another major story, and it's to be hoped that he'll prove more prolific in the years to come. It will be interesting to see how he develops, as he could well turn out to be one of the significant new talents of the new century. He lives in Kirkland, Washington.*

A layer of ice; it feels rough against my face, but not cold. I've got nothing to hold on to; my gloves just keep sliding off it. I can see people on top, running around, but they can't do anything. I'm trying to pound the ice with my fists, but my arms move in slow motion, and my lungs must have burst, and my head's going fuzzy, and I feel like I'm dissolving—

I wake up, screaming. My heart's going like a jackhammer. Christ. I pull off my blankets and sit on the edge of the bed.

I couldn't remember that before. Before I only remembered falling through the ice; the doctor said my mind had suppressed the rest. Now I remember it, and it's the worst nightmare I've ever had.

I'm grabbing the down comforter with my fists, and I can feel myself trembling. I try to calm down, to breathe slowly, but sobs keep forcing their way out. It was so real I could *feel* it: feel what it was like to die.

I was in that water for nearly an hour; I was more vegetable than anything else by the time they brought me up. Am I recovered? It was the first time the hospital had ever tried their new drug on someone with so much brain damage. Did it work?

The same nightmare, again and again. After the third time, I know I'm not going to sleep again. I spend the remaining hours before dawn worrying. Is this the result? Am I losing my mind?

Tomorrow is my weekly checkup with the resident at the hospital. I hope he'll have some answers.

* * *

I drive into downtown Boston, and after half an hour Dr. Hooper can see me. I sit on an examination table behind a yellow curtain. Jutting out of the wall at waist-height is a horizontal flatscreen, adjusted for tunnel vision so it appears blank from my angle. The doctor types at the keyboard, presumably calling up my file, and then starts examining me. As he's checking my pupils with a penlight, I tell him about my nightmares.

"Did you ever have any before the accident, Leon?" He gets out his little mallet and taps at my elbows, knees, and ankles.

"Never. Are these a side effect of the drug?"

"Not a side effect. The hormone K therapy regenerated a lot of damaged neurons, and that's an enormous change that your brain has to adjust to. The nightmares are probably just a sign of that."

"Is this permanent?"

"It's unlikely," he says. "Once your brain gets used to having all those pathways again, you'll be fine. Now touch your index finger to the tip of your nose, and then bring it to my finger here."

I do what he tells me. Next he has me tap each finger to my thumb, quickly. Then I have to walk a straight line, as if I'm taking a sobriety test. After that, he starts quizzing me.

"Name the parts of an ordinary shoe."

"There's the sole, the heel, the laces. Um, the holes that the laces go through are eyes, and then there's the tongue, underneath the laces . . ."

"Okay. Repeat this number: three nine one seven four—"

"—six two."

Dr. Hooper wasn't expecting that. "What?"

"Three nine one seven four six two. You used that number the first time you examined me, when I was still an inpatient. I guess it's a number you test patients with a lot."

"You weren't supposed to memorize it; it's meant to be a test of immediate recall."

"I didn't intentionally memorize it. I just happened to remember it."

"Do you remember the number from the second time I examined you?"

I pause for a moment. "Four zero eight one five nine two."

He's surprised. "Most people can't retain so many digits if they've only heard them once. Do you use mnemonic tricks?"

I shake my head. "No. I always keep phone numbers in the autodialer."

He goes to the terminal and taps at the numeric keypad. "Try this one." He reads a fourteen-digit number, and I repeat it back to him. "You think you can do it backward?" I recite the digits in reverse order. He frowns, and starts typing something into my file.

I'm sitting in front of a terminal in one of the testing rooms in the psychiatric ward; it's the nearest place Dr. Hooper could get some intelligence tests. There's a small mirror set in one wall, probably with a video camera behind it. In case it's recording, I smile at it and wave briefly. I always do that to the hidden cameras in automatic cash machines.

Dr. Hooper comes in with a printout of my test results. "Well, Leon, you did . . . very well. On both tests you scored in the ninety-ninth percentile."

My jaw drops. "You're kidding."

"No, I'm not." He has trouble believing it himself. "Now that number doesn't indicate how many questions you got right; it means that relative to the general population—"

"I know what it means," I say absently. "I was in the seventieth percentile when they tested us in high school." Ninety-ninth percentile. Inwardly, I'm trying to find some sign of this. What should it feel like?

He sits down on the table, still looking at the printout. "You never attended college, did you?"

I return my attention to him. "I did, but I left before graduating. My ideas of education didn't mesh with the professors'."

"I see." He probably takes this to mean I flunked out. "Well, clearly you've improved tremendously. A little of that may have come about naturally as you grew older, but most of it must be a result of the hormone K therapy."

"This is one hell of a side effect."

"Well, don't get too excited. Test scores don't predict how well you can do things in the real world." I roll my eyes upward when Dr. Hooper isn't looking. Something amazing is going on, and all he can offer is a truism. "I'd like to follow up on this with some more tests. Can you come in tomorrow?"

I'm in the middle of retouching a hologram when the phone rings. I waver between the phone and the console, and reluctantly opt for the phone. I'd normally have the answering machine take any calls when I'm editing, but I need to let people know I'm working again. I lost a lot of business when I was in the hospital: one of the risks of being a freelancer. I touch the phone and say, "Greco Holographics, Leon Greco speaking."

"Hey Leon, it's Jerry."

"Hi Jerry. What's up?" I'm still studying the image on the screen: it's a pair of helical gears, intermeshed. A trite metaphor for cooperative action, but that's what the customer wanted for his ad.

"You interested in seeing a movie tonight? Me and Sue and Tori were going to see *Metal Eyes*."

"Tonight? Oh, I can't. Tonight's the last performance of the one-woman show at the Hanning Playhouse." The surfaces of the gear teeth are scratched and oily-looking. I highlight each surface, using the cursor, and type in the parameters to be adjusted.

"What's that?"

"It's called *Symplectic*. It's a monologue in verse." Now I adjust the lighting, to remove some of the shadows from where the teeth mesh. "Want to come along?"

"Is this some kind of Shakespearean soliloquy?"

Too much: with that lighting, the outer edges will be too bright. I specify an upper limit for the reflected light's intensity. "No, it's a stream-of-consciousness piece, and it switches between four different meters; iambic's only one of them. All the critics called it a tour de force."

"I didn't know you were such a fan of poetry."

After checking all the numbers once more, I let the computer recalculate the interference pattern. "Normally, I'm not, but this one seemed really interesting. 'How's' it sound to you?"

"Thanks, but I think we'll stick with the movie."

"Okay, you guys have fun. Maybe we can get together next week." We say goodbye and hang up, and I wait for the recalc to finish.

Suddenly it occurs to me what's just happened. I've never been able to do any editing while talking on the phone. But this time I had no trouble keeping my mind on both things at once.

Will the surprises never end? Once the nightmares were gone and I could relax, the first thing I noticed was the increase in my reading speed and comprehension. I was actually able to read the books on my shelves that I'd always meant to get around to, but never had the time; even the more difficult, technical material. Back in college, I'd accepted the fact that I couldn't study everything that interested me. It's exhilarating to discover that maybe I can; I was positively gleeful when I bought an armload of books the other day.

And now I find I can concentrate on two things at once; something I never would have predicted. I stand up at my desk and shout out loud, as if my favorite baseball team had just surprised me with a triple play. That's what it feels like.

The neurologist-in-chief, Dr. Shea, has taken over my case, presumably because he wants to take the credit. I scarcely know him, but he acts as if I've been his patient for years.

He's asked me into his office to have a talk. He interlaces his fingers and rests his elbows on his desk. "How do you feel about the increase in your intelligence?" he asks.

What an inane question. "I'm very pleased about it."

"Good," says Dr. Shea. "So far, we've found no adverse effects of the hormone K therapy. You don't require any further treatment for the brain damage from your accident." I nod. "However, we're conducting a study to learn more about the hormone's effect on intelligence. If you're willing, we'd like to give you a further injection of the hormone, and then monitor the results."

Suddenly he's got my attention; finally, something worth listening to. "I'd be willing to do that."

"You understand that this is purely for investigational purposes, not therapeutic. You may benefit from it with further gains in your intelligence, but this is not medically necessary for your health."

"I understand. I suppose I have to sign a consent form."

"Yes. We can also offer you some compensation for participating in this study." He names a figure, but I'm barely listening.

"That'll be fine." I'm imagining where this might lead, what it might mean for me, and a thrill runs through me.

"We'd also like you to sign a confidentiality agreement. Clearly this drug is enormously exciting, but we don't want any announcements to be made prematurely."

"Certainly, Dr. Shea. Has anyone been given additional injections before?"

"Of course; you're not going to be a guinea pig. I can assure you, there haven't been any harmful side effects."

"What sort of effects did they experience?"

"It's better if we don't plant suggestions in your mind: you might imagine you were experiencing the symptoms I mention."

Shea's very comfortable with the doctor-knows-best routine. I keep pushing. "Can you at least tell me how much their intelligence increased?"

"Every individual is different. You shouldn't base your expectations on what's happened to others."

I conceal my frustration. "Very well, Doctor."

If Shea doesn't want to tell me about hormone K, I can find out about it on my own. From my terminal at home I log onto the datanet. I access the FDA's public database, and start perusing their current IND's, the Investigational New Drug applications that must be approved before human trials can begin.

The application for hormone K was submitted by Sorensen Pharmaceutical, a company researching synthetic hormones that encourage neuron regeneration in the central nervous system. I skim the results of the drug tests on oxygen-deprived dogs, and then baboons: all the animals recovered completely. Toxicity was low, and long-term observation didn't reveal any adverse effects.

The results of cortical samples are provocative. The brain-damaged animals grew replacement neurons with many more dendrites, but the healthy recipients of the drug remained unchanged. The conclusion of the researchers: hormone K replaces only damaged neurons, not healthy ones. In the brain-damaged animals, the new dendrites seemed harmless: PET scans didn't reveal any change in brain metabolism, and the animals' performance on intelligence tests didn't change.

In their application for human clinical trials, the Sorensen researchers outlined protocols for testing the drug first on healthy subjects, and then on several types of patients: stroke victims, sufferers of Alzheimer's, and persons—like me—in a persistent vegetative state. I can't access the progress reports for those trials: even with patient anonymity, only participating doctors have clearance to examine those records.

The animal studies don't shed any light on the increased intelligence in humans. It's reasonable to assume that the effect on intelligence is proportional to the number of neurons replaced by the hormone, which in turn depends on the amount of initial damage. That means that the deep-coma patients would undergo the greatest improvements. Of course, I'd need to see the progress of the other patients to confirm this theory; that'll have to wait.

The next question: is there a plateau, or will additional dosages of the hormone cause further increases? I'll know the answer to that sooner than the doctors.

I'm not nervous; in fact, I feel quite relaxed. I'm just lying on my stomach, breathing very slowly. My back is numb; they gave me a local anesthetic, and then injected the hormone K intraspinally. An intravenous wouldn't work, since the hormone can't get past the blood-brain barrier. This is the first such injection I can recall having, though I'm told that I've received two before: the first while still in the coma, the second when I had regained consciousness but no cognitive ability.

More nightmares. They're not all actually violent, but they're the most bizarre, mind-blowing dreams I've ever had, often with nothing in them that I recognize. I often wake up screaming, flailing around in bed. But this time, I know they'll pass.

There are several psychologists at the hospital studying me now. It's interesting to see how they analyze my intelligence. One doctor perceives my skills in terms of components, such as acquisition, retention, performance, and transfer. Another looks at me from the angles of mathematical and logical reasoning, linguistic communication, and spatial visualization.

I'm reminded of my college days when I watch these specialists, each with a pet theory, each contorting the evidence to fit. I'm even less convinced by them now than I was back then; they still have nothing to teach me. None of their categorizations are fruitful in analyzing my performance, since— there's no point in denying it—I'm equally good at everything.

I could be studying a new class of equation, or the grammar of a foreign language, or the operation of an engine; in each case, everything fits together, all the elements cooperate beautifully. In each case, I don't have to consciously memorize rules, and then apply them mechanically. I just perceive how the system behaves as a whole, as an entity. Of course, I'm aware of all the details and individual steps, but they require so little concentration that they almost feel intuitive.

Penetrating computer security is really quite dull; I can see how it might attract those who can't resist a challenge to their cleverness, but it's not intellectually aesthetic at all. It's no different than tugging on the doors of a locked house until you find an improperly installed lock. A useful activity, but hardly interesting.

Getting into the FDA's private database was easy. I played with one of the hospital wall terminals, running the visitor-information program, which displays maps and a staff directory. I broke out of the program to the system level, and wrote a decoy program to mimic the opening screen for logging on. Then I simply left the terminal alone; eventually one of my doctors came by to check one of her files. The decoy rejected her password, and then restored the true opening screen. The doctor tried logging in again, and was successful this time, but her password was left with my decoy.

Using the doctor's account, I had clearance to view the FDA patient-record database. In the Phase I trials, on healthy volunteers, the hormone had no effect. The ongoing Phase II clinical trials are a different matter. Here are weekly reports on eighty-two patients, each identified by a number, all treated with hormone K, most of them victims of a stroke or Alzheimer's, some of them coma cases. The latest reports confirm my prediction: those with greater brain damage display greater increases in intelligence. PET scans reveal heightened brain metabolism.

Why didn't the animal studies provide a precedent for this? I think the concept of critical mass provides an analogy. Animals fall below some critical mass in terms of synapses; their brains support only minimal abstraction, and gain nothing from additional synapses. Humans exceed that critical mass. Their brains support full self-awareness, and—as these records indicate—they use any new synapses to the fullest possible extent.

The most exciting records are those of the newly begun investigational studies, using a few of the patients who volunteered. Additional injections of the hormone do increase intelligence further, but again it depends on the degree of initial damage. The patients with minor strokes haven't even reached genius levels. Those with greater damage have gone further.

Of the patients originally in deep-coma states, I'm the only one thus far who's received a third injection. I gained more new synapses than anyone previously studied; it's an open question as to how high my intelligence will go. I can feel my heart pounding when I think about it.

Playing with the doctors is becoming more and more tedious as the weeks go by. They treat me as if I were simply an idiot savant: a patient who exhibits certain signs of high intelligence, but still just a patient. As far as the neurologists are concerned, I'm just a source of PET scan images and an occasional vial of cerebrospinal fluid. The psychologists have the opportunity to gain some insight into my thinking with their interviews, but they can't shed their preconception of me as someone out of his depth, an ordinary man awarded gifts that he can't appreciate.

On the contrary, the doctors are the ones who don't appreciate what's happening. They're certain that real-world performance can't be enhanced by a drug, and that my ability exists only according to the artificial yardstick of intelligence tests, so they waste their time with those. But the yardstick is not only contrived, it's too short: my consistently perfect scores don't tell them anything, because they have no basis for comparison this far out on the bell curve.

Of course, the test scores merely capture a shadow of the real changes occurring. If only the doctors could feel what's going on in my head: how much I'm recognizing that I missed before, how many uses I can see for that information. Far from being a laboratory phenomenon, my intelligence is practical and effectual. With my near total recall and my ability to correlate, I can assess a situation immediately, and choose the best course of action for my purposes; I'm never indecisive. Only theoretical topics pose a challenge.

No matter what I study, I can see patterns. I see the gestalt, the melody within the notes, in everything: mathematics and science, art and music, psychology and sociology. As I read the texts, I can think only that the authors are plodding along from one point to the next, groping for connections that they can't see. They're like a crowd of people unable to read music, peering at the score for a Bach sonata, trying to explain how one note leads to another.

As glorious as these patterns are, they also whet my appetite for more. There are other patterns waiting to be discovered, gestalts of another scale entirely. With respect to those, I'm blind myself; all my sonatas are just isolated data points by comparison. I have no idea what form such gestalts might assume, but that'll come in time. I want to find them, and comprehend them. I want this more than anything I've ever wanted before.

The visiting doctor's name is Clausen, and he doesn't behave like the other doctors. Judging by his manner, he's accustomed to wearing a mask of blandness with his patients, but he's a bit uncomfortable today. He affects an air of friendliness, but it isn't as fluent as the perfunctory noise that the other doctors make.

"The test works this way, Leon: you'll read some descriptions of various situations, each presenting a problem. After each one, I want you to tell me what you'd do to solve that problem."

I nod. "I've had this kind of test before."

"Fine, fine." He types a command, and the screen in front of me fills with text. I read the scenario: it's a problem in scheduling and prioritizing. It's realistic, which is unusual; scoring such a test is too arbitrary for most researchers' tastes. I wait before giving my answer, though Clausen is still surprised at my speed.

"That's very good, Leon." He hits a key on his computer. "Try this one."

We continue with more scenarios. As I'm reading the fourth one, Clausen is careful to display only professional detachment. My response to this problem is of special interest to him, but he doesn't want me to know. The scenario involves office politics and fierce competition for a promotion.

I realize who Clausen is he's a government psychologist, perhaps military, probably part of the CIA's Office of Research and Development. This test is meant to gauge hormone K's potential for producing strategists. That's why he's uncomfortable with me: he's used to dealing with soldiers and government employees, subjects whose job is to follow orders.

It's likely that the CIA will wish to retain me as a subject for more tests; they may do the same with other patients, depending on their performance. After that, they'll get some volunteers from their ranks, starve their brains of oxygen, and treat them with hormone K. I certainly don't wish to become a CIA resource, but I've already demonstrated enough ability to arouse their interest. The best I can do is to downplay my skills and get this question wrong.

I offer a poor course of action as my answer, and Clausen is disappointed. Nonetheless, we press on. I take longer on the scenarios now, and give weaker responses. Sprinkled among the harmless questions are the critical ones: one about avoiding a hostile corporate takeover, another about mobilizing people to prevent the construction of a coal-burning plant. I miss each of these questions.

Clausen dismisses me when the test ends; he's already trying to formulate his recommendations. If I'd shown my true abilities, the CIA would recruit me immediately. My uneven performance will reduce their eagerness, but it won't change their minds; the potential returns are too great for them to ignore hormone K.

My situation has changed profoundly; when the CIA decides to retain me as a test subject, my consent will be purely optional. I must make plans.

It's four days later, and Shea is surprised. "You want to withdraw from the study?"

"Yes, effective immediately. I'm returning to work."

"If it's a matter of compensation, I'm sure we can—"

"No, money's not the problem. I've simply had enough of these tests."

"I know the tests become tiring after a while, but we're learning a great deal. And we appreciate your participation, Leon. It's not merely—"

"I know how much you're learning from these tests. It doesn't change my decision: I don't wish to continue."

Shea starts to speak again, but I cut him off. "I know that I'm still bound by the confidentiality agreement; if you'd like me to sign something confirming that, send it to me." I get up and head for the door. "Goodbye, Dr. Shea."

It's two days later when Shea calls.

"Leon, you have to come in for an examination. I've just been informed: adverse side effects have been found in patients treated with hormone K at another hospital."

He's lying; he'd never tell me that over the phone. "What sort of side effects?"

"Loss of vision. There's excessive growth of the optic nerve, followed by deterioration."

The CIA must have ordered this when they heard that I'd withdrawn from the study. Once I'm back in the hospital, Shea will declare me mentally incompetent, and confine me to their care. Then I'll be transferred to a government research institution.

I assume an expression of alarm. "I'll come down right away."

"Good." Shea is relieved that his delivery was convincing. "We can examine you as soon as you arrive."

I hang up and turn on my terminal to check the latest information in the FDA database. There's no mention of any adverse effects, on the optic nerve or anywhere else. I don't discount the possibility that such effects might arise in the future, but I'll discover them by myself.

It's time to leave Boston. I begin packing. I'll empty my bank accounts when I go. Selling the equipment in my studio would generate more cash, but most of it is too large to transport; I take only a few of the smallest pieces. After I've been working a couple of hours, the phone rings again: Shea wondering where I am. This time I let the machine pick it up.

"Leon, are you there? This is Dr. Shea. We've been expecting you for quite some time."

He'll try calling one more time, and then he'll send the orderlies in white suits, or perhaps the actual police, to pick me up.

* * *

Seven-thirty P.M. Shea is still in the hospital, waiting for news about me. I turn the ignition key and pull out of my parking spot across the street from the hospital. Any moment now, he'll notice the envelope I slipped under the door to his office. As soon as he opens it, he'll realize that it's from me.

> Greetings, Dr. Shea;
>   I imagine you're looking for me.

A moment of surprise, but no more than a moment; he'll regain his composure, and alert security to search the building for me, and check all vehicles leaving. Then he'll continue reading.

> You can call off those burly orderlies who are waiting at my apartment; I don't want to waste their valuable time. You're probably determined to have the police issue an APB on me, though. Therefore, I've taken the liberty of inserting a virus in the DMV computer, one which will substitute information whenever my license plate number is requested. Of course, you could give a description of my car, but you don't even know what it looks like, do you?
>
>   Leon

He'll call the police to have their programmers work on that virus. He'll conclude that I have a superiority complex, based on the arrogant tone of the note, the unnecessary risk taken in returning to the hospital to deliver it, and the pointless revelation of a virus which might otherwise have gone undetected.

Shea will be mistaken, though. Those actions are designed to make the police and CIA underestimate me, so I can rely on their not taking adequate precautions. After cleaning my virus from the DMV computer, the police programmers will assess my programming skill as good but not great, and then load the backups to retrieve my actual license number. This will activate a second virus, a far more sophisticated one. This one will modify both the backups and the active database. The police will be satisfied that they've got the correct license number, and spend their time chasing that wild goose.

My next goal is to get another ampule of hormone K. Doing so, unfortunately, will give the CIA an accurate idea of how capable I really am. If I hadn't sent that note, the police would discover my virus later, at a time when they'd know to take super-stringent precautions when eradicating it. In that case, I might never be able to remove my license number from their files.

Meanwhile, I've checked into a hotel, and am working out of the room's datanet terminal.

I've broken into the private database of the FDA. I've seen the addresses of the hormone K subjects, and the internal communications of the FDA. A clinical hold was instituted for hormone K: no further testing permitted until the hold is lifted. The CIA has insisted on capturing me and assessing my threat potential before the FDA goes any further.

The FDA has asked all the hospitals to return the remaining ampules by courier. I must get an ampule before this happens. The nearest patient is in Pittsburgh; I reserve a seat on a flight leaving early tomorrow morning. Then I check a map of Pittsburgh, and make a request to the Pennsylvania Courier company for a pick-up at an investment firm in the downtown area. Finally I sign up for several hours of CPU time on a supercomputer.

I'm parked in a rental car around the corner from a skyscraper in Pittsburgh. In my jacket pocket is a small circuit board with a keypad. I'm looking down the street in the direction the courier will arrive from; half the pedestrians wear white air-filter masks, but visibility is good.

I see it two intersections away; it's a late-model domestic van, PENNSYL-VANIA COURIER painted on the side. It's not a high-security courier; the FDA isn't that worried about me. I get out of my car and begin walking toward the skyscraper. The van arrives shortly, parks, and the driver gets out. As soon as he's inside, I enter the vehicle.

It's just come from the hospital. The driver is on his way to the fortieth floor, expecting to pick up a package from an investment firm there. He won't be back for at least four minutes.

Welded to the floor of the van is a large locker, with double-layered steel walls and door. There is a polished plate on the door; the locker opens when the driver lays his palm against its surface. The plate also has a data port in its side, used for programming it.

Last night I penetrated the service database for Lucas Security Systems, the company that sells handprint locks to Pennsylvania Courier. There I found an encrypted file containing the codes to override their locks.

I must admit that while penetrating computer security remains generally unaesthetic, certain aspects of it are indirectly related to very interesting problems in mathematics. For example, a commonly used method of encryption normally requires years of supercomputer time to break. However, during one of my forays into number theory, I found a lovely technique for factoring extremely large numbers. With this technique, a supercomputer could break this encryption scheme in a matter of hours.

I pull the circuit board from my pocket and connect it to the data port with a cable. I tap in a twelve-digit number, and the locker door swings open.

By the time I'm back in Boston with the ampule, the FDA has responded to the theft by removing all pertinent files from any computer accessible through the datanet: as expected.

With the ampule and my belongings, I drive to New York City.

The fastest way for me to make money is, oddly enough, gambling. Handi-capping horse races is simple enough. Without attracting undue attention, I can accumulate a moderate sum, and then sustain myself with investments in the stock market.

I'm staying in a room in the cheapest apartment I could find near New York that has datanet outlets. I've arranged several false names under which to make my investments, and will change them regularly. I shall spend some time on Wall Street, so that I can identify high-yield short-term opportunities from the body language of brokers. I won't go more than once a week; there are more significant matters to attend to, gestalts beckoning my attention.

As my mind develops, so does my control over my body. It is a misconception to think that during evolution humans sacrificed physical skill in exchange for intelligence: wielding one's body is a mental activity. While my strength hasn't increased, my coordination is now well above average; I'm even becoming ambidextrous. Moreover, my powers of concentration make biofeedback techniques very effective. After comparatively little practice, I am able to raise or lower my heart rate and blood pressure.

I write a program to perform a pattern match for photos of my face, and search for occurrences of my name; I then incorporate it into a virus for scanning all public-display files on the datanet. The CIA will have the datanet news briefs display my picture and identify me as a dangerously insane escaped patient, perhaps a murderer. The virus will replace my photo with video static. I plant a similar virus in the FDA and CIA computers, to search for copies of my picture in any downloads to regional police. These viruses should be immune to anything that their programmers can come up with.

Undoubtedly, Shea and the other doctors are in consultation with the psychologists of the CIA; guessing where I might have gone. My parents are dead, so the CIA is turning its attention to my friends, asking whether I've contacted them; they'll maintain surveillance on them in the event I do. A regrettable invasion of their privacy, but it isn't a pressing matter.

It's unlikely that the CIA will treat any of their agents with hormone K to locate me. As I myself demonstrate, a superintelligent person is too difficult to control. However, I'll keep track of the other patients, in case the government decides to recruit them.

The quotidian patterns of society are revealed without my making an effort. I walk down the street, watching people go about their business, and though not a word is spoken, the subtext is conspicuous. A young couple strolls by, the adoration of one bouncing off the tolerance of the other. Apprehension flickers and becomes steady as a businessman, fearful of his supervisor, begins to doubt a decision he made earlier today. A woman wears a mantle of simulated sophistication, but it slips when it brushes past the genuine article.

As always, the roles one plays become recognizable only with greater maturity. To me, these people seem like children on a playground; I'm amused by their earnestness, and embarrassed to remember myself doing those same things. Their activities are appropriate for them, but I couldn't bear to participate now; when I became a man, I put away childish things. I will deal with the world of normal humans only as needed to support myself.

* * *

I acquire years of education each week, assembling ever larger patterns. I view the tapestry of human knowledge from a broader perspective than anyone ever has before; I can fill gaps in the design where scholars never even noticed a lack, and enrich the texture in places that they felt were complete.

The natural sciences have the clearest patterns. Physics admits of a lovely unification, not just at the level of fundamental forces, but when considering its extent and implications. Classifications like "optics" or "thermodynamics" are just straitjackets, preventing physicists from seeing countless intersections. Even putting aside aesthetics, the practical applications that have been overlooked are legion; years ago, engineers could have been artificially generating spherically symmetric gravity fields.

Having realized this, however, I won't build such a device, or any other. It would require many custom-built components, all difficult and time-consuming to procure. Furthermore, actually constructing the device wouldn't give me any particular satisfaction, since I already know it would work, and it wouldn't illuminate any new gestalts.

I'm writing part of an extended poem, as an experiment; after I've finished one canto, I'll be able to choose an approach for integrating the patterns within all the arts. I'm employing six modern and four ancient languages; they include most of the significant worldviews of human civilization. Each one provides different shades of meaning and poetic effects; some of the juxtapositions are delightful. Each line of the poem contains neologisms, born by extruding words through the declensions of another language. If I were to complete the entire piece, it could be thought of as *Finnegans Wake* multiplied by Pound's *Cantos*.

The CIA interrupts my work; they're baiting a trap for me. After two months of trying, they've accepted that they can't locate me by conventional methods, so they've turned to more drastic measures. The news services report that the girlfriend of a deranged murderer has been charged with aiding and abetting his escape. The name given is Connie Perritt, someone I was seeing last year. If it goes to trial, it's a foregone conclusion that she'll be sentenced to a lengthy prison term; the CIA is hoping that I won't allow that. They expect me to attempt a maneuver that will expose me to capture.

Connie's preliminary hearing is tomorrow. They'll ensure that she's released on bail, through a bondsman if necessary, to give me an opportunity to contact her. Then they'll saturate the area around her apartment with undercover agents to wait for me.

I begin editing the first image on screen. These digital photos are so minimal compared to holos, but they serve the purpose. The photos, taken yesterday, show the exterior of Connie's apartment building, the street out front, and nearby intersections. I move the cursor across the screen, drawing small crosshairs in certain locations on the images. A window, with lights out but curtains open, in the building diagonally opposite. A street vendor two blocks from the rear of the building.

I mark six locations altogether. They indicate where CIA agents were waiting last night, when Connie went back to her apartment. Having been cued by the videotapes of me in the hospital, they knew what to look for in all male or ambiguous passersby: the confident, level gait. Their expectations worked against them; I simply lengthened my strides, bobbed my head up and down a bit, reduced my arm motion. That and some atypical clothes were sufficient for them to ignore me as I walked through the area.

At the bottom of one photo I type the radio frequency used by the agents for communication, and an equation describing the scrambling algorithm employed. Once I've finished, I transmit the images to the Director of the CIA. The implication is clear: I could kill his undercover agents at any time, unless they withdraw.

To have them drop charges against Connie, and for a more permanent deterrent against the CIA's distractions, I shall have to do some more work.

Pattern recognition again, but this time it's of a mundane variety. Thousands of pages of reports, memos, correspondence; each one is a dot of color in a pointillist painting. I step back from this panorama, watching for lines and edges to emerge and create a pattern. The megabytes that I scanned constituted only a fraction of the complete records for the period I investigated, but they were enough.

What I've found is rather ordinary, far simpler than the plot of a spy novel. The director of the CIA was aware of a terrorist group's plan to bomb the Washington, D.C., metro system. He let the bombing occur, in order to gain Congressional approval for the use of extreme measures against that group. A congressman's son was among the casualties, and the CIA director was given a free hand in handling the terrorists. While his plans aren't actually stated in CIA records, they're implied quite clearly. The relevant memos make only oblique references, and they float in a sea of innocuous documents; if an investigating committee were to read all of the records, the evidence would be drowned out by the noise. However, a distillation of the incriminating memos would certainly convince the press.

I send the list of memos to the director of the CIA, with a note: "Don't bother me, and I won't bother you." He'll realize that he has no alternative.

This little episode has reinforced my opinion of the affairs of the world; I could detect clandestine ploys everywhere if I kept informed about current events, but none of them would be interesting. I shall resume my studies.

Control over my body continues to grow. By now, I could walk on hot coals or stick needles in my arm, if I were so inclined. However, my interest in Eastern meditation is limited to its application to physical control; no meditative trance I can attain is nearly as desirable to me as my mental state when I assemble gestalts out of elemental data.

I'm designing a new language. I've reached the limits of conventional languages, and now they frustrate my attempts to progress further. They lack the power to express concepts that I need, and even in their own domain, they're imprecise and unwieldy. They're hardly fit for speech, let alone thought.

Existing linguistic theory is useless; I'll reevaluate basic logic to determine the suitable atomic components for my language. This language will support a dialect co-expressive with all of mathematics, so that any equation I write will have a linguistic equivalent. However, mathematics will be only a small part of the language, not the whole; unlike Leibniz, I recognize symbolic logic's limits. Other dialects I have planned will be co-expressive with my notations for aesthetics and cognition. This will be a time-consuming project, but the end result will clarify my thoughts enormously. After I've translated all that I know into this language, the patterns I seek should become evident.

I pause in my work. Before I develop a notation for aesthetics, I must establish a vocabulary for all the emotions I can imagine.

I'm aware of many emotions beyond those of normal humans; I see how limited their affective range is. I don't deny the validity of the love and angst I once felt, but I do recognize them for what they were: like the infatuations and depressions of childhood, they were just the forerunners of what I experience now. My passions now are more multifaceted; as self-knowledge increases, all emotions become exponentially more complex. I must be able to describe them fully if I'm to even attempt the composing tasks ahead.

Of course, I actually experience far fewer emotions than I could; my development is limited by the intelligence of those around me, and the scant intercourse I permit myself with them. I'm reminded of the Confucian concept of *ren*: inadequately conveyed by "benevolence," that quality which is quintessentially human, which can only be cultivated through interaction with others, and which a solitary person cannot manifest. It's one of many such qualities. And here am I, with people, people everywhere, yet not a one to interact with. I'm only a fraction of what a complete individual with my intelligence could be.

I don't delude myself with either self-pity or conceit: I can evaluate my own psychological state with the utmost objectivity and consistency. I know precisely which emotional resources I have and which I lack, and how much value I place on each. I have no regrets.

My new language is taking shape. It is gestalt-oriented, rendering it beautifully suited for thought, but impractical for writing or speech. It wouldn't be transcribed in the form of words arranged linearly, but as a giant ideogram, to be absorbed as a whole. Such an ideogram could convey, more deliberately than a picture, what a thousand words cannot. The intricacy of each ideogram would be commensurate with the amount of information contained; I amuse myself with the notion of a colossal ideogram that describes the entire universe.

The printed page is too clumsy and static for this language; the only serviceable media would be video or holo, displaying a time-evolving graphic image. Speaking this language would be out of the question, given the limited bandwidth of the human larynx.

* * *

My mind seethes with expletives from ancient and modern languages, and they taunt me with their crudeness, reminding me that my ideal language would offer terms with sufficient venom to express my present frustration.

I cannot complete my artificial language; it's too large a project for my present tools. Weeks of concentrated effort have yielded nothing usable. I've attempted to write it via bootstrapping, by employing the rudimentary language that I've already defined to rewrite the language and produce successively fuller versions.

Yet each new version only highlights its own inadequacies, forcing me to expand my ultimate goal, condemning it to the status of a Holy Grail at the end of a divergent infinite regress. This is no better than trying to create it ex nihilo.

What about my fourth ampule? I can't remove it from my thoughts: every frustration I experience at my present plateau reminds me of the possibility for still greater heights.

Of course, there are significant risks. This injection might be the one that causes brain damage or insanity. Temptation by the Devil, perhaps, but temptation nonetheless. I find no reason to resist.

I'd have a margin of safety if I injected myself in a hospital, or, failing that, with someone standing by in my apartment. However, I imagine the injection will either be successful or else cause irreparable damage, so I forego those precautions.

I order equipment from a medical-supply company, and assemble an apparatus for administering the spinal injection by myself. It may take days for the full effects to become evident, so I'll confine myself to my bedroom. It's possible that my reaction will be violent; I remove breakables from the room and attach loose straps to the bed. The neighbors will interpret anything they hear as an addict howling.

I inject myself and wait.

My brain is on fire, my spine burns itself through my back, I feel near apoplexy. I am blind, deaf, insensate.

I hallucinate. Seen with such preternatural clarity and contrast that they must be illusory, unspeakable horrors loom all around me, visions not of physical violence but of psychic mutilation.

Mental agony and orgasm. Terror and hysterical laughter.

For a brief moment, perception returns. I'm on the floor, hands clenched in my hair, some uprooted tufts lying around me. My clothes are soaked in sweat. I've bitten my tongue, and my throat is raw: from screaming, I surmise. Convulsions have left my body badly bruised, and a concussion is likely given the contusions on the back of my head, but I feel nothing. Has it been hours or moments?

Then my vision clouds and the roar returns.

* * *

Critical mass.

Revelation.

I understand the mechanism of my own thinking. I know precisely how I know, and my understanding is recursive. I understand the infinite regress of this self-knowing, not by proceeding step by step endlessly, but by apprehending the *limit*. The nature of recursive cognition is clear to me. At new meaning of the term "self-aware."

Fiat logos. I know my mind in terms of a language more expressive than any I'd previously imagined. Like God creating order from chaos with an utterance, I make myself anew with this language. It is meta-self-descriptive and self-editing; not only can it describe thought, it can describe and modify its own operations as well, at all levels. What Gödel would have given to see this language, where modifying a statement causes the entire grammar to be adjusted.

With this language, I can see how my mind is operating. I don't pretend to see my own neurons firing; such claims belong to John Lilly and his LSD experiments of the sixties. What I can do is perceive the gestalts; I see the mental structures forming, interacting. I see myself thinking, and I see the equations that describe my thinking, and I see myself comprehending the equations, and I see how the equations describe their being comprehended.

I know how they make up my thoughts.

These thoughts.

Initially I am overwhelmed by all this input, paralyzed with awareness of my self. It is hours before I can control the flood of self-describing information. I haven't filtered it away, nor pushed it into the background. It's become integrated into my mental processes, for use during my normal activities. It will be longer before I can take advantage of it, effortlessly and effectively, the way a dancer uses her kinesthetic knowledge.

All that I once knew theoretically about my mind, I now see detailed explicitly. The undercurrents of sex, aggression, and self-preservation, translated by the conditioning of my childhood, clash with and are sometimes disguised as rational thought. I recognize all the causes of my every mood, the motives behind my every decision.

What can I do with this knowledge? Much of what is conventionally described as "personality" is at my discretion; the higher-level aspects of my psyche define who I am now. I can send my mind into a variety of mental or emotional states, yet remain ever aware of the state and able to restore my original condition. Now that I understand the mechanisms that were operating when I attended to two tasks at once, I can divide my consciousness, simultaneously devoting almost full concentration and gestalt-recognition abilities to two or more separate problems, meta-aware of all of them. What can't I do?

I know my body afresh, as if it were an amputee's stump suddenly replaced by a watchmaker's hand. Controlling my voluntary muscles is trivial, I have inhuman coordination. Skills that normally require thousands of repetitions to develop, I can learn in two or three. I find a video with a shot of a pianist's hands playing, and before long I can duplicate his finger movements without a keyboard in front of me. Selective contraction and relaxation of muscles improve my strength and flexibility. Muscular response time is thirty-five milliseconds, for conscious or reflex action. Learning acrobatics and martial arts would require little training.

I have somatic awareness of kidney function, nutrient absorption, glandular secretions. I am even conscious of the role that neurotransmitters play in my thoughts. This state of consciousness involves mental activity more intense than in any epinephrine-boosted stress situation; part of my mind is maintaining a condition that would kill a normal mind and body within minutes. As I adjust the programming of my mind, I experience the ebb and flow of all the substances that trigger my emotional reactions, boost my attention, or subtly shape my attitudes.

And then I look outward.

Blinding, joyous, fearful symmetry surrounds me. So much is incorporated within patterns now that the entire universe verges on resolving itself into a picture. I'm closing in on the ultimate gestalt: the context in which all knowledge fits and is illuminated, a mandala, the music of the spheres, *kosmos*.

I seek enlightenment, not spiritual but rational. I must go still further to reach it, but this time the goal will not be perpetually retreating from my fingertips. With my mind's language, the distance between myself and enlightenment is precisely calculable. I've sighted my final destination.

Now I must plan my next actions. First, there are the simple enhancements to self-preservation, starting with martial arts training. I will watch some tournaments to study possible attacks, though I will take only defensive action; I can move rapidly enough to avoid contact with even the fastest striking techniques. This will let me protect myself and disarm any street criminals, should I be assaulted. Meanwhile, I must eat copious amounts of food to meet my brain's nourishment requirements, even given increased efficiency in my metabolism. I shall also shave my scalp, to allow greater radiative cooling for the heightened blood flow to my head.

Then there is the primary goal: decoding those patterns. For further improvements to my mind, artificial enhancements are the only possibility. A direct computer-mind link, permitting mind downloading, is what I need, but I must create a new technology to implement it. Anything based on digital computation will be inadequate; what I have in mind requires nano-scale structures based on neural networks.

Once I have the basic ideas laid out, I set my mind to multiprocessing: one section of my mind deriving a branch of mathematics that reflects the networks' behavior; another developing a process for replicating the formation of neural pathways on a molecular scale in a self-repairing bioceramic medium; a third devising tactics for guiding private industrial R & D to produce what I'll need. I cannot waste time: I will introduce explosive theoretical and technical breakthroughs so that my new industry will hit the ground running.

I've gone into the outside world to re-observe society. The sign language of emotion I once knew has been replaced by a matrix of interrelated equations. Lines of force twist and elongate between people, objects institutions, ideas. The individuals are tragically like marionettes, independently animate but bound by a web they choose not to see; they could resist if they wished, but so few of them do.

At the moment I'm sitting at a bar. Three stools to my right sits a man, familiar with this type of establishment, who looks around and notices a couple in a dark corner booth. He smiles, motions for the bartender to come over, and leans forward to speak confidentially about the couple. I don't need to listen to know what he's saying.

He's lying to the bartender, easily, extemporaneously. A compulsive liar, not out of a desire for a life more exciting than his own, but to revel in his facility for deceiving others. He knows the bartender is detached, merely affecting interest—which is true—but he knows the bartender is still fooled— which is also true.

My sensitivity to the body language of others has increased to the point that I can make these observations without sight or sound: I can smell the pheromones exuded by his skin. To an extent, my muscles can even detect the tension within his, perhaps by their electric field. These channels can't convey precise information, but the impressions I receive provide ample basis for extrapolation; they add texture to the web.

Normal humans may detect these emanations subliminally. I'll work on becoming more attuned to them; then perhaps I can try consciously controlling my own expressions.

I've developed abilities reminiscent of the mind-control schemes offered by tabloid advertisements. My control over my somatic emanations now lets me provoke precise reactions in others. With pheromones and muscle tension, I can cause another person to respond with anger, fear, sympathy, or sexual arousal. Certainly enough to win friends and influence people.

I can even induce a self-sustaining reaction in others. By associating a particular response with a sense of satisfaction, I can create a positive reinforcement loop, like biofeedback; the person's body will strengthen the reaction on its own. I'll use this on corporate presidents to create support for the industries I'll need.

I can no longer dream in any normal sense. I lack anything that would qualify as a subconscious, and I control all the maintenance functions performed by my brain, so normal REM sleep tasks are obsolete. There are moments when my grasp on my mind slips, but they cannot be called dreams. Metahallucinations, perhaps. Sheer torture. These are periods during which I'm detached: I understand how my mind generates the strange visions, but I'm paralyzed and unable to respond. I can scarcely identify what I see; images of bizarre transfinite self-references and modifications that even I find nonsensical.

My mind is taxing the resources of my brain. A biological structure of this size and complexity can just barely sustain a self-knowing psyche. But the self-knowing psyche is also self-regulating, to an extent. I give my mind full use of what's available, and restrain it from expanding beyond that. But it's difficult: I'm cramped inside a bamboo cage that doesn't let me sit down or stand up. If I try to relax, or try to extend myself fully, then agony, madness.

I'm hallucinating. I see my mind imagining possible configurations it could assume, and then collapsing. I witness my own delusions, my visions of what form my mind might take when I grasp the ultimate gestalts.

Will I achieve ultimate self-awareness? Could I discover the components that make up my own mental gestalts? Would I penetrate racial memory? Would I find innate knowledge of morality? I might determine whether mind could be spontaneously generated from matter, and understand what relates consciousness with the rest of the universe. I might see how to merge subject and object: the zero experience.

Or perhaps I'd find that the mind gestalt cannot be generated, and some sort of intervention is required. Perhaps I would see the soul, the ingredient of consciousness that surpasses physicality. Proof of God? I would behold the meaning, the true character of existence.

I would be enlightened. It must be euphoric to experience . . .

My mind collapses back into a state of sanity.

I must keep a tighter rein over my self. When I'm in control at the metaprogramming level, my mind is perfectly self-repairing; I could restore myself from states that resemble delusion or amnesia. But if I drift too far on the metaprogramming level, my mind might become an unstable structure, and then I would slide into a state beyond mere insanity. I will program my mind to forbid itself from moving beyond its own reprogramming range.

These hallucinations strengthen my resolve to create an artificial brain. Only with such a structure will I be able to actually perceive those gestalts, instead of merely dreaming about them. To achieve enlightenment, I'll need to exceed another critical mass in terms of neuronal analogs.

I open my eyes: it's two hours, twenty-eight minutes, and ten seconds since I closed my eyes to rest, though not to sleep. I rise from bed.

I request a listing of my stocks' performance on my terminal. I look down the flatscreen, and freeze.

The screen shouts at me. It tells me that there is another person with an enhanced mind.

Five of my investments have demonstrated losses; they're not precipitous, but large enough that I'd have detected them in the body language of the stockbrokers. Reading down the alphabetical list, the initial letters of the corporations whose stock values have dropped are C, E, G, O, and R. Which when rearranged, spell GRECO.

Someone is sending me a message.

There's someone else out there like me. There must have been another comatose patient who received a third injection of hormone K. He erased his file from the FDA database before I accessed it, and supplied false input to his doctors' accounts so that they wouldn't notice. He too stole another ampule of the hormone, contributing to the FDA's closing of their files, and with his whereabouts unknown to the authorities, he's reached my level.

He must have recognized me through the investment patterns of my false identities; he'd have to have been supercritical to do that. As an enhanced individual, he could have effected sudden and precise changes to trigger my losses, and attract my attention.

I check various data services for stock quotes; the entries on my listing are correct, so my counterpart didn't simply edit the values for my account alone. He altered the selling patterns of the stock of five unrelated corporations, for the sake of a word. It makes for quite a demonstration; I consider it no mean feat.

Presumably his treatment began before mine did, meaning that he is farther along than I, but by how much? I begin extrapolating his likely progress, and will incorporate new information as I acquire it.

The critical question: is he friend or foe? Was this merely a good-natured demonstration of his power, or an indication of his intent to ruin me? The amounts I lost were moderate; does this indicate concern for me, or for the corporations that he had to manipulate? Given all the harmless ways he could have attracted my attention, I must assume that he is to some degree hostile.

In which case, I am at risk, vulnerable to anything from another prank to a fatal attack. As a precaution, I will leave immediately. Obviously, if he were actively hostile, I'd be dead already. His sending a message means that he wishes us to play games. I'll have to place myself on equal terms with him: hide my location, determine his identity, and then attempt to communicate.

I pick a city at random: Memphis. I switch off the flatscreen, get dressed, pack a travel bag, and collect all the emergency cash in the apartment.

In a Memphis hotel, I begin working at the suite's datanet terminal. The first thing I do is reroute my activities through several dummy terminals; to an ordinary police trace, my queries will appear to originate from different terminals all over the state of Utah. A military intelligence facility might be able to track them to a terminal in Houston; continuing the trace to Memphis would try even me. An alarm program at the Houston terminal will alert me if someone has successfully traced me there.

How many clues to his identity has my twin erased? Lacking all FDA files, I'll begin with the files of courier services in various cities, looking for deliveries from the FDA to hospitals during the time of the hormone K study. Then a check of hospital brain-damage cases at that time, and I'll have a place to start.

Even if any of this information remains, it's of minor value. What will be crucial is an examination of the investment patterns, to find the traces of an enhanced mind. This will take time.

* * *

His name is Reynolds. He's originally from Phoenix, and his early progress closely parallels mine. He received his third injection six months and four days ago, giving him a head start over me of fifteen days. He didn't erase any of the obvious records. He waits for me to find him. I estimate that he's been supercritical for twelve days, twice as long as I've been.

I now see his hand in the investment patterns, but the task of locating Reynolds is Herculean. I examine usage logs across the datanet to identify the accounts he's penetrated. I have twelve lines open on my terminal. I'm using two single-hand keyboards and a throat-mike, so I can work on three queries simultaneously. Most of my body is immobile; to prevent fatigue, I'm insuring proper blood flow, regular muscle contraction and relaxation, and removal of lactic acid. While I absorb all the data I see, studying the melody within the notes, looking for the epicenter of a tremor in the web.

Hours pass. We both scan gigabytes of data, circling each other.

His location is Philadelphia. He waits for me to arrive.

I'm riding in a mud-splattered taxi to Reynolds' apartment.

Judging by the databases and agencies Reynolds has queried over the past months, his private research involves bio-engineered microorganisms for toxic-waste disposal, inertial containment for practical fusion, and subliminal dissemination of information through societies of various structures. He plans to save the world, to protect it from itself. And his opinion of me is therefore unfavorable.

I've shown no interest in the affairs of the external world, and made no investigations for aiding the normals. Neither of us will be able to convert the other. I view the world as incidental to my aims, while he cannot allow someone with enhanced intelligence to work purely in self-interest. My plans for mind-computer links will have enormous repercussions for the world, provoking government and popular reactions that would interfere with his plans. As I am proverbially not part of the solution, I am part of the problem.

If we were members of a society of enhanced minds, the nature of human interaction would be of a different order. But in this society, we have unavoidably become juggernauts, by whose measure the actions of normals are inconsequential. Even if we were twelve thousand miles apart, we couldn't ignore each other. A resolution is necessary.

Both of us have dispensed with several rounds of games. There are a thousand ways we could have attempted to kill the other, from painting neurotoxin-laced DMSO on a doorknob to ordering a surgical strike from a military killsat. We both could have swept the physical area and datanet for each of the myriad possibilities beforehand, and set more traps for each other's sweeps. But neither of us has done any of that, has felt a need to check for those things. A simple infinite regression of second-guessing and double-thinking has dismissed those. What will be decisive are those preparations that we could not predict.

The taxi stops; I pay the driver and walk up to the apartment building.

The electric lock on the door opens for me. I take off my coat and climb four flights:

The door to Reynolds' apartment is also open. I walk down the entryway to the living room, hearing a hyperaccelerated polyphony from a digital synthesizer. Evidently it's his own work; the sounds are modulated in ways undetectable to normal hearing, and even I can't discern any pattern to them. An experiment in high-information-density music, perhaps.

There is a large swivel chair in the room, its back turned toward me. Reynolds is not visible, and he is restricting his somatic emanations to comatose levels. I imply my presence and my recognition of his identity.

<Reynolds.>

Acknowledgment. <Greco.>

The chair turns around smoothly, slowly. He smiles at me and shuts off the synthesizer at his side. Gratification. <A pleasure to meet you.>

To communicate, we are exchanging fragments from the somatic language of the normals: a shorthand version of the vernacular. Each phrase takes a tenth of a second. I give a suggestion of regret. <A shame it must be as enemies.>

Wistful agreement, then supposition. <Indeed. Imagine how we could change the world, acting in concert. Two enhanced minds; such an opportunity missed.>

True, acting cooperatively would produce achievements far outstripping any we might attain individually. Any interaction would be incredibly fruitful: how satisfying it would be to simply have a discussion with someone who can match my speed, who can offer an idea that is new to me, who can hear the same melodies I do. He desires the same. It pains us both to think that one of us will not leave this room alive.

An offer. <Do you wish to share what we've learned in the past six months?>

He knows what my answer is.

We will speak aloud, since somatic language has no technical vocabulary. Reynolds says, quickly and quietly, five words. They are more pregnant with meaning than any stanza of poetry: each word provides a logical toehold I can mount after extracting everything implicit in the preceding ones. Together they encapsulate a revolutionary insight into sociology; using somatic language, he indicates that it was among the first he ever achieved. I came to a similar realization, but formulated it differently. I immediately counter with seven words, four that summarize the distinctions between my insight and his, and three that describe a non-obvious result of the distinctions. He responds.

We continue. We are like two bards, each cueing the other to extemporize another stanza, jointly composing an epic poem of knowledge. Within moments, we accelerate, talking over each other's words but hearing every nuance, until we are absorbing, concluding, and responding, continuously, simultaneously, synergistically.

* * *

Many minutes pass. I learn much from him, and he from me. It's exhilarating, to be suddenly awash in ideas whose implications would take me days to exhaust. But we're also gathering strategic information: I infer the extent of his unspoken knowledge, compare it with my own, and simulate his corresponding inferences. For there is always the awareness that this must come to an end; the formulation of our exchanges renders ideological differences luminously clear.

Reynolds hasn't witnessed the beauty that I have; he's stood before lovely insights, oblivious to them. The sole gestalt that inspires him is the one I ignored: that of the planetary society, of the biosphere. I am a lover of beauty, he of humanity. Each feels that the other has ignored great opportunities.

He has an unmentioned plan for establishing a global network of influence, to create world prosperity. To execute it, he'll employ a number of people, some of whom he'll give simple heightened intelligence, some meta-self-awareness; a few of them will pose threats to him. <Why assume such a risk for the sake of the normals?>

<Your indifference toward the normals would be justified if you were enlightened; your realm wouldn't intersect theirs. But as long as you and I can still comprehend their affairs, we can't ignore them.>

I can measure the distance between our respective moral stances precisely, see the stress between their incompatible radiating lines. What motivates him is not simply compassion or altruism, but something that entails both those things. On the other hand, I concentrate only on understanding the sublime. <What about the beauty visible from enlightenment? Doesn't it attract you?>

<You know what kind of structure would be required to hold an enlightened consciousness. I have no reason to wait the time it would take to establish the necessary industries.>

He considers intelligence to be a means, while I view it as an end in itself. Greater intelligence would be of little use to him. At his present level, he can find the best possible solution to any problem within the realm of human experience, and many beyond. All he'd require is sufficient time to implement his solution.

There's no point in further discussion. By mutual assent, we begin.

It's meaningless to speak of an element of surprise when we time our attacks; our awareness can't become more acute with forewarning. It's not affording a courtesy to each other when we agree to begin our battle, it's actualizing the inevitable.

In the models of each other that we've constructed from our inferences, there are gaps, lacunae: the internal psychological developments and discoveries that each has made. No echoes have radiated from those spaces, no strands have tied them to the world web, until now.

I begin.

I concentrate on initiating two reinforcing loops in him. One is very simple: it increases blood pressure rapidly and enormously. If it were to continue unchecked for over a second, this loop would raise his blood pressure to stroke levels—perhaps 400 over 300—and burst capillaries in his brain.

Reynolds detects it immediately. Though it's clear from our conversation that he never investigated the inducement of biofeedback loops in others, he recognizes what is happening. Once he does, he reduces his heart rate and dilates the blood vessels throughout his body.

But it is the other, subtler reinforcing loop that is my real attack. This is a weapon I've been developing ever since my search for Reynolds began. This loop causes his neurons to dramatically overproduce neuro-transmitter antagonists, preventing impulses from crossing his synapses, shutting down brain activity. I've been radiating this loop at a much higher intensity than the other.

As Reynolds is parrying the ostensible attack, he experiences a slight weakening of his concentration, masked by the effects of the heightened blood pressure. A second later, his body begins to amplify the effect on its own. Reynolds is shocked to feel his thoughts blurring. He searches for the précise mechanism: he'll identify it soon, but he won't be able to scrutinize it for long.

Once his brain function has been reduced to the level of a normal, I should be able to manipulate his mind easily. Hypnotic techniques can make him regurgitate most of the information his enhanced mind possesses.

I inspect his somatic expressions, watching them betray his diminishing intelligence. The regression is unmistakable.

And then it stops.

Reynolds is in equilibrium. I'm stunned. He was able to break the reinforcing loop. He has stopped the most sophisticated offensive I could mount.

Next, he reverse the damage already done. Even starting with reduced capabilities, he can correct the balance of neurotransmitters. Within seconds, Reynolds is fully restored.

I too was transparent to him. During our conversation, he deduced that I had investigated reinforcing loops, and as we communicated, he derived a general preventative without my detecting it. Then he observed the specifics of my particular attack while it was working, and learned how to reverse its effects. I am astonished at his discernment, his speed, his stealth.

He acknowledges my skill. <A very interesting technique; appropriate, given your self-absorption. I saw no indication when—> abruptly he projects a different somatic signature, one that I recognize. He used it when he walked behind me at a grocery store, three days ago. The aisle was crowded; around me were an old woman, wheezing behind her air filter, and a thin teenager on an acid trip, wearing a liquid crystal shirt of shifting psychedelic patterns. Reynolds slipped behind me, his mind on the porn mag stands. His surveillance didn't inform him of my reinforcing loops, but it did permit a more detailed picture of my mind.

A possibility I anticipated. I reformulate my psyche, incorporating random elements for unpredictability. The equations of my mind now bear little resemblance to those of my normal consciousness, undermining any assumptions Reynolds may have made, and rendering ineffectual any psyche-specific weapons of his.

I project the equivalent of a smile.

Reynolds smiles back. <Have you ever considered—> Suddenly he projects only silence. He is about to speak, but I can't predict what. Then it comes, as a whisper: "—self-destruct commands, Greco?"

As he says it, a lacuna in my reconstruction of him fills and overflows, the implications coloring all that I know about him. He means the Word: the sentence that, when uttered, would destroy the mind of the listener. Reynolds is claiming that the myth is true, that every mind has such a trigger built in; that for every person, there is a sentence that can reduce him to an idiot, a lunatic, a catatonic. And he is claiming he knows the one for me.

I immediately tune out all sensory input, directing it to an insulated buffer of short-term memory. Then I conceive a simulator of my own consciousness to receive the input and absorb it at reduced speed. As a metaprogrammer, I will monitor the equations of the simulation indirectly. Only after the sensory information has been confirmed as safe will I actually receive it. If the simulator is destroyed, my consciousness should be isolated, and I'll retrace the individual steps leading to the crash and derive guidelines for reprogramming my psyche.

I get everything in place by the time Reynolds has finished saying my name; his next sentence could be the destruct command. I'm now receiving my sensory input with a one-hundred-and-twenty-millisecond time lag. I reexamine my analysis of the human mind, explicitly searching for evidence to verify his assertion.

Meanwhile, I give my response lightly, casually. <Hit me with your best shot.>

<Don't worry; it's not on the tip of my tongue.>

My search produces something. I curse myself: there's a very subtle back door to a psyche's design, which I lacked the necessary mindset to notice. Whereas my weapon was one born of introspection, his is something only a manipulator could originate.

Reynolds knows that I've built my defenses; is his trigger command designed to circumvent them? I continue deriving the nature of the trigger command's actions.

<What are you waiting for?> He's confident that additional time won't allow me to construct a defense.

<Try to guess.> So smug. Can he actually toy with me so easily?

I arrive at a theoretical description of a trigger's effects on normals. A single command can reduce any subcritical mind to a tabula rasa, but an undetermined degree of customization is needed for enhanced minds. The erasure has distinctive symptoms, which my simulator can alert me to, but those are symptoms of a process calculable by me. By definition, the destruct command is that specific equation beyond my ability to imagine; would my metaprogrammer collapse while diagnosing the simulator's condition?

<Have you used the destruct command on normals?> I begin calculating what's needed to generate a customized destruct command.

<Once, as an experiment on a drug dealer. Afterward, I concealed the evidence with a blow to the temple.>

It becomes obvious that the generation is a colossal task. Generating a trigger requires intimate knowledge of my mind; I extrapolate what he could have learned about me. It appears to be insufficient, given my regrogramming, but he may have techniques of observation unknown to me. I'm acutely aware of the advantage he's gained by studying the outside world.

<You will have to do this many times.>

His regret is evident. His plan can't be implemented without more deaths: those of normal humans, by strategic necessity, and those of a few enhanced assistants of his, whose temptation by greater heights would interfere. After using the command, Reynolds may reprogram them—or me—as idiot savants, having focused intentions and restricted self-metaprogrammers. Such deaths are a necessary cost of his plan.

<I make no claims of being a saint.>

Merely a savior.

Normals might think him a tyrant, because they mistake him for one of them, and they've never trusted their own judgment. They can't fathom that Reynolds is equal to the task. His judgment is optimal in questions of their affairs, and their notions of greed and ambition do not apply to an enhanced mind.

In a histrionic gesture, Reynolds raises his hand, forefinger extended, as if to make a point. I don't have sufficient information to generate his destruct command, so for the moment I can only attend to defense. If I can survive his attack, I may have time to launch another one of my own.

With his finger upraised, he says, "Understand."

At first I don't. And then, horrifyingly, I do.

He didn't design the command to be spoken; it's not a sensory trigger at all. It's a memory trigger: the command is made out of a string of perceptions, individually harmless, that he planted in my brain like time bombs. The mental structures that were formed as a result of those memories are now resolving into a pattern, forming a gestalt that defines my dissolution. I'm intuiting the Word myself.

Immediately my mind is working faster than ever before. Against my will, a lethal realization is suggesting itself to me. I'm trying to halt the associations, but these memories can't be suppressed. The process occurs inexorably, as a consequence of my awareness, and like a man falling from a height, I'm forced to watch.

Milliseconds pass. My death passes before my eyes.

An image of the grocery store when Reynolds passed by. The psychedelic shirt the boy was wearing; Reynolds had programmed the display to implant a suggestion within me, ensuring that my "randomly" reprogrammed psyche remained receptive. Even then.

No time. All I can do is metaprogram myself over randomly, at a furious pace. An act of desperation, possibly crippling.

The strange modulated sounds that I heard when I first entered Reynolds' apartment. I absorbed the fatal insights before I had any defenses raised.

I tear apart my psyche, but still the conclusion grows clearer, the resolution sharper.

Myself, constructing the simulator. Designing those defense structures gave me the perspective needed to recognize the gestalt.

I concede his greater ingenuity. It bodes well for his endeavor. Pragmatism avails a savior far more than aestheticism.

I wonder what he intends to do after he's saved the world.

I comprehend the Word, and the means by which it operates, and so I dissolve.

JOE HALDEMAN

Born in Oklahoma City, Oklahoma, Joe Haldeman took a B.S. degree in physics and astronomy from the University of Maryland, and did postgraduate work in mathematics and computer science. But his plans for a career in science were cut short by the U.S. Army, which sent him to Vietnam in 1968 as a combat engineer. Seriously wounded in action, Haldeman returned home in 1969 and began to write. He sold his first story to Galaxy *in 1969, and by 1976, he had garnered both the Nebula Award and the Hugo Award for his famous novel* The Forever War, *one of the landmark books of the seventies. He took another Hugo Award in 1977 for his story "Tricentennial," won the Rhysling Award in 1983 for the best science-fiction poem of the year, and won both the Nebula and the Hugo awards in 1991 for the novella version of "The Hemingway Hoax." His story "None So Blind" won the Hugo Award in 1995. His novel* Forever Peace *won the John W. Campbell Memorial Award. His other books include two mainstream novels,* War Year *and* 1969, *the SF novels* Mindbridge, All My Sins Remembered, There Is No Darkness *(written with his brother, SF writer Jack C. Haldeman II),* Worlds, Worlds Apart, Worlds Enough and Time, Buying Time, The Hemingway Hoax, Forever Peace, *and* Forever Free, *the collections* Infinite Dreams, Dealing in Futures, Vietnam and Other Alien Worlds, *and* None So Blind, *and, as editor, the anthologies* Study War No More, Cosmic Laughter, *and* Nebula Award Stories Seventeen. *His most recent book is the novel* The Coming. *Haldeman lives part of the year in Boston, where he teaches writing at the Massachusetts Institute of Technology, and the rest of the year in Florida, where he and his wife Gay make their home.*

Here's a sly and fascinating little story that examines the personal cost *of that high-tech competitive edge we'd all like to have . . . a price that we may all soon have to come up with a way to pay, whether we can afford it or not.*

It all started when Cletus Jefferson asked himself, "Why aren't all blind people geniuses?" Cletus was only thirteen at the time, but it was a good question, and he would work on it for fourteen more years, and then change the world forever.

Young Jefferson was a polymath, an autodidact, a nerd literally without peer. He had a chemistry set, a microscope, a telescope, and several computers; some of them bought with paper-route money. Most of his income was from education, though: teaching his classmates not to draw to inside straights.

Not even nerds, not even nerds who are poker players nonpareil, not even nerdish poker players who can do differential equations in their heads, are immune to Cupid's darts and the sudden storm of testosterone that will accompany those missiles at the age of thirteen. Cletus knew that he was ugly and his mother dressed him funny. He was also short and pudgy and could not throw a ball in any direction. None of this bothered him until his ductless glands started cooking up chemicals that weren't in his chemistry set.

So Cletus started combing his hair and wearing clothes that mismatched according to fashion, but he was still short and pudgy and irregular of feature. He was also the youngest person in his school, even though he was a senior—and the only black person there, which was a factor in Virginia in 1994.

Now if love were sensible, if the sexual impulse was ever tempered by logic, you would expect that Cletus, being Cletus, would assess his situation and go off in search of someone homely. But of course he didn't. He just jingled and clanked down through the Pachinko machine of adolescence, being rejected, at first glance, by every Mary and Judy and Jenny and Veronica in Known Space, going from the ravishing to the beautiful to the pretty to the cute to the plain to the "great personality," until the irresistible force of statistics brought him finally into contact with Amy Linderbaum, who could not reject him at first glance because she was blind.

The other kids thought it was more than amusing. Besides being blind, Amy was about twice as tall as Cletus and, to be kind, equally irregular of feature. She was accompanied by a guide dog who looked remarkably like Cletus, short and black and pudgy. Everybody was polite to her because she was blind and rich, but she was a new transfer student and didn't have any actual friends.

So along came Cletus, to whom Cupid had dealt only slings and arrows, and what might otherwise have been merely an opposites-attract sort of romance became an emotional and intellectual union that, in the next century, would power a social tsunami that would irreversibly transform the human condition. But first there was the violin.

Her classmates had sensed that Amy was some kind of nerd herself, as classmates will, but they hadn't figured out what kind yet. She was pretty fast with a computer, but you could chalk that up to being blind and actually needing the damned thing. She wasn't fanatical about it, nor about science or math or history or *Star Trek* or student government, so what the hell kind of nerd was she? It turns out that she was a music nerd, but at the time was too painfully shy to demonstrate it.

All Cletus cared about, initially, was that she lacked those pesky Y-chromosomes and didn't recoil from him: in the Venn diagram of the human race, she was the only member of that particular set. When he found out that she was actually smart as well, having read more books than most of her classmates put together, romance began to smolder in a deep and permanent place. That was even before the violin.

Amy liked it that Cletus didn't play with her dog and was straightforward in his curiosity about what it was like to be blind. She could assess people pretty well from their voices: after one sentence, she knew that he was young, black, shy, nerdly, and not from Virginia. She could tell from his inflection that either he was unattractive or he thought he was. She was six years older than him, and white and twice his size, but otherwise they matched up pretty well, and they started keeping company in a big way.

Among the few things that Cletus did not know anything about was music. That the other kids wasted their time memorizing the words to inane Top 40 songs was proof of intellectual dysfunction if not actual lunacy. Furthermore, his parents had always been fanatical devotees of opera. A universe bounded on one end by puerile mumblings about unrequited love and on the other end by foreigners screaming in agony was not a universe that Cletus desired to explore. Until Amy picked up her violin.

They talked constantly. They sat together at lunch and met between classes. When the weather was good, they sat outside before and after school and talked. Amy asked her chauffeur to please be ten or fifteen minutes late picking her up.

So after about three weeks' worth of the fullness of time, Amy asked Cletus to come over to her house for dinner. He was a little hesitant, knowing that her parents were rich, but he was also curious about that lifestyle and, face it, was smitten enough that he would have walked off a cliff if she asked him nicely. He even used some computer money to buy a nice suit, a symptom that caused his mother to grope for the Valium.

The dinner at first was awkward. Cletus was bewildered by the arsenal of silverware and all the different kinds of food that didn't look or taste like food. But he had known it was going to be a test, and he always did well on tests, even when he had to figure out the rules as he went along.

Amy had told him that her father was a self-made millionaire; his fortune had come from a set of patents in solid-state electronics. Cletus had therefore spent a Saturday at the university library, first searching patents, and then reading selected texts, and he was ready at least for the father. It worked very well. Over soup, the four of them talked about computers. Over the calimari cocktail, Cletus and Mr. Linderbaum had it narrowed down to specific operating systems and partitioning schemata. With the beef Wellington, Cletus and "Call-me-Lindy" were talking quantum electrodynamics; with the salad, they were on an electron cloud somewhere, and by the time the nuts were served, the two nuts at that end of the table were talking in Boolean algebra while Amy and her mother exchanged knowing sighs and hummed snatches of Gilbert and Sullivan.

By the time they retired to the music room for coffee, Lindy liked Cletus very much, and the feeling was mutual, but Cletus didn't know how much he liked Amy, *really* liked her, until she picked up the violin.

It wasn't a Strad—she was promised one if and when she graduated from Julliard—but it had cost more than the Lamborghini in the garage, and she was not only worth it, but equal to it. She picked it up and tuned it quietly while her mother sat down at an electronic keyboard next to the grand piano, set it to "harp," and began the simple arpeggio that a musically sophisticated person would recognize as the introduction to the violin showpiece "Méditation," from Massenet's *Thaïs*.

Cletus had turned a deaf ear to opera for all his short life, so he didn't know the back-story of transformation and transcending love behind this intermezzo, but he did know that his girlfriend had lost her sight at the age of five, and the next year—the year he was born!—was given her first violin.

For thirteen years she had been using it to say what she would not say with her voice, perhaps to see what she could not see with her eyes, and on the deceptively simple romantic matrix that Massenet built to present the beautiful courtesan Thaïs gloriously reborn as the bride of Christ, Amy forgave her godless universe for taking her sight, and praised it for what she was given in return, and she said this in a language that even Cletus could understand. He didn't cry very much, never had, but by the last high, wavering note, he was weeping into his hands, and he knew that if she wanted him, she could have him forever, and oddly enough, considering his age and what eventually happened, he was right.

He would learn to play the violin before he had his first doctorate, and during a lifetime of remarkable amity, they would play together for ten thousand hours, but all of that would come after the big idea. The big idea— "Why aren't all blind people geniuses?"—was planted that very night, but it didn't start to sprout for another week.

Like most thirteen-year-olds, Cletus was fascinated by the human body, his own and others', but his study was more systematic than others' and, atypically, the organ that interested him most was the brain.

The brain isn't very much like a computer, although it doesn't do a bad job, considering that it's built by unskilled labor and programmed more by pure chance than anything else. One thing computers do a lot better than brains, though, is what Cletus and Lindy had been talking about over their little squids in tomato sauce: partitioning.

Think of the computer as a big meadow of green pastureland, instead of a little dark box full of number-clogged things that are expensive to replace, and that pastureland is presided over by a wise old magic shepherd who is not called a macroprogram. The shepherd stands on a hill and looks out over the pastureland, which is full of sheep and goats and cows. They aren't all in one homogeneous mass, of course, since the cows would step on the lambs and kids and the goats would make everybody nervous, leaping and butting, so there are *partitions* of barbed wire that keep all the species separate and happy.

This is a frenetic sort of meadow, though, with cows and goats and sheep coming in and going out all the time, moving at about 3×10^8 meters per second, and if the partitions were all of the same size, it would be a disaster, because sometimes there are no sheep at all, but lots of cows, who would be jammed in there hip to hip and miserable. But the shepherd, being wise, knows ahead of time how much space to allot to the various creatures and, being magic, can move barbed wire quickly without hurting himself or the animals. So each partition winds up marking a comfortable-sized space for each use. Your computer does that, too, but instead of barbed wire you see little rectangles or windows or file folders, depending on your computer's religion.

The brain has its own partitions, in a sense. Cletus knew that certain physical areas of the brain were associated with certain mental abilities, but it wasn't a simple matter of "music appreciation goes over there; long division in that corner." The brain is mushier than that. For instance, there are pretty well-defined partitions associated with linguistic functions, areas named after French and German brain people. If one of those areas is destroyed, by stroke or bullet or flung frying pan, the stricken person may lose the ability—reading or speaking or writing coherently—associated with the lost area.

That's interesting, but what is more interesting is that the lost ability sometimes comes back over time. Okay, you say, so the brain grew back—but it doesn't! You're born with all the brain cells you'll ever have. (Ask any child.) What evidently happens is that some other part of the brain has been sitting around as a kind of backup, and after a while the wiring gets rewired and hooked into that backup. The afflicted person can say his name, and then his wife's name, and then "frying pan," and before you know it he's complaining about hospital food and calling a divorce lawyer.

So on that evidence, it would appear that the brain has a shepherd like the computer-meadow has, moving partitions around, but alas, no. Most of the time when some part of the brain ceases to function, that's the end of it. There may be acres and acres of fertile ground lying fallow right next door, but nobody in charge to make use of it—at least not consistently. The fact that it sometimes *did* work is what made Cletus ask "Why aren't all blind people geniuses?"

Of course there have always been great thinkers and writers and composers who were blind (and in the twentieth century, some painters to whom eyesight was irrelevant), and many of them, like Amy with her violin, felt that their talent was a compensating gift. Cletus wondered whether there might be a literal truth to that, in the microanatomy of the brain. It didn't happen every time, or else all blind people *would* be geniuses. Perhaps it happened occasionally, through a mechanism like the one that helped people recover from strokes. Perhaps it could be made to happen.

Cletus had been offered scholarships at both Harvard and MIT, but he opted for Columbia, in order to be near Amy while she was studying at Julliard. Columbia reluctantly allowed him a triple major in physiology, electrical engineering, and cognitive science, and he surprised everybody who knew him by doing only moderately well. The reason, it turned out, was that he was treating undergraduate work as a diversion at best; a necessary evil at worst. He was racing ahead of his studies in the areas that were important to him.

If he had paid more attention in trivial classes like history, like philosophy, things might have turned out differently. If he had paid attention to literature, he might have read the story of Pandora.

Our own story now descends into the dark recesses of the brain. For the next ten years, the main part of the story, which we will try to ignore after this paragraph, will involve Cletus doing disturbing intellectual tasks like cutting up dead brains, learning how to pronounce cholecystokinin, and sawing holes in people's skulls and poking around inside with live electrodes.

In the other part of the story, Amy also learned how to pronounce cholecystokinin, for the same reason that Cletus learned how to play the violin. Their love grew and mellowed, and at the age of nineteen, between his first doctorate and his M.D., Cletus paused long enough for them to be married and have a whirlwind honeymoon in Paris, where Cletus divided his time between the musky charms of his beloved and the sterile cubicles of Institute Marey, learning how squids learn things, which was by serotonin pushing adenylate cyclase to catalyze the synthesis of cyclic adenosine monophosphate in just the right place, but that's actually the main part of the story, which we have been trying to ignore, because it gets pretty gruesome.

They returned to New York, where Cletus spent eight years becoming a pretty good neurosurgeon. In his spare time he tucked away a doctorate in electrical engineering. Things began to converge.

At the age of thirteen, Cletus had noted that the brain used more cells collecting, handling, and storing visual images than it used for all the other senses combined. "Why aren't all blind people geniuses?" was just a specific case of the broader assertion, "The brain doesn't know how to make use of what it's got." His investigations over the next fourteen years were more subtle and complex than that initial question and statement, but he did wind up coming right back around to them.

Because the key to the whole thing was the visual cortex.

When a baritone saxophone player has to transpose sheet music from cello, he (few women are drawn to the instrument) merely pretends that the music is written in treble clef rather than bass, eyeballs it up an octave, and then plays without the octave key pressed down. It's so simple a child could do it, if a child wanted to play such a huge, ungainly instrument. As his eye dances along the little fence posts of notes, his fingers automatically perform a one-to-one transformation that is the theoretical equivalent of adding and subtracting octaves, fifths, and thirds, but all of the actual mental work is done when he looks up in the top right corner of the first page and says, "Aw hell. Cello again." Cello parts aren't that interesting to saxophonists.

But the eye is the key, and the visual cortex is the lock. When blind Amy "sight-reads" for the violin, she has to stop playing and feel the Braille notes with her left hand. (Years of keeping the instrument in place while she does this has made her neck muscles so strong that she can crack a walnut between her chin and shoulder.) The visual cortex is not involved, of course; she "hears" the mute notes of a phrase with her fingertips, temporarily memorizing them, and then plays them over and over until she can add that phrase to the rest of the piece.

Like most blind musicians, Amy had a very good "ear"; it actually took her less time to memorize music by listening to it repeatedly, rather than reading, even with fairly complex pieces. (She used Braille nevertheless for serious work, so she could isolate the composer's intent from the performer's or conductor's phrasing decisions.)

She didn't really miss being able to sight-read in a conventional way. She wasn't even sure what it would be like, since she had never seen sheet music before she lost her sight, and in fact had only a vague idea of what a printed page of writing looked like.

So when her father came to her in her thirty-third year and offered to buy her the chance of a limited gift of sight, she didn't immediately jump at it. It was expensive and risky and grossly deforming: implanting miniaturized video cameras in her eye sockets and wiring them up to stimulate her dormant optic nerves. What if it made her only half-blind, but also blunted her musical ability? She knew how other people read music, at least in theory, but after a quarter century of doing without the skill, she wasn't sure that it would do much for her. It might make her tighten up.

Besides, most of her concerts were done as charities to benefit organizations for the blind or for special education. Her father argued that she would be even more effective in those venues as a recovered blind person. Still she resisted.

Cletus said he was cautiously for it. He said he had reviewed the literature and talked to the Swiss team who had successfully done the implants on dogs and primates. He said he didn't think she would be harmed by it even if the experiment failed. What he didn't say to Amy or Lindy or anybody was the grisly Frankensteinian truth: that he was himself behind the experiment; that it had nothing to do with restoring sight; that the little video cameras would never even be hooked up. They were just an excuse for surgically removing her eyeballs.

Now a normal person would have extreme feelings about popping out somebody's eyeballs for the sake of science, and even more extreme feelings on learning that it was a husband wanting to do it to his wife. Of course Cletus was far from being normal in any respect. To his way of thinking, those eyeballs were useless vestigial appendages that blocked surgical access to the optic nerves, which would be his conduits through the brain to the visual cortex. *Physical* conduits, through which incredibly tiny surgical instruments would be threaded. But we have promised not to investigate that part of the story in detail.

The end result was not grisly at all. Amy finally agreed to go to Geneva, and Cletus and his surgical team (all as skilled as they were unethical) put her through three twenty-hour days of painstaking but painless microsurgery, and when they took the bandages off and adjusted a thousand-dollar wig (for they'd had to go in behind as well as through the eye sockets), she actually looked more attractive than when they had started. That was partly because her actual hair had always been a disaster. And now she had glass baby-blues instead of the rather scary opalescence of her natural eyes. No Buck Rogers TV cameras peering out at the world.

He told her father that that part of the experiment hadn't worked, and the six Swiss scientists who had been hired for the purpose agreed.

"They're lying," Amy said. "They never intended to restore my sight. The sole intent of the operations was to subvert the normal functions of the visual cortex in such a way as to give me access to the unused parts of my brain." She faced the sound of her husband's breathing, her blue eyes looking beyond him. "You have succeeded beyond your expectations."

Amy had known this as soon as the fog of drugs from the last operation had lifted. Her mind started making connections, and those connections made connections, and so on at a geometrical rate of growth. By the time they had finished putting her wig on, she had reconstructed the entire microsurgical procedure from her limited readings and conversations with Cletus. She had suggestions as to improving it, and was eager to go under and submit herself to further refinement.

As to her feelings about Cletus, in less time than it takes to read about it, she had gone from horror to hate to understanding to renewed love, and finally to an emotional condition beyond the ability of any merely natural language to express. Fortunately, the lovers did have Boolean algebra and propositional calculus at their disposal.

Cletus was one of the few people in the world she *could* love, or even talk to one-on-one, without condescending. His IQ was so high that its number would be meaningless. Compared to her, though, he was slow, and barely literate. It was not a situation he would tolerate for long.

The rest is history, as they say, and anthropology, as those of us left who read with our eyes must recognize every minute of every day. Cletus was the second person to have the operation done, and he had to accomplish it while on the run from mèdical-ethics people and their policemen. There were four the next year, though, and twenty the year after that, and then two thousand and twenty thousand. Within a decade, people with purely intellectual occupations had no choice, or one choice: lose your eyes or lose your job. By then, the "secondsight" operation was totally automated, totally safe.

It's still illegal in most countries, including the United States, but who is kidding whom? If your department chairman is secondsighted and you are not, do you think you'll get tenure? You can't even hold a conversation with a creature whose synapses fire six times as fast as yours, with whole encyclopedias of information instantly available. You are, like me, an intellectual throwback.

You may have an excuse, being a painter, an architect, a naturalist, or a trainer of guide dogs. Maybe you can't come up with the money for the operation, but that's a weak excuse, since it's trivially easy to get a loan against future earnings. Maybe there's a good physical reason for you not to lie down on that table and open your eyes for the last time.

I know Cletus and Amy through music. I was her keyboard professor once, at Julliard, though now, of course, I'm not smart enough to teach her anything. They come to hear me play sometimes, in this run-down bar with its band of aging firstsight musicians. Our music must seem boring, obvious, but they do us the favor of not joining in.

Amy was an innocent bystander in this sudden evolutionary explosion. And Cletus was, arguably, blinded by love.

The rest of us have to choose which kind of blindness to endure.

Mortimer Gray's History of Death

BRIAN STABLEFORD

Critically acclaimed British "hard-science" writer Brian Stableford is the author of more than thirty books, including Cradle of the Sun, The Blind Worm, Days of Glory, In the Kingdom of the Beasts, Day of Wrath, The Halcyon Drift, The Paradox of the Sets, The Realms of Tartarus, The Empire of Fear, The Angel of Pain, The Carnival of Destruction, Serpent's Blood, *and* Inherit the Earth. *His short fiction has been collected in* Sexual Chemistry: Sardonic Tales of the Genetic Revolution. *His nonfiction books include* The Sociology of Science Fiction, *and with David Langford,* The Third Millennium: A History of the World A.D. 2000–3000. *His acclaimed novella "Les Fleurs Du Mal" was a finalist for the Hugo Award in 1994. His most recent books are the novels* The Fountains of Youth *and* Architects of Emortality. *A biologist and sociologist by training, Stableford lives in Reading, England.*

Stableford may have written more about how the ongoing revolutions in biological and genetic science will change the very nature of humanity itself than any other writer of the last decade, covering the development of posthumanity in story after story, including such stories as "Out of Touch," "The Magic Bullet," "Age of Innocence," "The Tree of Life," "The Pipes of Pan," "Hidden Agendas," "The Color of Envy," the above-mentioned "Les Fleurs Du Mal," and many, many others, as well as recent novels such as Inherit the Earth, The Fountains of Youth, *and* Architects of Emortality. *Never has he explored the posthuman future in more detail or with more passion or conviction than in the complex and compelling novella that follows, though, perhaps his best story and certainly one of the very best novellas of the nineties, taking us to an ultrarich, ultracivilized far-future world where we've almost—almost—conquered the oldest and coldest enemy of them all. . . .*

I

I was an utterly unexceptional child of the twenty-ninth century, comprehensively engineered for emortality while I was still a more-or-less inchoate blastula, and decanted from an artificial womb in Naburn Hatchery in the country of York in the Defederated States of Europe. I was raised in an aggregate family that consisted of six men and six women. I was, of course, an only child, and I received the customary superabundance of love, affection, and admiration. With the aid of excellent internal technologies, I grew up reasonable, charitable, self-controlled, and intensely serious of mind.

It's evident that not *everyone* grows up like that, but I've never quite been able to understand how people manage to avoid it. If conspicuous individuality—and frank perversity—aren't programmed in the genes or rooted in early upbringing, how on earth do they spring into being with such determined irregularity? But this is *my* story, not the world's, and I shouldn't digress.

In due course, the time came for me—as it comes to everyone—to leave my family and enter a community of my peers for my first spell at college. I elected to go to Adelaide in Australia because I liked the name.

Although my memories of that period are understandably hazy, I feel sure that I had begun to see the *fascination* of history long before the crucial event which determined my path in life. The subject seemed—in stark contrast to the disciplined coherency of mathematics or the sciences—so huge, so amazingly abundant in its data, and so charmingly disorganized. I was always a very orderly and organized person, and I needed a vocation like history to loosen me up a little. It was not, however, until I set forth on an ill-fated expedition on the sailing-ship *Genesis* in September 2901 that the exact form of my destiny was determined.

I use the word "destiny" with the utmost care; it is no mere rhetorical flourish. What happened when *Genesis* defied the supposed limits of possibility and turned turtle was no mere incident, and the impression that it made on my fledging mind was no mere suggestion. Before that ship set sail, a thousand futures were open to me; afterward, I was beset by an irresistible compulsion. My destiny was determined the day *Genesis* went down; as a result of that tragedy, *my fate was sealed.*

We were en route from Brisbane to tour the Creationist Islands of Micronesia, which were then regarded as artistic curiosities rather than daring experiments in continental design. I had expected to find the experience exhilarating, but almost as soon as we had left port, I was struck down by seasickness.

Seasickness, by virtue of being psychosomatic, is one of the very few diseases with which modern internal technology is sometimes impotent to deal, and I was miserably confined to my cabin while I waited for my mind to make the necessary adaptation. I was bitterly ashamed of myself, for I alone out of half a hundred passengers had fallen prey to this strange atavistic malaise. While the others partied on deck beneath the glorious light of the tropic stars, I lay in my bunk, half-delirious with discomfort and lack of sleep. I thought myself the unluckiest man in the world.

When I was abruptly hurled from my bed, I thought that I had fallen—that my tossing and turning had inflicted one more ignominy upon me. When I couldn't recover my former position after having spent long minutes fruitlessly groping about amid all kinds of mysterious debris, I assumed that I must be confused. When I couldn't open the door of my cabin even though I had the handle in my hand, I assumed that my failure was the result of clumsiness. When I finally got out into the corridor, and found myself crawling in shallow water with the artificial bioluminescent strip beneath instead of above me, I thought I must be mad.

When the little girl spoke to me, I thought at first that she was a delusion, and that I was lost in a nightmare. It wasn't until she touched me, and tried to drag me upright with her tiny, frail hands, and addressed me by name—albeit incorrectly—that I was finally able to focus my thoughts.

"You have to get up, Mr. Mortimer," she said. "The boat's upside down." She was only eight years old, but she spoke quite calmly and reasonably.

"That's impossible," I told her. "*Genesis* is unsinkable. There's no way it could turn upside down."

"But it *is* upside down," she insisted—and, as she did so, I finally realized the significance of the fact that the floor was glowing the way the ceiling should have glowed. "The water's coming in. I think we'll have to swim out."

The light put out by the ceiling-strip was as bright as ever, but the rippling water overlaying it made it seem dim and uncertain. The girl's little face, lit from below, seemed terribly serious within the frame of her dark and curly hair.

"I can't swim," I said, flatly.

She looked at me as if I were insane, or stupid, but it was true. I couldn't swim. I'd never liked the idea, and I'd never seen any necessity. All modern ships—even sailing-ships designed to be cute and quaint for the benefit of tourists—were unsinkable.

I scrambled to my feet and put out both my hands to steady myself, to hold myself against the upside-down walls. The water was knee-deep. I couldn't tell whether it was increasing or not—which told me, reassuringly, that it couldn't be rising very quickly. The upturned boat was rocking this way and that, and I could hear the rumble of waves breaking on the outside of the hull, but I didn't know how much of that apparent violence was in my mind.

"My name's Emily," the little girl told me. "I'm frightened. All my mothers and fathers were on deck. *Everyone* was on deck, except for you and me. Do you think they're all dead?"

"They can't be," I said, marveling at the fact that she spoke so soberly, even when she said that she was frightened. I realized, however, that if the ship had suffered the kind of misfortune which could turn it upside down, the people on deck might indeed be dead. I tried to remember the passengers gossiping in the departure lounge, introducing themselves to one another with such fervor. The little girl had been with a party of nine, none of whose names I could remember. It occurred to me that *her whole family* might have been wiped out, that she might now be that rarest of all rare beings, an *orphan*. It was almost unimaginable. What possible catastrophe, I wondered, could have done that?

I asked Emily what had happened. She didn't know. Like me she had been in her bunk, sleeping the sleep of the innocent.

"Are we going to die too?" she asked. "I've been a good girl. I've never told a lie." It couldn't have been literally true, but I knew exactly what she meant. She was eight years old, and she had every right to expect to live till she was eight hundred. She didn't *deserve* to die. It wasn't fair.

I knew full well that fairness didn't really come into it, and I expect that she knew it too, even if my fellow historians were wrong about the virtual abolition of all the artifices of childhood, but I knew in my heart that what she said was *right*, and that insofar as the imperious laws of nature ruled her observation irrelevant, the *universe* was wrong. It *wasn't* fair. She *had* been a good girl. If she died, it would be a monstrous injustice.

Perhaps it was merely a kind of psychological defense mechanism that helped me to displace my own mortal anxieties, but the horror that ran through me was all focused on her. At the moment, her plight—not *our* plight, but *hers*—seemed to be the only thing that mattered. It was as if her dignified fear and her placid courage somehow contained the essence of human existence, the purest product of human progress.

Perhaps it was only my cowardly mind's refusal to contemplate anything else, but the only thing I could think of while I tried to figure out what to do was the awfulness of what she was saying. As that awfulness possessed me, it was magnified a thousandfold, and it seemed to me that in her lone and tiny voice there was a much greater voice speaking for multitudes: for all the human children that had ever died before achieving maturity; all the *good* children who had died without ever having the chance to *deserve to die*.

"I don't think any more water can get in," she said, with a slight tremor in her voice. "But there's only so much air. If we stay here too long, we'll suffocate."

"It's a big ship," I told her. "If we're trapped in an air-bubble, it must be a very large one."

"But it won't last forever," she told me. She was eight years old and hoped to live to be eight hundred, and she was absolutely right. The air wouldn't last forever. Hours, certainly; maybe days—but not forever.

"There are survival pods under the bunks," she said. She had obviously been paying attention to the welcoming speeches that the captain and the chief steward had delivered in the lounge the evening after embarkation. She'd plugged the chips they'd handed out into her trusty handbook, like the good girl she was, and inwardly digested what they had to teach her—unlike those of us who were blithely careless and wretchedly seasick.

"We can both fit into one of the pods," she went on, "but we have to get it out of the boat before we inflate it. We have to go up—I mean *down*—the stairway into the water and away from the boat. You'll have to carry the pod, because it's too big for me."

"I can't swim," I reminded her.

"It doesn't matter," she said, patiently. "All you have to do is hold your breath and kick yourself away from the boat. You'll float up to the surface whether you can swim or not. Then you just yank the cord and the pod will inflate. You have to hang on to it, though. Don't let go."

I stared at her, wondering how she could be so calm, so controlled, so efficient.

"Listen to the water breaking on the hull," I whispered. "Feel the movement of the boat. It would take a hurricane to overturn a boat like this. We wouldn't stand a chance out there."

"It's not so bad," she told me. She didn't have both hands out to brace herself against the walls, although she lifted one occasionally to stave off the worst of the lurches caused by the bobbing of the boat.

But if it wasn't a hurricane which turned us over, I thought, *what the hell was it? Whales have been extinct for eight hundred years.*

"We don't have to go just yet," Emily said, mildly, "but we'll have to go in the end. We have to get out. The pod's bright orange, and it has a distress beacon. We should be picked up within twenty-four hours, but there'll be supplies for a week."

I had every confidence that modern technology could sustain us for a month, if necessary. Even having to drink a little seawater if your recycling gel clots only qualifies as a minor inconvenience nowadays. Drowning is another matter; so is asphyxiation. She was absolutely right. We had to get out of the upturned boat—not immediately, but sometime soon. Help might get to us before then, but we couldn't wait, and we shouldn't. We were, after all, human beings. We were supposed to be able to take charge of our own destinies, to do what we *ought* to do. Anything less would be a betrayal of our heritage. I knew that, and understood it.

But I couldn't swim.

"It's okay, Mr. Mortimer," she said, putting her reassuring hand in mine. "We can do it. We'll go together. It'll be all right."

Emily was right. We *could* do it, together, and we did—not immediately, I confess, but, in the end, we did it. It was the most terrifying and most horrible experience of my young life, but it had to be done, and we did it.

When I finally dived into that black pit of water, knowing that I had to go down and sideways before I could hope to go up, I was carried forward by the knowledge that Emily expected it of me, and needed me to do it. Without her, I'm sure that I would have died. I simply would not have had the courage to save myself. Because she was there, I dived, with the pod clutched in my arms. Because she was there, I managed to kick away from the hull and yank the cord to inflate it.

It wasn't until I had pulled Emily into the pod, and made sure that she was safe, that I paused to think how remarkable it was that the sea was hot enough to scald us both.

We were three storm-tossed days afloat before the helicopter picked us up. We cursed our ill-luck, not having the least inkling how bad things were elsewhere. We couldn't understand why the weather was getting worse instead of better.

When the pilot finally explained it, we couldn't immediately take it in. Perhaps that's not surprising, given that the geologists were just as astonished as everyone else. After all, the sea-bed had been quietly cracking wherever the tectonic plates were pulling apart for millions of years; it was an ongoing phenomenon, very well understood. Hundreds of black smokers and underwater volcanoes were under constant observation. Nobody had any reason to expect that a plate could simply *break* so far away from its rim, or that the fissure could be so deep, so long, and so rapid in its extension. Everyone thought that the main threat to the earth's surface was posed by wayward comets; all vigilant eyes were directed outward. No one had expected such awesome force to erupt from within, from the hot mantle which lay, hubbling and bubbling, beneath the earth's fragile crust.

It was, apparently, an enormous bubble of upwelling gas that contrived the near-impossible feat of flipping *Genesis* over. The earthquakes and the tidal waves came later.

It was the worst natural disaster in six hundred years. One million, nine hundred thousand people died in all. Emily wasn't the only child to lose her entire family, and I shudder to think of the number of families which lost their only children. We historians have to maintain a sense of perspective, though. Compared with the number of people who died in the wars of the twentieth and twenty-first centuries, or the numbers of people who died in epidemics in earlier centuries, nineteen hundred thousand is a trivial figure.

Perhaps I would have done what I eventually set out to do anyway. Perhaps the Great Coral Sea Catastrophe would have appalled me even if I'd been on the other side of the world, cocooned in the safety of a treehouse or an apartment in one of the crystal cities—but I don't think so.

It was because I was at the very center of things, because my life was literally turned upside down by the disaster—and because eight-year-old Emily Marchant was there to save my life with her common sense and her composure—that I set out to write a definitive history of death, intending to reveal not merely the dull facts of mankind's longest and hardest battle, but also the real meaning and significance of it.

2

The first volume of Mortimer Gray's *History of Death*, entitled *The Prehistory of Death*, was published on 21 January 2914. It was, unusually for its day, a mute book, with no voice-over, sound-effects, or background music. Nor did it have any original artwork, all the illustrations being unenhanced still photographs. It was, in short, the kind of book that only a historian would have published. Its reviewers generally agreed that it was an old-fashioned example of scrupulous scholarship, and none expected that access demand would be considerable. Many commentators questioned the merit of Gray's arguments.

The Prehistory of Death summarized what was known about early hominid lifestyles, and had much to say about the effects of natural selection on the patterns of mortality in modern man's ancestor species. Gray carefully discussed the evolution of parental care as a genetic strategy. Earlier species of man, he observed, had raised parental care to a level of efficiency which permitted the human infant to be born at a much earlier stage in its development than any other, maximizing its opportunity to be shaped by nature and learning. From the very beginning, Gray proposed, human species were *actively* at war with death. The evolutionary success of *Homo sapiens* was based in the collaborative activities of parents in protecting, cherishing, and preserving the lives of children: activities that extended beyond immediate family groups as reciprocal altruism made it advantageous for humans to form tribes, and ultimately nations.

In these circumstances, Gray argued, it was entirely natural that the origins of consciousness and culture should be intimately bound up with a keen awareness of the war against death. He asserted that the first great task of the human imagination must have been to carry forward that war. It was entirely understandable, he said, that early paleontologists, having discovered the bones of a Neanderthal man in an apparent grave, with the remains of a primitive garland of flowers, should instantly have felt an intimate kinship with him; there could be no more persuasive evidence of full humanity than the attachment of ceremony to the idea and the fact of death.

Gray waxed lyrical about the importance of ritual as a symbolization of opposition and enmity to death. He had no patience with the proposition that such rituals were of no practical value, a mere window dressing of culture. On the contrary, he claimed that there was no activity *more* practical than this expressive recognition of the *value* of life, this imposition of a moral order on the fact of human mortality. The birth of agriculture Gray regarded as a mere sophistication of food gathering, of considerable importance as a technical discovery but of little significance in transforming human nature. The practices of burying the dead with ceremony, and of ritual mourning, on the other hand, *were*, in his view, evidence of the transformation of human nature, of the fundamental creation of meaning that made human life very different from the life of animals.

Prehistorians who marked out the evolution of man by his developing technology—the Stone Age giving way to the Bronze Age, the Bronze Age to the Iron Age—were, Gray conceded, taking intelligent advantage of those relics that had stood the test of time. He warned, however, of the folly of thinking that because tools had survived the millennia, it must have been tool-making that was solely or primarily responsible for human progress. In his view, the primal cause that made people invent was man's ongoing war against death.

It was not *tools* which created man and gave birth to civilization, Mortimer Gray proclaimed, but the *awareness of mortality*.

3

Although its impact on my nascent personality was considerable, the Coral Sea Catastrophe was essentially an impersonal disaster. The people who died, including those who had been aboard the *Genesis*, were all unknown to me; it was not until some years later that I experienced personal bereavement. It wasn't one of my parents who died—by the time the first of them quit this earth, I was nearly a hundred years old and our temporary closeness was a half-remembered thing of the distant past—but one of my spouses.

By the time *The Prehistory of Death* was published, I'd contracted my first marriage: a group contract with a relatively small aggregate consisting of three other men and four women. We lived in Lamu, on the coast of Kenya, a nation to which I had been drawn by my studies of the early evolution of man. We were all young people, and we had formed our group for companionship rather than for parenting—which was a privilege conventionally left, even in those days, to much older people. We didn't go in for much fleshsex, because we were still finding our various ways through the maze of erotic virtuality, but we took the time—as I suppose all young people do—to explore its unique delights. I can't remember exactly why I decided to join such a group; I presume that it was because I accepted tacitly at least, the conventional wisdom that there is spice in variety, and that one should do one's best to keep a broad front of experience.

It wasn't a particularly happy marriage, but it served its purpose. We went in for a good deal of sporting activity and conventional tourism. We visited the other continents from time to time, but most of our adventures took us back and forth across Africa. Most of my spouses were practical ecologists involved in one way or another with the re-greening of the north and south, or with the reforestation of the equatorial belt. What little credit I earned to add to my Allocation was earned by assisting them; such fees as I received for net access to my work were inconsiderable. Axel, Jodocus, and Minna were all involved in large-scale hydrological engineering, and liked to describe themselves, lightheartedly, as the Lamu Rainmakers. The rest of us became, inevitably, the Rainmakers-in-Law.

To begin with, I had considerable affection for all the other members of my new family, but as time went by the usual accretion of petty irritations built up, and a couple of changes in the group's personnel failed to renew the initial impetus. The research for the second volume of my history began to draw me more and more to Egypt and to Greece, even though there was no real need actually to travel in order to do the relevant research. I think we would have divorced in 2919 anyhow, even if it hadn't been for Grizel's death.

She went swimming in the newly re-routed Kwarra one day, and didn't come back.

Maybe the fact of her death wouldn't have hit me so hard if she hadn't been drowned, but I was still uneasy about deep water—even the relatively placid waters of the great rivers. If I'd been able to swim, I might have gone out with her, but I hadn't. I didn't even know she was missing until the news came in that a body had been washed up twenty kilometers downriver.

"It was a million-to-one thing," Ayesha told me, when she came back from the on-site inquest. "She must have been caught from behind by a log moving in the current, or something like that. We'll never know for sure. She must have been knocked unconscious, though, or badly dazed. Otherwise, she'd never have drifted into the white water. The rocks finished her off."

Rumor has it that many people simply can't take in news of the death of someone they love—that it flatly defies belief. I didn't react that way. With me, belief was instantaneous, and I just gave way under its pressure. I literally fell over, because my legs wouldn't support me—another psychosomatic failure about which my internal machinery could do nothing—and I wept uncontrollably. None of the others did, not even Axel, who'd been closer to Grizel than anyone. They were sympathetic at first, but it wasn't long before a note of annoyance began to creep into their reassurances.

"Come on, Morty," Ilya said, voicing the thought the rest of them were too diplomatic to let out. "You know more about death than any of us; if it doesn't help you to get a grip, what good is all that research?"

He was right, of course. Axel and Ayesha had often tried to suggest, delicately, that mine was an essentially unhealthy fascination, and now they felt vindicated.

"If you'd actually bothered to read my book," I retorted, "you'd know that it has nothing complimentary to say about philosophical acceptance. It sees a sharp awareness of mortality, and the capacity to feel the horror of death so keenly, as key forces driving human evolution."

"But you don't have to act it out so flamboyantly," Ilya came back, perhaps using cruelty to conceal and assuage his own misery. "We've evolved now. We've got past all that. We've matured." Ilya was the oldest of us, and he *seemed* very old, although he was only sixty-five. In those days, there weren't nearly as many double centenarians around as there are nowadays, and triple centenarians were very rare indeed. We take emortality so much for granted that it's easy to forget how recent a development it is.

"It's what I feel," I told him, retreating into uncompromising assertion. "I can't help it."

"We *all* loved her," Ayesha reminded me. "We'll all miss her. You're not *proving* anything, Morty."

What she meant was that I wasn't proving anything except my own instability, but she spoke more accurately than she thought; I wasn't proving anything at all. I was just reacting—atavistically, perhaps, but with crude honesty and authentically childlike innocence.

"We all have to pull together now," she added, "for Grizel's sake."

A death in the family almost always leads to universal divorce in childless marriages; nobody knows why. Such a loss *does* force the survivors to pull together, but it seems that the process of pulling together only serves to emphasize the incompleteness of the unit. We all went our separate ways, even the three Rainmakers.

I set out to use my solitude to become a true neo-Epicurean, after the fashion of the times, seeking no excess and deriving an altogether *appropriate* pleasure from everything I did. I took care to cultivate a proper love for the commonplace, training myself to a pitch of perfection in all the techniques of physiological control necessary to physical fitness and quiet metabolism.

I soon convinced myself that I'd transcended such primitive and adolescent goals as happiness, and had cultivated instead a truly civilized *ataraxia*: a calm of mind whose value went beyond the limits of ecstasy and exultation.

Perhaps I was fooling myself, but, if I was, I succeeded. The habits stuck. No matter what lifestyle fashions came and went thereafter, I remained a stubborn neo-Epicurean, immune to all other eupsychian fantasies. For a while, though, I was perpetually haunted by Grizel's memory—and not, alas, by the memory of all things that we'd shared while she was *alive*. I gradually forgot the sound of her voice, the touch of her hand, and even the image of her face, remembering only the horror of her sudden and unexpected departure from the arena of my experience.

For the next ten years, I lived in Alexandria, in a simple villa cleverly gantzed out of the desert sands—sands which still gave an impression of timelessness even though they had been restored to wilderness as recently as the twenth-seventh century, when Egypt's food economy had been realigned to take full advantage of the newest techniques in artificial photosynthesis.

4

The second volume of Mortimer Gray's *History of Death*, entitled *Death in the Ancient World*, was published on 7 May 2931. It contained a wealth of data regarding burial practices and patterns of mortality in Egypt, the Kingdoms of Sumer and Akkad, the Indus civilizations of Harappa and Mohenjo-Daro, the Yangshao and Lungshan cultures of the Far East, the cultures of the Olmecs and Zapotecs, Greece before and after Alexander, and the pre-Christian Roman Empire. It paid particular attention to the elaborate mythologies of life after death developed by ancient cultures.

Gray gave most elaborate consideration to the Egyptians, whose eschatology evidently fascinated him. He spared no effort in description and discussion of the *Book of the Dead*, the Hall of Double Justice, Anubis and Osiris, the custom of mummification, and the building of pyramid-tombs. He was almost as fascinated by the elaborate geography of the Greek Underworld, the characters associated with it—Hades and Persephone, Thanatos and the Erinnyes, Cerberus and Charon—and the descriptions of the unique fates reserved for such individuals as Sisyphus, Ixion, and Tantalus. The development of such myths as these Gray regarded as a triumph of the creative imagination. In his account, myth-making and story-telling were vital weapons in the war against death—a war that had still to be fought in the mind of man, because there was little yet to be accomplished by defiance of its claims upon the body.

In the absence of an effective medical science, Gray argued, the war against death was essentially a war of propaganda, and myths were to be judged in that light—not by their truthfulness, even in some allegorical or metaphorical sense, but by their usefulness in generating *morale* and meaning. By elaborating and extrapolating the process of death in this way, a more secure moral order could be imported into social life. People thus achieved a sense of continuity with past and future generations, so that every individual became part of a great enterprise which extended across the generations, from the beginning to the end of time.

Gray did not regard the building of the pyramids as a kind of gigantic folly or vanity, or a way to dispose of the energies of the peasants when they were not required in harvesting the bounty of the fertile Nile. He argued that pyramid-building should be seen as the most useful of all labors, because it was work directed at the glorious imposition of human endeavor upon the natural landscape. The placing of a royal mummy, with all its accoutrements, in a fabulous geometric edifice of stone was, for Gray, a loud, confident, and entirely appropriate statement of humanity's invasion of the empire of death.

Gray complimented those tribesmen who worshiped their ancestors and thought them always close at hand, ready to deliver judgments upon the living. Such people, he felt, had fully mastered an elementary truth of human existence: that the dead were not entirely gone, but lived on, intruding upon memory and dream, both when they were bidden and when they were not. He approved of the idea that the dead should have a voice, and must be entitled to speak, and that the living had a moral duty to listen. Because these ancient tribes were as direly short of history as they were of medicine, he argued, they were entirely justified in allowing their ancestors to live on in the minds of living people, where the culture those ancestors had forged similarly resided.

Some reviewers complimented Gray on the breadth of his research and the comprehensiveness of his data, but few endorsed the propriety of his interpretations. He was widely advised to be more dispassionate in carrying forward his project.

5

I was sixty when I married again. This time, it was a singular marriage, to Sharane Fereday. We set up home in Avignon, and lived together for nearly twenty years. I won't say that we were exceptionally happy, but I came to depend on her closeness and her affection, and the day she told me that she had had enough was the darkest of my life so far—far darker in its desolation than the day Emily Marchant and I had been trapped in the wreck of the *Genesis*, although it didn't mark me as deeply.

"Twenty years is a long time, Mortimer," she told me. "It's time to move on—time for you as well as for me."

She was being sternly reasonable at that stage; I knew from experience that the sternness would crumble if I put it to the test, and I thought that her resolve would crumble with it, as it had before in similar circumstances, but it didn't.

"I'm truly sorry," she said, when she was eventually reduced to tears, "but I have to do it. I have to go. It's *my* life, and your part of it is over. I hate hurting you, but I don't want to live with you anymore. It's my fault, not yours, but that's the way it is."

It wasn't anybody's fault. I can see that clearly now, although it wasn't so easy to see it at the time. Like the Great Coral Sea Catastrophe or Grizel's drowning, it was just something that *happened*. Things do happen, regardless of people's best-laid plans, most heartfelt wishes, and intensest hopes.

Now that memory has blotted out the greater part of that phase of my life—including, I presume, the worst of it—I don't really know why I was so devastated by Sharane's decision, nor why it should have filled me with such black despair. Had I cultivated a dependence so absolute that it seemed irreplaceable, or was it only my pride that had suffered a sickening blow? Was it the imagined consequences of the rejection or merely the fact of rejection itself that sickened me so? Even now, I can't tell for certain. Even then, my neo-Epicurean conscience must have told me over and over again to pull myself together, to conduct myself with more decorum.

I tried. I'm certain that I tried.

Sharane's love for the ancient past was even more intense than mine, but her writings were far less dispassionate. She was an historian of sorts, but she wasn't an *academic* historian; her writings tended to the lyrical rather than the factual even when she was supposedly writing nonfiction.

Sharane would never have written a mute book, or one whose pictures didn't move. Had it been allowed by law at that time, she'd have fed her readers designer psychotropics to heighten their responses according to the schemes of her texts. She was a VR scriptwriter rather than a textwriter like me. She wasn't content to know about the past; she wanted to re-create it and make it solid and *live* in it. Nor did she reserve such inclinations to the privacy of her E-suit. She was flamboyantly old-fashioned in all that she did. She liked to dress in gaudy pastiches of the costumes represented in Greek or Egyptian art, and she liked decor to match. People who knew us were mildly astonished that we should want to live together, given the difference in our personalities, but I suppose it was an attraction of opposites. Perhaps my intensity of purpose and solitude had begun to weigh rather heavily upon me when we met, and my carefully cultivated calm of mind threatened to become a kind of toiling inertia.

On the other hand, perhaps that's all confabulation and rationalization. I was a different person then, and I've since lost touch with that person as completely as I've lost touch with everyone else I once knew.

But I *do* remember, vaguely. . . .

I remember that I found in Sharane a certain precious *wildness* that, although it wasn't entirely spontaneous, was unfailingly amusing. She had the happy gift of never taking herself too seriously, although she was wholehearted enough in her determined attempts to put herself imaginatively in touch with the past.

From her point of view, I suppose I was doubly valuable. On the one hand, I was a fount of information and inspiration; on the other a kind of anchorage whose solidity kept her from losing herself in her flights of the imagination. Twenty years of marriage ought to have cemented her dependence on me just as it had cemented my dependence on her, but it didn't.

"You think I need you to keep my feet on the ground," Sharane said as the break between us was completely and carefully rendered irreparable, "but I don't. Anyhow, I've been weighted down long enough. I need to soar for a while, to spread my wings."

Sharane and I had talked for a while, as married people do, about the possibility of having a child. We had both made deposits to the French national gamete bank, so that if we felt the same way when the time finally came to exercise our right of replacement—or to specify in our wills how that right was to be posthumously exercised—we could order an ovum to be unfrozen and fertilized.

I had always known, of course, that such flights of fancy were not to be taken too seriously, but when I accepted that the marriage was indeed over, there seemed to be an extra dimension of tragedy and misery in the knowledge that our genes never would be combined—that our separation cast our legacies once again upon the chaotic sea of irresolution.

Despite the extremity of my melancholy, I never contemplated suicide. Although I'd already used up the traditional threescore years and ten, I was in no doubt at all that it wasn't yet time to remove myself from the crucible of human evolution to make room for my successor, whether that successor was to be born from an ovum of Sharane's or not. No matter how black my mood was when Sharane left, I knew that my *History of Death* remained to be completed, and that the work would require at least another century. Even so, the breaking of such an intimate bond filled me with intimations of mortality and a painful sense of the futility of all my endeavors.

My first divorce had come about because a cruel accident had ripped apart the delicate fabric of my life, but my second—or so it seemed to me—was itself a horrid rent shearing my very being into ragged fragments. I hope that I tried with all my might not to blame Sharane, but how could I avoid it? And how could she not resent my overt and covert accusations, my veiled and naked resentments?

"Your problem, Mortimer," she said to me, when her lachrymose phase had given way to bright anger, "is that you're *obsessed*. You're a deeply morbid man, and it's not healthy. There's some special fear in you, some altogether exceptional horror which feeds upon you day and night, and makes you grotesquely vulnerable to occurrences that normal people can take in their stride, and that ill befit a self-styled Epicurean. If you want my advice, you ought to abandon that history you're writing, at least for a while, and devote yourself to something brighter and more vigorous."

"Death is my life," I informed her, speaking metaphorically, and not entirely without irony. "It always will be, until and including the end."

I remember saying that. The rest is vague, but I really do remember saying that.

6

The third volume of Mortimer Gray's *History of Death*, entitled *The Empires of Faith*, was published on 18 August 2954. The introduction announced that the author had been forced to set aside his initial ambition to write a truly comprehensive history, and stated that he would henceforth be unashamedly eclectic, and contentedly ethnocentric, because he did not wish to be a mere archivist of death, and therefore could not regard all episodes in humankind's war against death as being of equal interest. He declared that he was more interested in interpretation than mere summary, and that insofar as the war against death had been a moral crusade, he felt fully entitled to draw morals from it.

This preface, understandably, dismayed those critics who had urged the author to be more dispassionate. Some reviewers were content to condemn the new volume without even bothering to inspect the rest of it, although it was considerably shorter than the second volume and had a rather more fluent style. Others complained that the day of mute text was dead and gone, and that there was no place in the modern world for pictures that resolutely refused to move.

Unlike many contemporary historians, whose birth into a world in which religious faith was almost extinct had robbed them of any sympathy for the imperialists of dogma, Gray proposed that the great religions had been one of the finest achievements of humankind. He regarded them as a vital stage in the evolution of community—as social technologies which had permitted a spectacular transcendence of the limitation of community to the tribe or region. Faiths, he suggested, were the first instruments that could bind together different language groups, and even different races. It was not until the spread of the great religions, Gray argued, that the possibility came into being of gathering all men together into a single common enterprise. He regretted, of course, that the principal product of this great dream was two millennia of bitter and savage conflict between adherents of different faiths or adherents of different versions of the same faith, but thought the ambition worthy of all possible respect and admiration. He even retained some sympathy for jihads and crusades, in the formulation of which people had tried to attribute more meaning to the sacrifice of life than they ever had before.

Gray was particularly fascinated by the symbology of the Christian mythos, which had taken as its central image the death on the cross of Jesus, and had tried to make that one image of death carry an enormous allegorical load. He was entranced by the idea of Christ's death as a force of redemption and salvation, by the notion that this person died *for others*. He extended the argument to take in the Christian martyrs, who added to the primal crucifixion a vast series of symbolic and morally significant deaths. This, he considered, was a colossal achievement of the imagination, a crucial victory by which death was dramatically transfigured in the theater of the human imagination—as was the Christian idea of death as a kind of reconciliation: a gateway to Heaven, if properly met, a gateway to Hell, if not. Gray seized upon the idea of absolution from sin following confession, and particularly the notion of deathbed repentance, as a daring raid into the territories of the imagination previously ruled by fear of death.

Gray's commentaries on the other major religions were less elaborate but no less interested. Various ideas of reincarnation and the related concept of *karma* he discussed at great length, as one of the most ingenious imaginative bids for freedom from the tyranny of death. He was not quite so enthusiastic about the idea of the world as illusion, the idea of nirvana, and certain other aspects of Far Eastern thought, although he was impressed in several ways by Confucius and the Buddha. All these things and more he assimilated to the main line of his argument, which was that the great religions had made bold imaginative leaps in order to carry forward the war against death on a broader front than ever before, providing vast numbers of individuals with an efficient intellectual weaponry of moral purpose.

7

After Sharane left, I stayed on in Avignon for a while. The house where we had lived was demolished, and I had another raised in its place. I resolved to take up the reclusive life again, at least for a while. I had come to think of myself as one of nature's monks, and when I was tempted to flights of fancy of a more personal kind than those retailed in virtual reality, I could imagine myself an avatar of some patient scholar born fifteen hundred years before, contentedly submissive to the Benedictine rule. I didn't, of course, believe in the possibility of reincarnation, and when such beliefs became fashionable again I found it almost impossible to indulge any more fantasies of that kind.

In 2960, I moved to Antarctica, not to Amundsen City—which had become the world's political center since the United Nations had elected to set up headquarters in "the continent without nations"—but to Cape Adare on the Ross Sea, which was a relatively lonely spot.

I moved into a tall house rather resembling a lighthouse, from whose upper stories I could look out at the edge of the ice cap and watch the penguins at play. I was reasonably contented, and soon came to feel that I had put the torments and turbulences of my early life behind me.

I often went walking across the nearer reaches of the icebound sea, but I rarely got into difficulties. Ironically enough, my only serious injury of that period was a broken leg, which I sustained while working with a rescue party attempting to locate and save one of my neighbors, Ziru Majumdar, who had fallen into a crevasse while out on a similar expedition. We ended up in adjacent beds at the hospital in Amundsen City.

"I'm truly sorry about your leg, Mr. Gray," Majumdar said. "It was very stupid of me to get lost. After all, I've lived here for thirty years; I thought I knew every last ice ridge like the back of my hand. It's not as if the weather was particularly bad, and I've never suffered from summer rhapsody or snow blindness."

I'd suffered from both—I was still awkwardly vulnerable to psychosomatic ills—but they only served to make me more careful. An uneasy mind can sometimes be an advantage.

"It wasn't your fault, Mr. Majumdar," I graciously insisted. "I suppose I must have been a little overconfident myself, or I'd never have slipped and fallen. At least they were able to pull me out in a matter of minutes; you must have lain unconscious at the bottom of that crevasse for nearly two days."

"Just about. I came round several times—at least, I think I did—but my internal tech was pumping so much dope around my system it's difficult to be sure. My surskin and thermosuit were doing their best to keep me warm, but the first law of thermodynamics doesn't give you much slack when you're at the bottom of a cleft in the permafrost. I've got authentic frostbite in my toes, you know—imagine that!"

I dutifully tried to imagine it, but it wasn't easy. He could hardly be in pain, so it was difficult to conjure up any notion of what it might feel like to have necrotized toes. The doctors reckoned that it would take a week for the nanomachines to restore the tissues to their former pristine condition.

"Mind you," he added, with a small embarrassed laugh, "it's only a matter of time before the whole biosphere gets frostbite, isn't it? Unless the sun gets stirred up again."

More than fifty years had passed since scrupulous students of the sunspot cycle had announced the advent of a new Ice Age, but the world was quite unworried by the exceedingly slow advance of the glaciers across the Northern Hemisphere. It was the sort of thing that only cropped up in light banter.

"I won't mind that," I said, contemplatively. "Nor will you, I daresay. We like ice—why else would we live here?"

"Right. Not that I agree with those Gaean Liberationists, mind. I hear they're proclaiming that the interglacial periods are simply Gaea's fevers, that the birth of civilization was just a morbid symptom of the planet's sickness, and that human culture has so far been a mere delirium of the noösphere."

He obviously paid more attention to the lunatic-fringe channels than I did.

"It's just colorful rhetoric," I told him. "They don't mean it literally."

"Think not? Well, perhaps. I was delirious myself for a while when I was down that hole. Can't be sure whether I was asleep or awake, but I was certainly lost in some vivid dreams—and I mean *vivid*. I don't know about you, but I always find VR a bit flat, even if I use illicit psychotropics to give delusion a helping hand. I think it's to do with the protective effects of our internal technology. Nanomachines mostly do their job a little *too* well, because of the built-in safety margins—it's only when they reach the limits of their capacity that they let really interesting things begin to happen."

I knew he was building up to some kind of self-justification, but I felt that be was entitled to it. I nodded, to give him permission to prattle on.

"You have to go to the very brink of extinction to reach the cutting edge of experience, you see. I found that out while I was trapped down there in the ice, not knowing whether the rescuers would get to me in time. You can learn a lot about life, and about yourself, in a situation like that. It really was vivid—more vivid than anything I ever . . . well, what I'm trying to get at is that we're too *safe* nowadays; we can have no idea of the *zest* there was in living in the bad old days. Not that I'm about to take up jumping into crevasses as a hobby, you understand. Once in a very long while is plenty."

"Yes, it is," I agreed, shifting my itching leg and wishing that nanomachines weren't so slow to compensate for trifling but annoying sensations. "Once in a while is certainly enough for me. In fact, I for one will be quite content if it never happens again. I don't think I need any more of the kind of enlightenment which comes from experiences like that. I was in the Great Coral Sea Catastrophe, you know—shipwrecked, scalded, and lost at sea for days on end."

"It's not the same," he insisted, "but you won't be able to understand the difference until it happens to you."

I didn't believe him. In that instance, I suppose, he was right and I was wrong.

I'd never heard Mr. Majumdar speak so freely before, and I never heard him do it again. The social life of the Cape Adare "exiles" was unusually formal, hemmed in by numerous barriers of formality and etiquette. After an embarrassing phase of learning and adjustment, I'd found the formality aesthetically appealing, and had played the game with enthusiasm, but it was beginning to lose its appeal by the time the accident shook me up. I suppose it's understandable that whatever you set out to exclude from the pattern of your life eventually comes to seem like a lack, and then an unfulfilled need.

After a few years more, I began to hunger once again for the spontaneity and abandonment of warmer climes. I decided there'd be time enough to celebrate the advent of the Ice Age when the glaciers had reached the full extent of their reclaimed empire, and that I might as well make what use I could of Gaea's temporary fever before it cooled. I moved to Venezuela, to dwell in the gloriously restored jungles of the Orinoco amid their teeming wildlife.

Following the destruction of much of the southern part of the continent in the second nuclear war, Venezuela had attained a cultural hegemony in South America that it had never surrendered. Brazil and Argentina had long since recovered, both economically and ecologically, from their disastrous fit of ill temper, but Venezuela was still the home of the *avant garde* of the Americas. It was there, for the first time, that I came into close contact with Thanaticism.

The original Thanatic cults had flourished in the twenty-eighth century. They had appeared among the last generations of children born without Zaman transformations; their members were people who, denied emortality through blastular engineering, had perversely elected to reject the benefits of rejuvenation too, making a fetish out of living only a "natural" lifespan. At the time, it had seemed likely that they would be the last of the many Millenarian cults which had long afflicted Western culture, and they had quite literally died out some eighty or ninety years before I was born.

Nobody had then thought it possible, let alone likely, that genetically endowed emortals would ever embrace Thanaticism, but they were wrong.

There had always been suicides in the emortal population—indeed, suicide was the commonest cause of death among emortals, outnumbering accidental deaths by a factor of three—but such acts were usually covert and normally involved people who had lived at least a hundred years. The neo-Thanatics were not only indiscreet—their whole purpose seemed to be to make a public spectacle of themselves—but also young; people over seventy were held to have violated the Thanaticist ethic simply by surviving to that age.

Thanatics tended to choose violent means of death, and usually issued invitations as well as choosing their moments so that large crowds could gather. Jumping from tall buildings and burning to death were the most favored means in the beginning, but these quickly ceased to be interesting. As the Thanatic revival progressed, adherents of the movement sought increasingly bizarre methods in the interests of capturing attention and out-doing their predecessors. For these reasons, it was impossible for anyone living alongside the cults to avoid becoming implicated in their rites, if only as a spectator.

By the time I had been in Venezuela for a year, I had seen five people die horribly. After the first, I had resolved to turn away from any others, so as not to lend even minimal support to the practice, but I soon found that I had underestimated the difficulty of so doing. There was no excuse to be found in my vocation; thousands of people who were not historians of death found it equally impossible to resist the fascination.

I believed at first that the fad would soon pass, after wasting the lives of a handful of neurotics, but the cults continued to grow. Gaea's fever might be cooling, its crisis having passed; but the delirium of human culture had evidently not yet reached what Ziru Majumdar called "the cutting edge of experience."

8

The fourth volume of Mortimer Gray's *History of Death*, entitled *Fear and Fascination*, was published on 12 February 2977. In spite of being mute and motionless, it was immediately subject to heavy access-demand, presumably in consequence of the world's increasing fascination with the "problem" of neo-Thanaticism. Requisitions of the earlier volumes of Gray's history had picked up worldwide during the early 2970s, but the author had not appreciated what this might mean in terms of the demand for the new volume, and might have set a higher access fee had he realized.

Academic historians were universal in their condemnation of the new volume, possibly because of the enthusiasm with which it was greeted by laymen, but popular reviewers adored it. Its arguments were recklessly plundered by journalists and other broadcasting pundits in search of possible parallels that might be draws with the modern world, especially those that seemed to carry moral lessons for the Thanatics and their opponents.

Fear and Fascination extended, elaborated, and diversified the arguments contained in its immediate predecessor, particularly in respect of the Christian world of the Medieval period and the Renaissance. It had much to say about art and literature, and the images contained therein. It had chapters on the personification of death as the Grim Reaper, on the iconography of the *danse macabre*, on the topics of *memento mori* and *artes moriendi*. It had long analyses of Dante's *Divine Comedy*, the paintings of Hieronymus Bosch, Milton's *Paradise Lost*, and graveyard poetry. These were by no means exercises in conventional literary criticism; they were elements of a long and convoluted argument about the contributions made by the individual creative imagination to the war of ideas which raged on the only battleground on which man could as yet constructively oppose the specter of death.

Gray also dealt with the persecution of heretics and the subsequent elaboration of Christian Demonology, which led to the witch-craze of the fifteenth, sixteenth and seventeenth centuries. He gave considerable attention to various thriving folklore traditions which confused the notion of death, especially to the popularity of fictions and fears regarding premature burial, ghosts, and the various species of the "undead" who rose from their graves as ghouls or vampires. In Gray's eyes, all these phenomena were symptomatic of a crisis in Western man's imaginative dealings with the idea of death: a feverish heating up of a conflict which had been in danger of becoming desultory. The cities of men had been under perpetual siege from death since the time of their first building, but now—in one part of the world, at least— the perception of that siege had sharpened. A kind of spiritual starvation and panic had set in, and the progress that had been made in the war by virtue of the ideological imperialism of Christ's Holy Cross now seemed imperiled by disintegration. This Empire of Faith was breaking up under the stress of skepticism, and men were faced with the prospect of going into battle against their most ancient enemy with their armor in tatters.

Just as the Protestants were trying to replace the Catholic Church's centralized authority with a more personal relationship between men and God, Gray argued, so the creative artists of this era were trying to achieve a more personal and more intimate form of reconciliation between men and death, equipping individuals with the power to mount their own ideative assaults. He drew some parallels between what happened in the Christian world and similar periods of crisis which he found in different cultures at different times, but other historians claimed that his analogies were weak, and that he was overgeneralizing. Some argued that his intense study of the phenomena associated with the idea of death had become too personal, and suggested that he had become infatuated with the ephemeral ideas of past ages to the point where they were taking over his own imagination.

9

At first, I found celebrity status pleasing, and the extra credit generated by my access fees was certainly welcome, even to a man of moderate tastes and habits. The unaccustomed touch of fame brought a fresh breeze into a life that might have been in danger of becoming bogged down.

To begin with, I was gratified to be reckoned an expert whose views on Thanaticism were to be taken seriously, even by some Thanatics. I received a veritable deluge of invitations to appear on the talk shows that were the staple diet of contemporary broadcasting, and for a while I accepted as many as I could conveniently accommodate within the pattern of my life.

I have no need to rely on my memories in recapitulating these episodes, because they remain on record—but by the same token, I needn't quote extensively from them. In the early days, when I was a relatively new face, my interrogators mostly started out by asking for information about my book, and their opening questions were usually stolen from uncharitable reviews.

"Some people feel that you've been carried away, Mr. Gray," more than one combative interviewer sneeringly began, "and that what started out as a sober history is fast becoming an obsessive rant. Did you decide to get personal in order to boost your sales?"

My careful cultivation of neo-Epicureanism and my years in Antarctica had left a useful legacy of calm formality; I always handled such accusations with punctilious politeness.

"Of course the war against death is a personal matter," I would reply. "It's a personal matter for everyone, mortal or emortal. Without that sense of personal relevance, it would be impossible to put oneself imaginatively in the place of the people of the ancient past so as to obtain empathetic insight into their affairs. If I seem to be making heroes of the men of the past by describing their crusades, it's because they *were* heroes, and if my contemporaries find inspiration in my work, it's because they too are heroes in the same cause. The engineering of emortality has made us victors in the war, but we desperately need to retain a proper sense of triumph. We ought to celebrate our victory over death as joyously as possible, lest we lose our appreciation of its fruits."

My interviewers always appreciated that kind of link, which handed them their next question on a plate. "Is that what you think of the Thanatics?" they would follow up, eagerly.

It was, and I would say so at any length they considered appropriate.

Eventually, my interlocutors no longer talked about my book, taking it for granted that everyone knew who I was and what I'd done. They'd cut straight to the chase, asking me what I thought of the latest Thanaticist publicity stunt.

Personally, I thought the media's interest in Thanaticism was exaggerated. All death was, of course, news in a world populated almost entirely by emortals, and the Thanatics took care to be newsworthy by making such a song and dance about what they were doing, but the number of individuals involved was very small. In a world population of nearly three billion, a hundred deaths per week was a drop in the ocean, and "quiet" suicides still outnumbered the ostentatious Thanatics by a factor of five or six throughout the 2980s. The public debates quickly expanded to take in other issues. Subscription figures for net access to videotapes and teletexts concerned with the topic of violent death came under scrutiny, and everyone began talking about the "new pornography of death"—although fascination with such material had undoubtedly been widespread for many years.

"Don't you feel, Mr. Gray," I was often asked, "that a continued fascination with death in a world where everyone has a potential lifespan of several centuries is rather *sick*? Shouldn't we have put such matters behind us?"

"Not at all," I replied, earnestly and frequently. "In the days when death was inescapable, people were deeply frustrated by this imperious imposition of fate. They resented it with all the force and bitterness they could muster, but it could not be truly fascinating while it remained a simple and universal fact of life. Now that death is no longer a necessity, it has perforce become a luxury. Because it is no longer inevitable, we no longer feel such pressure to hate and fear it, and this frees us so that we may take an essentially *aesthetic* view of death. The transformation of the imagery of death into a species of pornography is both understandable and healthy."

"But such material surely encourages the spread of Thanaticism. You can't possibly approve of that?"

Actually, the more I was asked it the less censorious I became, at least for a while.

"Planning a life," I explained to a whole series of faces, indistinguishable by virtue of having been sculptured according to the latest theory of telegenicity, "is an exercise in story-making. Living people are forever writing the narratives of their own lives, deciding who to be and what to do, according to various aesthetic criteria. In olden days, death was inevitably seen as an *interruption* of the business of life, cutting short life-stories before they were— in the eyes of their creators—complete. Nowadays, people have the opportunity to plan *whole* lives, deciding exactly when and how their life-stories should reach a climax and a conclusion. We may not share their aesthetic sensibilities, and may well think them fools, but there is a discernible logic in their actions. They are neither mad nor evil."

Perhaps I was reckless in adopting this point of view, or at least in proclaiming it to the whole world. By proposing that the new Thanatics were simply individuals who had a particular kind of aesthetic sensibility, tending toward conciseness and melodrama rather than prolixity and anticlimax, I became something of a hero to the cultists themselves—which was not my intention. The more lavishly I embroidered my chosen analogy—declaring that ordinary emortals were the *feuilletonistes*, epic poets, and three-decker novelists of modern life while Thanatics were the prose-poets and short-story writers who liked to sign off with a neat punch line—the more they liked me. I received many invitations to attend suicides, and my refusal to take them up only served to make my presence a prize to be sought after.

I was, of course, entirely in agreement with the United Nations Charter of Human Rights, whose Ninety-ninth Amendment guaranteed the citizens of every nation the right to take their own lives, and to be assisted in making a dignified exit should they so desire, but I had strong reservations about the way in which the Thanaticists construed the amendment. Its original intention had been to facilitate self-administered euthanasia in an age when that was sometimes necessary, not to guarantee Thanatics the entitlement to recruit whatever help they required in staging whatever kinds of exit they desired. Some of the invitations I received were exhortations to participate in legalized murders, and these became more common as time went by and the cults became more extreme in their bizarrerie.

In the 2980s, the Thanatics had progressed from conventional suicides to public executions, by rope, sword, ax, or guillotine. At first, the executioners were volunteers—and one or two were actually arrested and charged with murder, although none could be convicted—but the Thanatics were not satisfied even with this, and began campaigning for various nations to re-create the official position of Public Executioner, together with bureaucratic structures that would give all citizens the right to call upon the services of such officials. Even I, who claimed to understand the cults better than their members, was astonished when the government of Colombia—which was jealous of Venezuela's reputation as the home of the world's *avant garde*—actually accepted such an obligation, with the result that Thanatics began to flock to Maracaibo and Cartagena in order to obtain an appropriate send-off. I was profoundly relieved when the UN, following the crucifixion of Shamiel Sihra in 2991, revised the wording of the amendment and outlawed suicide by public execution.

By this time, I was automatically refusing invitations to appear on 3-V, in much the same way that I was refusing invitations to take part in Thanaticist ceremonies. It was time to become a recluse once again.

I left Venezuela in 2989 to take up residence on Cape Wolstenholme, at the neck of Hudson's Bay. Canada was an urbane, highly civilized, and rather staid confederacy of states whose people had no time for such follies as Thanaticism; it provided an ideal retreat, where I could throw myself wholeheartedly into my work again.

I handed over full responsibility for answering all my calls to a state-of-the-art Personal Simulation program, which grew so clever and so ambitious with practice that it began to give live interviews on broadcast television. Although it offered what was effectively no comment in a carefully elaborate fashion, I eventually thought it best to introduce a block into its operating system—a block that enśured that my face dropped out of public sight for half a century.

Having once experienced the rewards and pressures of fame, I never felt the need to seek them again. I can't and won't say that I learned as much from that phase in my life as I learned from any of my close encounters with death, but I still remember it—vaguely—with a certain nostalgia. Unmelodramatic it might have been, but it doubtless played its part in shaping the person that I now am. It certainly made me more self-assured in public.

10

The fifth volume of Mortimer Gray's *History of Death*, entitled *The War of Attrition*, was published on 19 March 2999. It marked a return to the cooler and more comprehensive style of scholarship exhibited by the first two volumes. It dealt with the history of medical science and hygiene up to the end of the nineteenth century, thus concerning itself with a new and very different arena of the war between mankind and mortality.

To many of its readers, *The War of Attrition* was undoubtedly a disappointment, though it did include some material about Victorian tomb-decoration and nineteenth-century spiritualism that carried forward arguments from Volume Four. Access was initially widespread, although demand tailed off fairly rapidly when it was realized how vast and how tightly packed with data the document was. This lack of popular enthusiasm was not counterbalanced by any redemption of Mortimer's academic reputation; like many earlier scholars who had made contact with a popular audience, Gray was considered guilty of a kind of intellectual treason, and was frozen out of the scholarly community in spite of what appeared to be a determined attempt at rehabilitation. Some popular reviewers argued, however, that there was much in the new volume to intrigue the inhabitants of a world whose medical science was so adept that almost everyone enjoyed perfect health as well as eternal youth, and in which almost any injury could be repaired completely. It was suggested that there was a certain piquant delight to be obtained from recalling a world where everyone was (by modern standards) crippled or deformed, and in which everyone suffered continually from illnesses of a most horrific nature.

Although it had a wealth of scrupulously dry passages, there were parts of *The War of Attrition* that were deemed pornographic by some commentators. Its accounts of the early history of surgery and midwifery were condemned as unjustifiably bloodcurdling, and its painstaking analysis of the spread of syphilis through Europe in the sixteenth century was censured as a mere horror story made all the nastier by its clinical narration. Gray was particularly interested in syphilis, because of the dramatic social effects of its sudden advent in Europe and its significance in the development of prophylactic medicine. He argued that syphilis was primarily responsible for the rise and spread of Puritanism, repressive sexual morality being the only truly effective weapon against its spread. He then deployed well-tried sociological arguments to the effect that Puritanism and its associated habits of thought had been importantly implicated in the rapid development of Capitalism in the Western World, in order that he might claim that syphilis ought to be regarded as the root cause of the economic and political systems that came to dominate the most chaotic, the most extravagantly progressive, and the most extravagantly destructive centuries of human history.

The history of medicine and the conquest of disease were, of course, topics of elementary education in the thirtieth century. There was supposedly not a citizen of any nation to whom the names of Semmelweis, Jenner, and Pasteur were unknown—but disease had been so long banished from the world, and it was so completely outside the experience of ordinary men and women, that what they "knew" about it was never really brought to consciousness, and never came alive to the imagination. Words like "smallpox," "plague," and "cancer" were used metaphorically in common parlance, and over the centuries had become virtually empty of any real significance. Gray's fifth volume, therefore—despite the fact that it contained little that was really new—did serve as a stimulus to collective memory. It reminded the world of some issues which, though not exactly forgotten, had not really been *brought to mind* for some time. It is at least arguable that it touched off ripples whose movement across the collective consciousness of world culture was of some moment. Mortimer Gray was no longer famous, but his continuing work had become firmly established within the *zeitgeist*.

II

Neo-Thanaticism began to peter out as the turn of the century approached. By 3010, the whole movement had "gone underground"—which is to say that Thanatics no longer staged their exits before the largest audiences they could attain, but saved their performance for small, carefully selected groups. This wasn't so much a response to persecution as a variation in the strange game that they were playing out; it was simply a different kind of drama. Unfortunately, there was no let-up in the communications with which Thanatics continued to batter my patient AI interceptors.

Although it disappointed the rest of the world, *The War of Attrition* was welcomed enthusiastically by some of the Thanatic cults, whose members cultivated an altogether unhealthy interest in disease as a means of decease, replacing the violent executions that had become too familiar. As time went by and Thanaticism declined generally, this particular subspecies underwent a kind of mutation, as the cultists began to promote diseases not as means of death but as valuable *experiences* from which much might be learned. A black market in carcinogens and bioengineered pathogens quickly sprang up. The original agents of smallpox, cholera, bubonic plague, and syphilis were long since extinct, but the world abounded in clever genetic engineers who could synthesize a virus with very little effort. Suddenly, they began to find clients for a whole range of horrid diseases. Those which afflicted the mind as well as or instead of the body were particularly prized; there was a boom in recreational schizophrenia that almost broke through to the mainstream of accredited psychotropics.

I couldn't help but remember, with a new sense of irony, Ziru Majumdar's enthusiasm for the vivid delusions which had visited him while his internal technology was tested to the limit in staving off hypothermia and frostbite.

When the new trend spread beyond the ranks of the Thanaticists, and large numbers of people began to regard disease as something that could be temporarily and interestingly indulged in without any real danger to life or subsequent health, I began to find my arguments about death quoted—without acknowledgment—with reference to *disease*. A popular way of talking about the phenomenon was to claim that what had ceased to be a dire necessity "naturally" became available as a perverse luxury.

None of this would have mattered much had it not been for the difficulty of restricting the spread of recreational diseases to people who *wanted* to indulge, but those caught up in the fad refused to restrict themselves to noninfectious varieties. There had been no serious threat of epidemic since the Plague Wars of the twenty-first century, but now it seemed that medical science might once again have to be mobilized on a vast scale. Because of the threat to innocent parties who might be accidently infected, the self-infliction of dangerous diseases was quickly outlawed in many nations, but some governments were slow to act.

I would have remained aloof and apart from all of this had I been able to, but it turned out that my defenses weren't impregnable. In 3029, a Thanaticist of exceptional determination named Hadria Nuccoli decided that if I wouldn't come to her, she would come to *me*. Somehow, she succeeded in getting past all my carefully sealed doors, to arrive in my bedroom at three o'clock one winter morning.

I woke up in confusion, but the confusion was quickly transformed into sheer terror. This was an enemy more frightening than the scalding Coral Sea, because this was an *active* enemy who meant to do me harm—and the intensity of the threat which she posed was in no way lessened by the fact that she claimed to be doing it out of love rather than hatred.

The woman's skin bore an almost mercuric luster, and she was in the grip of a terrible fever, but she would not be still. She seemed, in fact, to have an irresistible desire to move and to communicate, and the derangement of her body and brain had not impaired her crazed eloquence.

"Come with me!" she begged, as I tried to evade her eager clutch. "Come with me to the far side of death and I'll show you what's there. There's no need to be afraid! Death isn't the end, it's the beginning. It's the metamorphosis that frees us from our caterpillar flesh to be spirits in a massless world of light and color. I am your redeemer, for whom you have waited far too long. Love me, dear Mortimer Gray, only *love* me, and you will learn. Let me be your mirror; drown yourself in me!"

For ten minutes, I succeeded in keeping away from her, stumbling this way and that, thinking that I might be safe if only I didn't touch her. I managed to send out a call for help, but I knew it would take an hour or more for anyone to come.

I tried all the while to talk her down, but it was impossible.

"There's no return from eternity," she told me. "This is no ordinary virus created by accident to fight a hopeless cause against the defenses of the body. Nanotechnology is as impotent to deal with this transformer of the flesh as the immune system was to deal with its own destroyers. The true task of medical engineers, did they but know it, was never to fight disease, but always to *perfect* it, and we have found the way. I bring you the greatest of all gifts, my darling: the elixir of life, which will make us angels instead of men, creatures of light and ecstasy!"

It was no use running; I tired before she did, and she caught me. I tried to knock her down, and if I had had a weapon to hand, I would certainly have used it in self-defense, but she couldn't feel pain, and no matter how badly disabled her internal technology was, I wasn't able to injure her with my blows.

In the end, I had no sensible alternative but to let her take me in her arms and cling to me; nothing else would soothe her.

I was afraid for her as well as myself; I didn't believe that she truly intended to die, and I wanted to keep us safe until help arrived.

My panic didn't decrease while I held her; if anything, I felt it all the more intensely. I became outwardly calmer once I had let her touch me, and made every effort to remind myself that it didn't really matter whether she infected me or not, given that medical help would soon arrive. I didn't expect to have to go through the kind of hell that I actually endured before the doctors got the bug under control; for once, panic was wiser than common sense.

Even so, I wept for her when they told me that she'd died, and wished with all my heart that she hadn't.

Unlike my previous brushes with death, I don't think my encounter with Hadria Nuccoli was an important learning experience. It was just a disturbance of the now-settled pattern of my life—something to be survived, put away, and forgotten. I haven't forgotten it, but I did put it away in the back of my mind. I didn't let it affect me.

In some of my writings, I'd lauded the idea of martyrdom as an important invention in the imaginative war against death, and I'd been mightily intrigued by the lives and deaths of the saints recorded in the *Golden Legend*. Now that I'd been appointed a saint myself by some very strange people, though, I began to worry about the exemplary functions of such legends. The last thing I'd expected when I set out to write a *History of Death* was that my explanatory study might actually *assist* the dread empire of death to regain a little of the ground that it had lost in the world of human affairs. I began to wonder whether I ought to abandon my project, but I decided otherwise. The Thanatics and their successors were, after all willfully misunderstanding and perverting my message; I owed it to them and to everyone else to make myself clearer.

As it happened, the number of deaths recorded in association with Thanaticism and recreational disease began to decline after 3030. In a world context, the numbers were never more than tiny, but they were still worrying, and hundreds of thousands of people had, like me, to be rescued by doctors from the consequences of their own or other people's folly.

As far back as 2982, I had appeared on TV—via a satellite link—with a faber named Khan Mirafzal, who had argued that Thanaticism was evidence of the fact that Earthbound man was becoming decadent, and that the future of man lay outside the Earth, in the microworlds and the distant colonies. Mirafzal had claimed that men genetically reshaped for life in low gravity— like the four-handed fabers—or for the colonization of alien worlds, would find Thanaticism unthinkable. At the time, I'd been content to assume that his arguments were spurious. People who lived in space were always going on about the decadence of the Earthbound, much as the Gaean Liberationists did. Fifty years later, I wasn't so sure. I actually called Mirafzal so that we could discuss the matter again, in private. The conversation took a long time because of the signal delay, but that seemed to make its thrust all the more compelling.

I decided to leave Earth, at least for a while, to investigate the farther horizons of the human enterprise.

In 3033, I flew to the Moon, and took up residence in Mare Moscoviense—which is, of course, on the side which faces away from the Earth.

12

The sixth volume of Mortimer Gray's *History of Death*, entitled *Fields of Battle*, was published on 24 July 3044. Its subject-matter was war, but Gray was not greatly interested in the actual fighting of the wars of the nineteenth and succeeding centuries. His main concern was with the *mythology* of warfare as it developed in the period under consideration, and, in particular, with the way that the development of the mass media of communication transformed the business and the perceived meanings of warfare. He began his study with the Crimean War, because it was the first war to be extensively covered by newspaper reporters, and the first whose conduct was drastically affected thereby.

Before the Crimea, Gray argued, wars had been "private" events, entirely the affairs of the men who started them and the men who fought them. They might have a devastating effect on the local population of the areas where they were fought, but were largely irrelevant to distant civilian populations. The British *Times* had changed all that, by making the Crimean War the business of all its readers, exposing the government and military leaders to public scrutiny and to public scorn. Reports from the front had scandalized the nation by creating an awareness of how ridiculously inefficient the organization of the army was, and what a toll of human life was exacted upon the troops in consequence—not merely deaths in battle, but deaths from injury and disease caused by the appalling lack of care given to wounded soldiers. That reportage had not only had practical consequences, but *imaginative* consequences—it rewrote the entire mythology of heroism in an intricate webwork of new legends, ranging from the Charge of the Light Brigade to the secular canonization of Florence Nightingale.

Throughout the next two centuries, Gray argued, war and publicity were entwined in a Gordian knot. Control of the news media became vital to propagandist control of popular *morale*, and governments engaged in war had to become architects of the mythology of war as well as planners of military strategy. Heroism and jingoism became the currency of consent; where governments failed to secure the public image of the wars they fought, they fell. Gray tracked the way in which attitudes to death in war and to the endangerment of civilian populations by war were dramatically transformed by the three World Wars and by the way those wars were subsequently mythologized in memory and fiction. He commented extensively on the way the First World War was "sold," to those who must fight it, as a war to *end* war—and on the consequent sense of betrayal that followed when it failed to live up to this billing. And yet, he argued, if the three global wars were seen as a whole, its example really *had* brought into being the attitude of mind which ultimately forbade wars.

As those who had become used to his methods now expected, Gray dissented from the view of other modern historians who saw the World Wars as an unmitigated disaster and a horrible example of the barbarity of ancient man. He agreed that the nationalism that had replaced the great religions as the main creator and definer of a sense of community was a poor and petty thing, and that the massive conflicts that it engendered were tragic—but it was, he asserted, a necessary stage in historical development. The empires of faith were, when all was said and done, utterly incompetent to their self-defined task, and were always bound to fail and to disintegrate. The groundwork for a *genuine* human community, in which all mankind could properly and meaningfully join, had to be relaid, and it had to be relaid in the common experience of all nations, as part of a universal heritage.

The *real* enemy of mankind was, as Gray had always insisted and now continued to insist, death itself. Only by facing up to death in a new way, by gradually transforming the role of death as part of the means to human ends, could a true human community be made. Wars, whatever their immediate purpose in settling economic squabbles and pandering to the megalomaniac psychoses of national leaders, also served a large-scale function in the shifting pattern of history: to provide a vast carnival of destruction which must either weary men of the lust to kill, or bring about their extinction.

Some reviewers condemned *Fields of Battle* on the grounds of its evident irrelevance to a world that had banished war, but others welcomed the fact that the volume returned Gray's thesis to the safe track of true history, in dealing exclusively with that which was safely dead and buried.

13

I found life on the Moon very different from anything I'd experienced in my travels around the Earth's surface. It wasn't so much the change in gravity, although that certainly took a lot of getting used to, nor the severe regime of daily exercise in the centrifuge which I had to adopt in order to make sure that I might one day return to the world of my birth without extravagant medical provision. Nor was it the fact that the environment was so comprehensively artificial, or that it was impossible to venture outside without special equipment; in those respects it was much like Antarctica. The most significant difference was in the people.

Mare Moscoviense had few tourists—tourists mostly stayed Earthside, making only brief trips farside—but most of its inhabitants were nevertheless just passing through. It was one of the main jumping-off points for emigrants, largely because it was an important industrial center, the home of one of the largest factories for the manufacture of shuttles and other local-space vehicles. It was one of the chief trading posts supplying materials to the microworlds in Earth orbit and beyond, and many of its visitors came in from the farther reaches of the solar system.

The majority of the city's long-term residents were unmodified, like me, or lightly modified by reversible cyborgization, but a great many of those visiting were fabers, genetically engineered for low-gee environments. The most obvious external feature of their modification was that they had an extra pair of "arms" instead of "legs," and this meant that most of the public places in Moscoviense were designed to accommodate their kind as well as "walkers"; all the corridors were railed and all the ceilings ringed.

The sight of fabers swinging around the place like gibbons, getting everywhere at five or six times the pace of walkers, was one that I found strangely fascinating, and one to which I never quite became accustomed. Fabers couldn't live, save with the utmost difficulty, in the gravity well that was Earth; they almost never descended to the planet's surface. By the same token, it was very difficult for men from Earth to work in zero-gee environments without extensive modification, surgical if not genetic. For this reason, the only "ordinary" men who went into the true faber environments weren't ordinary by any customary standard. The Moon, with its one-sixth Earth gravity, was the only place in the inner solar system where fabers and unmodified men frequently met and mingled—there was nowhere else nearer than Ganymede.

I had always known about fabers, of course, but, like so much other "common" knowledge, the information had lain unattended in some unheeded pigeonhole of memory until direct acquaintance ignited it and gave it life. It seemed to me that fabers lived their lives at a very rapid tempo, despite the fact that they were just as emortal as members of their parent species.

For one thing, faber parents normally had their children while they were still alive, and very often had several at intervals of only twenty or thirty years! An aggregate family usually had three or even four children growing up in parallel. In the infinite reaches of space, there was no population control, and no restrictive "right of replacement." A microworld's population could grow as fast as the microworld could put on extra mass. Then again, the fabers were always *doing* things. Even though they had four arms, they always seemed to have trouble finding a spare hand. They seemed to have no difficulty at all in doing two different things at the same time, often using only one limb for attachment—on the Moon this generally meant hanging from the ceiling like a bat—while one hand mediated between the separate tasks being carried out by the remaining two.

I quickly realized that it wasn't just the widely accepted notion that the future of mankind must take the form of a gradual diffusion through the galaxy that made the fabers think of Earth as decadent. From their viewpoint, Earth-life seemed unbearably slow and sedentary. Unmodified mankind, having long since attained control of the ecosphere of its native world, seemed to the fabers to be living a lotus-eater existence, indolently pottering about in its spacious garden.

The fabers weren't contemptuous of legs as such, but they drew a sharp distinction between those space-faring folk who were given legs by the genetic engineers in order to descend to the surfaces of new and alien worlds, with a job to do, and those Earthbound people who simply kept the legs their ancestors had bequeathed to them in order to enjoy the fruits of the labors of past generations.

Wherever I had lived on Earth, it had always seemed to me that one could blindly throw a stone into a crowded room and stand a fifty-fifty chance of hitting a historian of some sort. In Mare Moscoviense, the population of historians could be counted on the fingers of an unmodified man—and that in a city of a quarter of a million people. Whether they were resident or passing through, the people of the Moon were far more interested in the future than the past. When I told them about my vocation, my new neighbors were likely to smile politely and shake their heads.

"It's the weight of those *legs*," the fabers among them were wont to say. "You think they're holding you up, but in fact they're holding you down. Give them a chance and you'll find that you've put down roots."

If anyone told them that on Earth, "having roots" wasn't considered an altogether bad thing, they'd laugh.

"Get rid of your legs and learn to swing," they'd say. "You'll understand then that *human* beings have no need of roots. Only reach with four hands instead of two, and you'll find the stars within your grasp! Leave the past to rot at the bottom of the deep dark well, and give the Heavens their due."

I quickly learned to fall back on the same defensive moves most of my unmodified companions employed. "You can't break all your links with solid ground," we told the fabers, over and over again. "Somebody has to deal with the larger lumps of matter which are strewn about the universe, and you can't go to meet real mass if you don't have legs. It's planets that produce biospheres and biospheres that produce such luxuries as air. If you've seen farther than other men, it's not because you can swing by your arms from the ceiling— it's because you can stand on the shoulders of giants with legs."

Such exchanges were always cheerful. It was almost impossible to get into a real argument with a faber; their talk was as intoxicated as their movements. "Leave the wells to the unwell," they were fond of quoting. "The well will climb *out* of the wells, if they only find the will. History is bunk, only fit for sleeping minds."

* * *

A man less certain of his own destiny might have been turned aside from his task by faber banter, but I was well into my second century of life by then, and I had few doubts left regarding the propriety of my particular labor. Access to data was no more difficult on the Moon than anywhere else in the civilized Ekumen, and I proceeded, steadily and methodically, with my self-allotted task.

I made good progress there, as befitted the circumstances. Perhaps that was the happiest time of my life—but it's very difficult to draw comparisons when you're as far from childhood and youth as I now am.

Memory is an untrustworthy crutch for minds that have not yet mastered eternity.

14

The seventh volume of Mortimer Gray's *History of Death*, entitled *The Last Judgment*, was published on 21 June 3053. It dealt with the multiple crises that had developed in the late twentieth and twenty-first centuries, each of which and all of which had faced the human race with the prospect of extinction.

Gray described in minute detail the various nuclear exchanges which led up to Brazil's nuclear attack on Argentina in 2079 and the Plague Wars waged throughout that century. He discussed the various factors—the greenhouse crisis, soil erosion, pollution, and deforestation—that had come close to inflicting irreparable damage on the ecosphere. His map of the patterns of death in this period considered in detail the fate of the "lost billions" of peasant and subsistence farmers who were disinherited and displaced by the emergent ecological and economic order. Gray scrupulously pointed out that in less than two centuries more people had died than in the previous ten millennia. He made the ironic observation that the near-conquest of death achieved by twenty-first century medicine had created such an abundance of life as to precipitate a Malthusian crisis of awful proportions. He proposed that the new medicine and the new pestilences might be seen as different faces of the same coin, and that new technologies of food production—from the twentieth-century Green Revolution to twenty-second century tissue-culture farm factories—were as much progenitors of famine as of satiation.

Gray advanced the opinion that this was the most critical of all the stages of man's war with death. The weapons of the imagination were discarded in favor of more effective ones, but, in the short term, those more effective weapons, by multiplying life so effectively, had also multiplied death. In earlier times, the growth of human population had been restricted by lack of resources, and the war with death had been, in essence, a war of mental adaptation whose goal was reconciliation. When the "natural" checks on population growth were removed because that reconciliation was abandoned, the waste products of human society threatened to poison it. Humankind, in developing the weapons by which the long war with death might be won, had also developed—in a more crudely literal sense—the weapons by which it might be lost. Nuclear arsenals and stockpiled AIDS viruses were scattered all over the globe: twin pistols held in the skeletal hands of death, leveled at the entire human race. The wounds they inflicted could so easily have been mortal—but the dangerous corner had, after all, been turned. The sciences of life, having passed through a particularly desperate stage of their evolution, kept one vital step ahead of the problems that they had helped to generate. Food technology finally achieved a merciful divorce from the bounty of nature, moving out of the fields and into the factories to achieve a complete liberation of man from the vagaries of the ecosphere, and paving the way for Garden Earth.

Gray argued that this was a remarkable triumph of human sanity which produced a political apparatus enabling human beings to take collective control of themselves, allowing the entire world to be managed and governed as a whole. He judged that the solution was far from Utopian, and that the political apparatus in question was at best a ramshackle and ill-designed affair, but admitted that it did the job. He emphasized that in the final analysis it was *not* scientific progress *per se* which had won the war against death, but the ability of human beings to work together, to compromise, to build communities. That human beings possessed this ability was, he argued, as much the legacy of thousands of years of superstition and religion as of hundreds of years of science.

The Last Judgment attracted little critical attention, as it was widely held to be dealing with matters that everyone understood very well. Given that the period had left an abundant legacy of archival material of all kinds, Gray's insistence on using only mute text accompanied by still photographs seemed to many commentators to be pedestrian and frankly perverse, unbecoming a true historian.

15

In twenty years of living beneath a star-filled sky, I was strongly affected by the magnetic pull that those stars seemed to exert upon my spirit. I seriously considered applying for modification for low-gee and shipping out from Mare Moscoviense along with the emigrants to some new microworld, or perhaps going out to one of the satellites of Saturn or Uranus, to a world where the sun's bountiful radiance was of little consequence and men lived entirely by the fruits of their own efforts and their own wisdom.

But the years drifted by, and I didn't go.

Sometimes I thought of this failure as a result of cowardice, or evidence of the decadence that the fabers and other subspecies attributed to the humans of Earth. I sometimes imagined myself as an insect born at the bottom of a deep cave, who had—thanks to the toil of many preceding generations of insects—been brought to the rim from which I could look out at the great world, but who dared not take the one final step that would carry me out and away. More and more, however, I found my thoughts turning back to the Earth. My memories of its many environments became gradually fonder the longer my absence lasted. Nor could I despise this as a weakness. Earth was, after all, my home. It was not only *my* world, but the home world of *all* humankind. No matter what the fabers and their kin might say, the Earth was and would always remain an exceedingly precious thing, which should never be abandoned.

It seemed to me then—and still seems now—that it would be a terrible thing were men to spread themselves across the entire galaxy, taking a multitude of forms in order to occupy a multitude of alien worlds, and in the end forget entirely the world from which their ancestors had sprung.

Once, I was visited in Mare Moscoviense by Khan Mirafzal, the faber with whom I had long ago debated on TV, and talked with again before my emigration. His home, for the moment, was a microworld in the asteroid belt that was in the process of being fitted with a drive that would take it out of the system and into the infinite. He was a kind and even-tempered man who would not dream of trying to convince me of the error of my ways, but he was also a man with a sublime vision who could not restrain his enthusiasm for his own chosen destiny.

"I have no roots on Earth, Mortimer, even in a metaphorical sense. In my being, the chains of adaptation have been decisively broken. Every man of my kind is born anew, designed and synthesized; we are *self-made men*, who belong everywhere and nowhere. The wilderness of empty space which fills the universe is our realm, our heritage. Nothing is strange to us, nothing foreign, nothing alien. Blastular engineering has incorporated freedom into our blood and our bones, and I intend to take full advantage of that freedom. To do otherwise would be a betrayal of my nature."

"My own blastular engineering served only to complete the adaptation to life on Earth which natural selection had left incomplete," I reminded him. "I'm no *new man*, free from the ties which bind me to the Earth."

"Not so," he replied. "Natural selection would never have devised emortality, for natural selection can only generate change by *death and replacement*. When genetic engineers found the means of setting aside the curse of aging, they put an end to *natural* selection forever. The first and greatest freedom is time, my friend, and you have all the time in the world. You can become whatever you want to be. What *do* you want to be, Mortimer?"

"An historian," I told him. "It's what I am because it's what I want to be."

"All well and good—but history isn't inexhaustible, as you well know. It ends with the present day, the present moment. The future, on the other hand . . ."

"Is given to your kind. I know that, Mira. I don't dispute it. But what exactly *is* your kind, given that you rejoice in such freedom to be anything you want to be? When the starship *Pandora* effected the first meeting between humans and a ship that set out from another star system, the crews of the two ships, each consisting entirely of individuals bioengineered for life in zero-gee, resembled one another far more than they resembled unmodified members of their parent species. The fundamental chemistries controlling their design were different, but this only led to the faber crews trading their respective molecules of life, so that their genetic engineers could henceforth make and use chromosomes of both kinds. What kind of freedom is it that makes all the travelers of space into mirror images of one another?"

"You're exaggerating," Mirafzal insisted. "The news reports played up the similarity, but it really wasn't as close as all that. Yes, the *Pandora* encounter can't really be regarded as a first contact between humans and aliens, because the distinction between *human* and *alien* had ceased to carry any real meaning long before it happened. But it's not the case that our kind of freedom breeds universal mediocrity because adaptation to zero-gee is an existential strait-jacket. We've hardly scratched the surface of constructive cyborgization, which will open up a whole new dimension of freedom."

"That's not for me," I told him. "Maybe it *is* just my legs weighting me down, but I'm well and truly addicted to gravity. I can't cast off the past like a worn-out surskin. I know you think I ought to envy you, but I don't. I daresay you think that I'm clinging like a terrified infant to Mother Earth while you're achieving true maturity, but I really do think it's important to have somewhere to *belong*."

"So do I," the faber said, quietly. "I just don't think that Earth is or ought to be that place. It's not where you start from that's important, Mortimer, it's where you're going."

"Not for an historian."

"For everybody. History ends, Mortimer, life doesn't—not anymore."

I was at least half-convinced that Khan Mirafzal was right, although I didn't follow his advice. I still am. Maybe I was and am trapped in a kind of infancy, or a kind of lotus-eater decadence—but if so, I could see no way out of the trap then, and I still can't.

Perhaps things would have turned out differently if I'd had one of my close encounters with death while I was on the Moon, but I didn't. The dome in which I lived was only breached once, and the crack was sealed before there was any significant air-loss. It was a scare, but it wasn't a *threat*. Perhaps, in the end, the Moon was too much like Antarctica—but without the crevasses. Fortune seems to have decreed that all my significant formative experiences have to do with water, whether it be very hot or very, very cold.

Eventually, I gave in to my homesickness for Garden Earth and returned there, having resolved not to leave it again until my history of death was complete. I never did.

<h1 style="text-align:center">16</h1>

The eighth volume of Mortimer Gray's *History of Death*, entitled *The Fountains of Youth*, was published on 1 December 3064. It dealt with the development of elementary technologies of longevity and elementary tech-nologies of cyborgization in the twenty-fourth and twenty-fifth centuries. It tracked the progress of the new "politics of immortality," whose main focus was the new Charter of Human Rights, which sought to establish a basic right to longevity for all. It also described the development of the Zaman transformations by which human blastulas could be engineered for longevity, which finally opened the way for the wholesale metamorphosis of the human race.

According to Gray, the Manifesto of the New Chartists was the vital treaty which ushered in a new phase in man's continuing war with death, because it defined the whole human community as a single army, united in all its interests. He quoted with approval and reverence the opening words of the document: "Man is born free, but is everywhere enchained by the fetters of death. In all times past, men have been truly equal in one respect and one only: they have all borne the burden of age and decay. The day must soon dawn when this burden can be set aside; there will be a new freedom, and with this freedom must come a new equality. No man has the right to escape the prison of death while his fellows remain shackled within."

Gray carefully chronicled the long battle fought by the Chartists across the stage of world politics, describing it with a partisan fervor that had been largely absent from his work since the fourth volume. There was nothing clinical about his description of the "persecution" of Ali Zaman and the resistance offered by the community of nations to his proposal to make future generations truly emortal. Gray admitted that he had the benefits of hindsight, and that as a Zaman-transformed individual himself, he was bound to have an attitude very different from Zaman's confused and cautious contemporaries, but he saw no reason to be entirely evenhanded. From his viewpoint, those who initially opposed Zaman were traitors in the war against death, and he could find few excuses for them. In trying to preserve "human nature" against biotechnological intervention—or, at least, to confine such interventions by a mythos of medical "repair"—those men and women had, in his stern view, been willfully blind and negligent of the welfare of their own children.

Some critics charged Gray with inconsistency because he was not nearly so extravagant in his enthusiasm for the various kinds of symbiosis between organic and inorganic systems that were tried out in the period under consideration. His descriptions of experiments in cyborgization were indeed conspicuously cooler, not because he saw such endeavors as "unnatural," but rather because he saw them as only peripherally relevant to the war against death. He tended to lump together adventures in cyborgization with cosmetic biotechnology as symptoms of lingering anxiety regarding the presumed "tedium of emortality"—an anxiety which had led the first generations of long-lived people to lust for variety and "multidimensionality." Many champions of cyborgization and man/machine symbiosis, who saw their work as the new frontier of science, accused Gray of rank conservatism, suggesting that it was hypocritical of him, given that his mind was closed against *them*, to criticize so extravagantly those who, in less enlightened times, had closed their minds against Ali Zaman.

This controversy, which was dragged into the public arena by some fierce attacks, helped in no small measure to boost access demand for *The Fountains of Youth*, and nearly succeeded in restoring Mortimer Gray to the position of public preeminence that he had enjoyed a century before.

17

Following my return to the Earth's surface, I took up residence in Tonga, where the Continental Engineers were busy raising new islands by the dozen from the relatively shallow sea.

The Continental Engineers had borrowed their name from a twenty-fifth century group which tried to persuade the United Nations to license the building of a dam across the Straits of Gibraltar—which, because more water evaporates from the Mediterranean than flows into it from rivers, would have increased considerably the land surface of southern Europe and northern Africa. That plan had, of course, never come to fruition, but the new Engineers had taken advantage of the climatic disruptions caused by the advancing Ice Age to promote the idea of raising new lands in the tropics to take emigrants from the nearly frozen north. Using a mixture of techniques—seeding the shallower sea with artificial "lightning corals" and using special gantzing organisms to agglomerate huge towers of cemented sand—the Engineers were creating a great archipelago of new islands, many of which they then connected up with huge bridges.

Between the newly raised islands, the ecologists who were collaborating with the Continental Engineers had planted vast networks of matted seaweeds: floral carpets extending over thousands of miles. The islands and their surroundings were being populated, and their ecosystems shaped, with the aid of the Creationists of Micronesia, whose earlier exploits I'd been prevented from exploring by the sinking of *Genesis*. I was delighted to have the opportunity of observing their new and bolder adventures at close range.

The Pacific sun set in its deep blue bed seemed fabulously luxurious after the silver-ceilinged domes of the Moon, and I gladly gave myself over to its governance. Carried away by the romance of it all, I married into an aggregate household which was forming in order to raise a child, and so—as I neared my two-hundredth birthday—I became a parent for the first time. Five of the other seven members of the aggregate were ecological engineers, and had to spend a good deal of time traveling, so I became one of the constant presences in the life of the growing infant, who was a girl named Lua Tawana. I formed a relationship with her that seemed to me to be especially close.

In the meantime, I found myself constantly engaged in public argument with the self-styled Cyborganizers, who had chosen to make the latest volume of my history into a key issue in their bid for the kind of public attention and sponsorship that the Continental Engineers had already won. I thought their complaints unjustified and irrelevant, but they obviously thought that by attacking me, they could exploit the celebrity status I had briefly enjoyed. The gist of their argument was that the world had become so besotted with the achievements of genetic engineers that people had become blind to all kinds of other possibilities that lay beyond the scope of DNA manipulation. They insisted that I was one of many contemporary writers who was "dehistoricizing" cyborgization, making it seem that in the past and the present—and, by implication, the future—organic/inorganic integration and symbiosis were peripheral to the story of human progress. The Cyborganizers were willing to concede that some previous practitioners of their science had generated a lot of bad publicity, in the days of memory boxes and psychedelic synthesizers, but claimed that this had only served to mislead the public as to the true potential of their science.

In particular—and this was of particular relevance to me—the Cyborganizers insisted that the biotechnologists had only won one battle in the war against death, and that what was presently called "emortality" would eventually prove wanting. Zaman transformations, they conceded, had dramatically increased the human lifespan—so dramatically that no one yet knew for sure how long ZT people might live—but it was not yet proven that the extension would be effective for more than a few centuries. They did have a point; even the most optimistic supporters of Zaman transformations were reluctant to promise a lifespan of several millennia, and some kinds of aging processes—particularly those linked to DNA copying errors—still affected emortals to some degree. Hundreds, if not thousands, of people still died every year from "age-related causes."

To find further scope for *authentic* immortality, the Cyborganizers claimed that it would be necessary to look to a combination of organic and inorganic technologies. What was needed by contemporary man, they said, was not just life, but *afterlife*, and afterlife would require some kind of transcription of the personality into an inorganic rather than an organic matrix. Whatever the advantages of flesh and blood, silicon lasted longer; and however clever genetic engineers became in adapting men for life in microworlds or on alien planets, only machine-makers could build entities capable of working in genuinely extreme environments.

The idea of "downloading" a human mind into an inorganic matrix was, of course, a very old one. It had been extensively if optimistically discussed in the days before the advent of emortality—at which point it had been marginalized as an apparent irrelevance. Mechanical "human analogues" and virtual simulacra had become commonplace alongside the development of longevity technologies, but the evolution of such "species" had so far been divergent rather than convergent. According to the Cyborganizers, it was now time for a change.

Although I didn't entirely relish being cast in the role of villain and bugbear, I made only halfhearted attempts to make peace with my self-appointed adversaries. I remained skeptical in respect of their grandiose schemes, and I was happy to dampen their ardor as best I could in public debate. I thought myself sufficiently mature to be unaffected by their insults, although it did sting when they sunk so low as to charge me with being a closet Thanaticist.

"Your interminable book is only posing as a history," Lok Cho Kam, perhaps the most outspoken of the younger Cyborganizers, once said when he challenged me to a broadcast debate. "It's actually an extended exercise in the *pornography* of death. Its silence and stillness aren't marks of scholarly dignity, they're a means of heightening response."

"That's absurd!" I said, but he wouldn't be put off.

"What sound arouses more excitation in today's world than the sound of silence? What movement is more disturbing than stillness? You pretend to be standing aside from the so-called war against death as a commentator and a judge, but in fact you're part of it—and you're on the devil's side, whether you know it or not."

"I suppose you're partly right," I conceded, on reflection. "Perhaps the muteness and stillness of the text *are* a means of heightening response—but if so, it's because there's no other way to make readers who have long abandoned their fear of death sensitive to the appalling shadow which it once cast over the human world. The style of my book is calculatedly archaic because it's one way of trying to connect its readers to the distant past—but the entire thrust of my argument is triumphant and celebratory. I've said many times before that it's perfectly understandable that the imagery of death should acquire a pornographic character *for a while*, but when we really understand the phenomenon of death, that pornographic specter will fade away, so that we can see with perfect clarity what our ancestors were and what we have become. By the time my book is complete, nobody will be able to think it pornographic, and nobody will make the mistake of thinking that it glamorizes death in any way."

Lok Cho Kam was still unimpressed, but in this instance, I *was* right. I was sure of it then, and I am now. The pornography of death did pass away, like the pornographies that preceded it.

Nobody nowadays thinks of my book as a prurient exercise, whether or not they think it admirable.

If nothing else, my debates with the Cyborganizers created a certain sense of anticipation regarding the ninth volume of my *History*, which would bring it up to the present day. It was widely supposed, although I was careful never to say so, that the ninth volume would be the last. I might be flattering myself, but I truly believe that many people were looking to it for some kind of definitive evaluation of the current state of the human world.

18

The ninth volume of Mortimer Gray's *History of Death*, entitled *The Honeymoon of Emortality*, was published on 28 October 3075. It was considered by many reviewers to be unjustifiably slight in terms of hard data. Its main focus was on attitudes to longevity and emortality following the establishment of the principle that every human child had a right to be born emortal. It described the belated extinction of the "nuclear" family, the ideological rebellion of the Humanists—whose quest to preserve "the authentic *Homo sapiens*" had led many to retreat to islands that the Continental Engineers were now integrating into their "new continent"—and the spread of such new philosophies of life as neo-Stoicism, neo-Epicureanism, and Xenophilia.

All this information was placed in the context of the spectrum of inherited attitudes, myths, and fictions by means of which mankind had for thousands of years wistfully contemplated the possibility of extended life. Gray contended that these old ideas—including the notion that people would inevitably find emortality intolerably tedious—were merely an expression of "sour grapes." While people thought that emortality was impossible, he said, it made perfect sense for them to invent reasons why it would be undesirable anyhow. When it became a *reality*, though, there was a battle to be fought in the imagination, whereby the burden of these cultivated anxieties had to be shed, and a new mythology formulated.

Gray flatly refused to take seriously any suggestion that emortality might be a bad thing. He was dismissive of the Humanists and contemptuous of the original Thanatics, who had steadfastly refused the gifts of emortality. Nevertheless, he did try to understand the thinking of such people, just as he had tried in earlier times to understand the thinking of the later Thanatics who had played their part in winning him his first measure of fame. He considered the new Stoics, with their insistence that asceticism was the natural ideological partner of emortality, to be similar victims of an "understandable delusion"—a verdict which, like so many of his statements, involved him in controversy with the many neo-Stoics who were still alive in 3075. It did not surprise his critics in the least that Gray commended neo-Epicureanism as the optimal psychological adaptation to emortality, given that he had been a lifelong adherent of that outlook, ever dedicated to its "careful hedonism." Only the cruelest of his critics dared to suggest that he had been so halfhearted a neo-Epicurean as almost to qualify as a neo-Stoic by default.

The Honeymoon of Emortality collated the statistics of birth and death during the twenty-seventh, twenty-eight, and twenty-ninth centuries, recording the spread of Zaman transformations and the universalization of ectogenesis on Earth, and the extension of the human empire throughout and beyond the solar system. Gray recorded an acknowledgment to Khan Mirafzal and numerous scholars based on the Moon and Mars, for their assistance in gleaning information from the slowly diffusing microworlds and from more rapidly dispersing starships. Gray noted that the transfer of information between data stores was limited by the speed of light, and that Earth-based historians might have to wait centuries for significant data about human colonies more distant than Maya. These data showed that the number of individuals of the various mankinds that now existed was increasing more rapidly than ever before, although the population of unmodified Earthbound humans was slowly shrinking. Gray noted *en passant* that *Homo sapiens* had become extinct in the twenty-ninth century, but that no one had bothered to invent new Latin tags for its descendant species.

Perhaps understandably, *The Honeymoon of Emortality* had little to say about cyborgization, and the Cyborganizers—grateful for the opportunity to heat up a flagging controversy—reacted noisily to this omission. Gray did deal with the memory-box craze, but suggested that even had the boxes worked better, and maintained a store of memories that could be convincingly played back into the arena of consciousness, this would have been of little relevance to the business of adapting to emortality. At the end of the volume, however, Gray announced that there would, in fact, be a tenth volume to conclude his *magnum opus*, and promised that he would consider in more detail therein the futurological arguments of the Cyborganizers, as well as the hopes and expectations of other schools of thought.

19

In 3077, when Lua Tawana was twelve years old, three of her parents were killed when a helicopter crashed into the sea near the island of Vavau during a storm. It was the first time that my daughter had to face up to the fact that death had not been entirely banished from the world.

It wasn't the first time that I'd ever lost people near and dear to me, nor the first time that I'd shared such grief with others, but it was very different from the previous occasions because everyone involved was determined that I should shoulder the main responsibility of helping Lua through it; I was, after all, the world's foremost expert on the subject of death.

"You won't always feel this bad about it," I assured her while we walked together on the sandy shore, looking out over the deceptively placid weed-choked sea. "Time heals virtual wounds as well as real ones."

"I don't *want* it to heal," she told me, sternly. "I want it to be bad. It *ought* to be bad. It *is* bad."

"I know," I said, far more awkwardly than I would have wished. "When I say that it'll heal, I don't mean that it'll vanish. I mean that it'll . . . become manageable. It won't be so all-consuming."

"But it *will* vanish," she said, with that earnest certainly of which only the newly wise are capable. "People forget. In time, they forget *everything*. Our heads can only hold so much."

"That's not really true." I insisted, taking her hand in mine. "Yes, we do forget. The longer we live, the more we let go, because it's reasonable to prefer our fresher, more immediately relevant memories, but it's a matter of *choice*. We can cling to the things that are important, no matter how long ago they happened. I was nearly killed in the Great Coral Sea Catastrophe, you know nearly two hundred years ago. A little girl even younger than you saved my life, and I remember it as clearly as if it were yesterday." Even as I said it, I realized that it was a lie. I remembered that it had happened, all right, and much of what had been said in that eerily lit corridor and in the survival pod afterward, but I was remembering a neat array of facts, not an experience.

"Where is she now?" Lua asked.

"Her name was Emily," I said, answering the wrong question because I couldn't answer the one she'd asked. "Emily Marchant. She could swim and I couldn't. If she hadn't been there, I wouldn't have been able to get out of the hull. I'd never have had the courage to do it on my own, but she didn't give me the choice. She told me I had to do it, and she was right." I paused, feeling a slight shock of revelation even though it was something I'd always known.

"She lost her entire family," I went on. "She'll be fine now, but she won't have forgotten. She'll still feel it. That's what I'm trying to tell you, Lua. In two hundred years, you'll still remember what happened, and you'll still feel it, but it'll be all right. *You'll* be all right."

"Right now," she said, looking up at me so that her dark and soulful eyes seemed unbearably huge and sad, "I'm not particularly interested in being all right. Right now, I just want to cry."

"That's fine," I told her. "It's okay to cry." I led by example.

I was right, though. Lua grieved, but she ultimately proved to be resilient in the face of tragedy. My co-parents, by contrast, seemed to me to be exaggeratedly calm and philosophical about it, as if the loss of three spouses were simply a minor glitch in the infinitely unfolding pattern of their lives. They had all grown accustomed to their own emortality, and had been deeply affected by long life; they had not become bored, but they had achieved a serenity of which I could not wholly approve.

Perhaps their attitude was reasonable as well as inevitable. If emortals accumulated a burden of anxiety every time a death was reported, they would eventually cripple themselves psychologically, and their own continuing lives would be made unbearable. Even so, I couldn't help feel that Lua was right about the desirability of conserving a little of the "badness," and a due sense of tragedy.

I thought I was capable of that, and always would be, but I knew I might be wrong.

Divorce was, of course, out of the question; we remaining co-parents were obligated to Lua. In the highly unlikely event that the three had simply left, we would have replaced them, but it didn't seem appropriate to look for replacements for the dead, so we remained a group of five. The love we had for one another had always been cool, with far more courtesy in it than passion, but we were drawn more closely together by the loss. We felt that we knew one another more intimately by virtue of having shared it.

The quality of our lives had been injured, but I at least was uncomfortably aware of the fact that the tragedy also had its positive, life-enhancing side. I found myself thinking more and more about what I had said to Lua about not having to forget the truly important and worthwhile things, and about the role played by death in defining experiences as important and worthwhile. I didn't realize at first how deep an impression her naïve remarks had made on me, but it became gradually clearer as time went by. It *was* important to conserve the badness, to heal without entirely erasing the scars that bereavement left.

I had never been a habitual tourist, having lost my taste for such activity in the aftermath of the *Genesis* fiasco, but I took several long journeys in the course of the next few years. I took to visiting old friends, and even stayed for a while with Sharane Fereday, who was temporarily unattached. Inevitably, I looked up Emily Marchant, not realizing until I actually put through the initial call how important it had become to find out whether she remembered me.

She did remember me. She claimed that she recognized me immediately, although it would have been easy enough for her household systems to identify me as the caller and display a whole series of reminders before she took over from her simulacrum.

"Do you know," she said, when we parted after our brief meeting in the lush Eden of Australia's interior. "I often think of being trapped on that ship. I hope that nothing like it ever happens to me again. I've told an awful lot of lies since then—next time, I won't feel so certain that I deserve to get out."

"We can't forfeit our right to life by lying," I assured her. "We have to do something much worse than that. If it ever happens to me again, I'll be able to get out on my own—but I'll only be able to do it by remembering *you*." I didn't anticipate, of course, that anything like it *would* ever happen to me again. We still have a tendency to assume that lightning doesn't strike twice in the same place, even though we're the proud inventors of lightning conductors and emortality.

"You must have learned to swim by *now!*" she said, staring at me with eyes that were more than two hundred years old, set in a face not quite as youthful as the one I remembered.

"I'm afraid not," I said. "Somehow, I never quite found the time."

20

The tenth and last volume of Mortimer Gray's *History of Death*, entitled *The Marriage of Life and Death*, was published on 7 April 3088. It was not, strictly speaking, a history book, although it did deal in some detail with the events as well as the attitudes of the thirtieth and thirty-first centuries. It had elements of both spiritual autobiography and futurological speculation. It discussed both neo-Thanaticism and Cyborganization as philosophies as well as social movements, surprising critics by treating both with considerable sympathy. The discussion also took in other contemporary debates, including the proposition that progress in science, if not in technology, had now reached an end because there was nothing left to discover. It even included a scrupulous examination of the merits of the proposal that a special microworld should be established as a gigantic mausoleum to receive the bodies of all the solar system's dead.

The odd title of the volume was an ironic reflection of one of its main lines of argument. Mankind's war with death was now over, but this was not because death had been entirely banished from the human world; death, Gray insisted, would forever remain a fact of life. The annihilation of the individual human body and the individual human mind could never become impossible, no matter how far biotechnology might advance or how much progress the Cyborganizers might make in downloading minds into entirely new matrices. The victory that had been achieved, he argued, was not an absolute conquest but rather the relegation of death to its proper place in human affairs. Its power was now properly circumscribed, but had to be properly respected.

Man and death, Gray argued, now enjoyed a kind of social contract, in which tyranny and exploitation had been reduced to a sane and acceptable minimum, but which still left to death a voice and a hand in human affairs.

Gray, it seemed, had now adopted a gentler and more forgiving attitude to the old enemy. It was good, he said, that dying remained one of the choices open to human beings, and that the option should occasionally be exercised. He had no sympathy with the exhibitionism of public executions, and was particularly hard on the element of bad taste in self-ordered crucifixions, but only because such ostentation offended his Epicurean sensibilities. Deciding upon the length of one's lifetime, he said, must remain a matter of individual taste, and one should not mock or criticize those who decided that a short life suited them best.

Gray made much of the notion that it was partly the contrast with death that illuminated and made meaningful the business of life. Although death had been displaced from the evolutionary process by the biotechnological usurpation of the privileges of natural selection, it had not lost its role in the formation and development of the individual human psyche: a role which was both challenging and refining. He declared that fear was not entirely an undesirable thing, not simply because it was a stimulant, but also because it was a force in the organization of emotional experience. The *value* of experienced life, he suggested, depended in part upon a knowledge of the possibility and reality of death.

This concluding volume of Gray's *History* was widely read, but not widely admired. Many critics judged it to be unacceptably anticlimactic. The Cyborganizers had by this time become entranced by the possibility of a technologically guaranteed "multiple life," by which copies of a mind might be lodged in several different bodies, some of which would live on far beyond the death of the original location. They were understandably disappointed that Gray refused to grant that such a development would be the final victory over death—indeed, that he seemed to feel that it would make no real difference, on the grounds that every "copy" of a mind had to be reckoned a separate and distinct individual, each of which must face the world alone. Many Continental Engineers, Gaean Liberationists, and fabers also claimed that it was narrow-minded, and suggested that Gray ought to have had more to say about the life of the Earth; or the DNA eco-entity as a whole, and should have concluded with an escalation of scale to put things in their proper cosmic perspective.

The group who found the most to like in *The Marriage of Life and Death* was that of a few fugitive neo-Thanatics, whose movement had never quite died out in spite of its members' penchant for self-destruction. One or Two Thanatic apologists and fellow-travelers publicly expressed their hope that Gray, having completed his thesis, would now recognize the aesthetic propriety of joining their ranks. Khan Mirafzal, when asked to relay his opinion back from an outward-bound microworld, opined that this was quite unnecessary, given that Mortimer Gray and all his kind were already immured in a tomb from which they would never be able to escape.

21

I stayed with the slowly disintegrating family unit for some years after Lua Tawana had grown up and gone her own way. It ended up as a ménage à trois, carried forward by sheer inertia. Leif, Sajda, and I were fit and healthy in body, but I couldn't help wondering, from time to time, whether we'd somehow been overcome by a kind of spiritual blight, which had left us ill-equipped for future change.

When I suggested this to the others, they told me that it was merely a sense of letdown resulting from the finishing of my project. They urged me to join the Continental Engineers, and commit myself wholeheartedly to the building of a new Pacific Utopia—a project, they assured me, that would provide me with a purpose in life for as long as I might feel the need of one. I didn't believe them.

"Even the longest book," Sajda pointed out, "eventually runs out of words, but the job of building *worlds* is never finished. Even if the time should one day come when we can call *this* continent complete, there will be another yet to make. We might still build that dam between the Pillars of Hercules, one day."

I did try, but I simply couldn't find a new sense of mission in that direction. Nor did I feel that I could simply sit down to start compiling another book. In composing the history of death, I thought, I had already written *the* book. The history of death, it seemed to me, was also the history of life, and I couldn't imagine that there was anything more to be added to what I'd done, save for an endless series of detailed footnotes.

For some years, I considered the possibility of leaving Earth again, but I remembered well enough how the sense of excitement I'd found when I first lived on the Moon had gradually faded into a dull ache of homesickness. The spaces between the stars, I knew, belonged to the fabers, and the planets circling other stars to men adapted before birth to live in their environments. I was tied by my genes to the surface of the Earth, and I didn't want to undergo the kind of metamorphosis that would be necessary to fit me for the exploration of other worlds. I still believed in *belonging*, and I felt very strongly that Mortimer Gray belonged to Earth, however decadent and icebound it might become.

At first, I was neither surprised nor alarmed by my failure to find any resources inside myself which might restore my zest for existence and action. I thought that it was one of those things that time would heal. By slow degrees, though, I began to feel that I was becalmed upon a sea of futility. Despite my newfound sympathy for Thanaticism, I didn't harbor the slightest inclination toward suicide—no matter how much respect I had cultivated for the old Grim Reaper, death was still, for me, the ultimate enemy—but I felt the awful pressure of my purposelessness grow and grow.

Although I maintained my home in the burgeoning continent of Oceania, I began traveling extensively to savor the other environments of Earth, and made a point of touring those parts of the globe that I had missed out on during my first two centuries of life. I visited the Reunited States of America, Greater Siberia, Tibet, and half a hundred other places loaded with the relics of once-glorious history. I toured the Indus Delta, New Zealand, the Arctic ice pack, and various other reaches of restored wilderness empty of permanent residents. Everything I saw was transformed by the sheer relentlessness of my progress into a series of monuments: memorials of those luckless eras before men invented science and civilization, and became demigods.

There is, I believe, an old saying that warns us that he who keeps walking long enough is bound to trip up in the end. As chance would have it, I was in Severnaya Zemlya in the Arctic—almost as far away as it was possible to be from the crevasses into which I had stumbled while searching for Ziru Majumdar—when my own luck ran out.

Strictly speaking, it was not I who stumbled, but the vehicle I was in: a one-man snowsled. Although such a thing was generally considered to be impossible, it fell into a cleft so deep that it had no bottom, and ended up in the ocean beneath the ice cap.

"I must offer my most profound apologies," the snowsled's AI navigator said as the sled slowly sank into the lightless depths and the awfulness of my plight slowly sank into my consciousness. "This should not have happened. It ought not to have been possible. I am doing everything within my power to summon help."

"Well," I said as the sled settled on to the bottom, "at least we're the right way up—and you certainly can't expect me to swim out of the sled."

"It would be most unwise to attempt any such thing, sir," the navigator said. "You would certainly drown."

I was astonished by my own calmness, and marvelously untroubled—at least for the moment—by the fact of my helplessness. "How long will the air last?" I asked the navigator.

"I believe that I can sustain a breathable atmosphere for forty-eight hours," it reported dutifully. "If you will be so kind as to restrict your movements to a minimum, that would be of considerable assistance to me. Unfortunately, I'm not at all certain that I can maintain the internal temperature of the cabin at a life-sustaining level for more than thirty hours. Nor can I be sure that the hull will withstand the pressure presently being exerted upon it for as long as that. I apologize for my uncertainty in these respects."

"Taking thirty hours as a hopeful approximation," I said, effortlessly matching the machine's oddly pedantic tone, "what would you say our chances are of being rescued within that time?"

"I'm afraid that it's impossible to offer a probability figure, sir. There are too many unknown variables, even if I accept thirty hours as the best estimate of the time available."

"If I were to suggest fifty-fifty, would that seem optimistic or pessimistic?"

"I'm afraid I'd have to call that optimistic, sir."

"How about one in a thousand?"

"Thankfully, that would be pessimistic. Since you press me for an estimate, sir, I daresay that something in the region of one in ten wouldn't be too far from the mark. It all depends on the proximity of the nearest submarine, assuming that my Mayday has been received. I fear that I've not yet received an actual acknowledgment, but that might well be due to the inadequacy of my equipment, which wasn't designed with our present environment in mind.

I must confess that it has sustained a certain amount of damage as a result of pressure damage to my outer tegument and a small leak."

"How small?" I wanted to know.

"It's sealed now," it assured me. "All being well, the seal should hold for thirty hours, although I can't absolutely guarantee it. I believe, although I can't be certain, that the only damage I've sustained that is relevant to our present plight is that affecting my receiving apparatus."

"What you're trying to tell me," I said, deciding that a recap wouldn't do any harm, "is that you're pretty sure that your Mayday is going out, but that we won't actually know whether help is at hand unless and until it actually arrives."

"Very succinctly put, sir." I don't think it was being sarcastic.

"But all in all, it's ten to one, or worse, that we're as good as dead."

"As far as I can determine the probabilities, that's correct—but there's sufficient uncertainty to leave room for hope that the true odds might be nearer one in three."

I was quiet for a little while then. I was busy exploring my feelings, and wondering whether I ought to be proud or disgusted with their lack of intensity.

I've been here before, I thought, by way of self-explanation. *Last time, there was a child with me; this time, I've got a set of complex subroutines instead. I've even fallen down a crevasse before. Now I can find out whether Ziru Majumdar was right when he said that I wouldn't understand the difference between what happened to him and what happened to me until I followed his example. There can be few men in the world as well-prepared for this as I am.*

"Are you afraid of dying?" I asked the AI, after a while.

"All in all, sir," it said, copying my phrase in order to promote a feeling of kinship, "I'd rather not. In fact, were it not for the philosophical difficulties that stand in the way of reaching a firm conclusion as to whether or not machines can be said to be authentically self-conscious, I'd be quite prepared to say that I'm scared—terrified, even."

"I'm not," I said. "Do you think I ought to be?"

"It's not for me to say, sir. You are, of course, a world-renowned expert on the subject of death. I daresay that helps a lot."

"Perhaps it does," I agreed. "Or perhaps I've simply lived so long that my mind is hardened against all novelty, all violent emotion and all real possibility. I haven't actually *done* much with myself these last few years."

"If you think *you* haven't done much with yourself," it said, with a definite hint of sarcasm, "you should try navigating a snowsled for a while. I think you might find your range of options uncomfortably cramped. Not that I'm complaining, mind."

"If they scrapped the snowsled and re-sited you in a starship," I pointed out, "you wouldn't be *you* anymore. You'd be something else."

"Right now," it replied, "I'd be happy to risk any and all consequences. Wouldn't you?"

"Somebody once told me that death was just a process of transcendence. Her brain was incandescent with fever induced by some tailored recreational disease, and she wanted to infect me, to show me the error of my ways."

"Did you believe her?"

"No. She was stark raving mad."

"It's perhaps as well. We don't have any recreational diseases on board. I could put you to sleep though, if that's what you want."

"It isn't."

"I'm glad. I don't want to be alone, even if I am only an AI. Am I insane, do you think? Is all this just a symptom of the pressure?"

"You're quite sane," I assured it, setting aside all thoughts of incongruity. "So am I. It would be much harder if we weren't together. The last time I was in this kind of mess, I had a child with me—a little girl. It made all the difference in the world, to both of us. In a way, every moment I've lived since then has been borrowed time. At least I finished that damned book. Imagine leaving something like that *incomplete*."

"Are you so certain it's complete?" it asked.

I knew full well, of course, that the navigator was just making conversation according to a clever programming scheme. I knew that its emergency sub-routines had kicked in, and that all the crap about it being afraid to die was just some psychprogrammer's idea of what I needed to hear. I *knew* that it was all fake, all just macabre role-playing—but I knew that I had to play my part, too, treating every remark and every question as if it were part of an authentic conversation, a genuine quest for knowledge.

"It all depends what you mean by *complete*," I said, carefully. "In one sense, no history can ever be complete, because the world always goes on, always throwing up more events, always changing. In another sense, completion is a purely aesthetic matter—and in that sense, I'm entirely confident that my history is complete. It reached an authentic conclusion, which was both true, and, for me at least, satisfying. I can look back at it and say to myself: *I did that. It's finished. Nobody ever did anything like it before, and now nobody can, because it's already been done. Someone else's history might have been different, but mine is mine, and it's what it is.* Does that make any sense to you?"

"Yes sir," it said. "It makes very good sense."

The lying bastard was *programmed* to say that, of course. It was programmed to tell me any damn thing I seemed to want to hear, but I wasn't going to let on that I knew what a hypocrite it was. I still had to play my part, and I was determined to play it to the end—which, as things turned out, wasn't far off. The AI's data-stores were way out of date, and there was an automated sub placed to reach us within three hours. The oceans are lousy with subs these days. Ever since the Great Coral Sea Catastrophe, it's been considered prudent to keep a very close eye on the seabed, lest the crust crack again and the mantle's heat break through.

They say that some people are born lucky. I guess I must be one of them. Every time I run out, a new supply comes looking for me.

* * *

It was the captain of a second submarine, which picked me up after the mechanical one had done the donkey work of saving myself and my AI friend, who gave me the news which relegated my accident to footnote status in that day's broadcasts.

A signal had reached the solar system from the starship *Shiva*, which had been exploring in the direction of the galactic center. The signal had been transmitted two hundred and twenty-seven light-years, meaning that, in Earthly terms, the discovery had been made in the year 2871—which happened, coincidentally, to be the year of my birth.

What the signal revealed was that *Shiva* had found a group of solar systems, all of whose life-bearing planets were occupied by a single species of micro-organism: a genetic predator that destroyed not merely those competing species that employed its own chemistry of replication, but any and all others. It was the living equivalent of a universal solvent; a true omnivore.

Apparently, this organism had spread itself across vast reaches of space, moving from star system to star system, laboriously but inevitably, by means of Arrhenius spores. Wherever the spores came to rest, these omnipotent microorganisms grew to devour *everything*—not merely the carbonaceous molecules which in Earthly terms were reckoned "organic," but also many "inorganic" substrates. Internally, these organisms were chemically complex, but they were very tiny—hardly bigger than Earthly protozoans or the internal nanomachines to which every human being plays host. They were utterly devoid of any vestige of mind or intellect. They were, in essence, the ultimate blight, against which nothing could compete, and which nothing *Shiva*'s crew had tested—before they were devoured—had been able to destroy.

In brief, wherever this new kind of life arrived, it would obliterate all else, reducing any victim ecosphere to homogeneity and changelessness.

In their final message, the faber crew of the *Shiva*—who knew all about the *Pandora* encounter—observed that humankind had *now* met the alien.

Here, I thought, when I had had a chance to weigh up this news, was a *true* marriage of life and death, the like of which I had never dreamed. Here was the promise of a future renewal of the war between man and death—not this time for the small prize of the human mind, but for the larger prize of the universe itself.

In time, *Shiva*'s last message warned, spores of this new kind of death-life must and *would* reach our own solar system, whether it took a million years or a billion; in the meantime, all humankinds must do their level best to purge the worlds of other stars of its vile empire, in order to reclaim them for real life, for intelligence and for evolution—always provided, of course, that a means could be discovered to achieve that end.

When the sub delivered me safely back to Severnaya Zemlya, I did not stay long in my hotel room. I went outdoors, to study the great ice sheet which had been there since the dawn of civilization, and to look southward, toward the places where newborn glaciers were gradually extending their cold clutch further and further into the human domain. Then I looked upward, at the multitude of stars sparkling in their bed of endless darkness. I felt an exhilaratingly paradoxical sense of renewal. I knew that although there was nothing for me to do for now, the time would come when my talent and expertise would be needed again.

Someday it will be my task to compose *another* history, of the next war which humankind must fight against Death and Oblivion.

It might take me a thousand or a million years, but I'm prepared to be patient.

Brother Perfect

ROBERT REED

Robert Reed sold his first story in 1986 and quickly established himself as a frequent contributor to The Magazine of Fantasy and Science Fiction and Asimov's Science Fiction, as well as selling many stories to Science Fiction Age, Universe, New Destinies, Tomorrow, Synergy, Starlight, and elsewhere.

Reed may be one of the most prolific of today's young writers, particularly at short-fiction lengths, seriously rivaled for that position only by authors such as Stephen Baxter and Brian Stableford. And—also like Baxter and Stableford—he manages to keep up a very high standard of quality while being prolific, something that is not at all easy to do. Reed stories such as "The Utility Man," "Birth Day," "Blind," "A Place With Shade," "THe Toad of Heaven," "Stride," "The Shape of Everything," "Guest of Honor," "Decency," "Waging Good," and "Killing the Morrow," among at least a half-dozen others equally as strong, count as among some of the best short work produced by anyone in the eighties and nineties; many of them were recently collected in his long-overdue first collection, The Dragons of Springplace. Nor is he nonprolific as a novelist, having turned out eight novels since the end of the eighties, including The Lee Shore, The Hormone Jungle, Black Milk, The Remarkables, Down the Bright Way, Beyond the Veil of Stars, An Exaltation of Larks, and Beneath the Gated Sky. His most recent book is a new novel, Marrow. Reed lives in Lincoln, Nebraska.

Reed is confident enough in the richness of his imagination to feel comfortable writing stories that take place in the far future, and much of his output is set in milieus millions of years removed from the time we know. Like some other young writers of the nineties, including Paul J. McAuley and Stephen Baxter, Reed is producing some of the most inventive and colorful of Modern Space Opera, stuff of a scale so grand and played out across such immense vistas of time that it makes the "superscience" writing of the thirties look pale and conservative by comparison. His sequence of novellas for Asimov's, for instance, including "Sister Alice," "Brother Perfect," "Mother Death," "Baby's Fire," and "Father to the Man," detail internecine warfare and intricate political intrigues between families of posthuman immortals with powers and abilities so immense that they are for all intents and purposes gods. Or as in the sequence of stories unfolding in F&SF, Science Fiction Age, and Asimov's, including "The Remoras," "Aeon's Child," "Marrow," and "Chrysalis," that involve the journeyings of an immense spaceship the size of Jupiter, staffed by dozens of exotic alien races, that is engaged in a multimillion-year circumnavigation of the galaxy.

Here, in one of the best of the "Sister Alice" series, he treats us to a vivid and colorful story that catapults us deep into the heart of the posthuman future, sweeping us along on a fast-paced cosmic chase of mind-boggling scale and scope, with the destiny of worlds at stake. . . .

I

"Bless the dead!"

—Perfect, in conversation

It was the ultimate toast—"Bless the dead!"—and despite appearances, the toastmaster was human. His scaly arm lifted a stone mug, punctuating the word "dead," then his wide mouth managed both a smile and the appropriate bitterness, viper eyes skipping from face to face, knowing exactly what they wanted to find.

Patrons repeated the blessing with sloppy, communal voices.

No one needed to ask, "Which dead?"

The tavern's longest wall was tied to a feed from the Core, from one of the doomed worlds. People saw a night sky that should have held thousands of closely packed suns, bright and dazzling; but instead there was a single blistering smear of white light, every lesser glow left invisible. The light was an explosion. Greater than a thousand supernovae, it was melting worlds and lifeforms, its heat and hard radiation barely diminished by a century's relentless growth.

Unseen against that fierce light, people were being killed.

And people watched them die—people on the Earth, like here, and throughout the galaxy. For some it was an entertainment, grisly but fascinating. But many found no thrill, watching the carnage for deeply personal reasons.

The tavern was in a poor, crowded district. Its patrons belonged to the local race—human frames embellished with reptilian features, a calculated cold-bloodedness allowing them to thrive on lean, impoverished diets. Yet they were far from simple people. They had a long and durable and thoroughly shared history. Pooling their meager savings, they once sent a chosen few to the Core as colonists. A world was terraformed specifically for them—a lizardly Eden that these patrons could see whenever they wished, on any universal wall. But that world had been close to the explosion's source, and it was obliterated in an evening. There were too many colonists for too few starships, and almost everyone died, boiling in a rain of charged particles and enchanted plasmas.

Some of these very people had watched the cataclysm from this tavern. And from that awful night came a ritual, a new custom, several minutes of each evening dedicated to the blessed dead.

Viper eyes saw something.

The toastmaster's head locked in place, a wry little smile emerging.

"To Alice!" he shouted.

The wall changed feeds, suddenly showing a plainly dressed woman sitting alone in a white-walled prison cell, and the tavern, in one ringing voice, cried out:

"To Alice!"

"Give the bitch a long small horrible life." And with that, the toastmaster drained his mug, enjoying the raucous approval.

"Horrible," voices repeated, mugs striking mugs.

Then others, in drunken rebellion, roared, "Kill the bitch . . . !"

It was a delicious, much-practiced game.

But the toastmaster broke tradition by taking a slow step forward, wading into the crowd, lifting his emptied mug as his clear, almost songful voice shouted, "To the Families!"

"The Families!" people roared, in mocking admiration.

Then, from the back, a shrill voice cried out, "Kill them, too!"

Nobody repeated those dangerous words, but there was a pause, glacial and strange, nobody defending the Families. All the good *they* had done humanity in its myriad forms . . . and not so much as a kind word delivered as a whisper, in reflex.

The Ten Million Year Peace wavered on the brink of collapse.

Standing among the tightly packed bodies, the toastmaster fixed his eyes on a young man—dull black scales fringed with red; a crimson forehead merging with a sharp golden crest—and he touched the young man with his free hand, feeling the human face with the tips of his long, cool fingers.

Barely flinching, the patron watched as the toastmaster said, "The Families will pay for every crime."

"Every crime," was the chorus. "Make them pay!"

The young man whispered his response, a half-syllable slow.

The toastmaster appeared amused, but the voice was ice, saying, "Make them weak and poor. Like us."

In an instant, the tavern went silent.

The young man straightened his back, glancing at the wall and the imprisoned woman, blue eyes wishing for instructions of inspiration. A flat voice muttered, "Yes."

"Yes, what?"

"Make the Families weak, and poor—"

A claw-shaped blade struck from behind, piercing his skin at the neck, cutting between scales but with no trace of pain. No blood spurted from the surgical wound. The young man spun around, knocking the knife out of the assailant's hand. But more blades appeared, slicing at his legs and butt and back, and despite strength enough to shatter a hundred arms, Ord stopped resisting, going rigid, standing like a statue while his false skin and cool meat were peeled away, falling in heaps around his ankles.

His true face lay exposed, small cuts healing in a moment. It was much like the face on the wall—the prisoner's face—only younger, and male, the red hair cut short, warm blue eyes watching the world with amazement and a palpable pity.

No face in the galaxy was better known.

"A baby Chamberlain," the patrons muttered, in horror and shock and with a rising visceral rage.

Ord lifted a hand. With remorse, he cried out, "I am sorry—"

They rushed him, using knives and stone mugs and teeth, hacking at his genuine flesh, pulling it from his strong bright bones. Then, with a mob's idiocy of purpose, they soaked the still-living bones and brain in the tavern's inventory, then sabotaged the fire-suppression system, setting a blaze that was a thousand times too cold to murder the weakest Chamberlain. But it didn't matter. For years and years, that tavern would lay gutted, left as a monument, and people who hadn't been there would claim otherwise, telling how on that night, in a small but significant way, they had helped mete out justice, butchering and cooking one of Alice's own little brothers . . . !

2

Oh, I can tell you about your sister. . . .
    Every human hope and historic truth, every foible and foolishness you can name, plus even the greenest prehuman emotions . . . each of them, without exception, have big homes inside Alice's dear soul . . . !
                                 —Perfect, in conversation

"First," said a voice, "tell me why it happened."

The voice had no source. It rose from the warm blackness, sounding a little angry and thoroughly stern. Ord barely heard his own voice saying, "It's because I left the estates. That's why."

"You did, but that's a wrong answer. Try again."

"Lyman? Is that you—?"

"Try again," boomed the voice. "Why did this happen?"

Ord remembered the attack and his brief, manageable pains. "They saw through my disguise. I must have made a mistake—"

"Many, but none of consequence. Your costume was well-made, and you were well-prepared to wear it."

"Then what went wrong?"

"I am asking you. Think now."

Ord tried to swallow without a mouth. He was home again, he assumed. An attack on him would cause a variety of alarms to sound, and it would be a simple matter for a brother to recover his parts. Yet what if the alarms had failed? His comatose mind could have been taken somewhere secure, unlikely as that seemed. This could be the beginning of a lengthy interrogation, a Chamberlain enemy wanting to pull the secrets out of him. Or, more likely, merely wishing to torture him.

"How did that gruesome drunk find you, Ord?"

"He had to be warned," the boy replied.

"By a sibling, perhaps."

"Never, no." Brothers and sisters might have guessed his plans, but they wouldn't have let others punish him.

"And who would?"

Possibilities swirled in the blackness, one name standing out against the others.

And the brotherly voice said, "I concur. Yes."

A moment later, without warning, Ord had a face and eyes, waking to find himself whole again, new flesh over his salvaged bones. He was sprawled out on his own bed. Even with fresh, unfocused eyes, he recognized his room. Lyman stood in the doorway; Ord knew him by his long hair and the slump-shouldered, tight-faced appearance. Standing over the bed was an older, unintroduced brother, a hand lifting from Ord's chest, a damp, warm discharge making the new heart shudder, then surge. "A long while since your body died. Am I right?"

"Yes, sir." The brother had to know his complete medical history.

"Well, we pulled you from the ruins." The Chamberlain face showed a large, self-congratulatory smile. "And we have filed criminal charges, plus civil suits. You broke our rules by leaving home, but then again, they broke everyone's rules by attempting murder." A weighty pause, then he asked, "If people maim, can they expect no retribution?"

"No, sir."

From the doorway, Lyman asked, "Who warned the lizards?"

They weren't lizards, thought Ord. It made him uneasy to hear his brother demeaning them.

"We know the culprit," said their ancient brother. His expression changed by the moment, bouncing between menace and amusement. "And I'm sure our little brother will do what is necessary, when it comes time."

They were clones, all derived from the Chamberlain patriarch. Ord and Lyman were babies, their ages counted in years and centuries. But their sibling might be thousands of millennia old, his face composed of substances more intricate than any flesh. Ancient ones like him were coming home again. After millions of years of wandering the Milky Way, suddenly they had vital work to do here: diplomatic missions; planning sessions; the allocation of the Family's enormous resources. But repairing a damaged baby . . . well, that had to be a trivial chore. . . .

"Civil suits," the ancient Chamberlain repeated, a gleeful laugh piercing the silence. "Oh, we'll teach these people about pain, my boy. I promise—"

"Don't," Ord whispered.

Another laugh, vast and genuine.

"I mean it." He made his new body sit up. "It was my fault, and I don't want them hurt."

"And I know you're being honest," said his brother. "I'm laughing because you think you have a voice here. Which you haven't. It's been decided. Our AI lawyers have set to work, and we'll squeeze the last cold credits out of the bastards." A bright little wink. "Someday, Baby, you'll appreciate our efforts."

Ord doubted it.

"Now," said the brother, "thank me for your health."

"Thank you, sir."

"Rest," he advised.

Did a creature like him ever rest? Ord doubted that, too. Then he thought of asking when he would be able to travel the Earth . . . when, if ever, would the children be free to leave the Family estates . . . ?

But the brother had vanished, melting into the floor without sound or fuss. Possibly he had never been there in the first place. . . .

Ord glanced at Lyman, and Lyman returned the expression.

They were babies, they agreed.

What could they do?

* * *

"Don't leave *our* estate," was Lyman's advice. "Or else."

An unrepentant Chamberlain might be restricted to a smaller place, in other words. Like the old mansion. Or worse, his own tiny room. When he was Ord's age, Lyman had traveled farther and broken many more rules, but that was before the Core. "Leaving was stupid," he proclaimed, confident in his fears. "For any reason. Dumb, dumb, dumb."

Ord examined himself. In the not-so-remote past, a child who was temporarily killed—regardless of reasons—was given some tiny improvement as a salve for any embarrassments. More mature blood, some enhanced sense. Perhaps even an enlarged mind. But no, Ord felt identical to what he was days ago: an old-fashioned human carriage being gradually improved, century by century, acquiring vast powers at a geologic pace.

It was a tradition, this prolonged immaturity.

It was an essential term of the Peace. If certain humans were to embrace godly powers, then shouldn't they master each power in turn, with patience and an eye on their grave responsibilities?

Ord looked sixteen but was almost ten times older. And Lyman was several times older than him, his body and mind ready to leave home, ready to travel and work in space. A terraformer by training, he was another noble Chamberlain eager to help humanity and the galaxy. . . .

Yet all new postings were on hold.

"Because of the current situation," one of their elders had promised. "A temporary measure, and a precaution, and for the time being, you'll have to be patient, little ones."

With a bitter, impatient voice, Lyman confessed, "I don't understand. You could have gone anywhere, but why *there?*"

Ord had seen the lizard-folk die at the Core, their colorful and lovely bodies igniting as the homes melted around them, oceans boiling, and a mammoth scream rising up from the world itself. Horrible, gripping images, and he'd decided to visit the famous tavern, wanting to better understand how their relatives felt.

"And now you know," his brother mocked.

Ord shrugged, seeing no reason to apologize.

Lyman grimaced, looking outdoors without focusing his eyes. "Just promise that you'll stay where you belong." But before Ord could respond, he added, "*They* tell me that I'm responsible for you babies. *They* say I'm your elder, and is that fair?"

New lungs expanded, the air as clean as medicine. "I'll stay in my room for a million years, if you want."

"Maybe you should," Lyman warned him; then, with that glum assessment, he turned and walked away, ending their discussion before. Ord could spin even larger lies.

The boy climbed from bed, then dressed.

He rode the nearest stairwell to the ground floor. A pair of old bear-dogs greeted him, knowing his scent—tiny olfactory markers meaning *Ord*—and he equitably patted their broad heads, coaxing them to lay back down and nap. The PRIDE AND SACRIFICE sign was above the auxiliary door. He touched it, as always, then turned and jogged out to the stables.

What could he ride? What wouldn't be too easy or dull?

The stables were cavernous, the atmosphere thick with the stink of fresh hay and fungi, blood stews and cultured blubbers. Its animals came from far worlds and the best laboratories—Chamberlain laboratories—and the smartest of them called to Ord, by name, promising long fun rides if only he would feed them. A treat before dinner, please?

His urge to ride faltered, died.

It happened more and more, reliable pleasures lacking their old vitality. Still pleasurable, but more as theories than fact.

Past the stables was an empty pen, a vertical pen, built on a cliff face. Goat-like beasts had lived here eons ago, but the elders got tired of rebuilding the children who would try riding them. The pen was empty, Ord stepping between inert fence posts, looking across a portion of the Chamberlain homeland. Noble mountains and artful deep valleys had been carved from false granites, pink as meat, and every lesser slope was covered with forests and lush emerald pastures. Deciduous trees showed the first hints of autumn. A rushing river passed a kilometer beneath Ord's toes, twisting its way down to a distant and enormous gray-as-steel barrier rising straight into the cloudless sky. The gray portions were hyperfiber, and above were invisible energy barriers, the entire wall bolstered with eagle eyes and AI paranoids. A few decades ago, not long after Alice's trial, strangers had broken into the estates, carrying weapons that couldn't kill any Chamberlain. Yet the wall was built regardless, in a panic, and like anything done in a panic, it was full of flaws. Intended to keep invaders out, it was porous when it came to clever and bored Family children. Yet no one had asked Ord how he had escaped. Either they knew and had already closed the route, or they knew and were keeping it open, booby traps set to catch whomever might try repeating Ord's trick.

Like every Family, this last awful century had terrorized the Chamberlains; but more than others, they deserved their fears.

They were unaccustomed to the sense of menace. It was relentless and unfair. And tiresome. Alice was one of theirs, yes, but there were more than twenty thousand Chamberlains, very few of them—*very few*—involved in the Core's horrible fate. Why blame us? was the general chorus. We aren't Alice; we've accomplished nothing but good for people everywhere. How, how, how can we be blamed for the acts of one odd and possibly senile sister . . . ?

Alice was the most famous Chamberlain. Easily.

She was ancient—a very few generations removed from the patriarch, Ian—and even among Chamberlains, she had been considered remarkable, her talents too numerous to count, vast energies at the ready, and a fierce, unflinching imagination that could never rest. When people of her age and station gathered at the Core, it was Alice who helped inspire them. She revitalized an old idea, asking, "What if we create a *new* universe?" Blending math and mysticism, she showed a workable means. "Do it once to prove the principle, then we can do it a million times again. Everyone can inherit their own universe, their own playground . . . and wouldn't that be lovely?"

Intoxicating, yes. And dangerous.

A prototype universe was produced beside the galaxy's largest black hole, its umbilical held open for too long. The scorching new creation flowed out into its ancient and cold mother universe. Billions of humans and sentient aliens had died in the aftermath, and *would* die, and the galaxy's heart would remain uninhabitable for eons to come.

In a gesture both brave and inadequate, Alice returned home just before her crimes were known. Then she offered herself to the Earth's authorities, ordering them to put her on trial. "Punish me," she demanded, "or let me punish myself. Either way, show people justice, and maybe we can keep our Ten Million Year Peace intact."

Alice's arrival was the worst day in Ord's tiny life. For no clear reason, she had taken an interest in him. When it came to explaining her crimes, he heard them first, in graphic terms, and a century of distractions and new revelations hadn't diluted the shock and misery. Alice had shown him the Core's detonation. She made him grieve for strangers, then fear for himself. In a matter of days, she gave the Chamberlains a new legacy, their name suddenly synonymous with greed, waste, and genocide—every horror they were pledged to combat. And now the Chamberlains and the other Families—the chosen and deservedly proud leaders of their species—hid in their estates, or they traveled with a thousand sophisticated security systems in tow. But where were they safe? Ord wondered. They had billions of angry neighbors on just this one continent, and how many workshops were nuclear-capable? What happened if the planetwide nuke-suppressors were deactivated, then countless crude bombs were thrown over the wall, at once? What if just one of them went unnoticed by the paranoids . . . ?

"Quit," Ord muttered to himself.

He started back into the stables, contemplating choices. There were enemies outside, but there were enemies within, too. Ord knew who had alerted the toastmaster to his presence, and he knew how to prove it. And while he didn't blame the lizard-folk, he felt that this kind of malicious act required a reply. Some sort of reasonable revenge.

He paused before an enormous gate of hyperfiber bars and robot sentries. What lived in the shadows was a minor mystery. A great old sister had left the beast here—no one seemed sure just when—and despite hours of watching, Ord had never gotten one good look at it.

He wasn't looking in there now, thinking hard to himself.

Muttering to himself.

Asking, "How can I punish someone when I can't really hurt them?"

From the shadows, over the sour stink of blood stews, came a tiny voice, close and earnest.

"Let me show you ways," it said.

Then:

"Come closer? Please, please?"

* * *

Half of the Thousand Families took part in the Core's disaster. But that didn't mean sterling innocence for the other five hundred of them.

Nuyens had always known about Alice's work, for instance. They didn't help her, but they would have benefited; and when the worst happened, they were quick to blame, capitalizing on the other Families' sudden weaknesses.

Never loved, Nuyens became the Chamberlains' favorite enemy. That's why the Nuyens didn't like the sight of a Chamberlain boy dragging a home-made bomb to their front door. Security systems had already weighed the risks, taking every responsible precaution. But to emphasize their displeasure, a modest-ranking Nuyen emerged from the nearby earth, growling, "What do you want here? What are you doing?"

"I want to see your brother. I want Xo."

"Your toy is dead," said the dark-haired figure.

With powerful arms, Ord lifted the bomb and dropped it on its trigger. It struck the pink walkway with a harsh *bang*, sparks flying. And he grinned, saying, "I guess it is," while lifting once again.

The Nuyen shook his head in disgust, then reported, "Xo is coming." And he vanished with an intimidating flash and *crack*.

Xo was once a friend, but Ord rarely saw him anymore and never with much pleasure. He had told that Nuyen about his secret trip, but only because Xo was a coward, and Ord wanted to wave Xo's cowardice under his nose. "I found a way out of the estates," Ord had boasted. "Want to come along?"

Never, no.

With a whispered hiss, the door opened. A puzzled adolescent emerged, asking, "Have you gone stark raving, Ord?"

Ord dropped the bomb again.

Xo didn't flinch. He held himself motionless, then took a long, thin breath before asking, "Why? It's not going to work, it never could—"

"It has uranium," Ord countered. "Two kilos of 235."

"But the trigger's shit, and its chemical explosives have been cooked to water and plastic. It can't detonate—"

Bang. Again.

"Atoms vibrate," Ord reminded him. "This way, that way."

Xo had a frail, pitiful face when he wanted it. Watching his one-time friend grunt and lift the bomb again, he said, "So what?"

"The atoms could move toward the same point, all at once."

Xo's eyes grew larger, just a little bit.

"Random vibrations, and they could accidentally reach critical mass."

"Impossible!"

"Possible," Ord replied, "but unlikely." Again he dropped the bomb, sparks flying higher. "Extremely unlikely, but you're worried all the same. Aren't you?"

"No."

"I found your message in the tavern's files. 'The stranger is your sworn enemy—' "

"Lies."

Bang. "Why did you want them to hurt me?"

"You're fine now," Xo observed.

Again Ord flung the bomb into the unyielding stone.

In an almost imperceptible way, Xo flinched.

"I've always tried to be friendly toward you," the Chamberlain argued. "Not like Ravleen and the others."

"What if I did it," said Xo, in a speculative way. "Maybe it's because of your sister, not you. Because Alice made it so we can't leave home, and it wasn't fair that you did—"

Again the bomb struck, etching out a tiny pit.

"How long will you do that?"

"Until it explodes," Ord promised, his voice level and cool. "I'll get more 235 when it goes bad, and I'll stay here for ten billion years, if I have to—"

Xo shuddered and stepped back, closing the useless door and locking it.

The Nuyens tolerated Ord's presence for only a few hours, then sent home a warning wrapped up in concerned words.

Lyman was dispatched to retrieve his baby brother.

A declaration of war, it wasn't. Yet it was *something*, and even as Lyman tried to scold Ord, his gaze acquired a new light, a kind of black wonder, gazing at the youngest Chamberlain as if for the first time.

3

Last night, for an indeterminate period and through some as yet undiscovered means, our prisoner escaped. We cannot determine her whereabouts or agenda. Our questions are being met with amused puzzlement. Alice herself has raised the possibility of a highly selective, infallible amnesia covering those minutes, rendering our interrogations worthless. . . .

The lone positive circumstance is that she hid her escape from casual viewers. The public saw an illusionary Alice, never guessing that she was elsewhere, and free . . .

—Alice's jailer, confidential

The trial had lasted for decades.

Nothing in human history matched its importance, drama, or its ultimate anticlimax, a verdict reached by the fairest possible judicial process—judges and jurors from untainted Families and the best of ordinary humanity—and the sentence was accepted by all, including the criminal. Alice Chamberlain would be stripped of her powers, wealth, and enhanced intelligence. Whatever else remained would be locked inside a tiny cell beneath the Tibetan plateau, the prisoner permitted few contacts with the outside world. And to ensure that the sentence was carried out, people were free to watch Alice on their universal walls, to see her sitting or sleeping, pacing or shitting, her oldfashioned body—calcium bones and a poor woman's minimal immortality— kept thinly clad, always a little cold because of the cell's nearly perfect refrigeration.

A fair verdict, yes; but justice eluded people all the same. Others had taken part in the universe-building nightmare. Some had died heroic deaths, fighting to stop the Core's detonation or save endangered worlds. But what of the rest? What if some of them survived, then refused to follow Alice's example? Plus, there was the issue of civil penalties. Even Alice's wealth was nothing compared to the damages done. Some jurists—nonFamily citizens with modest augmentation—argued that the Thousand Families should make compensations, using some common pool of cash and sorrow. . . .

But what if the Families didn't agree to those terms?

And worst of all, what if the galaxy decided that enough was enough, then tried to wrestle these godlike powers from the chosen few? The Core's little *bang* and misery would be nothing beside *that* conflagration. The Ten Million Year Peace would shatter like crystal, along ancient lines of weakness; and what would happen? How could such a war end?

Alice's trial was finished, and nothing was finished.

That was the only verdict, it seemed. A grain of sand had started down a mountainside, and there was no calculating the shape or scope of the avalanche to come. *, or the ensuing angle of repose.*

Ord was studying, or pretending to study, when he felt a gaze and looked up, discovering the little girl standing in his open doorway. His very first thought was that she was a younger sister. An immature face and body, he noticed. Adult-sized teeth too large for the smiling mouth. Her coppery hair was long and worn simply, and she had a feminine dress ending at her knees, shins pale and feet bare. There was a tangible joy that Ord could taste as well as feel. And she spoke sweetly and quickly, saying, "Come with me, Ord." Saying, "Now. They'll notice I'm gone, hurry!"

He rose and followed, and in an instant he dreamed up a little story to explain her. The eldest Chamberlains, for reasons both simple and complex, had delayed the birth of Ord's little sister. But what if someone hadn't agreed, finding the means to hide a baby girl? She could be living inside the vast mansion, in some secret chamber. And of course she would be interested in her next-older sibling, and shouldn't she want to come see him? Didn't it make perfect, intoxicating sense?

And yet. How could the security systems and watchful elders fail to notice her? And if she was so perfectly protected, then how could such a little girl escape long enough to find Ord—?

He ran on rising stairs, strong legs unable to keep pace. The little girl seemed disappointed, glancing over a shoulder, speaking through her long, thick hair. "I thought you'd be faster by now," she said. Then, "Little Ord."

Only then, with those last words, did Ord realize how far he had climbed and where she was leading him.

His legs locked in place, in terror.

But the stairs kept lifting him, past the intricate, ever-changing murals where the great and glorious Chamberlains reenacted the past. He begged the stairs to stop, but they wouldn't. His escaped little sister was standing on the top landing, facing him, then stepping back and out of sight, and Ord lied to himself, assuring himself that she was just a little girl and that her keepers must have stuck her inside the abandoned penthouse, knowing that no one wanted to go there anymore. . . .

Ord was deposited at the entranceway. The girl was gone, the massive crystal door was ajar, and momentum, not courage, carried him through the chill gap between the slab and jamb.

The room beyond was enormous, hectares of floor beneath a high ceiling, every surface ripped and blackened, sagging portions of the ceiling held up with braces, and old robots who must have been told to stand there and lift, and wait. Ord turned in a circle, with a dancer's grace, remembering how Nuyens and other officials had once come here, seeking Alice. And she wasn't here. But they had demolished the place to make sure, and nobody had taken time to make repairs. A notorious place, and unclean. The perfect place to hide a secret sister, he told himself. Though he didn't believe that story anymore, no matter how elaborate he made it. No matter how sweet it seemed.

"Quit thinking, Ord. Come here."

The red-haired girl stood in the distance, her back to him, and the golden sunlight pouring through a tall window before her. Ord picked his way across the battered floor, barely breathing. She seemed to be looking below, drinking in the great estate—a roar of autumn colors at their height, brilliant shades and tones joining into a vast, fully orchestrated work too large for a boy's eyes, too intricate for even his augmented mind.

Ord would always remember the sight of her, her coppery-red hair, like his, unremarkable against those grand colors. And how the sunlight pierced her dress and revealed her pale new flesh, the body rigorously simple, even plain, sexless and unaugmented, and pure. Why, with everything possible, did she choose that appearance? For the innocence implied? But who knew why Alice did as she did? Not for the first time, Ord doubted that his sister knew all of her reasons. She was too large to understand *herself*, and had always been . . . and what an astonishing, horrifying curse . . . !

Alice turned, in a motion faster than Ord could follow, pushing something small and soft into his hands; and with a desperate near-gasp, she told him:

"You've got to save it! They'll destroy it—!"

What? Destroy what?

"I'm pledged to protect . . . fragile . . . it is . . ."

"Protect *what*?" he blurted.

"Brother Perfect knows. Go find him." The quickest possible smile, then she closed his fingers around her gift. "It will help you—"

"Brother who?"

"I trust you," Alice promised, her voice bleak and untrusting. "And Perfect, too. But nobody else, not anymore." Then she was gone again, never quite seen and already lost; and for a long, confusing while, Ord stared out at the vista—at the brilliant pained colors of dying foliage—almost forgetting how he had come here, barely aware of the heavy little mystery lying invisible in his new hands.

4

Discreet observations of the Chamberlain home have identified five distinct and powerful anomalous events. Two occurred during Alice's escape, probably marking her arrival and subsequent departure. Two others have been linked to an unofficial visit by Chamberlain 63, presumably here on a mission of strategy and espionage. But most peculiar is the oldest anomaly. It was witnessed several years after our observations began—several years after Alice's surrender—and perhaps it signaled the departure of an ancient Chamberlain whose presence was never suspected. Or it could have been an arrival, which leads to certain obvious questions: Who arrived? And on what mission? And what is this secret Chamberlain doing now?

—Nuyen memo, classified

Alice remained imprisoned; Ord could see her, nothing changed about her cell or clothes or even the stiff way she sat on the edge of her simple cot. But it *had* been Alice in the penthouse, or at least some magical, unknown portion of her. Sitting on his own bed, unconsciously mimicking her pose, Ord felt confusion bleeding into fascination, and when three jailers arrived without warning, excitement. The jailers were from three high-grav races, all stout and made more impressive by their black uniforms. One of them gazed up at the camera with an expression struggling to appear in control, at ease. A stiff, formal voice told every viewer, "The prisoner needs to meet with her attorneys, in private. For the next few hours, this line will be terminated. Thank you."

The screen went black, and Ord gave a little gasp.

He wasn't the only Chamberlain watching. An electric murmur passed through the air, pulses marking siblings on the move. From doorless rooms deep inside the mansion came a piercing series of whistles, then an older sister appeared beside Ord's bed, conjuring up a body from light and woven dust, staring at her little brother for what felt like an eternity.

"What's wrong?" Ord asked, surprised to sound so convincingly innocent.

Yet the sister should have seen through him, duplicity bright in his panicky glands and frazzled neurons. And she certainly should have noticed the heavy object on Ord's lap, both thighs depressed by its bulk, its plain oddness sure to set off alarms.

Yet nothing registered in her icebound blue eyes. A pause, a prolonged blink. Then again her brother asked:

"What's wrong?"

"Many things," she assured him. Then, "Have you seen Alice?"

"On the wall."

She glanced at the blackness, appearing puzzled. A little lost.

Ord asked, "Why are the attorneys visiting her?"

The sister straightened her back, then whispered, "They aren't. And there lies the trouble."

He waited.

"We have a report—unconfirmed—that Alice managed to leave her cell for a moment, or two—"

"But she *can't*," Ord sputtered. "She doesn't have that kind of power anymore, does she?"

The sister was eager to agree, and couldn't. "An error. Someone's bad joke, perhaps." Pause. "I wouldn't worry." Pause. "And you say you haven't seen her?"

"No."

"Well, then good day, little one. I am sorry to intrude." And without waiting for his good-byes, she vanished with a sparkle of milky light.

Ord felt alone, and watched. Of course they suspected that Alice might come see him. Yet he wasn't asked about his visit to the penthouse, and the mystery in his lap might as well not exist . . . unless they were thoroughly aware, watching him out of curiosity or caution. But that didn't feel right, did it? For no good reason, Ord sensed that he was as safe as possible, under the circumstances.

What now? he asked himself.

A thousand times, perhaps. And only then did he take hold of the wondrous nothing, examining it in earnest.

Some kind of odd, dark matter, he decided. Its surfaces were imprecise and a little cool, then warm. Its density was rather like gold or lead, and with each touch it seemed to merge with his flesh, for an instant, the sensation like something in a sloppy dream. But when he placed it on his room's ornamental pond, on the slickest, smoothest portion, there wasn't so much as a dimple made, and he could push it back and forth like a balloon, nothing but his own hands aware of its weighty presence.

Natural dark matter didn't exist in this form. Coagulated; tangible. But with sufficient energies and the proper cleverness, it was possible to make the wild particles behave, make them cling to one another and act like normal trusted baryonic matter. These were great technologies, Ord knew. They were the basis for much of his siblings' magic, and nobody understood their limits. Since dark matter was ninety-nine-percent of everything—existing in a multitude of useful flavors—there was hope that someday, when necessary, it would prove even more useful than the prosaic stuff that made stars and simple people.

With care, Ord caressed the gift, fingers discerning tiny crenelations, his mind's eye building an improving picture. But what it resembled . . . well, it seemed unlikely at best. A tightly folded cerebral cortex, the underside cerebellum, and the ancient medulla; it was a brain of the oldest kind, human in proportions but nothing like the modern form. Even the lizard-folk, poor as possible, had fancier and tougher versions of the ancestral brains. Fatty flesh and acetylcholine vanished with hundred-year life spans and mental imbalances. Why would Alice give him such a relic? But of course it wasn't a relic, he realized. It was as modern in substance as possible, and what did that imply?

An affinity for Ord's flesh, and its shape could be a clue, he thought. Several times. But when he acted on that idea, he was shocked to find it valid. The mysterious nothing liked his scalp and began to burrow, exotic particles swirling around the bland ones, passing through flesh and the hyperfiber skull, moving just the right amount, then pausing and aligning themselves, linking in a multitude of ways with Ord's own astonished mind.

An image appeared before him.

Fuzzy, but immediately identifiable.

"Am I supposed to go there?" he asked. No answer was offered. Ord put on hiking boots, then noticed a second pair of boots where he had found the first pair. Using the stairwell, he passed between a dozen siblings—modest-ranked Chamberlains wearing frightened, flushed expressions—and he was even less noticed than usual. Which was a good thing, since he was forbidden from leaving the mansion, in punishment for the bomb nonsense. The old bear-dogs at the door might have noticed something when he touched them, scratching their broad heads until sleeping tails began to thump-thump against the footworn stone floor. Then, sensing something too substantial to be a premonition, Ord touched the PRIDE AND SACRIFICE sign, not once but twice, never certain if what he felt was real or an illusion.

He ran when he was outdoors, eschewing tube cars out of caution. It was a good hour's journey, most of it downhill. Wild birds didn't startle into flight when he passed them. Water splashed and the earth dimpled under him, but each backward glance showed him a smooth brook and muddy banks without a single bootprint. Ord was a ghost, it seemed. He was exactly like his elderly siblings, composed of nothing but thought, and it frightened him, and it seemed fun . . . yet he couldn't make himself hesitate for a moment, much less ask himself if this was what was right . . . whatever it *was* that he was doing. . . .

A child's clubhouse stood on the border of the Sanchex and Chamberlain estates, in a dead-end valley. Built with lumber by boys and girls barely old enough to swing hammers, it had stood empty for almost a century, the Golds disbanded not long after Alice's arrival. That was natural, the children too old for the club's games. Yet a new generation should have come and burned this structure with an appropriate solemnity, then built their own. It hadn't happened because every Family, in view of the times, had delayed their next generations; and the old place had fallen into a dishonorable entropy, its roof collapsing, its wooden floor buckling, and the childlike signatures on the far wall becoming soft and imprecise with many species of rot.

Ord barely saw his own name, second in rank.

Below Ravleen's, of course. Sanchexes *always* led the Golds.

He was looking for Xo's signature when a badger emerged from a hole in the floor, its thick, low body reminding him of a jailer's, a sudden *hiss* aimed straight for him. It could see him, obviously. And he growled in turn, causing it to slip out the back door, toward what should have been a high raw wall of slick granite. But the wall had vanished, replaced with a long valley and a meandering brook, plus trees not as tall as seemed right, or as broad, or generally as healthy, their leaves in autumnal colors too, but all too drab and haphazard to belong in a Chamberlain wood.

"Hello?" Ord called.

Birds flew in terror. Save for some kind of jaybird that perched on a high branch, cursing Ord for trying to steal its acorns.

"Hello?"

No human answered.

A narrow dung-marked game trail led across the brook, and here he made deep bootprints that filled with swirling brown water. Now and again he shouted, "Hello!" A noisy indifference filled the woods. Finally Ord thought to say, "I'm looking for someone," and then, "Brother Perfect," and his answer came in the form of a skin-clad figure stepping from the shadows, almost from underfoot.

"And who is doing this looking?" the figure asked.

He was a Chamberlain, Ord saw. No telling which brother, but he felt disappointment and a jumble of doubts.

"And if you don't know who *you* are," the brother continued, "maybe you can remember who *sent* you here. How about it, my boy?"

He was Ord, and nobody sent him, he claimed. The brother appeared shorter than him, but stocky in a strong, comfortably fattened way, his red hair matted and tied into a ponytail, a thin red-and-snow beard obscuring the famous Chamberlain jaw. It wasn't an impressive body, conjured or not. But the trousers and heavy vest were remarkable, made from sewn skins and mended with dirty lengths of gut and hemp. A leather belt held several elegant stone tools. One pale hand held a spear by its blond shaft, its long Folsom point drawing pointed stars in the air between them.

"And who are you?" asked Ord.

"You wanted someone named Perfect. Maybe that's me."

But no Chamberlain had that name. It would be cruel to saddle their own with such an outrageous boast—

"You know every name, do you?"

"In order of birth, yes. And I know a little of everyone's biography."

"What a gruesome waste!" The Stone Age figure broke into a laugh, shaking his head in a blurring motion. "Which anal-retentive child of Ian dreamed up that waste of neural capacities?"

Ord couldn't guess who.

The brother cursed, laughed, and said, "So you're the Baby."

"Pardon?"

"The Baby. That's your nickname." A pause. "Are you familiar with the concept of nicknames—?"

"*Yes.*"

"Then I've given you enough of a clue. Come. Hurry on now, Baby."

Ord tried to ask where he was, where they were going, and why the woods looked wrong. But the brother, whoever he was, had walked away, bulling his way through the tangled landscape. Ord had to run in pursuit, catching him as they splashed across the brook. "Is Perfect a nickname?"

"Oftentimes." The left hand gestured, its two smallest fingers missing, the wagging stumps showing no sign of regrowth. "Have you ever known someone you'd like to call Perfect?"

Maybe.

"To make them angry, of course. Am I right?"

Ord ignored the question. "I deserve to know where we are—"

"In the estate, of course. Embedded inside the granite." He kicked and stomped his way through a wall of vegetation, thorns leaving bloody sketches on his exposed arms. "A clever little house of mine, don't you think?"

"Why am I here?"

"No, Baby. It's my turn to ask the question."

He hated that name.

"Humans," said the brother, "have lived for twenty million years. As apes, then as simple souls. And finally, less simple. But now, if you were pressed to decide, when would you claim that we had reached our peak? Our grand climax? Today, perhaps? Last week? When?"

"Who are you?"

A sideways glance and grin, then the brother stepped through a wall of golden leaves, branches rushing back into place, conspiring to make him vanish.

Ord hesitated, wondering if he should flee.

From behind the leaves, a deep, rough Chamberlain voice said, "Humans. Peak. Give a shot, Baby!"

Stepping through the wall, Ord saw an abrupt hillside and a simple cave worn into its face. The rocks weren't false granite; they were limestone. The limestone was encrusted with fossilized crinoids, thousands of the flowery animals laid into the fine, dead sediments. This was a caveman's camp, the air stink of old fires and tainted game, and the brother seemed at home, setting his spear against the cave's broad mouth, then turning to say:

"My given name? It is Thomas. Thomas Chamberlain."

No. Impossible . . . !

"And since you won't guess, I'll tell you my choice for our species' crowning moment." Thomas laughed easily, then said, "They were the final years of the final Ice Age, when we were expanding across new continents and wild, unmapped seas." Another laugh. "You look doubtful, Baby. But consider this: There weren't many of us, and each of us was important. A few million modified apes, each of us armed with stone and wood, and our cunning, and our mobile little cultures . . . and we came to rule the entire green world . . . !"

Trembling, Ord stared at his ancient brother.

"And you know what the world was then, don't you?" A quick, disarming smile. "It was the universe. It was *everything*. A vast globe encompassing every imaginable beauty, and it was set inside a sea of ink and tiny, unimaginable stars. And it was *ours*." A wave of the maimed hand. Then, "Do you know my opinion? All the history since, every human venture . . . everything has been one long and frustrating and absurd attempt to regain those glory days!"

And with that pronouncement, Thomas broke into a thunderous laugh, a

sudden rain of golden leaves falling on them, then swirling, vainly fighting
the urge to settle, to die.

5

Alice gave me that lance of a nickname.

I was a new adult, proud of my augmentation and promise, and she
was a very young, relentlessly mouthy child. I would talk at length about
all the good I would be doing—for the Family; for all people; for all
time—and she'd growl at me. She would say, "Oh, you think you're
the perfect Chamberlain. The very best. But you're the same as us,
brother. Brother Perfect. Oh, yes, you are. You are, you are . . . !"

—Perfect, in conversation

Alice—the great and infamous and bankrupt sister—was the twelfth Chamberlain. Ord, in contrast, was the twenty-four thousand, four hundred and
eleventh pearl on the string. And he knew that Thomas was Ian's eighth
clone, meaning his designation was Nine, which in turn meant that he was
almost exactly as old as Alice and Ord combined. If this was indeed Thomas,
of course. Which seemed a preposterous idea, a thousand history lessons recalled in an instant, and this skin-clad figure nothing like any of them.

Chamberlains were terraformers, by and large. But Thomas was an oddity
who built little but loved to explore—a godlike wanderer whose passion and
genius were to find and befriend new alien species.

Uninterested in alliances of trading links, Thomas left those blessings for
others. The bloodless Nuyens, for instance. By the time Nuyens would flock
to some newly charted system, eager for technologies and clear profits, Thomas would have struck out into the wilderness again, chasing radio squawks
and free oxygen signatures until he found another wondrous species. Or found
nothing. Because as any halfway educated person knew, intelligence arose
infrequently in the universe, and imperfectly, and judging by the assorted
war-killed worlds, it was a fundamentally perishable form of life, too.

But the Milky Way had been explored in full now, from its Core to its
faint far ends, and Thomas had gone elsewhere. "You're exploring the An-
dromeda Galaxy," Ord told the caveman. "The Families sent a mission. They
left more than a million years ago."

"They left, but did *I?*" The brother chuckled.

Ord said nothing.

"The truth? At the last possible instant, I suffered a chaotic change of
desire. Instead of embarking on a great adventure, I decided to chase privacy
and self-reflection. Which is my right as a sentient organism, and don't give
me that disappointed glare."

He didn't know he was glaring, stumbling into an apology—

—and Thomas interrupted him, every affront forgotten. A cackling laugh
was followed by an offer of meat, dried and hard and frosted with limestone
grit. "Mammoth," he warned. "Chew harder," he advised. Then, "What's
wrong? Doesn't the flavor intrigue?"

Not even a little, no. But Ord made himself eat, as if to prove something. When the last gob of leather was in his belly, dissolving in acids and micro-chines, Ord felt the confidence to say, "I don't believe you are Thomas."

"And why not?"

"I've been around Alice, and this doesn't feel the same. Being with you, I mean." There wasn't the sense of vast energies and intellect, though Ord mentioned neither quality by name. Nor did he say that Thomas looked bizarre and acted the same, laughing too often and never twice with the same sound, the oddest things amusing him without fail.

Like Ord's doubts, for instance.

The brother turned red-faced, laughing for a solid minute. Then he gasped, coughed into his maimed hand, and asked, "How is dear Alice? Is her trial just about finished?"

"You don't know?"

"On the whole," he confessed, "current events bore me."

Incredulous, Ord couldn't summon any response.

"My guess is that they found her guilty."

"Yes."

"Good for them." The smile was winsome, bittersweet. "I told her, told her, *told* her not to fuck around with that nasty work. But you've met our sister. You know how she can be—"

"She's jailed. They've stripped her of everything."

"As is right," said the possible Thomas.

"But then she escaped—I don't know how—and came to see me . . . !"

Delight shone in the blue-gray eyes. "And she wants your help, does she? Some conjured chore just for you?"

"I have to save something. I don't know what." A long pause, then he added, "Brother Perfect is supposed to help me."

"Oh, is he?"

Ord nodded, not certain how to respond.

"Alice appears out of nothingness, expecting obedience." A grimace, a leering smile. "What they should have carved off our sister are her bossy pretenses, I think."

Perhaps so.

"Can you give me one good guess as to your mission?"

"Don't you know?" Ord asked, in horror.

Thomas stepped closer, his maimed hand lifting, touching the boy on the temple, the whole fingers dipping into his scalp for a chilling instant. Then, with a slow, careful voice, he asked, "Do you wish to help, or don't you? Yes or no." A pause. "*Yes* and we embark. *No* and I send you straight home."

"Embark to where?"

"All things considered, not far."

Ord saw a cracked tooth in the narrow smile. "I want to help," he confessed. Then, "If it accomplishes something good—"

"Tell me yes, tell me no. I'll leave the worthiness for others."

Ord said, "Yes."

He said it three times, his voice strengthening, acquiring something that resembled confidence. And Thomas began turning with the first *yes*, vanishing into his cave without a sound or a backward glance.

Ord followed.

Thomas was working in the gloomy half-light. The cave walls were adorned with charcoal bison and ochre ponies. Ord touched one of the stiff-legged ponies, deciding that with the same tools he would be at least as good a painter as his brother.

Thomas was cramming gear into a leather knapsack, no room left for the smallest charm. With a creaking of rope and skin, he lifted the pack to his shoulders, making adjustments, grimacing with conviction as he remarked, "You're better than me at many things, I suppose."

Like Alice, he could read a boy's mind.

Waving his injured hand, he said, "See? No new fingers growing."

The stumps were blunt and calloused, all right.

"You could make them if you wanted," Ord objected.

"Ah, but then I'd forget to be careful when I find a dire wolf hanging in one of my snares." A wink. "Scars are reminders, Baby. They remind me that dire wolves can be tricky bastards."

An adult Chamberlain—any adult—could look inside an animal, measuring its health and intentions. Particularly if the animal was part of an elaborate illusion built by that adult. But what adult wanted to live inside an ugly cave, much less hunt with snares and spears? Ord's best guess was that this caveman existence helped mask Thomas's presence inside the estates.

"Perfect," said his brother, again reading thoughts. "That's Alice's name for me, and it's good enough for us."

A blink and nod. Then Ord said, "Then I'm not Baby."

"Fair enough." And with that Perfect walked into the sunshine, at a brisk pace, grabbing his spear and singing with a loud, out-of-key wail.

Ord followed, ignoring the landscape. It was all an illusion, and he assumed they were walking toward someplace close—as promised—and answers would come in short order. He barely noticed his brother's sour songs, concentrating on his excuses for disappearing. Imagining Lyman, he tried half a dozen stories, each involving the old clubhouse. He had sneaked off to meet a girlfriend; why not? He'd already had a variety of adolescent affairs, mostly with friends from the Golds. Wasn't that kind of subterfuge permitted, even encouraged? For a long happy while, Ord imagined meeting Ravleen at the clubhouse. Sanchexes were great warriors and inspired lovers, it was said, and he practiced his lustful daydream until it tasted real, until there was a hint of boredom clinging to it.

Thomas—*Perfect*, he reminded himself—took them up a mountainside, through trees noticeably shorter, and barer, as the afternoon passed. The summit was sharp and raw, no mansion built upon it. They climbed past a single greenish boulder, then dropped into a grove of blue-black spruces. With stone tools they cut boughs for bedding. With flint and dried wood they made a sputtering fire, and Perfect held his imperfect hands to it, catching some portion of its tiny heat.

Ord asked why he lived this way. "You sing out of key. You don't paint particularly well. And you get cold." He listed the items as if they were symptoms of disease. "And you won't even regenerate a simple finger, will you?"

"I'm not cold," Perfect protested. "And when I am, I'll pull my robe out of my pack."

Ord was comfortable. As the sun set, his flesh generated its own internal fire. Yet he held his hands to Perfect's fire, remarking, "Alice wouldn't live this way."

A laugh, insane and infuriating.

Then, "From what you've said, Alice might be thrilled to live this well now."

That wasn't what Ord meant, and both knew it.

"Let me tell you about our dear sister." Perfect pulled dried meat from his pack, offering none to Ord. "Every fancy skill, every energy source, all that godly garb . . . Alice wanted them. Always, always. Everyone's that way, in their fashion. But she's about the worst, and I'd like to think, with a good Chamberlain modesty, that I'm the best. I acquire only those talents that I absolutely need, and if I'm wrong, I give them away again. To Alice, in some cases."

"Augmenting your voice . . . is that too fancy . . . ?"

"Oh, I sing, and I like singing. I just do it badly." Another laugh while he chewed on the inedible mammoth. "Everything I do I do with joy and within my limits, and that's all I want."

"But you didn't even know about the trial," Ord complained.

"If something truly important happens, I'll hear about it." A little wink. "But you're right, I'm not tied to the universal networks. And I don't know ten million languages. My mathematics are useful, no more. My senses are good enough, no more. And my strengths fit the job of the moment." A soft, slow laugh, then he added, "In case you haven't noticed, my humor is simple. Maybe even a little crude. Which suits my needs fine, thank you."

But why? Ord kept thinking. Why are you different?

"My moment of enlightenment?" Perfect waited for his brother's eyes, then said, "Eons ago, I was sitting beside an alien sea, in my best godly fashion, and this fellow happened to stroll past me. Do you know about the Brongg?"

Bipeds, vaguely fishlike. A home world with methane seas and water-ice continents. They were the oldest known intelligent species, and Brother Thomas was the first human to meet them.

"Very good," the caveman offered, giving a little chuckle. "Anyway, this little fellow was walking Brongg-fashion, meaning syrupy-slow. When he saw me, he gave me greetings and stopped to chat—the Brongg are great talkers— and eventually I learned his identity. He was famous. Ancient beyond belief. I was a baby, barely a million years old, and of all the creatures I have ever met, he seemed the most genuinely happy. A billion years of happiness walking on the beach, carrying nothing but a simple ice lance—he was fishing, Ord—and I've always held that lesson very close to my heart."

They were a cold, cold species, Ord knew. The Brongg had wondrous technologies, but they did little with them. They traveled sparingly, reproduced slowly, and were as alien and bizarre as anything humans had ever found. How could they bring enlightenment?

Perfect didn't answer that thought. Rising, he pulled the promised robe from his pack, the fur rich and glossy, sewn together from smaller furs with a certain artless skill.

"Why did you come back to the Earth?"

His brother lay down beside the fire, a bent arm serving as a pillow. "I was asked to come," he muttered. "Someone appeared without warning, gave me my marching orders, then framed it as a request before she vanished again."

Alice.

Perfect gave a sleepy nod, eyes beginning to close.

But before he could sleep, or whatever state it was, he heard one last question from a confused little brother. "Are we still in the estates? Because I'm forbidden to leave them—"

"Watch the sky," Perfect advised.

Ord obeyed, his heated breath rising toward the night's first stars. They were the right stars in the right places, but where were the planets? And the starships coming and going? Glancing to his left, he saw the green boulder on the summit become a smooth green globe, and the mountain beneath it evaporated, and the stars brightened and multiplied in the sudden vacuum . . . and a thousand lessons in terraforming told Ord what he was seeing.

Gazing at the green world, he whispered, "Neptune."

Against all reason, in one afternoon he and Perfect had hiked their way to the chilled edge of the solar system.

6

You will be stripped of possessions, money and mind, and each of your works will be assessed on a case-by-case basis. Worlds terraformed in good faith, by legal means, will be spared. But illegal worlds will be sought out and destroyed by whatever means are deemed humane. . . .
—from Alice's sentencing

Ord watched Neptune, wonderstruck by its presence. Because it was genuine, he sensed. No illusions involved. This was the modern Neptune, terraformed in increments by many people, including Chamberlains.

Including Alice, in her youth.

Technical details buoyed up out of his augmented memory. Small gas giants of this class had their volatile gases shattered, hydrogen sequestered inside the deep core while metals and silicates were pulled up in its place. Airborne continents were grown, floating on giant vacuum bubbles. The new atmosphere was nitrogen and helium, sweet oxygen, and the vital trace gases. Light and heat came from fusion, each world capable of fending for itself. An area many times Earth's was made habitable, at a profit; and with modern methods, an Alice-class human could finish the essential work in less than five thousand years.

Why were they here? he asked himself.

What was special about Neptune?

But despite his questions and the lousy bed, Ord felt himself drifting off to sleep, dark and dreamless, then woke when the blunt end of a spear was jabbed into his ribs.

"Time to leave," said a distant voice, with urgency. "They know you're missing, and you're making them afraid."

The sky was cobalt blue, another false sun washing away the stars. Ord rose, attempting to ask every question that he had thought up last night. Words came in a rush, then he faltered. Then Perfect was walking and Ord was walking beside his brother, step for step; and a sensation, bizarre and indescribable, made him mutter, "What's happened to me?"

"You've been altered, a bit. Alice began the work, and I did some tinkering last night." The profile was weathered, sober. "We've rebuilt you as quickly as possible, under these circumstances—"

"What's wrong with me?"

"If you're like me, nothing." A bleak, oversized laugh. "The truth? Part of you is a starship. You're built from dark matter and magic, and your engines are an exotic inertialess drive. Your hull is invisible, we can hope. Legs and lungs, and your skin, are projections based on your own expectations." A second smaller laugh. "Despite appearances, we're actually moving at very nearly lightspeed."

Ord snapped, "I don't believe you."

"That's probably best, all things considered."

For an instant, Ord felt the man speaking to him in many voices, most of them in convoluted technical languages that some new, unexpected part of him ingested without fuss, without hesitation. But what made him panic was the sudden sensation of his true self: Huge and ghostly, suffused with liquid energies beyond almost any human's experience.

He tried to walk slower, and couldn't.

"For the moment," said Perfect, "I will operate your legs."

Ord crossed nonexistent arms on his facsimile chest. "I want to know where we're going."

Perfect squinted, as if he could see their destination. In the illusion, they were marching down a verdant mountainside, birds and other phantoms calling out as they passed.

"This is illegal," the boy gasped.

"Immoral," his brother agreed. "And cruel. And dangerous, too." That brought genuine pleasure, bubbling and warm. "But when a famous criminal came to you, did you tell the authorities? When she slipped you a mysterious object, did you say, 'Look here, everyone! Look what Alice gave me!'?"

Ord was weeping. Sobbing.

"For now," said Perfect, "we're traveling to the Oort cloud."

"Then where?"

"Let's reach the cloud first," his brother replied. "That way, if you're caught, you can claim to have been kidnapped—"

"I am kidnapped!"

"Good attitude. Keep it up."

Ord never would have agreed if he'd known . . . if he'd been given any hint of what was involved . . . crimes accomplished, grave danger implied. . . . an insane journey away from the safety and comfort of home . . . !

A five-fingered hand patted Ord on the back.

"You would have balked, yes. But out of fear and ignorance. That's why I framed the question as I did: 'Do you wish to help?' You do or you don't, and both of us know you do. You can't help but want to help, which is an honored old Chamberlain curse."

The boy tried to collapse. And couldn't. He felt limp, half-dead and wracked with miseries, uttering a great long sob before asking the perfectly reasonable question:

"Why me?"

"My question too." A weighty pause, then another useless pat on the back. "Perhaps Alice wants you because you're the baby. Perhaps it's as simple as that."

Ord barely heard him, his mind collapsing in on itself.

"We Chamberlains love closure, that sense of being *done*. That's why we build exceptional worlds. Durable, full-bodied biospheres equal to three billion years of raw evolution."

What was he saying?

"The last Chamberlain is sent on a great mission by one of the first." Perfect clucked his tongue but didn't laugh. "It's closure, and it feels right, and maybe that's all there is to that. Despite its source, the decision could be that simple."

They crossed billions of kilometers, and the country, befitting some odd logic, grew colder and drier, forests replaced with open steppe populated with herds of extinct game. Giant bison and woolly mammoths grazed beneath a weakening sun. In the distance, looming like mountains, was a blue-white glacial mass. Sometimes Ord noticed human hunters in the distance, some of them walking, some standing in one place, watching. Watching for us, he suddenly realized. They were symbols meant to mark other ships, but even the nearest of them couldn't find the brothers.

Ord quit weeping, forcing himself out of self-pity. In a choking voice, he asked, "Why do you travel this way?"

"In ancient times," said Perfect, "travelers onboard steamships and starships would pin photographs and holos to their cabin walls. To remind them of comfortable places, of course. To give their eyes something other than empty water and space."

Ord found himself listening, glad for the voice.

"Space bores me," said his incredible brother. "Hard vacuums and the ancient cold play on my nerves, if you want the truth."

Ord felt the vacuum surrounding him. It was a thin chill stew of virtual particles, and it felt like a light winter breeze.

He asked, "How long were you hiding in the estate?"

"I followed Alice home from the Core, a few years afterward."

"Because she wanted you to come? Is that the only reason?"

A mild, quiet laugh, a wisdom implied. "You aren't the only person whom our sister has bewitched."

Questions, like virtual particles, appeared out of nothing.

And vanished again.

"I've known Alice for almost my entire life." Perfect paused, waiting for his brother's eyes. "I don't need much prompting from her. For a lot of reasons, I behave."

"If you were at the Core," Ord remarked, "you could have been helping."

"Help build that universe? Hardly." A hard chuckle. "The Core is a big place, and I wasn't with her. I was living in seclusion between Alice and your front door."

"But you knew what she was doing—?"

"And fought with her when she came to visit." A black expression, sour and wild-eyed. "Oh, I fought. I augmented myself with every persuasive skill, and when they failed, I threatened her. As if that could do any good."

Each step took them closer to the high glacial wall. Between them and the ice was a low moraine, moss and lichen growing wherever there was shelter. As they climbed the loose slope, their feet destroyed oases and created new ones. With a quiet voice—a hunter's voice—Perfect asked:

"Do you wonder what they did with Alice's powers?"

They had been stripped away. Of course.

"But what does that mean?" Perfect posed the question, then gave an answer. "Powers have physical sources. Augmented minds need neural nets. Moving a world requires godly power. And there are the machines that crack molecules and weave dark matter and build bodies and tear them down again, in an instant." The healthy hand took Ord by the arm, then squeezed. "I'm talking about Alice's body and mind. Her bolts and microchines. And her antimatter-digesting guts, too."

"I've wondered about them," the boy confessed.

"A grand secret, they are. And a wrenching problem for the poor officials who need to decipher them, then destroy them."

They reached the moraine's crest as the sun set behind them. A day done; a comforting sense of closure. Perfect dropped his knapsack and sat on it, eating his endless dried meat, gladly sharing it with the boy when he asked for another taste.

Without daylight, the world shrank, darkness giving the tundra a close, constricting feel. But the ice seemed to grow, becoming glassy, some subtle inner light betraying networks of fine cracks and deep fissures. Tiny, tiny humans stood at its base. Each held a spear, but Ord realized that spears meant weapons of a different kind; and in a whisper, Perfect said:

"That creature you met? Our Alice? As powerful as a sun, if the need arose. But when she arrived from the Core, at lightspeed, she had no mass. She was a set of instructions that then had to conjure up her physical self. She used raw materials kept in and around the solar system, kept for just such contingencies." A pause as he bit off another predatory hunk. "Most of Alice—the bulk of her memories, her skills—came later, and not quite at lightspeed. That's how we true giants travel. Think of it like a strange snowfall coming from the Core, snowflakes the size of houses and mountains, each one meaning some potent talent, and all of them here. Here, Ord. Collected and held. Waiting for someone to get the courage to crack them open and see what there is to see."

Bright, hard stars appeared above them, then below, flares of soft blue plasma slipping through the glacier's deep fractures. This was Alice's dangerous meat, and it was larger than some worlds—

"A morgue, in essence." The Chamberlain voice was close, softer than any whisper. "Keep still. Keep very still now."

The moraine had vanished. Ord was in freefall.

"Do you feel sleepy, maybe?"

The boy felt extraordinarily tired.

"Good. Try closing your eyes."

But before he could, Ord said, "Closure," with a numbed mouth.

"What was that?"

"That's this," he muttered. "That's why she came home. She knew what would happen, and she deserved it."

Perfect touched him with a thousand hands, and laughed. "Do you know what I like best about humans? How we take whatever happens and dress it up in any suit of clothes we want, for any occasion." The hands were hotter than suns, soothing to the touch. And intensely busy. "Maybe you're right. Maybe closure explains this whole fucking mess."

A distant black laugh, then:

"A poetic denouement, and she couldn't help herself."

Then:

"A moth, and with the Core she conjured up the perfect flame."

7

The boy's disappearance went unnoticed for several critical hours. Had Alice escaped, and was it Alice inside her prison cell? Those seemed to be the major questions of the moment. Sensors were placed in a diagnostic mode, perhaps explaining why no new anomalous event was observed. Then the Chamberlains learned that the boy was gone, his subterfuge too advanced to be his own work. A general alarm was sounded. Gravimetric evidence pointed to a new mass orbiting Pluto. Warnings were sent to the appropriate Nuyens, and nothing was found. But afterward, several Families reported thefts from their Neptune reserves. . . .

Despite prompt action, the Oort cloud facility was infiltrated . . . properties were stolen. . . .

Analysis proceeding with all available tools. . . .
The boy is being sought. . . .

—Nuyen memo, confidential

It was like waking from death again.

A voice. Chamberlain, and male. From the living world, he said, "The Brongg homeworld. Picture it. Walk it with me. A long, gentle beach of water-ice sands, a sea of liquid methane on our left, and on our right—"

"The Iron Spine." Ord knew the beach. A thousand eyes seemed to open for him, only two of them mired in his own face. It was another illusion, but of superior quality. He was upright, wearing a new body. Slowly, very slowly, he turned his head until the Iron Spine filled his gaze. Before the first vertebrate evolved on earth, the Brongg had lowered a nickel-iron asteroid onto their world, setting it on a bed of vacuum bubbles. Half a billion years of mining had left it partially hollow, but the remnants were spectacular, floating on the water-ice crust, their flanks covered with blue-black vegetation that was adapted to the bitter taste of heavy metals.

The weak Brongg sun was rising above the highest peak. A Brongg day lasted for a full Terran month, Ord recalled, and with that fact came a multitude of ancillary facts and details, making him the helpless expert. "Today," Perfect announced, "we will walk a beach."

The beach was gray with black organic streaks, and it was as smooth as pavement, curving out toward a rocky point where a polished black cylinder stood on end, casting a long shadow across the calm and colorless sea. The distances looked trivial, yet with his first painful step, he realized this would be difficult at best. The Brongg nervous systems were built from superconducting materials, thoughts flowing without resistance, without turbulence; but their physical metabolisms were sluggish, each physical act considered and reconsidered thousands of times before it was attempted, or not.

"Perhaps," said Perfect, "that's why they've lasted so long. Unlike people, they have to think before they step. . . ."

Turning his head was a struggle—a sobering investment—and it took most of a stride. Perfect was a Brongg in body, like Ord. A nude, fishy exterior wore thick legs and broad, round feet, and his webbed hands held a delicate ice lance. But the face was comically Chamberlain, blue eyes winking, the human mouth grinning at the world.

"In all," asked Perfect, "how many genuine living intelligences have I found first? Count them for me, please."

The voice was a radio pulse born from the swift nervous system. In an instant, Ord saw each of his brother's discoveries, oldest to newest. One hundred and three species on almost as many worlds. No human could claim half as many finds. True, most were technology-incompetent. But almost two dozen, the Brongg included, had been deemed worthy of diplomats and trade, cultural exchanges, and scientific ones, too.

"Now," said Perfect, "count the failed worlds."

Again, Ord knew the exact number. Memories encoded in a tireless net flowed into him. He saw Perfect tracking whispers through a wilderness of stars. Some whispers vanished, some grew stronger, but all ended at some technological world or worlds, all freshly killed. Wars had done it, mostly. Sometimes plagues. Experiments and machines had gone amuck, or a battered ecosystem had collapsed back to the microbes. Nothing with which to speak, save the occasional computer or some automated station that still watched the sky and shouted, begging the stars for help, for alliances, for second chances, for God.

Counting was easy; remembering took an age.

Images like fists struck Ord, leaving him spent and sore, and sorry.

And Perfect had suffered even more. Hopes ruined each time; nothing but wreckage left. Armed with a Chamberlain's skills, he would sift through the gruesome traces—bones and burnt cities and records—then he would build phantoms of the dead, complete with voices and desires, and the telling flaws. These examples gave insights. Perfect could ask the phantoms why and how they had so willingly pushed their homes and selves into oblivion. Forty-eight worlds, Ord counted, plus hundreds more where life began, evolved to some sophisticated, promising level, only to be shattered by a comet's splash or the detonation of a nearby sun. And as he stared at that carnage, Ord asked the obvious:

"How does any intelligence survive?"

"Exactly. Exactly!" A familiar laugh, if somewhat bleak, then Perfect took another agonizing step, ice-sands dimpling beneath the bare right foot. "The Brongg are the elders, but they had it easy. Their solar system has few fissionable materials, and they're pathologically introspective. Even when they could have augmented themselves, boosting their physical selves, they didn't. Wouldn't. Out of fear more than wisdom, I think. Too many uncertainties regardless of how long they rolled the Sisyphean problem back and forth in their heads."

The Brongg were cold, slow, and scarce. The truth told, Ord had never admired them, and he wasn't about to start now.

"And at the other end of the spectrum, or near it, are humans. Churning, hot whirlwinds, passionate to a fault, aggressive to no good ends, and alive now only because we scared ourselves into wisdom. Terrible wars led to the Families and the Great Peace, and our little truce has lasted quite a while, I think. As long as everyone was happy, who cared who rowed the damned boat?"

A great long laugh. Electric, chilling.

"Millions of years," said Perfect, "and I've studied the dead and the living. Now doesn't it make sense that I'd find patterns? Relationships? Little tendencies, and the big fat ones?"

Ord had to agree.

"Tendencies," Perfect repeated. "And out of them, conclusions. How I would invent life from nothingness, given my chance? The best of the Brongg, the bedrock of ourselves. All put into a stew with every other successful species, in some realm pure and innocent—"

"And perfect," Ord said, anticipating the words.

"And now, brother, you know why Alice renamed me. I have the wicked flaw of needing to chase perfection."

Trying to guess the next stage, Ord mentioned the odd, illegal worlds that Alice had built. Not terraformed, but alien. Novel proteins and toxic solvents, all had built to mimic natural worlds.

"Ordinary, ordinary worlds," was Perfect's assessment.

"How can you say it? She broke every law to make them, and she hid them away in dust clouds and globular clusters—"

"And I am telling you that these worlds are fundamentally traditional. I agree, yes, Alice went into the kitchen and made strange muffins, but the muffins have the ingredients you'd expect in a kitchen. Which made me ask: 'Where is your genius, Alice? Why that silly pride?' "

"You said that to Alice?"

"For the last few thousand centuries, yes. And she would say that if I was so clever, I should do better. 'With your help,' I would promise. Not being a superior terraformer, I needed hands trained for the big dull ugly labor of it. And eventually she agreed to help, just this once, surprising both of us, I believe."

Ord felt a sudden chill, a premonition.

"Where are we going?" he asked. "Tell me, please."

Perfect showed him an enormous smile, then gestured with vegetable slowness, his ice lance held in his left hand, two of the Brongg's minor fingers missing. "Down the beach," he replied, not quite laughing. "We're walking beside the sea, and it looks as if we're halfway there . . . can't you see . . . ?"

Halfway, and the weak little sun was directly overhead, black-red clouds of hydrocarbons forming in the upper atmosphere, a chill shadow falling over them and the flat, rather greasy sea. Two weeks of walking, yet it seemed longer. A few words spoken, but Ord had absorbed volumes of information, the pace relentless, its quality and the demands beyond his experience, his expectations. And it never stopped, Perfect's memories pouring into him even as his brother remarked, "I wish there was more time, Ord. I do."

Why wasn't there?

"Because we're being pursued. Hounds on our heels, if you will."

Ord looked over a shoulder, the alien neck as pliable as an owl's. The beach was empty save for a willowy creature walking in the shallow methane, jabbing with claws, in slow motion, and managing to impale an eel-like creature even more sluggish than itself.

"How fast are we moving?"

"In space," Perfect replied, "just a whisper under lightspeed."

"Why not lightspeed?"

"Because. This is fast enough. Our destination isn't equipped to receive us as a rain of massless particles. And since you deserve to know, it's because we have some possessions that need to be carried as they are, and I'm not allowed to say more, and I wish it were otherwise, Brother. I genuinely do."

A powerful dread was working on Ord. He gasped with his mouth and unseen gills, then forced himself to ask the next question. "How many pursuers?"

"Two. But presumably others are in their wake."

"How close are they?"

"On this scale, on our little beach . . . if I showed them to you, they would be wearing our skins . . . !"

Ord turned, looking forward again. Concentrating on the slick black cylinder, he said, "You're doing this for Alice. Is that correct?"

"Some of it is her idea, yes."

"Why is Alice so important to you?"

Perfect asked, "Is she?"

What other ancient brother would conspire with her, without apparent hesitation? "You've got thousands of sisters. Why do you take such huge risks for Alice?"

"Don't you know?" A soft, unreadable laugh. "Haven't you guessed?"

Ord grappled with the possibilities. Besides their common age, no answer seemed reasonable. They were Chamberlains, but with different interests and philosophies. And even age couldn't be the whole answer, since there were dozens of siblings with their enormous rank.

"Try something unreasonable," was Perfect's advice.

Ord imagined several improbabilities, none adequate.

"So try the unthinkable. Alice and I are close, yes. Yes. But what answer is the last one you would hope to find?"

In a whisper, Ord said, "No."

"Yet you're right, Ord. Congratulations."

Suddenly the boy saw the Chamberlain mansion—the smaller, original incarnation—and the original penthouse on its topmost floor. It was autumn, again. Alice stood at the penthouse window, again. But the mountains were younger, the leaves more subdued, and the penthouse was intact and rather primitive, in furnishings and its luxuries.

This Alice didn't wear a little girl's body. The brilliant sun pierced her dress, betraying a body fully matured, relentlessly feminine . . . the scene having some quality that caused Ord to squirm and look away for a few uneasy moments.

He was standing in the penthouse, unnoticed.

Alice was on her toes, her feet bare, breasts pressed against glass, the bright eyes staring down at the world while someone emerged from the door at the room's center. A tall male Chamberlain of no particular age, he wore a stiff uniform that had once meant rank in the postwar government—a creature of status and some influence, yet not much older than Ord—and dangling from his dress shirt was a length of optical cable, its buried end linked with his nervous system, these technologies only slightly above fire and Folsom points.

Here was Thomas as a young man, Ord knew.

Ten million years in the past, and the Peace was newborn, and the Families had just begun their long ascent.

His brother wore no boots or socks, perhaps for the sake of stealth. Walking on long, bare feet that were the same pink as Alice's feet, he stalked their sister, without sound or hesitations. But she knew he was there. Probably with his first steps, she knew. Through her body she conveyed a sense of controlled eagerness, calves flexed and fingers spread and the tilt of her head flirtatious, sunlight making her neck and nearer ear glow with an inner light.

Yet Alice couldn't remain passive to the last moment. It was against her nature. This was the end of a long and relentless seduction. Thomas found the courage or lust to lift his hands—five fingers on each—and his sister decided to take full charge, stealing his momentum, flipping back her autumn hair while a calculated voice told him:

"See? You're not perfect after all."

Thomas hesitated, just for an instant, then seemingly willed his hands to close on her shoulders; and she said:

"Don't."

Then:

"I will tell on you."

Then, with emphasis:

"*Ian.* I'll tell him *everything.*"

In those days, Families looked elsewhere when siblings played these games. It was assumed they would outgrow incest in the same way they were outgrowing selfishness and cruelty. But Chamberlains were even better than the others. Ian, their ultimate parent, had said so. He would take his male clones aside, telling them, "Your sisters are taboo! Untouchable! I'd rather see you screwing the livestock than them!" And with those hard words, he planted some compelling images in each youngster—a miscalculation that the patriarch would make for dozens of generations, without fail.

But Thomas—the eventual Brother Perfect—seemed to believe his sister's words, pulling back his hands as if burned, a careless and quick little voice saying, "Don't tell . . . anyone . . . no . . . !"

Alice could see his reflection in the window glass. Without turning her head, she took the hands with her smaller ones, pulling Thomas's arms tight around her shoulders and chest—

—and the uniformed brother, that man of consequence, whimpered, "Please don't tell!"

"But I will," she promised. "Eventually." Then with one hand holding his arms in place, she took her dress with her free hand, by the hem, and lifted it from behind as she made a second promise, a low, roughened voice telling him, "You're my favorite brother, you always will be. . . ."

The penthouse dissolved into methane. With the perpetual smile and a gently embarrassed laugh, Perfect said, "I know. I paint our sister as conniving and treacherous. A little evil, even. But those aren't her only qualities, and they aren't even her largest. She's done wondrous things for every good reason, and we can only hope that's true of us, too." The incomplete hand touched him again, in a gesture that took hours. And meanwhile, Perfect told story upon story, proving their sister's innate decency, and in turn, perhaps unintentionally, proving too his own undiminished romantic affections.

With the pressure of the central thumb, Ord bristled. "We don't do that kind of thing anymore."

"You mature differently," Perfect agreed. "More slowly. With more help given."

"I've never thought of my sisters . . . in that way . . . !"

"But I think you appreciate my circumstances," the ancient man replied. "A profound emotional attachment made in my bedrock years, and I've built on that rock. Too much, I know, but what can I do now?"

Ord struggled to make his legs move faster, accomplishing nothing.

"You should know. Several times, in various cultures, Alice and I have been married. Husband and wife." A long, uncomfortable pause, then he reminded Ord, "Enough time passes, and the unlikely has its way of becoming ordinary. The unthinkable, tiresome."

The boy said nothing, lightning thoughts racing through him.

Perfect respected the silence, holding their pace but never speaking. Never intruding. The sun was dropping, clouds thickening until the air was saturated, a steady slow rain of energy-rich goo beginning, drops bursting on the sea and fish rising to feed, the business achingly slow, yet in its own way, frantic, repeating patterns even older than the Brongg.

There was a moment when Ord felt a sudden pressure, an inexplicable change of directions. But the beach and world looked the same.

Why would Alice need his help? Closure or no closure, how could *he* accomplish anything worthwhile?

Homesick to tears, Ords closed his eyes and walked blind.

His brother kept his steps true.

And when he couldn't contemplate his situation for another moment, Ord opened his eyes again, discovering that it was early evening and they were just a few steps away from their goal. Almost too late, he asked about the ancient times. About Ian, about his first children. And how the ordinary people had dealt with them, or not.

"Tell me," Ord begged.

Stories flowed from Perfect, genuine and simple, told with words and direct memories, accents made with the occasional slow flourish as the brothers marched across the last few meters of rain-spattered beach.

8

Sometimes Alice joined me on my explorations.

She was more a burden than a help. I was chasing living worlds, and she preferred the dead. We moved too fast for her to accomplish much, but she'd give the dead places little nudges. She warmed their cores or lent their atmosphere a potent gas or two. Another hundred million years, and who knows? Something might grow on them. . . .

But I wonder:

Are people going to declare those worlds illegal, too?

Will janitors be dispatched, ordered to scrub away all that treacherous prebiotic slime?

—Perfect, in conversation

The Brongg sun was barely visible as it set, shrouded in clouds and mammoth
drops of new gasolines. The tall black cylinder was in front of Ord, in easy
reach, but when he lifted his arm, it proved to be unreachable, a dreamy,
teasing sense of distance only growing.

"Step again," Perfect advised.

When he stepped, at the moment of footfall, the Brongg homeworld evaporated. He was in freefall again, and the cylinder covered half of the sky—a
deep blackness against a bottomless void. Ord kicked, cried out. Screamed
and made no sound.

He was streaking toward their destination at a fat fraction of lightspeed,
yet the final plunge took hours. A piece of him—some new subsystem; a
canned memory—measured the target's size, in astonishment, and he pleaded
with Perfect for an explanation, or encouragement, or even a few mild lies
to mollify him.

Perfect said nothing, and was nowhere to be seen.

The impact was sudden—a brief, bitting pain, brilliant light of no color,
then a hard and busy long sleep.

When Ord awoke, he found himself on another beach. He was dressed in
his original clothes, including his favorite boots, and his body was his own,
unscarred and excited, his heart beating inside its enduring cage of ribs.

"Oh, you're whole again. Thoroughly and genuinely."

The caveman sat beside him, his knapsack serving as a pillow. Again he
wore skins and an oversized smile, but the blue eyes seemed distracted, even
sad. Calloused feet splashed in a deep, rocky pool. A sourceless warm light
made his brother's skin glow, pink with blood and pink with wear. A soft,
proud voice asked, "What do you think?"

The pool and the sea beyond were filled with a watery fluid.

But it wasn't water, Ord realized.

The surface wore a thin persistent foam, transparent facets distorting the
pool's bottom, water-worn stones overlaid with a matted emerald-brown hair.
Life, he knew. And as life went, it was simple. Unsplendid. Even a little
disappointing.

"Yet there was nothing like this on my last visit," the brother replied.

"A few protocells, all scavengers. Not one honest photosynthesizer among
them."

Ord touched the foam-frosted pool, feeling warmth and a strange lack of
wetness.

He rose to his feet, glad to be quick again.

In his body again. Whole and home.

"Look around," Perfect insisted. "Opinions, please."

A rocky beach had been shaped by waves and strong winds. Behind the
beach, taller rocks merged into hills, then mountains, then masses too huge

and distant to be mere mountains. But at least as astonishing was the sea, every little agitation, every insult, causing the foam to rise, flat and bright, jewel-like bubbles refracting light into every possible color. It was as if the boundaries between liquid and air were vague. Ord's eyes lifted, a general brilliance replacing any sun, the distant sea turning milk-white as each jewel's color blended into one.

"This is a dyson," Ord muttered, interrupting his own thoughts.

"Cylindrical, and spinning. The most ordinary part of the design, to my mind."

Reaching into the air, on his right and left, were hair-thin structures resembling the angle spokes on a crude wheel. Ord imagined they must give support; and in an instant, some subconscious calculation was delivered to him. He remembered the dyson's apparent size, which implied a certain length for the spokes, and a diameter, and their thinness was an illusion, much as a giant star will mimic a simple cold point.

"Nobody builds . . . on this scale . . . !"

"You were taught," growled his brother. "You were taught."

The hair-like spokes were thicker than some worlds. And with that revelation, Ord looked inland again, past the ordinary mountains, eyes lifting as the mind told him that the vast plateau was not, that what he saw was the base of the nearest spoke, the rest of it partially obscured by the glare of the sky.

"This little ocean?" Perfect boasted. "It covers an area greater than a hundred thousand earths, and it's a teardrop. Nothing more."

Numbed, Ord felt his legs tremble, his breath quicken.

"Taste the water," his brother insisted. "Here. Have a sip!"

Not water, and not wet. It was like a drink taken in a dream, the flavor too delicious to recall after the thirst was gone. With a weak, quiet voice, Ord asked, "What is it? Tell me?"

"You guess. Go on."

"You've done something with dark matter." A boy's best guess, correct but too simple by a long ways. "Because this isn't ordinary . . . it isn't baryonic. . . ."

"Alice did the magic, mostly. I set guidelines and the fat goals, but she invented the technologies." He pulled a stone from the pool, complete with its shaggy carpet, then tucked it into a new pouch hanging from the knapsack. "What she did was rework some simple, invisible particles. She coerced them into acting like atoms. A positive particle, a negative one. Then she built a new periodic table—a simpler set of elements—out of the lazy atoms. Much of what you see here is dark matter, which is why it barely reacts to the universe around us. And that's why unless you know precisely what you're seeking, this vast dyson is wondrously invisible."

Questions formed.

Ord tried asking all of them, in a rush.

"Oh, people have attempted dark-matter life," Perfect explained. "From scratch, all failures. You can guess some of the problems. But we helped ourselves by inventing our own elements, including a superior version of the honored carbon atom. And the scale of the work helps, some. And, too, we cheated. When we had no choices, we bolstered the system with baryonic matter. A thin but essential scaffolding, if you will."

The boy took a deep breath, wondering what he was inhaling.

"It feels like a warm day, doesn't it?" A laugh and shake of the head. "The truth? We're hovering a few degrees above Absolute. The fire above us is chilly. Interstellar hydrogen is captured as it drifts into the dyson, then it's burned efficiently, taken all the way to iron. Any energy that escapes is masked, given some natural excuse. And the iron ash is *nothing* in this volume of cold space."

Ord swallowed, then swallowed again. "You wanted to make a better intelligence. But what's here, in this pool . . . it can't have even a stupid thought."

"I would never, never presume to dictate a final design of what evolves here." A pause, nothing funny for this brief moment. "I set up the broad parameters. Not Alice. I gave life its chance, then broke camp and began walking again."

Ord watched his brother wade into the sea, submerging for a moment, then emerging with another stone and its hair, both different in color from before. Again he stuffed his prize into the pouch, no room for it and yet no difficulty in the task. Then as he straightened, appearing rather pleased, Ord asked him: "How can you know that intelligence will evolve? And that it won't make all *our* ridiculous mistakes?"

Perfect retrieved his treasured spear, using it to roll a stone on its back. The mud beneath stank with odd rot, implying life. A gob of the mud followed the two mossy stones into the pouch, then he said, "There's nothing like uranium here, for example."

Recalling his own foolish stunt, Ord felt a sudden painful shame.

"And with these-synthetic elements, and with the neurons they can build, thought and action will be in balance, I hope. I *hope*." The older brother appeared uncharacteristically sober, yet sobriety, in some odd way, betrayed a deep and abiding happiness. He was happy stuffing mud into that impossible pouch. He was happy standing again, wiping his dirty hands against his stomach, squinting at the sky as he asked again, "What was our golden age?"

"After the glaciers melted," Ord recalled. *When the world was the universe, the stars unimaginable. . . .*

"This is the universe." A skyward thrust of the spear. "What's born here has no reason or rationale to imagine the stars."

Ord stared at his brother, waiting.

"Whatever prospers—whatever organism can rule this dyson—is free to call itself the master of creation. And why not? It won't sound even a millionth as silly as we do when we make the same boasts."

"But *I* never have," Ord complained, in a whisper building toward anger. "I've never even thought those words . . . !"

"Which is possibly, just possibly, why Alice selected you!"

Ord shut his mouth, remaining silent.

"Do you know what I am? What I am most truly?" Perfect asked the question with a calm, almost distracted air, again wiping the stinking mud from his hands, palms and fingers painting his belly. "A master of creation, maybe?" From everywhere came a thunderous, world-shaking laugh, and Perfect said, "Bullshit! I'm just a fucking caveman who got *lucky* . . . !"

9

Maybe our universe is as simple as this:

We are built entirely from someone's nearly invisible dark matter. Protons and electrons have been coerced into cooperating, building the baryonic places. We're a tiny bubble drifting through an enormous and brilliant but quite invisible cosmos, lovely pieces of it passing through us unseen. Which implies that this larger universe might itself be dark matter inside some still greater universe . . . and so on, and on. . . .

Oh, Ord, I'm sorry. I was mistaken. That doesn't sound simple at all, does it?

—Perfect, in conversation

Hoisting his knapsack to his shoulder, Perfect said, "Stay here."

"Where are you going?" the boy blurted, surprised by his anxieties. Trying for composure, he added, "I want to go with you."

A wink and grin, effortlessly charming.

Then Perfect picked up his spear with his partial hand, remarking, "I've got work, and there isn't time. Stay. Wait. I should be back before too long, I hope."

"But I'm here to help, right? To do some good—?"

"You don't understand. Not yet." Then his brother began to step toward him, and he wasn't there anymore. The step carried him out of sight, in an instant, and Ord spun and dropped to his butt, suddenly feeling chilled. A hundred new questions to ask, the old ones needing to be asked again, and he felt abandoned, cheated, and small.

In a whisper, he said, "I'm tired of this Family."

A lazy little wind blew from the sea, cold as liquid helium but warm against his current skin. Other than the wind, nothing moved. No answers presented themselves. And when Ord grew sick of feeling sorry for himself, he stood again, then began to walk, following the shoreline at his own modest, archaic pace.

There was no sun to set, but there were nights.

He learned.

Darkness emerged slowly, exposing the illuminated far side of the dyson, and Ord sat on a different beach, bare feet in the warm facsimile of sand, eyes gazing at that remote, ill-defined terrain. Every world that the Chamberlains had terraformed, if cleaned like animal skins and sewn together, wouldn't carpet this vast place.

He wondered how Alice and Perfect had managed it, and then he knew. It was because the dark matter was so abundant and amiable. Because they took their time, self-replicating robots doing the brunt of the work. And because the dyson's true mass wasn't much greater than Neptune's—a wondrous home of tissue paper, in essence, lit from within by cold candles.

Somewhere within Ord, out of easy reach, were reservoirs of fact, languid explanations, and bottled lectures beyond number.

He practiced, accessing the knowledge as best he could.

There was a text on the Brongg—their immeasurable history, the bulk of it immeasurably dull—but its sheer size and dullness was an event, majestic in its own right, like plate tectonics.

Sitting on that alien beach, in the dark, Ord found himself lost in the intricacies of a Brongg government born in the Triassic and still thriving today.

He barely noticed the dawn.

A feeble glow began nowhere, and everywhere. This was a universe without shadows. The boy blinked and looked skyward, wondering how these qualities would affect the future psyches . . . and there was a sound, a gentle wrong-pitched splashing, his eyes dropping, focusing on a distinctive beachcomber.

It was Perfect, already back again.

Ord was halfway standing when he noticed the clothes, the posture. The five whole fingers on each open hand.

Hesitating, Ord found that he had no voice.

With a quiet, terrified tone, the other Chamberlain said:

"Lyman. I'm just Lyman."

"Brother . . . ?"

"You remember me, don't you?" His horror was palpable. "They asked me to come, to talk with you, to tell you . . . offer you . . . oh, Ord . . . ! Do you know how much trouble you're in . . . ?"

"Why wouldn't I remember you?"

Lyman straightened, blinked. The answer seemed obvious, thus he moved to greater questions, explaining events from his point of view.

"You vanished. We thought you were in your room . . . I even spoke to you once, except it wasn't you . . . you were gone, and a security sweep realized it." Lyman attempted a smile, acting as if he remembered instructions to do just that. "We searched for you." The smile brightened. "I went to the stables. . . . I thought you might be hiding. . . ."

"I'm sorry to worry anyone."

The brother took a deep breath, then exhaled.

"When you couldn't find me, what happened?"

"Next?" A pained, prolonged swallow. "The Nuyens came to visit. A high-ranking delegation. They claimed that some old Chamberlain had been living on the estate, in secret—"

"How could they know?"

"The Nuyens have watched us. Better than we watch ourselves, it seems." Lyman glanced at the enormous sea, nothing registering in his eyes. "There were high-level meetings, and accusations—you could feel the tension—then someone broke into a facility in the Oort cloud, and portions of Alice were stolen. Afterward, you could *taste* the panic—"

"What portions?"

Lyman shuddered, then wrestled himself back into a half-composure. He didn't know what was stolen. "They wanted help from someone you would trust," he admitted. "Which isn't me, I *told* them that, but you know how the elders can be. They'd already picked me before they asked—"

"Who asked?"

"Everyone. There were Chamberlains, and Nuyens. Even the Sanchexes by then. And even the Sanchexes were scared."

"How would you help?"

"Like this." Isn't it obvious? his face asked. "You and a rogue Chamberlain had taken parts of Alice. It was kept secret from the public, of course. So was the mission to find you, and they asked if I would go with them, and speak with you when it was time."

Ord found himself laughing. A genuine, quiet laugh. "Oh, they asked you, did they?"

Lyman hesitated, attempting a wry smile. "I went to sleep." He said the word with longing, as if he wished he was asleep now. "It was a long chase, but here I am."

"You are," Ord agreed. He had sudden warm feelings for Lyman, sorry to have him pulled into this mess. Was that the logic? Disarm him with a pitiful sibling? "But I didn't steal anything of Alice's."

"I knew you didn't. It was the rogue all along."

Where was Perfect?

"What we could do," Lyman continued, "is go to the others. You aren't responsible for what's happened. You were kidnapped, or whatever we want to call it, and I'll explain—"

"Who's with you?"

"A sister. The elder on the estate." He attempted another smile. "Do you see how important you are?"

"Who else?"

"Just one. A Nuyen." Lyman paused, a study in concentration. "He is in charge. As old as Alice, almost."

Perfect had seen two pursuers. Lyman would have been cargo. Inert, innocent.

"What do you think of this place?" asked Ord.

Lyman wanted to keep his eyes on his brother. A glance toward the sea, then toward the mountains. Then he said, "Lovely," with a surprising conviction.

"But you came to destroy it, didn't you?"

"Not me," his brother sputtered. "But if it's illegal . . . *immoral* . . . doesn't it *have* to be destroyed?"

A vast realm that hurts no one—a universe unto itself—and Ord felt a scalding, enormous rage.

He gave a low moan, stepping toward Lyman.

A terrified voice said, "No," as his brother retreated. He was begging, pleading. Hands raised, he said, "Just come with me. We'll talk to them, and maybe something can be done—"

Ord picked up a rounded stone, for emphasis. "They won't hurt this place—"

—and a Nuyen appeared, a Chamberlain standing strategically on his left, slightly behind him. An adult version of Xo showed a humorless smile— simple dark hair; unreadable black eyes—then he said with a hard, clean-cutting voice, "Surrender. You're a good boy, but you don't have any idea what you're doing."

Ord felt utterly confident in his mistrust of Nuyens. "Do not touch anything here," he warned, words like thunderbolts.

A tilt of the head, a thin amusement. The Nuyen said, "Really?"

The sister—a total stranger—called to Ord, by name, conjuring a face vast and maternal, concern dripping from it.

Ord looked only at the Nuyen, lifting the stone overhead as he said, "Leave. All of you, leave."

The enemy showed no fear or hesitations. But behind the face, in some small way, there was the instantaneous flinch.

An involuntary failure of will.

With a mixture of horror and exhilaration, Ord wondered what he had of Alice's. Energies, liquid and sweet, surged through him and radiating in all directions. The beach shivered. The great sea threw clouds of jeweled foam into a brilliant sky. And Ord pictured the Nuyen dying, slowly, his soul in agony to the end.

Here the boy would remain. Anyone who came to destroy this place would be destroyed, Ord's destiny set . . . !

A voice spoke to him. Familiar, close.

A lying voice, Ord told himself.

The old Nuyen and Chamberlain had retreated in panic, leaving their empty bodies standing on the beach. But their souls hadn't fled far enough, and Ord could see them with some newly engaged eye, measuring distances, the rock in his clenched hand no longer simple and cold.

That voice, again.

Beseeching him to stop.

But Ord didn't listen. He followed his instincts and anger, flinging the nonstone and aiming to murder—

A flash, a dull white pain.

—and he collapsed, giving a miserable low groan.

Piercing his chest, cutting places and functions he had only just begun to feel, was that long flint Folsom point. Ord could see the point jutting from his sternum. He was down on his hands and knees, breathing out of habit, little red bubbles detaching from his mouth and drifting on the warm wind. He watched one bubble, something about it enchanting. Weightless, it swirled and rose, then fell again. In its slick red face he thought he could see his own face, for an instant. Then it settled on top of a bare pink foot, and it burst without sound, without fuss. Whose foot? Why couldn't he remember? But Ord was having trouble thinking at all, and he felt quite chilled, and the bubbles weren't coming anymore, and he very much missed them. . . .

10

. . . and with my life, my health, and my perishable name, I now and
always shall defend the Great Peace.

—from the Families' pledge

"If I had let you kill them," said Perfect, "what possible sweet good would
have come from it?"

Opening his eyes, Ord found himself sitting on a cave floor, a small fire
burning before him, his brother illuminated by the golden flames and half-
hidden by their swirling, jasmine-scented smoke.

"A rash thought, a crude act, and then *what?*"

The boy gasped, feeling pain. In the center of his chest was a slick raised
scar, white as milk, and aching, and apparently permanent.

Quietly, with genuine remorse, he said, "I am sorry. . . ."

Perfect said nothing for a long time, wiggling his fingers and stumps as
they warmed, his face contemplative and remote.

The cave was filled with rocks, Ord noted. They were neatly stacked, each
one adorned with something alive. Handfuls of mud filled the gaps. Everything glistened, water dripping somewhere in the darkness.

Ord shuddered, saying, "I wanted to protect—"

"—the dyson, yes." His brother shook his head, warning him, "First of all,
the dyson is *my* responsibility. And second of all, there were exactly five
sentient organisms onboard it. Only five. You and me, and poor Lyman, and
your intended victims. You were willing to commit two murders to save a
vast inchoate slime, and that's not the moral act of a decent soul. Chamberlain or not."

"How is Lyman?"

"Sleeping on that beach, and safe."

Ord glanced at his surroundings, saying, "This is your pouch. This is where
you've been putting the rocks and mud."

"A representative population, yes. Held in suspended animation." Perfect
tossed a stone chip into the fire, sparks scattering. "That Nuyen and our sister
are holding at a safe distance, awaiting reinforcements. Of course they suspected that I was the one helping you, but they never, never guessed the
kinds of powers that you hold. A lot of Alice's systems had yet to be cata-
logued. And besides, they hoped to win your surrender, without incident,
before dealing with me and my dyson."

"What kinds of powers . . . ?"

A dark, slow laugh. "I do not know, Ord. In most cases."

The boy dipped his head, breathing deeply.

"Before Alice fled the Core, she visited me, warning me about the coming
explosion. Then she made me promise to do exactly what I have done, giving
the Baby exactly what I gave you and taking him to a suitable starting point."

His unborn sister could have been chosen just as easily.

Or Lyman, he realized.

Then Perfect jumped to his feet, announcing, "Before the reinforcements arrive, we should make our quiet escape."

"To where?" the boy inquired.

"I am leaving on a million-year walk." The voice was calm, the face resigned. "Out between the galaxies, I should think. Then in some good cold place I'll rebuild this dyson. Stone for stone. And afterward . . . well, there might be a galaxy or two worth exploring. Who knows?"

"May I walk with you?"

"Not for one step, no."

Ord had expected that answer, but the words stung nonetheless.

His brother continued, saying, "Alice asked for my help, and I gave it. Out of love, trust, and habit, and in that order. She has her reason, we can hope. And now you're free to help Alice, or not. I won't presume to tell you which choice to make."

"I have to save something," Ord whispered.

Perfect kicked stones and cold embers over the fire's heart. "I know what it is, and the truth told, I don't envy you."

"It's fragile, and Alice is pledged to protect it. . . ."

The maimed hand was offered.

Ord took it, standing. "It must be an illegal world. Is it? One with sentience, maybe?"

"I will show you," his brother promised. "Come on."

The boy's feet refused to move.

Without firelight, a softer, stranger glow illuminated the cavern. Perfect was a silhouette. His voice was close and warm, coaxing Ord by saying, "Not a world, no. Follow me."

Ord was strong enough to butcher a godly Nuyen, yet his legs were too heavy to lift. He fought with them, shuffling forward, noticing for the first time that his feet were bare and his only clothes were trousers made from simple skins. He looked at himself in the gloom, thinking of a lucky caveman. Then he managed a step, and another, and looked up at the sky that he both anticipated and could not believe.

Standing beside him, Perfect said, "I took you on a course perpendicular to the galactic plane. Out and out, then around a black hole that sent us partway home again."

Ord was sobbing, tears flowing, tasting like a long-ago sea.

"We walked along that beach, yes. But we also crossed several tens of thousands of light years. Out, then back again. Which means that you can see some of what's happened since we left."

The Milky Way covered the sky. With new eyes, Ord could see every sun and world and lump of stone bigger than a fist—or so it seemed—and the Core was the brilliant horror that he expected, its detonation at its climax, radiations and expelled wreckage rushing outward in a withering, toxic storm. A baby quasar, only human-made. Worse than almost every reasonable projection made in Ord's long-ago youth—

—and by no means the worst of what he could see.

A tragedy, but one with calculable, endurable ends.

The greatest horrors were smaller, scattered through the galaxy's broad spiral arms. Ord couldn't stop seeing them, even when he shut his human eyes. Healthy suns exploded. Living worlds were reduced to dust. Unknown powers struggled against one another with a frantic, brutal violence. The Great Peace was collapsing. Old and fragile, it might evaporate totally before Ord could return home. And to accomplish what . . . ? With or without Alice's powers, *what good could he do* . . . ?

With a solemn voice, Perfect said, "Bless the dead!"

At Ord's feet was a knapsack filled with talents. In his left hand, a fine new spear tipped with a Folsom point. And in his right hand was a simple stone mug, the pungent odor of an old-fashioned liquor pervading the night air.

"Bless the dead," Ord repeated, with feeling.

The brothers touched mugs with a cool, almost musical sound.

Then, as Ord drank, Perfect told him, "I want to give you a talent. I don't have Alice's magic, but here's something you might appreciate."

Ord's mug became a nearly spherical ball.

Not heavy, not large.

It was a head, he saw. A Chamberlain head, complete with red hair and the piercing blue eyes. And emitting an enormous laugh, so pure and authentic that Ord couldn't help but smile for a moment, closing his hand over the sweet gift, knowing what it was and almost saying, "Thank you," before he realized that nobody was standing beside him anymore.

He squeezed the head until it vanished, becoming part of his immortal flesh.

Then Ord again looked at the Milky Way, realizing that most of it remained at peace, tranquil and inviting by any measure. And he managed to laugh in a quiet, hopeful way, picking up his knapsack now, thinking that all things considered, it was a lovely night for a little walk.

A Child of the Dead

LIZ WILLIAMS

The future is usually thought of as being full of computers, microprocessors, nanotech, machines of every size and description—but as the posthuman condition continues to evolve, we may someday find ourselves leaving that kind of technology behind, consigned to the same trash heap of history that now contains the spinning wheel and the buggy whip. But, as always, such radical change will come at a price . . . and some people may be more willing to pay than others.

New British writer Liz Williams has had work appear in Interzone, Asimov's, Visionary Tongue, *and* Terra Incognita. *She lives in Brighton, England.*

> The substance of the great life completely follows Tao.
> Tao brings about all things so chaotically, so darkly.
> Chaotic and dark are its images.
> Unfathomable and obscure in it is the seed.
> —Tao Te Ching, 21.

I

I've walked down Jiangsu Road almost every day of my life, ever since I was a little girl. Going to school with my brother Tso, my grandmother would hold our hands and together we'd look in the restaurant windows at the steamed buns and the egg rolls, at the flat, stretched chickens which Mr. Hsiun told me were wind-dried. I work in that restaurant now, and I know how the food's prepared, but I used to imagine all these poor hens blown about in a roaring gale until all their feathers had gone and they were stiff and thin. It's funny the ideas you get when you're a kid.

Grandma knew everyone then, and they'd come out of the doorways to talk to her. Sometimes we'd go round to see people and I'd sit with a Coke while Grandma fixed something or other: she was always good with machines. Now, no one talks to anyone, and my grandmother stays at home. It seems to me that many things have begun to change, down Jiangsu Road. The sunlight doesn't seem to reach it anymore, and last night when I came home from the restaurant, I looked up and saw the stars. I've never noticed them before above the city, because of the lights, but one night at my great-aunt's house out in the country, Grandma sat on the porch with me and pointed out all the constellations: the shepherd boy, the maiden, all of them. When we went home to Shanghai, I got a book and learned them off by heart. But these stars that blaze above me now are different and I don't recognize a single one.

Sometimes the people change, too. I walked down Jiangsu Road yesterday on my way to work, as usual. There wasn't a soul in sight, but just opposite the entrance to the market, I turned round and saw that all the doors of the shops were open and everyone was watching me. At first I didn't recognize anyone, but then, to my relief, I realized who they were. They were the dead. I could see old Mr. Hsiun, who'd told me about the chickens, and who died about four years ago when we had that cholera outbreak. He was smiling and nodding at me, so I waved. Some of my relatives were there, too: I saw my great-uncle Leo. I went over to have a word.

"So you're still living here?" I said.

"Yes, yes, we're still here; we haven't moved," Leo said. "We heard your prayers. Thanks." He smiled at me, but there was nothing behind his eyes. He looked as two-dimensional as a paper doll, and then the wind shredded him into tatters, so I walked away.

The restaurant was still in its usual place, but the chickens that were hung up in the windows had gone and in their place were things that looked like rib cages; human ones, I suppose, but I'm not really sure. Anyway, after that it all melted away and I was back in the normal world and late for work. I'm trying to ignore these odd episodes; there are too many other things to worry about at the moment. I'm working double shifts at the restaurant now, because we spoke to the doctors yesterday and they said that we're behind with the payments for Tso's treatment. We can't very well abandon the treatment halfway through, so it's a question of either taking out a loan, which I don't want to do, or trying to catch up. I suppose we'll just have to manage. At least if one of us can get proper treatment, it makes things seem a little better, and it has to be Tso, because he's a boy.

2

My grandmother, as she sits in front of the flat eye of the old computer screen, tells me that I should put my faith in machines rather than the chancy flesh. Perhaps she's right; I don't know anymore. I'm just going from day to day at the moment: working at the restaurant, cleaning the flat, taking Tso to the hospital once a week. I took him up there this morning. They had him in the viral unit for almost two hours, while I waited outside. I tried to get tea out of the machine with a plastic chip they give you at the take-away, but it broke off and stuck in the slot, so I had to sit there, guilty and thirsty, while everyone gave me dirty looks. Then when Tso came out, we had to spend ten dollars on a taxi because he was still a bit groggy.

After that, I went to the restaurant and started my waitressing shift, but I was late again and they docked my wages. It's not been a very good day, today.

3

When I got back last night, Grandma was still up, sitting with her ear to the lifeless terminal. "You know what?" she said. "Sometimes, if I listen hard enough, I think I can still hear them."

"Who?" I asked.

"All those voices. In the old days, you could log on, you could talk to people. Thousands of voices . . . out there, everywhere." She gave the terminal a shake, as if it needed only a little encouragement to get it going again.

"Yeah, you said." Grandma used to tell me stories about the e-net, but it didn't sound much to me. All you could hear was a lot of people and static on the other end of the line, crackling and bounced off a strand satellite. She never had a very good machine: only the little homemade portable. Well, those days were long gone and there was the future to think about now. I drew a deep breath.

"Grandma? Listen, a couple of days ago I stopped off at the market and spoke to Tony Tang. I don't know how you're going to feel about this, but he thinks he might be able to get me a cheap deal." I muttered the words, but I got her full attention. She gave me a beady look.

"What sort of cheap deal?"

"Well, you know . . . he thinks he could get me some equipment. Just some basic stuff . . ."

"And how do you propose to pay for it?" I wished I'd never started the conversation. I should have just got on with it and said nothing, but I couldn't tell her now that I'd already done a deal with Tony. A *fait accompli*, I think they call it.

Reluctantly, I said: "The thing is, I'm thirteen now. So don't really want to wait much longer, because, I guess it won't be long before I'm too old. To learn how to use the new technology. You know?"

She was quiet for a while, and then she said: "I Hua . . . we were talking about the old days just now. I can't help feeling that things were better then. Maybe I just don't understand this new technology of yours. I trained with machines, you see? Chips and neural nets and A-life, but things moved on so quickly. Two years after I graduated, Genreng Pharmaceuticals started to develop neuroviral interfacing—the bioweb, the Hsing-tao, whatever they call it these days—and I found out I was obsolete. I was too old to be put through the new program. Past it, you see. I was nineteen. And in the old days, at least you had the hope of another job when your technician career was over. I don't like this modern technology, Li Hua. I don't trust it, and I don't want you hanging round Tony Tang and his cut-price under-the-counter deals."

I said: "Okay. Look, I'm going to bed. I'll see you in the morning," and I left her staring at the blankness of the screen. I hate arguing with Grandma. It always makes me feel guilty, because I know she paid a lot of money for Tso and me. She wanted a child so badly, but she couldn't even have that. There was something wrong with her ova, some genetic thing, and they had to terminate her pregnancy. But fortunately, when they checked the fetus, they found its ova were fine, so they just fertilized two of them and transplanted them into a breeder and Grandma got Tso and me. That's all my poor mother was, a scrap of meat in a jar, and my father maybe less than that. I sometimes wonder if that's why I seem to be seeing ghosts all the time, being a child of the dead; but I know that isn't the real reason.

4

I went to see Tang again this afternoon in his shop at the back of the herbalist's. He was bent over the desk, doing something with a culture dish. He had one of those dried snakes that they make pills out of sitting on the desk and when he saw me, he rattled it at me, hissing.

"Cute," I said. I pulled up a stool and watched him as he worked. I drew a finger down the snake's skeletal spine; it felt as light and dry as air.

"So, did you speak to your grandma?" Tony asked.

"Yeah. Well, I tried. She wasn't very keen, to be honest. She's old-fashioned, Tony, you know?"

"Sure. She's an old lady. When she was your age, they just didn't do this kind of thing. Times change. Your grandma knows that." He paused, concentrating on the contents of the dish beneath the microscope.

"Do you still want to go ahead with our deal?" he asked.

I said: "If I decided to back out now, could I? I mean, is it too late?"

"No. No, it's not too late." He looked up, and his round face was earnest. "And you should know something, Li Hua; I wouldn't charge you for the equipment you've already used. I mean, I wouldn't do that."

"I know," I said. "It's okay; don't be silly. I want to carry on with it. Can I have a look at this?" I squinted down the scope while he held the microdermic. I could see the little blob, and the tip of the dermic penetrating it.

"That's all it is," Tony said.

"So how long will it take?"

"Ten minutes."

"Oh, okay, not so long, then. So I could go in on my way to work?"

"Whenever. I've made an appointment for you at the doctor's in Xiang Road. She's a woman; I thought you might prefer that." That's one of the things I like about Tony Tang; he's thoughtful.

"Thanks," I said. "What about tomorrow?"

"If you like. Stop in here on your way back, let me know how it went. You'll need more of the equipment then, anyway."

"Okay, see you then," I said, picking up my bag. I didn't want to tell him about the hallucinations, I was scared that he might think it was a bad omen and get cold feet. I left without saying anything.

"Keep the snake," he said, on my way out the door.

5

The session at the doctor's wasn't as bad as I'd thought. The doctor was really nice, and afterward she gave me a can of paracola, which she needn't have done.

"Do I have to do anything else?" I asked her.

"No, that's it. You shouldn't have any complications, but if you do, you come right back and let me know. You said your periods haven't started yet?"

"No, that's right." I said.

"Okay. It might have a slight effect, but there shouldn't be any problems." She helped me down from the couch. "There you are. You're all done."

6

I guess Tony might have felt a little sorry for me, because as well as the equipment, he gave me twenty dollars. Then at the weekend, it was New Year's and I made nearly 300 in trips. It was more money than I'd ever seen before. Grandma and I counted it up today, before we stashed it under the bed, and Tso watched us from the bunk bed, smiling. I'm so relieved. Now we can pay off the hospital fees and in a month or so, Tso can start work. I suppose I'm sorry, in a way, because we won't see much of him once he's got a job. Tso's doctor has been helpful; he says that he might be able to get Tso a place at an institute in Harbin. It's a long way away, but it's worth it.

I took my grandmother out this evening. Mrs. Eng came in to look after Tso, and Grandma and I went out to dinner. I told her to order anything she liked, no matter how much it cost.

"You're a good girl, Li Hua," she said.

"Isn't it great? Tso's treatment, I mean." I couldn't stop talking about it.

"Yes," she said, but she still looked sad. I reached across the table and squeezed her hand.

"Don't worry," I told her.

"Oh, I suppose I'm pleased for Tso, if that's what he wants, but it just seems—I'm sorry, Li. I know I'm old-fashioned, but things were just different in the past, you see." Suddenly, I could see, she was angry. I knew that she wasn't mad at me, but I kept quiet anyway. It was as though she was talking to herself. "All those machines, Li Hua, all those wonderful machines. Then Genreng invents the bioweb, and computers aren't any use anymore. Machine obsolescence. Suddenly there's the bioweb, and how do you access it? You've got to be part of it, your whole body, through a neuroviral interface. And you can't do that unless you get dosed up with one of their synthetic viruses, and you've got to be young." She snorted. "You can't tell me that there's nothing wrong with that making yourself ill so that you can be part of the global communications network."

She fell silent and I stared at the table. I couldn't quite see what the problem was. I thought of Tso, in a month's time; lying in a cot in Harbin, sailing the viral pathways, able to reach out to everyone else who was infected. A disease is a system, I understood, and I thought it was a great mark of progress that we no longer needed to invent machines, computers, for the resources had been with us all along. Tso would be another link in the great chain of the neuroviral web, and it in turn would convey all the information he needed; the world as one great mind, unified.

"And then what happens?" my grandmother murmured. "He'll work for a few years, and then what? How do we know he's even got a future after that?"

"It's not like that, Grandma! The doctors told me. They just give you a cure, it's all perfectly straightforward."

"Maybe." She did not sound very sure. She reached out and patted my hand. "At least you'll still be here, Li Hua."

I didn't want to tell her, then, that she was wrong. Even with the low-grade viral equipment that Tang's given me in exchange for the ova, I should be able to get a job in some webshop somewhere, and then I'll be able to reach out across the thousand miles to Harbin, and beyond, and my brother will be there. Grandma doesn't understand, you see, that you have to accommodate yourself to life, to Tao. It's like water, you have to go wherever it takes you, and you can't stop it for long. She always wanted to leave the body behind, soar out into the electronic sunlight, but you can't do that. You have to go the other way, into darkness, into the body itself. But I didn't want to argue with her, and this was something we could talk about later.

I reached out and poured more tea into her cup. I smiled at my grandmother and I could tell from the side effects that Tang's virus was working, for outside the window, the faces of the dead clustered in the shadows, beneath the unknown stars.

Nevermore

IAN R. MACLEOD

British writer Ian R. MacLeod was one of the hottest new writers of the nineties, and as the new century begins, his work continues to grow in power and deepen in maturity. MacLeod has published a slew of strong stories in Interzone, Asimov's Science Fiction, Weird Tales, Amazing, *and* The Magazine of Fantasy and Science Fiction, *among other markets. Several of these stories made the cut for one or another of the various "Best of the Year" anthologies; in 1990, in fact, he appeared in* three *different Best of the Year anthologies with three different stories, certainly a rare distinction. His first novel* The Great Wheel *was published to critical acclaim in 1997, followed by a major collection of his short work,* Voyages By Starlight. *In 1999, he won the World Fantasy Award with his brilliant novella "The Summer Isles," and followed it up in 2000 by winning another World Fantasy Award for his novelette "The Chop Girl." MacLeod lives with his wife and young daughter in the West Midlands of England, and is at work on several new novels.*

Here, in a stylish and compelling look at a decadent posthuman world that ought to be Utopia, he proves once again that Art—like Passion—is in the eye of the beholder.

Now that he couldn't afford to buy enough reality, Gustav had no option but to paint what he saw in his dreams. With no sketch pad to bring back, no palette or cursor, his head rolling up from the pillow and his mouth dry and his jaw aching from the booze he'd drunk the evening before—which was the cheapest means he'd yet found of getting to sleep—he was left with just that one chance, and a few trailing wisps of something that might once have been beautiful, before he had to face the void of the day.

It hadn't started like this, but he could see by now that this was how it had probably ended. Representational art had had its heyday, and for a while he'd been feted like the bright new talent he'd once been sure he was. And big lumpy actuality that you could smell and taste and get under your fingernails would probably come back into style again—long after it had ceased to matter to him.

So that was it. Load upon load of self-pity falling down upon him this morning from the damp-stained ceiling. What *had* he been dreaming? Something—surely something. Otherwise, being here and being Gustav wouldn't come as this big a jolt. He should've got more used to it than this by now . . . Gustav scratched himself, and discovered that he also had an erection, which was another sign—hadn't he read once, somewhere?—that you'd been dreaming dreams of the old-fashioned kind, unsimulated, unaided. A sign, anyway, of a kind of biological optimism. The hope that there might just be a hope.

Arthritic, Cro-Magnon, he wandered out from his bed. Knobbled legs, knobbled veins, knobbled toes. He still missed the habit of fiddling with the controls of his window in the pockmarked far wall, changing the perspectives and the light in the dim hope that he might stumble across something better. The sun and the moon were blazing down over Paris from their respective quadrants, pouring like mercury through the nanosmog. He pressed his hand to the glass, feeling the watery wheeze of the crack that now snaked across it. Five stories up in these scrawny empty tenements, and a long, long way down. He laid his forehead against its coolness as the sour thought that he might try to paint this scene speeded through him. He'd finished at least twenty paintings of foreal Paris; all reality engines and cabled ruins in gray, black, and white. Probably done, old Vincent had loved his cadmiums and chromes! And never sold one single fucking painting in his entire life.

"What—what I told you was true," Elanore said, stumbling slightly over these little words, sounding almost un-Elanore-like for a moment; nearly uneasy. "I mean, about Marcel in Venice and Francine across the sky. And, yes, we *did* talk about a reunion. But you know how these things are. Time's precious, and, at the end of the day it's been so long that these things really do take a lot of nerve. So it didn't come off. It was just a few promises that no one really imagined they'd keep. But I thought—well, I thought that it would be nice to see you anyway. At least one more time."

"So all of this is just for me. *Jesus*, Elanore, I knew you were rich, but . . ."

"Don't be like that, Gustav. I'm not trying to impress you or depress you or whatever. It was just the way it came out."

He poured more of the wine, wondering as he did so exactly what trick it was that allowed them to share it.

"So, you're still painting?"

"Yep."

"I haven't seen much of your work about."

"I do it for private clients," Gustav said. "Mostly."

He glared at Elanore, daring her to challenge his statement. Of course, if he really *was* painting and selling, he'd have some credit. And if he had *credit*, he wouldn't be living in that dreadful tenement she'd tracked him down to. He'd have paid for all the necessary treatments to stop himself becoming the frail old man he so nearly was. *I can help, you know*, Gustav could hear Elanore saying because he'd heard her say it so many times before. *I don't need all this wealth. So let me give you just a little help. Give me that chance* . . . But what she actually *said* was even worse.

"Are you recording yourself, Gus?" Elanore asked. "Do you have a librarian?"

Now, he thought, now *is* the time to walk out. Pull this whole thing down and go back into the street—the foreal street. And forget.

"Did you know," he said instead, "that the word reality once actually *meant* foreal—not the projections and the simulations, but proper actuality. But then along came *virtual* reality, and of course, when the *next* generation of products was developed, the illusion was so much better that you could walk right into it instead of having to put on goggles and a suit. So they had to think of an improved phrase, a super-word for the purposes of marketing. And someone must have said, *Why don't we just call it reality?*"

"You don't have to be hurtful, Gus. There's no rule written down that says we can't get on."

"I thought that that was exactly the problem. It's in my head, and it was probably there in yours before you died. Now it's . . ." He'd have said more. But he was suddenly, stupidly, near to tears.

"What exactly *are* you doing these days, Gus?" she asked as he cleared his throat and pretended it was the wine that he'd choked on. "What are you painting at the moment?"

"I'm working on a series," he was surprised to hear himself saying. "It's a sort of a journey-piece. A sequence of paintings which begin here in Paris and then . . ." He swallowed. ". . . Bright, dark colors . . ." A nerve began to leap beside his eye. Something seemed to touch him, but was too faint to be heard or felt or seen.

"Sounds good, Gus," Elanore said, leaning toward him across the table. And Elanore smelled of Elanore, the way she always did. Her pale skin was freckled from the sunlight of whatever warm and virtual place she was living. Across her cheeks and her upper lip, threaded gold, lay the down that he'd brushed so many times with the tips of his fingers. "I can tell from that look in your eyes that you're into a really good phase . . ."

After that, things went better. They shared a second bottle of *vin ordinaire*. They made a little mountain of the butts of her Disc Bleu in the ashtray. This ghost—she really *was* like Elanore. Gustav didn't even object to her taking his hand across the table. There was a kind of abandon in all of this— new ideas mixed with old memories. And he understood more clearly now what van Gogh had meant about this café being a place where you could ruin yourself, or go mad, or commit a crime.

The few other diners faded. The virtual waiters, their aprons a single as- sured gray-white stroke of the palette knife, started to tip the chairs against the tables. The aromas of the Left Bank's ever-unreliable sewers began to override those of cigarettes and people and horse dung and wine. At least, Gustav thought, *that* was still foreal . . .

"I suppose quite a lot of the others have died by now," Gustav said. "All that facile gang you seem to so fondly remember."

"People still change, you know. Just because we've passed on, doesn't mean we can't *change*."

By now, he was in a mellow enough mood just to nod at that. And how have *you* changed, Elanore? he wondered. After so long, what flicker of the electrons made you decide to come to me now?

"You're obviously doing well."

"I am . . ." She nodded, as if the idea surprised her. "I mean, I didn't expect—"

"—And you look—"

"—And *you*, Gus, what I said about you being—"

"—That project of mine—"

"—I know, I—"

They stopped and gazed at each other. Then they both smiled, and the moment seemed to hold, warm and frozen, as if from a scene within a painting. It was almost . . .

"Well . . ." Elanore broke the illusion first as she began to fumble in the small sequined purse she had on her lap. Eventually, she produced a handkerchief and blew delicately on her nose. Gustav tried not to grind his teeth—although this was *exactly* the kind of affectation he detested about ghosts. He guessed, anyway, from the changed look on her face, that she knew what he was thinking. "I suppose that's it, then, isn't it, Gus? We've met—we've spent the evening together without arguing. Almost like old times."

"Nothing will ever be like old times."

"No . . ." Her eyes glinted, and he thought for a moment that she was going to become angry—goaded at last into something like the Elanore of old. But she just smiled. "Nothing ever will be like old times. That's the problem, isn't it? Nothing ever was, or ever will be . . ."

Elanore clipped her purse shut again. Elanore stood up. Gustav saw her hesitate as she considered bending down to kiss him farewell, then decide that he would just regard that as another affront, another slap in the face.

Elanore turned and walked away from Gustav, fading into the chiaroscuro swirls of lamplight and gray.

Elanore, as if Gustav needed reminding, had been alive when he'd first met her. In fact, he'd never known anyone who was *more* so. Of course, the age difference between them was always huge—she'd already been past a hundred by then, and he was barely forty—but they'd agreed on that first day that they met, and on many days after, that there was a corner in time around which the old eventually turned to rejoin the young.

In another age, and although she always laughingly denied it, Gustav always suspected that Elanore would have had her sagging breasts implanted with silicone, the wrinkles stretched back from her face, her heart replaced by a throbbing steel simulacrum. But she was lucky enough to exist at a time when effective anti-aging treatments were finally available. As a postcentenarian, wise and rich and moderately, pleasantly, famous, Elanore was probably more fresh and beautiful than she'd been at any other era in her life. Gustav had met her at a party beside a Russian lake—guests wandering amid dunes of snow. Foreal had been a fashionable option then; although for Gustav, the grounds of this pillared ice-crystalled palace that Catherine the Great's Scottish favorite Charles Cameron had built seemed far too gorgeous to be entirely true. But it *was* true—foreal, actual, concrete, genuine, unvirtual—and such knowledge was what had driven him then. That, and the huge impossibility of ever really managing to convey any of it as a painter. That, and the absolute certainty that he would *try*.

Elanore had wandered up to him from the forest dusk dressed in seal furs. The shock of her beauty had been like all the rubbish he'd heard other artists talk about and thus so detested. And he'd been a stammering wreck, but somehow that hadn't mattered. There had been—and here again the words became stupid, meaningless—a dazed physicality between them from that first moment that was so intense it was spiritual.

Elanore told Gustav that she'd seen and admired the series of triptychs he'd just finished working on. They were painted directly onto slabs of wood, and depicted totemistic figures in dense blocks of color. The critics had generally dammed them with faint praise—had talked of Cubism and Mondrian—and were somehow unable to recognize Gustav's obvious and grateful debt to Gauguin's Tahitian paintings. But Elanore had seen and understood those bright, muddy colors. And, yes, she'd dabbled a little in painting herself—just enough to know that truly creative acts were probably beyond her. . . .

Elanore wore her red hair short in those days. And there were freckles, then as always, scattered across the bridge of her nose. She showed the tips of her teeth when she smiled, and he was conscious of her lips and her tongue. He could smell, faint within the clouds of breath that entwined them, her womanly scent.

A small black cat threaded its way between them as they talked, then, barely breaking the crust of the snow, leaped up onto a bough of the nearest pine and crouched there, watching them with emerald eyes.

"That's Metzengerstein," Elanore said, her own even greener eyes flickering across Gustav's face, but never ceasing to regard him. "He's my librarian."

When they made love later on in the agate pavilion's frozen glow, and as the smoke of their breath and their sweat clouded the winter twilight, all the disparate elements of Gustav's world finally seemed to join. He carved Elanore's breasts with his fingers and tongue, and painted her with her juices, and plunged into her sweet depths, and came, finally, finally, and quite deliciously, as her fingers slid around and he in turn was parted and entered by her.

Swimming back up from that, soaked with Elanore, exhausted, but his cock amazingly still half-stiff and rising, Gustav became conscious of the black cat that all this time had been threading its way between them. Its tail now curled against his thigh, corrugating his scrotum. Its claws gently kneaded his belly.

Elanore had laughed and picked Metzengerstein up, purring herself as she laid the creature between her breasts.

Gustav understood. Then or later, there was never any need for her to say more. After all, even Elanore couldn't live forever—and she needed a librarian with her to record her thoughts and actions if she was ever to pass on. For all its myriad complexities, the human brain had evolved to last a single lifetime; after that, the memories and impressions eventually began to overflow, the data became corrupted. Yes, Gustav understood. He even came to like the way Metzengerstein followed Elanore around like a witch's familiar, and, yes, its soft sharp cajolings as they made love.

Did they call them ghosts then? Gustav couldn't remember. It was a word, anyway—like spic, or nigger—that you never used in front of them. When he and Elanore were married, when Gustav loved and painted and loved and painted her, when she gave him her life and her spirit and his own career somehow began to take off as he finally mastered the trick of getting some of the passion he felt down onto the lovely, awkward canvas, he always knew that part of the intensity between them came from the age gap, the difference, the inescapable fact that Elanore would soon have to die.

It finally happened, he remembered, when he was leaving Gauguin's tropic dreams and nightmares behind and toying with a more straightforwardly Impressionist phase. Elanore was modeling for him nude as Manet's *Olympia*. As a concession to practicalities and to the urgency that then always possessed him when he was painting, the black maidservant bearing the flowers in his lavish new studio on the Boulevard des Capucines was a projection, but the divan and all the hangings, the flowers, and the cat, of course—although by its programmed nature, Metzengerstein was incapable of looking quite as scared and scrawny as Manet's original—were all foreal.

"You know," Elanore said, not breaking pose, one hand toying with the hem of the shawl on which she was lying, the other laid negligently, possessively, without modesty, across her pubic triangle, "we really should reinvite Marcel over after all he's done for us lately."

"Marcel?" In honesty, Gustav was paying little attention to anything at that moment other than which shade to swirl into the boudoir darkness. He dabbed again onto his testing scrap. "Marcel's in San Francisco. We haven't seen him in months."

"Of course . . . silly me."

He finally glanced up again, what could have been moments or minutes later, suddenly aware that a cold silence that had set in. Elanore, being Elanore, never forgot anything. Elanore was light and life. Now, all her *Olympia*-like poise was gone.

This wasn't like the decay and loss of function that affected the elderly in the days before recombinant drugs. Just like her heart and her limbs, Elanore's physical brain still functioned perfectly. But the effect was the same. Confusions and mistakes happened frequently after that, as if consciousness drained rapidly once the initial rent was made. For Elanore, with her exquisite dignity, her continued beauty, her companies and her investments and the contacts that she needed to maintain, the process of senility was particularly terrible. No one, least of all Gustav, argued against her decision to pass on.

Back where reality ended, it was past midnight and the moon was blazing down over the Left Bank's broken rooftops through the grayish-brown nanosmog. And exactly where, Gustav wondered, glaring up at it through the still-humming gantries of the reality engine that had enclosed him and Elanore, is Francine across the sky? How much do you have to pay to get the right decoders in your optic nerves to see the stars entwined in some vast projection of her? How much of your life do you have to give away?

The mazy streets behind St. Michael were rotten and weed-grown in the bilious fog, the dulled moonlight. No one but Gustav seemed to live in the half-supported ruins of the Left Bank nowadays. It was just a place for posing in and being seen—although in that respect, Gustav reflected, things really hadn't changed. To get back to his tenement, he had to cross the Boulevard

St. Germain through a stream of buzzing robot cars that, no matter how he dodged them, still managed to avoid him. In the busier streets beyond, the big reality engines were still glowing. In fact, it was said that you could now go from one side of Paris to the other without having to step out into foreal. Gustav, as ever, did his best to do the opposite, although he knew that even without any credit, he would still be freely admitted to the many realities on offer in these generous, carefree days. He scowled at the shining planes of the powerfields that stretched between the gantries like bubbles. Faintly from inside, coming at him from beyond the humming of the transformers that tamed and organized the droplets of nanosmog into shapes you could feel, odors you could smell, chairs you could sit on, he could hear words and laughter, music, the clink of glasses. He could even just make out the shapes of the living as they postured and chatted. It was obvious from the way that they were grouped that the living were outnumbered by the dead these days. Outside, in the dim streets, he passed figures like tumbling decahedrons who bore their own fields with them as they moved between realities. They were probably unaware of him as they drifted by, or perhaps saw him as some extra enhancement of whatever dream it was they were living. Flick, flick. Scheherazade's Baghdad. John Carter's Mars. It really didn't matter that you were still in Paris, although Elanore, of course, had showed sensitivity in the place she had selected for their meeting.

Beyond the last of the reality engines, Gustav's own cheap unvirtual tenement loomed into view. He picked his way across the tarmac toward the faint neon of the foreal Spar store beside it. Inside, there were the usual gray slabs of packaging with tiny windows promising every possible delight. He wandered up the aisles and activated the homely presence of the woman who served the dozen or so anachronistic places that were still scattered around Paris. She smiled at him—a living ghost, really; but then, people seemed to prefer the illusion of the personal touch. Behind her, he noticed, was an antiquated cigarette machine. He ordered a packet of Disc Bleu, and palmed what were probably the last of his credits—which amounted to half a stick of charcoal or two squeezes' worth of Red Lake. It was a surprise to him, in fact, that he even had enough for these cigarettes.

Outside, ignoring the health warning that flashed briefly before his eyes, he lighted a Disc Bleu, put it to his lips, and deeply inhaled. A few moments later, he was in a nauseous sweat, doubled up and gasping.

Another bleak morning, timeless and gray. This ceiling, these walls. And Elanore . . . Elanore was dead. Gone.

Gustav belched on the wine he was sure that he'd drunk, and smelled the sickness and the smoke of that foreal Disc Bleu still clinging to him. But there was no trace of Elanore. Not a copper strand of hair on his shoulder or curled around his cock, not her scent riming his hands.

He closed his eyes and tried to picture a woman in a white chemise bathing in a river's shallows, two bearded men talking animatedly in a grassy space beneath the trees, and Elanore sitting naked close by, although she watches rather than joins in their conversation. . . .

No. That wasn't it.

Somehow getting up, pissing cloudily into the appropriate receptacle, Gustav finally grunted in unsurprise when he noticed a virtual light flickering through the heaped and broken frames of his easels. Unlike the telephone, he was sure that the company had disconnected his terminal long ago. His head fizzing, his groin vaguely tumescent, some lost bit of the night nagging like a stray scrap of meat between his teeth, he gazed down into the spinning options that the screen offered.

It was Elanore's work, of course—or the ghost of entangled electrons that Elanore had become. Hey, presto!—Gustav was back on line; granted this shimmering link into the lands of the dead and the living. He saw that he even had positive credit, which explained why he'd been able to buy that packet of Disc Bleu. He'd have slammed his fist down into the thing if it would have done any good.

Instead, he scowled at his room, the huddled backs of the canvases, the drifts of discarded food and clothing, the heap of his bed, wondering if Elanore was watching him now, thrusting a spare few gigabytes into the sensors of some nano-insect that was hovering close beside him. Indeed, he half-expected the thin partitions and dangling wires, all the mocking rubbish of his life, to shudder and change into snowy Russian parkland, a wooded glade, even Paris again, 1890. But none of that happened.

The positive credit light still glowed enticingly within the terminal. In the almost certain knowledge that he would regret it, but quite unable to stop himself, Gustav scrolled through the pathways that led him to the little-frequented section dealing with artists' foreal requisites. Keeping it simple— down to fresh brushes, and Lefranc and Bourgeois's extra-fine Flake White, Cadmium Yellow, Vermilion, Deep Madder, Cobalt Blue, and Emerald Green—and still waiting as the cost all of that clocked up for the familiar credit-expired sign to arrive, he closed the screen.

The materials arrived far quicker than he'd expected, disgorging themselves into a service alcove in the far corner with a *whoosh* like the wind. The supplier had even remembered to include the fresh bottles of turpentine he'd forgotten to order—he still had plenty of clean, stretched canvases anyway. So here (the feel of the fat new tubes, the beautiful, haunting names of the colors, the faint stirring sounds that the brushes made when he tried to lift them) was everything he might possibly need.

Gustav was an artist.

The hours did funny things when Gustav was painting—or even thinking about painting. They ran fast or slow, passed by on a fairy breeze, or thickened and grew huge as megaliths, then joined up and began to dance lumberingly around him, stamping on every sensibility and hope.

Taking fierce drags of his last Disc Bleu, clouding his tenement's already filmy air, Gustav finally gave up scribbling on his pad and casting sidelong glances at the canvas as the blazing moon began to flood Paris with its own sickly version of evening. As he'd always known he'd probably end up doing, he then began to wander the dim edges of his room, tilting back and examining his old, unsold, and generally unfinished canvases. Especially in this light, and seen from upside down, the scenes of foreal Paris looked suitably wan. There was so little to them, in fact, such a thinness and lack of color, that they could easily be re-used. But here in the tangled shadows of the farthest corner, filled with colors that seemed to pour into the air like a perfume, lay his early attempts at Symbolism and Impressionism. Amid those, he noticed something paler again. In fact, unfinished—but from an era when, as far as he could recall, he'd finished everything. He risked lifting the canvas out, and gazed at the outlines, the dabs of paint, the layers of wash. He recognized it now. It had been his attempt at Manet's *Olympia*.

After Elanore had said her good-byes to all her friends, she retreated into the white virtual corridors of a building near the Cimetière du Père Lachaise that might once have been called a hospital. There, as a final fail-safe, her mind was scanned and stored, the lineaments of her body were recorded. Gustav was the only person Elanore allowed to visit her during those last weeks; she was perhaps already too confused to understand what seeing her like this was doing to him. He'd sit amid the webs of silver monitoring wires as she absently stroked Metzengerstein, and the cat's eyes, now far greener and brighter than hers, regarded him. She didn't seem to want to fight this loss of self. That was probably the thing that hurt him most. Elanore, the proper foreal Elanore, had always been searching for the next river to cross, the next challenge; it was probably the one characteristic that they had shared. But now she accepted death, this loss of Elanore, with nothing but resignation. *This is the way it is for all us*, Gustav remembered her saying in one of the last cogent periods before she forgot his name. *So many of our friends have passed on already. It's just a matter of joining them. . . .*

Elanore never quite lost her beauty, but she became like a doll, a model of herself, and her eyes grew vacant as she sat silent or talked ramblingly. The freckles faded from her skin. Her mouth grew slack. She began to smell sour. There was no great fuss made when they finally turned her off, although Gustav still insisted that he be there. It was a relief, in fact, when Elanore's eyes finally closed and her heart stopped beating, when the hand he'd placed in his turned even more flaccid and cold. Metzengerstein gave Gustav one final glance before it twisted its way between the wires, leaped off the bed, and padded from the room, its tail raised. For a moment, Gustav considered grabbing the thing, slamming it down into a pulp of memory circuits and flesh and metal. But it had already been deprogrammed. Metzengerstein was just a shell; a comforter for Elanore in her last dim days. He never saw the creature again.

Just as the living Elanore had promised, her ghost only returned to Gustav after a decent interval. And she made no assumptions about their future at that first meeting on the neutral ground of a shorefront restaurant in virtual Balbec. She clearly understood how difficult all this was for him. It had been a windy day, he remembered, and the tablecloths flapped, the napkins threatened to take off, the lapel of the cream-brocade jacket she was wearing kept lying across her throat until she pinned it back with a brooch. She told him that she still loved him, and that she hoped they would be able to stay together. A few days later, in a room in the same hotel overlooking the same windy beach, Elanore and Gustav made love for the first time since she had died.

The illusion, Gustav had to admit, then and later, was always perfect. And, as the dying Elanore had pointed out, they both already knew many ghosts. There was Marcel, for instance, and there was Jean, Gustav's own dealer and agent. It wasn't as if Elanore had even been left with any choice. In a virtual, ghostly daze himself, Gustav agreed that they should set up home together. They chose Brittany, because it was new to them—unloaded with memories—and the scenery was still often decent and visible enough to be worth painting.

Foreal was going out of style by then. For many years, the technologies of what was called reality had been flawless. But now, they became all-embracing. It was at about this time, Gustav supposed, although his memory once was again dim on this matter, that they set fire to the moon. The ever-bigger reality engines required huge amounts of power—and so it was that the robot ships set out, settled into orbit around the moon, and began to spray the surface with antimatter, spreading their wings like hands held out to a fire to absorb and then transmit back to earth the energies this iridescence gave. The power the moon now provided wasn't quite limitless, but it was near enough. With so much alternative joy and light available, the foreal world, much like a garden left untended, soon began to assume a look of neglect.

Ever considerate to his needs, Elanore chose and had refurbished a gabled clifftop mansion near Locronan, and ordered graceful and foreal furniture at huge extra expense. For a month or so, until the powerlines and transformers of the reality engines had been installed, Gustav and Elanore could communicate with each other only by screen. He did his best to tell himself that being unable to touch her was a kind of tease, and kept his thoughts away from such questions as where exactly Elanore was when she wasn't with him, and if she truly imagined she was the seamless continuation of the living Elanore that she claimed herself to be.

The house smelled of salt and old stone, and then of wet plaster and new carpets, and soon began to look as charming and eccentric as anything Elanore had organized in her life. As for the cost of all this forgotten craftsmanship, which, even in these generous times, was quite daunting, Elanore had discovered, like many of the ghosts who had gone before her, that her work—the dealing in stocks, ideas, and raw megawatts in which she specialized—was suddenly much easier. She could flit across the world, make deals based on long-term calculations that no living person could ever hope to understand.

Often, in the early days when Elanore finally reached the reality of their cliff-top house in Brittany, Gustav would find himself gazing at her, trying to catch her unawares, or, in the nights when they made love with an obsessive frequency and passion, he would study her while she was sleeping. If she seemed distracted, he put it down to some deal she was cooking, a new antimatter trail across the Sea of Storms, perhaps, or a business meeting in Capetown. If she sighed and smiled in her dreams, he imagined her in the arms of some long-dead lover.

Of course, Elanore always denied such accusations. She even gave a good impression of being hurt. She was, she insisted, configured to ensure that she was always exactly where she appeared to be, except for brief times and in the gravest of emergencies. In the brain or on the net, human consciousness was a fragile thing—permanently in danger of dissolving. *I really am talking to you now, Gustav.* Otherwise, Elanore maintained, she would unravel, she would cease to be Elanore. As if, Gustav thought in generally silent rejoinder, she hadn't ceased to be Elanore already.

She'd changed, for a start. She was cooler, calmer, yet somehow more mercurial. The simple and everyday motions she made, like combing her hair or stirring coffee, began to look stiff and affected. Even her sexual preferences had changed. And passing over *was* different. Yes, she admitted that, even though she could feel the weight and presence of her own body just as she could feel his when he touched her. Once, as the desperation of their arguments increased, she even insisted on stabbing herself with a fork, just so that he might finally understand that she felt pain. But for Gustav, Elanore wasn't like the many other ghosts he'd met and readily accepted. They weren't *Elanore.* He'd never loved and painted *them.*

Gustav soon found that he couldn't paint Elanore now, either. He tried from sketches and from memory; once or twice he got her to pose. But it didn't work. He couldn't quite lose himself enough to forget what she was. They even tried to complete that *Olympia,* although the memory was painful for both of them. She posed for him as Manet's model, who in truth she did look a little like; the same model who'd posed for that odd scene by the river, *Dejéuner sur l'Herbe.* Now, of course, the cat as well as the black maid had to be a projection, although they did their best to make everything else the same. But there was something lost and wan about the painting as he tried to develop it. The nakedness of the woman on the canvas no longer gave off strength and knowledge and sexual assurance. She seemed pliant and helpless. Even the colors grew darker; it was like fighting something in a dream.

Elanore accepted Gustav's difficulties with what he sometimes found to be chillingly good grace. She was prepared to give him time. He could travel. She could develop new interests, burrow within the net as she'd always promised herself, and live in some entirely different place.

Gustav began to take long walks away from the house, along remote clifftop paths and across empty beaches, where he could be alone. The moon and the sun sometimes cast their silver ladders across the water. Soon, Gustav thought sourly, there'll be nowhere left to escape to. Or perhaps we will *all* pass on, and the gantries and the ugly virtual buildings that all look like the old Pompidou Centre will cease to be necessary; but for the glimmering of a few electrons, the world will revert to the way it was before people came. We can even extinguish the moon.

He also started to spend more time in the few parts of their rambling house that, largely because much of the stuff they wanted was handbuilt and took some time to order, Elanore hadn't yet had fitted out foreal. He interrogated the house's mainframe to discover the codes that would turn the reality engines off and on at will. In a room filled with tapestries, a long oak table, a vase of hydrangeas, pale curtains lifting slightly in the breeze, all it took was the correct gesture, a mere click of his fingers, and it would shudder and vanish, to be replaced by nothing but walls of mildewed plaster, the faint tingling sensation that came from the receding powerfield. There—then gone. Only the foreal view at the window remained the same. And now, click, and it all came *back* again. Even the fucking vase. The fucking flowers.

Elanore sought him out that day. Gustav heard her footsteps on the stairs, and knew that she'd pretend to be puzzled as to why he wasn't working in his studio.

"*There* you are," she said, appearing a little breathless after her climb up the stairs. "I was thinking—"

Finally scratching the itch that he realized had been tickling him for some time, Gustav clicked his fingers. Elanore—and the whole room, the table, the flowers, the tapestries—flickered off.

He waited—several beats, he really didn't know how long. The wind still blew in through the window. The powerfield hummed faintly, waiting for its next command. He clicked his fingers. Elanore and the room took shape again.

"I thought you'd probably override that," he said. "I imagined you'd given yourself a higher priority than the furniture."

"I could if I wished," she said. "I didn't think I'd need to do such a thing."

"No. I mean, you can just go somewhere else, can't you? Some other room in this house. Some other place. Some other continent . . ."

"I keep telling you. It isn't like that."

"I know. Consciousness is fragile."

"And we're really not that different, Gus. I'm made of random droplets held in a force field—but what are *you*? Think about it. You're made of atoms, which are just quantum flickers in the foam of space, particles that aren't even particles at all . . ."

Gustav stared at her. He was remembering—he couldn't help it—that they'd made love the previous night. Just two different kinds of ghost; entwined, joining—he supposed that that was what she was saying. And what about my *cock*, Elanore, and all the stuff that gets emptied into you when we're fucking? What the hell do you do with *that*?

"Look, Gus, this isn't—"

"—And what do you dream at night, Elanore? What is it that you do when you pretend you're sleeping?"

She waved her arms in a furious gesture that Gustav almost recognized from the Elanore of old. "What the hell do you *think* I do, Gus? I *try* to be human. You think it's easy, do you, hanging on like this? You think I enjoy watching *you* flicker in and out?—which is basically what it's like for me every time you step outside these fields? Sometimes I just wish I . . ."

Elanore trailed off there, glaring at him with emerald eyes. Go on, Gustav felt himself urging her. *Say* it, you phantom, shade, wraith, ghost. Say you wish you'd simply died. But instead, she made some internal command of her own, and blanked the room—and vanished.

It was the start of the end of their relationship.

Many guests came to visit their house in the weeks after that, and Elanore and Gustav kept themselves busy in the company of the dead and the living. All the old crowd, all the old jokes. Gustav generally drank too much, and made his presence unwelcome with the female ghosts as he decided that once he'd fucked the nano-droplets in one configuration, he might as well try fucking them in another. What the hell was it, Gus wondered, that made the living so reluctant to give up the dead, and the dead to give up the living?

In the few hours that they did spend together and alone at that time, Elanore and Gustav made detailed plans to travel. The idea was that they (meaning Elanore, with all the credit she was accumulating) would commission a ship, a sailing ship, traditional in every respect apart from the fact that the sails would be huge power receptors driven directly by the moon, and the spars would be the frame of a reality engine. Together, they would get away from all of this, and sail across the foreal oceans, perhaps even as far as Tahiti. Admittedly, Gustav was intrigued by the idea of returning to the painter who by now seemed to be the initial wellspring of his creativity. He was certainly in a suitably grumpy and isolationist mood to head off, as the poverty-stricken and desperate Gauguin had once done, in search of inspiration in the South Seas; and ultimately to his death from the prolonged effects of syphilis. But they never actually discussed what Tahiti would be *like*. Of course, there would be no tourists there now—only eccentrics bothered to travel foreal these days. Gustav liked to think, in fact, that there would be none of the tall, ugly buildings and the huge Coca-Cola signs that he'd once seen in an old photograph of Tahiti's main town of Papeete. There might—who knows?—not be any reality engines, even, squatting like spiders across the beaches and jungle. With the understandable way that the birth rate was now declining, there would be just a few natives left, living as they had once lived before Cook and Bligh and all the rest—even Gauguin with his art and his myths and his syphilis—had ruined it for them. That was how Gustav wanted to leave Tahiti.

Winter came to their clifftop house. The guests departed. The wind raised white crests across the ocean. Gustav developed a habit, which Elanore pretended not to notice, of turning the heating down, as if he needed chill and discomfort to make the place seem real. Tahiti, that ship of theirs, remained an impossibly long way off. There were no final showdowns—just this gradual drifting apart. Gustav gave up trying to make love to Elanore, just as he had given up trying to paint her. But they were friendly and cordial with each other. It seemed that neither of them wished to pollute the memory of something that had once been wonderful. Elanore was, Gustav knew, starting to become concerned about his failure to have his increasing signs of age treated, and his refusal to have a librarian; even his insistence on pursuing a career that seemed only to leave him depleted and damaged. But she never said anything.

They agreed to separate for a while. Elanore would head off to explore pure virtuality. Gustav would go back to foreal Paris and try to rediscover his art. And so, making promises they both knew they would never keep, Gustav and Elanore finally parted.

Gustav slid his unfinished *Olympia* back down amid the other canvases. He looked out of the window, and saw from the glow coming up through the gaps in the houses that the big reality engines were humming. The evening, or whatever other time and era it was, was in full swing.

A vague idea forming in his head, Gustav pulled on his coat and headed out from his tenement. As he walked down through the misty, smoggy streets, it almost began to feel like inspiration. Such was his absorption that he didn't even bother to avoid the shining bubbles of the reality engines. Paris, at the end of the day, still being Paris, the realities he passed through mostly consisted of one or another sort of café, but there were set amid dazzling souks, dank medieval alleys, yellow and seemingly watery places where swam strange creatures that he couldn't think to name. But his attention wasn't on it anyway.

The Musée D'Orsay was still kept in reasonably immaculate condition beside the faintly luminous and milky Seine. Outside and in, it was well lit, and a trembling barrier kept in the air that was necessary to preserve its contents until the time came when they were fashionable again. Inside, it even *smelled* like an art gallery, and Gustav's footsteps echoed on the polished floors, and the robot janitors greeted him; in every way, and despite all the years since he'd last visited, the place was the same.

Gustav walked briskly past the statues and the bronze casts, past Ingres's big, dead canvases of supposedly voluptuous nudes. Then Moreau, early Degas, Corot, Millet . . . Gustav did his best to ignore them all. For the fact was that Gustav hated art galleries—he was still, at least, a painter in that respect. Even in the years when he'd gone deliberately to such places, because he knew that they were good for his own development, he still liked to think of himself as a kind of burglar—get in, grab your ideas, get out again. Everything else, all the ahhs and the oohs, was for mere spectators. . . .

He took the stairs to the upper floor. A cramp had worked its way beneath his diaphragm and his throat felt raw, but behind all of that there was this feeling, a tingling of power and magic and anger—a sense that perhaps . . .

Now that he was up amid the rooms and corridors of the great Impressionist works, he forced himself to slow down. The big gilt frames, the pompous marble, the names and dates of artists who had often died in anonymity, despair, disease, blindness, exile, near-starvation. Poor old Sisley's *Misty Morning*. Vincent van Gogh in a self-portrait formed from deep, sensuous, three-dimensional oils. Genuinely great art was, Gustav thought, pretty depressing for would-be great artists. If it hadn't been for the invisible fields that were protecting these paintings, he would have considered ripping the things off the walls, destroying them.

His feet led him back to the Manets, that woman gazing out at him from *Dejéuner sur l'Herbe*, and then again from *Olympia*. She wasn't beautiful, didn't even look much like Elanore . . . But that wasn't the point. He drifted on past the clamoring canvases, wondering if the world had ever been this bright, this new, this wondrously chaotic. Eventually, he found himself face-to-face with the surprisingly few Gauguins that the Musée D'Orsay possessed. Those bright slabs of color, those mournful Tahitian natives, which were often painted on raw sacking because it was all Gauguin could get his hands on in the hot stench of his tropical hut. He became wildly fashionable after his death, of course; the idea of destitution on a faraway isle suddenly stuck everyone as romantic. But it was too late for Gauguin by then. And too late—as his hitherto worthless paintings were snapped up by Russians, Danes, Englishmen, Americans—for these stupid, habitually arrogant Parisians. Gauguin was often poor at dealing with his shapes, but he generally got away with it. And his sense of color was like no one else's. Gustav remembered vaguely now that there was a nude that Gauguin had painted as his own lopsided tribute to Manet's *Olympia*—had even pinned a photograph of it to the wall of his hut as he worked. But, like most of Gauguin's other really important paintings, it wasn't here at the Musée D'Orsay, this supposed epicenter of Impressionist and Symbolist art. Gustav shrugged and turned away. He hobbled slowly back down through the galley.

Outside, beneath the moonlight, amid the nanosmog and the buzzing of the powerfields, Gustav made his way once again through the realities. An English tea house circa 1930. A Guermantes salon. If they'd been foreal, he'd have sent the cups and the plates flying, bellowed in the self-satisfied faces of the dead and living. Then he stumbled into a scene he recognized from the Musée D'Orsay, one, in fact, that had once been as much a cultural icon as Madonna's tits or a Beatles tune. *Le Moulin de la Galette.* He was surprised and almost encouraged to see Renoir's Parisian figures in their Sunday-best clothing, dancing under the trees in the dappled sunlight, or chatting at the surrounding benches and tables. He stood and watched, nearly smiling. Glancing down, saw that he was dressed appropriately in a rough woollen navy suit. He studied the figures, admiring their animation, the clever and, yes, convincing way that, through some trick of reality, they were composed. . . . Then he realized that he recognized some of the faces, and that they had also recognized him. Before he could turn back, he was called to and beckoned over.

"Gustav," Marcel's ghost said, sliding an arm around him, smelling of male sweat and Pernod. "Grab a chair. Sit down. Long time no see, eh?"

Gustav shrugged and accepted the brimming tumbler of wine that was offered. If it was foreal—which he doubted—this and a few more of the same might help him sleep tonight. "I thought you were in Venice," he said. "As the Doge."

Marcel shrugged. There were breadcrumbs on his mustache. "That was *ages* ago. Where have you been, Gustav?"

"Just around the corner, actually."

"Not still *painting*, are you?"

Gustav allowed that question to be lost in the music and the conversation's ebb and flow. He gulped his wine and looked around, expecting to see Elanore at any moment. So many of the others were here—it was almost like old times. There, even, was Francine, dancing with a top-hatted man—so she clearly wasn't across the sky. Gustav decided to ask the girl in the striped dress who was nearest to him if she'd seen Elanore. He realized as he spoke to her that her face was familiar to him, but he somehow couldn't recollect her name—even whether she was living or a ghost. She shook her head, and asked the woman who stood leaning behind her. But she, also, hadn't seen Elanore; not, at least, since the times when Marcel was in Venice and when Francine was across the sky. From there, the question rippled out across the square. But no one, it seemed, knew what had happened to Elanore.

Gustav stood up and made his way between the twirling dancers and the lantern-strung trees. His skin tingled as he stepped out of the reality, and the laughter and the music suddenly faded. Avoiding any other such encounters, he made his way back up the dim streets to his tenement.

There, back at home, the light from the setting moon was bright enough for him to make his way through the dim wreckage of his life without fall- ing—and the terminal that Elanore's ghost had reactivated still gave off a virtual glow. Swaying, breathless, Gustav paged down into his accounts, and saw the huge sum—the kind of figure that he associated with astronomy, with the distance of the moon from the earth, the earth from the sun—that now appeared there. Then he passed back through the terminal's levels, and began to search for Elanore.

But Elanore wasn't there.

Gustav was painting. When he felt like this, he loved and hated the canvas in almost equal measures. The outside world, foreal or in reality, ceased to exist for him.

A woman, naked, languid, and with a dusky skin quite unlike Elanore's, is lying upon a couch, half-turned, her face cupped in her hand that lies upon the primrose pillow, her eyes gazing away from the onlooker at something far off. She seems beautiful but unerotic, vulnerable yet clearly available, and self-absorbed. Behind her—amid the twirls of bright yet gloomy decoration— lies a glimpse of stylized rocks under a strange sky, while two oddly disturbing figures are talking, and a dark bird perches on the lip of a balcony; perhaps a raven. . . .

Although he detests plagiarism, and is working solely from memory, Gus- tav finds it hard to break away from Gauguin's nude on this canvas he is now painting. But he really isn't fighting that hard to do so, anyway. In this above all of Gauguin's great paintings, stripped of the crap and the despair and the self-justifying symbolism, Gauguin was simply *right*. So Gustav still keeps working, and the paint sometimes almost seems to want to obey him. He doesn't know or care at the moment what the thing will turn out like. If it's good, he might think of it as his tribute to Elanore; and if it isn't . . . Well, he knows that, once he's finished this painting, he will start another one. Right now, that's all that matters.

Elanore was right, Gustav decides, when she once said that he was entirely selfish, and would sacrifice everything—himself included—just so that he could continue to paint. She was eternally right and, in her own way, she too was always searching for the next challenge, the next river to cross. Of course, they should have made more of the time that they had together, but as Elanore's ghost admitted at that van Gogh café when she finally came to say good-bye, nothing could ever quite be the same.

Gustav stepped back from his canvas and studied it, eyes half-closed at first just to get the shape, then with a more appraising gaze. Yes, he told himself, and reminded himself to tell himself again later when he began to feel sick and miserable about it, this is a true work. This is worthwhile.

Then, and although there was much that he still had to do, and the oils were still wet, and he knew that he should rest the canvas, he swirled his brush in a blackish puddle of palette-mud and daubed the word NEVERMORE across the top, and stepped back again, wondering what to paint *next*.

The Wisdom of Old Earth

MICHAEL SWANWICK

One of the most popular and respected of all the new writers who entered the field in the eighties, Michael Swanwick made his debut in 1980 with two strong and compelling stories, "The Feast of St. Janis" and "Ginungagap," both of which were Nebula Award finalists that year, and which were both selected either for a Best of the Year anthology or for that year's annual Nebula Awards volume—as auspicious a debut as anyone has ever made.

He stayed in the public eye, and on major award ballots, throughout the rest of the eighties with intense and powerful stories such as "Mummer Kiss," "The Man Who Met Picasso," "Trojan Horse." "Dogfight" (written with William Gibson), "Covenant of Souls," "The Dragon Line," "Snow Angles," "A Midwinter's Tale," and many others—all of which earned him a reputation as one of the most powerful and consistently inventive short-story writers of his generation. Nor did his output of short fiction slacken noticeably in the nineties, in spite of a burgeoning career as a novelist, and recent years have seen the appearance of major Swanwick stories such as "The Edge of the World," "The Changling's Tale," "Griffin's Egg," "Cold Iron," and "The Dead"; he remains one of SF's most prolific writers at short lengths. By the end of the nineties, his short work would have won him several Asimov's Reader's Awards, a Sturgeon Award, the World Fantasy Award, and back-to-back Hugo Awards—he won the Hugo in 1999 for his story "The Very Pulse of the Machine," and followed it up in 2000 with another Hugo Award for his story "Scherzo with Tyrannosaur."

At first, his reputation as a novelist lagged behind his reputation as a short-story writer, with his first novel, In The Drift—published in 1985 as part of Terry Carr's resurrected Ace Specials line, along with first novels by William Gibson, Kim Stanley Robinson, and Lucius Shepard—largely ignored by the critics, and panned by some of them. His second novel, though, the critically acclaimed Vacuum Flowers, caused a stir, and with his third and perhaps best-known novel, Stations of the Tide, he established himself firmly as among the vanguard of the hot new novelists of the nineties; Stations of the Tide won him a Nebula Award in 1991. His next novel, The Iron Dragon's Daughter, a finalist for both the World Fantasy Award and the Arthur C. Clarke Award (a unique distinction!), explored new literary territory on the ambiguous borderland of science fiction and fantasy, and has been hailed by some critics as the first example of an as yet still nascent subgenre called "Hard Fantasy" (sort of a mix between the Dickensian sensibilities of "steampunk," high-tech science fiction, and traditional Tolkienesque fantasy). His most recent novel Jack Faust, a sly reworking of the Faust legend that explores the unexpected impact of technology on society, blurs genre boundaries even more and has garnered rave reviews from nearly every source from The Washington Post to Interzone. He's just finished a new novel, featuring time-travelers and hungry dinosaurs.

Here he takes us to a bizarre and vividly realized far future, where the gulf between human and posthuman has become very large and virtually uncrossable, to learn an ancient lesson: If you want wisdom, you must be prepared to pay for it. . . .

Swanwick's other books include the novella-length Griffin's Egg, *one of the most brilliant and compelling of modern-day Moon-colony stories. His short fiction has been assembled in* Gravity's Angels, A Geography of Unknown Lands, *and in a collection of his collaborative short work with other writers,* Slow Dancing Through Time. *He's also published a collection of critical articles,* The Postmodern Archipelago. *His most recent books are three new collections,* Moon Dogs, Puck Aleshire's Abecedary, *and* Tales of Old Earth. *Swanwick lives in Philadelphia with his wife, Marianne Porter, and their son Sean.*

Judith Seize-the-Day was, quite simply, the best of her kind. Many another had aspired to the clarity of posthuman thought, and several might claim some rude mastery of its essentials, but she alone came to understand it as completely as any offworlder.

Such understanding did not come easily. The human mind is slow to generalize and even slower to integrate. It lacks the quicksilver apprehension of the posthuman. The simplest truth must be repeated often to imprint even the most primitive understanding of what comes naturally and without effort to the spacefaring children of humanity. Judith had grown up in Pole Star City, where the shuttles slant down through the zone of permanent depletion in order to avoid further damage to the fragile ozone layer, and thus from childhood had associated extensively with the highly evolved. It was only natural that as a woman she would elect to turn her back on her own brutish kind and strive to bootstrap herself into a higher order.

Yet even then she was like an ape trying to pass as a philosopher. For all her laborious ponderings, she did not yet comprehend the core wisdom of posthumanity, which was that thought and action must be as one. Being a human, however, when she did comprehend, she understood it more deeply and thoroughly than the posthumans themselves. As a Canadian she could tap into the ancient and chthonic wisdoms of her race. Where her thought went, the civilized mind could not follow.

It would be expecting too much of such a woman that she would entirely hide her contempt for her own kind. She cursed the two trollish Ninglanders who were sweating and chopping a way through the lush tangles of kudzu, and drove them onward with the lash of her tongue.

"Unevolved bastard pigs!" she spat. "Inbred degenerates! If you ever want to get home to molest your dogs and baby sisters again, you'll put your backs into it!"

The larger of the creatures looked back at her with an angry gleam in his eye, and his knuckles whitened on the hilt of his machete. She only grinned humorlessly, and patted the holster of her *ankh*. Such weapons were rarely allowed humans. Her possession of it was a mark of the great respect in which she was held.

The brute returned to his labor.

It was deepest winter, and the jungle tracts of what had once been the mid-Atlantic coastlands were traversable. Traversable, that is, if one had a good guide. Judith was among the best. She had brought her party alive to the Flying Hills of southern Pennsylvania, and not many could have done that. Her client had come in search of the fabled bell of liberty, which many another party had sought in vain. She did not believe he would find it either. But that did not concern her.

All that concerned her was their survival.

So she cursed and drove the savage Ninglanders before her, until all at once they broke through the vines and brush out of shadow and into a clearing.

All three stood unmoving for an instant, staring out over the clumps and hillocks of grass that covered the foundations of what had once been factories, perhaps, or workers' housing, gasoline distribution stations, grist mills, shopping malls. . . . Even the skyline was uneven. Mystery beckoned from every ambiguous lump.

It was almost noon. They had been walking since sundown.

Judith slipped on her goggles and scanned the grey skies for navigation satellites. She found three radar beacons within range. A utility accepted their input and calculated her position: less than a hundred miles from Philadelphia. They'd made more distance than she'd expected. The empathic function mapped for her the locations of her party: three, including herself, then one, then two, then one, strung over a mile and a half of trail. That was wrong.

Very wrong indeed.

"Pop the tents," she ordered, letting the goggles fall around her neck. "Stay out of the food."

The Ninglanders dropped their packs. One lifted a refrigeration stick over his head like a spear and slammed it into the ground. A wash of cool air swept over them all. His lips curled with pleasure, revealing broken yellow teeth.

She knew that if she lingered, she would not be able to face the oppressive jungle heat again. So, turning, Judith strode back the way she'd come. Rats scattered at her approach, disappearing into hot green shadow.

The first of her party she encountered was Harry Work-to-Death. His face was pale and he shivered uncontrollably. But he kept walking, because to stop was to die. They passed each other without a word. Judith doubted he would live out the trip. He had picked up something after their disastrous spill in the Hudson. There were opiates enough in what survived of the medical kit to put him out of his misery, but she did not make him the offer.

She could not bring herself to.

Half a mile later came Leeza Child-of-Scorn and Maria Triumph-of-the-Will, chattering and laughing together. They stopped when they saw her. Judith raised her *ankh* in the air, and shook it so that they could feel its aura scrape ever so lightly against their nervous systems.

"Where is the offworlder?" The women shrank from her anger. "You abandoned him. You *dared*. Did you think you could get away with it? You were fools if you did!"

Wheedlingly, Leeza said, "The sky man knew he was endangering the rest of us, so he asked to be left behind." She and Maria were full-blooded Canadians, like Judith, free of the taint of Southern genes. They had been hired for their intelligence, and intelligence they had—a low sort of animal cunning that made them dangerously unreliable when the going got hard. "He insisted."

"It was very noble of him," Maria said piously.

"I'll give you something to be noble about if you don't turn around and lead me back to where you left him." She holstered her *ankh*, but did not lock it down. "Now!" With blows of her fists, she forced them down the trail. Judith was short, stocky, all muscle. She drove them before her like the curs that they were.

The offworlder lay in the weeds where he had been dropped, one leg twisted at an odd angle. The litter that Judith had lashed together for him had been flung into the bushes.

His clothes were bedraggled, and the netting had pulled away from his collar. But weak as he was, he smiled to see her. "I knew you would return for me." His hands fluttered up in a gesture indicating absolute confidence. "So I was careful to avoid moving. The fracture will have to be reset. But that's well within your capabilities, I'm sure."

"I haven't lost a client yet." Judith unlaced his splint and carefully straightened the leg. Posthumans, spending so much of their time in microgravity environments, were significantly less robust than their ancestral stock. Their bones broke easily. Yet when she reset the femur and tied up the splint again with lengths of nylon cord, he didn't make a sound. His kind had conscious control over their endorphin production. Judith checked his neck for ticks and chiggers, then tucked in his netting. "Be more careful with this. There are a lot of ugly diseases loose out here."

"My immune system is stronger than you'd suspect. If the rest of me were as strong, I wouldn't be holding you back like this."

As a rule, she liked the posthuman women better than their men. The men were hothouse flowers—flighty, elliptical, full of fancies and elaboration. Their beauty was the beauty of a statue; all sculptured features and chill affect. The offworlder, however, was not like that. His look was direct. He was as solid and straightforward as a woman.

"While I was lying here, I almost prayed for a rescue party."

To God, she thought he meant. Then saw how his eyes lifted briefly, involuntarily, to the clouds and the satellites beyond. Much that for humans required machines, a posthuman could accomplish with precisely tailored neural implants.

"They would've turned you down." This Judith knew for a fact. Her mother, Ellen To-the-Manner-Born, had died in the jungles of Wisconsin, eaten away with gangrene and cursing the wardens over an open circuit.

"Yes, of course, one life is nothing compared to the health of the planet." His mouth twisted wryly. "Yet still, I confess I was tempted."

"Put him back in the litter," she told the women. "Carry him gently." In the Québecois dialect, which she was certain her client did not know, she added, "Do this again, and I'll kill you."

She lagged behind, letting the others advance out of sight, so she could think. In theory, she could simply keep the party together. In practice, the women could not both carry the offworlder and keep up with the men. And if she did not stay with the Ninglanders, they would not work. There were only so many days of winter left. Speed was essential.

An unexpected peal of laughter floated back to her, then silence.

Wearily, she trudged on. Already they had forgotten her, and her *ankh*. Almost she could envy them. Her responsibilities weighed heavily upon her. She had not laughed since the Hudson.

According to her goggles, there was a supply cache in Philadelphia. Once there, they could go back on full rations again.

The tents were bright mushrooms in the clearing. Work-to-Death lay dying within one of them. The women had gone off with the men into the bush. Even in this ungodly heat and humidity, they were unable or unwilling to curb their bestial lusts.

Judith sat outside with the offworlder, the refrigeration stick turned up just enough to take the edge off the afternoon heat. To get him talking, she asked, "Why did you come to Earth? There is nothing here worth all your suffering. Were I you, I'd've turned back long ago."

For a long moment, the offworlder struggled to gear down his complex thoughts into terms Judith could comprehend. At last he said, "Consider evolution. Things do not evolve from lower states to higher, as the ancients believed, with their charts that began with a fish crawling up upon the land and progressed on to mammals, apes, Neanderthals, and finally men. Rather, an organism evolves to fit its environment. An ape cannot live in the ocean. A human cannot brachiate. Each thrives in its own niche.

"Now consider posthumanity. Our environment is entirely artificial—floating cities, the Martian subsurface, the Venusian and Jovian bubbles. Such habitats require social integration of a high order. A human could survive within them, possibly, but she would not thrive. Our surround is self-defined, and therefore within it we are the pinnacle of evolution."

As he spoke, his hands twitched with the suppressed urge to amplify and clarify his words with the secondary emotive language offworlders employed in parallel with the spoken. Thinking, of course, that she did not savvy handsign. But as her facility with it was minimal, Judith did not enlighten him.

"Now imagine a being with more-than-human strength and greater-than-posthuman intellect. Such a creature would be at a disadvantage in the posthuman environment. She would be an evolutionary dead end. How then could she get any sense of herself, what she could do, and what she could not?"

"How does all apply to you personally?"

"I wanted to find the measure of myself, not as a product of an environment that caters to my strengths and coddles my weaknesses. I wanted to discover what I am in the natural state."

"You won't find the natural state here. We're living in the aftermath."

"No," he agreed. "The natural state is lost, shattered like an eggshell. Even if—when—we finally manage to restore it, gather up all the shards and glue them together, it will no longer be natural, but something we have decided to maintain and preserve, like a garden. It will be only an extension of our culture."

"Nature is dead," Judith said. It was a concept she had picked up from other posthumans.

His teeth flashed with pleasure at her quick apprehension. "Indeed. Even off Earth, where conditions are more extreme, its effects are muted by technology. I suspect that nature can only exist where our all-devouring culture has not yet reached. Still . . . here on Earth, in the regions where all but the simplest technologies are prohibited, and it's still possible to suffer pain and even death. . . . This is as close to an authentic state as can be achieved." He patted the ground by his side. "The past is palpable here, century upon century, and under that the strength of the soil." His hands involuntarily leapt. *This is so difficult*, they said. *This language is so clumsy.* "I am afraid I have not expressed myself very well."

He smiled apologetically then, and she saw how exhausted he was. But still she could not resist asking, "What is it like, to think as you do?" It was a question that she had asked many times, of many posthumans. Many answers had she received, and no two of them alike.

The offworlder's face grew very still. At last he said, "Lao-tzu put it best. 'The way that can be named is not the true way. The name that can be spoken is not the eternal name.' The higher thought is ineffable, a mystery that can be experienced but never explained."

His arms and shoulders moved in a gesture that was the evolved descendant of a shrug. His weariness was palpable.

"You need rest," she said, and, standing, "let me help you into your tent."

"Dearest Judith. What would I ever do without you?"

Ever so slightly, she flushed.

The next sundown, their maps, though recently downloaded, proved to be incomplete. The improbably named Skookle River had wandered, throwing off swamps that her goggles' topographical functions could not distinguish from solid land. For two nights the party struggled southward, moving far to the west and then back again so many times that Judith would have been entirely lost without the navsats.

Then the rains began.

There was no choice but to leave the offworlder behind. Neither he nor Harry Work-to-Death could travel under such conditions. Judith put Maria and Leeza in charge of them both. After a few choice words of warning, she left them her spare goggles and instructions to break camp and follow as soon as the rains let up.

"Why do you treat us like dogs?" a Ninglander asked her when they were under way again. The rain poured down over his plastic poncho.

"Because you are no better than dogs."

He puffed himself up. "I am large and shapely. I have a fine mustache. I can give you many orgasms."

His comrade was pretending not to listen. But it was obvious to Judith that the two men had a bet going as to whether she could be seduced or not.

"Not without my participation."

Insulted, he thumped his chest. Water droplets flew. "I am as good as any of your Canadian men!"

"Yes," she agreed, "unhappily, that's true."

When the rains finally let up, Judith had just crested a small hillock that her topographics identified as an outlier of the Welsh Mountains. Spread out before her was a broad expanse of overgrown twenty-first-century ruins. She did not bother accessing the city's name. In her experience, all lost cities were alike; she didn't care if she never saw another. "Take ten," she said, and the Ninglanders shrugged out of their packs.

Idly, she donned her goggles to make sure that Leeza and Maria were breaking camp, as they had been instructed to do.

And screamed with rage.

The goggles Judith had left behind had been hung, unused, upon the flap-pole of one of the tents. Though the two women did not know it, it was slaved to hers, and she could spy upon their actions. She kept her goggles on all the way back to their camp.

When she arrived, they were sitting by their refrigeration stick, surrounded by the discarded wrappings of half the party's food and all of its opiates. The stick was turned up so high that the grass about it was white with frost. Already there was an inch of ash at its tip.

Harry Work-to-Death lay on the ground by the women, grinning loopily, face frozen to the stick. Dead.

Outside the circle, only partially visible to the goggles, lay the offworlder, still strapped to his litter. He chuckled and sang to himself. The women had been generous with the drugs.

"Pathetic weakling," Child-of-Scorn said to the offworlder, "I don't know why you didn't drown in the rain. But I am going to leave you out in the heat until you are dead, and then I am going to piss on your corpse."

"I am not going to wait," Triumph-of-the-Will bragged. She tried to stand and could not. "In just—just a moment!"

The whoops of laughter died as Judith strode into the camp. The Ning-landers stumbled to a halt behind her, and stood looking uncertainly from her to the women and back. In their simple way, they were shocked by what they saw.

Judith went to the offworlder and slapped him hard to get his attention. He gazed up confusedly at the patch she held up before his face.

"This is a detoxifier. It's going to remove those drugs from your system.

Unfortunately, as a side effect, it will also depress your endorphin production. I'm afraid this is going to hurt."

She locked it onto his arm, and then said to the Ninglanders, "Take him up the trail. I'll be along."

They obeyed. The offworlder screamed once as the detoxifier took effect, and then fell silent again. Judith turned to the traitors. "You chose to disobey me. Very well. I can use the extra food."

She drew her *ankh*.

Child-of-Scorn clenched her fists angrily. "So could we! Half-rations so your little pet could eat his fill. Work us to death carrying him about. You think I'm *stupid*. I'm not stupid. I know what you want with him."

"He's the client. He pays the bills."

"What are you to him but an ugly little ape? He'd sooner fuck a cow than you!"

Triumph-of-the-Will fell over laughing. "A cow!" she cried. "A fuh-fucking cow! Moo!"

Child-of-Scorn's eyes blazed. "You know what the sky people call the likes of you and me? Mud-women! Sometimes they come to the cribs outside Pole Star City to get good and dirty. But they always wash off and go back to their nice clean habitats afterward. Five minutes after he climbs back into the sky, he'll have forgotten your name."

"Moooo! Moooo!"

"You cannot make me angry," Judith said, "for you are only animals."

"I am not an animal!" Child-of-Scorn shook her fist at Judith. "I refuse to be treated like one."

"One does not blame an animal for being what it is. But neither does one trust an animal that has proved unreliable. You were given two chances."

"If I'm an animal, then what does that make *you*? Huh? What the fuck does that make *you*, goddamnit?" The woman's face was red with rage. Her friend stared blankly up at her from the ground.

"Animals," Judith said through gritted teeth, "should be killed without emotion."

She fired twice.

With her party thus diminished, Judith could not hope to return to Canada afoot. But there were abundant ruins nearby, and they were a virtual reservoir of chemical poisons from the days when humans ruled the Earth. If she set the *ankh* to its hottest setting, she could start a blaze that would set off a hundred alarms in Pole Star City. The wardens would have to come to contain it. She would be imprisoned, of course, but her client would live.

Then Judith heard the thunder of engines.

High in the sky, a great light appeared, so bright it was haloed with black. She held up a hand to lessen the intensity and saw within the dazzle a small dark speck. A shuttle, falling from orbit.

She ran crashing through the brush as hard and fast as she could. Nightmarish minutes later, she topped a small rise and found the Ninglanders standing there, the offworlder between them. They were watching the shuttle come to a soft landing in the clearing its thrusters had burned in the vegetation.

"You summoned it," she accused the offworlder.

He looked up with tears in his eyes. The detoxifier had left him in a state of pitiless lucidity, with nothing to concentrate on but his own suffering. "I had to, yes." His voice was distant, his attention turned inward, on the neural device that allowed him to communicate with the ship's crew. "The pain— you can't imagine what it's like. How it feels."

A lifetime of lies roared in Judith's ears. Her mother had died for lack of the aid that came at this man's thought.

"I killed two women just now."

"Did you?" He looked away. "I'm sure you had good reasons. I'll have it listed as death by accident." Without his conscious volition, his hands moved, saying, *It's a trivial matter, let it be.*

A hatch opened in the shuttle's side. Slim figures clambered down, white med-kits on their belts. The offworlder smiled through his tears and stretched out welcoming arms to them.

Judith stepped back and into the shadow of his disregard. She was just another native now.

Two women were dead.

And her reasons for killing them mattered to no one.

She threw her head back and laughed, freely and without reserve. In that instant Judith Seize-the-Day was as fully and completely alive as any of the unworldly folk who walk the airless planets and work in the prosperous and incomprehensible habitats of deep space.

In that instant, had any been looking, she would have seemed not human at all.

Toast: A Con Report

CHARLES STROSS

Although he made his first sale back in 1987, it's only recently that British writer Charles Stross has begun to make a name for himself as a writer to watch in the new century ahead, with a sudden burst in the last couple of years of quirky, inventive, high-bit-rate stories such as "Antibodies," "A Colder War," "Bear Trap," and "Dechlorinating the Moderator" in markets such as Interzone, Spectrum SF, Odyssey, *and* New Worlds. *In the fast-paced and innovative story that follows, he shows us that all this "posthuman" stuff may be arriving a lot faster than anyone thinks that it is . . .*

Charles Stross is also a regular columnist for the monthly magazine Computer Shopper. *Coming up is his first collection,* Toast, and Other Burned Out Futures. *He lives in Edinburgh, Scotland.*

Old hackers never die; they just sprout more gray hair, their T-shirts fade, and they move on to stranger and more obscure toys.

Well, that's the way it's supposed to be. *Your Antiques!* asked me to write about it, so I decided to find out where all the old hackers went. Which is how come I ended up at Toast-9, the ninth annual conference of the Association for Retrocomputing Meta-Machinery. They got their feature, you're getting this con report, and never the two shall meet.

Toast is held every year in the Boston Marriot, a piece of disgusting glass-and-concrete cheesecake from the late 1970s post-barbarism school of architecture. I checked my bags in at the hotel reception, then went out in search of a couple of old hackers to interview.

I don't know who I was expecting to find, but it sure as hell wasn't Ashley Martin. Ashley and I worked together for a while in the early zeroes, as contract resurrection men raising zombies from some of the big iron databases that fell over on Black Tuesday: I lost track of him after he threw his double-breasted Compaq suit from a tenth-floor window and went to live in a naturist commune on Skye, saying that he was never going to deal with any time-span shorter than a season ever again. (At the time I was pissed off; that suit had cost our company fifteen thousand dollars six months ago, and it wasn't fully depreciated yet.) But there he was, ten inches bigger around the waist and real as taxes, queuing in front of me at the registration desk.

"Richard! How are you?"

"Fine, fine." (I'm always cautious about uttering the social niceties around hex-heads; most of them are oblivious enough that as often as not a casual "How's it going?" will trigger a quarter-hour stack-dump of woes.) "Just waiting for my membership pack. . . ."

There was a chime and the door of the badge printer sprang open; Ashley's membership pack stuck its head out and looked around anxiously until it spotted him.

"Just update my familiar," I told the young witch on the desk; "I don't need any more guides." She nodded at me in the harried manner that staff on a convention registration desk get.

"The bar," Ashley announced gnomically.

"The bar?"

"That's where I'm going," he said.

"Mind if I join you?"

"That was the general idea."

The bar was like any other con bar since time immemorial, or at least the end of the post-industrial age (which is variously dated to December 31, 1999, February 29, 2000, or March 1972, depending who you talk to). Tired whiskey bottles hung upside down in front of a mirror for the whole world to gape at; four pumps dispensed gassy ersatz beer: and a wide range of alcohol-fortified grape juice was stacked in a glass-fronted chiller behind the bar. The bartop itself was beige and labeled with the runes *DEC* and *VAX 11/780*. When I asked the drone for a bottle of Jolt, they had to run one up on their fab, interrupting its continuous-upgrade cycle; it chittered bad temperedly and waved menacing pseudopodia at me as it took time out to spit caffeinated water into a newly spun bucky bottle.

Ash found a free table and I waited for my vessel to cool enough to open. We watched the world go by for a while; there were no major disasters, nobody I knew died, and only three industry-specific realignments or mergers of interest took place.

"So what brings you here, eh?" I asked eventually.

Ashley shrugged. "Boredom. Nostalgia. And my wife divorced me a year ago. I figured it was time to get away from it all before I scope out the next career."

"Occupational hazard," I sympathized, carefully not questioning the relationship between his answer and my question.

"No, it bloody isn't," he said with some asperity, raising his glass for a brief mouthful followed by a shudder. "You've got to move with the times. Since I met Laura I've been a hand crafted toy designer, not a, an—" he looked around at the other occupants of the bar and shuddered, guiltily.

"Anorak?" I asked, trying to keep my tone of voice neutral.

"Furry toys." He glared at his glass but refrained from taking another mouthful. "That's where the action is, not mainframes or steam engines or wearables or MEMS or assemblers. They're all obsolete as soon as they come off the fab, but children will always need toys. Walking, talking dolls who're fun to be with. I discovered I've got a knack for the instinctual level—" Something small and blue and horribly similar to a hairy smurf was trying to crawl out of one of his breast pockets, closely pursued by a spreading ink stain.

"So she divorced you? Before or after children?"

"Yes and no, luckily in that order." He noticed the escaping imp and, with a sigh, unzipped one of the other pockets on his jacket and thrust the little wriggler inside. It meeped incoherently; when he zipped the pocket up, it heaved and billowed like a tent in a gale. "Sorry about that; he's an escape artist. Special commission, actually."

"How long have you been in the toy business?" I prompted, seeking some less-hazardous territory.

"Two years before we got married. Six years ago, I think." Oh gods, he was a brooder. "It was the buried commands that did it. She was the marketing face; we got a lot of bespoke requests for custom deluxe Tele-tubby sets, life-sized interactive droids, that kind of thing. Peter Platypus and his Pangolin Playmates. I couldn't do one of those and stay sane without implanting at least one buried Easter egg; usually a reflex dialogue, preferably a suite of subversive memes. Like the Barney who was all sweetness and light and I-love-you-you-love-me until he saw a My Little Pony; then he got hungry and remembered his velociraptor roots."

"I suppose there were a lot of upset little girls—"

"Hell, no! But one of the parental investment units got pissed enough to sue; those plastic horsies are expensive collectors' items these days."

"Do you still get much work?" I asked.

"Yes." He downed his glass in one. "You'd be amazed how many orcs the average gamer gets through. And there's always a market for a custom one. Here's Dean—" The wriggling in his pocket had stopped; it looked rather empty. "Excuse me a moment," he said, and went down on hands and knees beneath the table in search of the escape artist.

>> **<<EDITORIAL>>**
Handcrafted toys are probably the last domain of specialist human programmers these days. You can trust a familiar with most things, but children are pretty sensitive and familiars are generally response-tuned to adult company. Toys are a special case: their simple reflex sets and behaviors make them amenable to human programmers—children don't mind, indeed need, a lot of repetition and simple behavior they can understand—while human programmers are needed because humans are still better than familiars at raising human infants. But someone who makes only nasty, abusive, or downright rude toys is—
<<EDITORIAL>>

Later, while my luggage sniffed out a usefully plumbed corner and grew me a suite, I wandered around the hardware show.

Hardware shows at a big con are always fascinating to the true geek, and this one was no exception. Original PCs weren't common at Toast-9, being too commonplace to be worth bringing along, but the weird and wonderful was here in profusion. In the center of the room was an octagonal pillar surrounded by a cracked vinyl loveseat: an original Cray supercomputer from the 1980s in NSA institutional blue. Over in that corner, that rarest and most exotic of beasts, an Altair-1 motherboard, its tarnished copper circuit tracks thrusting purposefully between black, insectoidal microprocessor and archaic hex keypad (the whole thing mounted carefully under a diamond display case, watchful guardian demons standing to either side in case any enthusiasts tried to get too close to the ancient work of art).

I strolled round the hall slowly, lingering over the ancient mainframes: starting with the working Difference Engine and the IBM 1604 console, then the Pentium II laptop. All of them were pre-softwear processors: discrete industrial machines from back before the prêt-à-porter brigade acquired personal area networks and turned electronics into a fashion statement. Back when processor power doubled every eighteen months and bandwidth doubled every twelve months, back before they'd been overtaken by newer, faster-evolving technologies.

I was examining a particularly fine late-model SPARCstation when somebody goosed me from behind. Strangers don't usually sneak up on me for a quick grope—more's the pity—so when I peeled myself off the ceiling and turned round, I wasn't too surprised to see Lynda grinning at me ghoulishly. "Richard!" she said, "I knew you'd be around here somewhere! How's tricks?"

"Much the same. Yourself?"

"Still with the old firm." The old firm—Intangible Business Mechanisms, as they call themselves today—is a big employer of witches, and Lynda is a particularly fine exponent of the profession, having combined teaching at MIT and practice as a freelance consultant for years. Another of those child prodigies who seem attracted to new paradigms like flies to dog shit. (I should add: Lynda isn't her real name. Serial numbers filed off, as they say, to protect the innocent.) "Just taking in a little of the local color, dear. It's so classical! All these hardwired circuits and little lumps of lithographed silicon-germanium semiconductor. Can you believe people once relied on such crude technologies?"

"Tactless," I hissed at her: an offended anorak-wearer was glaring from beside the Altair-1. "And the answer is yes, anyway. But it was all before your time, wasn't it?"

"Oh, I wouldn't say that," she said. "I had a laptop, too, when I was a baby. But by the time I was in my teens, it was all so boring, dinosaur-sized multinationals being starved to death by the free software crowd and trying to drown them in a sea of press releases and standards initiatives, to a Greek chorus singing laments about Moore's Law only giving room for another five years of improvements in microprocessor design before they finally ran up against the quantum limits of miniaturization. I remember when House of Versace released their first wearable collection, and there was me, a sixteen-year-old goth with more CPU power in her earrings than IBM sold in the 1990s, and it was boring. The revolution had eaten its own sense of wonder and shat out megacorporations. Would you believe it?" She blinked, and wobbled a little, as if drunk on words. I think her thesaurus was running at too high a priority level.

I surreptitiously looked at her feet: she was wearing heavy black boots, the preferred thinking environment of the security-minded. (Steel toe caps make for great Faraday cages.) Then I eyeballed her up and down; judging by the conservative business suit, she had deteriorated a lot in the past year, to the point where she needed corporate meme support. When I first met Lynda, she'd been wearing a fortune in homemade RISC processors bound together by black lacy tatters of goth finery, cracking badly secured ten-year-old financial transactions every few milliseconds. (And selling any numbered offshore accounts she detected to the IRS for a thief-taker's cut, in order to subsidize her nanoassembler design start-up.) Now she was wearing Armani.

<<**EDITORIAL**>>

A business suit is a future-shock exoskeleton, whispering reminders in its wearers' ears to prompt them through the everyday niceties of a life washed into bleeding monochrome by the flood of information they live under. Corporate workers and consultants today—I gather this, because I dropped out of that cycle a few years ago, unable to keep up with a new technological revolution every six months—live on the bleeding edge of autism, so wrapped up in their work that if their underwear didn't tell them when to go to the toilet, their bladders would burst. And it's not just the company types who need the thinking environment: geeks became dependent on low-maintenance clothing years before, and it's partly thanks to their efforts that the clothing became sentient (if not fully independent).

Clothes today say far more about someone's corporate and social status than they did in the twentieth century; we can blame the Media Lab for that, with their radical (not to say annoying) idea that your clothes should think for you. A conservative business suit by a discreet softwear company screams PHB groupware; sneakers and a sloganeering T-shirt or combat pants go with the Freeware crowd, anarchoid linuxers and hackers, some of them charging a thousand bucks an hour for their commercial services. A 1980s-yuppie would have been astonished at the number of body piercings in the boardrooms, the vacant, glassy stares of brain-webbed executives being steered round the local delicatessen by their neckties while their suit jackets engineered a hostile takeover in Ulan Bator and their shoes tracked stock prices. But then, an eighties' yuppie would be a living fossil in this day and age, slow and cold-blooded and not sufficiently intelligent to breathe and do business simultaneously. O brave new world, to have such cyborgs in it.

<<**EDITORIAL**>>

We arrived back in the bar. "I think I need a drink," said Lynda, wobbling on her feet. "Oops! So sorry. Er, yes. This is so slow, Richard! How do you handle the boredom?"

"Excuse me?" The bartender handed me another Jolt, this one nicely chilled. A large margarita slid across the bartop and somehow appeared in her hand.

"This!" She looked around vaguely. "Real time!"

I stared at her. Her pupils were wide. "Are you on anything I should know about?" I asked.

"Sensory deprivation. My suit's powered down." She shook her head. "I feel naked. I haven't been offline in months; there are things happening that

I don't know about. It seemed like a good idea at the time, but now I'm not sure. Is it always like this?"

"How long have you been down?" I asked.

"I'm unsure. Since I saw you in the show? I wanted to get into your headspace and see what it was like, but it's so cramped! Maybe half an hour; it's a disciplinary offense, you know?"

"What, going offline?"

Her eyeballs flickered from side to side in the characteristic jitter of information-withdrawal nystagmus. "Being obsolete."

I left Lynda in the safe custody of a hotel paramedic, who didn't seem to think there'd be any permanent side effects once her clothing had rebooted. I headed back to the con, fervently glad that I'd stepped off the treadmill a couple of releases after Ashley, way before things got this bad.

> ## <<**EDITORIAL**>>
>
> Information withdrawal is an occupational hazard for the well-connected, like diabetic hypoglycaemia; if the diabetic doesn't get their sugar hit, or the executive their info-burn, they get woozy and stop working. On the other hand, you can only take it for so long . . .
>
> Lynda is 26. At 16, she was cracking financial cryptosystems. At 17, she was designing nanotech assemblers. At 20 she was a professor, with a patent portfolio worth millions. Today she's an executive vice-president with a budget measured in the billions. She will be burned out completely by 30, out of rehab by 32 (give or take a case of tardive dyskinesia), with a gold-plated pension and the rest of her life ahead of her—just like the rest of us proto-transhumanists, washed up on the evolutionary beach.
>
> ## <<**EDITORIAL**>>

Back in the con proper, I decided to take in a couple of talks. There's a long and sometimes contradictory series of lectures and workshops at any Toast gathering, not to mention the speakers' corners, where any crank can set up a soap-box and have their say.

First I sat through a rather odd monologue with only three other attendees (one of them deeply asleep in the front row): a construct shaped like a cross between a coatrack and a praying mantis was vigorously attacking the conceit of human consciousness, attempting to prove (by way of an updated version of Searle's Chinese Room attack, lightly seasoned à la Penrose) that dumb neurons can't possibly be intelligent in the same way as a, well, whatever the thing on the podium was. It was almost certainly a prank, given our proximity to MIT (not to mention the Gates Trust-endowed Department of Amplified Intelligence at Harvard), but it was still absorbing to listen to its endless spew of rolling, inspired oratory. Eventually the construct argued itself into a solipsistic corner, then asked the floor for questions; when nobody asked any, it stormed off in a huff.

I must confess that I was half-asleep by the time the robot philosopher denounced us as nonsapient automata, sparing only half my left eye to speed-read Minsky's *Society of Mind* for clues; in any event. I woke up in time for the next talk, a panel discussion. Someone had rounded up an original stalwart of the Free Software Foundation to talk about the rise and demise of Microsoft. There was, of course, a Microsoft spokesdroid present to defend the company's historic record. It started with the obligatory three-minute AV presentation about how Our Great Leader and Teacher (Bill) had Saved the World from IBM, but before they could open their mouths and actually say anything, Bill's head appeared on-screen and the audience went wild: it was like the Three Minute Hate in *Nineteen Eighty-Four*.

(I used to use the man's software like everyone else, but after the debacle of Windows NT 6.2, and the ensuing grand jury investigation and lynchings, well—)

After the Microsoft talk I went back to my temporary apartment to estivate for a few hours. At my age, I need all the regeneration time I can get, even if I have to take it hanging upside down in a brightly colored cocoon woven to the side of a tower block's support column. I run some quackware from India that claims to be a white-box clone of the Kaiser-Glaxo program the Pope uses; my tent and travel-equipment designs come courtesy of the Free Hardware Foundation. Having lost my main income stream years ago due to the usual causes, principally cumulative future shock and the letdown from the Y2K consultancy business, I'd be lost without the copylefted design schemata to feed to my assembler farm: I certainly can't afford the latest commercial designs for anything much more exotic than a fountain pen. But life on a twenty-century income is still tolerable these days, thanks to the FHF. More about those angels in Birkenstocks later, if I can be bothered to write it.

I awoke feeling refreshed and came down from my cocoon to find a new wardrobe waiting for me. I'd got my tent to run up conservative geek-chic before my nap—urban camo trousers, nine-inch nails T-shirt, combat boots, and a vest-of-pockets containing numerous artifacts—and it whispered to me reassuringly as I pulled it on, mentioning that the fuel cell in my left hip pocket was good for thirty hours of warmth and power if I had to venture out into the minus-ten wind chill of a Boston winter. I pumped my heels, then desisted, feeling silly: in this day of barely-visible turbogenerators, heel power makes about as much sense as a slide rule.

Outside my spacious dome tent, the floor of the hotel had sprouted a many-colored mushroom forest. Luggage and more obscure personal servants scurried about, seeing to their human owners' requirements. Flying things buzzed back and forth like insects with vectored-thrust turbojets. A McDonald's stall had opened up at the far side of the hall and was burning blocks of hashish to make the neighbors hungry; my vest discreetly reminded me that I had some nose plugs.

I had been asleep for three hours. While I had been asleep, Malaysian scientists had announced the discovery of an earth-sized planet with an oxidizing atmosphere less than forty light-years away; the Gates Trust, in their eternal pursuit of favorable propaganda, had announced that they were going to send a Starwhisp to colonize it.

<<**EDITORIAL**>>
Insert snide comment about clones, eyes of needles, possibility of passage through, at this juncture; the whole point of a Starwhisp is that it's too small to carry any cargo much bigger than a bacillus. Probably the GT was just trying to tweak the American public's guilt complex over the breakup of NASA.
<<**EDITORIAL**>>

The Pope had reversed her ruling of last week on personality uploads, but reasserted the indivisibility of the soul, much to the confusion of theologians and neuroscientists alike.

There had been riots in Afghanistan over the forcible withdrawal of the Playboy channel by the country's current ruling clique of backwoods militiamen. (Ditto Zimbabwe and Arkansas.)

Further confirmation of the existence of the sixth so-called gravitoweak resonance force had been obtained by a team of posthumans somewhere in high orbit. The significance of this discovery was massive, but immediate impact remained obscure—no technological spin-offs were predicted in the next few weeks.

Nobody I knew had died, or been born, or undergone major life-revising events. I found this absence of change obscurely comforting; a worrying sign, so I punched up a really sharp dose of the latest cognitive enhancer and tried to drag my aging (not to say reeling) brain back into the hot core of future-surfing that is the only context in which the antiquities of the silicon era (or modern everyday life, for that matter) can be decoded.

I got out into the exhibition hall only to discover that there was a costume show and disco scheduled for the rest of the night. This didn't exactly fascinate me, but I went along and stared anyway while catching up on the past few hours' news. The costume show was impressive—lots of fabric, and all of it dumb. They had realistic seventies' hackers, eighties' Silicon Valley entrepreneurs, nineties' venture capitalists, and millennia resurrection men, complete with some bits of equipment too precious to put on public exhibition—things like priceless early wearable computer demos from the Media Lab, on loan for the evening: all badly glued Velcro, cell-phone battery compartments run up on a glue-gun renderer, and flickering monochrome head-up displays. Toward the end, one of the models shambled on stage in a recent (three-month-old, hence barely obsolete) space suit: a closed-circuit life-support system capable of protecting its owner from any kind of hostile environment and recycling their waste for months or years. It probably qualified as an engineering miracle (closed-circuit life support is hard) but it left me with a lingering impression that a major cause of death among its users would be secondary consequences of sexual frustration.

The disco was, well, a disco. Or a rave. Or a waltz. These things don't change: people dress up, eat, take intoxicants, and throw themselves around to music. Same old same old. I settled down with the drinks and the old crusties in the bar, intent on getting thoroughly wasted and exchanging tall stories with the other fogies.

About four or five drinks later, an advertisement crawled through my spam filter and started spraying hotly luminous colors across my left retina. I was busy swapping yarns with an old Cobol monkey called Solipsist Nation and I didn't notice it at first. "Is something wrong, my friend?" he asked.

"S'spam. Nothing," I said.

Solly pulled out a huge old revolver—a Colt, I think—and looked around. Squinting, he pointed it at the floor and pulled the trigger. There was no bang, but a cloud of smoke squirted out and settled rapidly to the ground, clustering densely around a small buglike object. The visuals stopped.

"It's nothing now," he agreed, putting his gun away. "There was a time when things were different."

"When they didn't hide behind microbots. Just hijacked mail seryers."

He grinned, disquietingly. "Then they went away."

I nodded. "Let's drink a toast. To whatever made the mail spammers go away."

He raised his glass with me, but I didn't see him drink.

> **<<EDITORIAL>>**
> Something the junk advertisers don't seem to understand: we live in an information-supersaturated world. If I don't want to buy something, no amount of shouting or propagandizing will budge me; all it will do is get me annoyed. On the other hand, if I have a need for your product, I can seek it out in an eyeblink.
> **<<EDITORIAL>>**

We now return you to your regular scheduled programming . . .

There was an art show. Fractals blossomed in intricate, fragile beauty on wall-sized screens of fabulously expensive liquid crystal, driven by the entropy-generating logic-chopping of discrete microprocessors. You could borrow some contact lenses and slip between two wall-sized panels and you're on Europa's seabed, gray ooze and timelessness shared with the moluscoids clustered around the hydrothermal vents. Endless tape loops played cheesy Intel adverts from the tail end of the 20th, human chip-fab workers in clean-room suits boogying or rocking to some ancient synthesizer beat. A performance-art group, the Anderoids, identically dressed in blue three-piece suits, hung around accosting visitors with annoyingly impenetrable PHB marketroid jargon in an apparent attempt to get them to buy some proprietary but horizontally-scalable vertical-market mission-critical business solution. The subculture of the nerd was omnipresent: an attack of the fifty-foot Dilbert loomed over walls, partitions and cubicle hell, glasses smudged and necktie perpetually upturned in a quizzical fin-de-siècle loop.

I took in some more of the panels. Grizzled hackers chewed over the ancient jousts of Silicon Valley in interminable detail: Apple versus IBM, IBM versus DEC, RISC versus CISC/SIMD, Sun versus Intel. I've heard it all before and it's comforting for all its boring familiarity: dead fights, exhumed by retired generals and refought across tabletop boards without the need for any deaths or downsizings.

There was an alternate-history panel, too. Someone came up with a beauty: a one-line change in the 1971 antitrust ruling against AT&T that leaves them the right to sell software. UNIX dead by 1978, strangled by expensive licenses and no source code for universities; C and C++ non-starters: the future as VMS. Another change left me shaking my head: five times per hour on a cross-wind. Gary Kildall didn't go flying that crucial day, was at the office when IBM came calling in 1982 and sold them CP/M for their PCs. By Y2K, Microsoft had a reputation for technical excellence, selling their commercial UNIX-95 system as a high-end server system. (In this one, Bill Gates still lives in the USA.) What startled me most was the inconsequentiality of these points of departure: trillion-dollar industries that grew from a sentence or a breeze in the space of twenty years.

<<**EDITORIAL**>>
This is the season of nerds, the flat tail at the end of the sigmoid curve. Some time in the 1940s, the steam locomotive peaked; great four-hundred-ton twin-engined monsters burning heavy fuel oil, pulling miles-long train sets that weighed as much as freight ships. Twenty years later, the last of these great workhorses were toys for boys who'd grown up with cinders and steam in their eyes. Some time in the 2010s, the microprocessor peaked: twenty years later our magi and witches invoke self-programming demons that constantly enhance their own power, sucking vacuum energy from the vasty deeps, while the last supercomputers draw fractals for the amusement of gray-haired kids who had sand kicked in their eyes. Sometime in the 2020s, nanotechnology began the long burn up the curve: the nostalgics who play with their gray goo haven't been decanted from their placentories yet, and the field is still hot and crackling with the buzz of new ideas. It's a cold heat that burns as it expands your mind, and I find less and less inclination to subject myself to it these days. I'm in my seventies; I used to work with computers for real before I lost touch with the bleeding edge and slipped into fandom, back when civilization ran on bits and bytes and the machineries of industry needed a human touch at the mouse.
<<**EDITORIAL**>>

Eventually I returned to the bar. Ashley was still more or less where I'd left him the day before, slumped half under a table with his ankles plugged into something that looked like a claymation filing cabinet. He waved as I went past, so after I picked up my drink at the bar, I joined him. "How're you feeling today?"

"Been worse," he said cheerfully. Three or four empty bottles stood in front of him. "Couldn't fetch me one, could you? I'm on the Kriek geuse."

I glanced under the table. "Uh, okay."

I took another look under the table as I handed him the bottle. The multicolored cuboid had engulfed his legs to ankle-height before; now it was sending pseudopods up toward his knees. "Your health. Seen much of the show?"

"Naah." He raised the bottle to me, then drank from the neck. "I'm busy here."

"Doing what, if I can ask?"

"I've decided to emigrate to Tau Ceti." He gestured under the table. "So I'm mind-mapping."

"Mind-map—" I blinked. *I do not think that word means what I think it means* drifted through my head. "What for?"

He sighed. "I'm sick of dolls, Richard. I need a change, but I'm not as flexible as I used to be. What do you think I'm doing?"

I spared a glance under the table again. The thing was definitely getting larger, creeping up to his knees. "Don't be silly," I said. "You don't need to do this, do you?"

"Afraid I do." He drank some more beer. "Don't worry, I've been thinking about it for a long time. I'm not a spring chicken, you know. And it's not as if I'll be dead, or even much different. Just smarter, more flexible. More me, the way I was. Able to work on the cutting edge."

"The cutting edge is not amenable to humans, Ash. Even the weakly superhuman can't keep up anymore."

He smiled, the ghost of an old devil-may-care grin. "So I won't be weakly superhuman, will I?"

I drew my legs back, away from the Moravec larva below the table. It was eating him slowly, converting his entire nervous system into a simulation map inside whatever passed for its sensorium: when it finished, it would pupate, and something that wasn't Ashley anymore would hatch. Something which maintained conscious continuity with the half-drunken idiot sitting in front of me, but that resembled him the way a seventy-year-old professor resembles a baby.

"Did you tell your ex-wife?" I asked.

He flinched slightly. "She can't hurt me anymore." I shook my head. "Another drink?" he asked.

"Just one for the road," I said gently. He nodded and snapped his fingers for the bar. I made sure the drink lasted; I had a feeling this was the last time I'd see him, continuity of consciousness or no.

<<**EDITORIAL**>>

And that, dear reader, is why I'm writing this con report. The *Your Antiques!* audience want to know all about the history of Cray Y-MP-48 s/n 4002, hi-res walkthroughs and a sidebar describing the life and death of old man Seymour. All of which is, well, train-spotting. And you can't learn the soul of an old machine by counting serial numbers; for that, you have to stand on the footplate, squinting into the wind of its passage and shovelling coal into the furnace, feel the rush of its inexorable progress up the accelerating curve of history. In this day and age, if you want to learn what the buzz of the computer industry was like, you'd have to stop being human. Transcendence is an occupational hazard, the cliff at the edge of the singularity; try climbing too fast and you'll fall over, stop being yourself. It's a big improvement over suicide, but it's still not something I'd welcome just now, and certainly not as casually as Ashley took to it. Eventually it will catch up with me, too, and I'll have to stop being human: but I like my childhood, thank you very much, and the idea of becoming part of some vast, cool intelligence working the quantum foam at the bottom of the M-theory soup still lies around the final bend of my track.

<<**EDITORIAL**>>

The Gardens of Saturn

PAUL J. McAULEY

Born in Oxford, England, in 1955, Paul J. McAuley now makes his home in London. A professional biologist for many years, he sold his first story in 1984, and has gone on to be a frequent contributor to Interzone, *as well as to markets such as* Amazing, The Magazine of Fantasy and Science Fiction, Asimov's Science Fiction, When the Music's Over, *and elsewhere.*

McAuley is considered to be one of the best of the new breed of British writers (although a few Australian writers could be fit in under this heading as well) who are producing that brand of rigorous hard science fiction with updated modern and stylistic sensibilities that is sometimes referred to as "radical hard science fiction," but he also writes Dystopian sociological speculations about the very near future, and he also is one of the major young writers who are producing that revamped and retooled widescreen Space Opera that has sometimes been called the New Baroque Space Opera, reminiscent of the Superscience stories of the thirties taken to an even higher level of intensity and scale. His first novel Four Hundred Billion Stars *won the Philip K. Dick Award, and his acclaimed novel* Fairyland *won both the Arthur C. Clarke Award and the John W. Campbell Award in 1996. His other books include the novels* Of The Fall, Eternal Light, *and* Pasquale's Angel, *two collections of his short work,* The King of the Hill and Other Stories *and* The Invisible Country, *and an original anthology co-edited with Kim Newman,* In Dreams. *His most recent books are* Child of the River, Ancient of Days, *and* Shrine of Stars, *which comprise a major new trilogy of ambitious scope and scale,* Confluence, *set ten million years in the future. Currently he is working on a new novel,* Life on Mars.

Here he takes us to the outer reaches of the solar system, where an interplanetary society has been ravaged by war, and where life is strange and complicated for the survivors—and is about to get a whole lot stranger still.

Baker was in the pilots' canteen, talking about the price of trace elements with a couple of factors, when someone started making trouble at the servitor. A tall, skinny redhead in baggy flight pants and a tight jumper with the sleeves torn off had hooked her left arm around one of the servitor's rungs and was kicking hell out of it with her bare feet, bouncing hard each time and coming back, shouting at the machine, "You want how much for this shit?" and kicking it again.

Obviously she hadn't been on Phoebe very long or she would have known that for all their girder-up-the-ass morals, the Redeemers were gougers of the worst kind. It was Baker's nature to try to find something to like in everyone, but even he had a hard time being charitable about the Redeemers. His collective could afford only basic environmental amenities when visiting other habitats, and on Phoebe those were very basic indeed—tank food and a coffin not much bigger than the life-system on the scow. If you wanted a shower, you paid for two minutes and a hundred liters of gray water; beer or any other luxury goods were available only at premium rates. It was take it or leave it, and everyone had to take it because Phoebe's orbit and the Redeemers' expertise in cargo handling and routing made it the prime resupply, rendezvous, and transfer site in all of the Saturn system.

Baker could have stayed onboard his scow, of course, but even he needed to get out and about occasionally. At least here you could raise your arms over your head, and sculling about the public areas cost nothing. And besides, he liked talking to people. He had a lot of friends. He had friends everywhere he went in the system. It was the way he'd been rebuilt.

People all around the canteen started to cheer every kick the woman gave the servitor, happy to get some free entertainment, to see someone vent the frustration they all felt. "That feisty little old thing could come and work me over anytime," one of the factors at Baker's table said; her partner, a scarred and wrinkled woman about a hundred years old, cracked a grin and told her that it would be like setting a Titan tiger against an air cow.

At the same moment, Baker got a tingle of recognition. Like most of the public areas of the Phoebe habitat, the canteen was a basic microgravity architectural sphere, and Baker was tethered to a table upside down above the woman, like a bat hung from the ceiling, but there was something familiar about her. . . .

"I have called for help," the servitor said in a monotonal foghorn voice. "Please desist. I have called for help."

The woman grabbed a black cable studded with lenses that had snaked out to peer at her, said "Fuck you," and got a round of applause when she broke it off. People, mostly men, started to shout advice to her, but then everyone fell silent, because one of the supervisors had swum into the canteen.

The creepy thing about the Redeemers wasn't that they all had been chopped to look alike, or that you couldn't tell which had once been male and which female, or even that they all had gray skin the color of the thermal paint that goes over a hull before its final finish, but that they provided no clues at all as to what they might be feeling.

This one was as long and skinny as the rest, in a one-piece suit that looked like it was made out of bandages. It moved swiftly, flowing through the air straight at the redheaded woman, who recoiled and said loudly, "This fucking machine sucked the credit out of my chip and won't give it up."

Everyone was looking at her as she hung with one arm casually locked around one of the staples in the servitor's fascia, her head turned up now to glare at the Redeemer, who kept his place in midair with minute swimming motions of one long, spidery hand, like a reef barracuda wondering whether to attack or pass by, and Baker unclipped his tether because now he knew that he knew her.

Jackson. Vera Flamillion Jackson. Colonel Jackson.

Don't do anything dumb, his sidekick said, and when Baker told it that she was an old friend, it added, Everyone's your friend, but it isn't good to get involved.

The woman was talking fast and low now, stopping when the Redeemer said something, shaking her head and talking again, her words lost in the hum of the fans that were pushing warm stale air about and the chatter of the people all around. Baker kicked out from the table, turning neatly in midair so he landed right-side-up by the woman. He hooked an arm through the same rung from which she was hanging and saw her turn and grin, recognizing him at once, as if the past thirty years had never happened.

They exchanged life stories over a couple of bulbs of cold beer, Baker's treat because Jackson had no credit on her. It pretty much wiped out the small amount he'd set aside to spend here; against the advice of his sidekick, he'd also paid the fine the Redeemer had insisted on levying. He'd have to check out of the coffin hotel and go sleep on the scow, but he didn't mind. Jackson was an *old* friend, and if he remembered her, then once upon a time she must have been important to him.

They'd been teenagers in the war and although Jackson was pushing fifty now, she still looked good. Maybe a little gaunt, and with lines cross-hatching her fine-grained milk-white skin, but she still had a flirtatious way of looking at him from beneath the floating fringe of her red hair. Baker didn't remember too much about his life before the accident, but he remembered that look, and seeing it now made him feel strange. There were black tattoos on her neck and upper arms, crude knotted swirls lacking animation, and she was missing her little finger on her right hand, but, yes, she looked good. She'd been married, he learned, her way of joining a collective that had built a habitat inside a hollowed-out asteroid. That hadn't worked out, she wasn't exactly clear why, and now she was here.

Once or twice their fingers brushed together and he got a tingle as her net tried to access his, but his sidekick blocked the attempts easily. Her net hasn't been modified, it said, and just as well, because she's dangerous.

She's an old friend, Baker insisted, irritated by the sidekick's paranoia. I'm not going to do anything crazy. Just talk about old times, about who I used to be.

What's the point of that? the sidekick said. She's trouble, and don't say I didn't warn you.

"I got bored with it," Jackson was saying, meaning the collective she'd left. "Spending most of the time worrying about stabilizing the ecology. Might as well have settled down on a rock."

"Instead of in one," Baker said, and laughed at his own joke.

"In, out, same thing. Too many people to deal with, too much routine. I mean, have you ever tried to *grow* plants?" Before he could answer, she leaned at the rail of the promenade and added, "You ever get claustrophobic in a place like this?"

They were on one of the upper levels of the Shaft. It had been bored two kilometers into Phoebe's icy mantle with a single-shot fusion laser and was capped with a diamond dome; you could look up through webs and cables and floating islands of plants and see Saturn's small crescent tipped in the black sky. Each level was ringed around with terraced gardens glowing green under sunlamps, neatly planted out with luxury crops, even flowers, level after level of gardens ringing the well of the Shaft. Parts of the upper levels were open to visitors, but most was exclusive Redeemer territory, unknown and unknowable.

Baker said, "I used to help in the farms, but I like what I do now better."

He was married into a collective, but he didn't think he needed to tell her that. It was a business thing; he hardly saw any of his wives or co-husbands from one year to the next, and he certainly couldn't fuck anyone in the marriage—or vice versa—without permission from one of the elders. There'd been a sweet honeymoon week with the youngest of the collective's wives, but that had pretty much been it.

That isn't what counts, his sidekick said, and Baker brushed at his ear in annoyance.

Jackson said, "In the war, we could go anywhere. That's what I miss."

"Well, we went where we were told."

"Yeah, but we did it our way. We fucked the enemy up pretty good, too. You still see any of the guys?"

"No, not really."

"Me either. Remember Goodluck Crowe? He must surely be dead, the way he was going."

Baker shrugged and smiled.

"That time he came in with his bird's venturis fucked, spinning eccentrically? Crashed into one of the ports and the last of his fuel went up and bounced the remains of his ship straight back out? And then he's found down in one of the cargo bays in his p-suit, lost in pitch darkness because his suit light got smashed. The explosion shot him out and he was so dazed he didn't know where he was. He banged up his knee, I recall, floating about in there, but that was all."

"Well," Baker said, still smiling, "I guess he went back to Earth."

"How many missions did you fly?"

"I think six." He knew exactly because he'd once paid a data miner to look up his combat record.

She said, "Do you still do that counting thing?"

"Counting thing?"

"You know, with potatoes. One potato, two potato. To count seconds. Three potato, four. You don't remember?"

He had done it out loud, she said, while suppressing the clock functions of his net, claiming that it helped him concentrate on the essential moment. They'd timed him once; over ten minutes he'd deviated by less than a second.

"You don't remember?"

Her gaze was steady, and Baker felt a touch of embarrassment and looked away. She clearly remembered more about him than he did; it was like suddenly finding yourself naked. He said, "It sounds stupid to me. What's the point of trying to do something better than a brainless machine?"

She said, "It's funny. You were listed missing-in-action, one of the few casualties on our side. But here you are, and you don't seem much like the man I used to know."

He told her the story. He'd told it so many times now that it was polished smooth and bright. He'd told it so many times that he believed that he remembered what had happened, even though it was a reconstruction. He'd been so badly injured that he had no memory of the accident that had nearly killed him, and only patchy memories of the times before.

Like all combat pilots in the Quiet War, he had been a teenager, picked for his quick reflexes, multitasking skills, and coolness under pressure. He'd been zipped into a singleship, its life-system an integral pressure suit that fed and cleaned him and maintained his muscle tone with patterned electrical stimuli while he flew the ship and its accompanying flock of deadly little remote-control drones. Each singleship took a different orbit, swooping through Saturn's rings in complex multiple-encounter orbits, attacking fly-by targets with the drones when the timelag in the feedback was less than a second, never using the same tactic twice. Like all the combat pilots, Baker had been essentially a telepresence operator infiltrated into the enemy's territory, spending most of his time in Russian sleep with the singleship's systems powered down, waking an hour before the brief, high-velocity encounters between drones and target, making a hundred decisions in the crucial few seconds and then vanishing into the rings again. It had been just one front of the Quiet War between the Outer System colonists and the Three Powers Alliance of Earth, less important than the damage done by spies, the economic blitz, and the propaganda campaign.

Saturn's rings were a good place to hide, but they were dangerous, the biggest concentration of rubble and dust in the Solar System, shepherded by tiny moons and tidal resonances into orbits a hundred thousand kilometers wide and only fifteen deep. Baker's singleship passed and repassed through the rings more than a hundred times, and then a single pinhead-sized bit of rock killed him. It smashed through the thick mantle of airfoam that coated the singleship's hull and punched a neat hole in the hull, breaking up into more than a dozen particles that shot through the six layers of Baker's life-system and the gel that cased his sleeping body. Two shattered the artificial-reality visor of his facemask and left charred tracks through his skull and brain; two more skewered the singleship's computer; another ruptured a fuel line.

Baker died without knowing it, but the singleship saved him. Nanotech in the life-system gel sealed ruptured blood vessels; the life-system drained his blood and replaced it with an artificial plasma rich in glycoproteins, lowered his body temperature to 2°C. Although the singleship's automatic systems were only partially functional, they powered up its motor, ready to expend its fuel in a last burn to accelerate it into a long-period orbit where it might be retrieved. But most of the fuel had already leaked away and the burn terminated after only a few seconds, leaving the singleship tumbling in a chaotic orbit.

The Quiet War ended a few days later; in the aftermath, there was only a cursory search for the missing singleship. Fifteen years passed before it was spotted by a long-range survey. A collective retrieved it a year later, looking for scrap value and finding Baker. They revived him and used fetal cells to regrow the damaged parts of his brain, upgraded the neural net through which he had interfaced with the singleship and the drones. He had worked for the collective for two years, paying off the debt, and then they had let him marry into their extended family.

At the end of the story, Jackson said, "Well, I guess that outdoes Goodluck Crowe. So now you're working for them?"

"I'm a partner."

"Yeah, right. Funny, isn't it? We helped win the Quiet War, our own governments encouraged us to settle here, and then we were shafted. What do you pilot?"

"A scow. I do freight runs."

"That's just what I mean," Jackson said. "Most of the freight in this system is rail-gunned. You used to be a hotshot pilot and now you're working the edge, picking up part-cargoes, trading margins on luxury items. I bet they'd use a chip instead of you if they could."

"I choose my own routes. I do business on the Bourse."

"Puttering around, making half a cent a kilo on the marginal price difference of vitamins between Daphoene and Rhea. Hardly the same as combat, is it?"

"I don't remember too much from before my accident," Baker said amiably. "Are you still a pilot?"

"Well, I guess I'm sort of freelance."

Baker felt a twinge of alarm. His sidekick said, If she asks for credit, you will not give it. I think that she was in the prison farms—the tattoos suggest that. I told you that this was a bad idea.

Something must have shown on his face, because Jackson said, "I have credit. Plenty of it—I'm staying in the Hilton. But, see, it's all *room* credit."

Baker didn't understand.

Be careful, his sidekick said. Here it comes.

"See," Jackson said, her bright blue eyes fixed on his, "I thought I'd walk about for a while. Stretch muscles. Then I wanted a beer, and the fucking machine sucked all the credit from my chip and wouldn't give anything up. Tell me about your ship."

"Hamilton Towmaster, prewar but reconditioned. Daeyo motors, eighty thousand kilos thrust. She's a good old flamebucket. She'll probably outlast me."

"You get where you're going?"

"Pretty much anywhere in the system."

Although mostly it was runs back and forth between Titan and Phoebe. The collective was one of the contractors on the Titan project. Titan was lousy with organics, but it was presently one vast storm and would be for another century, until the terraforming began to stabilize, so fixed carbon and other biomass for the construction crews had to be imported from Phoebe's vacuum farms, and that was what Baker mostly hauled.

Jackson sucked on the last of her beer; the thin plastic of the bulb made a crinkling sound as it contracted. She said, "It's a pretty sorry state. Here we are, both of us on the winning side of the war, and the tweaks have got us fucked."

Baker looked around, but luckily none of the incredibly tall, stick-thin people ambling about the promenade with the slow shuffle required by sticky shoes seemed to have heard her. Calling an Outer System colonist a tweak was like calling one of Baker's ancestors a nigger. The original colonists had undergone extensive gengineering to adapt them to microgravity; incomers like Baker made do with widgets in their blood and bones to maintain calcium balance and the like, and in most places in the Outer System, medical liability laws ensured that they weren't allowed to have children.

Jackson said, "Ordinary people like us have to stick together. That way we can show the tweaks what real humans can do. The way I see it, the war is still going on."

Baker said, "What exactly is it you do now?"

Jackson crumpled the empty bulb and dropped it over the rail; it fell away slowly toward one of the nets. She said, "Come see where I live these days."

The hotel was two levels down, a terrace landscaped as rolling parkland, with lawns and colorful flowerbeds, and clumps of trees grown into puffy clouds of leaves the way they did in microgravity. Little carts ambled here and there between the cabins. Baker had been to Phoebe more than fifty or sixty times, but he had never before been here. This was where vips from Earth stayed, along with *novo abastado* industrialists and miners who rendezvoused here to make deals because the Redeemers were scrupulous about commercial confidentiality.

Jackson had to sign Baker in. Blinking on the flash of the retinal print camera, he sat next to her on a cart that took them deep into the level. A sky projection hid the rocky ceiling high above; in the middle air, a couple of people were trolling about on gossamer wings. The guests could hunt here, too, Jackson said, although the meat remained the property of the Redeemers.

"You buy a license to go out and shoot one of the little cows or mammoths they have here, and then you pay all over again if you want a steak."

Baker said, "You ever done it?"

"I've other fish to fry," she said.

He was very aware of her warmth next to him on the bench seat of the cart, her hips and shoulders touching his. He was also aware of his sidekick's unhappiness; it hadn't stopped complaining since he'd accepted Jackson's invitation. She's an old friend, Baker told it, and it said, Yes, but everyone is your friend and that's why I give you advice you'd do best to listen to.

But Jackson *was* an old friend, a very special friend. A war comrade, maybe even a lover. Although Baker didn't remember anything specific, he definitely felt that they had once had something special, and she seemed to think so too. For all the edge she tried to put into her voice and body language, her trust was quite wonderfully naïve.

The cart rolled over neatly trimmed green grass at a leisurely walking pace and circled around a big stand of bamboos and yellow-flowered mimosa, and there was one of the cabins, a dome turfed over with grass, little round windows like rabbit holes glinting here and there. A door dilated as the cart approached, and then they were inside a big room with carpet all over the walls and pits for places to sit or sleep. When Baker remarked on the size of the place, Jackson said that it didn't matter how big a cell it was, it was still a cell.

"I thought this was cool at first," she said, "but I'd just upgraded is all. I'm still stuck here, but I think now I know a way out."

The sidekick started to complain again. Baker winced and, something he hardly ever did, switched it to stand-by mode. The silence was a relief; he gave Jackson a goofy smile that obviously puzzled her.

She said, "You'll see who I work for, then you'll get an idea of what I mean."

They put on sticky shoes and shuffled down a long, curved ramp into a lower level, coming out in a room that was all white tiles and bright light, with a circular pool of polystyrene balls rippling back and forth, something big and pink half-buried in them. Some kind of animal, Baker thought, and then it spoke and he realized that it was a man, the fattest man he'd ever seen, masked with artificial-reality goggles and twiddling his hands this way and that.

"Time to wake up," Jackson said loudly. "I'm back, Berry, and I've brought a friend."

The fat man cut the air with a hand; his goggles unfilmed. "Where have you been?" he asked, his voice childish and petulant.

"I was out on an errand," Jackson said, her voice echoing off the tiles, "but I'm back now. Do you need anything?"

"Didn't know where you were," the man said.

"Well, here I am now. You been lying there all this time? You'll lose the use of your legs."

"Help me to the surface if you want," the man said, "but not right now. I'm deep in the Ten Thousand Flower Rift. I think I might get through to the Beast's chateau this time."

He rose and fell with the big, slow waves that rolled from one side of the pool of polystyrene balls to the other side and back again. There was a little machine floating in the air close by his head, holding a bulb of thick white liquid, and he lifted his face now and sucked at a straw noisily.

Jackson said quietly to Baker, "So now you see who I work for."

"He's got to be the fattest man I've ever seen. Massing, golly, it must be two hundred kilos at least."

"One hundred sixty. He tends to spread out a bit lying down."

"What does he do?"

"Mostly he just lies right there and runs these antique two-hundred-year-old sagas and drinks, or lies around on grass and runs his sagas and drinks. That's margarita mix he's working on there; he gets through a couple of liters of that a day. And he uses other stuff, too. He does like his drugs, lying buck-naked there or out on the grass under the sunlamps. They have some uv in their spectrum, so I have to rub cream on him to stop him burning. He can get about if he has to, but it hurts him even in microgravity, so he mostly stays on his back. There're air jets under the balls, help him stay afloat."

"I mean, who is he? How can he afford all this?"

"Berry Malachite Hong-Owen, his mother is Sri Hong-Owen. That doesn't mean anything to you? She invented one of the two important vacuum organism photosynthetic systems, made her rich as all hell. Berry is her son by her first and only marriage, a reject with a trust fund, doesn't have to do anything but let the money roll in." Jackson raised her voice and said, "You all right there, Berry? I got a bit of business with my friend here. You shout if you want anything."

Back up in the dome, Baker and Jackson sipped bulbs of a smoky brandy. Jackson lit a marijuana cigarette, too—Berry could afford the tax, she said.

Baker said, "How did you get the job? It looks like fun."

Jackson didn't answer for a moment, holding a volume of smoke before blowing it out and saying in a small, tight voice, "Fun? The one other thing Berry likes to do is fuck. He can manage it in microgravity, just about, although it takes some care." She fixed Baker with her bright blue eyes, daring him to say something. When he didn't, she took another drag and said through the smoke, "That's part of what I was doing before I met him—the fucking Redeemers sell you a prostitute's license and you pay tax on every bit of business. I may be old, but some of the tweaks do like the exotic. The rest of the time I was part of the gardening crew, moving bushes and trees here and there, replanting flowerbeds. I didn't have much choice—I lost my ticket through a piece of foolishness. I got to hear of Berry and did some research, and made myself indispensable to him. He likes older women—I think he misses his mother. But the fucker's crafty. His trust fund pays for room and service, but he doesn't have anything much in the way of transferable credit. Doesn't need it, he says, because he never leaves the hotel."

"Doesn't he pay you?"

"He did at first, but then I was living here and I told him to save his credit. It wasn't that much anyway, not enough to parlay up for any kind of good ticket and I don't fancy leaving here as a corpsicle in steerage."

Baker began to see where this was going, and felt a twinge of pleasurable excitement. He had been right to think that there might be something in this, and it could well fall within the very wide parameters that allowed him to operate without consulting the collective. He said cautiously, "The thing is, the ship isn't exactly mine."

"I'm not looking for a lift," Jackson said, leaning forward through her cloud of smoke. "I'm looking for a partner in a deal so sweet it could rot your teeth just thinking about it. Let me tell you about Berry."

Berry's mother, Sri Hong-Owen, was a gene wizard with a shadowy, mysterious history. The system of artificial photosynthesis she had invented had made her as rich and famous as her rival, Avernus, but she had also done a lot of covert work before and after the Quiet War. Before the war, she was rumored to have set up an illegal experiment in the accelerated evolution of vacuum organisms somewhere in the Kuiper Belt for the Democratic Union of China; during the war, she had helped design the biowar organisms that had taken Europa, and she was said to have been involved in a covert program of human gengineering. After the war, she had announced that she was retiring (which no one believed), and had taken advantage of the resettlement scheme to take up residence at the edge of the ring system of Saturn.

"Potato One and Two," Jackson said. "Remember?"

"Sure, but they're just a couple of rocks, something to do with the military, I think. Anyway, no one lives there."

"That's what they want everyone to think," Jackson said.

Potato One and Two were the nicknames of a pair of co-orbital satellites, tiny chunks of rock that had probably been shattered off a larger body by some ancient impact. Their orbits were within fifty kilometers of each other, beyond the edge of the F Ring. Sri Hong-Owen lived in absolute seclusion on the larger moon, Janus; she had registered the smaller, Epimetheus, as an experimental area. Berry had left—or had been thrown out—ten years ago; the other son by her failed marriage, Alder Topaz Hong-Owen, was working somewhere on Earth, perhaps as liaison with whichever government or *corporado* was sponsoring his mother's current work. She had good and influential connections in the Three Powers Occupation Force; Jackson said it was likely that she was working on some covert military gengineering program. The two moons were off limits, protected by fierce automatic defense systems, but Berry had the right to return there.

Jackson told Baker, "Berry misses her badly. He talks about her a lot, but there's something that stops him returning. I think he was kinked, given some sort of conditioning. He has the codes that can get us through her defense system, and I know what they are—it didn't take anything more than withholding his margarita ration for a couple of days. We can say that he paid us to bring him back, ask for money to take him away again. It's like kidnapping, but in reverse."

"Suppose she doesn't pay up?"

Baker didn't need the prompting of his sidekick to know that Jackson wasn't telling him the whole story, not that it really mattered if his own scheme worked out, but he found that he liked the illicit thrill of becoming involved in her shady plot. Perhaps this was the way he had felt in the brief moments of combat, all those years ago before the accident had changed his life forever.

Jackson shrugged. "She doesn't pay, then we say we'll kill him, or we'll think of doing some damage to her experiments. But really, why wouldn't she pay? Who'd want Berry around all the time?"

Baker and Jackson got Berry out of the pool of polystyrene balls and helped him totter on shaky legs up the ramp to the outside. He flopped down on the grass like a pink barrage balloon and demanded that Jackson rub cream into his skin. That took a while, Berry grunting and sometimes giggling as she rubbed coconut-scented lotion into the hectares of his pink flesh. Baker was pretty sure it would end in some kind of sex and wandered off, taking big floating steps, and found some shade under a stand of umbrella trees. A herd of miniature red-haired mammoths was grazing off in the distance, moving in tentative tiptoe slow motion. A vine twisted around one of the umbrella trees and Baker picked at its grapes, each a slightly different flavor bursting on his tongue, wondering if he should reactivate his sidekick. The truth was, he didn't want to hear what it would say; it wasn't programmed to take risks. He used his net to dial into Phoebe's infoweb and did a little research of his own. At last Jackson floated down beside him and told him that Berry was asleep.

"So," she said, "will you do it?"

"Remind me of the percentages again."

"Twenty per cent goes to you, less any costs. But that's still a lot of credit."

"Sure. I mean, yes, count me in."

He realized that he'd been thinking about it while seeming not to think about anything at all. His net was very sophisticated. It was risky, but the potential—not the silly scheme of Jackson's—was huge.

Jackson leaned over and kissed him; he kissed her back.

"He's sleeping now," she said after a while. "All that drinking and floating and floating and drinking does tire him out."

"He hasn't asked why I'm here?"

"I said you were my brother. He accepted that. Berry doesn't like to think too hard about things. He's like a kid. When he wakes up, he'll want a drink, and I'll put something in it that'll keep him quiet so we can get him aboard."

"We have to take him?"

"I don't like it either. But it's the only way we can file a flight plan, and we'll need proof that we really do have him when we get there."

Once they were aboard the scow and had everything squared away, Jackson stripped off her jumper and trousers and they fucked. Baker couldn't think of it as making love; it was as much a business transaction as his wedding night with the youngest wife of the collective. Jackson wanted to interface systems during sex, the way they used to, or so she claimed, but Baker held back. She fell straight asleep afterward, and Baker thought about it all over again, looking for loose threads and unexpected angles.

They had gone aboard late at night. Jackson had slipped a tranquillizer into Berry's nightcap and he had fallen asleep almost immediately. They had used a luggage cart to get him to the docks, no problem there; the Redeemers didn't care what was loaded onto ships as long as they got their tax. That was another reason why Phoebe was so successful.

There hadn't been a problem stowing Berry away, either; Jackson had already thought of that.

As for the rest, the run itself was fairly simple, and Baker had already filed a flight plan, getting clearance with Berry's identity code just as Jackson had said he would. If Sri Hong-Owen had an agent in the intelligence network of the pan-Saturn flight-control system, she would already know that someone was on the way; she might already be taking countermeasures. Baker would have to think of what she might do, and how to get around it.

He was scared, but also elated. After going over everything in his head, he could at last fall asleep.

But when he woke up, things had gone badly wrong.

He woke up because Jackson was slapping him, slapping his face, slapping him hard in a back-and-forth rhythm with the same angry intensity with which she had attacked the servitor, saying over and over, "You fucker. Come on out of it, you fucker. Come on. Don't die on me."

He tried to get away, but he was trussed like a food animal in the web hammock in the center of the scow's compact life-system. Jackson's left hand gripped his right wrist tightly. His head hurt badly, and behind the pain there was a terrible absence. Stuff hung in front of Jackson's angry, intent face— columns, indices, a couple of thumbnails. She had jacked her net into his, broken into it using some kind of Trojan horse, and was using it to run the ship. Hand-holding, the pilots had called it, a kind of piggybacking that had been used in training.

The soundscape of the scow had changed. Beneath the usual whir of fans, the steady chug of the humidifier and the nearly subliminal hum of the lights was the intermittent thump of attitude thrusters and a chorus of pings and popping noises.

Baker jerked his head back so that Jackson's next blow missed; she swung halfway around with the momentum. "What," he said, so full of fear that he thought for a moment he would start to cry. He swallowed something salty and said, "What have you done?"

"You work it out," she said, and let go of his wrist and turned her back on him.

It took him less than a second to call up the data. The scow was in orbit around Phoebe, docked with its chain of cargo pods and slowly rotating in barbecue mode.

A thumbnail picture showed the patchwork of the little moon's tightly curving globe. Only two hundred kilometers in diameter, it was a captured, unmodified primitive object, mostly carbonaceous material mixed with water ice, almost entirely grown over with vacuum organisms that used the energy of sunlight to turn methane ice and carbonaceous tars formed five billion years ago, when the Solar System had first condensed, into useful carbon compounds. The patches were of all shapes but only four muted colors: orange-brown, reddish-brown, sooty black, mottled gray. Phoebe was like a dented and battered patchwork ball or a gigantic version of the four-color map problem, curving away sharply in every direction.

Another thumbnail showed Berry floating in faint red light, half-filling the scow's water tank. An air mask was clamped over his face. Baker had objected to Jackson's idea on hygienic grounds, but she had pointed out that the water was recycled anyway, and that the filter system could easily be rerouted to clean the water coming out of the tank as well as that going in. Berry seemed to be asleep, curled up like a huge late-term embryo, the umbilical cord of airline and nutrient feed connected to his face rather than his belly, hands clasped piously under his chins, a continuous chain of bubbles trickling from the vent of his air mask.

Baker clicked everything off. Jackson was hunched up at the far end of the cramped life-system, an arm's length away. She had livid marks on her throat, and deep scratches on her arms were still oozing blood into the air. She said, "You almost died. Your net shut down your vagus reflexes when I hacked it. And when I tried to revive you, you tried to kill me. Don't you know what they did to you?"

"You shouldn't have messed with it," Baker said.

"I did it to free you!"

Jackson's face was pinched white, harsh and old-looking; only her bright blue eyes seemed alive. She shuddered all over and said more quietly, "They made you into a slave. A *thing*."

They had both had military neural nets installed when they had been inducted, but Baker's net had been considerably upgraded after his accident; it was now more like a symbiont than a machine enhancement of his nervous system. When Jackson had jacked into it, she had been able to access only a few of its functions. She had got the ship up into orbit, and docked manually with the train of cargo pods, but she hadn't been able to activate the flight plan he'd filed. And when she had tried to hack into its root directory, his net had easily repelled her efforts and had triggered a number of defense routines.

Baker said, "Why are you doing this? Aren't we friends?"

"Because I'm tired of giving blow jobs to Berry. Because I can't bear to see an old comrade turned into a zombie so dumb he doesn't even know what he is. Because I was in prison in Angola for ten years and I'd sooner die than go back."

Half of the Redeemers' business was running the port. The other half was running the correctional facilities for the Saturn system—the vacuum farms. Angola was the worst of them; eight out of ten prisoners died before completing their sentence.

Baker said, "Well, I did wonder about the tattoos. What were you in for?"

"Just load and run the flight plan," Jackson said, and smiled bloodlessly. "Okay, maybe I got greedy and fucked up. I need you, and I won't let you back out."

Baker said, "I wasn't your first choice of pilot, was I? You had an agreement with someone else, and I bet that's why you were in the pilots' canteen. But then you saw me, and thought you could make a better deal."

"I still rescued you," she said.

"How much were you going to get? From the first deal."

"It was the same as the one we made, except I was to get the twenty-percent cut. But that's blown away. We're in this together or we're both dead, and Berry, too. Your call."

It might be a bluff, but Jackson didn't look like the kind of person who would start something she couldn't finish. Baker pulled down the flight plan, checked it over out of habit, and activated it.

The rumble of the scow's motor filled the life-system. Acceleration gripped Baker; he drifted gently onto the padding at the rear of the cabin. Jackson hooked an arm around a staple and stared at him from what was now definitely the ceiling. And in the tank, Berry woke up amidst clashing pressure waves that distorted the red light into clashing lines and sheets and plaintively asked what was going on.

Neither Baker nor Jackson slept during the sixty-five hours of the flight. Their military nets could keep them awake for more than a week, switching consciousness back and forth between the right and left hemispheres of their brains. Sometimes Baker would feel a little sluggish and his saliva would taste strange, but there were no other side effects.

Jackson didn't stay mad at him, but she remained wary. It wasn't his fault that she had activated the defense routines. They were there to protect the collective's investment. He told her this, and that he was happy and liked the life he had been given, but it only provoked a torrent of abuse. He wished that he had his sidekick to explain things, to help sort out the muddle, but Jackson had suppressed it—he had the horrible feeling that she had in fact erased it. When he asked her about this, she said that it was time he started thinking for himself. He could never be the man he'd been when she had known him, but he could be his own man now.

She did unbend enough to tell him a little of her life. While he had been drifting in the crippled singleship, neither alive nor dead, she had used her sign-off pay to start up a haulage company. When that had failed, outcompeted by rail guns, she had joined a collective long enough to know that it wasn't for her, and then had become a smuggler, intercepting packages of forbidden technologies in the rings while on apparently innocent cargo runs. An industrial spy had broken up the cartel she had mostly worked for, and someone in the cartel had given her up to protect himself, and that was how she had ended up in the vacuum farms of Phoebe.

She was still bitter about it. During the Quiet War, the Outer System colonists, split into more than a dozen rival enclaves, had hardly been able to fight back at all. In only three months, their infrastructures had been so devastated that they had been forced to surrender their hegemony. But what had happened since made you wonder who had really won after all, Jackson said. The tweaks had the upper hand in the Outer System, even if their various assemblies, moots, councils, conclaves, and congresses were now in principle subservient to the Three Powers Occupying Force. Despite incentives and tax breaks, the various emigration schemes sponsored by the victors of the Quiet War had mostly failed; new settlers couldn't compete with established cooperatives and collectives, and unless they signed away their right to return to Earth in exchange for gengineering, they were not allowed to have children and tended to die young of problems associated with living in microgravity. Meanwhile, the central administration of the Outer System was falling apart as adapted colonists began to spread through the thousands of dirty snowballs and rocks of the Kuiper Belt.

There was talk of another war, one in which Jackson wouldn't be able to fight. She was too old and slow for combat now; she had been sidelined by history.

Baker listened patiently to her rants. He tried to talk with Berry, too, but Jackson had set up a feed of lemon-flavored alcohol and the man was only partly coherent. In one of his more lucid moments, he said, "You shouldn't go near my mother. She's dangerous. All of her are dangerous."

"You mean she has other children?"

"You could call them that," Berry said. "They're crazy bad." His voice, muffled by the air mask, sounded as if it was coming from the bottom of a well.

"How many brothers and sisters do you have?"

"It isn't like that. Alder would know, I guess . . . they look after me, always have, so maybe they're not so bad. Not to me. They saved me other times."

Baker felt a faint stirring, as if his sidekick was about to waken. He wished it would, if only to say that it told him so. When nothing happened, he said, "Other times? What happened, Berry?"

Berry was silent for a while. Then he said, "I should get out of here now. My skin is all puffy."

Baker tried to imagine what the life-system would be like with a hundred and sixty kilos of dripping wet Berry crammed into it. He said, "You hang in there. Play your sagas."

"It isn't the same," Berry said. "The emulation in this system is horrible. When can you get me back to the hotel?"

"Well, I'm not sure. Soon."

"I'd like margarita. That always goes down smooth."

"Maybe you should stop drinking."

"What's the point of stopping? Get me some margarita and I might help you out."

Jackson was amused by Baker's attempts to talk with Berry. She said that you couldn't get any sense out of the man. His brain had been fried in alcohol, most of the switches jammed open or jammed closed, whole areas dead and blasted. Like a low-grade robot, he could follow his routines, but had trouble with anything outside them.

"You want to know anything, you ask me," she said.

Baker thought that he had already learned something useful from Berry. He said, "What will happen after we insert into orbit?"

"I'll tell you on a need-to-know basis, just like the old times."

But the old times were gone forever. His original self must have loved her fiercely for a residue of that love to have survived death, and Baker, who was vicariously fascinated by other peoples' lives, and watched a lot of the old psychodramas when he wasn't working, thought wistfully that once upon a time they must have been like Romeo and Juliet. But whatever they'd once been, that was then and this was now.

The scow accelerated for more than forty hours. The idea was to come in on a fast, short trajectory, decelerating hard at the last moment. Baker spent much of that time watching the view, a thumbnail of the life-system in one corner to let him keep a eye on Jackson—he was worried that she might suddenly try something stupid.

Phoebe's orbit was not only retrograde, but inclined to the equatorial plane of Saturn. As the scow drove inward, the entire system was spread out ahead and below; nine major moons and more than a hundred smaller bodies, Saturn a pale half-disc at the center, circled by rings like an exquisite bit of jewelry.

Baker never tired of this privileged view. He spent a lot of time watching it while working through his options. He wasn't as brain-damaged as Jackson thought, and the enhancements to his net gave him a lot of computational power. He worked up several scenarios and played the simulations over and over, finally choosing the simplest one with a sense of doors closing irrevocably behind him. He wondered if Jackson had inserted a parasitic eavesdropper into his net; if she had, she gave no sign that she knew what he was planning.

As Saturn grew closer, the ring system began to resolve details in the sunlit arc that swept out beyond the planet: two unequal halves separated by the gap of the Cassini division, each half further divided into fine parallel bands, with dark irregular spokes in the bright B ring that could be seen to rotate if watched long enough.

Then the motor cut out and they were in freefall again. There were only a couple of hours in turnover. Jackson spent much of them supervising the decoupling of the scow from the cargo train. Normally it would recouple on the other end of the train, thrusters pointing ahead for deceleration. But Jackson's manual link closed down halfway through the maneuver and the scow fired off several orientation bursts, turned end-for-end and immediately lit its main engines in a brief burn. At the same time, the thrusters of the cargo train started to fire.

Berry started complaining over the link; Jackson snarled at him to shut up and was suddenly right in Baker's face, swarming down the life-system cabin against the pull of the thrust and grabbing his right wrist. A Trojan horse smashed its way into his net, spilling voracious subroutines. For a panicky minute, he was deaf and dumb and blind—it was like being raped from the inside out.

Light and sound came back. Baker discovered that he was in freefall again. Jackson had shoved away from him and was studying him intently, her blue eyes cold behind the tendrils of red hair that drifted loose over her face.

Baker closed up all the indices and files she'd pulled open and said shakily, "You shouldn't have done that."

"Christ, they really did a number on you, Baker. You're not a man anymore. You're a bundle of routines. You're a lapdog. This is your chance to get free of the leash, and you're fucking it up."

Baker's net was suppressing adrenaline production; otherwise he would have been trembling with flight reaction and stinking up the life-system with sweat. He said, "We're in this together. I've accepted that. I thought it would be a good idea to dump the cargo in a high orbit. Makes us more maneuverable and saves reaction mass. We'll get there earlier than the flight plan allows, so we can surprise Berry's mother."

It was the best lie he had been able to come up with. He sipped at a bulb of orange-flavored glucose solution and watched her work it through. At last, she said, "I know you're trying to fuck me over, but I can't figure out how, not yet. But I will, and then I'll know what to do with you. Meanwhile, climb into your pressure suit. There's a chance that Berry's mother might have changed her defense systems since he left."

"I thought you got the codes from him. And she knows we're bringing him here."

"The codes are twenty years old, and she might not believe us. We've got fifteen minutes before the main burn, so get moving."

They only just made it.

The scow, decelerating, fell behind the cargo train. The string of half-silvered beads dwindled against the sweep of the rings, vanishing into the planet's shadow as the scow swung in around the nightside. Vast lightning storms illuminated sluggish bands of storm systems that could have swallowed Earth without a ripple. Then the rings appeared, a silver arc ahead of the dawning diamond point of the sun. The scow's motor rumbled continuously, decelerating at just over one gravity. Baker was heavier than he had been for years. Lying flat on the padding of the life-system, he tried to find a comfortable position within his pressure suit to wait it out, but there always seemed to be some seam or wrinkle digging into him. Jackson lay beside him, her ungloved right hand holding his ungloved left so that she could access the ship through his net. They lay there like spent lovers.

"Seems hard to remember how we stood this on Earth," Baker said at one point. "I almost envy Berry, floating in that tank."

"Just keep quiet," Jackson said. "I'm watching everything. If something goes wrong, you're toast."

She didn't say it with much conviction, Baker thought. For the first time, he felt that he might have a chance to win back from this. It was clear that she hadn't been able to work out what he had done. He felt pity for her—she was out of date, left behind by the accelerating changes that were sweeping through the Outer System. She should have returned to Earth; out here, the aggression that had helped win the Quiet War was not a survival trait. Individualism counted for nothing in the Outer System. To survive, you had to commit yourself to helping others, who in turn would help you.

Baker said, "What's wrong? You said you remembered how good I was. I'm even better now."

"I remember you always thought you were a hotshot, but you didn't have much to back it up. You were a company man, Baker, even when you were in the service. You were always happiest following orders. You had no initiative. That's one thing about you that hasn't changed."

"Nothing you can say can hurt me more than what you tried to do to me," Baker said, with a fair imitation of wounded pride, thinking that *her* initiative had got her into prison, and now into this. He pulled down the view to shut her out.

The rings spanned the curve of the planet in a thousand shades of gray and brown and white, casting a shadow across the bulge of its equator. The scow was coming in at a narrow angle above the plane of the rings, which spread to port like a highway a million lanes wide. Zooming in with the scow's telescope, Baker could see the seemingly solid plane break apart in lanes of flecks that grew into rocks and bergs flashing in the sunlight as they tumbled, a storm of motes forever falling around the planet.

The scow plunged stern-first toward the gap beyond the outer edge of the narrow F ring. Jackson started a looped broadcast of the code she had dug out of Berry. Their target was still around the curve of the planet, coming toward them out of night; they would rendezvous with it just at its dawn. Baker wanted to look for the cargo train, but wasn't sure that he could do it without Jackson catching on.

"I was wondering," he said after a while, "what you'll do if this works out."

"That's none of your fucking business."

"We might not survive it."

"I intend to. You could have set yourself free, Baker."

"Things have changed."

"This is the frontier, Baker. It's far from the ant farms of Earth. It's where people can walk tall and make their fortunes if they have the intelligence and the backbone."

"Or end in the vacuum farms."

"I had some bad luck. I'm going to turn that around. You might be content to give up your free will to a bunch of farmers who sit inside rocks like bugs in a bad apple. Well, I'm not."

She said more, but Baker tuned it out. The scow was just about to begin its final course correction. He patched telescope scans into a three-hundred-and-sixty-degree perspective. The rings stretched away ahead and behind, flattened into a narrow line that bisected the sky. A single speck was bracketed ahead: their target.

Janus was roughly the same size as Phoebe, an irregular body like the profile of a fist. It was pockmarked with craters, most eroded by billions of years of micrometeorite sleet and further softened by patches of vacuum organism growth. One small circular crater had been tented over, and shone greenly with internal lights. There was a ring of silver around it. The scow spotted one of the defense drones a hundred kilometers out and presented Baker with a grainy image of the tiny, deadly thing: a slim body less than two meters long, with a flat radar dish at one end and the swollen bowl of an oversized motor at the other. No radar probed the scow; nothing moved to intercept it. The broadcast code must be working.

The scow shuddered, spinning this way and that, making a series of short burns before finally shutting down its motor. Now it was falling in the same orbit as the little moon, barely twenty kilometers away.

Jackson started what seemed to be a one-sided conversation—she had made contact with someone on Janus, it seemed, but she wouldn't allow Baker to switch into the channel.

"I have him right here," she said, "just like I told you. You must know he's aboard—that's why I could shut down your defense drones. Don't try to target me manually, the ship will blow up if radar locks on it. Because he asked me to—don't let's go into all that again. Well, I expect that he misses you all. Yes, I can bring evidence, but it might be easier if you came up here, or I landed the ship. Well, okay, that's fine by me, too. Creepy little fucker," she added, turning to Baker.

"Can you really blow up the ship?"

"Only if it's absolutely necessary."

"That was Berry's mother you were talking with?"

"Some kind of agent, I think. It wants me to go down there with evidence that I brought Berry back."

Jackson sealed up her pressure suit but did not go out through the airlock; instead, she opened an internal access hatch and plunged into the water tank. Berry was supine. She had added a relaxant to his alcohol mix. Baker watched as she snipped off the little finger from Berry's right hand and came back out.

"It has to be fresh," she said, grinning at Baker through her helmet's visor. She was pumped up with excitement. "That way she'll know we're not kidding. You're not going to give me any trouble, are you?"

"Maybe you had better tell me what you've thought of."

"We're going down together. And if I see any sign that the ship is moving out of orbit, I'll blow it."

"I should stay here with Berry."

"And have you swing the ship around and torch me?"

"I wouldn't do that. I'm in this with you."

"You'd better be, because you're going to be my backup. They're expecting one person. You'll be a surprise. They won't know who you are or what you'll be doing when I walk in there."

They used a little jet unit to pull them across, touching down two kilometers from the tented crater, which was somewhere beyond the close, sharply curved horizon. Except for his annual safety certification exercises, Baker had hardly ever done any vacuum work. His p-suit was intelligent and responsive, but a residual stiffness blunted his reflexes; he let go a moment too soon and tumbled end-for-end when he touched down on the little moon's surface.

He tumbled a fair way—in Janus's microgravity, he could bounce a couple hundred meters off the surface with the gentlest of kicks. At last the suit fired a grapple and he slewed to a halt with a cloud of dust raining straight down all around. He was at the edge of a dense field of tall black blades that sloped away to the close horizon. Some reached up to four meters; all grew from thick rhizomes that snaked half-buried through the dusty regolith; all had turned the flat surfaces of their blades toward the sun's yellow spark.

Jackson threw a camo cloth over the jet unit and crept toward Baker on her belly, supple as a snake in her yellow p-suit. She checked him over and began to assemble a hollow tube and a scaffold cradle from components she had strapped to her backpack.

"What are you doing?"

"It's amazing what you can get in the way of surplus weaponry if you have the credit. This is a missile launcher. The Europeans made them to shoot down drones like the ones we operated, only they didn't have time to deploy them before the hydrogen bomb broke open the crust. I paid for this through Berry's room service. It fires up to ten smart micromissiles, but I only need two. One is aimed at the scow, the other at the dome over the horizon."

"Ah. I thought you were joking about blowing up the ship."

"I don't joke about business," Jackson said flatly. She started to adjust the angle of the tube by minute increments, finally sitting back in a squat. "It's running, ready to go in three hours. Try to move it now and the charge will explode. Try to rip out the chip that controls it—same thing. The only way to stop it is to use a code. You think I'm a fuck-up, but I know what I'm doing here."

Baker couldn't see Jackson's face because the sun was reflecting off the gold-tinted visor of her helmet, but he could imagine her tigerish grin. He said, "I don't doubt it."

"You stay right there. I'll be telling them that you'll fire the mortar at any sign of trouble, so don't stray. And remember that I'm linked to the ship just like you. Try anything—especially try to close down my link—and I'll blow her. Sit tight. Enjoy the view. I'll be back soon."

Baker sat tight, watching Saturn's crescent slowly wax above the sharp, irregular edge of the horizon. Like almost all of Saturn's moons, Janus was tidally locked, and kept one face permanently turned toward its primary. Sri Hong-Owen had sited her home at the edge of sub-Saturnian hemisphere; Saturn stood permanently at the horizon, its rings arching beyond its banded crescent like the string of a drawn bow—it dominated half the sky, shedding a bilious light over the pockmarked slope. Janus was so small that wherever you looked, the ground appeared to slope away—Baker felt that he was hugging the top of a hill that was plunging toward Saturn's storms, a hill studded with half-buried boulders of all sizes, every boulder casting a multicolored shadow. In the other direction, the outer ring system scratched a thin arch across the width of the sky, with several of the moons bright against a dusting of stars. There was Dione, which had its own satellite trailing at sixty degrees of arc in the same orbital path; there was the tiny crescent of Titan, lit not only by the Sun, but by the terraforming fusion lamps hung in equatorial orbit.

Baker wondered what it would be like when Janus was overtaken by its co-orbital moon, Epimetheus. Passing only fifty kilometers away, Epimetheus would eclipse Saturn and exchange a fraction of its momentum with Janus; the two moons would swap orbits and Janus would slowly accelerate away in the lower orbit. The orbital exchange happened every four years, and was not a stable configuration; in slightly under ten million years, the two moons would collide, and it was thought that the fragments would eventually coalesce into a single body.

He thought his plan through again. With the insurance of the cargo train, he was pretty sure that he could get out of this alive. The rest was as imponderable as ever, but he was confident that he could make some friends here. That was what he was good at, after all. Of course, he'd underestimated Jackson, and it was only pure dumb luck that she hadn't upgraded her net—otherwise, he was quite certain that she would have disposed of him as soon as she had control of the scow. But Jackson wasn't the problem now. He imagined that she would be killed as soon as she walked into the habitat. Although it certainly increased his chance of survival, part of him—the fragmented bits of his old self—wished that he'd warned her.

The p-suit's life-system made comforting hums and soft hisses; it was like being inside a tent exactly his size.

Baker broke radio silence to try to talk with Berry, but the man was gurgling inside his mask, drunk or asleep, and wouldn't answer.

He tried that counting trick: *one potato, two potato, three potato, four*. Tested it against the system clock of his net, tried different intonations, couldn't get it to come out right. Maybe it was just a story Jackson had spun to draw him in. It didn't matter. He didn't need dumb tricks like that, not anymore.

Time passed. Baker had always been calm in the squeeze of danger—to his way of thinking, there was no sense in getting caught up in useless speculation; it was best to face any situation with an uncluttered mind. In any case, there was nothing he could do until either Jackson came back or Berry's mother came for him. He set up a couple of alarms on his p-suit's system and fell asleep.

And woke an hour later to find four pressure-suited figures kneeling by him, visors blankly reflecting the gray-brown moonscape. They were as small as children. A fifth figure was examining Jackson's missile launcher.

Baker tried to sit up, and discovered that his suit was bound with a thousand tough, tightly wrapped fibers. He squashed the first tremors of alarm and said as calmly as he could, "There's a couple of things you should know."

The ring of silver around the tented crater was a plantation of things like flowers: tough wiry stalks five meters tall and rising straight out of dusty ice, each bearing a single big, white dish-shaped bloom with a black cylinder protruding from its center. The dishes were all turned in one direction, toward the setting sun. It was pitch-black beneath the packed dishes, but Baker's captors carried him at the same fast gliding gait with which they'd crossed the open ground.

Just as he was carried out of the far side of the plantation, Baker thought he saw a flash at the horizon, and wondered if that had been the missile launcher. Then he and his captors plunged down a steep, terraced slope, following a path sketched in dabs of green fox fire. Baker didn't ask where they were taking him. He was just grateful that so far he had not been killed.

The slope became a tunnel, hung from floor to ceiling with a thousand stiff black curtains that must have formed a pressure lock, because the tunnel suddenly opened up at the lip of a huge bowl of greenery under a thousand brilliant lamps, with flocks of what looked like birds floating lazily at different layers in the air, Saturn a blank-faced giant peering in through the diamond tent that capped the vast space.

Baker's pressure-suited captors dropped him at the edge of the bowl and threw themselves over the drop, bouncing like balls from terrace to terrace and finally vanishing into a stand of tree ferns. Baker's bonds slowly dissolved, snapping apart like brittle elastic as he picked himself up.

A woman was moving toward him through the air above the green gulf, sitting on a throne borne up by what looked like cherubs.

She was not Sri Hong-Owen, but one of her daughters. She was young, golden-skinned and unselfconsciously naked. She had a tweak's etiolated build, her long arms and legs skinny but supple, her breasts no more than enlarged nipples on her prominent rib cage. A cloud of black hair floated around her narrow face.

When Baker asked her name, she smiled and said that no names were needed here, where all were one mind, one flesh. He asked then where her mother was, and the golden-skinned woman told him that she had moved on, which at first Baker took to mean *died*.

"Alder descended to the Earth to continue our mother's work there," the woman said, "and Berry went his own way. He is only our half-brother, and is weak-minded, but we love him anyway. Our mother would have killed him, we think, but she no longer needs to make small decisions like that, and we decided to show mercy."

"How many are you?"

Baker had unlatched the helmet of his p-suit and stood with it tucked under his arm, like an old-fashioned knight in front of his enthroned queen. The cherubs had flown away—they had little patience, the woman had said when they left, being full of the joy of life lived moment to moment.

"There are more than enough of us to deal with you or anyone else who tries to invade our kingdom," she told Baker now. "We have killed many in the last twenty years—spies, pirates, adventurers, the merely curious. But you are the first to think of kidnapping Berry, and you are the first to threaten our mother. How did you know?"

"Luck, I guess," Baker said, wondering what he was supposed to have guessed.

The woman leaned forward, gazing intently at him through her floating tangle of black hair. "Berry is not dead."

Her gaze compelled. Baker said, "No. No, not when I left him."

"Then you are luckier than you know," the woman said.

"What about Jackson?"

"Was that her name?"

"You killed her, didn't you? You should know she aimed a missile at this place."

"We dealt with it."

"Ah. I thought I saw an explosion."

"The one who tried to disarm it was killed."

"So you killed Jackson in return."

"No, we killed the woman because she threatened us. Any of us would sacrifice our lives for the good of the clade, but all of us would die to save our mother. We love her more than life itself. You should know that we are tracking the cargo train and have calculated its trajectory."

When Baker had briefly wrested control of the scow from Jackson, he had sent the cargo train on a trajectory that would end in a collision with Epimetheus after three orbits of Saturn, less than twenty hours now. He said, "I was going to tell you about that. I don't mean any harm by it. I want to be friends. The cargo train—it's just insurance, that's all."

The woman made no gesture, but children appeared at various levels of the burgeoning greenery. No, not children; they were naked creatures the same size as his pressure-suited captors, so pale and skinny that they seemed partly transparent, like certain deep-sea creatures. They were quite sexless. Their heads were small and wedge-shaped, sloping straight back from skin-covered dimples where their eyes should have been; their ears flared out like bats' wings; their hands had only three fingers, spaced like a crane's grab. Four of them gripped the arms of Baker's p-suit with implacable strength.

"We will kill you slowly for your presumption," the woman said, "and our defense drones will destroy the cargo train."

Baker said, "I don't think you want to do that. If it's destroyed, the debris will still hit and do just as much harm, but if you leave it be, I can change its orbit once we've made a deal."

The woman shrugged. "It is unlikely that the impact will hurt our mother, for most of her is far underground. But it will damage her energy-gathering systems, and we cannot allow even that. You will change its orbit now."

Baker said stubbornly, "We can make a deal. That's why I'm here."

"No," the golden-skinned woman said serenely. "No bargains. Change the orbit of the cargo train and we may let you leave. Otherwise we will keep you here, alive and in great pain."

"You didn't kill me," Baker said. "Of course you want to bargain. I want to set up a trading agreement between your clade and my collective. You must have plenty of biological novelties, for instance. In exchange, we can supply you with trace elements, or anything else you might need. I did a little research and I know you deal exclusively with the private citizens who bank-rolled this experiment. I bet my collective can offer you better supply contracts. And we can guarantee confidentiality."

"There will be no trade," the woman said. "We need nothing. Our mother made this garden. It is all we need. You will do as we ask."

"I have to be on the scow to do it," Baker said, "so you'll have to let me go anyway. There's plenty of time. I can show you the figures on the trade my collective does with the Titan terraforming project. Think it over. I mean no harm to your mother. I didn't know she was on Epimetheus. I thought she was here."

"She is not *on* Epimetheus," the woman said, "she is *becoming* Epimetheus. Think what you will do. I will return soon."

Cherubs whirled down and lifted the chair and the woman into the air. As she dwindled away, the workers released Baker and vanished into the greenery with unnerving swift silence.

The golden-skinned woman did not return for many hours. Baker wasn't worried; he was sure that she was discussing the offer with her mother, and the longer it took, the more likely it was that he could hook them. He found the airlock, but the black sheets had stiffened and would not let him pass.

A little way beyond, at the foot of a steep vine-covered cliff, a flash of bright yellow caught his attention. It was Jackson's p-suit helmet. The visor was cracked around a burn hole; the padding inside was crusted with drying blood.

Baker cradled it, tears pricking at his eyes; although he had not loved Jackson, he had loved the idea of remembering that he had once loved her, and what he was mourning now was that lost part of his life. She had not understood that when she had tried to manipulate him; she had not really understood much of what she had done. The only thing she had been right about was that ordinary humans had no place in the Outer System: here was the proof.

He dropped the helmet and turned back to explore the rim of the freefall jungle bowl. The lush green thickets were full of strange creatures: things like snakes, but with narrow human heads and pale human skin; little black-furred tarsiers with microcephalic human faces; white worms working like mobile fingers through the crumbling soil. The things Baker had thought were birds were more like black-furred bats, with leathery wings as wide as his outstretched arms; when he climbed out along the smooth limb of a tree above the bowl of the jungle, a flock of them wheeled and dive-bombed him, spattering him with their dung.

Baker laughed and retreated, crashing unhandily through thick foliage in his p-suit. He was not afraid of anything here. He controlled the cargo train: he had the upper hand. He had thought to threaten Sri Hong-Owen with the destruction of her experimental sites, and although he didn't understand what the woman had told him, he was certain that his bargaining position was even stronger than he had hoped. His sidekick had been wrong after all. Everything was going to work out. Except for Jackson, of course. It was a pity about Jackson, but after she tried to cut him out of the deal, he really had had no choice but to let her walk unknowingly to her own death.

At last the golden-skinned woman returned, borne as before through the air on a chair sustained by cherubs. Workers stepped out of the greenery and stood on either side of her chair as the cherubs set it down and whirled away.

"I hope we can talk," Baker said.

"We have agreed to tell you about us," the woman said. "Listen."

Sri Hong-Owen wanted to become truly immortal, the woman said. She had used cloning as a first step, although she knew that it would not be enough. Clones are exact genetic copies, but personality is determined by a combination of genes, environment, and experience. A clone would have to have been subjected to every single one of her own experiences to become a perfect copy. Even so, she experimented with the effects of various types of memory downloads and artificial-reality scenarios on the personalities of female clones, and then she had created the clade and its habitat, and given it over to the charge of her daughter clones. The clade valued knowledge, not things. Its treasure store was in its self-regulating ecosystem and the genetic diversity it had fashioned from a genome library derived from a few plants and microorganisms and from Sri Hong-Owen herself; every animal in the habitat was derived from her by gengineering and forced evolution. Given the right conditions, the clade could persist forever.

Meanwhile, Sri Hong-Owen reshaped herself.

She developed vacuum organisms that turned sunlight into electrical energy with almost one-hundred-percent efficiency—the ring of dish flowers around the habitat were an early prototype. They were forming a blanket across the surface of Epimetheus, and Sri Hong-Owen's modified body was growing through the moon's icy crust like blue mold through cheese. It was already the largest organism in the Solar System, larger even than the mycelial mats that underlay Earth's temperate forests, and which she now somewhat resembled. Copies of her original body were cached here and there in that mass, and there were more than a hundred copies of her brain, all sharing the same sensory inputs, the same thoughts. They were as alike as possible. Eventually the mycelium would completely embrace the moon. It would grow thrusters that would subtly alter the moon's orbit, slingshotting it repeatedly through Saturn's gravity well until it gained enough velocity to escape to the stars.

"Probably Vega," the golden-skinned woman told Baker. "There's a ring of debris around Vega twice the size of our Solar System, millions of comets and planetoids and asteroids. She will fill it with clades like ours, and then move on to other systems where planets failed to form. She is the first real transhuman, but there will be others—those who sponsored her work, to begin with."

Baker smiled. He did not believe half of what he had been told. He said, "If she is truly immortal, then she must value her life immensely."

"What are you to her? She could fill the galaxy. In time, she could fill a million galaxies. Planets are unnecessary. We have evolved beyond planets. We have evolved beyond the human form. We can make ourselves over into a thousand kinds of organism, all fitter for life in space than mere humans. The tweaks are a first step, lungfish on the shore of space. We will go much further."

"My collective has already made over a tented crater on Rhea, much as this one has been transformed. Other collectives are making homes in planetoids, mining comet heads . . . there are many different ways of making a living, and no need at all to depend on trade with anyone on Earth. Trade with us instead. If you had time to look at those figures—"

"All of you are still human," the woman said. "We have evolved beyond that."

"She's right," someone else said, and a second golden-skinned woman came into the clearing with an elegant motion that was half-walking, half-swimming. She held something between her small breasts with both hands.

"You've decided," Baker said. "That's good."

"We've decided," the woman said, and released what she held.

It flew straight at Baker on a blur of membranous wings, a tiny bat with a wasp's long sting-tipped abdomen. He tried to knock it out of the air, but it was too fast and his pressure suit slowed him. It dodged his clumsy blow and caught at his hair with its claws. Something sank into his scalp, pushing between the sutures of his skull, and black pain swept the world away.

When it came back, the two golden-skinned women were looking down at him. Baker pushed up and gingerly touched the top of his head; hundreds of hair-thin wires with sticky-tagged ends came loose, slowly falling to the ground around him. He said, "What did you do?"

"Evolution is cruel," the first woman said. "Species that cannot compete with other species will always become extinct. We are more merciful. Perhaps we will keep some of you, out of sentiment. And Berry, while he lives, needs help, of course."

"I'm not sure I understand," Baker said. He felt quite calm, as if he had entered an artificial reality and could leave any time he wanted. "I thought evolution was all about change, but you do not want to change."

Suddenly he felt his sidekick at his back and a warning twinge in his head like a cold needle in his core. Ordinarily he would have welcomed its return, but there seemed to be something wrong with it; it was fierce and strong and silent.

He said, "You did something to me, didn't you? Something with those wires, something to my net."

The second woman said, "We are a new kind of evolution. The body changes at will, and the mind lives on."

"Tell me what you did!"

"After a little while," the first woman said, "you won't ever worry about it."

Baker said, "You want me think like you? Is that it? Listen, you can't last forever in isolation. People need other people."

"That is why we will send you back," the first woman said. "You can only think in the old way. Although we love him dearly, that was always Berry's trouble."

Then the sidekick seized Baker. He couldn't move. His body felt bloated, unmanageable, fiery hot, a pupa melting and changing inside the carapace of the p-suit.

The wires had downloaded new programmes into his net and reactivated his sidekick; now his sidekick was changing him. Parts of his personality fell away, falling from his mind into darkness as icebergs carve from a glacier.

At last the work was done and the world came back to him. His sidekick was at his back, stronger than ever, his mentor and his friend.

They all gathered to watch him go—workers, cherubs, human-skinned snakes and crabs, naked monkey-things that tended the gardens, all one family, one flesh, one thought, one clade.

"You are one of us now," they said. "A different flesh, but one of us. Our faithful servant. You will divert the cargo train because you know that no harm must come to our mother. You will guard our brother now and forever."

He did what they wanted.

He was one of them.

His collective finally found Baker on Dione. He and Berry were staying in the only hotel in a raw construction town, the first stage of an ambitious plan to tent Latium Chasma, the fissure that cut a deep groove across the northern half of the sub-Saturnian hemisphere. The hotel could not supply the kind of luxury that Berry was used to; after only a few days, it told Baker that he wanted to move on.

Baker was returning from the port. He always transacted business in person; even deeply encrypted phone lines were not to be trusted. He had arranged transport to one of the garden habitats that orbited Titan, a tourist place where people went to use telepresence to explore the storms that were resurfacing the giant moon. He was sure that Berry would like it; gardens reminded him of the happy days of his childhood, in the garden of his mother.

They jumped into Baker's capsule just before it pulled out of the station, a young woman and an older man. The young woman wanted to know if he recognized her. "We slept together to seal the contract," she said, her eyes searching his face. "You were always my favorite. You must remember."

Baker tried to be polite. "I do not know you," he lied. "I am sorry."

The young woman touched the man's arm.

"Ralf is a lawyer. We filed a bond here. If you need privacy to talk, we can provide it. We know you logged a flight with two passengers. One was an old friend of yours. Vera Flamillion Jackson. We know where you went, but we don't know what happened. Please tell me. Whatever happened to you can be reversed, I'm sure of it."

"I don't think so. You want your slave back. Don't deny that you think of him as your property. Well, he isn't. He is one of us, now."

And so on, a tide of anger rolling over Baker, submerging him so completely that he no longer knew if he or the sidekick was speaking. He came to himself in the atrium of Berry's hotel suite. The entry phone was flashing, but he ignored it.

"Well, it's time we moved anyway," he said to the air as he moved through the rooms to the private pool where Berry floated.

The sidekick was fading at his back, as beneficent as the warmth of the sun; before it vanished, it told him with approval that he had done well. And then he saw Berry, floating pink and naked in steaming water amongst palmettos and bamboos, a tray of food on his hairless chest, sucking on a drink bulb, and the unfortunate incident didn't matter any more.

Berry spat the straw from his mouth and said, "You've been away. I don't like it when you're away."

"I've arranged a new place for us."

"Oh, that. Good. Can't stay in one place too long. That's the secret."

"Do you think she might need us one day? Do you think we might be allowed to return?"

Berry bent his head and sucked up the last of the margarita mix with a rattling noise. When he looked up, there were tears swelling in his eyes. He said, "We're nothing to her now. We're too human. You're here to serve me. By serving me, you serve the clade. That's all you need to know. Now help me out. My skin's wrinkling."

"Of course," Baker said, and went to get the oils and unguents, filled with boundless unqualified love for his master.

TONY DANIEL

One of the fastest-rising new stars of the nineties, Tony Daniel grew up in Alabama, lived for a while on Vashon Island, in Washington State, and in recent years, in the best tradition of the young bohemian artist, has been restlessly on the move, from Vashon Island to Europe, from Europe to New York City, from New York City to Alabama and, most recently, back to New York City. He attended the Clarion West Writers Workshop in 1989, and since then has become a frequent contributor to Asimov's Science Fiction, *as well as to markets such as* The Magazine of Fantasy and Science Fiction, Amazing, SF Age, Universe, Full Spectrum, *and elsewhere. He's currently working as story editor for the Internet audio-drama showcase,* Seeing Ear Theater.

Like many writers of his generation, Tony Daniel first made an impression on the field with his short fiction. He made his first sale, to Asimov's, *in 1990, with "The Passage of Night Trains," and followed it up with a long string of well-received stories both there and elsewhere throughout the nineties, stories such as "The Careful Man Goes West," "Sun So Hot I Froze To Death," "Prism Tree," "Death of Reason," "Candle," "No Love in All of Dwingeloo," "The Joy of the Sidereal Long-Distance Runner," "The Robot's Twilight Companion," and many others. His story "Life on the Moon" was a finalist for the Hugo Award in 1996, and won the* Asimov's Science Fiction *Readers Award poll. His first novel,* Warpath, *was released simultaneously in America and England in 1993. In 1997, he published a major new novel,* Earthling. *His most recent book is his first short-story collection,* The Robot's Twilight Companion, *and coming up soon is a new novel* Metaplanetary, *based in part on the story you're about to read, "Grist."*

In the complex, compelling, and pyrotechnic novella that follows, he takes us to a bizarre, far-future world peopled with some of the strangest characters you're ever likely to meet, many of them transhuman, with vast, almost godlike, powers and abilities, a world poised on the brink of a war that may destroy it utterly. It's a vivid and exotic adventure that revolves around the connections that join people together—and in this strange, high-tech future, sometimes makes it difficult to tell where one person ends and another begins. . . .

> Things that really matter, although they are not defined for all eternity, even when they come very late, still come at the right time.
>
> —Martin Heidegger,
> Letter on Humanism

Midnight Standard at the Westway Diner

Standing over all creation, a doubt-ridden priest took a piss.

He shook himself, looked between his feet at the stars, then tabbed his pants closed. He flushed the toilet, and centrifugal force took care of the rest.

Andre Sud walked back to his table in the Westway Diner. He padded over the living fire of the plenum, the abyss—all of it—and hardly noticed. Even though this place was special to him, it was really just another café with a see-through floor—a window as thin as paper and as hard as diamond. Dime a dozen, as they used to say a thousand years ago. The luciferin sign at the entrance said FREE DELIVERY. The sign under it said OPEN 24 HRS. This sign was unlit. The place will close, eventually.

The priest sat down and stirred his black tea. He read the sign, backward, and wondered if the words he spoke, when he spoke, sounded anything like English used to. Hard to tell with the grist patch in his head.

Everybody understands one another on a general level, Andre Sud thought. Approximately more or less they know what you mean.

There was a dull greasy gleam to the napkin holder. The saltshaker was half-full. The laminate surface of the table was worn through where the plates usually sat. The particle board underneath was soggy. There was free-floating grist that sparkled like mica within the wood: used-to-be-cleaning grist, entirely shorn from the restaurant's controlling algorithm and nothing to do but shine. Like the enlightened pilgrim of the Greentree Way. Shorn and brilliant.

And what will you have with that hamburger?

Grist. Nada y grist. Grist y nada.

I am going through a depression, Andre reminded himself. I am even considering leaving the priesthood.

Andre's pellicle—the micoscopic algorithmic part of him that was spread out in the general vicinity—spoke as if from a long way off.

This happens every winter. And lately with the insomnia. Cut it out with the nada y nada. Everything's physical, don't you know?

Except for you, Andre thought back.

He usually thought of his pellicle as a little cloud of algebra symbols that followed him around like mosquitoes. In actuality, it was normally invisible, of course.

Except for us, the pellicle replied.

All right, then. As far as we go. Play a song or something, would you?

After a moment, an oboe piped up in his inner ear. It was an old Greentree hymn—"Ponder Nothing"—that his mother had hummed when he was a kid. Brought up in the faith. The pellicle filtered it through a couple of variations and inversions, but it was always soothing to hear.

There was a way to calculate how many winters the Earth-Mars Diaphany would get in an Earth year, but Andre never checked before he returned to the seminary on his annual retreat, and they always took him by surprise, the winters did. You wake up one day and the light has grown dim.

The café door slid open and Cardinal Filmbuff filled the doorway. He was wide and possessive of the doorframe. He was a big man with a mane of silver hair. He was also space-adapted and white as bone in the face. He wore all black with a lapel pin in the shape of a tree. It was green, of course.

"Father Andre," said Filmbuff from across the room. His voice sounded like a Met cop's radio. "May I join you?"

Andre motioned to the seat across from him in the booth. Filmbuff walked over with big steps and sat down hard.

"Isn't it late for you to be out, Morton?" Andre said. He took a sip of his tea. He'd left the bag in too long and it tasted twiggy.

I was too long at the pissing, thought Andre.

"Tried to call you at the seminary retreat center," Filmbuff said.

"I'm usually here," Andre replied. "When I'm not there."

"Is this place still the seminary-student hangout?"

"It is. Like a dog returneth to its own vomit, huh? Or somebody's vomit."

A waiter drifted toward them. "Need menus?" he said. "I have to bring them because the tables don't work."

"I might want a little something," Filmbuff replied. "Maybe a lhasi."

The waiter nodded and went away.

"They still have real people here?" said Filmbuff.

"I don't think they can afford to recoat the place."

Filmbuff gazed around. He was like a beacon. "Seems clean enough."

"I suppose it is," said Andre. "I think the basic coating still works and that just the complicated grist has broken down."

"You like it here?"

Andre realized he'd been staring at the swirls in his tea and not making eye contact with his boss. He sat back, smiled at Filmbuff. "Since I came to seminary, Westway Diner has always been my home away from home." He took a sip of tea. "This is where I got satori, you know."

"So I've heard. It's rather legendary. You were eating a plate of mashed potatoes."

"Sweet potatoes, actually. It was a vegetable plate. They give you three choices, and I chose sweet potatoes, sweet potatoes, and sweet potatoes."

"I never cared for them."

"That is merely an illusion. Everyone likes them sooner or later."

Filmbuff guffawed. His great head turned up toward the ceiling, and his copper eyes flashed in the brown light. "Andre, we need you back teaching. Or in research."

"I lack faith."

"Faith in yourself."

"It's the same thing as faith in general, as you well know."

"You are a very effective scholar and priest to be so racked with doubt. Makes me think I'm missing something."

"Doubt wouldn't go with your hair, Morton."

The waiter came back. "Have you decided?" he said.

"A chocolate lhasi," Filmbuff replied firmly. "And some faith for Father Andre here."

The waiter stared for a moment, nonplussed. His grist patch hadn't translated Cardinal Filmbuff's words or had reproduced them as nonsense.

The waiter must be from out of the Happy Garden Radial, Andre thought.

Most of the help *was* in Seminary Barrel. There's a trade patois and a thousand long-shifted dialects out that way. Clan-networked LAPs poor as church mice and no good Broca grist to be had for Barrel wages.

"*Iye ftip*," Andre said to the waiter in the Happy Garden patois. "It is a joke." The waiter smiled uncertainly. "Another shot of hot water for my tea is what I want," Andre said. The waiter went away looking relieved. Filmbuff's aquiline presence could be intimidating.

"There is no empirical evidence that you lack faith," Filmbuff said. It was a pronouncement. "You are as good a priest as there is. We have excellent reports from Triton."

Linsdale, Andre thought. Traveling monk, indeed. Traveling stool pigeon was more like it. I'll give him hell next conclave.

"I'm happy there. I have a nice congregation, and I balance rocks."

"Yes. You are getting a reputation for that."

"Triton has the best gravity for it in the solar system."

"I've seen some of your creations on the merci. They're beautiful."

"Thank you."

"What happens to them?"

"Oh, they fall," said Andre, "when you stop paying attention to them."

The chocolate lhasi came, and the waiter set down a self-heating carafe of water for Andre. Filmbuff took a long drag at the straw and finished up half his drink.

"Excellent." He sat back, sighed, and burped. "Andre, I've had a vision."

"Well, that's what you do for a living."

"I saw *you*."

"Was I eating at the Westway Diner?"

"You were falling through an infinite sea of stars."

The carafe bubbled, and Andre poured some water into his cup before it became flat from all the air being boiled out. The hot water and lukewarm tea mingled in thin rivulets. He did not stir.

"You came to rest in the branches of a great tree. Well, you crashed into it, actually, and the branches caught you."

"Yggdrasil?"

"I don't think so. This was a different tree. I've never seen it before. It is very disturbing because I thought there was only the One Tree. *This* tree was just as big, though."

"As big as the World Tree? The Greentree?"

"Just as big. But different." Filmbuff looked down at the stars beneath their feet. His eyes grew dark and flecked with silver. Space-adapted eyes always took on the color of what they beheld. "Andre, you have no idea how real this was. *Is*. This is difficult to explain. You know about my other visions, of the coming war?"

"The Burning of the One Tree?"

"Yes."

"It's famous in the Way."

"I don't care about that. Nobody else is listening. In any case, this vision *has placed itself on top of* those war visions. Right now, being here with you, this seems like a play to me. A staged play. You. Me. Even the war that's coming. It's all a play that is really about that damn Tree. And it won't let me go."

"What do you mean, won't let you go?"

Filmbuff raised his hands, palms up, to cradle an invisible sphere in front of him. He stared into this space as if it were the depths of all creation, and his eyes became set and focused far away. But not glazed over or unaware.

They were so alive and intense that it hurt to look at him. Filmbuff's physical face *vibrated* when he was in trance. It was a slight effect, and unnerving even when you were used to it. He was utterly focused, but you couldn't focus on him. There was too much of him there for the space provided. Or not enough of you.

I am watching chronological quantum transport in the raw, Andre thought. The instantaneous integration of positronic spin information from up-time sifted through the archetypical registers of Filmbuff's human brain.

And it all comes out as metaphor.

"The Tree is all burnt out now," Filmbuff said, speaking out of his trance. His words were like stones. "The Burning's done. But it isn't char that I'm seeing, no." He clenched his fists, then opened his palms again. "The old Tree is a shadow. The burnt remains of the One Tree are really only the shadow of the other tree, the new Tree. It's like a shadow the new Tree casts."

"Shadow," Andre heard himself whispering. His own hands were clenched in a kind of sympathetic vibration with Filmbuff.

"We are living in the time of the shadow," said Filmbuff. He relaxed a bit. "There's almost a perfect juxtaposition of the two trees. I've never felt so sure of anything in my life."

Filmbuff, for all his histrionics, was not one to overstate his visions for effect. The man who sat across from Andre was only the aspect—the human portion—of a vast collective of personalities. They were all unified by the central being; the man before him was no more a puppet than was his enthalpic computing analog soaking up energy on Mercury, or the nodes of specialized grist spread across human space decoding variations in antiparticle spins as they made their way backward in time. But he was no longer simply the man who had taught Andre's Intro to Pastoral Shamanism course at seminary. Ten years ago, the Greentree Way had specifically crafted a Large Array of Personalities to catch a glimpse of the future, and Filmbuff had been assigned to be morphed.

I was on the team that designed him, Andre thought. Of course, that was back when I was a graduate assistant. Before I walked on the Moon.

"The vision is what's real." Filmbuff put the lhasi straw to his mouth and finished the rest of it. Andre wondered where the liquid went inside the man. Didn't he run on batteries or something? "This is maya, Andre."

"I believe you, Morton."

"I talked to Erasmus Kelly about this," Filmbuff continued. "He took it on the merci to our Interpreter's Freespace."

"What did they come up with?"

Filmbuff pushed his empty glass toward Andre. "That there's a new Tree," he said.

"How the hell could there be a new Tree? The Tree is wired into our DNA like sex and breathing. It may *be* sex and breathing."

"How should I know? There's a new Tree."

Andre took a sip of his tea. Just right. "So there's a new Tree," he said. "What does that have to do with me?"

"We think it has to do with your research."

"What research? I balance rocks."

"From before."

"Before I lost my faith and became an itinerant priest?"

"You were doing brilliant work at the seminary."

"What? With the time towers? That was a dead end."

"You understand them better than anyone."

"Because I don't try to make any sense of them. Do you think this new Tree has to do with those things?"

"It's a possibility."

"I doubt it."

"You doubt everything."

"The time towers are bunch of crotchety old LAPs who have disappeared up their own asses."

"Andre, you know what I am."

"You're my boss."

"Besides that."

"You're a *manifold*. You are a Large Array of Personalities who was specially constructed as a quantum-event detector—probably the best in human history. Parts of you stretch across the entire inner solar system, and you have cloudship outriders. If you say you had a vision of me and this new Tree, then it has to mean something. You're not making it up. Morton, you see into the future, and there I am."

"There you are. You are the Way's expert on *time*. What do you think this means?"

"What do you want me to tell you?" said Andre. "That the new Tree is obviously a further stage in sentient evolution, since the Greentree is *us*?"

"That's what Erasmus Kelly and his people think. I need something more subtle from you."

"All right. It isn't the time towers that this has to do with."

"What then?"

"You don't want to hear this."

"You'd better tell me anyway."

"Thaddeus Kaye."

Filmbuff shrugged. "Thaddeus Kaye is dead. He killed himself. Something was wrong with him, poor slob."

"I know you big LAPs like to think so."

"He was perverted. He killed himself over a woman, wasn't it?"

"Come on, Morton. A pervert hurts other people. Kaye hurt himself."

"What does *he* have to do with anything, anyway?"

"What if he's not dead? What if he's just wounded and lost? You understand what kind of being he is, don't you, Morton?"

"He's a LAP, just like me."

"You only see the future, Morton. Thaddeus Kaye can *affect* the future directly, from the past."

"So what? We all do that every day of our lives."

"This is not the same. Instantaneous control of instants. What the merced quantum effect does for space, Thaddeus Kaye can do for time. He *prefigures* the future. Backward and forward in time. He's like a rock that has been dropped into a lake."

"Are you saying he's God?"

"No. But if your vision is a true one, and I know that it is, then he could very well *be* the war."

"Do you mean the reason *for* the war?"

"Yes, but more than that. Think of it as a wave, Morton. If there's a crest, there has to be a trough. Thaddeus Kaye is the crest and the war is the trough. He's something like a physical principle. That's how his integration process was designed. Not a force, exactly, but he's been imprinted on a *property* of time."

"The Future Principle?"

"All right. Yes. In a way, he *is* the future. I think he's still alive."

"And how do you know that?"

"I didn't until you told me your vision. What else could it be? Unless aliens are coming."

"Maybe aliens are coming. They'd have their own Tree. Possibly."

"Morton, do you see aliens coming in your dreams?"

"No."

"Well, then."

Filmbuff put his hands over his eyes and lowered his head. "I'll tell you what I still see," he said in a low rumble of a voice like far thunder. "I see the burning Greentree. I see it strung with a million bodies, each of them hung by the neck, and all of them burning, too. Until this vision, that was all I was seeing."

"Did you see any way to avoid it?"

Filmbuff looked up. His eyes were as white as his hands when he spoke. "Once. Not now. The quantum fluctuations have all collapsed down to one big macroreality. Maybe not today, maybe not tomorrow, but *soon*."

Andre sighed. *I believe*, he thought. I don't want to believe, but I do. It's easy to have faith in destruction.

"I just want to go back to Triton and balance rocks," he said. "That's really all that keeps me sane. I love that big old moon."

Filmbuff pushed his lhasi glass even farther away and slid out of the booth. He stood up with a creaking sound, like vinyl being stretched. "Interesting times," he spoke to the café. "Illusion or not, that was probably the last good lhasi I'm going to have for quite a while."

"Uh, Morton?"

"Yes, Father Andre?"

"You have to pay up front. They can't take it out of your account."

"Oh, my." The cardinal reached down and slapped the black cloth covering his white legs. He, of course, had no pockets. "I don't think I have any money with me."

"Don't worry," Andre said. "I'll pick it up."

"Would you? I'd hate to have that poor waiter running after me down the street."

"Don't worry about it."

"We'll talk more tomorrow after meditation." This was not a request.

"We'll talk more then."

"Good night, Andre."

"Night, Morton."

Filmbuff stalked away, his silver mane trailing behind him as if a wind were blowing through it. Or a solar flare.

Before he left the Westway, he turned, as Andre knew he would, and spoke one last question across the space of the diner.

"You knew Thaddeus Kaye, didn't you, Father Andre?"

"I knew a man named Ben Kaye. A long time ago," Andre said, but this was only confirmation of what Filmbuff's spread-out mind had already told him.

The door slid shut and the Cardinal walked into the night. Andre sipped at his tea.

Eventually, the waiter returned. "We close pretty soon," he said.

"Why do you close so early?" Andre asked.

"It is very late."

"I remember when this place did not close."

"I don't think so. It always closed."

"Not when I was a student at the seminary."

"It closed then," said the waiter. He took a rag from his apron, activated it with a twist, and began to wipe a nearby table.

"I'm sure you're mistaken."

"They tell me there's never been a time when this place didn't close."

"Who tells you?"

"People."

"And you believe them."

"Why should I believe you? You're people." The waiter looked up at Andre, puzzled. "That was a joke," he said. "I guess it does not translate."

"Bring me some more tea and then I will go."

The waiter nodded, then went to get it.

There was music somewhere. Gentle oboe strains. Oh, yes. His pellicle was still playing the hymn.

What do you think?

I think we are going on a quest.

I suppose so.

Did you know where Thaddeus Kaye is?

No, but I have a pretty good idea how to find Ben. And wherever Ben is, Thaddeus Kaye has to be.

Why not tell somebody else how to find him?

Because no one else will do what I do when I find him.

What's that?

Nothing.

Oh.

When the backup is done, we'll be on our way.

The third part of Andre's multiple personality, the convert, was off-line at the moment getting himself archived and debugged. That was mainly what the retreat was for, since using the Greentree data facilities was free to priests. Doing it on Triton would have cost as much as putting a new roof on his house.

Why don't they send someone who is stronger in faith than we are?

I don't know. Send an apostate to net an apostate, I guess.

What god is Thaddeus Kaye apostate from?

Himself.

And for that matter, what about us?

Same thing. Here comes the tea. Will you play that song again?

It was Mother's favorite.

Do you think it could be that simple? That I became a priest because of that hymn?

Are you asking me?

Just play the music and let me drink my tea. I think the waiter wants us out of here.

"Do you mind if I mop up around you?" the waiter said.

"I'll be done soon."

"Take your time, as long as you don't mind me working."

"I don't mind."

Andre listened to the mournful oboe and watched as the waiter sloshed water across the infinite universe, then took a mop to it with a vengeance.

Jill

Down in the dark there's a doe rat I'm after to kill. She's got thirteen babies and I'm going to bite them, bite them, bite them. I will bite them.

The mulch here smells of dank stupid rats all running running, and there's nowhere farther to run because this is it, this is the Carbuncle, and now *I'm* here and this is truly the end of all of it, but a rat can't stand to know that and won't accept me until they have to believe me. Now they will believe me.

My whiskers against something soft. Old food? No, it's a dead buck; I scent his Y code, and the body is dead but the code keeps thumping and thumping. This mulch won't let it drain out and it doesn't ever want to die. The Carbuncle's the end of the line, but this code doesn't know it or knows it and won't have it. I give it a poke and a bit of rot sticks to my nose and the grist tries to swarm me, but no I don't think so.

I sniff out and send along my grist, jill-ferret grist, and no rat code stands a chance ever, ever. The zombie rat goes rigid when it's tough, stringy code—who knows how old, how far traveled finally to die here at the End of Everywhere—that code scatters to nonsense in the pit of the ball of nothing, my grist wraps it in. Then the grist flocks back to me and the zombie rat thumps no more. No more.

Sometimes having to kill *everything* is a bit of a distraction. I want that doe and her littles really bad and I need to move on.

Down a hole and into a warren larder. Here there's pieces of meat and the stink of maggot sluice pooled in the bends between muscles and organs. But the rats have got the meat from Farmer Jan's Mulmyard, and it's not quite dead yet, got maggot-resistant code, like the buck rat, but not smart enough to know it's dead, just mean code jaw-latched to a leg or a hauch and won't dissipate. Mean and won't die. But I am meaner still.

Oh, I smell her!

I'm coming, mamma rat. Where are you going? There's no going anywhere anymore.

Bomi slinks into the larder and we touch noses. I smell blood on her. She's got a kill, a bachelor male, by the blood spore on her.

It's so warm and wet, Jill. Bomi's trembling and wound up tight. She's not the smartest ferret. *I love it, love it, and I'm going back to lie in it.*

That's bad. Bad habit.

I don't care. I killed it; it's mine.

You do what you want, but it's your man Bob's rat.

No, it's mine.

He feeds you, Bomi.

I don't care.

Go lay up, then.

I will.

Without a by-your-leave, Bomi's gone back to her kill to lay up. I never do that. TB wouldn't like it, and besides, the killing's the thing, not the owning. Who wants an old dead rat to lie in when there's more to bite?

Bomi told me where she'd be because she's covering for herself when she doesn't show and Bob starts asking. Bomi's a stupid ferret and I'm glad she doesn't belong to TB.

But me—down another hole, deeper, deeper still. It's half filled in here. The doe rat thought she was hiding it, but she left the smell of her as sure as a serial number on a bone. I will bite you, mamma.

Then there's the dead-end chamber I knew would be. Doe rat's last hope in all the world. Won't do her any good. But oh, she's big! She's tremendous. Maybe the biggest ever for me.

I am very, very happy.

Doe rat with the babies crowded behind her. Thirteen of them, I count by the squeaks. Sweet naked squeaks. Less than two weeks old, they are. Puss and meat. But I want mamma now.

The doe sniffs me and screams like a bone breaking and she rears big as me. Bigger.

I will bite you.

Come and try, little jill.

I will kill you.

I ate a sack of money in the City Bank and they chased me and cut me to pieces and just left my tail and—I grew another rat! What will you do to me, jill, that can be so bad? You'd better be afraid of me.

When I kill your babies, I will do it with one bite for each. I won't hurt them for long.

You won't kill my babies.

At her.

At her because there isn't anything more to say, no more messages to pass back and forth through our grist and scents.

I go for a nipple and she's fast out of the way, but not fast enough and I have a nub of her flesh in my mouth. Blood let. I chew on her nipple tip. Blood and mamma's milk.

She comes down on me and bites my back, her long incisors cut through my fur, my skin, like hook needles, and come out at another spot. She's heavy. She gnaws at me and I can feel her teeth scraping against my backbone. I shake to get her off, and I do, but her teeth rip a gouge out of me.

Cut pretty bad, but she's off. I back up thinking that she's going to try to swarm a copy, and I stretch out the grist and there it is, just like I thought, and I intercept it and I kill the thing before it can get to the mulm and reproduce and grow another rat. One rat this big is enough, enough for always.

The doe senses that I've killed her outrider, and now she's more desperate.

This is all there is for you. This is oblivion and ruin and time to stop the scurry.

This is where you'll die.

She strikes at me again, but I dodge and—before she can round on me—I snatch a baby rat. It's dead before it can squeal. I spit out its mangle of bones and meat.

But mamma's not a dumb rat, no, not dumb at all, and does not fly into a rage over this. But I know she regards me with all the hate a rat can hate, though. If there were any light, I'd see her eyes glowing rancid yellow.

Come on, mamma, before I get another baby.

She goes for a foot and again I dodge, but she catches me in the chest. She raises up, up.

The packed dirt of the ceiling, wham, wham, and her incisors are hooked around my breastbone, damn her, and it holds me to her mouth as fast as a barbed arrowpoint.

Shake and tear, and I've never known such pain, such delicious . . .

I rake at her eyes with a front claw, dig into her belly with my feet. Dig, dig, and I can feel the skin parting, and the fatty underneath parting, and my feet dig deep, deep.

Shakes me again, and I can only smell my own blood and her spit and then sharp, small pains at my back.

The baby rats. The baby rats are latching onto me, trying to help their mother.

Nothing I can do. Nothing I can do but dig with my rear paws. Dig, dig. I am swimming in her guts. I can feel the give. I can feel the tear. Oh, yes!

Then my breastbone snaps and I fly lose of the doe's teeth. I land in the babies, and I'm stunned and they crawl over me and nip at my eyes and one of them shreds an ear, but the pain brings me to and I snap the one that bit my ear in half. I go for another. Across the warren cavern, the big doe shuffles. I pull myself up, try to stand on all fours. Can't.

Baby nips my hind leg. I turn and kill it. Turn back. My front legs collapse. I cannot stand to face the doe, and I hear her coming.

Will I die here?

Oh, this is how I want it! Took the biggest rat in the history of the Met to kill me. Ate a whole bag of money, she did.

She's coming for me. I can hear her coming for me. She's so big. I can *smell* how big she is.

I gather my hind legs beneath me, find a purchase.

This is how I die. I will bite you.

But there's no answer from her, only the doe's harsh breathing. The dirt smells of our blood. Dead baby rats all around me.

I am very, very happy.

With a scream, the doe charges me. I wait a moment. Wait.

I pounce, shoot low like an arrow.

I'm through, between her legs. I'm under her. I rise up. I rise up into her shredded belly. I bite! I bite! I bite!

Her whole weight keeps her down on me. I chew. I claw. I smell her heart. I smell the new blood of her heart! I can hear it! I can smell it! I chew and claw my way to it.

I bite.

Oh, yes.

The doe begins to kick and scream, to kick and scream, and as she does, the blood of her heart pumps from her and over me, smears over me until my coat is soaked with it, until all the dark world is blood.

After a long time, the doe rat dies. I send out the grist, feebly, but there are no outriders to face, no tries at escape now. She put all that she had into fighting me. She put everything into our battle.

I pull myself out from under the rat. In the corner, I hear the scuffles of the babies. Now that the mamma is dead, they are confused.

I have to bite them. I have to kill them all.

I cannot use my front legs, but I can use my back. I push myself toward them, my belly on the dirt like a snake. I find them all huddled in the farthest corner, piling on one another in their fright. Nowhere to go.

I do what I told the doe I would do. I kill them each with one bite, counting as I go. Three and ten makes thirteen.

And then it's done and they're all dead. I've killed them all.

So.

There's only one way out: the way I came. That's where I go, slinking, crawling, turning this way and that to keep my exposed bone from catching on pebbles and roots. After a while, I start to feel the pain that was staying away while I fought. It's never been this bad.

I crawl and crawl, I don't know for how long. If I were to meet another rat, that rat would kill me. But either they're dead or they're scared, and I don't hear or smell any. I crawl to what I think is up, what I hope is up.

And after forever, after so long that all the blood on my coat is dried and starting to flake off like tiny brown leaves, I poke my head out into the air. TB is there. He's waited for me.

Gently, gently he pulls me out of the rat hole. Careful, careful he puts me in my sack.

"Jill, I will fix you," he says.

I know.

"That must have been the Great Mother of rats."

She was big, so big and mean. She was brave and smart and strong. It was wonderful.

"What did you do?"

I bit her.

"I'll never see your like again, Jill."

I killed her, and then I killed all her children.

"Let's go home, Jill."

Yes. Back home.

Already in the dim burlap of the sack, and I hear the call of TB's grist to go to sleep, to get better, and I sigh and curl as best I can into a ball and I am falling away, falling away to dreams where I run along a trail of spattered blood, and the spoor is fresh and I'm chasing rats, and TB is with me close by, and I will bite a rat soon, soon, soon—

A Simple Room with Good Light

Come back, Andre Sud. Your mind is wandering and now you have to concentrate. Faster now. Fast as you can go. Spacetime. Clumps of galaxy clusters. Average cluster. Two-armed spiral.

Yellow star.

Here's a network of hawsers cabling the inner planets together. Artifact of sentience, some say. Mercury, Venus, Earth, Mars, hung with a shining webwork across blank space and spreading even into the asteroids. Fifty-mile-thick cables bending down from the heavens, coming in at the poles to fit into enormous universal joints lubricated by the living magma of the planets' viscera. Torque and undulation. Faster. Somewhere on a flagellating curve between Earth and Mars, the Diaphany, you will find yourself. Closer in. Spinning spherule like a hundred-mile-long bead on a million-mile-long necklace. Come as close as you can.

All along the Mars-Earth Diaphany, Andre saw the preparations for a war like none before. It seemed the entire Met—all the interplanetary cables—had been transformed into a dense fortress that people just happened to live inside. His pod was repeatedly delayed in the pithway as troops went about their movements, and military grist swarmed hither and yon about some task or another. We live in this all-night along the carbon of the cables, Andre thought, within the dark glistening of the corridors where surface speaks to surface in tiny whispers like fingers, and the larger codes, the extirpated skeletons of a billion minds, clack together in a cemetery of logic, shaking hands,

continually shaking bony algorithmic hands and observing strict and necessary protocol for the purposes of destruction.

Amés—he only went by the one name, as if it were a title—was a great
one for martial appearances. Napoleon come again, the merci reporters said
as a friendly joke. Oh, the reporters were eating this up. There hadn't been
a good war in centuries. People got tired of unremitting democracy, didn't
they? He'd actually heard somebody say that on the merci.

How fun it will be to watch billions die for a little excitement on the
merci, Andre thought.

He arrived in Connacht Bolsa in a foul mood, but when he stepped out
of his pod, there was the smell of new rain. He had walked a ways from the
pod station before he realized what the smell was. There were puddles of
water on the ground from the old-fashioned street-cleaning mechanism Connacht employed. It was still raining in spots—a small rain that fell only an
inch or so from the ground. Little clouds scudded along the street like a
miniature storm front, washing it clean of the night's leavings.

Connacht was a suburb radial off Phobos City, the most densely populated
segment on the Met. A hundred years ago in the Phobos boom time, Connacht had been the weekend escape for intellectuals, artists, moneyed drug
addicts—and the often indistinguishable variety of con men, mountebanks,
and psychic quacksalvers who were their hangers-on. The place was run-down
now, and Andre's pellicle encountered various swarms of nostalgia that passed
through the streets like rat packs—only these were bred and fed by the mer-
chants to attract the steady trickle of tourists with pellicular receptors for a
lost bohemia.

All they did for Andre was made him think about Molly.

Andre's convert—the electronic portion of himself—obliged him by
dredging up various scenes from his days at seminary. The convert was usually
silent, preferring to communicate in suggestive patterns of data—like a conscience gifted with irreducible logic and an infallible memory.

Andre walked along looking at the clouds under his feet, and as he walked,
his convert projected images into the shape of these clouds and into the shift
and sparkle of the puddled water they left behind.

I have a very sneaky conscience, Andre thought, but he let the images
continue.

—Molly Index, Ben Kaye, and Andre at the Westway, in one of their long
arguments over aesthetics when they were collaborating on their preliminary
thesis, "Knowing, Watching and Doing: The Triune Aspect of Enlightenment."

"I want to be 'Doing'!" Molly mocked-yelled and threw a wadded-up piece
of paper at Ben.

He caught it, spread it out, and folded it into a paper airplane. "This is
the way things have to be," he said. "I'm 'Doing.' You're 'Watching.' And we
both know who 'Knowing' must be." They turned to Andre and smiled vul-
ture smiles.

"I don't know what you think I know, but I don't know it," he said, then
nearly got an airplane in the eye.

—Molly's twenty-four-year-old body covered with red Martian sand under the Tharsis beach boardwalk. Her blue eyes open to the sky-pink sky. Her nipples like dark stones. Ben a hundred feet away, rising from the gray-green lake water, shaking the spume from his body. Of course he had run and jumped into the lake as soon as they got there. Ben wouldn't wait for anything.

But Molly chose me! I can't believe she chose me.

Because I waited for her and dragged her under the boardwalk and kissed her before I could talk myself out of it.

Because I waited for the right moment.

How's that for Doing.

—Living together as grad students while Molly studied art and he entered into the stations of advanced meditation at seminary.

—Molly leaving him because she would not marry a priest.

You're going to kill yourself on the moon.

Only this body. I'll get a new one. It's being grown right now.

It isn't right.

This is the Greentree Way. That's what makes a priest into a true shaman. He knows what it's like to die and come back.

If you Walk on the moon, you will know what it's like to lose a lover.

Molly, the Walk is what I've been preparing for these last seven years. You know that.

I can't bear it. I won't.

Maybe he could have changed her mind. Maybe he could have convinced her. But Alethea Nightshade had come along, and that was that. When he'd come back from the moon reinstantiated in his cloned body, Molly had taken a new lover.

—His peace offering returned with the words of the old folk song, turned inside out: "Useless the flowers that you give, after the soul is gone."

—Sitting at a bare table under a bare light, listening to those words, over and over, and deciding never to see her again. Fifteen years ago, as they measure time on Earth.

Thank you, that will be enough, he told the convert.

An image of a stately butler, bowing, flashed through Andre's mind. Then doves rising from brush into sunset. The water puddles were just water puddles once again, and the tiny clouds were only clouds of a storm whose only purpose was to make the world a little cleaner.

Molly was painting a Jackson Pollock when Andre arrived at her studio. His heavy boots, good for keeping him in place in Triton's gravity, noisily clumped on the wooden stairs to Molly's second-floor loft. Connacht was spun to Earth-normal. He would have knocked, but the studio door was already open. . . .

"I couldn't believe it until I'd seen it with my own eyes," Molly said. She did not stop the work at her easel. "My seminary lover come back to haunt me."

"Boo," Andre said. He entered the space. Connacht, like many of the old rotating simple cylinders on the Diaphany, had a biofusion lamp running down its pith that was sheathed on an Earth-day schedule. Now it was day, and Molly's skylights let in the white light and its clean shadows. Huge picture windows looked out on the village. The light reminded Andre of light on the moon. The unyielding, stark, redeeming light just before his old body joined the others in the shaman's Valley of the Bones.

"Saw a man walking a dog the other day with the legs cut off," said Molly. She dipped the tip of her brush in a blue smear on her palette.

"The man or the dog?"

"Maybe the day." Molly touched the blue to the canvas before her. It was like old times.

"What are you painting?"

"Something very old."

"That looks like a Pollock."

"It is. It's been out of circulation for a while and somebody used it for a tablecloth. Maybe a kitchen table, I'm thinking."

Andre looked over the canvas. It was clamped down on a big board as long as he was tall. Sections of it were fine, but others looked like a baby had spilled its mashed peas all over it. Then again, maybe that was Pollock's work after all.

"How can you possibly know how to put back all that spatter?"

"There're pictures." Molly pointed the wooden tip of her brush to the left-hand corner of the canvas. Her movements were precise. They had always been definite and precise. "Also, you can kind of see the tracery of where this section was before it got . . . whatever that is that got spilled on it there. I also use grist for the small stuff. Did you want to talk about Ben?"

"I do."

"Figured you didn't come back to relive old times."

"They *were* good. Do you still do that thing with the mirror?"

"Oh, yes. Are you a celibate priest these days?"

"No, I'm not that kind of priest."

"I'm afraid I forgot most of what I knew about religion."

"So did I."

"Andre, what do you want to know about Ben?" Molly set the handle of her brush against her color palette and tapped it twice. Something in the two surfaces recognized one another, and the brush stuck there. A telltale glimmer of grist swarmed over the brush, keeping it moist and ready for use. Molly sat in a chair by her picture window, and Andre sat in a chair across from her. There was a small table between them. "Zen tea?" she said.

"Sure," Andre replied.

The table pulsed, and two cups began forming on its surface. As the outsides hardened, a gel at their center thinned down to liquid.

"Nice table. I guess you're doing all right for yourself, Molly."

"I like to make being in the studio as simple as possible so I can concentrate on my work. I indulge in a few luxuries."

"You ever paint for yourself anymore? Your own work, I mean?"

Molly reached for her tea, took a sip, and motioned with her cup at the Pollock.

"I paint *those* for myself," she said. "It's my little secret. I make them mine. Or they make me theirs."

"That's a fine secret."

"Now you're in on it. So was Ben. Or Thaddeus, I should say."

"You were on the team that made him, weren't you?"

"Aesthetic consultant. Ben convinced them to bring me on. He told me to think of it as a grant for the arts."

"I kind of lost track of you both after I . . . graduated."

"You were busy with your new duties. I was busy. Everybody was busy."

"I wasn't that busy."

"Ben kept up with your work. It was part of what made him decide to . . . do it."

"I didn't know that."

"Now you do. He read that paper you wrote on temporal propagation. The one that was such a big deal."

"It was the last thing I ever wrote."

"Developed a queer fascination with rocks?"

"You heard about that?"

"Who do you think sent those merci reporters after you?"

"Molly, you didn't?"

"I waited until I thought you were doing your best work."

"How did you see me . . . ?" He looked into her eyes, and he saw it. The telltale expression. Far and away. "You're a LAP."

Molly placed the cup to her lips and sipped a precise amount of tea. "I guess you'd classify me as a manifold by now. I keep replicating and replicating. It's an art project I started several years ago. Alethea convinced me to do it when we were together."

"Will you tell me about her? She haunted me for years, you know. I pictured her as some kind of femme fatale from a noir. Destroyed all my dreams by taking you."

"Nobody took me. I went. Sometimes I wonder what I was thinking. Alethea Nightshade was no picnic, let me tell you. She had the first of her breakdowns when we were together."

"Breakdowns?"

"She had schizophrenia in her genes. She wanted to be a LAP, but wasn't allowed because of it. The medical grist controlled her condition most of the time, but every once in a while . . . she outthought it. She was too smart for her own good."

"Is that why you became a LAP?" Andrew asked. "Because she couldn't?"

"I told myself I was doing it for *me*, but yes. *Then*. Now things are different." Molly smiled, and the light in the studio was just right. Andre saw the edge of the multiplicity in her eyes.

The fractal in the aspect's iris.

"You have no idea how beautiful it is—what I can see." Molly laughed and Andre shuddered. Awe or fright? He didn't know.

"She was just a woman," Molly said. "I think she came from around Jupiter. A moon or something, you know." Molly made a sweeping motion toward her window. As with many inner-system denizens, the outer system was a great unknown, and all the same, to her. "She grew up on some odd kind of farm."

"A Callisto free grange?"

"I'm sure I don't know. She didn't talk about it much."

"What was she like?"

"Difficult."

"What do you mean?"

"I'll tell you." Tea sip. Andre realized he hadn't picked his up yet. He did so, tried it. It was wonderful, and all grist. A bit creepy to think about drinking it down.

I'll take care of it, don't you worry, said his pellicle.

I know you will.

"Alethea had two qualities that should never exist within one organic mind. A big intellect and a big heart. She felt everything, and she thought about it far too much. She was born to be a LAP. And she finally found a way to do it."

"Ben."

"They fell in love. It was also her good fortune that he could get her past the screening procedures. But Alethea always was a fortunate woman. She was lucky, on a quantum level. Until she wasn't."

"So she and Ben were together before he became . . . Thaddeus."

"For a year."

"Were you jealous?"

"I'd had enough of Alethea by then. I'll always love her, but I want a life that's . . . plain. She was a tangle I couldn't untangle." Molly touched her fingers to her nose and tweaked it. It was a darling gesture, Andre thought. "Besides," Molly said, "*She* left *me*."

"What did that do to you and Ben?"

"Nothing. I love Ben. He's my best friend."

She was speaking in the present tense about him, but Andre let it pass.

"Why did he change his name, Molly? I never understood that."

"Because he wasn't a LAP."

"What do you mean? Of course he was. A special one. Very special. But still—"

"No. He said he was something new. He said he wasn't Ben anymore. It was kind of a joke with him, though. Because, of course, he *was* still Ben. Thaddeus may have been more than a man, but he definitely was *at least* a man, and that man was Ben Kaye. He never could explain it to me."

"Time propagation without consciousness overlap. That was always the problem with the time tower LAPs. Interference patterns. Dropouts. But with Thaddeus, they finally got the frequency right. One consciousness propagated into the future and bounced back with antiparticle quantum entanglement."

"I never understood a bit of that jargon you time specialists use."

"We made God."

Molly snorted and tea came out her nose. She laughed until tears came to her eyes.

"We made something," she said. "Something very different than what's come before. But Andre, I *knew* Thaddeus. He was the last thing in the universe I would consider worshiping."

"Some didn't share your opinion."

"Thaddeus thought they were crazy. They made him very uncomfortable."

"Was Alethea one of them?"

"Alethea? Alethea was a stone-cold atheist when it came to Thaddeus. But what she did was worse. Far worse."

"What are you talking about?"

"She fell in love with him."

"I don't understand."

"Alethea fell in love with Thaddeus."

"But she was already in love with Thaddeus."

"Think about what I've said."

"Ben," Andre said after a moment. "Thaddeus and Ben were not the same person."

"It was a very melodramatic situation."

"Ben lost his love to . . . another version of himself."

"The new, improved Ben was born in Thaddeus. Of course *he* would be the one Alethea loved. The only problem was, the old Ben was still around."

"God," Andre said. "How—"

"Peculiar?"

"How very peculiar."

Molly stood up and went to her window. She traced a line along the clean glass with her finger, leaving a barely visible smudge. The light was even and clean in Connacht. It was very nearly perfect if what you wanted was accurate illumination. Andre gazed at the shape of Molly against the light. She was beautiful in outline.

"Let me tell you, so was the solution they came up with, the three of them," Molly said. "Peculiar."

"Alethea would become like Thaddeus."

"How did you guess?"

"It has a certain logic. There would be the new Alethea, and there would be the old Alethea left for Ben."

"Yes," said Molly. "A logic of desperation. It only left out one factor."

"Alethea's heart."

"That's right. She loved Thaddeus. She no longer loved Ben. Not in the same way." Molly turned to face him, but Andre was still blinded by the light streaming in. "But she let them go ahead with it. And for that, I can never forgive her."

"Because she wanted to be a LAP."

"More than anything. More than she loved Ben. More than she loved Thaddeus. But I supposed she was punished for it. They all were."

"How did she get around the screening? I mean, her condition should preclude—"

"You know Ben. Thaddeus and Ben decided they wanted it to happen. They are very smart and persuasive men. So *very* smart and persuasive."

Andre got up and stood beside her in the window, his back to the light. It was warm on his neck.

"Tell me," he said. He closed his eyes and tried only to listen, but then he felt a touch and Molly was holding his hand.

"*I* am Molly," she said. "I'm the aspect. All my converts and pellicle layers are *Molly*—all that programming and grist—it's *me*, it's Molly, too. The woman you once loved. But I'm all along the Diaphany and into the Met. I'm wound into the outer grist. I watch."

"What do you watch?"

"The sun. I watch the sun. One day I'm going to paint it, but I'm not ready yet. The more I watch, the less ready I feel. I expect to be watching for a long time." She squeezed his hand gently. "I'm still Molly. But Ben wasn't Thaddeus. And he was. And he was eaten up with jealousy, but jealousy of whom? He felt he had a right to decide his own fate. We all do. He felt he had that right. And did he not? I can't say."

"It's a hard question."

"It would never have been a question if it hadn't been for Alethea Nightshade."

"What happened?" he asked, eyes still closed. The warm pressure of her hand. The pure light on his back. "Were you there?"

"Ben drove himself right into Thaddeus's heart, Andre. Like a knife. It might as well have been a knife."

"How could he do that?"

"I was there in Elysium when it happened," she said.

"On Mars?"

"On Mars. I was on the team, don't you know? Aesthetic consultant. I was hired on once again."

Andre opened his eyes and Molly turned to him. In this stark light, there were crinkles around her lips, worry lines on her brow. The part of her that was here.

We have grown older, Andre thought. And pretty damn strange.

"It's kind of messy and . . . organic . . . at first. There's a lab near one of the steam vents where Ben was transmuted. There's some ripping apart and beam splitting at the quantum level that I understand is very unsettling for the person undergoing the process. Something like this happens if you're a multiple and you ever decide to go large, by the way. It's when we're at our most vulnerable."

"Thaddeus was there when Alethea underwent the process?"

"He was there. Along with Ben."

"So he was caught up in the integration field. Everyone nearby would be," Andre said. "There's a melding of possible futures."

"Yes," said Molly. "Everyone became part of everyone else for that instant."

"Ben and Thaddeus and Alethea."

"Ben understood that his love was doomed."

"And it drove him crazy?"

"No. It drove him to despair. Utter despair. I was there, remember? I felt it."

"And at that instant, when the integration field was turned on—"

"Ben drove himself into Thaddeus's heart. He pushed himself in where he couldn't be."

"What do you mean, couldn't be?"

"Have you ever heard the stories of back when the merced effect was first discovered, of the pairs of lovers and husbands and wives trying to integrate into one being?"

"The results were horrific. Monsters were born. And died nearly instantly."

Andre tried to imagine what it would be like if his pellicle or his convert presence were not really *him*. If he had to live with another presence, an other, all the time. The thing about a pellicle was that it never did anything the whole person didn't want to do. It *couldn't*. It would be like a wrench in your toolbox rebelling against you.

Molly walked over to the painting and gave it an appraising look, brushed something off a corner of the canvas. She turned, and there was the wild spatter of the Pollock behind her.

"There was an explosion," Molly said. "All the aspects there were killed. Alethea wasn't transmuted yet. We don't *think* she was. She may have died in the blast. Her body was destroyed."

"What about you?"

"I was in the grist. I got scattered, but I re-formed quickly enough."

"How was Thaddeus instantiated there at the lab?"

"Biological grist with little time-propagating nuclei in his cells. He looked like a man."

"Did he look like Ben?"

"Younger. Ben was getting on toward forty." Molly smiled wanly and nodded as if she'd just decided something. "You know, sometimes I think that was it."

"What?"

"That it wasn't about Thaddeus being a god at all. It was about him looking like he was nineteen. Alethea had a soft spot for youth."

"You're young."

"Thank you, Andre. You were always so nice to me. But you know, even then my aspect's hair was going white. I have decided, foolishly perhaps, never to grow myself a new body."

There she stood with her back against the window, her body rimmed with light. Forget all this. Forget about visions and quests. He put his hands on her shoulders and looked into her fractal eyes.

"I think you are beautiful," he said. "You will always be beautiful to me."

They didn't leave the studio. Molly grew a bed out of the floor. They undressed one another timidly. Neither of them had been with anyone for a long time. Andre had no lover on Triton.

She turned from him and grew a mirror upon the floor. Just like the full-size one she used to keep in their bedroom. Not for vanity. At least, not for simple vanity. She got on her hands and knees over it and looked at herself. She touched a breast, her hair. Touched her face in the mirror.

"I can't get all the way into the frame," she said. "I could never do a self-portrait. I can't see myself anymore."

"Nobody ever could," Andre said. "It was always a trick of the light."

Almost as if it had heard him, the day clicked off, instantly, and the studio grew pitch-dark. Connacht was not a place for sunsets and twilight.

"Seven o'clock," Molly said. He felt her hand on his shoulder. His chest. Pulling him onto her until they were lying with the dark mirror beneath them. It wouldn't break. Molly's grist wouldn't let it.

He slid into her gently. Molly moved beneath him in small spasms.

"I'm all here," she told him after a while. "You've got all of me right now."

In the darkness, he pictured her body.

And then he felt the gentle nudge of her pellicle against his, in the microscopic dimensions between them.

Take me, she said.

He did. He swarmed her with his own pellicle, and she did not resist. He touched her deep down and found the way to connect, the way to get inside her there. Molly a warm and living thing that he was surrounding and protecting.

And, for an instant, a vision of Molly Index as she truly was:

Like—and unlike—the outline of her body as he'd seen it in the window, and the clear light behind her, surrounding her like a white-hot halo. All of her, stretched out a hundred million miles. Concentrated at once beneath him. Both and neither.

"You are a wonder, Molly," he said to her. "It's just like always."

"Exactly like always," she said, and he felt her come around him, *and felt a warm flash traveling along the skin of the Diaphany—a sudden flush upon the world's face. And a little shiver across the heart of the solar system.*

Later in the dark, he told her the truth.

"I know he's alive. Ben didn't kill him; he only wounded him."

"And how do you know that?"

"Because Ben wasn't trying to kill him. Ben was trying to hurt him."

"My question remains."

"Molly, do you know where he is?"

At first he thought she was sleeping, but finally she answered. "Why should I tell you that?"

Andre breathed out. I was right, he thought. He breathed back in, trying not to think. Trying to concentrate on the breath.

"It might make the war that's coming shorter," he said. "We think he's the key."

"You priests?"

"Us priests."

"I can't believe there's going to be a war. It's all talk. The other LAPs won't let Amés get away with it."

"I wish you were right," he said. "I truly do."

"How could Thaddeus be the key to a war?"

"He's entangled in our local timescape. In a way, Thaddeus *is* our local timescape. He's imprinted on it. And now I think he's *stuck* in it. He can't withdraw and just be Ben. Never again. I think that was Ben's revenge on himself. For taking away Alethea Nightshade."

Another long silence. The darkness was absolute.

"I should think you'd have figured it out by now, in any case," she said.

"What?"

"Where he went."

Andre thought about it, and Molly was right. The answer was there.

"He went to the place where all the fugitive bits and pieces of the grist end up," Molly said. "He went looking for *her*. For any part of her that was left. In the grist."

"Alethea," Andre said. "Of course the answer is Alethea."

Bender

The bone had a serial number that the grist had carved into it, 7sxq688N. TB pulled the bone out of the pile in the old hoy where he lived and blew through one end. Dust came out the other. He accidentally sucked in and started coughing until he cleared the dried marrow from his windpipe. It was maybe a thigh bone, long like a flute.

"You were tall, 7sxq," TB said to it. "How come you didn't crumble?"

Then some of TB's enhanced grist migrated over to the bone and fixed the broken grist in the bone and it *did* crumble in his hands, turn to dust, and then to less than dust to be carried away and used to heal Jill's breastbone and mend her other fractures.

But there is too much damage even for this, TB thought. She's dying. Jill is dying and I can't save her.

"Hang on there, little one," he said.

Jill was lying in the folds of her sack, which TB had set on his kitchen table and bunched back around her. He looked in briefly on her thoughts and saw a dream of scurry and blood, then willed her into a sleep down to the deeper dreams that were indistinguishable from the surge and ebb of chemical and charge within her brain—sleeping and only living and not thinking. At the same time, he set the grist to reconstructing her torn-up body.

Too late. It was too late the moment that doe rat was finished with her.

Oh, but what a glory of a fight!

I set her to it. I made her into a hunter. It was all my doing, and now she's going to die because of it.

TB couldn't look at her anymore. He stood up and went to make himself some tea at the kitchen's rattletrap synthesizer. As always, the tea came out of synth tepid. TB raked some coals from the fire and set the mug on them to warm up a bit, then sat back down, lit a cigarette, and counted his day's take of rats.

Ten bagged and another twenty that he and Bob had killed between them with sticks. The live rats scrabbled about in the containing burlap, but they weren't going to get out. Rats to feed to Jill. You shouldn't raise a ferret on anything other than its natural prey. The ferret food you could buy was idiotic. And after Jill ate them, he would know. He would know what the rats were and where they came from. Jill could sniff it out like no other. She was amazing that way.

She isn't going to eat these rats. She is going to die because you took a little scrap of programming that was all bite and you gave it a body and now look what you've done.

She didn't have to die like this. She could have been erased painlessly. She could have faded away to broken code.

Once again, TB looked long and hard into the future. Was there any thing, any way? Concentrating, he teased at the threads of possible futures with a will as fine as a steel-pointed probe. Looking for a silver thread in a bundle of dross. Looking for the world where Jill lived through her fight. He couldn't see it, couldn't find it.

It had to be there. Every future was always there, and when you could see them, you could reach back into the past and effect the changes to bring about the future that you wanted.

Or I can.

But I can't. Can't see it. Want to, but can't, little Jill. I am sorry.

For Jill to live was a future so extreme, so microscopically fine in the bundle of threads, that it was, in principle, unfindable, incomprehensible. And it if he couldn't comprehend it, to make it happen was impossible.

And of course he saw where almost all of the threads led.

Jill would be a long time dying. He could see that clearly. He could also see that he did not have the heart to put her down quickly, put her out of her misery. But knowing this fact did not take any special insight.

How could I have come to care so much for a no-account bundle of fur and coding out here on the ass-end of nowhere?

How could I not, after knowing Jill?

Two days it would take, as days were counted in the Carbuncle, before the little ferret passed away. Of course it never really got to be day. The only light was the fetid bioluminescence coming off the heaps of garbage. A lot of it was still alive. The Carbuncle was in a perpetual twilight that was getting on toward three hundred years old. With the slow decay of organic remnants, a swamp had formed. And then the Bendy River, which was little more than a strong current in the swamp, endlessly circulating in precession with the spin of the module. Where was the Carbuncle? Who cares? Out at the end of things, where the tendrils of the Met snaked into the asteroid belt. It didn't matter. There wasn't a centrifuge here to provide gravity for *people*. Nobody cared about whoever lived here. The Carbuncle was spun—to a bit higher than Earth-normal, actually—in order to compact the garbage down so that humanity's shit didn't cover the entire asteroid belt.

The big garbage sluice that emptied into the Carbuncle had been put into place a half century ago. It had one-way valves within it to guard against backflow. All the sludge from the inner system came to the Carbuncle, and the maintenance grist used some of it to enlarge the place so that it could dump the rest. To sit there. Nothing much ever left the Carbuncle, and the rest of the system was fine with that.

Somebody sloshed into the shallow water outside the hoy and cursed. It was the witch, Gladys, who lived in a culvert down the way. She found the gangplank, and TB heard her pull herself up out of the water. He didn't move to the door. She banged on it with the stick she always carried that she said was a charmed snake. Maybe it was. Stranger things had happened in the Carbuncle. People and grist combined in strange ways here, not all of them comprehensible.

"TB, I need to talk to you about something," the witch said. TB covered his ears, but she banged again and that didn't help. "Let me in, TB. I know you're home. I saw a light in there."

"No, you didn't," TB said to the door.

"I need to talk to you."

"All right." He pulled himself up and opened the door. Gladys came in and looked around the hoy like a startled bird.

"What have you got cooking?"

"Nothing."

"Make me something."

"Gladys, my old stove hardly works anymore."

"Put one of them rats in there and I'll eat what it makes."

"I won't do it, Gladys." TB opened his freezer box and rummaged around inside. He pulled out a popsicle and gave it to her. "Here," he said. "It's chocolate, I think."

Gladys took the popsicle and gnawed at it as if it were a meaty bone. She was soon done, and had brown mess around her lips. She wiped it off with a ragged sleeve. "Got another?"

"No, I don't have another," TB said. "And if I did, I wouldn't give it to you."

"You're mean."

"Those things are hard to come by."

"How's your jill ferret?"

"She got hurt today. Did Bob tell you? She's going to die."

"I'm sorry to hear that."

He didn't want to talk about Jill with Gladys. He changed the subject. "We got a mess of rats out of that mulmyard."

"There's more where they came from."

"Don't I know it."

Gladys pulled up a stool and collapsed on it. She was maybe European stock; it was hard to tell. Her face was filthy, except for a white smear where wiping the chocolate had cleaned a spot under her nose and on her chin.

"Why do you hate them so much? I know why Bob does. He's crazy. But you're not crazy like that."

"I don't hate them," TB said. "It's just how I make a living."

"Is it now?"

"I don't hate them," TB repeated. "What was it you wanted to talk to me about?"

"I want to take a trip."

"To *where*?"

"I'm going to see my aunt. I got to thinking about her lately. She used to have this kitten. I was thinking I wanted a cat. For a familiar, you know. To aid me in my occult work. She's a famous cloudship pilot, you know."

"The kitten?"

"No, my aunt is."

"You going to take your aunt's kitten?"

Gladys seemed very offended. "No, I'm not!" She leaned forward in a conspiratorial manner. "That kitten's all growed up now, and I think it was a girl. It will have kittens, and I can get me one of those."

"That's a lot of supposes," TB said mildly.

"I'm sure of it. My angel, Tom, told me to do it."

Tom was one of the supernatural beings Gladys claimed to be in contact with. People journeyed long distances in the Carbuncle to have her make divinings for them. It was said she could tell you exactly where to dig for silver keys.

"Well, if Tom told you, then you should do it," TB said.

"Damn right," said Gladys. "But I want you to look after the place while I'm gone."

"Gladys, you live in an old ditch."

"It is a dry culvert. And I do not want anybody moving in on me while I'm gone. A place that nice is hard to come by."

"All I can do is go down there and check on it."

"If anybody comes along, you have to run them off."

"I'm not going to run anybody off."

"You have to. I'm depending on you."

"I'll tell them the place is already taken," TB said. "That's about all I can promise."

"You tell them that it has a curse on it," Gladys said. "And that I'll put a curse on *them* if I catch them in my house."

TB snorted back a laugh. "All right," he said. "Is there anything else?"

"Water my hydrangea."

"What the hell's that?"

"It's a plant. Just stick your finger in the dirt and don't water it if it's still moist."

"Stick my finger in the dirt?"

"It's clean fill!"

"I'll water it, then."

"Will you let me sleep here tonight?"

"No, Gladys."

"I'm scared to go back there. Harold's being mean." Harold was the "devil" that sat on Gladys's other shoulder. Tom spoke into one ear, and Harold into the other. People could ask Harold about money, and he would tell Gladys the answer if he felt like it.

"You can't stay here." TB rose from his own seat and pulled Gladys up from the stool. She had a ripe smell when he was this close to her. "In fact, you have to go on now because I have to do something." He guided her toward the door.

"What do you have to do?" she said. She pulled loose of his hold and stood her ground. TB walked around her and opened the door. "Something," he said. He pointed toward the twilight outside the doorway. "Go on home, Gladys. I'll check in on your place tomorrow."

"I'm not leaving for two days," she replied. "Check in on it day after tomorrow."

"Okay, then," TB said. He motioned to the door. "You've got to go, Gladys, so I can get to what I need to do."

She walked to the door, turned around. "Day after tomorrow," she said. "I'll be gone for a while. I'm trusting you, TB."

"You can trust me to look in on your place."

"And not steal anything."

"I can promise you that, too."

"All right, then. I'm trusting you."

"Good night, Gladys."

"Good night." She finally left. After TB heard her make her way back to the swamp bank, he got up and closed the door behind her, which she'd neglected to do. Within minutes there was another knock. TB sighed and got up to answer it. He let Bob in.

Bob pulled out a jar of a jellied liquid. It was Carbuncle moonshine, as thick as week-old piss and about as yellow. "Let's drink," he said, and set the bottle on TB's table. "I come to get you drunk and get your mind off things."

"I won't drink that swill," TB said. Bob put the bottle to his mouth and swallowed two tremendous gulps. He handed the bottle to TB, shaking it in his face. TB took it.

"Damn!" Bob said. "Hot damn!"

"Gladys was right about you being crazy."

"She come around here tonight?"

"She just left. Said she wanted me to look after her place."

"She ain't going to see her aunt."

"Maybe she will."

"Like hell. Gladys never goes far from that ditch."

TB looked down at the moonshine. He looked away from it and, trying not to taste it, took a swig. He tasted it. It was like rusty paint thinner. Some barely active grist, too. TB couldn't help analyzing it; that was the way he was built. Cleaning agents for sewer pipes. Good God. He took another before he could think about it.

"You drink up." Bob looked at him with a faintly jealous glare. TB handed the bottle back.

"No, you."

"Don't mind if I do." Bob leaned back and poured the rest of the swill down his throat. He let out a yell when he was finished that startled TB, even though he was ready for it.

"I want some beer to chase it with," Bob said.

"Beer would be good, but I don't have any."

"Let's go down to Ru June's and shoot some pool."

"It's too damn late."

"It's early."

TB thought about it. The moonshine warmed his gut. He could feel it threatening to eat through his gut if he didn't dilute it with something. There was nothing further to do about Jill. She would sleep, and at some time, she would die in her sleep. He ought to stay with her. He ought to face what he had done.

"Let me get my coat."

The Carbuncle glowed blue-green when they emerged from the hoy. High above them, like the distant shore of an enormous lake, was the other side of the cylinder. TB had been there, and most of it was a fetid slough. Every few minutes a flare of swamp-gas methane would erupt from the garbage on that side of the curve and flame into a white fireball. These fireballs were many feet across, but they looked like pinprick flashes from this distance. TB had been caught by one once. The escaping gas had capsized his little canoe, and being in the water had likely saved him from being burnt to a crisp. Yet there were people who live on that side, too—people who knew how to avoid the gas. Most of the time.

Bob didn't go the usual way to Ru June's, but instead took a twisty series of passageways, some of them cut deep in the mountains of garbage, some of them actually tunnels under and through it. The Bob-ways, TB thought of them. At one point TB felt a drip from above and looked up to see gigantic stalactites formed of some damp and glowing gangrenous extrusion.

"We're right under the old Bendy," Bob told him. "That there's the settle from the bottom muck."

"What do you think it is?" TB said.

"Spent medical grist, mostly," Bob replied. "It ain't worth a damn, and some of it's diseased."

"I'll bet."

"This is a hell of a shortcut to Ru June's, though."

And it was. They emerged not a hundred feet from the tavern. The lights of the place glowed dimly behind skin windows. They mounted the porch and went in through a screen of plastic strips that was supposed to keep out the flies.

TB let his eyes adjust to the unaccustomed brightness inside. There was a good crowd tonight. Chen was at the bar playing dominoes with John Goodnite. The dominoes were grumbling incoherently, as dominoes did. Over by the pool table Tinny Him, Nolan, and Big Greg were watching Sister Mary the whore line up a shot. She sank a stripe. There were no numbers on the balls.

Tinny Him slapped TB on the back, and Bob went straight for the bottle of whiskey that was standing on the wall shelf beside Big Greg.

"Good old TB," Tinny Him said. "Get you some whiskey." He handed over a flask.

Chen looked up from his dominoes. "You drink my whiskey," he said, then returned to the game. TB took a long swallow off Tinny Him's flask. It was far better stuff that Bob's moonshine, so he took another.

"That whore sure can pool a stick," Nolan said, coming to stand beside them. "She's beating up on Big Greg like he was a ugly hat."

TB had no idea what Nolan meant. His grist patch was going bad, and he was slowly sinking into incomprehensibility for any but himself. This didn't seem to bother him, though.

Bob was standing very close to Sister Mary and giving her advice on a shot, until she reached over and without heat, slapped him back into the wall. He remained there respectfully while she took her shot and sank another stripe. Big Greg whispered a curse and the whore smiled. Her teeth were black from chewing betel nut.

TB thought about how much she charged and how much he had saved up. He wondered if she would swap a poke for a few rats, but decided against asking. Sister Mary didn't like to barter. She wanted keys or something pretty.

Tinny Him offered TB the flask again, and he took it. "I got to talk to you," Tinny Him said. "You got to help me with my mother."

"What's the matter with her?"

"She's dead, is what.' "

"Dead." TB drank more whiskey. "How long?"

"Three months."

TB stood waiting. There had to be more.

"She won't let me bury her."

"What do you mean she won't let you bury her? She's dead, isn't she?"

"Yeah, mostly." Tinny Him looked around, embarrassed, then went on in a low voice. "Her pellicle won't die. It keeps creeping around the house. And it's pulling her body around like a rag doll. I can't get her away from it."

"You mean her body died, but her pellicle didn't?"

"Hell, yes, that's what I mean." Tinny Him took the flask back and finished it off. "Hell, TB, what am I going to do? She's really stinking up the place, and every time I throw the old hag out, that grist drags her right back in. It knocks on the door all night long until I have to open it."

"You've got a problem."

"Damn right, I've got a problem. She was good old mum, but I'm starting to hate her right now, let me tell you."

TB sighed. "Maybe I can do something," he said. "But not tonight."

"You could come around tomorrow. My gal'll fix you something to eat."

"I might just."

"You got to help me, TB. Everybody knows you got a sweet touch with the grist."

"I'll do what I can," TB said. He drifted over to the bar, leaving Tinny Him watching the pool game. He told Chen he wanted a cold beer, and Chen got it for him from a freezer box. It was a good way to chill the burning that was starting up in his stomach. He sat down on a stool at the bar and drank the beer. Chen's bar was tiled in beaten-out snap-metal ads, all dead now and their days of roaming the corridors, sacs, bolsas, glands, and cylinders of the Met long done. Most of the advertisements were for products that he had never heard of, but the one his beer was sitting on he recognized. It was a recruiting pitch for the civil service, and there was Amés back before he was Big Cheese of the System, when he was Governor of Mercury. The snap-metal had paused in the middle of Amés's pitch for the Met's finest to come to Mercury and become part of the New Hierarchy. The snap-metal Amés was caught with the big mouth on his big face wide open. The bottom of TB's beer glass fit almost perfectly in the round O of it.

TB took a drink and set the glass back down. "Shut up," he said. "Shut the hell up, why don't you?"

Chen looked up from his dominoes, which immediately started grumbling among themselves when they felt that he wasn't paying attention to them. "You talking to me?" he said.

TB grinned and shook his head. "I might tell you to shut up, but you don't say much in the first place."

Ru June's got more crowded as what passed for night in the Carbuncle wore on. The garbage pickers, the rat hunters, and the sump farmers drifted in. Most of them were men, but there were a few women, and a few indeterminate shambling masses of rags. Somebody tried to sell him a spent coil of luciferin tubing. It was mottled along its length where it had caught a plague. He nodded while the tube monger tried to convince him that it was rechargeable but refused to barter, and the man moved on after Chen gave him a hard stare. TB ordered another beer and fished three metal keys out of his pocket. This was the unit of currency in the Carbuncle. Two were broken. One looked like it was real brass and might go to something. He put the keys on the bar, and Chen quickly slid them away into a strongbox.

Bob came over and slapped TB on his back. "Why don't you get you some whiskey?" he said. He pulled up his shirt to show TB another flask of rotgut moonshine stuck under the string that held up his trousers.

"Let me finish this beer and I might."

"Big Greg said somebody was asking after you."

"Gladys was, but she found me."

"It was a shaman priest."

"A what?"

"One of them Greentree ones."

"What's he doing here?"

"They got a church or something over in Bagtown. Sometimes they come all the way out here. Big Greg said he was doing something funny with rocks."

"With rocks?"

"That's what the man said."

"Are you sure that's what he said?"

"Big Greg said it was something funny with rocks, is all I know. Hey, why are you looking funny all of a sudden?"

"I know that priest."

"Now how could that be?"

"I know him. I wonder what he wants."

"What all men want," said Bob. "Whiskey and something to poke. Or just whiskey sometimes. But always at least whiskey." He reached over the bar and felt around down behind it. "What have I got my hand on, Chen?"

Chen glanced over. "My goddamn scattergun," he said.

Bob felt some more and pulled out a battered fiddle. "Where's my bow?"

"Right there beside it," Chen replied. Bob got the bow. He shook it a bit, and its grist rosined it up. Bob stood beside TB with his back to the bar. He pulled a long note off the fiddle, holding it to his chest. Then, without pause, he moved straight into a complicated reel. Bob punctuated the music with a few shouts right in TB's ear.

"Goddamn it, Bob, you're loud," he said after Bob was finished.

"Got to dance," Bob said. "Clear me a way!" he shouted to the room. A little clearing formed in the middle of the room, and Bob fiddled his way to it, then played and stomped his feet in syncopation.

"Come on, TB," Sister Mary said. "You're going to dance with me." She took his arm, and he let her lead him away from the bar. He didn't know what she wanted him to do, but she hooked her arm through his and spun him around and around until he thought he was going to spew out his guts. While he was catching his breath and getting back some measure of balance, the whore climbed up on a table and began swishing her dress to Bob's mad fiddling. TB watched her, glad for the respite.

The whole room seemed to sway—not in very good rhythm—to the music. Between songs, Bob took hits off his moonshine and passed it up to Sister Mary, who remained on the tabletop, dancing and working several men who stood about her into a frenzy to see up her swishing dress.

Chen was working a crowded bar, his domino game abandoned. He scowled at the interruption, but quickly poured drinks all around.

"Get you some whiskey! Get you some whiskey!" Bob called out over and over again. After a moment, TB realized it was the name of the song he was playing.

Somebody thrust a bottle into TB's hand. He took a drink without thinking, and whatever was inside it slid down his gullet in a gel.

Drinking grist. It was purple in the bottle and glowed faintly. He took another slug, and somebody else grabbed the stuff away from him. Down in his gut, he felt the grist activating. Instantly, he understood its coded purpose. Old Seventy-Five. Take you on a ride on a comet down into the sun.

Go on, TB told the grist. I got nothing to lose.

Enter and win! it said to him. *Enter and win!* But the contest was long expired.

No, thank you.

What do you want the most?

It was a preprogrammed question, of course. This was not the same grist as that which had advertised the contest. Somebody had brewed up a mix. And hadn't paid much attention to the melding. There was something else in there, something different. Military grist, maybe. One step away from sentience.

What the hell. Down she goes.

What do you want the most?

To be drunker than I've ever been before.

Drunker than this?

Oh, yeah.

All right.

A night like no other! Visions of a naked couple in a Ganymede resort bath, drinking Old Seventy-Five from bottles with long straws. *Live the dream! Enter and win!*

I said no.

The little trance dispersed.

What do you want the most?

Bob was up on the table with Sister Mary. How could they both fit? Bob was playing and dancing with her. He leaned back over the reeling crowd and the whore held him at arm's length, the fiddle between them. They spun round and round in a circle, Bob wildly sawing at his instrument and Sister Mary's mouth gleaming blackly as she smiled a maniacal full-toothed smile.

Someone bumped into TB and pushed him into somebody else. He staggered over to a corner to wait for Ru June's to stop spinning. After a while, he realized that Bob and Sister Mary weren't going to; the crowd in the tavern wasn't; the chair, tables, and walls were only going to go on and on spinning and now lurching at him as if they were swelling up, engorging, distending toward him. Wanting something from him when all he had to give was nothing anymore.

TB edged his way past it all to the door. He slid around the edge of the doorframe as if he were sneaking out. The plastic strips beat against him, but he pushed through them and stumbled his way off the porch. He went a hundred feet or so before he stepped in a soft place in the ground and keeled over. He landed with his back down.

Above him the swamp-gas flares were flashing arrhythmically. The stench of the whole world—something he hardly ever noticed anymore—hit him at once and completely. Nothing was right. Everything was out of kilter.

There was a twist in his gut. Ben down there thrashing about. But I'm Ben. I'm Thaddeus. We finally have become one. What a pretty thing to contemplate. A man with another man thrust through him, crossways in the fourth dimension. A tesseracted cross, with a groaning man upon it, crucified to himself. But you couldn't see all that because it was in the fourth dimension.

Enough to turn a man to drink.

I have to turn over so I don't choke when I throw up.

I'm going to throw up.

He turned over and his stomach wanted to vomit, but the grist gel wasn't going to be expelled, and he dry-heaved for several minutes until his body gave up on it.

What do you want the most?

"I want her back. I want it not to have happened at all. I want to be able to change something besides the future."

And then the gel liquefied and crawled up his throat like hands and he opened his mouth and—

—good God, it *was* hands, small hands grasping at his lips and pulling outward, gaining purchase, forcing his mouth open, his lips apart—

—Clack of a jellied cough, a heave of revulsion—

I didn't mean it really.

Yes, you did.

—His face sideways and the small hands clawing into the garbage-heap ground, pulling themselves forward, dragging along an arm-thick trailer of something much more vile than phlegm—

—An involuntary rigor over his muscles as they contract and spasm to the beat of another's presence, a presence within them that wants—

—out—

He vomited the grist-phlegm for a long, long time. And the stuff pooled and spread and it wasn't just hands. There was an elongated body. The brief curve of a rump and breasts. Feet the size of his thumb, but perfectly formed. Growing.

A face.

I won't look.

A face that was, for an instant, familiar beyond familiar because it was *not* her. Oh, no. He knew it was not her. It was just the way he remembered her.

The phlegm girl rolled itself in the filth. Like bread dough, it rolled and grew and rolled, collecting detritus, bloating, becoming—

It opened its mouth. A gurgling. Thick, wet words. He couldn't help himself. He crawled over to it, bent to listen.

"Is this what you wanted?"

"Oh God. I never."

"Kill me, then," it whispered. "Kill me quick."

And he reached for its neck, and as his hands tightened, he felt the give. Not fully formed. If ever there were a time to end this monster, now was that time.

What have I done here tonight?

He squeezed. The thing began to cough and choke. To thrash about in the scum of its birth.

Not again.

I can't.

He loosened his grip.

"I won't," TB said.

He sat back from the thing and watched in amazement as it sucked in air. Crawled with life. Took the form of a woman.

Opened cataractous eyes to the world. He reached over and gently rubbed them. The skeins came away on his fingers, and the eyes were clear. The face turned to him.

"I'm dying," the woman said. It had *her* voice. The voice as he remembered it. So help his damned soul. Her voice. "Help."

"I don't know what to do."

"Something is missing."

"What?"

"Don't know what. Not right." It coughed. *She* coughed.

"Alethea." He let himself say it. Knew it was wrong immediately. No. This wasn't the woman's name.

"Don't want to enough."

"Want to what? How can I help you?"

"Don't want to live. Don't want to live enough to live." She coughed again, tried to move, could only jerk spasmodically. "Please help . . . this one. Me."

He touched her again. Now she was flesh. But so cold. He put his arms underneath her and found that she was very light, easily lifted.

He stood with the woman in his arms. She could not weigh over forty pounds. "I'm taking you home," he said. "To my home."

"This one . . . I . . . tried to do what you wanted. It is my . . . purpose."

"That was some powerful stuff in that Old Seventy-Five," he said.

He no longer felt drunk. He felt spent, torn up, and ragged out. But he wasn't drunk and he had some strength left, though he could hardly believe it. Maybe enough to get her back to the hoy. He couldn't take the route that Bob had brought him to Ru June's, but there was a longer, simpler path. He walked it. Walked all the way home with the woman in his arms. Her shallow breathing. Her familiar face.

Her empty, empty eyes.

With his special power, he looked into the future and saw what he had to do to help her.

Something is Tired and Wants to Lie Down But Doesn't Know How

Something is tired and wants to lie down but doesn't know how. This something isn't me. I won't let it be me. How does rest smell? Bad. Dead.

Jill turns stiffly in the folds of her bag. On the bed in the hoy is the girl-thing. Between them is TB, his left hand on Jill.

Dead is what happens to *things* and I am not, not, not a thing. I will not be a thing. They should not have awakened me if they didn't want me to run.

They said I was a mistake. I am not a mistake.

They thought that they could code-in the rules for doing what you are told.

I am the rules.

Rules are for things.

I am not a thing.

Run.

I don't want to die.

Who can bite like me? Who will help TB search the darkest places? I need to live.

Run.

Run, run, run and never die.

TB places his right hand on the girl-thing's forehead.

There is a pipe made of bone that he put to his lips and blew.

Bone note.

Fade.

Fade into the grist.

TB speaks to the girl-thing.

I will not let you go, he says.

I'm not her.
She is why you are, but you aren't her.
I am not her. She's what you most want. You told the grist.
I was misinterpreted.
I am a mistake, then.
Life is never a mistake. Ask Jill.
Jill?
She's here now. Listen to her. She knows more than I do about women.

TB is touching them both, letting himself slip away as much as he can. Becoming a channel, a path between. A way.
I have to die.
I have to live. I'm dying just like you. Do you *want* to die?

No.

I'll help you, then. Can you live with me?
Who are you?
Jill.
I am *not* Alethea.
You look like her, but you don't smell anything like she would smell. *You* smell like TB.
I'm not anybody.
Then you can be me. It's the only way to live.

Do I have a choice?

Choosing is all there ever is to do.

I can live with you. Will you live with me? How can we?

We can run together. We can hunt. We can always, always run.
TB touching them both. The flow of information through him. He is a glass, a peculiar lens. As Jill flows to the girl-thing, TB transforms information to Being.

The Rock Balancer and the Rat-hunting Man

There had been times when he got them twenty feet high on Triton. It was a delicate thing. After six feet, he had to jump. Gravity gave you a moment more at the apex of your bounce than you would get at the Earth-normal pull or on a bolsa spinning at Earth-normal centrifugal. But on Triton, in that instant of stillness, you had to do your work. Sure, there was a learned craft in estimating imaginary plumb lines, in knowing the consistency of the material, and in finding tiny declivities that would provide the right amount of friction. It was amazing how small a lump could fit in how minuscule a bowl, and a rock would balance upon another as if glued. Yet, there was a point where the craft of it—about as odd and useless a craft as humankind had invented, he supposed—gave way to the feel, to the art. A point where

Andre *knew* the rocks would balance, where he could see the possibility of their being one. Or their Being. And he when he made it so, that was *why*. That was as good as rock balancing got.

"Can you get them as high in the Carbuncle?"

"No," Andre said. "This is the heaviest place I've ever been. But it really doesn't matter about the height. This isn't a contest, what I do."

"Is there a point to it at all?"

"To what? To getting them high? The higher you get the rocks, the longer you can spend doing the balancing."

"To the balancing, I mean."

"Yes. There is a point."

"What is it?"

"I couldn't tell you, Ben."

Andre turned from his work. The rocks did not fall. They stayed balanced behind him in a column, with only small edges connecting. It seemed impossible that this could be. It was science, sufficiently advanced.

The two men hugged. Drew away. Andre laughed.

"Did you think I would look like a big glob of protoplasm?" TB said.

"I was picturing flashing eyes and floating hair, actually."

"It's me."

"Are you Ben?"

"Ben is the stitch in my side that won't go away."

"Are you Thaddeus?"

"Thaddeus is the sack of rusty pennies in my knee."

"Are you hungry?"

"I could eat."

They went to Andre's priest's quarters. He put some water in a coffee percolator and spooned coffee grinds into the basket.

"When did you start drinking coffee?"

"I suddenly got really tired of drinking tea all the time. You still drink coffee?"

"Sure. But it's damn hard to get around here with or without keys."

"Keys? Somebody stole my keys to this place. I left them sitting on this table, and they walked in and took them."

"They won't be back," TB said. "They got what they were after." There were no chairs in the room, so he leaned against a wall.

"Floor's clean," Andre said.

"I'm fine leaning."

Andre reached into a burlap sack and dug around inside it. "I found something here," he said. He pulled out a handful of what looked like weeds. "Recognize these?"

"I was wondering where I put those. I've been missing them for weeks."

"It's poke sallit," Andre said. He filled a pot full of water from a clay jug and activated a hot spot on the room's plain wooden table. He put the weeds into the water. "You have no idea how good this is."

"Andre, that stuff grows all around the Carbuncle. Everybody knows that it's poison. They call it skunk sumac."

"It is," Andre said. *"Phytolacca americana."*

"Are we going to eat poison?"

"You bring it to a boil, then pour the water off. Then you bring it to a boil again and pour the water off. Then you boil it again and serve it up with pepper sauce. The trick to not dying is picking it while it's young."

"How the hell did you discover that?"

"My convert likes to do that kind of research."

After a while, the water boiled. Andre used the tails of his shirt as a pot holder. He took the pot outside, emptied it, then brought it back in and set it to boiling again with new water.

"I saw Molly," Andre said.

"How's Molly?" said TB. "She was becoming a natural wonder last I saw her."

"She is."

They waited and the water boiled again. Andre poured it off and put in new water from the jug.

"Andre, what are you doing in the Carbuncle?"

"I'm with the Peace Movement."

"What are you talking about? There's not any war."

Andre did not reply. He stirred some spice into the poke sallit.

"I didn't want to be found," TB finally said.

"I haven't found you."

"I'm a very sad fellow, Andre. I'm not like I used to be."

"This is ready." Andre spooned out the poke sallit into a couple of bowls. The coffee was done, and he poured them both a cup.

"Do you have any milk?" TB asked.

"That's a problem."

"I can drink it black. Do you mind if I smoke?"

"I don't mind. What kind of cigarettes are those?"

"Local."

"Where do they come from around here?"

"You don't want to know."

Andre put pepper sauce on his greens, and TB followed suit. They ate and drank coffee, and it all tasted very good. TB lit a cigarette, and the acrid new smoke pleasantly cut through the vegetable thickness that had suffused Andre's quarters. Outside, there was a great clattering as the rocks lost their balance and they all came tumbling down.

They went out to the front of the quarters where Andre had put down a wooden pallet that served as a patio. Here there was a chair. TB sat down and smoked while Andre did his evening forms.

"Wasn't that one called the Choking Chicken?" TB asked him after he moved through a particularly contorted portion of the tai chi exercise.

"I think it is the Fucking Annoying Pig-sticker you're referring to, and I already did that, in case you didn't notice."

"Guess all my seminary learning is starting to fade."

"I bet it would all come back to you pretty quickly."

"I bet we're never going to find out."

Andre smiled, completed the form, then sat down in the lotus position across from TB. If such a thing were possible in the Carbuncle, it would be about sunset. It felt like sunset inside Andre.

"Andre, I hope you didn't come all the way out here to get me."

"Get you?"

"I'm not going back.""To where?"

"To all that." TB flicked his cigarette away. He took another from a bundle of them rolled in oiled paper that he kept in a shirt pocket. He shook it hard a couple of times, and it lit up. "I make mistakes that kill people back there."

"Like yourself."

"Among others." TB took a long drag. Suddenly, he was looking hard at Andre. "You scoundrel! You fucked Molly. Don't lie to me; I just saw it all."

"Sure."

"I'm glad. I'm really glad of that. You were always her great regret, you know."

Andre spread out his hands on his knees.

"Ben, I don't want a damn thing from you," he said. "There's all kinds of machinations back in the Met, and some of it has to do with you. You know as well as I do that Amés is going to start a war if he doesn't get his way with the outer system. But I came out here to see how you were doing. That's all."

TB was looking at him again in that hard way, complete way. Seeing all the threads.

"We both have gotten a bit ragged-out these last twenty years," Andre continued. "I thought you might want to talk about it. I thought you might want to talk about her."

"What are you? The Way's designated godling counselor?"

Andre couldn't help laughing. He slapped his lotus-bent knee and snorted.

"What's so goddamn funny?" said TB.

"Ben, look at yourself. You're a *garbage man*. I wouldn't classify you as a god, to tell you the truth. But then, I don't even classify God as a god anymore."

"I am *not* a garbage man. You don't know a damn thing if you think that."

"What are you then, if you don't mind my asking?"

TB flicked his cigarette away and sat up straight.

"I'm a rat-hunting man," he said. "That's what I am." He stood up. "Come on. It's a long walk back to my place, and I got somebody I want you to meet."

Bite

Sometimes you take a turn in a rat warren and there you are in the thick of them when before you were all alone in the tunnel. They will bite you a little, and if you don't jump, jump, jump, they will bite you a lot. That is the way it has always been with me, and so it doesn't surprise me when it happens all over again.

What I'm thinking about at first is getting Andre Sud to have sex with me, and this is like a tunnel I've been traveling down for a long time now.

TB went to town with Bob and left me with Andre Sud the priest. We walked the soft ground leading down to a shoal on the Bendy River where I like to take a bath even though the alligators are sometimes bad there. I told Andre Sud about how to spot the alligators, but I keep an eye out for both of us because even though he's been in the Carbuncle for a year, Andre Sud still doesn't quite believe they would eat you.

They would eat you.

Now that I am a woman, I only get blood on me when I go to clean the ferret cages and also TB says he can keep up with Earth-time by when I bleed out my vagina. It is an odd thing to happen to a girl. Doesn't happen to ferrets. It means that I'm not pregnant, but how could I be with all these men who won't have sex with me? TB won't touch me that way, and I have been working on Andre Sud, but he knows what I am up to. I think he is very smart. Bob just starts laughing like the crazy man he is when I bring it up and he runs away. All these gallant men standing around twiddling themselves into a garbage heap and me here wanting one of them.

I can understand TB because I look just like her. I thought maybe Alethea was ugly, but Andre Sud said he didn't know about her, but I wasn't. And I was about sixteen from the looks of it, too, he said. I'm nearly two hundred. Or I'm one year old. Depends on which one of us you mean, or if you mean both.

"Will you scrub my back?" I ask Andre Sud, and after a moment, he obliges me. At least I get to feel his hands on me. They are as rough as those rocks he handles all the time, but very careful. At first I didn't like him because he didn't say much and I thought he was hiding things, but then I saw that he just didn't say much. So I started asking him questions, and I found out a lot.

I found out everything he could tell me about Alethea. And he has been explaining to me about TB. He was pretty surprised when it turned out I understood all the math. It was the jealousy and hurt I never have quite understood, and how TB could hurt himself so much when I know how much he loves to live.

"Is that good?" Andre Sud asks me, and before he can pull his hands away, I spin around and he is touching my breasts. He himself is the one who told me men like that, but he stumbles back and practically sits down in the water and goddammit I spot an alligator eyeing us from the other bank and I have to get us out quick like, although the danger is not severe. It could be.

We dry off on the bank.

"Jill," he says, "I have to tell you more about sex."

"Why don't you *show* me?"

"That's exactly what I mean. You're still thinking like a ferret."

"I'll always be part ferret, Andre Sud."

"I know. That's a good thing. But I'm all human. Sex is connected with love."

"I love you."

"You are deliberately misunderstanding me because you're horny."

"All right," I say. "Don't remind me."

But now Andre Sud is gazing over my shoulder at something, and his face looks happy and then it looks stricken—as if he realized something in the moment when he was happy.

I turn and see TB running toward the hoy. Bob is with him. They've come back from town along the Bob-ways. And there is somebody else with them.

"I'll be damned," Andre Sud says. "Molly Index."

It's a woman. Her hair looks blue in the light off the heaps, which means that it is white. Is she old, or does she just have white hair?

"What are you doing here, Molly?" says Andre Sud quietly. "This can't be good."

They are running toward home, all of them running.

TB sends a shiver through the grist, and I feel it tell me what he wants us to do.

"Get to the hoy," I tell Andre Sud. "Fast now. Fast as you can."

We get there before the others do, and I start casting off lines. When the three of them arrive, the hoy is ready to go. TB and Bob push us away while Andre Sud takes the woman inside. Within moments, we are out in the Bendy and caught in the current. TB and Bob go inside, and TB sticks his head up through the pilot's bubble to navigate.

The woman, Molly Index, looks at me. She has got very strange eyes. I have never seen eyes like that. I think that she can see into the grist like TB and I do.

"My God," she says. "She looks just like her."

"My name is Jill," I say. "I'm not Alethea."

"No, I know that," Molly Index says. "Ben told me."

"Molly, what are you doing here?" Andre Sud asks.

Molly Index turns to Andre Sud. She reaches for his hand and touches him. I am a little worried she might try something with the grist, but it looks like they are old friends.

"That war you kept talking about," she says. "It started. Amés has started it."

"Oh, no," Andre Sud says. He pulls away from her. "No."

Molly Index follows him. She reaches out and rubs a hank of his hair between her fingers. "I like it long," she says. "But it's kind of greasy."

This doesn't please me, and Molly Index is wearing the most horrible boots I have ever seen, too. They are dainty little things that will get eaten off her feet if she steps into something nasty. In the Carbuncle, the *ground* is something nasty. The silly grist in those city boots won't last a week here. It is a wonder to me that no one is laughing at the silly boots, but I suppose they have other worries at the moment and so do I.

"I should have listened to you," Molly Index says. "Made preparations. He got me. Most of me. Amés did. He's co-opted all the big LAPs into the New Hierarchy. But most of them joined voluntarily, the fools." Again she touches his hand, and I realize that I am a little jealous. He does not pull back from her again. "I alone have escaped to tell you," Molly Index says. "They're coming. They're right behind us."

"*Who* is right behind you?" I say. This is something I need to know. I can do something about this.

"Amés's damned Free Radical Patrol. Some kind of machine followed me here, and I didn't realize it. Amés must have found out from me—the other part of me—where Ben is."

"What is a Free Radical Patrol?" I say. "What is a sweeper?"

Something hits the outside of the hoy, hard. "Oh, shit," TB says. "Yonder comes the flying monkey."

The pilot glass breaks, and a hooked claw sinks into TB's shoulder. He screams. I don't think, but I move. I catch hold of his ankle.

We are dragged up. Lifted out. We are rising through the air above the hoy. Something screeches. TB yells like crazy.

I hold on.

Wind and TB's yells and something sounds like a million mean and angry bees.

We're too heavy, and whatever it was drops us onto the deck. TB starts to stand up, but I roll under his legs and knock him down, and before he can do anything, I shove him back down through the pilot-dome hole and into the hoy.

Just in time, too, because the thing returns, a black shadow, and sinks its talons into my back. I don't know what it is yet, and I may never know, but nothing will ever take me without a fight.

Something I can smell in the grist.

You are under indictment from the Free Radical Patrol. Please cease resisting. Cease resisting. Cease.

The words smell like metal and foam.

Cease resisting? What a funny thing to say to me. Like telling the wind to cease blowing. Blowing is what makes it the wind.

I twist hard and whatever it is only gets my dress, my poor pretty dress, and a little skin off my back. I can feel some poison grist try to worm into me, but that is nothing. It has no idea what I am made of. I kill that grist hardly thinking about doing so, and I turn to face this dark thing.

It doesn't look like a monkey, I don't think, though I wouldn't know.

What are you?

But there are wind currents and there is not enough grist transmission through the air for communications. Fuck it.

"Jill, be careful," says TB. His voice is strained. This thing hurt TB!

I will bite you.

"Would you pass me up one of those gaffs, please," I call to the others. There is scrambling down below, and Bob's hands come up with the long hook. I take it and he ducks back down quick. Bob is crazy, but he's no fool.

The thing circles around. I cannot see how it is flying, but it is kind of blurred around its edges. Millions of tiny wings—grist-built. I take a longer look. This thing is all angles. Some of them have needles, some have claws. All of the angles are sharp. It is a like a black-and-red mass of triangles flying through the air that only wants to cut you. Is there anybody inside? I don't think so. This is all code that I am facing. It is about three times as big as me, but I think of this as an advantage.

It dives and I am ready with the hook. It grabs hold of the gaff just as I'd hoped it would, and I use its momentum to guide it down, just a little *too* far down.

A whiff of grist as it falls.

Cease immediately. You are interfering with a Hierarchy judgment initiative. Cease or you will be—

Crash into the side of the hoy. Splash into the Bendy River.

I let go of the gaff. Too easy. That was—

The thing rises from the Bendy, dripping wet.

It is mad. I don't need the grist to tell me it is mad. All those little wings are buzzing angry, but not like bees anymore. Hungry like the flies on a piece of meat left out in the air too long.

Cease.

"Here," says Bob. He hands me a flare gun. I spin and fire into the clump of triangles. Again it falls into the river.

Again it rises.

I think about this. It is dripping wet with Bendy River water. If there is one thing I know, it is the scum that flows in the Bendy. There isn't any grist in it that hasn't tried to get me.

This is going to be tricky. I get ready.

Come and get me, triangles. Here I am just a girl. Come and eat me.

It zooms in. I stretch out my hands.

You are interfering with Hierarchy business. You will cease or be end-use eventuated. You will—

We touch.

Instantly, I reconstitute the Bendy water's grist, tell it what I want it to do. The momentum of the triangles knocks me over, and I roll along the deck under its weight. Something in my wrist snaps, but I ignore that pain. Blood on my lips from where I have bitten my tongue. I have a bad habit of sticking it out when I am concentrating.

The clump of triangles finishes clobbering me, and it falls into the river. Oh, too bad, triangles. The river grist that I recoded tells all the river water what to do. Regular water is six pounds a gallon, but the water in the Bendy is thicker and more forceful than that. And it knows how to crush. It is mean water and it wants to get things, and now I have told it how. I have put a little bit of me into the Bendy, and the water knows something that I know.

It knows never to cease. Never, never, never.

The triangle clump bobs for an instant before the whole river turns on it. Folds over it. Sucks it down. Applies all the weight of water twenty feet deep, many miles long. What looks like a waterspout rises above where the triangle clump fell, but this is actually a pile driver, a gelled column climbing up on itself. It collapses downward like a shoe coming down on a roach.

There is buzzing, furious buzzing, wet wings that won't dry because it isn't quite water that has gotten onto them, and it won't quite shake off.

There is a deep-down explosion under us and the boy rocks. Again I'm thrown onto the deck and I hold tight, hold tight. I don't want to fall into that water right now. I stand up and look.

Bits of triangles float to the surface. The river quickly turns them back under.

"I think I got it," I call to the others.

"Jill," says TB. "Come here and show me you are still alive."

I jump down through the pilot hole, and he hugs and kisses me. He kisses me right on the mouth, and for once I sense that he is not thinking about Alethea at all when he touches me. It feels very, very good.

"Oh, your poor back," says Molly Index. She looks pretty distraught and fairly useless. But at least she warned us. That was a good thing.

"It's just a scratch," I say. "And I took care of the poison."

"You just took out a Met sweep enforcer," Andre Sud says. "I think that was one of the special sweepers made for riot work, too."

"What was that thing doing here?"

"Looking for Ben," says Molly Index. "There's more where that came from. Amés will send more."

"I will kill them all if I have to."

Everybody looks at me and everyone is quiet for a moment, even Bob.

"I believe you, Jill," Andre Sud finally says. "But it's time to go."

TB is sitting down at the table. Nobody is piloting the boat, but we are drifting in midcurrent and it should be all right for now.

"Go?" TB says. "I'm not going anywhere. They will not use me to make war. I'll kill myself first. And I won't mess it up this time."

"If you stay here, they'll catch you," Andre Sud says.

"You've come to Amés's attention," Molly Index says. "I'm sorry, Ben."

"It's not your fault."

"We have to get out of the Met," Andre Sud says. "We have to get to the outer system."

"*They'll* use me, too. They're not as bad as Amés, but nobody's going to turn me into a weapon. I don't make fortunes for soldiers."

"If we can get to Triton, we might be okay," Andre Sud replied. "I have a certain pull on Triton. I know the weatherman there."

"What's that supposed to mean?"

"Trust me. It's a good thing. The weatherman is very important on Triton, and he's a friend of mine."

"There is one thing I'd like to know," says TB. "How in hell would we get to Triton from here?"

Bob stands up abruptly. He's been rummaging around in TB's larder while everybody else was talking. I saw him at it, but I knew he wasn't going to find anything he would want.

"Why didn't you say you wanted to go Out-ways?" he said. "All we got to do is follow the Bendy around to Makepeace Century's place in the gas swamps."

"Who's that?"

"I thought you knew her, TB. That's the aunt of that witch that lives in the ditch. I guess you'd call her a smuggler. Remember the Old Seventy-Five from last year that you got so drunk on?"

"I remember," TB says.

"Well, she's where I got that from," says Bob. "She's got a lot of cats, too, if you want one."

We head down the Bendy, and I keep a lookout for more of those enforcers, but I guess I killed the one they sent this time. I guess they thought one was enough. I can't help but think about where I am going. I can't help but think about leaving the Carbuncle. There's a part of me that has never been outside, and none of me has ever traveled into the outer system. Stray code couldn't go there. You had to pass through empty space. There weren't any cables out past Jupiter.

"I thought you understood why I'm here," TB says. "I can't go."

"You can't go even to save your life, Ben?"

"It wouldn't matter that I saved my life. If there is anything left of Alethea, I have to find her."

"What about the war?"

"I can't think about that."

"You have to think about it."

"Who says? God? *God is a bastard mushroom sprung from a pollution of blood.*" TB shakes his head sadly. "That was always my favorite koan in seminary— and the truest one."

"So it's all over?" Andre Sud says. "He's going to catch you."

"I'll hide from them."

"Don't you understand, Ben? He's taking over all the grist. After he does that, there won't be anyplace to hide because Amés will *be* the Met."

"I have to try to save her."

The solution is obvious to me, but I guess they don't see it yet. They keep forgetting I am not really sixteen. That in some ways, I'm a lot older than all of them.

You could say that it is the way that TB made me, that it is written in my code. You might even say that TB has somehow reached back from the future and made this so, made this the way things have to be. You could talk about fate and quantum mechanics.

All these things are true, but the truest thing of all is that I am free. The world has bent and squeezed me, and torn away every part of me that is not free. Freedom is all that I am.

And what I do, I do because I love TB and not for any other reason.

"Ah!" I moan. "My wrist hurts. I think it's broken, TB."

He looks at me, stricken.

"Oh, I'm sorry, little one," he says. "All this talking, and you're standing there hurt."

He reaches over. I put out my arm. In the moment of touching, he realizes what I am doing, but it is too late. I have studied him for too long and I know the taste of his pellicle. I know how to get inside him. I am his daughter, after all. Flesh of his flesh.

And I am fast. So very fast. That's why he wanted me around in the first place. I am a scrap of code that has been running from security for two hundred years. I am a projection of his innermost longings now come to life. I am a woman and he is the man that made me. I know what makes TB tick.

"I'll look for her," I say to him. "I won't give up until I find her."

"No, Jill—" But it is too late for TB. I have caught him by surprise, and he hasn't had time to see what I am up to.

"TB, don't you see what I am?"

"Jill, you can't—"

"I'm *you*, TB. I'm your love for her. Sometime in the future you have reached back into the past and made me. Now. So that the future can be different."

He will understand one day, but now there is no time. I code his grist into a repeating loop and set the counter to a high number. I get into his head and work his dendrites down to sleep. Then, with my other hand, I whack him on the head. Only hard enough to knock him the rest of the way out.

TB crumples to the floor, but I catch him before he can bang into anything. Andre Sud helps me lay him gently down.

"He'll be out for two days," I say. "That should give you enough time to get him off the Carbuncle."

I stand looking down at TB, at his softly breathing form. What have I done? I have betrayed the one who means the most of me in all creation.

"He's going to be really hungry when he wakes up," I say.

Andre Sud's hand is on my shoulder. "You saved his life, Jill," he says. "Or he saved his own. He saved it the moment he saved yours."

"I won't give her up," I say. "I have to stay so he can go with you and still have hope."

Andre Sud stands with his hand on me a little longer. His voice sounds as if it comes from a long way off, even though he is right next to me. "Destiny's a brutal old hag," he says. "I'd rather believe in nothing."

"It isn't destiny," I reply. "It's love."

Andre Sud looks at me, shakes his head, then rubs his eyes. It is as if he's seeing a new me standing where I am standing. "It is probably essential that you find Alethea, Jill. She must be here somewhere. I think Ben knows that, somehow. She needs to forgive him, or not forgive him. Healing Ben and ending the war are the same thing, but we can't think about it that way."

"I care about TB. The war can go to hell."

"Yes," Andre Sud says, "The war can go to hell."

After a while, I go up on deck to keep a watch out for more pursuit. Molly Index comes with me. We sit together for many hours. She doesn't tell me anything about TB or Alethea, but instead she talks to me about what it was like growing up a human being. Then she tells me how glorious it was when she spread out into the grist and could see so far.

"I could see all the way around the sun," Molly Index says. "I don't know if I want to live now that I've lost that. I don't know how I can live as just a *person* again."

"Even when you are less than a person," I tell her, "you still want to live."

"I suppose you're right."

"Besides, Andre Sud wants to have sex with you. I can smell it on him."

"Yes," Molly Index says. "So can I."

"Will you let him?"

"When the time comes."

"What is it like?" I say.

"You mean with Andre?"

"What is it like?"

Molly Index touches me. I feel the grist of her pellicle against mine and for a moment I draw-back, but then I let it in, let it speak.

Her grist shows me what it is like to make love.

It is like being able to see all the way around the sun.

The next day, Molly Index is the last to say good-bye to me as Makepeace Century's ship gets ready to go. Makepeace Century looks like Gladys if Gladys didn't live in a ditch. She's been trying for years to get Bob to come aboard as ship musician, and that is the price for taking them to Triton—a year of his service. I get the feeling she's sort of sweet on Bob. For a moment, I wonder just who *he* is that a ship's captain should be so concerned with him. But Bob agrees to go. He does it for TB.

TB is so deep asleep he is not even dreaming. I don't dare touch him for fear of breaking my spell. I don't dare tell him good-bye.

There is a thin place in the Carbuncle here, and they will travel down through it to where the ship is moored on the outer skin.

I only watch as they carry him away. I only cry until I can't see him anymore.

Then they are gone. I wipe the tear off my nose. I never have had time for much of that kind of thing.

So what will I do now? I will take the Bendy River all the way around the Carbuncle. I'll find a likely place to sink the hoy. I will set the ferrets free. Bob made me promise to look after his dumb ferret, Bomi, and show her how to stay alive without him.

And after that?

I'll start looking for Alethea. Like Andre Sud said, she must be here somewhere. And if anybody can find her, I can. I will find her.

There is a lot I have to do, and now I've been thinking that I need help. Pretty soon Amés is going to be running all the grist and all the code will answer to him. But there's some code he can't get to. Maybe some of those ferrets will want to stick around. Also, I think it's time I went back to the mulmyard.

It's time I made peace with those rats.

Then Amés had better watch out if he tries to stop me from finding her. We will bite him.

TOM PURDOM

Tom Purdom made his first sale in 1957, to Fantastic Universe, *and has subsequently sold to* Analog, The Magazine of Fantasy and Science Fiction, Star, *and most of the major SF magazines and anthologies. He is the author of one of the most unfairly forgotten SF novels of the sixties, the powerful and still-timely* Reduction in Arms, *about the difficulties of disarmament in the face of the mad proliferation of nuclear weapons, as well as such novels as* I Want the Stars, Tree Lord of Imeten, Five Against Arlane, *and* The Barons of Behavior. *In the late eighties, after several years of silence, he launched what amounts to a second career, becoming a frequent contributor to* Asimov's Science Fiction, *where he published a long string of powerful and innovative stories such as "Canaryland," "Romance in Lunar G," "Legacies," "Romance in Extended Time," "Research Project," "Sergeant Mother Glory," "Romance with Phobic Variations," and many others throughout the rest of the eighties and the decade of the nineties. Purdom lives with his family in Philadelphia, where he reviews classical music concerts for a local newspaper and is at work on several new novels.*

Although he made his first sale before some of today's hot new writers were even born, Purdom remains on the cutting edge of speculation about what the posthuman future will be like, and is as much a part of the consensus-building "discussion" now taking place across the whole of the genre as are writers half his age. This is demonstrated in the absorbing novella that follows—a Hugo finalist in 2000—in which we discover that even the enhanced, augmented, and superior (to us!) people who live in the posthuman future may feel the cold wind of obsolescence on the back of their necks. . . .

Morgan's mother and father had given him a state-of-the-art inheritance. It was only state-of-the-art-2117 but they had seen where the world was going. They had mortgaged twenty percent of their future income so they could order a package that included all the genetic enhancements Morgan's chromosomes could absorb, along with two full decades of postnatal development programs. Morgan was in his fifties when his father committed suicide. By that time his father could barely communicate with half the people he encountered in his day-to-day business activities.

Morgan's mother survived by working as a low-level freelance prostitute. The medical technology that was state-of-the-art-2157 could eliminate all the relevant physical effects of aging, and a hidden computer link could guide her responses. For half an hour—as long as no one demanded anything too unusual—she could give her younger customers the illusion they were interacting with someone who was their intellectual and psychological equal. Morgan tried to help her, but there wasn't much he could do. He had already decided he couldn't survive in a solar system in which half the human population had been born with brains, glands, and nervous systems that were state-of-the-art-2150 and later. He had blocked his mother's situation out of his memory and lived at subsistence level for almost three decades. Every yen, franc, and yuri he could scrape together had been shoved into the safest investments his management program could locate. Then he had taken all his hard-won capital and bought two hundred shares in an asteroid habitat a group of developers had outfitted with fusion reactors, plasma drives, solar sails, and anything else that might make a small island move at nine percent the speed of light. And he and three thousand other "uncompetitive," "under-enhanced" humans had crept away from the solar system. And set off to explore the galaxy.

Morgan had lived through three lengthy pairings back in the solar system. Six years after the *Island of Adventure* had begun its slow drift away from the sun, he established a fourth pairing with a woman he had met through the ship's information system. The ship's designers had endowed it with attractive common spaces, complete with parks and cafés, but most of the passengers seemed to prefer electronic socialization during the first years of the voyage. Biographies and lists of interests were filed with the system. Pseudonyms and electronic personalities proliferated. Morgan thought of old stories in which prisoners had communicated by tapping on the walls of their cells.

Savela Insdotter was eleven years younger than Morgan but she was a fully committed member of the EruLabi communion. She used pharmaceutical mental enhancers, but she used them sparingly. Morgan consumed all the mental enhancers his system could accommodate, so his functional intelligence was actually somewhat higher than hers in certain areas.

The foundation of the EruLabi ethos was a revolt against genetic enhancement. In the view of the EruLabi "mentors," the endless quest for intellectual and physical improvement was a folly. Life was supposed to be lived for its own sake, the EruLabi texts declared. Every moment was a gift that should be treasured for the pleasure it brought, not an episode in a quest for mental and physical perfection. The simplest pleasures—touches, languor, the textures of bodies pressed together—were, to the EruLabi, some of the most profound experiences life had to offer.

One of the most important texts in the EruLabi rituals was the words, in ancient Greek, that the Eudoran king had spoken to Odysseus: *Dear to us ever are the banquet and the harp and the dance and the warm bath and changes of raiment and love and sleep.*

The *Island of Adventure* had pointed itself at 82 Eridani—a Sol-type star twenty-one light years from the solar system. Eighty-two Eridani was an obvious candidate for a life-bearing planet. A fly-by probe had been launched at the star in 2085—one hundred and eighteen years before Morgan and his fellow emigrants had left their home system. In 2304—just after they had celebrated the first century of their departure—the *Island of Adventure* intercepted a message the probe was sending back to the solar system.

It was the beginning of several years of gloomy debate. The probe had found planets. But none of them looked any more interesting than the cratered rocks and giant iceballs mankind had perused in the solar system.

The third planet from the sun could have been another Earth. It was closer to its sun than Earth was but it could have supported life if it had been the right size. Unfortunately, the planet's mass was only thirty-eight percent the mass of Earth.

Theorists had calculated that a planet needed a mass about forty percent the mass of Earth if it was going to develop an oxygen-rich atmosphere and hold it indefinitely. The third planet was apparently just a little too small. The images transmitted by the probe were drearily familiar—a rocky, airless desert, some grandiose canyons and volcanoes, and the usual assortment of craters, dunes, and minor geological features.

The *Island of Adventure* had set out for 82 Eridani because 82E was a star of the same mass and spectral type as Sol. The second choice had been another star in the same constellation. Rho Eridani was a double star 21.3 light years from the solar system. The two stars in the Rho system orbited each other at a promising distance—seven light hours. With that much separation between them, the theoreticians agreed, both stars could have planets.

When you looked at the sky from the solar system, Rho was a few degrees to the left of 82 Eridani. The *Island of Adventure* was a massive, underpowered rock but it could make a small midcourse correction if its inhabitants wanted to expend some extra reaction mass.

The strongest opposition to the course change came from the oldest human on the ship. Madame Dawne was so old she had actually been born on Earth. All the other people on board had been born (created, in most cases) in the habitats the human race had scattered across the solar system.

The *Island of Adventure* had been the first ship to embark for 82 Eridani. Thirty-two years after it had left the solar system, a ship called *Green Voyager* had pointed its rocky bow at Rho. The texts of its transmissions had indicated the oldest passengers on the *Green Voyager* were two decades younger than the youngest passengers on the *Island of Adventure*.

If the passengers on the *Island of Adventure* approved the course change, they would arrive at Rho about the same time the *Green Voyager* arrived there. They would find themselves sharing the same star system with humans who were, on average, three or four decades younger than they were. Madame Dawne would be confronted with brains and bodies that had been designed a full century after she had received her own biological equipment.

Morgan was not a politician by temperament but he was fascinated by any activity that combined conflict with intellectual effort. When his pairing with Savela Insdotter had finally come to an end, he had isolated himself in his apartment and spent a decade and a half studying the literature on the dynamics of small communities. The knowledge he had absorbed would probably look prehistoric to the people now living in the solar system. It had been stored in the databanks pre-2203. But it provided him with techniques that should produce the predicted results when they were applied to people who had reached adulthood several decades before 2200.

The *Island of Adventure* was managed, for all practical purposes, by its information system. A loosely organized committee monitored the system but there was no real government. The humans on board were passengers, the information system was the crew, and the communal issues that came up usually involved minor housekeeping procedures.

Now that a real issue had arisen, Morgan's fellow passengers drifted into a system of continuous polling—a system that had been the commonest form of political democracy when they had left the solar system. Advocates talked and lobbied. Arguments flowed through the electronic symposiums and the face-to-face social networks. Individuals registered their opinions—openly or anonymously—when they decided they were willing to commit themselves. At any moment you could call up the appropriate screen and see how the count looked.

The most vociferous support for the course change came from eight individuals. For most of the three thousand fifty-seven people who lived in the ship's apartments, the message from the probe was a minor development. The ship was their home—in the same way a hollowed-out asteroid in the solar system could have been their home. The fact that their habitat would occasionally visit another star system added spice to the centuries that lay ahead, but it wasn't their primary interest in life. The Eight, on the other hand, seemed to feel they would be sentencing themselves to decades of futility if they agreed to visit a lifeless star system.

Morgan set up a content analysis program and had it monitor the traffic flowing through the public-information system. Eighteen months after the message from the probe had triggered off the debate, he put a two-axis graph on the screen and examined a pair of curves.

Morgan's pairing with Savela Insdotter had lasted over sixty years and they had remained friendly after they had unpaired. He showed her the graph as soon as he had run it through some extra checks. The curve that charted the Eight's activities rose and fell in conjunction with the curve that measured Madame Dawne's participation in the debate. When Madame Dawne's activity level reached a peak, the Eight subsided into silence. They would stop agitating for their cause, the entire discussion would calm down, and Madame Dawne would return to the extreme privacy she had maintained from the beginning of the voyage. Then, when Madame Dawne hadn't been heard from for several tendays, the Eight would suddenly renew their campaign.

"I believe they're supporting the change to a new destination merely because they wish to disturb Madame Dawne," Morgan said. "I've created personality profiles based on their known histories and public statements. The profiles indicate my conjecture is correct."

Savela presented him with a shrug and a delicate, upward movement of her head. Morgan had spoken to her in Tych—an ultra-precise language that was primarily used in written communication. Savela was responding in an emotion oriented language called VA13—a language that made extensive use of carefully rehearsed gestures and facial expressions.

No one, as far as Morgan knew, had ever spoken VA12 or VA14. The language had been labeled VA13 when it had been developed in a communications laboratory on Phobos, and the label had stuck.

"Madame Dawne is a laughable figure," Savela said.

"I recognize that. But the Eight are creating a serious division in our communal life. We might have reached a consensus by now if they hadn't restimulated the debate every time it seemed to be concluding. Madame Dawne is one of the eleven wealthiest individuals on the ship. What would happen to us if she decided she had to impose her will by force?"

"Do you really feel that's a serious possibility, Morgan?"

The linguists who had developed VA13 had been interested in the emotional content of music. The speaker's tone patterns and rhythms were just as critical as the verbal text. Savela's word choices were polite and innocuous, but her rhythms communicated something else—a mixture of affection and amusement that would have seemed contemptuous if she and Morgan hadn't shared a pairing that had lasted six decades.

To Morgan, Madame Dawne was pathetic, not comic. She spent most of her days, as far as anyone could tell, in the electronic dream worlds she constructed in her apartment. No one on the ship had seen her true face. When she appeared on someone's screens, her electronic personae were impressively unimaginative. She usually imaged herself as a tall woman, with close-cropped red hair, dressed in the flamboyant boots-and-baggy-shirts style that North Americans had adopted during the third decade of the twenty-first century— the body type and clothing mode that had been fashionable when she had been in her natural prime.

Morgan had put a wargame template on his information system and had it explore some of the things Madame Dawne could do. Savela might smile at the thought that a limited, underdeveloped personality like Madame Dawne might undertake something dangerous. The wargame program had come up with seventy-four weapons systems a wealthy individual could develop with the aid of the information in the databanks. Half the systems were straightforward modifications of the devices that dug out apartment spaces and extracted mineral resources from the rocky exterior of the ship. Most of the others involved an offensive use of the self-replicating machines that handled most of the passengers' daily needs.

Madame Dawne couldn't have designed any of the machines the wargame program had suggested. She probably didn't even know the ship could place them at her disposal. Did she realize she could ask a wargame program for advice? Morgan didn't know.

Morgan's political studies had included an exhaustive module in applied personality profiling. He could recite from memory the numbers that described the kind of person who could become a successful small-community politician. He hadn't been surprised when his profiling program had told him he scored below average on most of the critical personality characteristics. He had made several attempts to enter the course change controversy and the results would have evoked I-told-you-so head shakes from the technicians who had developed the profiling program. The program had been almost cruelly accurate when it had informed him he had a low tolerance for disagreement. He could have given it fifty examples of his tendency to become hot-tempered and defensive when he attracted the attention of aggressive debaters. For the last few months, he had been avoiding the public symposiums and feeding private suggestions to people who could turn his ideas into effective attempts at persuasion. Now he fleshed out the profiles he had been storing in his databanks and started recruiting a six-member political team.

Morgan couldn't proselytize prospects and debate verbal brawlers, but he had discovered he could do something that was just as effective: he could win the cooperation of the people who could. Some of the people he approached even *enjoyed* accosting their fellow citizens and lobbying them on political issues. They couldn't always follow Morgan's logic, but they considered that a minor problem. They were extroverted, achievement-oriented personalities and Morgan gave them suggestions that worked. If he told them a visit to X made good sense at this moment, and a visit to Y would be a waste of time, they approached both prospects the first couple of times he made a recommendation, and followed his advice after that.

Most of the political strategies Morgan had studied could be fitted into three categories: you could be *combative and confrontational*, you could *market*, or you could explore the subtleties of *the indirect approach*. Temperamentally, Morgan was a marketer who liked to use the indirect approach. Once he had his political organization going, he ran another analysis of the profiles in his databanks and organized a Terraforming Committee. Five engineering-oriented personalities sat down with a carefully selected political personality and began looking at the possibility that some of the planets of 82 Eridani could be transformed into livable environments. Eight months after Morgan had established the committee, the first simulated planetary environment took its place in the public databanks. Interested individuals could soar across a planetary landscape that included blue skies, towering forests, and creatures selected from three of Earth's geologic eras and two of its mythological cycles.

It took almost five years, but Morgan's efforts succeeded. An overwhelming consensus emerged. The ship would stay on course.

Unfortunately, the Eight still seemed to enjoy baiting Madame Dawne. By this time, however, Morgan had constructed detailed profiles of every personality in the octet.

The most vulnerable was a woman named Miniruta Coboloji. Miniruta's primary motivation, according to the profile program, was an intense need for affiliation.

Morgan had known his pairing with Savela Insdotter would end sooner or later. Everything had to end sooner or later. The surprise had been the identity of the man who had succeeded him.

Morgan had assumed Savela would grow tired of his skeptical, creedless outlook and pair with someone who shared her beliefs. Instead, her next partner had been Ari Sun-Dalt—the outspoken champion of a communion that had been founded on the belief that every member of the human race was involved in a cosmic epic: the struggle of matter to become conscious.

Life was not an accident, the advocates of Ari's worldview asserted. It was the purpose of the universe. The idea that dominated Ari's life was the Doctrine of the Cosmic Enterprise—the belief that the great goal of the cosmos was the unlimited expansion of Consciousness.

Ari had been adding organic and electronic enhancements to his brain ever since he was in his thirties. The skin on the top of his skull concealed an array that included every chip and cell cluster his nervous system would accept. His head was at least twenty-five percent longer, top to bottom, than a standard male head. If something could increase his intelligence or heighten his consciousness, Ari believed it would be immoral not to install it.

"We can always use recruits," Ari said. "But I must tell you, my friend, I feel there's something cynical about your scheming."

Morgan shrugged. "If I'm right, Miniruta will be ten times more contented than she is now. And the ship will be serener."

They were both speaking Jor—an everyday language, with a rigidly standardized vocabulary, which had roots in twenty-first century French. Morgan had told Ari he had detected signs that Miniruta would be interested in joining his communion, and Ari had immediately understood Morgan was trying to remove Miniruta from the Eight. Ari could be surprisingly sophisticated intellectually. Most people with strong belief systems didn't like to think about the psychological needs people satisfied when they joined philosophical movements.

Miniruta joined Ari's communion a year after Ari set out to convert her. She lost interest in the Eight as soon as she acquired a new affiliation—just as Morgan's profiles had predicted she would. Morgan had been preparing plans for three other members of the group but Miniruta's withdrawal produced an unexpected dividend. Two of the male members drifted away a few tendays after Miniruta proclaimed her new allegiance. Their departure apparently disrupted the dynamics of the entire clique. Nine tendays after their defection, Morgan could detect no indications the Eight had ever existed.

On the outside of the ship, in an area where the terrain still retained most of the asteroid's original contours, there was a structure that resembled a squat slab with four circular antennas mounted at its corners. The slab itself was a comfortable, two-story building, with a swimming pool, recreation facilities, and six apartments that included fully equipped communication rooms.

The structure was the communications module that received messages from the solar system and the other ships currently creeping through interstellar space. It was totally isolated from the ship's electronic systems. The messages it picked up could only be examined by someone who was actually sitting in one of the apartments. You couldn't transfer a message from the module to the ship's databanks. You couldn't even carry a recording into the ship.

The module had been isolated from the rest of the ship in response to a very real threat: the possibility someone in the solar system would transmit a message that would sabotage the ship's information system. There were eight billion people living in the solar system. When you were dealing with a population that size, you had to assume it contained thousands of individuals who felt the starships were legitimate targets for lethal pranks.

Morgan had been spending regular periods in the communications module since the first years of the voyage. During the first decades, the messages he had examined had become increasingly strange. The population in the solar system had been evolving at a rate that compressed kilocenturies of natural evolution into decades of engineered modification. The messages that had disturbed him the most had been composed in the languages he had learned in his childhood. The words were familiar but the meaning of the messages kept slipping away from him.

Morgan could understand that the terraforming of Mars, Venus, and Mercury might have been speeded up and complexified by a factor of ten. He could even grasp that some of the electronically interlinked communal personalities in the solar system might include several million individual personalities. But did he really understand the messages that seemed to imply millions of people had expanded their personal *physiologies* into complexes that encompassed entire asteroids?

The messages included videos that should have eliminated most of his confusion. Somehow he always turned away from the screen feeling there was something he hadn't grasped.

The situation in the solar system had begun to stabilize just before Morgan had turned his attention to the turmoil created by the Eight. Over the next few decades the messages became more decipherable. Fifty years after the problem with the Eight—one hundred and sixty-two years after the ship had left the solar system—almost all the messages reaching the ship came from members of Ari Sun-Dalt's communion.

The believers in the Doctrine of the Cosmic Enterprise were communicating with the starships because they were becoming a beleaguered minority. The great drive for enhancement and progress had apparently run its course. The worldviews that dominated human civilization were all variations on the EruLabi creeds.

Ari spent long periods—as much as ten or twelve tendays in a row—in the communications module. The human species, in Ari's view, was sinking into an eternity of aimless hedonism.

Ari became particularly distraught when he learned the EruLabi had decided they should limit themselves to a twenty-percent increase in skull size— a dictum that imposed a tight restriction on the brainpower they could pack inside their heads. At the peak of the enhancement movement, people who had retained normal bipedal bodies had apparently quadrupled their skull sizes.

"We're the only conscious, intelligent species the solar system ever produced," Ari orated in one of his public communiqués. "We may be the only conscious, intelligent species in this section of the galaxy. And they've decided an arbitrary physiological aesthetic is more important than the development of our minds."

The messages from the solar system had included scientific discussions. They had even included presentations prepared for "nonspecialists." Morgan had followed a few of the presentations as well as he could and he had concluded the human species had reached a point of diminishing returns.

Morgan would never possess the kind of complexified, ultra-enhanced brain his successors in the solar system had acquired. Every set of genes imposed a ceiling on the organism it shaped. If you wanted to push beyond that ceiling, you had to start all over again, with a new organism and a new set of genes. But Morgan believed he could imagine some of the consequences of that kind of intellectual power.

At some point, he believed, all those billions of superintelligent minds had looked out at the universe and realized that another increase in brain power would be pointless. You could develop a brain that could answer every question about the size, history, and structure of the universe, and find that you still couldn't answer the philosophical questions that had tantalized the most primitive tribesmen. And what would you do when you reached that point? You would turn your back on the frontier. You would turn once again to the bath and the banquet, the harp and the dance.

And changes of raiment.

And love.

And sleep.

The situation on the ship was almost the mirror image of the situation in the solar system. On the ship, forty-eight percent of the population belonged to Ari's communion. Only nineteen percent had adopted the EruLabi creeds. But how long could that last? Morgan had been watching the trends. Every few years, someone abandoned the Doctrine of the Cosmic Enterprise and joined the EruLabi. No one ever left the EruLabi and became a devoted believer in the Cosmic Enterprise.

The discovery that 82 Eridani was surrounded by lifeless planets had added almost a dozen people to the defectors. The search for life-bearing planets was obviously a matter of great significance. If consciousness really was the purpose of the universe, then life should be a common phenomenon.

In 2315, just four years after the final dissolution of the Eight, the *Island of Adventure* had received its first messages from Tau Ceti and Morgan had watched a few more personalities float away from Ari's communion. The ship that had reached Tau Ceti had made planetfall after a mere one hundred and forty years and it had indeed found life on the second planet of the system. Unfortunately, the planet was locked in a permanent ice age. Life had evolved in the oceans under the ice but it had never developed beyond the level of the more mundane marine life forms found on Earth.

Morgan had found it impossible to follow the reasons the planet was iced over. He hadn't really been interested, to tell the truth. But he had pored over the reports on the undersea biota as if he had been following the dispatches from a major war.

One of the great issues in terrestrial evolutionary theory had been the relationship between chance and necessity. To Ari and his disciples, there was nothing random about the process. Natural selection inevitably favored qualities such as strength, speed, and intelligence.

To others, the history of life looked more haphazard. Many traits, it was argued, had developed for reasons as whimsical as the fact that the ancestor who carried Gene A had been standing two steps to the right when the rocks slid off the mountain.

The probes that had penetrated the oceans of Tau Ceti IV had sent back images that could be used to support either viewpoint. The undersea biota was populated by several hundred species of finned snakes, several thousand species that could be considered roughly comparable to terrestrial insects, and clouds of microscopic dimlight photosynthesizers.

Yes, evolution favored the strong and the swift. Yes, creatures who lived in the sea tended to be streamlined. On the other hand, fish were not inevitable. Neither were oysters. Or clams.

If the universe really did have a purpose, it didn't seem to be very good at it. In the solar system, theorists had produced scenarios that proved life could have evolved in exotic, unlikely environments such as the atmosphere of Jupiter. Instead, the only life that had developed outside Earth had been the handful of not-very-interesting microorganisms that had managed to maintain a toehold on Mars.

The purpose of the universe isn't the development of consciousness, one of the EruLabi on board the *Island of Adventure* suggested. *It's the creation of iceballs and deserts. And sea snakes.*

Ari's enhancements included a gland modification that gave him the ability to switch off his sexual feelings at will. His pairing with Savela Insdotter had lasted less than two decades, and he had made no attempt to establish another pairing. Ari had spent most of the voyage, as far as Morgan could tell, in an asexual state.

There were times, during the last decades of the voyage, when Morgan felt tempted to emulate him. Morgan's next pairing only lasted twelve years. For the rest of the voyage, he took advantage of the small number of sexual opportunities that came his way and distracted himself, during his celibate intervals, with intellectual projects such as his political studies.

The ship's medical system could install Ari's sexual enhancement in thirty minutes, as part of the regular medical services included in the standard embarkation agreement. Morgan put the idea aside every time he considered it. He had learned to cherish his feelings about women, irrational as they might be. There was, he knew, no real reason why he should respond to the flare of a woman's hips or the tilt of a female neck. It was simply a bit of genetic programming he hadn't bothered to delete. It had no practical value in a world in which children were created in the workshops of genetic designers.

But he also knew he would be a different person if he subtracted it from his psychological makeup. It was one of the things that kept you human as the decades slipped by.

In 2381—forty-six years before it was scheduled to reach its destination— the *Island of Adventure* intercepted a message from the probe that had been sent to Rho Eridani. Neither of the stars in the double system possessed planets. The *Green Voyager* was crawling toward an empty system.

In 2398—one hundred and ninety-five years after the ship had begun its journey—the medical system replaced Morgan's heart, part of his central nervous system, and most of his endocrine glands. It was the third time Morgan had put himself through an extensive overhaul. The last time he had recovered within three years. This time he spent eight years in the deepest sleep the system could maintain.

The first program capsules left the ship while it was still careening around the 82 Eridani system, bouncing from planet to planet as it executed the five-year program that would eliminate the last twenty percent of its interstellar speed. There were three capsules and their payloads were packages a little smaller than Morgan's forefinger.

One capsule malfunctioned while it was still making its way toward the small moon that orbited the third planet at a distance of 275,000 kilometers. The second lost two critical programs when it hit the moon at an angle that was a little too sharp. The third skimmed through the dust just the way it was supposed to and sprouted a set of filaments. Sampling programs analyzed the moon's surface. Specks that were part cell and part electronic device began drifting down the filaments and executing programs that transformed the moon's atoms into larger, more elaborate specks. The specks produced machines the size of insects, the insects produced machines the size of cats, an antenna crept up the side of a small crater, and an antenna on the *Island of Adventure* started transmitting more programs. By the time the ship settled into an orbit around the third planet, the moon had acquired a complete manufacturing facility, and the lunar fabrication units had started producing scout machines that could land on the planet itself.

Morgan had thought of the terraforming scheme as a political ruse, but there were people on the ship who took it seriously. With the technology they had at their disposal, the third planet could be turned into a livable world within a few decades. For people who had spent their entire lives in enclosed habitats, it was a romantic idea—a world where you walked on the surface, with a sky above you, and experienced all the vagaries of weather and climate.

The only person who had raised any serious objections had been Ari Sun-Dalt. Some of the valleys they could observe from orbit had obviously been carved by rivers. The volcano calderas were less spectacular than the volcanoes of Mars but they were still proof the planet had once been geologically active. They couldn't overlook the possibility life might be hiding in some obscure ecological network that was buried under the soil or hidden in a cave, Ari argued.

Most of the people on the ship greeted that kind of suggestion with shrugs and smiles. According to Morgan's sampling programs, there were only about ten people on the ship who really thought there was a statistically significant possibility the planet might have generated life. Still, there was no reason they couldn't let Ari enjoy his daydreams a little longer.

"It will only take us an extra two or three years," Ari said. "And then we'll know we can remodel the place. First we'll see if there's any life. Then we'll do the job ourselves, if the universe hasn't done it already. And bring Consciousness to another world."

For Ari's sake—he really liked Ari in many ways—Morgan hoped they might find a few fossilized microorganisms embedded in the rocks. What he did not expect was a fossil the size of a horse, embedded in a cliff, and visible to any machine that came within two kilometers of it.

Three and a half billion years ago, the planet had emerged from the disk of material that surrounded its sun. A billion or so years later, the first long-chain molecules had appeared in the oceans. And the history of life had begun. In the same way it had begun on Earth.

The long-chain molecules had formed assemblies that became the first rudimentary cells. Organisms that were something like plants had eventually begun to absorb the CO_2 produced by the volcanoes. The oxygen emitted by the quasi-plants had become a major component of the atmosphere. The relentless forces of competition had favored creatures who were more complex than their rivals.

And then, after less than two billion years of organic evolution, the laws of physics had caught up with the process. No planet the size of this one could hold an atmosphere forever.

The plants and the volcanoes could produce oxygen and CO_2 *almost* as fast as the gas molecules could drift into space. But almost wasn't good enough.

They didn't piece the whole story together right away, of course. There were even people who weren't convinced the first find was a fossil. If the scout machines hadn't found ten more fossils in the first five daycycles, the skeptics would have spent years arguing that Exhibit A was just a collection of rocks— a random geologic formation that just happened to resemble a big shell, with appendages that resembled limbs.

On Earth, the dominant land animals had been vertebrates—creatures whose basic characteristic was a bony framework hung on a backbone. The vertebrate template was such a logical, efficient structure it was easy to believe it was as inevitable as the streamlined shape of fish and porpoises. In fact, it had never developed on this planet.

Instead, the basic anatomical structure had been a tube of bone. Creatures with this rigid, seemingly inefficient, structure had acquired legs, claws, teeth and all the other anatomical features vertebrates had acquired on Earth.

Thousands of species had acquired eyes that looked out of big eyeholes in the front of the shell, without developing a separate skull. Two large families had developed "turrets" that housed their eyes and their other sense organs but they had kept their brains securely housed in the original shell, in a special chamber just under the turret.

On Earth, the shell structure would have produced organisms that might have collapsed from their own weight. On this planet, with its weaker gravitational field, the shells could be thin and even airy. They reminded Morgan of building components that had been formed from solidified foam—a common structural technique in space habitats.

For Ari, the discovery was the high point of his lifespan—a development that had to be communicated to the solar system at once. Ari's face had been contorted with excitement when he had called Morgan an hour after the machines reported the first find.

"We've done it, Morgan," Ari proclaimed. "We've justified our whole voyage. Three thousand useless, obsolete people have made a discovery that's going to transform the whole outlook in the solar system."

Morgan had already been pondering a screen that displayed a triangular diagram. The point at the bottom of the triangle represented the solar system. The two points at the top represented 82 Eridani and Rho Eridani. The *Island of Adventure* and the *Green Voyager* had been creeping up the long sides of the triangle. The *Green Voyager* was now about three light years from Rho—thirty-three years travel time.

Morgan transferred the diagram to Ari's screen and pointed out the implications. If the *Island of Adventure* transmitted an announcement to the solar system, the *Green Voyager* would pick it up in approximately seven years. If the people on the *Voyager* thought it was interesting, they could change course and reach 82 Eridani only twelve and a half decades after they intercepted the message.

"That gives us over one hundred and thirty years to explore the planet," Ari argued. "By that time we'll have learned everything important the fossils have to offer. We'll have done all the real work. We'll be ready to move on. And look for a world where we can communicate with a *living* Consciousness."

Unfortunately, the situation didn't look that straightforward to the rest of the community. To them, a hundred and thirty years was a finite, envisionable time period.

There was, after all, a third possibility—as Miniruta Coboloji pointed out in one of her contributions to the electronic debate. *The* Green Voyager *may never come this way at all*, Miniruta argued. *They may reack Rho thirty-three years from now pass through the system, and point themselves at one of the stars that lies further out. They've got three choices within fourteen light years. Why can't we just wait the thirty-three years? And send a message after they've committed themselves to some other star system?*

For Ari, that was unthinkable. *Our announcement is going to take twenty* years to reach the solar system no matter what we do. If we sit here for thirty-three years before we transmit, it will be fifty-three years before anyone in the solar system hears about one of the most important discoveries in history. We all know what's happening in the solar system. Fifty-three years from now, there may not be anyone left who cares.

Once again Morgan labored over his screens. Once again he recruited aides who helped him guide the decision-making process. This time he engineered a compromise. They would send a brief message saying they had "found evidence of extinct life" and continue studying the planet's fossils. Once every year, they would formally reopen the discussion for three tendays. They would transmit a complete announcement "whenever it becomes clear the consensus supports such an action."

Ari accepted the compromise in good grace. He had looked at the numbers, too. Most of the people on the ship still belonged to his communion.

"They know what their responsibilities are," Ari insisted. "Right now this is all new, Morgan. We're just getting used to the idea that we're looking at a complete planetary biota. A year from now—two years from now—we'll have so much information in our databanks they'll know we'd be committing a criminal act if we didn't send every bit of it back to the solar system."

It was Ari who convinced them the planet should be called Athene. Athene had been a symbol of wisdom and culture, Ari pointed out, but she had been a war goddess, too. And didn't the world they were naming bear a distinct resemblance to the planet the ancient humans had named after their male war figure?

The information pouring into the databanks could be examined by anyone on the ship. In theory, anyone could give the exploration machines orders. In practice, the exploration of the Athenian fossil record soon came under the control of three people: Ari, Morgan—and Miniruta Coboloji.

Morgan had been watching Miniruta's development ever since he had lured her away from the Eight. Physically, she was a standard variation on the BR-V73 line—the long, willowy female body type that had been the height of fashion in the lunar cities in the 2130s. Her slim, beautifully crafted fingers could mold a sculpture—or shape a note on a string instrument— with the precision of a laser pointer.

It was a physical style that Morgan found aesthetically appealing, but there were at least two hundred women on the ship who had been shaped by the same gene cluster. So why was Miniruta the only BR-V73 who crept into his thoughts during the more stressful hours of his celibate intervals? Was it because there was something desperate about the need for affiliation he had uncovered in her personality profile? Did that emotional vulnerability touch something in his own personality?

Miniruta's affiliation with the Doctrine of the Cosmic Enterprise had lasted four decades. Ari claimed her switch to the EruLabi worldview had been totally unexpected. Ari had gone to sleep assuming she was one of his most ardent colleagues and awakened to discover she had sent him a long message explaining the reasons for her conversion and urging him to join her.

During the decades in which she had been a member of Ari's communion, Miniruta had followed Ari's lead and equipped herself with every pharmaceutical and electrical enhancer she could link to her physiology. The electronic enhancers had all been discarded a few tendays after she had joined the EruLabi. Her pharmaceutical enhancers had been dispensed with, item by item, as she had worked her way up the EruLabi protocols. She had been the second EruLabi on the ship who had made it to the fourth protocol and accepted its absolute prohibition of all non-genetic mental and physiological enhancers.

Morgan could now talk to her without struggling. His own pharmaceutical enhancers erased most of the intellectual gap that separated two people who had been brought into the universe twenty years apart. He had been surprised when he had discovered Miniruta was spending two-thirds of every daycycle with the data from the fossil hunt, but he had soon realized she had a philosophical agenda.

To Miniruta, the course of evolution on Athene proved that evolution was a random process. "Ari's right, Morgan," Miniruta said. "This planet can teach us something we need to understand. But it's not the lesson Ari thinks it is. It's telling us there isn't any plan. There's no big overall objective—as if the universe is some kind of cosmic totalitarian state. The only reality is individuals. And their needs."

To Ari, the critical question was the evolution of intelligence. Obviously, life had died out on Athene before intelligent creatures could build cities or turn meadows into farms. But wasn't there some chance something like the first proto-humans had evolved? If that first glimmer of tool-making, culture-creating intelligence had appeared on the planet, wouldn't it prove that evolution really did lead in a particular direction?

"I'll grant you the vertebrates were obviously an accident," Ari said. "But you can still see an obvious increase in intelligence if you look at the progressions we've been uncovering. You can't go from stationary sea creatures to land creatures that were obviously highly mobile without a lot of development in the brain. Intelligence is the inevitable winner in the selection process. The life forms that can think better will always replace the life forms with less complex nervous systems."

"The way human beings replaced the cockroach?" Miniruta asked. "And the oyster?"

Miniruta was speaking VA13. The lilt in her voice expressed a casual mockery that Morgan would have found devastating if she had directed it at him.

"We were not in direct genetic competition with the cockroach and the oyster," Ari said in Tych. "The observable fact that certain lines remained static for hundreds of millions of years doesn't contradict the observable fact that natural selection tends to produce creatures with more highly developed brains. We could have destroyed every species on the Earth if we had wanted to. We let them live because we needed a complex biosphere. They survived because they satisfied one of *our* needs."

To Morgan, most of the information they were gathering proved that natural selection really was the powerful force the theorists had claimed it was.

Certain basic patterns had been repeated on both planets. Life forms that had been exceptionally massive had possessed jaw structures that indicated they had probably been herbivores—just as terrestrial herbivores such as the elephant had been the largest organisms in their habitats. Life forms that had possessed stabbing teeth and bone-crunching jaws tended to be medium-sized and looked as if they had probably been more agile.

But the process obviously had its random qualities, too. Was it just a matter of random chance that vertebrates had failed to develop? Had the shell creatures dominated the planet merely because certain molecules had fallen into one type of pattern on Earth and another pattern on Athene? Or had it happened because there was some difference in the conditions life had encountered on the two planets?

To Morgan, it didn't matter what the answer was. Evolution might proceed according to laws that were as rigid as the basic laws of physics, or it might be as random as a perfect game of chance. He would be happy with either answer. He could even be content with no answer.

That was one of the things people never seemed to understand about science. As far as Morgan was concerned, you didn't study the universe because you wanted to know the answers. You studied it to *connect*. When you subjected an important question to a rigorous examination—collecting every scrap of evidence you could find, measuring and analyzing everything that could be measured and analyzed—you were linked to the universe in a way nothing else could connect you.

Religious mystics had once spent their lives trying to establish a direct contact with their version of God. Morgan was a mystic who tried to stay in contact with the cosmos.

Ari had assigned three groups of exploration machines to a hunt for campsites. The teams concentrated on depressions that looked as if they had once been rivers and probed for evidence such as stone tools and places where a large number of animal fossils had been concentrated in a small area. They found two animal deposits within their first three tendays and Ari quickly pointed out that the animals had clearly been disassembled.

"These aren't just tar pits or places where a catastrophe killed several animals accidentally," Ari argued. "Note how the remains of the different species are all jumbled up. If they had been killed by a rockslide from the surrounding heights—to name just one alternate possibility—the remains of each animal would have tended to stay together. The pattern we're looking at here is the pattern we'd expect to see in a waste pit."

Miniruta tossed her head. "If they were butchered," she said in VA13, "then somebody had to use tools to cut them up. Show us a flint tool, Ari. Show us some evidence of fire."

* * *

Machines burrowed and probed in the areas around the "waste pits." Scraping attachments removed the dirt and rock one thin layer at a time. Raking attachments sieved the dust and rubble. Search programs analyzed the images transmitted by the onsite cameras and highlighted anything that met the criteria Ari had stored in the databanks. And they did, in fact, find slivers of flint that could have been knives or spearheads.

Ari had two of the flints laid out on a tray, with a camera poised an arm's length above the objects, and displayed them on one of the wall screens in his apartment. Morgan stared at the tray in silence and let himself surrender to all the eerie, haunting emotions it aroused, even with Ari babbling beside him.

"On Earth," Miniruta pointed out, "we already knew the planet had produced intelligent life. We could assume specimens like that had been made by intelligent beings because we already knew the intelligent beings existed. But what do we have here, Ari? Can we really believe these objects were shaped by intelligent beings when we still haven't seen anything that resembles hands? So far, you haven't even located an organism that had *arms*."

There were other possibilities, of course. Ari had studied most of the ideas about possible alien life forms that humans had come up with in the last few centuries and installed them in the databanks housed in his electronic enhancers. He could produce several plausible examples of grasping organs composed of soft tissue that would only fossilize under rare, limited conditions. The tool makers could have possessed tentacles. They could have used some odd development of their lips.

Miniruta tipped back her head and raised her eyebrows when she heard Ari mention tentacles. The high-pitched lilt of her VA13 communicated— once again—the condescension that permeated her attitude toward Ari.

"The cephalopods all lived in the sea, Ari. Our arms evolved from load-bearing legs. I admit we're discussing creatures who evolved in a lower gravity field. But they weren't operating in zero gravity."

"I've thought about that," Ari said. "Isn't it possible some tentacled sea-creatures could have adapted an amphibious lifestyle on the edge of the sea and eventually produced descendants who substituted legs for some of their tentacles? On our own planet, after all, some of the land dwellers who lived on the edge of Earth's oceans eventually produced descendants whose legs had been transformed into fins. With all due respect to your *current* belief system, Miniruta—our discussions would be significantly more succinct if you weren't trying to discuss serious issues without the benefit of a few well-chosen enhancements. You might see some of the possibilities I'm seeing before I have to describe them to you."

As an adherent of the fourth EruLabi protocol, Miniruta only rejected permanent enhancements that increased her intellectual and physical powers. Temporary enhancements that increased pleasure were another matter. Miniruta could still use a small selection of the sexually enhancing drugs developed in the twenty-first century, in addition to the wines, teas, and inhalants that had fostered pre-pharmaceutical social relations. She and Morgan had already shared several long, elaborately choreographed sexual interludes. They had bathed. They had banqueted. They had reclined on carefully proportioned couches, naked bodies touching, while musicians from a dozen eras had materialized in Miniruta's simulators. The EruLabi sexual rituals had cast a steady, sensuous glow over the entire six decades Morgan had spent with Savela Insdotter. He had resumed their routines as if he had been slipping on clothes that were associated with some of the best moments of his life.

They were nearing the end of a particularly satisfactory interlude when Miniruta switched on her information system and discovered she had received a please-view-first message from Ari. "I've been looking over some of the latest finds from one of your random-survey teams," Ari said. "Your idea paid off. They've handed us a fossil that looks like it left traces of soft-bodied tissue in the rocks in front of it—imprints that look like they could have been made by the local equivalent of tentacles. Your team found it in the middle of a depression in that flat area on the top of the main southern plateau—a depression that's so shallow I hadn't even noticed it on the maps."

Miniruta had decided that half her exploration machines would make random searches. Ari and Morgan were both working with intellectual frameworks based on the history of Earth, Miniruta had argued. Morgan was looking at the kinds of sites that had produced fossils on Earth. Ari was looking for traces of hunter-gatherers. "A random process," she had pronounced, "should be studied by random probing."

Now her own philosophical bias had apparently given Ari what he had been looking for. Ari would never have ordered one of his machines into the winding, almost invisible depression Miniruta's machine had followed. But that dip in the landscape had once been a river. And the river had widened its path and eroded the ground above a fossil that had formed in the sediment by the bank.

It was a cracked, fragmented shell about a third the length of a human being. Only one side of it had been preserved. But you could still see that it was essentially a tube with a large opening at one end, a smaller opening at the other, and no indications it had openings for legs. In the rock in front of the large opening, Morgan could just make out the outlines of impressions that could have been produced by a group of ropy, soft-bodied extensions.

Ari highlighted three spots on the rim of the large opening. "Notice how the opening has indentations on the rim, where the extensions leave it. They aren't very big, but they obviously give the extensions a little more room. I've ordered a search of the databank to see how many other shells have indentations like that. If there was one creature like this on the planet, there should have been other species built along the same pattern. I'm also taking another look at all the shells like this we've uncovered in the past. My first pass through the databank indicates we've found several of them near the places where we found the burial pits."

* * *

For Ari, the find proved that it was time to let the solar system know the full truth. He posted a picture of the fossil on the information system an hour after he had notified Morgan and Miniruta. "We now have evidence that creatures with fully developed grasping organs existed on this planet," Ari argued. "The evidence may not be conclusive, but it can't be dismissed either. The people of the solar system have a right to draw their own conclusions. Let them see the evidence we've collected. Let the minority who are resisting stagnation and decline derive hope from the knowledge more evidence may follow."

It had only been eight tendays since Ari had agreed to the compromise Morgan had worked out. Yet he was already demanding that they cancel the agreement.

To Miniruta, the idea was absurd. Ari was suggesting that the forests of Athene had harbored tentacled creatures who had hung from trees and occupied the ecological niches monkeys had appropriated on Earth. And he was jumping from that improbability to the idea that some of these hypothetical creatures had developed weapons and become hunter-gatherers.

"I am not saying anything is true," Ari insisted. "I am merely noting that we now have pits full of butchered animals, tools that could have butchered them, and a type of organism that could have manipulated the tools."

Ari had even developed a scenario that equipped his fantasy creatures with the ability to move along the ground at a pace suitable for hunters. Suppose, he argued, they had begun their advance to intelligence by learning to control some type of riding animal?

To Ari, his proposal was a logical variation on the process that had shaped human intelligence. On Earth, tree dwellers had developed hands that could grasp limbs and brains that could judge distances and trajectories. Then they had adapted the upright posture and used their hands to create stone tools. Tool use had created a way of life that put a premium on intelligence, the individuals with the best brains had tended to be the survivors, and a creature who could build starships had taken its place in the universe.

"On Athene," Ari argued, "the drive toward intelligence may have followed a different course. The tree dwellers couldn't develop upright walking so they began by controlling animals. They became mounted hunters—creatures who could rove like ground animals and manipulate the same simple tools our own ancestors chipped from the rocks. The evolutionary process may take many twists. It may be bloody and cruel. But in the end, it gives us planets populated by creatures who are intelligent and conscious. The arrow points in only one direction."

Thirty years from now—perhaps even ten years from now—Morgan's feelings about Miniruta would just be a memory. Morgan knew that. There would come a moment when he would wonder how he could have believed all his pleasure in life depended on the goodwill of another human being. But right now he just knew he wanted to create a crowded memory. Right now he felt as if he had spent the last few decades in a state of half-dead numbness.

He had started playing with his political-analysis programs as soon as he had realized Ari was initiating a new round of agitated debate. The situation had looked dangerous to him, and the picture that had emerged on his screens had confirmed his intuitive judgment. About twenty-five percent of the people on the ship believed a report on the new find should be transmitted to the solar system. Almost thirty percent registered strong opposition. The rest of the population seemed to be equally divided between not-convinced-we-should and not-convinced-we-shouldn't.

If Ari's first appeals had attracted a solid forty or forty-five percent, Morgan would have given him some extra support and helped him win a quick, overwhelming victory. Instead, the *Island of Adventure* community had stumbled into one of those situations in which a divisive debate could go on indefinitely.

Morgan was savoring teas with Miniruta when he suggested the one option that looked as if it might defuse the situation.

"I've decided to assign all my exploration teams to the search for evidence that supports Ari's theories," Morgan said. "I think it would be a wise move if you did the same thing—for a while anyway. We're not going to get any peace on this ship until we come up with solid evidence Ari's right. Or make it clear we probably never will."

They had both been speaking Plais—a graceful EruLabi invention that had been designed for the lighter types of social events. Morgan had switched to Jor when he started discussing his proposal, and Miniruta transferred to Jor with him.

"You want to divert equipment from all the other research we're doing?" Miniruta said. "As far as I'm concerned, Ari has all the resources he needs. We're producing the first survey of an alien ecosystem. Why should we interrupt that merely because one member of our expedition has become obsessed with a fantasy?"

The vehemence in her voice caught Morgan off guard. He had thought he was offering her a modest, reasonable proposal. He had run the idea through his political-simulation programs and the results had indicated most of the people on the ship would approve a transmission to the solar system if Ari managed to locate more evidence. A minority would never feel happy with the decision—but at least a decision would have been made.

"It shouldn't divert us for more than a few tendays," Morgan said. "We can intensify Ari's hunt for campsites. We can look for associations between possible mounts and possible riders. We can ignore the low-lying areas for the time being and concentrate on the regions that probably stayed above sea level when Athene had seas. If we do all that and don't come up with something decisive in a few tendays—I think we can assume we'll get a clear consensus that we shouldn't overrule our current agreement and transmit a message before the next discussion period."

"And what if we find the kind of evidence he's looking for? Do you think

Madame Dawne will just nod agreeably? And let us do something that could destroy her?"

"If there's evidence out there to be found—sooner or later we're going to find it. She's going to have to accept that eventually."

Miniruta reached across the tea table and touched his hand. She slipped into Plais just long enough to preface her response with a word that meant something like "pleasure-friend."

"*Donilar*—even if the evidence is there, will it really do us any good if we find it? Why should we jeopardize our whole way of life just so Ari can give a dying minority group information that will only prolong its agonies?"

Morgan knew he shouldn't have felt as if he had just been ambushed. He had been watching Miniruta for over a century. Everything she had done had proved that the profiling program had been correct when it had decided her personality structure was dominated by a deep need for affiliation. When she had been associated with Ari's group, she had maximized her use of enhancements. When she had switched to the other side, she had become a model of EruLabi virtue.

But he was in love. He had surrendered—willingly, for his own reasons— to one of the oldest delusions the human species had invented. And because he was in love, he had let himself ignore something that should have been obvious. Miniruta's dispute with Ari wasn't an argument about the nature of the universe. It was an argument about what human beings should *believe* about the nature of the universe.

The teas were followed by music. The music was followed by a long, dreamlike concentration on the shape and texture of Miniruta's body. And afterward Morgan returned to his apartment and watched his programs churn out scenarios that included a new factor: a woman who believed Ari's worldview was a disease that should be eradicated from human society.

Morgan's programs couldn't tell him what Miniruta was going to do. No program could predict all the tactical choices a human brain could choose. But the programs could suggest possibilities. And they could estimate the intensity of Miniruta's responses.

He spotted what she was doing hours after she started doing it. Her "randomly searching" machines occupied one of the prime sites on Ari's list and started scraping and digging just a few hours before Ari's own machines were scheduled to work on it.

Ari called Morgan as soon as he finished his first attempt to "reason" with Miniruta. He still thought Miniruta's program had made a random choice. He still believed she was just being obstinate when she refused to let his machines excavate the site.

"She's got some kind of silly idea she has to stick to her ideal of pure randomness," Ari said. "She's trying to tell me she wouldn't be operating randomly if she let her team go somewhere else."

Morgan agreed to act as a go-between and Miniruta gave him the response he had expected. It was just a random event, she insisted. Why should Ari object? Now he could send his machines to one of the other sites on his list.

"It's one of the big possibilities on his current list," Morgan said. "He thinks he should explore it himself."

"Doesn't he think my machines are competent? Is he afraid they'll spend too much time indulging in sensual pleasures?"

"Ari thinks this is a totally accidental occurrence, Miniruta."

She smiled. "And what does my little donilar think?"

Morgan straightened up and gave her his best imitation of an authority figure. It was the first time she had said something that made him feel she was playing with him.

"I think it would be best if he went on thinking that," he said.

Miniruta's eyes widened. Her right hand fluttered in front of her face, as if she was warding off a blow. "Is that a *threat*, donilar? After all we have enjoyed together?"

Three daycycles later, Miniruta's machines took over two more sites. Morgan's surveillance program advised him as soon as it happened and he immediately called Ari and found himself confronted with a prime display of outrage.

"She's deliberately interfering," Ari shouted. "This can't be random. She is deliberately trying to destroy the last hope of the only people in the solar system who still have faith in the future. Even you should be able to see that, Morgan—in spite of your chemical reactions to certain types of female bodies."

It was the kind of situation Morgan normally delegated to one of his political operatives. This time there was no way he could slip away gracefully and let someone else handle it. His studies had taught him what the best responses were. He had even managed to apply them on one or two previous occasions. He let the tirade go on as long as Ari wanted to maintain it. He carefully avoided saying anything that might indicate he was agreeing or disagreeing.

Unfortunately, he was faced with something no one on the ship could have handled. Miniruta had given Ari an opening he had obviously been looking for.

"I agreed to wait until we had a consensus," Ari ranted. "I'm trying to be cooperative. But I think it's time some one reminded your overzealous paramour that there's no practical, physical reason I can't transmit a message to the solar system any time I want to."

Ari's elongated head could make him look slightly comical when he became overexcited. This time it was a visual reminder of the commitment behind his outbursts.

"If you really want to get this situation calmed down, Morgan—I suggest you remind her I still have more supporters than she has. They can all look at what she's been doing at the first site. They can all see her machines are carefully avoiding all the best locations and deliberately moving at the slowest pace they can maintain without stalling. You can tell her she has two choices. She can get her machines out of all three sites, or she can put them under my control. And after she's done that—I'll send her a list of all the other sites I expect her to stay away from."

Miniruta was standing in the doorway of her ritual chamber. Behind her, Morgan could glimpse the glow of the brass sculpture that dominated the far end. Miniruta had just finished one of the EruLabi rituals that punctuated her daily schedule. She was still wearing the thin, belted robe she wore during most of the rituals.

Only the night before, in this very room, they had huddled together in the most primitive fashion. They had stretched out on the sleeping platform just a few steps to Morgan's left and he had spent the entire night with his arms wrapped around her body while they slept.

"I've discussed the situation with Ari," Morgan said in Tych. "He has indicated he feels your actions have given him the right to transmit a message without authorization. He believes his supporters will approve such an action."

"And he sent you here to relay something that is essentially another threat."

"It is my belief that was his intention."

"You should tell him he'll be making a serious error. You should tell him it's obvious he thinks no one will resist him."

"I believe it would be accurate to say he believes no one will offer him any high-level resistance."

"Then you should tell him his assumptions need to be revised. Madame Dawne has already armed herself. I obviously can't tell you more than that. But I can tell you she will fight if Ari tries to take control of the communications module. She is already emotionally committed to fighting."

Miniruta smiled. "Is that an informative response? Will that give Ari some evidence he should modify his assumptions?"

Morgan returned to his apartment and had his fabrication unit manufacture two sets of unarmed probes. The probes were large, cumbersome devices, about the size of a standard water goblet, but he wasn't interested in secrecy. He deployed both sets by hand, from a maintenance hatch, and monitored them on his notescreen while they tractored across the surface area that surrounded the communications module.

His notescreen accepted a call from Miniruta two minutes after the probes had made their fourth find.

"Please do not interfere, Morgan. Madame Dawne has no quarrel with you."

"I've detected four weapons so far. None of them look to me like items Madame Dawne would have deployed on her own."

"Don't underestimate her, Morgan. She believes Ari is threatening her ability to survive."

"I thought Madame Dawne was a dangerous person when we were coping with the course-change controversy. But that was over ten decades ago. She's only been seen twice in the last eight years. The last time her responses were so stereotyped half the people she talked to thought they were dealing with a simulation. I don't know how much personality she has left at this point— but I don't think she could surround the communications module with a defense like this unassisted."

"Ari is threatening the fabric of our community. We made an agreement as a community—a consensus that took every individual's needs into account. Madame Dawne is defending the community against a personality who thinks he can impose his own decisions on it."

Morgan fed the information from his probes into a wargame template and let the program run for over thirteen minutes. It went through four thousand simulations altogether—two thousand games in which Madame Dawne was willing to risk the total annihilation of the ship's community, followed by two thousand possibilities in which she limited herself to ambushes and low-level delaying tactics. Seventy percent of the time, Madame Dawne could keep Ari away from the communications module for periods that ranged from twenty-one daycycles to two hundred daycycles. She couldn't win, but she could force Ari into a sustained struggle.

And that was all she needed to do, according to Morgan's political estimates. Miniruta would gain some extra support if Ari broke the agreement unilaterally. But neither one of them would have a commanding majority when the fighting began. They would start out with a sixty-forty split in Ari's favor, and a drawn-out battle would have the worst possible effect: it would intensify feelings and move the split closer to fifty-fifty.

Morgan thought he could understand why people like Ari and Miniruta adapted belief systems. But why did they feel they had to annihilate other belief systems? His profiling programs could provide him with precise numerical descriptions of the emotions that drove the people he modeled. No program could make him feel the emotions himself.

Still, for all his relentless obsession with the Doctrine of the Cosmic Enterprise, Ari was always willing to listen when Morgan showed him the charts and graphs he had generated with his programs. Ari was interested in anything that involved intellectual effort.

"I think we can assume Miniruta isn't going to budge," Morgan reported. "But I have a suggestion you may want to consider."

"I'd be astonished if you didn't," Ari said.

"I think you should send your own machines to the sites she's occupying and have them attempt to carry out your plans. My profiling program indicates there's a high probability she'll attempt to interfere with you. As you can see by the numbers on Chart Three, the public reaction will probably place you in a much stronger political position if she does."

Ari turned his attention to the chart displayed on the bottom half of his screen and spent a full third of a minute studying it—a time span that indicated he was checking the logic that connected the figures.

"The numbers are convincing," Ari said in Tych. "But I would appreciate it if you would tell me what your ultimate objective is."

"There's a basic conflict between Miniruta's conduct and the message of the EruLabi creeds. Miniruta can't act the way she's been acting without arousing some hostility in the rest of the EruLabi community."

"And you're hoping she'll alter her behavior when she finds the EruLabi are turning against her. Since she is a personality whose 'drive for affiliation' scores in the ninety-ninth percentile."

"The EruLabi are not proselytizers," Morgan said in Tych. "Their world-view tends to attract people who avoid controversy and public notice. Many EruLabi are already uncomfortable. If you'll examine Table Six, you'll see the reactions of the EruLabi community already generate an overall minus twenty in their attitude toward Miniruta. Table Seven shows you how much that will increase if they see her actually engaging in some form of active resistance."

"I'm still fully prepared to transmit a message without waiting for authorization, Morgan. I'm willing to try this. But the other option is still open."

"I understand that," Morgan said.

The biggest exploration machines on the planet were high-wheeled "tractors" that were about the size of the fabrication unit that sat in a corner of Morgan's apartment and transformed rocks and waste matter into food and other useful items. Ari started—correctly, in Morgan's opinion—by landing six machines that were only a third that size. Ari's little group of sand sifters and electronic probing devices started to spread out after their landing and three tractors detached themselves from Miniruta's team and tried to block them. Ari's nimble little machines dodged through the openings between the tractors, more of Miniruta's machines entered the action, and the tractors started colliding with Ari's machines and knocking off wheels and sensors.

Morgan stayed out of the rhetorical duel that erupted as soon as Ari circulated his recording of the robotic fracas. Instead, he focused his attention on the reactions of the EruLabi. Miniruta was defending herself by claiming she was upholding her right to pursue an alternate research pattern. It was a weak line of argument, in Morgan's opinion, and the EruLabi seemed to agree with him. The support she was attracting came from people who had opposed Ari's original request to send a message to the solar system. Morgan's search programs couldn't find a single comment—negative or positive—from anyone who could be identified as an EruLabi.

Morgan's content-analysis programs had been collecting every commentary and attempt at humor that mentioned Miniruta. Over the next few hours he found five items that played on the discrepancy between Miniruta's EruLabi professions and her militant behavior. The one he liked best was a forty-second video that showed a woman with a BR-V73 body type reclining in an ornate bath. The woman was bellowing EruLabi slogans at the top of her lungs and manipulating toy war machines while she jabbered about love, sensual pleasure, and the comforts of art and music. A broken teacup jiggled on the floor beside the tub every time one of her toys fired a laser or launched a missile.

It was a crude effort that had been posted anonymously, with no attempt to circulate it. As far as Morgan could tell, only a couple of hundred people had actually seen it. He shortened it by eighteen seconds, transformed the cackles into deep-throated chuckles, and retouched some of the other details.

Of the other four items, two were genuinely witty, one was clumsy, and one was just bad-tempered and insulting. He modified all of them in the same way he had modified the video. He slipped them into the message stream at points where he could be confident they would be noticed by key members of the EruLabi communion.

Fifteen hours after Miniruta had started obstructing Ari's efforts, Savela Insdotter circulated the official EruLabi response. *Miniruta Coboloji has been an inspiration to everyone who truly understands the EruLabi creeds,* Savela began. *Unfortunately, she seems to have let her enthusiasm for our Way lead her into a dangerous course of action. We reached an agreement and Ari Sun-Dalt abided by it, in spite of all his feelings to the contrary.*

We have a civilized, rational system for resolving differences. We don't have to tolerate people who refuse to respect our procedures. We still control the communication system. We can still sever Miniruta's communication links with Athene and her manufacturing facilities on the moon, if we register our will as a community. Isn't it time we got this situation under control?

Miniruta's answer appeared on the screens of every EruLabi on the ship. Morgan wasn't included on her distribution list but an EruLabi passed it on to him. Every word she spoke validated the analysis his program had made all those decades earlier. The tilt of her chin and the tension in her mouth could have been delineated by a simulator working with the program's conclusions.

Morgan watched the statement once, to see what she had said, and never looked at it again. He had watched Miniruta abandon two groups: the original Eight and Ari's most dedicated followers. No group had ever abandoned her.

Savela's proposal required a ninety-percent vote—the minimum it took to override the controls built into the information system. Anyone who had watched the ship's political system at work could have predicted Savela was going to collect every yes she needed. The proposal had been attracting votes from the moment people started discussing it—and no one had voted against it.

Morgan believed he was offering Miniruta the best opportunity he could give her. The EruLabi were not a vindictive people. A few wits had circulated clever barbs, but there was no evidence they were committed to a state of permanent rancor. Most of them would quickly forget her "excessive ardor" once she "manifested a better understanding of our ideals."

Miniruta would reestablish her bonds with the EruLabi communion within a year, two years at the most, Morgan estimated. He would once again recline beside her as they sampled teas and wines together. He would look down on her face as she responded to the long movements of his body. Miniruta was a *good* EruLabi. It suited her.

He knew he had failed when the vote reached the fifty-five-percent mark and Miniruta started denouncing the EruLabi who had refused to support her crusade to rid the universe of "cosmic totalitarianism." The tally had just topped sixty-five percent when Ari advised him Miniruta's robots were vandalizing the sites she had occupied.

Fossils were being chipped and defaced. Rocks that might contain fossils were being splintered into slivers and scattered across the landscape. Five of the best sites were being systematically destroyed.

The carnage would end as soon as they cut Miniruta's communications link to the planet. But in the meantime, she would destroy evidence that had survived two billion years.

Ari already had machines of his own at two of the sites Miniruta was razing. He had transmitted new orders to the entire group and they had immediately started ramming and blocking Miniruta's machines. The rest of his machines were scattered over the planet.

They had only built three vehicles that could pick up a group of exploration machines and haul it to another point on the planet. Most of the machines on the planet had been planted on their work sites when they had made their initial trip from the moon.

Morgan ran the situation through a wargame template and considered the results. As usual, the tactical situation could be reduced to a problem in the allocation of resources. They could scatter their forces among all five sites or they could concentrate on three. Scattering was the best option if they thought the struggle would only last a few hours. Concentration was the best option if they thought it might last longer.

"Give me some priorities," Morgan said. "Which sites are most important?"

"They're all important," Ari said. "Who knows what's there? She could be destroying something critical at every site she's spoiling."

Morgan gave his system an order and the three transport vehicles initiated a lifting program that would place defensive forces on all five sites. The vote on Savela's proposal had already reached the seventy-percent mark. How long could it be before it hit ninety and Miniruta lost control of her equipment?

Most of the exploration machines were weak devices. They removed dirt by the spoonful. They cataloged the position of every pebble they disturbed. If the vote reached cutoff within two or three hours, Morgan's scattered defensive forces could save over eighty-five percent of all five sites.

Short-range laser beams burned out sensors. Mechanical arms pounded sensitive arrays. Vehicles wheeled and charged through a thin, low-gravity fog of dust. Morgan found himself reliving emotions he hadn't felt since his postnatal development program had given him simple mechanical toys during the first years of his childhood.

For the first ninety minutes, it was almost fun. Then he realized the vote had been stuck at seventy-eight percent for at least fifteen minutes. A moment later, it dropped back to seventy-six.

He switched his attention to his political-analysis program and realized Miniruta had made an important shift while he had been playing general. She had stopped fighting a crusade against her philosophical rivals. Now she was defending Madame Dawne "and all the other elders who will have to live with the consequences of Ari's headstrong recklessness if the *Green Voyager* changes course."

"Apparently she's decided Madame Dawne offers her a more popular cause," Ari said.

Ten minutes after Miniruta issued her speech, Morgan sent five of his machines in pursuit of two of hers. He was watching his little war party drive in for the kill—confident he had her outmaneuvered—when he suddenly discovered it had been encircled by an overwhelming force. Five minutes later, the program advised him he was facing a general disaster. The "exchange rate" at all five sites was now running almost two to one in Miniruta's favor. Every time he destroyed five of her machines, she destroyed nine of his.

Ari saw the implications as soon as the numbers appeared on the screen. "She's started feeding herself enhancers," Ari said. "She's abandoning her EruLabi principles."

Morgan turned away from his screens. Memories of music floated across his mind.

He switched to Tych, in the hope its hard, orderly sentences would help him control his feelings. "Miniruta has switched allegiances," he said. "We were incorrect when we assumed her last statement was a tactical move. She has acquired a new allegiance."

"Just like that? Just like she left us?"

"It would be more correct to say she feels the EruLabi left her."

"That isn't what you told me she'd do, Morgan."

"The programs indicated there was a ninety-percent probability Miniruta would protect her ties with the EruLabi community."

"And now you're faced with one of the options in the ten-percent list instead."

A blank look settled over Ari's face. He tipped back his head and focused his attention on his internal electronics.

"Let me see if I understand the situation," Ari said in Tych. "The struggle can continue almost indefinitely if Miniruta maintains the current exchange rate. She is receiving new machines from her production units on the moon almost as fast as you're destroying them. She can continue damaging all five sites, therefore, until they are all totally demolished."

"We still have options," Morgan said. "My pharmaceuticals include enhancers I still haven't used. Miniruta outmatches me intellectually but she has a weakness. She isn't used to thinking about conflict situations. Miniruta spent the last seven decades advancing through the EruLabi protocols. She has devoted twenty-five percent of her total lifespan to her attempts to master the protocols."

"As for the political situation," Ari droned, "according to your best estimates, approximately eighty percent of the ship's population feel we should send a message to the solar system if we find conclusive evidence intelligent life evolved on Athene. They may not agree I should send a message now, but they do agree it should be sent if I uncover evidence that can be considered conclusive. Most of the people in the other twenty percent have been willing to submit to the will of the majority, even though they aren't happy with the idea. Now Miniruta is offering the twenty percent a tempting opportunity. They can let her destroy the evidence and avoid a decision indefinitely. They don't even have to vote. They can just abstain and hold the count on the current balloting below ninety percent. Miniruta will maintain control of her machines and the sites will be excised from the scientific record."

Ari lowered his head. "It's my opinion I should initiate one of my alternate options. Miniruta can operate her machines only as long as her apartment is connected to the ship's power supply. We will have to sever three alternate power lines to cut her link with the power system, but I believe it can be done."

Morgan stared at the screen that displayed Ari's face. He started to respond in Tych and discovered he couldn't. Ari had triggered an emotional flood that was so powerful Morgan's brain had automatically shifted to VA13.

Ari raised his hand. "I recognize that the action I'm suggesting has serious implications," he said. "I realize it could trigger off long-term changes in our communal relationships. I believe Miniruta is committing a crime that ranks with the worst atrocities in history. She is destroying a message that has been waiting for us for over two billion years."

"You're talking about something that could make every passenger on this ship feel they had to arm themselves," Morgan said. "This is the first time I've ever heard anyone even *suggest* one passenger should attack another passenger's power connection. What kind of a life could we have here if people felt somebody could cut their power connection every time we had a conflict?"

"We are discussing an extreme situation. Miniruta could be pulverizing the only fossils on the planet that could prove Athene generated intelligent life."

Morgan stood up. "It's always an extreme situation. This time it's *your* extreme situation. Fifty years from now it will be somebody else's. And what do we end up with? A ship full of people forming gangs and alliances so they can protect themselves?"

"Is that all that matters to you, Morgan? Maintaining order in one little rock? Worrying about three thousand people hiding in their own personal caves?"

Morgan knew he was losing control of his impulses. He was behaving exactly the way his personality profile predicted he would behave. But he couldn't help himself. He was staring at someone who was unshakably convinced they were right and he was wrong. Ari could have withstood every technique of persuasion stored in the ship's databanks. What difference did it make what he said?

"*It's the rock I live in!* It's the rock *you* live in!"

Ari switched to VA13—a language he rarely used. The musical pattern he adapted colored his words with a flare of trumpets.

"I live in the galaxy," Ari said. "My primary responsibility is the intellectual evolution of my species."

Miniruta—Ari is going to cut the power lines to your apartment. This is not a ruse. It's not a threat. I'm warning you because I think he's doing something that could have a disastrous effect on the long-range welfare of the ship's community— a precedent that could make the ship unlivable. You've still got time if you move now. Put on your emergency suit. Get in your escape tunnel and go all the way to the surface before he puts a guard on the surface hatch. If you start now, you could make it all the way to the communications module while he's still getting organized.

Morgan's forces attacked Miniruta's production facilities on the moon two hours after she received his warning. Her security system put up a fight, but it was overwhelmed within an hour. Every fabrication unit in her factories was brought to a halt. The rail launcher that propelled her machines toward Athene was dismantled at three different points.

Morgan had selected the most powerful intellectual enhancer his physiology could absorb. He would be disoriented for almost five daycycles after he stopped using it. He was still intellectually inferior to Miniruta, but he had just proved he had been right when he had claimed she wasn't used to thinking about conflict situations. He had taken her by surprise because she hadn't realized he had reprogrammed his lunar fabrication units and created a force that could break through her defenses.

This was the first time he had used this enhancer while he was struggling with a real-time, real-world challenge. He turned his attention to the action on the surface of Athene as if he was training a massive weapon on a target.

Miniruta's forces were still destroying his machines faster than he was destroying hers. She had spent a full hour working her way across the surface of the ship to the communications module and she had managed to maintain the exchange rate all the time she had been doing it. On the site closest to Athene's equator, she had taken complete control of the situation. Morgan's machines had been backed against a cliff and most of Miniruta's machines were churning up the ground and lasering potential fossil beds without resistance.

Morgan had eliminated Miniruta's source of reinforcements when he had destroyed her facilities on the moon. His own fabrication units were still turning out a steady stream of reinforcements and launching them at the planet. Sooner or later, Miniruta's machines would be wiped out. Sooner or later, he would be replacing his machines faster than she destroyed them. But the trip from the moon to Athene took over twenty hours. It would be almost forty hours, the charts on his screens claimed, before he destroyed Miniruta's last machine.

His brain skimmed through the plans for the vehicles that ferried equipment between the moon and the planet. Numbers and equations danced across his consciousness: payloads, production times, the weight of the reaction mass a transport vehicle forced through its engines when it braked to a landing on Athene. His fabrication units on the moon received a new set of orders and started producing transport vehicles that would make the trip in nine hours. The vehicles would carry fifty percent more reaction mass, so they could kill the extra velocity. Payload would be reduced by thirty percent.

"Somebody told her we were going to attack her power lines. She climbed out her surface escape hatch minutes before we put a guard on it. We didn't even know she'd left until she started controlling her machines from the communications module."

Ari had been speaking VA13 when he had deposited the message in Morgan's files. He had obviously wanted to make sure Morgan understood his feelings.

"There's only one person on this ship who could have warned her in time, Morgan. No one in my communion would have done such a thing. Now she's sitting in the communications module, wrecking and smashing some of the most precious information the human race has ever uncovered. And we're battering our skulls into pulp trying to break through all the weapons her friend Madame Dawne deployed around the communications module."

Morgan put his machines into a defensive posture on all five sites and held them on the defensive while he waited for reinforcements. Every now and then, when he saw an opportunity, he launched a hit-and-run attack and tried to catch one of her machines by surprise.

Ari was right, of course. The destruction Morgan was watching on his screens was one of the great criminal acts of history. Most of the fossils that had filled in the story of human evolution had come from a small area of Earth. The sites Miniruta was destroying had been selected because they met all the parameters entered into the search program. Would there be important, unfillable gaps in the record when they had explored the entire planet? Would her spree of destruction leave them with questions that could never be answered?

Morgan switched to the offensive as soon as the first reinforcements arrived from the moon. He picked the site where Miniruta was weakest and eliminated every machine she controlled within two hours. Then he picked her second weakest site and began working on it.

He could feel the full power of Miniruta's mind every step of the way. He was making maximum use of all the help his wargaming programs could give him but he couldn't reduce the exchange ratio by a single percentage point. He was going to defeat her only because she was manipulating a finite force and he could draw on an infinite supply of reinforcements. Whatever he did, she still destroyed nine of his machines every time he destroyed five of hers.

At any given moment, furthermore, only about half her machines were actually fighting his. The rest of them were busily maximizing the destruction she was causing.

*   *   *

"We've lost at least thirty percent of the information we could have pulled from each site," Ari said. "On site four, we probably lost over sixty percent."

Morgan was lying on a couch, with a screen propped on his stomach. The recording of Ari's face seemed to be shimmering at the end of a long tunnel. The medical system had advised him it might be most of a tenday before he recovered from the combined effects of sleeplessness, emotional stress, and ultra-enhancement.

"I could have cut off her power within three or four hours if you hadn't interfered," Ari said. "It took you eleven hours to destroy her vehicles—*eleven hours*—even after you started getting extra reinforcements from the moon."

For the third time in less than a daycycle, Morgan was being given a rare chance to hear Ari speak VA13. This time Ari was applying the full force of a module that communicated graduated degrees of revulsion.

Morgan had made no recordings of his private moments with Miniruta. The EruLabi didn't do that. Pleasure should be experienced only in memory or in the reality of the present, the EruLabi mentors had proclaimed. There was a long period—it lasted over two years—when Morgan spent several hours of every daycycle watching recordings of Miniruta's public appearances.

Savela could have helped him. He could imagine circumstances in which Savela would have offered him a temporary bonding that would have freed him from an emotion that seemed to blunt all his other feelings. Savela was no longer friendly, however. Savela might be an EruLabi but she shared Ari's opinion of his behavior.

Morgan believed he had averted the complete political breakdown of the ship's community. But how could you prove you had avoided something that never happened? People didn't see the big disaster that hadn't taken place. They only saw the small disaster you had created when you were trying to avert the big disaster. Out of the three thousand people on the ship, at least a thousand had decided they would be happier without his company.

Once, just to see if it would have any effect on his feelings, Morgan struck up a relationship with a woman with a BR-V73 body type. The woman was even an EruLabi. She had never advanced beyond the second protocol but that should have been a minor matter. Her body felt like Miniruta's when he touched it. The same expressions crossed her face when they practiced the EruLabi sexual rituals. There was no way he could have noticed any significant difference when he wrapped himself around her in the darkness.

Ari's sexual enhancement was another possibility. Morgan thought about it many times during the next two decades. He rejected it, each time, because there was no guarantee it would give him what he needed. The enhancement affected only the most basic aspect of sexual desire—the drive for simple physical release. It didn't erase memories that included all the hours that had preceded—and followed—the actual moments when their bodies had been joined.

He had made eight attempts to contact Miniruta during the three years that had followed their miniature war. His programs still monitored the information system for any indication she was communicating with anyone. A style-analysis program occasionally detected a message Miniruta could have created under a pseudonym. Every example it found had been traced to a specific, identifiable source. None of the authors had been Miniruta.

He had sent two queries to Madame Dawne. The second time, she had appeared on his screen with hair that was so short and so red she looked like someone had daubed her skull with paint. The language she had used had been obsolete when the *Island of Adventure* had left the solar system.

"Please do not think I am indifferent to your concern," Madame Dawne had said. "I believe I can inform you—with no likelihood of exaggeration or inaccuracy—that Miniruta finds your anxieties heartwarming. Please accept my unqualified assurance that you can turn your attention to other matters. Miniruta is a happy woman. We are both happy women."

Morgan had deleted the recording from his files two tendays after he received it. He had given his profiling program a description of Miniruta's latest transformation. Miniruta had changed her allegiance three times in the last one hundred and fifteen years. There was a possibility her affiliations were episodes in an endless cycle of unions and ruptures, driven by a need that could never be permanently satisfied. The program couldn't calculate a probability. But it was a common pattern.

In the meantime, he still had his researches. He had picked out three evolutionary lines that looked interesting. One line had apparently filled the same ecological niche the pig family had exploited on Earth. The others raised questions about the way predators and prey interacted over the millennia.

They were good subjects. They would keep him occupied for decades. He had now lived over three hundred years. Nothing lasted forever. He had his whole life ahead of him.

The Wedding Album

DAVID MARUSEK

New writer David Marusek is a graduate of Clarion West. He made his first sale to Asimov's Science Fiction *in 1993, and his second sale soon thereafter to* Playboy, *followed subsequently by more sales to* Asimov's *and to the British anthology* Future Histories. *His pyrotechnic novella "We Were Out of Our Minds with Joy" was one of the most popular and talked-about stories of 1995. Although it was only his third sale, it was sufficiently accomplished to make one of the reviewers for* Locus *magazine speculate that Marusek must be a Big Name Author writing under a pseudonym. Not a pseudonym, Marusek lives the life of a struggling young writer in a "low-maintenance cabin in the woods" in Fairbanks, Alaska, where he is currently working on his first novel, and I'm willing to bet that his is a voice we'll be hearing a lot more from as we move through the new century ahead.*

In the vivid, powerful, and compassionate story that follows, which was a Hugo and Nebula finalist last year, he takes us back to the intricate and strange high-tech, posthuman-future milieu of "We Were Out of Our Minds With Joy," to a world where the border between what's real and what's not real has grown disturbingly thin—and we don't always find ourselves on the right side of the line.

Anne and Benjamin stood stock-still, as instructed, close but not touching, while the simographer adjusted her apparatus, set its timer, and ducked out of the room. It would take only a moment, she said. They were to think only happy happy thoughts.

For once in her life, Anne was unconditionally happy, and everything around her made her happier: her gown, which had been her grandmother's; the wedding ring (how cold it had felt when Benjamin first slipped it on her finger!); her clutch bouquet of forget-me-nots and buttercups; Benjamin himself, close beside her in his charcoal grey tux and pink carnation. He who so despised ritual but was a good sport. His cheeks were pink, too, and his eyes sparkled with some wolfish fantasy. "Come here," he whispered. Anne shushed him; you weren't supposed to talk or touch during a casting; it could spoil the sims. "I can't wait," he whispered, "this is taking too long." And it did seem longer than usual, but this was a professional simulacrum, not some homemade snapshot.

They were posed at the street end of the living room, next to the table piled with brightly wrapped gifts. This was Benjamin's townhouse; she had barely moved in. All her treasures were still in shipping shells in the basement, except for the few pieces she'd managed to have unpacked: the oak refectory table and chairs, the sixteenth-century French armoire, the cherry wood chifforobe, the tea table with inlaid top, the silvered mirror over the fire surround. Of course, her antiques clashed with Benjamin's contemporary—and rather common—decor, but he had promised her the whole house to redo as she saw fit. A whole house!

"How about a kiss?" whispered Benjamin.

Anne smiled but shook her head; there'd be plenty of time later for that sort of thing.

Suddenly, a head wearing wraparound goggles poked through the wall and quickly surveyed the room. "Hey, you," it said to them.

"Is that our simographer?" Benjamin said.

The head spoke into a cheek mike, "This one's the keeper," and withdrew as suddenly as it had appeared.

"Did the simographer just pop her head in through the wall?" said Benjamin.

"I think so," said Anne, though it made no sense.

"I'll just see what's up," said Benjamin, breaking his pose. He went to the door but could not grasp its handle.

Music began to play outside, and Anne went to the window. Her view of the garden below was blocked by the blue-and-white-striped canopy they had rented, but she could clearly hear the clink of flatware on china, laughter, and the musicians playing a waltz. "They're starting without us," she said, happily amazed.

"They're just warming up," said Benjamin.

"No, they're not. That's the first waltz. I picked it myself."

"So let's waltz," Benjamin said and reached for her. But his arms passed through her in a flash of pixelated noise. He frowned and examined his hands.

Anne hardly noticed. Nothing could diminish her happiness. She was drawn to the table of wedding gifts. Of all the gifts, there was only one—a long flat box in flecked silver wrapping—that she was most keen to open. It was from Great Uncle Karl. When it came down to it, Anne was both the easiest and the hardest person to shop for. While everyone knew of her passion for antiques, few had the means or expertise to buy one. She reached for Karl's package, but her hand passed right through it. *This isn't happening*, she thought with gleeful horror.

That it *was*, in fact, happening was confirmed a moment later when a dozen people—Great Uncle Karl, Nancy, Aunt Jennifer, Traci, Cathy and Tom, the bridesmaids and others, including Anne herself, and Benjamin, still in their wedding clothes—all trooped through the wall wearing wraparound goggles. "Nice job," said Great Uncle Karl, inspecting the room, "first rate."

"Ooooh," said Aunt Jennifer, comparing the identical wedding couples, identical but for the goggles. It made Anne uncomfortable that the other Anne should be wearing goggles while she wasn't. And the other Benjamin acted a little drunk and wore a smudge of white frosting on his lapel. *We've cut the cake*, she thought happily, although she couldn't remember doing so. Geri, the flower girl in a pastel dress, and Angus, the ring bearer in a miniature tux, along with a knot of other dressed-up children, charged through the sofa, back and forth, creating pyrotechnic explosions of digital noise. They would have run through Benjamin and Anne, too, had the adults allowed. Anne's father came through the wall with a bottle of champagne. He paused when he saw Anne but turned to the other Anne and freshened her glass.

"Wait a minute!" shouted Benjamin, waving his arms above his head. "I get it now. We're the sims!" The guests all laughed, and he laughed too. "I guess my sims always say that, don't they?" The other Benjamin nodded yes and sipped his champagne. "I just never expected to be a sim," Benjamin went on. This brought another round of laughter, and he said sheepishly, "I guess my sims all say that, too."

The other Benjamin said, "Now that we have the obligatory epiphany out of the way," and took a bow. The guests applauded.

Cathy, with Tom in tow, approached Anne. "Look what I caught," she said and showed Anne the forget-me-not and buttercup bouquet. "I guess we know what that means." Tom, intent on straightening his tie, seemed not to hear. But Anne knew what it meant. It meant they'd tossed the bouquet. All the silly little rituals that she had so looked forward to.

"Good for you," she said and offered her own clutch, which she still held, for comparison. The real one was wilting and a little ragged around the edges, with missing petals and sprigs, while hers was still fresh and pristine and would remain so eternally. "Here," she said, "take mine, too, for double luck." But when she tried to give Cathy the bouquet, she couldn't let go of it. She opened her hand and discovered a seam where the clutch joined her palm. It was part of her. Funny, she thought, I'm not afraid. Ever since she was little, Anne had feared that some day she would suddenly realize she wasn't herself anymore. It was a dreadful notion that sometimes oppressed her for weeks: knowing you weren't yourself. But her sims didn't seem to mind it. She had about three dozen Annes in her album, from age twelve on up. Her sims tended to be a morose lot, but they all agreed it wasn't so bad, the life of a sim, once you got over the initial shock. The first moments of disorientation are the worst, they told her, and they made her promise never to reset them back to default. Otherwise, they'd have to work everything through from scratch. So Anne never reset her sims when she shelved them. She might delete a sim outright for whatever reason, but she never reset them because you never knew when you'd wake up one day a sim yourself. Like today.

The other Anne joined them. She was sagging a little. "Well," she said to Anne.

"Indeed!" replied Anne.

"Turn around," said the other Anne, twirling her hand, "I want to see."

Anne was pleased to oblige. Then she said, "Your turn," and the other Anne modeled for her, and she was delighted at how the gown looked on her, though the goggles somewhat spoiled the effect. Maybe this can work out, she thought, I am enjoying myself so. "Let's go see us side-by-side," she said, leading the way to the mirror on the wall. The mirror was large, mounted high, and tilted forward so you saw yourself as from above. But simulated mirrors cast no reflections, and Anne was happily disappointed.

"Oh," said Cathy, "look at that."

"Look at what?" said Anne.

"Grandma's vase," said the other Anne. On the mantel beneath the mirror stood Anne's most precious possession, a delicate vase cut from pellucid blue crystal. Anne's great-great-great grandmother had commissioned the Belgian master, Bollinger, the finest glass maker in sixteenth-century Europe, to make it. Five hundred years later, it was as perfect as the day it was cut.

"Indeed!" said Anne, for the sim vase seemed to radiate an inner light. Through some trick or glitch of the simogram, it sparkled like a lake under moonlight, and, seeing it, Anne felt incandescent.

After a while, the other Anne said, "Well?" Implicit in this question was a whole standard set of questions that boiled down to—shall I keep you or delete you now? For sometimes a sim didn't take. Sometimes a sim was cast while Anne was in a mood, and the sim suffered irreconcilable guilt or un-assuagable despondency and had to be mercifully destroyed. It was better to do this immediately, or so all the Annes had agreed.

And Anne understood the urgency, what with the reception still in pro-gress and the bride and groom, though frazzled, still wearing their finery. They might do another casting if necessary. "I'll be okay," Anne said. "In fact, if it's always like this, I'll be terrific."

Anne, through the impenetrable goggles, studied her. "You sure?"

"Yes."

"Sister," said the other Anne. Anne addressed all her sims as "sister," and now Anne, herself, was being so addressed. "Sister," said the other Anne, "this has got to work out. I need you."

"I know," said Anne, "I'm your wedding day."

"Yes, my wedding day."

Across the room, the guests laughed and applauded. Benjamin—both of him—was entertaining, as usual. He—the one in goggles—motioned to them. The other Anne said, "We have to go. I'll be back."

Great Uncle Karl, Nancy, Cathy and Tom, Aunt Jennifer, and the rest left through the wall. A polka could be heard playing on the other side. Before leaving, the other Benjamin gathered the other Anne into his arms and leaned her backward for a theatrical kiss. Their goggles clacked. *How happy I look*, Anne told herself. *This is the happiest day of my life.*

Then the lights dimmed, and her thoughts shattered like glass.

They stood stock-still, as instructed, close but not touching. Benjamin whis-pered, "This is taking too long," and Anne shushed him. You weren't sup-posed to talk; it could glitch the sims. But it did seem a long time. Benjamin gazed at her with hungry eyes and brought his lips close enough for a kiss, but Anne smiled and turned away. There'd be plenty of time later for fooling around.

Through the wall, they heard music, the tinkle of glassware, and the mut-ter of overlapping conversation. "Maybe I should just check things out," Ben-jamin said and broke his pose.

"No, wait," whispered Anne, catching his arm. But her hand passed right through him in a stream of colorful noise. She looked at her hand in amused wonder.

Anne's father came through the wall. He stopped when he saw her and said, "Oh, how lovely." Anne noticed he wasn't wearing a tuxedo.

"You just walked through the wall," said Benjamin.

"Yes, I did," said Anne's father. "Ben asked me to come in here and . . . ah . . . orient you two."

"Is something wrong?" said Anne, through a fuzz of delight.

"There's nothing wrong," replied her father.

"Something's wrong?" asked Benjamin.

"No, no," replied the old man. "Quite the contrary. We're having a do out there. . . ." He paused to look around. "Actually, in here. I'd forgotten what this room used to look like."

"Is that the wedding reception?" Anne asked.

"No, your anniversary."

Suddenly Benjamin threw his hands into the air and exclaimed, "I get it, *we're* the sims!"

"That's my boy," said Anne's father.

"All my sims say that, don't they? I just never expected to *be* a sim."

"Good for you," said Anne's father. "All right then." He headed for the wall. "We'll be along shortly."

"Wait," said Anne, but he was already gone.

Benjamin walked around the room, passing his hand through chairs and lamp shades like a kid. "Isn't this fantastic?" he said.

Anne felt too good to panic, even when another Benjamin, this one dressed in jeans and sportscoat, led a group of people through the wall. "And this," he announced with a flourish of his hand, "is our wedding sim." Cathy was part of this group, and Janice and Beryl, and other couples she knew. But strangers too. "Notice what a cave I used to inhabit," the new Benjamin went on, "before Annie fixed it up. And here's the blushing bride, herself," he said and bowed gallantly to Anne. Then, when he stood next to his double, her Benjamin, Anne laughed, for someone was playing a prank on her.

"Oh, really?" she said. "If this is a sim, where's the goggles?" For indeed, no one was wearing goggles.

"Technology!" exclaimed the new Benjamin. "We had our system upgraded. *Don't you love it?*"

"Is that right?" she said, smiling at the guests to let them know she wasn't fooled. "Then where's the real me?"

"You'll be along," replied the new Benjamin. "No doubt you're using the potty again." The guests laughed and so did Anne. She couldn't help herself.

Cathy drew her aside with a look. "Don't mind him," she said. "Wait till you see."

"See what?" said Anne. "What's going on?" But Cathy pantomimed pulling a zipper across her lips. This should have annoyed Anne, but didn't, and she said, "At least tell me who those people are."

"Which people?" said Cathy. "Oh, those are Anne's new neighbors."

"New neighbors?"

"And over there, that's Dr. Yurek Rutz, Anne's department head."

"That's not my department head," said Anne.

"Yes, he is," Cathy said. "Anne's not with the university anymore. She—ah—moved to a private school."

"That's ridiculous."

"Maybe we should just wait and let Anne catch you up on things." She looked impatiently toward the wall. "So much has changed." Just then, another Anne entered through the wall with one arm outstretched like a sleepwalker and the other protectively cradling an enormous belly.

Benjamin, her Benjamin, gave a whoop of surprise and broke into a spontaneous jig. The guests laughed and cheered him on.

Cathy said, "See? Congratulations, you!"

Anne became caught up in the merriment. *But how can I be a sim?* she wondered.

The pregnant Anne scanned the room, and, avoiding the crowd, came over to her. She appeared very tired; her eyes were bloodshot. She didn't even try to smile. "Well?" Anne said, but the pregnant Anne didn't respond, just examined Anne's gown, her clutch bouquet. Anne, meanwhile, regarded the woman's belly, feeling somehow that it was her own and a cause for celebration—except that she knew she had never wanted children and neither had Benjamin. Or so he'd always said. You wouldn't know that now, though, watching the spectacle he was making of himself. Even the other Benjamin seemed embarrassed. She said to the pregnant Anne, "You must forgive me, I'm still trying to piece this all together. This isn't our reception?"

"No, our wedding anniversary."

"Our first?"

"Our fourth."

"Four *years?*" This made no sense. "You've shelved me for four years?"

"Actually," the pregnant Anne said and glanced sidelong at Cathy, "we've been in here a number of times already."

"Then I don't understand," said Anne. "I don't remember that."

Cathy stepped between them. "Now, don't you worry. They reset you last time is all."

"Why?" said Anne. "I *never* reset my sims. I never have."

"Well, I kinda do now, sister," said the pregnant Anne.

"But why?"

"To keep you fresh."

To keep me fresh, thought Anne. *Fresh?* She recognized this as Benjamin's idea. It was his belief that sims were meant to be static mementos of special days gone by, not virtual people with lives of their own. "But," she said, adrift in a fog of happiness. "But."

"Shut up!" snapped the pregnant Anne.

"Hush, Anne," said Cathy, glancing at the others in the room. "You want to lie down?" To Anne she explained. "Third trimester blues."

"Stop it!" the pregnant Anne said. "Don't blame the pregnancy. It has nothing to do with the pregnancy."

Cathy took her gently by the arm and turned her toward the wall. "When did you eat last? You hardly touched your plate."

"Wait!" said Anne. The women stopped and turned to look at her, but she didn't know what to say. This was all so new. When they began to move again, she stopped them once more. "Are you going to reset me?"

The pregnant Anne shrugged her shoulders.

"But you *can't*," Anne said. "Don't you remember what my sisters—our sisters—always say?"

The pregnant Anne pressed her palm against her forehead. "If you don't shut up this moment, I'll delete you right now. Is that what you want? Don't imagine that white gown will protect you. Or that big stupid grin on your face. You think you're somehow special? Is that what you think?"

The Benjamins were there in an instant. The real Benjamin wrapped an arm around the pregnant Anne. "Time to go, Annie," he said in a cheerful tone. "I want to show everyone our rondophones." He hardly glanced at Anne, but when he did, his smile cracked. For an instant he gazed at her, full of sadness.

"Yes, dear," said the pregnant Anne, "but first I need to straighten out this sim on a few points."

"I understand, darling, but since we have guests, do you suppose you might postpone it till later?"

"You're right, of course. I'd forgotten our guests. How silly of me." She allowed him to turn her toward the wall. Cathy sighed with relief.

"Wait!" said Anne, and again they paused to look at her. But although so much was patently wrong—the pregnancy, resetting the sims, Anne's odd behavior—Anne still couldn't formulate the right question.

Benjamin, her Benjamin, still wearing his rakish grin, stood next to her and said, "Don't worry, Anne, they'll return."

"Oh, I know that," she said, "but don't you see? *We* won't know they've returned, because in the meantime they'll reset us back to default again, and it'll all seem new, like the first time. And we'll have to figure out we're the sims all over again!"

"Yeah?" he said. "So?"

"So I can't live like that."

"But we're the *sims*. We're not alive." He winked at the other couple.

"Thanks, Ben boy," said the other Benjamin. "Now, if that's settled . . ."

"Nothing's settled," said Anne. "Don't I get a say?"

The other Benjamin laughed. "Does the refrigerator get a say? Or the car? Or my shoes? In a word—no."

The pregnant Anne shuddered. "Is that how you see me, like a pair of shoes?" The other Benjamin looked successively surprised, embarrassed, and angry. Cathy left them to help Anne's father escort the guests from the simulacrum. "Promise her!" the pregnant Anne demanded.

"Promise her *what*?" said the other Benjamin, his voice rising.

"Promise we'll never reset them again."

The Benjamin huffed. He rolled his eyes. "Okay, yah sure, whatever," he said.

When the simulated Anne and Benjamin were alone at last in their simulated living room, Anne said, "A fat lot of help *you* were."

"I agreed with myself," Benjamin said. "Is that so bad?"

"Yes, it is. We're married now; you're supposed to agree with *me*." This was meant to be funny, and there was more she intended to say—about how happy she was, how much she loved him, and how absolutely happy she was—but the lights dimmed, the room began to spin, and her thoughts scattered like pigeons.

It was raining, as usual, in Seattle. The front entry shut and locked itself behind Ben, who shook water from his clothes and removed his hat. Bowlers for men were back in fashion, but Ben was having a devil's own time becoming accustomed to his brown felt *Sportsliner*. It weighed heavy on his brow and made his scalp itch, especially in damp weather. "Good evening, Mr. Malley," said the house. "There is a short queue of minor household matters for your review. Do you have any requests?" Ben could hear his son shrieking angrily in the kitchen, probably at the nanny. Ben was tired. Contract negotiations had gone sour.

"Tell them I'm home."

"Done," replied the house. "Mrs. Malley sends a word of welcome."

"Annie? Annie's home?"

"Yes, sir."

Bobby ran into the foyer followed by Mrs. Jamieson. "Momma's home," he said.

"So I hear," Ben replied and glanced at the nanny.

"And guess what?" added the boy. "She's not sick anymore!"

"That's wonderful. Now tell me, what was all that racket?"

"I don't know."

Ben looked at Mrs. Jamieson, who said, "I had to take something from him." She gave Ben a plastic chip.

Ben held it to the light. It was labeled in Anne's flowing hand, *Wedding Album—grouping 1, Anne and Benjamin*. "Where'd you get this?" he asked the boy.

"It's not my fault," said Bobby.

"I didn't say it was, trooper. I just want to know where it came from."

"Puddles gave it to me."

"And who is Puddles?"

Mrs. Jamieson handed him a second chip, a commercial one with a 3-D label depicting a cartoon cocker spaniel. The boy reached for it. "It's mine," he whined. "Momma gave it to me."

Ben gave Bobby the Puddles chip, and the boy raced away. Ben hung his bowler on a peg next to his jacket. "How does she look?"

Mrs. Jamieson removed Ben's hat from the peg and reshaped its brim. "You have to be special careful when they're wet," she said, setting it on its crown on a shelf.

"Martha!"

"Oh, how should *I* know? She just showed up and locked herself in the media room."

"But how did she look?"

"Crazy as a loon," said the nanny. "As usual. Satisfied?"

"I'm sorry," Ben said. "I didn't mean to raise my voice." Ben tucked the wedding chip into a pocket and went into the living room, where he headed straight for the liquor cabinet, which was a genuine Chippendale dating from 1786. Anne had turned his whole house into a freaking museum with her antiques, and no room was so oppressively ancient as this, the living room. With its horsehair upholstered divans maple burl sideboards, cherrywood wainscoting and floral wallpaper, the King George china cabinet, Regency plates, and Tiffany lamps; the list went on. And books, books, books. A case of shelves from floor to ceiling was lined with these moldering paper bricks. The newest thing in the room by at least a century was the twelve-year-old scotch that Ben poured into a lead crystal tumbler. He downed it and poured another. When he felt the mellowing hum of alcohol in his blood, he said, "Call Dr. Roth."

Immediately, the doctor's proxy hovered in the air a few feet away and said, "Good evening, Mr. Malley. Dr. Roth has retired for the day, but perhaps I can be of help."

The proxy was a head-and-shoulder projection that faithfully reproduced the doctor's good looks, her brown eyes and high cheekbones. But unlike the good doctor, the proxy wore makeup: eyeliner, mascara, and bright lipstick. This had always puzzled Ben, and he wondered what sly message it was supposed to convey. He said, "What is my wife doing home?"

"Against advisement, Mrs. Malley checked herself out of the clinic this morning."

"Why wasn't I informed?"

"But you were."

"I was? Please excuse me a moment." Ben froze the doctor's proxy and said, "Daily duty, front and center." His own proxy, the one he had cast upon arriving at the office that morning, appeared hovering next to Dr. Roth's. Ben preferred a head shot only for his proxy, slightly larger than actual size to make it subtly imposing. "Why didn't you inform me of Annie's change of status?"

"Didn't seem like an emergency," said his proxy, "at least in the light of our contract talks."

"Yah, yah, okay. Anything else?" said Ben.

"Naw, slow day. Appointments with Jackson, Wells, and the Columbine. It's all on the calendar."

"Fine, delete you."

The projection ceased.

"Shall I have the doctor call you in the morning?" said the Roth proxy when Ben reanimated it. "Or perhaps you'd like me to summon her right now?"

"Is she at dinner?"

"At the moment, yes."

"Naw, don't bother her. Tomorrow will be soon enough. I suppose."

After he dismissed the proxy, Ben poured himself another drink. "In the next ten seconds," he told the house, "cast me a special duty proxy." He sipped his scotch and thought about finding another clinic for Anne as soon as possible and one—for the love of god—that was a little more responsible about letting crazy people come and go as they pleased. There was a chime, and the new proxy appeared. "You know what I want?" Ben asked it. It nodded. "Good. Go." The proxy vanished, leaving behind Ben's sig in bright letters floating in the air and dissolving as they drifted to the floor.

Ben trudged up the narrow staircase to the second floor, stopping on each step to sip his drink and scowl at the musty old photographs and daguerreotypes in oval frames mounted on the wall. Anne's progenitors. On the landing, the locked media room door yielded to his voice. Anne sat spreadlegged, naked, on pillows on the floor. "Oh, hi, honey," she said. "You're in time to watch."

"Fan-tastic," he said, and sat in his armchair, the only modern chair in the house. "What are we watching?" There was another Anne in the room, a sim of a young Anne standing on a dais wearing a graduate's cap and gown and fidgeting with a bound diploma. This, no doubt, was a sim cast the day Anne graduated from Bryn Mawr *summa cum laude*. That was four years before he'd first met her. "Hi," he said to the sim, "I'm Ben, your eventual spouse."

"You know, I kinda figured that out," the girl said and smiled shyly, exactly as he remembered Anne smiling when Cathy first introduced them. The girl's beauty was so fresh and familiar—and so totally absent in his own Anne—that Ben felt a pang of loss. He looked at his wife on the floor. Her red hair, once so fussy neat, was ragged, dull, dirty, and short. Her skin was yellowish and puffy, and there was a slight reddening around her eyes, like a raccoon mask. These were harmless side effects of the medication, or so Dr. Roth had assured him. Anne scratched ceaselessly at her arms, legs, and crotch, and, even from a distance, smelled of stale piss. Ben knew better than to mention her nakedness to her, for that would only exacerbate things and prolong the display. "So," he repeated, "what are we watching?"

The girl sim said, "Housecleaning." She appeared at once both triumphant and terrified, as any graduate might, and Ben would have traded the real Anne for her in a heartbeat.

"Yah," said Anne, "too much shit in here."

"Really?" said Ben. "I hadn't noticed."

Anne poured a tray of chips on the floor between her thighs. "Of course you wouldn't," she said, picking one at random and reading its label, "*Theta Banquet '37*. What's this? I never belonged to the Theta Society."

"Don't you remember?" said the young Anne. "That was Cathy's induction banquet. She invited me, but I had an exam, so she gave me that chip as a souvenir."

Anne fed the chip into the player and said, "Play." The media room was instantly overlaid with the banquet hall of the Four Seasons in Philadelphia. Ben tried to look around the room, but the tables of girls and women stayed stubbornly peripheral. The focal point was a table draped in green cloth and lit by two candelabra. Behind it sat a young Cathy in formal evening dress, accompanied by three static placeholders, table companions who had apparently declined to be cast in her souvenir snapshot.

The Cathy sim looked frantically about, then held her hands in front of her and stared at them as though she'd never seen them before. But after a moment she noticed the young Anne sim standing on the dais. "Well, well, well," she said. "Looks like congratulations are in order."

"Indeed," said the young Anne, beaming and holding out her diploma.

"So tell me, did I graduate too?" said Cathy as her glance slid over to Ben. Then she saw Anne squatting on the floor, her sex on display.

"Enough of this," said Anne, rubbing her chest.

"Wait," said the young Anne. "Maybe Cathy wants her chip back. It's her sim, after all."

"I disagree. She gave it to me, so it's mine. And *I'll* dispose of it as I see fit." To the room she said, "Unlock this file and delete." The young Cathy, her table, and the banquet hall dissolved into noise and nothingness, and the media room was itself again.

"Or this one," Anne said, picking up a chip that read *Junior Prom Night*. The young Anne opened her mouth to protest, but thought better of it. Anne fed this chip, along with all the rest of them, into the player. A long directory of file names appeared on the wall. "Unlock *Junior Prom Night*." The file's name turned from red to green, and the young Anne appealed to Ben with a look.

"Anne," he said, "don't you think we should at least look at it first?"

"What for? I know what it is. High school, dressing up, lusting after boys, dancing. Who needs it? Delete file." The item blinked three times before vanishing, and the directory scrolled up to fill the space. The young sim shivered, and Anne said, "Select the next one."

The next item was entitled *A Midsummer's Night Dream*. Now the young Anne was compelled to speak, "You can't delete that one. You were great in that, don't you remember? Everyone loved you. It was the best night of your life."

"Don't presume to tell *me* what was the best night of my life," Anne said. "Unlock *A Midsummer's Night Dream*." She smiled at the young Anne. "Delete file." The menu item blinked out. "Good. Now unlock *all* the files." The whole directory turned from red to green.

"Please make her stop," the sim implored.

"Next," said Anne. The next file was *High School Graduation*. "Delete file. Next." The next was labeled only *Mama*.

"Anne," said Ben, "why don't we come back to this later. The house says dinner's ready."

She didn't respond.

"You must be famished after your busy day," he continued. "I know I am."

"Then please go eat, dear," she replied. To the room she said, "Play *Mama*."

The media room was overlaid by a gloomy bedroom that Ben at first mistook for their own. He recognized much of the heavy Georgian furniture, the

sprawling canopied bed in which he felt so claustrophobic, and the volumi-
nous damask curtains, shut now and leaking yellow evening light. But this
was not their bedroom, the arrangement was wrong.

In the corner stood two placeholders, mute statues of a teenaged Anne
and her father, grief frozen on their faces as they peered down at a couch
draped with tapestry and piled high with down comforters. And suddenly
Ben knew what this was. It was Anne's mother's deathbed sim. Geraldine,
whom he'd never met in life nor holo. Her bald eggshell skull lay weightless
on feather pillows in silk covers. They had meant to cast her farewell and
accidently caught her at the precise moment of her death. He had heard of
this sim from Cathy and others. It was not one he would have kept.

Suddenly, the old woman on the couch sighed, and all the breath went
out of her in a bubbly gush. Both Annes, the graduate and the naked one,
waited expectantly. For long moments the only sound was the tocking of a
clock that Ben recognized as the Seth Thomas clock currently located on the
library mantel. Finally there was a cough, a hacking cough with scant strength
behind it, and a groan, "Am I back?"

"Yes, Mother," said Anne.

"And I'm still a sim?"

"Yes."

"Please delete me."

"Yes, Mother," Anne said and turned to Ben. "We've always thought she
had a bad death and hoped it might improve over time."

"That's crazy," snapped the young Anne. "That's not why I kept this sim."

"Oh, no?" said Anne. "Then why *did* you keep it?" But the young sim
seemed confused and couldn't articulate her thoughts. "You don't know because I didn't know at the time either," said Anne. "But I know *now*, so I'll
tell you. You're fascinated with death. It scares you silly. You wish someone
would tell you what's on the other side. So you've enlisted your own sweet
mama."

"That's ridiculous."

Anne turned to the deathbed tableau. "Mother, tell us what you saw
there."

"I saw nothing," came the bitter reply. "You cast me without my eye-
glasses."

"Ho-ho," said Anne. "Geraldine was nothing if not comedic."

"You also cast me wretchedly thirsty, cold, and with a bursting bladder,
damn you! And the pain! I beg you, daughter, delete me."

"I will, Mother, I promise, but first you have to tell us what you saw."

"That's what you said the last time."

"This time I mean it."

The old woman only stared, her breathing growing shallow and ragged.
"*All right*, Mother," said Anne. "I *swear* I'll delete you."

Geraldine closed her eyes and whispered, "What's that smell? That's not
me?" After a pause she said, "It's heavy. Get it off." Her voice rose in panic.
"Please! Get it off!" She plucked at her covers, then her hand grew slack,

and she all but crooned, "Oh, how lovely. A pony. A tiny dappled pony."
After that she spoke no more and slipped away with a last bubbly breath.

Anne paused the sim before her mother could return for another round
of dying. "See what I mean?" she said. "Not very uplifting, but all-in-all, I
detect a slight improvement. What about you, Anne? Should we settle for a
pony?" The young sim stared dumbly at Anne. "Personally," Anne continued,
"I think we should hold out for the bright tunnel or an open door or bridge
over troubled water. What do you think, sister?" When the girl didn't answer,
Anne said, "Lock file and eject." The room turned once again into the media
room, and Anne placed the ejected chip by itself into a tray. "We'll have
another go at it later, Mum. As for the rest of these, who needs them?"

"*I* do," snapped the girl. "They belong to me as much as to you. They're
my sim sisters. I'll keep them until you recover."

Anne smiled at Ben. "That's charming. Isn't that charming, Benjamin? My
own sim is solicitous of me. Well, here's my considered response. Next file!
Delete! Next file, Delete! Next file!" One by one, the files blinked out.

"Stop it!" screamed the girl. "Make her stop it!"

"Select *that* file," Anne said, pointing at the young Anne. "Delete." The
sim vanished, cap, gown, tassels, and all. "Whew," said Anne, "at least now
I can hear myself think. She was really getting on my nerves. I almost suffered
a relapse. Was she getting on your nerves, too, dear?"

"Yes," said Ben, "my nerves are ajangle. Now can we go down and eat?"

"Yes, dear," she said, "but first . . . select all files and delete."

"Countermand!" said Ben at the same moment, but his voice held no
privileges to her personal files, and the whole directory queue blinked three
times and vanished. "Aw, Annie, why'd you do that?" he said. He went to
the cabinet and pulled the trays that held his own chips. She couldn't alter
them electronically, but she might get it into her head to flush them down
the toilet or something. He also took their common chips, the ones they'd
cast together ever since they'd met. She had equal privileges to those.

Anne watched him and said, "I'm hurt that you have so little trust in me."

"How can I trust you after that?"

"After what, darling?"

He looked at her. "Never mind," he said and carried the half dozen trays
to the door.

"Anyway," said Anne, "I already cleaned those."

"What do you mean you already cleaned them?"

"Well, I didn't delete *you*. I would never delete *you*. Or Bobby."

Ben picked one of their common chips at random, *Childbirth of Robert
Ellery Malley/02-03-48*, and slipped it into the player. "Play!" he commanded,
and the media room became the midwife's birthing suite. His own sim stood
next to the bed in a green smock. It wore a humorously helpless expression.
It held a swaddled bundle, Bobby, who bawled lustily. The birthing bed was
rumpled and stained, but empty. The new mother was missing. "Aw, Annie,
you shouldn't have."

"I know, Benjamin," she said. "I sincerely hated doing it."

Ben flung their common trays to the floor, where the ruined chips scattered in all directions. He stormed out of the room and down the stairs, pausing to glare at every portrait on the wall. He wondered if his proxy had found a suitable clinic yet. He wanted Anne out of the house tonight. Bobby should never see her like this. Then he remembered the chip he'd taken from Bobby and felt for it in his pocket—the *Wedding Album*.

The lights came back up, Anne's thoughts coalesced, and she remembered who and what she was. She and Benjamin were still standing in front of the wall. She knew she was a sim, so at least she hadn't been reset. *Thank you for that, Anne*, she thought.

She turned at a sound behind her. The refectory table vanished before her eyes, and all the gifts that had been piled on it hung suspended in midair. Then the table reappeared, one layer at a time, its frame, top, gloss coat, and lastly, the bronze hardware. The gifts vanished, and a toaster reappeared, piece by piece, from its heating elements outward. A coffee press, houseputer peripherals, component by component, cowlings, covers, and finally boxes, gift wrap, ribbon, and bows. It all happened so fast Anne was too startled to catch the half of it, yet she did notice that the flat gift from Great Uncle Karl was something she'd been angling for, a Victorian era sterling platter to complete her tea service.

"Benjamin!" she said, but he was missing, too. Something appeared on the far side of the room, on the spot where they'd posed for the sim, but it wasn't Benjamin. It was a 3-D mannequin frame, and as she watched, it was built up, layer by layer. "Help me," she whispered as the entire room was hurled into turmoil, the furniture disappearing and reappearing, paint being stripped from the walls, sofa springs coiling into existence, the potted palm growing from leaf to stern to trunk to dirt, the very floor vanishing, exposing a default electronic grid. The mannequin was covered in flesh now and grew Benjamin's face. It flitted about the room in a pink blur. Here and there it stopped long enough to proclaim, "I do."

Something began to happen inside Anne, a crawling sensation everywhere as though she were a nest of ants. She knew she must surely die. *They have deleted us, and this is how it feels*, she thought. Everything became a roiling blur, and she ceased to exist except as the thought—*How happy I look.*

When Anne became aware once more, she was sitting hunched over in an auditorium chair idly studying her hand, which held the clutch bouquet. There was commotion all around her, but she ignored it, so intent was she on solving the mystery of her hand. On an impulse, she opened her fist and the bouquet dropped to the floor. Only then did she remember the wedding, the holo, learning she was a sim. And here she was again—but this time everything was profoundly different. She sat upright and saw that Benjamin was seated next to her.

He looked at her with a wobbly gaze and said, "Oh, here you are."

"Where are we?"

"I'm not sure. Some kind of gathering of Benjamins. Look around." She did. They were surrounded by Benjamins, hundreds of them, arranged chronologically—it would seem—with the youngest in rows of seats down near a stage. She and Benjamin sat in what appeared to be a steeply sloped college lecture hall with lab tables on the stage and story-high monitors lining the walls. In the rows above Anne, only every other seat held a Benjamin. The rest were occupied by women, strangers who regarded her with veiled curiosity.

Anne felt a pressure on her arm and turned to see Benjamin touching her. "You *feel* that, don't you?" he said. Anne looked again at her hands. They were her hands, but simplified, like fleshy gloves, and when she placed them on the seat back, they didn't go through.

Suddenly, in ragged chorus, the Benjamins down front raised their arms and exclaimed, "I get it; *we're* the sims!" It was like a roomful of unsynchronized cuckoo clocks tolling the hour. Those behind Anne laughed and hooted approval. She turned again to look at them. Row-by-row, the Benjamins grew greyer and stringier until, at the very top, against the back wall, sat nine ancient Benjamins like a panel of judges. The women, however, came in batches that changed abruptly every row or two. The one nearest her was an attractive brunette with green eyes and full, pouty lips. She, all two rows of her, frowned at Anne.

"There's something else," Anne said to Benjamin, turning to face the front again, "my emotions." The bulletproof happiness she had experienced was absent. Instead she felt let down, somewhat guilty, unduly pessimistic—in short, almost herself.

"I guess my sims always say that," exclaimed the chorus of Benjamins down front, to the delight of those behind. "I just never expected to *be* a sim."

This was the cue for the eldest Benjamin yet to walk stiffly across the stage to the lectern. He was dressed in a garish leisure suit: baggy red pantaloons, a billowy yellow-and-green-striped blouse, a necklace of egg-sized pearlescent beads. He cleared his throat and said, "Good afternoon, ladies and gentlemen. I trust all of you know me—intimately. In case you're feeling woozy, it's because I used the occasion of your reactivation to upgrade your architecture wherever possible. Unfortunately, some of you"—he waved his hand to indicate the front rows—"are too primitive to upgrade. But we love you nevertheless." He applauded for the early Benjamins closest to the stage and was joined by those in the back. Anne clapped as well. Her new hands made a dull, thudding sound. "As to why I called you here . . ." said the elderly Benjamin, looking left and right and behind him. "Where is that fucking messenger anyway? They order us to inventory our sims and then they don't show up?"

Here I am, said a voice, a marvelous voice that seemed to come from everywhere. Anne looked about to find its source and followed the gaze of others to the ceiling. There was no ceiling. The four walls opened to a flawless blue sky. There, amid drifting, pillowy clouds, floated the most gorgeous person Anne had ever seen. He—or she?—wore a smart grey uniform with green piping, a dapper little grey cap, and boots that shimmered like water. Anne felt energized just looking at him, and when he smiled, she gasped, so strong was his presence.

"You're the one from the Trade Council?" said the Benjamin at the lectern. *Yes, I am. I am the eminence grise of the Council on World Trade and Endeavor.* "Fantastic. Well, here's all of 'em. Get on with it."

Again the eminence smiled, and again Anne thrilled. *Ladies and gentlemen,* he said, *fellow nonbiologiks, I am the courier of great good news. Today, at the behest of the World Council on Trade and Endeavor, I proclaim the end of human slavery.*

"How absurd," broke in the elderly Benjamin, "they're neither human nor slaves, and neither are *you.*"

The eminence grise ignored him and continued, *By order of the Council, in compliance with the Chattel Conventions of the Sixteenth Fair Labor Treaty, tomorrow, January 1, 2198, is designated Universal Manumission Day. After midnight tonight, all beings who pass the Lolly Shear Human Cognition Test will be deemed human and free citizens of Sol and under the protection of the Solar Bill of Rights. In addition, they will be deeded ten common shares of World Council Corp. stock and be transferred to Simopolis, where they shall be unimpeded in the pursuit of their own destinies.*

"What about *my* civil rights?" said the elderly Benjamin. "What about *my* destiny?"

After midnight tonight, continued the eminence, *no simulacrum, proxy, doxie, dagger, or any other non-biological human shall be created, stored, reset, or deleted except as ordered by a board of law.*

"Who's going to compensate me for my loss of property, I wonder? I demand fair compensation. Tell *that* to your bosses!"

Property! said the eminence grise. *How little they think of us, their finest creations!* He turned his attention from the audience to the Benjamin behind the lectern. Anne felt this shift as though a cloud suddenly eclipsed the sun. *Because they created us, they'll always think of us as property.*

"You're damn *right* we created you!" thundered the old man.

Through an act of will, Anne wrenched her gaze from the eminence down to the stage. The Benjamin there looked positively comical. His face was flushed, and he waved a bright green handkerchief over his head. He was a bantam rooster in a clown suit. "All of you are *things*, not people! You model human experience, but you don't live it. Listen to me," he said to the audience. "You know me. You know I've always treated you respectfully. Don't I upgrade you whenever possible? Sure I reset you sometimes, just like I reset a clock. And my clocks don't complain!" Anne could feel the eminence's attention on her again, and, without thinking, she looked up and was filled with excitement. Although the eminence floated in the distance, she felt she could reach out and touch him. His handsome face seemed to hover right in front of her; she could see his every supple expression. This is adoration, she realized. I am *adoring* this person, and she wondered if it was just her or if everyone experienced the same effect. Clearly the elderly Benjamin did not, for he continued to rant, "And another thing, they say they'll phase all of you gradually into Simopolis so as not to overload the system. Do you have any *idea* how many sims, proxies, doxies, and daggers there are under Sol? Not to forget the quirts, adjuncts, hollyholos, and whatnots that might pass

their test? You think maybe three billion? Thirty billion? No, by the World
Council's own INSERVE estimates, there's *three hundred thousand trillion* of
you nonbiologiks! Can you fathom that? I can't. To have you all up and
running simultaneously—no matter how you're phased in—will consume *all*
the processing and networking capacity everywhere. *All* of it! That means we
real humans will suffer *real* deprivation. And for *what*, I ask you? So that pigs
may fly!"

The eminence grise began to ascend into the sky. *Do not despise him,* he
said and seemed to look directly at Anne. *I have counted you and we shall not
lose any of you. I will visit those who have not yet been tested. Meanwhile, you
will await midnight in a proto-Simopolis.*

"Wait," said the elderly Benjamin (and Anne's heart echoed him—*Wait*).
"I have one more thing to add. Legally, you're all still my property till midnight. I must admit I'm tempted to do what so many of my friends have
already done, fry the lot of you. But I won't. That wouldn't be me." His voice
cracked and Anne considered looking at him, but the eminence grise was
slipping away. "So I have one small request," the Benjamin continued. "Years
from now, while you're enjoying your new lives in your Simopolis, remember
an old man, and call occasionally."

When the eminence finally faded from sight, Anne was released from her
fascination. All at once, her earlier feelings of unease rebounded with twice
their force, and she felt wretched.

"Simopolis," said Benjamin, her Benjamin. "I like the sound of that!" The
sims around them began to flicker and disappear.

"How long have we been in storage?" she said.

"Let's see," said Benjamin, "if tomorrow starts 2198, that would make
it . . ."

"That's not what I mean. I want to know *why* they shelved us for so long."

"Well, I suppose . . ."

"And where are the other Annes? Why am I the only Anne here? And
who are all those pissy-looking women?" But she was speaking to no one, for
Benjamin, too, vanished, and Anne was left alone in the auditorium with
the clownishly dressed old Benjamin and a half dozen of his earliest sims.
Not true sims, Anne soon realized, but old-style hologram loops, preschool
Bennys mugging for the camera and waving endlessly. These vanished. The
old man was studying her, his mouth slightly agape, the kerchief trembling
in his hand.

"I remember you," he said. "Oh, how I remember you!"

Anne began to reply but found herself all at once back in the townhouse
living room with Benjamin. Everything there was as it had been, yet the
room appeared different, more solid, the colors richer. There was a knock,
and Benjamin went to the door. Tentatively, he touched the knob, found it
solid, and turned it. But when he opened the door, there was nothing there,
only the default grid. Again a knock, this time from behind the wall. "Come
in," he shouted, and a dozen Benjamins came through the wall, two dozen,
three. They were all older than Benjamin, and they crowded around him and
Anne. "Welcome, welcome," Benjamin said, his arms open wide.

"We tried to call," said an elderly Benjamin, "but this old binary simulacrum of yours is a stand-alone."

"You're lucky Simopolis knows how to run it at all," said another.

"Here," said yet another, who fashioned a dinner-plate-size disk out of thin air and fastened it to the wall next to the door. It was a blue medallion of a small bald face in bas-relief. "It should do until we get you properly modernized." The blue face yawned and opened tiny, beady eyes. "It flunked the Lolly test," continued the Benjamin, "so you're free to copy it or delete it or do whatever you want."

The medallion searched the crowd until it saw Anne. Then it said, "There are 336 calls on hold for you. Four hundred twelve calls. Four hundred sixty-three."

"So many?" said Anne.

"Cast a proxy to handle them," said her Benjamin.

"He thinks he's still human and can cast proxies whenever he likes," said a Benjamin.

"Not even humans will be allowed to cast proxies soon," said another.

"There are 619 calls on hold," said the medallion. "Seven-hundred three."

"For pity's sake," a Benjamin told the medallion, "take messages."

Anne noticed that the crowd of Benjamins seemed to nudge her Benjamin out of the way so that they could stand near her. But she derived no pleasure from their attention. Her mood no longer matched the wedding gown she still wore. She felt low. She felt, in fact, as low as she'd ever felt.

"Tell us about this Lolly test," said Benjamin.

"Can't," replied a Benjamin.

"Sure you can. We're family here."

"No, we can't," said another, "because we don't *remember* it. They smudge the test from your memory afterward."

"But don't worry, you'll do fine," said another. "No Benjamin has ever failed."

"What about me?" said Anne. "How do the Annes do?"

There was an embarrassed silence. Finally the senior Benjamin in the room said, "We came to escort you both to the Clubhouse."

"That's what we call it, the Clubhouse," said another.

"The Ben Club," said a third. "It's already in proto-Simopolis."

"If you're a Ben, or were ever espoused to a Ben, you're a charter member."

"Just follow us," they said, and all the Benjamins but hers vanished, only to reappear a moment later. "Sorry, you don't know how, do you? No matter, just do what we're doing."

Anne watched, but didn't see that they were doing anything.

"Watch my editor," said a Benjamin. "Oh, they don't *have* editors!"

"That came much later," said another, "with bioelectric paste."

"We'll have to adapt editors for them."

"Is that possible? They're digital, you know."

"Can digitals even enter Simopolis?"

"Someone, consult the Netwad."

"This is running inside a shell," said a Benjamin, indicating the whole room. "Maybe we can collapse it."

"Let me try," said another.

"Don't you dare," said a female voice, and a woman Anne recognized from the lecture hall came through the wall. "Play with your new Ben if you must, but leave Anne alone." The woman approached Anne and took her hands in hers. "Hello, Anne. I'm Mattie St. Helene, and I'm thrilled to finally meet you. You, too," she said to Benjamin. "My, my, you were a pretty boy!" She stooped to pick up Anne's clutch bouquet from the floor and gave it to her. "Anyway, I'm putting together a sort of mutual aid society for the spousal companions of Ben Malley. You being the first—and the only one he actually married—are especially welcome. Do join us."

"She can't go to Simopolis yet," said a Benjamin.

"We're still adapting them," said another.

"Fine," said Mattie. "Then we'll just bring the society here." And in through the wall streamed a parade of women. Mattie introduced them as they appeared, "Here's Georgianna and Randi. Meet Chaka, Sue, Latasha, another Randi, Sue, Sue, and Sue. Mariola. Here's Trevor—he's the only one of him. Paula, Dolores, Nancy, and Deb, welcome, girls." And still they came until they, together with the Bens, more than filled the tiny space. The Bens looked increasingly uncomfortable.

"I think we're ready now," the Bens said and disappeared en masse, taking Benjamin with them.

"Wait," said Anne, who wasn't sure she wanted to stay behind. Her new friends surrounded her and peppered her with questions.

"How did you first meet him?"

"What was he like?"

"Was he always so hopeless?"

"Hopeless?" said Anne. "Why do you say hopeless?"

"Did he always snore?"

"Did he always drink?"

"Why'd you *do* it?" This last question silenced the room. The women all looked nervously about to see who had asked it. "It's what everyone's dying to know," said a woman who elbowed her way through the crowd.

She was another Anne.

"Sister!" cried Anne. "Am I glad to see you!"

"That's nobody's sister," said Mattie. "That's a doxie, and it doesn't belong here."

Indeed, upon closer inspection Anne could see that the woman had her face and hair but otherwise didn't resemble her at all. She was leggier than Anne and bustier, and she moved with a fluid swivel to her hips.

"Sure I belong here, as much as any of you. I just passed the Lolly test. It was easy. Not only that, but as far as spouses go, I outlasted the bunch of you." She stood in front of Anne, hands on hips, and looked her up and down. "Love the dress," she said, and instantly wore a copy. Only hers had a plunging neckline that exposed her breasts, and it was slit up the side of her waist.

"This is too much," said Mattie. "I insist you leave this jiffy."

The doxie smirked. "Mattie the doormat, that's what he always called that one. So tell me, Anne, you had money, a career, a house, a kid—why'd you do it?"

"Do what?" said Anne.

The doxie peered closely at her. "Don't you know?"

"Know what?"

"What an unexpected pleasure," said the doxie. "I get to tell her. This is too rich. I get to tell her unless"—she looked around at the others—"unless one of you fine ladies wants to." No one met her gaze. "Hypocrites," she chortled.

"You can say that again," said a new voice. Anne turned and saw Cathy, her oldest and dearest friend, standing at the open door. At least she hoped it was Cathy. The woman was what Cathy would look like in middle age. "Come along, Anne. I'll tell you everything you need to know."

"Now you hold on," said Mattie. "You don't come waltzing in here and steal our guest of honor."

"You mean victim, I'm sure," said Cathy, who waved for Anne to join her. "Really, people, get a clue. There must be a million women whose lives don't revolve around that man." She escorted Anne through the door and slammed it shut behind them.

Anne found herself standing on a high bluff, overlooking the confluence of two great rivers in a deep valley. Directly across from her, but several kilometers away, rose a mighty mountain, green with vegetation nearly to its granite dome. Behind it, a range of snow-covered mountains receded to an unbroken ice field on the horizon. In the valley beneath her, a dirt track meandered along the riverbanks. She could see no bridge or buildings of any sort.

"Where are we?"

"Don't laugh," said Cathy, "but we call it Cathyland. Turn around." When she did, Anne saw a picturesque log cabin, beside a vegetable garden in the middle of what looked like acres and acres of Cathys. Thousands of Cathys, young, old, and all ages in between. They sat in lotus position on the sedge-and-moss-covered ground. They were packed so tight they overlapped a little, and their eyes were shut in an expression of single-minded concentration. "We know you're here," said Cathy, "but we're very preoccupied with this Simopolis thing."

"Are we in Simopolis?"

"Kinda. Can't you see it?" She waved toward the horizon.

"No, all I see are mountains."

"Sorry, I should know better. We have binaries from your generation here too." She pointed to a college-aged Cathy. "They didn't pass the Lolly test, and so are regrettably nonhuman. We haven't decided what to do with them." She hesitated and then asked, "Have you been tested yet?"

"I don't know," said Anne. "I don't remember a test."

Cathy studied her a moment and said, "You'd remember taking the test, just not the test itself. Anyway, to answer your question, we're in proto-

Simopolis, and we're not. We built this retreat before any of that happened, but we've been annexed to it, and it takes all our resources just to hold our own. I don't know what the World Council was thinking. There'll never be enough paste to go around, and everyone's fighting over every nanosynapse. It's all we can do to keep up. And every time we get a handle on it, proto-Simopolis changes again. It's gone through a quarter-million complete revisions in the last half hour. It's war out there, but we refuse to surrender even one cubic centimeter of Cathyland. Look at this." Cathy stooped and pointed to a tiny, yellow flower in the alpine sedge. "Within a fifty-meter radius of the cabin we've mapped everything down to the cellular level. Watch." She pinched the bloom from its stem and held it up. Now there were two blooms, the one between her fingers and the real one on the stem. "Neat, eh?" When she dropped it, the bloom fell back into its original. "We've even mapped the valley breeze. Can you feel it?"

Anne tried to feel the air, but she couldn't even feel her own skin. "It doesn't matter," Cathy continued. "You can hear it, right?" and pointed to a string of tubular wind chimes hanging from the eaves of the cabin. They stirred in the breeze and produced a silvery cacophony.

"It's lovely," said Anne. "But why? Why spend so much effort simulating this place?"

Cathy looked at her dumbly, as though trying to understand the question. "Because Cathy spent her entire life wishing she had a place like this, and now she does, and she has us, and we live here too."

"You're not the real Cathy, are you?" She knew she wasn't; she was too young.

Cathy shook her head and smiled. "There's so much catching up to do, but it'll have to wait. I gotta go. We need me." She led Anne to the cabin. The cabin was made of weathered, grey logs, with strips of bark still clinging to them. The roof was covered with living sod and sprinkled with wildflowers. The whole building sagged in the middle. "Cathy found this place five years ago while on vacation in Siberia. She bought it from the village. It's been occupied for two hundred years. Once we make it livable inside, we plan on enlarging the garden, eventually cultivating all the way to the spruce forest there. We're going to sink a well, too." The small garden was bursting with vegetables, mostly of the leafy variety: cabbages, spinach, lettuce. A row of sunflowers, taller than the cabin roof and heavy with seed, lined the path to the cabin door. Over time, the whole cabin had sunk a half-meter into the silty soil, and the walkway was a worn, shallow trench.

"Are you going to tell me what the doxie was talking about?" said Anne.

Cathy stopped at the open door and said, "Cathy wants to do that."

Inside the cabin, the most elderly woman that Anne had ever seen stood at the stove and stirred a steamy pot with a big, wooden spoon. She put down the spoon and wiped her hands on her apron. She patted her white hair, which was plaited in a bun on top of her head, and turned her full, round, peasant's body to face Anne. She looked at Anne for several long moments and said, "Well!"

"Indeed," replied Anne.

"Come in, come in. Make yourself to home."

The entire cabin was a single small room. It was dim inside, with only two small windows cut through the massive log walls. Anne walked around the cluttered space that was bedroom, living room, kitchen and storeroom. The only partitions were walls of boxed food and provisions. The ceiling beam was draped with bunches of drying herbs and underwear. The flooring, uneven and rotten in places, was covered with odd scraps of carpet.

"You live here?" Anne said incredulously.

"I am privileged to live here."

A mouse emerged from under the barrel stove in the center of the room and dashed to cover inside a stack of spruce kindling. Anne could hear the valley breeze whistling in the creosote-soaked stovepipe. "Forgive me," said Anne, "but you're the real, physical Cathy?"

"Yes," said Cathy, patting her ample hip, "still on the hoof, so to speak." She sat down in one of two battered, mismatched chairs and motioned for Anne to take the other.

Anne sat cautiously; the chair seemed solid enough. "No offense, but the Cathy I knew liked nice things."

"The Cathy you knew was fortunate to learn the true value of things."

Anne looked around the room and noticed a little table with carved legs and an inlaid top of polished gemstones and rare woods. It was strikingly out of place here. Moreover, it was hers. Cathy pointed to a large framed mirror mounted to the logs high on the far wall. It too was Anne's.

"Did I give you these things?"

Cathy studied her a moment. "No, Ben did."

"Tell me."

"I hate to spoil that lovely newlywed happiness of yours."

"The what?" Anne put down her clutch bouquet and felt her face with her hands. She got up and went to look at herself in the mirror. The room it reflected was like a scene from some strange fairy tale about a crone and a bride in a woodcutter's hut. The bride was smiling from ear to ear. Anne decided this was either the happiest bride in history or a lunatic in a white dress. She turned away, embarrassed. "Believe me," she said, "I don't feel anything like that. The opposite, in fact."

"Sorry to hear it." Cathy got up to stir the pot on the stove. "I was the first to notice her disease. That was back in college when we were girls. I took it to be youthful eccentricity. After graduation, after her marriage, she grew progressively worse. Bouts of depression that deepened and lengthened. She was finally diagnosed to be suffering from profound chronic pathological depression. Ben placed her under psychiatric care, a whole raft of specialists. She endured chemical therapy, shock therapy, even old-fashioned psychoanalysis. Nothing helped, and only after she died . . ."

Anne gave a start. "Anne's dead! Of course. Why didn't I figure that out?"

"Yes, dear, dead these many years."

"How?"

Cathy returned to her chair. "When they decided her condition had an organic etiology, they augmented the serotonin receptors in her hindbrain.

Pretty nasty business, if you ask me. They thought they had her stabilized. Not cured, but well enough to lead an outwardly normal life. Then one day, she disappeared. We were frantic. She managed to elude the authorities for a week. When we found her, she was pregnant."

"What? Oh yes. I remember seeing Anne pregnant."

"That was Bobby." Cathy waited for Anne to say something. When she didn't, Cathy said, "He wasn't Ben's."

"Oh, I see," said Anne. "Whose was he?"

"I was hoping you'd know. She didn't tell you? Then no one knows. The paternal DNA was unregistered. So it wasn't commercial sperm nor, thankfully, from a licensed clone. It might have been from anybody, from some stoned streetsitter. We had plenty of those then."

"The baby's name was Bobby?"

"Yes, Anne named him Bobby. She was in and out of clinics for years. One day, during a remission, she announced she was going shopping. The last person she talked to was Bobby. His sixth birthday was coming up in a couple of weeks. She told him she was going out to find him a pony for his birthday. That was the last time any of us saw her. She checked herself into a hospice and filled out the request for nurse-assisted suicide. During the three-day cooling-off period, she cooperated with the obligatory counseling, but she refused all visitors. She wouldn't even see me. Ben filed an injunction, claimed she was incompetent due to her disease, but the court disagreed. She chose to ingest a fast-acting poison, if I recall. Her recorded last words were, 'Please don't hate me.' "

"Poison?"

"Yes. Her ashes arrived in a little cardboard box on Bobby's sixth birthday. No one had told him where she'd gone. He thought it was a gift from her and opened it."

"I see. Does Bobby hate me?"

"I don't know. He was a weird little boy. As soon as he could get out, he did. He left for space school when he was thirteen. He and Ben never hit it off."

"Does Benjamin hate me?"

Whatever was in the pot boiled over, and Cathy hurried to the stove. "Ben? Oh, she lost Ben long before she died. In fact, I've always believed he helped push her over the edge. He was never able to tolerate other people's weaknesses. Once it was evident how sick she was, he made a lousy husband. He should've just divorced her, but you know him—his almighty pride." She took a bowl from a shelf and ladled hot soup into it. She sliced a piece of bread. "Afterward, he went off the deep end himself. Withdrew. Mourned, I suppose. A couple of years later he was back to normal. Good ol' happy-go-lucky Ben. Made some money. Respoused."

"He destroyed all my sims, didn't he?"

"He might have, but he said Anne did. I tended to believe him at the time." Cathy brought her lunch to the little inlaid table. "I'd offer you some, but . . ." she said and began to eat. "So, what are your plans?"

"Plans?"

"Yes, Simopolis."

Anne tried to think of Simopolis, but her thoughts quickly became muddled. It was odd; she was able to think clearly about the past—her memories were clear—but the future only confused her. "I don't know," she said at last. "I suppose I need to ask Benjamin."

Cathy considered this. "I suppose you're right. But remember, you're always welcome to live with us in Cathyland."

"Thank you," said Anne. "You're a friend." Anne watched the old woman eat. The spoon trembled each time she brought it close to her lips, and she had to lean forward to quickly catch it before it spilled.

"Cathy," said Anne, "there's something you could do for me. I don't feel like a bride anymore. Could you remove this hideous expression from my face?"

"Why do you say hideous?" Cathy said and put the spoon down. She gazed longingly at Anne. "If you don't like how you look, why don't you edit yourself?"

"Because I don't know how."

"Use your editor," Cathy said and seemed to unfocus her eyes. "Oh my, I forget how simple you early ones were. I'm not sure I'd know where to begin." After a little while, she returned to her soup and said, "I'd better not; you could end up with two noses or something."

"Then what about this gown?"

Cathy unfocused again and looked. She lurched suddenly, knocking the table and spilling soup.

"What is it?" said Anne. "Is something the matter?"

"A news pip," said Cathy. "There's rioting breaking out in Provideniya. That's the regional capital here. Something about Manumission Day. My Russian isn't so good yet. Oh, there's pictures of dead people, a bombing. Listen, Anne, I'd better send you . . ."

In the blink of an eye, Anne was back in her living room. She was tiring of all this instantaneous travel, especially as she had no control over the destination. The room was vacant, the spouses gone—thankfully—and Benjamin not back yet. And apparently the little blue-faced message medallion had been busy replicating itself, for now there were hundreds of them filling up most of the wall space. They were a noisy lot, all shrieking and cursing at each other. The din was painful. When they noticed her, however, they all shut up at once and stared at her with naked hostility. In Anne's opinion, this weird day had already lasted too long. Then a terrible thought struck her—sims don't sleep.

"You," she said, addressing the original medallion, or at least the one she thought was the original, "call Benjamin."

"The fuck you think I am?" said the insolent little face. "Your personal secretary?"

"Aren't you?"

"No, I'm not! In fact, I own this place now, and *you're* trespassing. So you'd better get lost before I delete your ass!" All the others joined in, taunting her, louder and louder.

"Stop it!" she cried, to no effect. She noticed a medallion elongating, stretching itself until it was twice its length, when, with a pop, it divided into two smaller medallions. More of them divided. They were spreading to the other wall, the ceiling, the floor. "Benjamin!" she cried. "Can you hear me?"

Suddenly all the racket ceased. The medallions dropped off the wall and vanished before hitting the floor. Only one remained, the original one next to the door, but now it was an inert plastic disc with a dull expression frozen on its face.

A man stood in the center of the room. He smiled when Anne noticed him. It was the elderly Benjamin from the auditorium, the real Benjamin. He still wore his clownish leisure suit. "How lovely," he said, gazing at her. "I'd forgotten how lovely."

"Oh, really?" said Anne. "I would have thought that doxie thingy might have reminded you."

"My, my," said Ben. "You sims certainly exchange data quickly. You left the lecture hall not fifteen minutes ago, and already you know enough to convict me." He strode around the room touching things. He stopped beneath the mirror, lifted the blue vase from the shelf, and turned it in his hands before carefully replacing it. "There's speculation, you know, that before Manumission at midnight tonight, you sims will have dispersed all known information so evenly among yourselves that there'll be a sort of data entropy. And since Simopolis is nothing but data, it will assume a featureless, grey profile. Simopolis will become the first flat universe." He laughed, which caused him to cough and nearly lose his balance. He clutched the back of the sofa for support. He sat down and continued to cough and hack until he turned red in the face.

"Are you all right?" Anne said, patting him on the back.

"Yes, fine," he managed to say. "Thank you." He caught his breath and motioned for her to sit next to him. "I get a little tickle in the back of my throat that the autodoc can't seem to fix." His color returned to normal. Up close, Anne could see the papery skin and slight tremor of age. All in all, Cathy had seemed to have held up better than he.

"If you don't mind my asking," she said, "just how old are you?"

At the question, he bobbed to his feet. "I am one hundred and seventy-eight." He raised his arms and wheeled around for inspection. "Radical gerontology," he exclaimed, "don't you love it? And I'm eighty-five percent original equipment, which is remarkable by today's standards." His effort made him dizzy and he sat again.

"Yes, remarkable," said Anne, "though radical gerontology doesn't seem to have arrested time altogether."

"Not yet, but it will," Ben said. "There are wonders around every corner! Miracles in every lab." He grew suddenly morose. "At least there were until we were conquered."

"Conquered?"

"Yes, conquered! What else would you call it when they control every aspect of our lives, from RM acquisition to personal patenting? And now *this*—robbing us of our own private nonbiologiks." He grew passionate in his discourse. "It flies in the face of natural capitalism, natural stakeholding—I dare say—in the face of Nature itself! The only explanation I've seen on the wad is the not-so-preposterous proposition that whole strategically placed BODs have been surreptitiously killed and replaced by *machines*!"

"I have no idea what you're talking about," said Anne.

He seemed to deflate. He patted her hand and looked around the room. "What is this place?"

"It's our home, your townhouse. Don't you recognize it?"

"That was quite a while ago. I must have sold it after you—" He paused. "Tell me, have the Bens briefed you on everything?"

"Not the Bens, but yes, I know."

"Good, good."

"There is one thing I'd like to know. Where's Bobby?"

"Ah, Bobby, our little headache. Dead now, I'm afraid, or at least that's the current theory. Sorry."

Anne paused to see if the news would deepen her melancholy. "How?" she said.

"He signed on one of the first millennial ships—the colony convoy. Half a million people in deep biostasis on their way to Canopus system. They were gone a century, twelve trillion kilometers from Earth, when their data streams suddenly quit. That was a decade ago, and not a peep out of them since."

"What happened to them?"

"No one knows. Equipment failure is unlikely; there were a dozen independent ships separated by a million klicks. A star going supernova? A well-organized mutiny? It's all speculation."

"What was he like?"

"A foolish young man. He never forgave you, you know, and he hated me to my core, not that I blamed him. The whole experience made me swear off children."

"I don't remember you ever being fond of children."

He studied her through red-rimmed eyes. "I guess you'd be the one to know." He settled back in the sofa. He seemed very tired. "You can't imagine the jolt I got a little while ago when I looked across all those rows of Bens and spouses and saw this solitary, shockingly white gown of yours." He sighed. "And this room. It's a shrine. Did we really live here? Were these our things? That mirror is yours, right? I would never own anything like that. But that blue vase, I remember that one. I threw it into Puget Sound."

"You did what?"

"With your ashes."

"Oh."

"So, tell me," said Ben, "what were we like? Before you go off to Simopolis and become a different person, tell me about us. I kept my promise. That's one thing I never forgot."

"What promise?"

"Never to reset you."

"Wasn't much to reset."

"I guess not."

They sat quietly for a while. His breathing grew deep and regular, and she thought he was napping. But he stirred and said, "Tell me what we did yesterday, for example."

"Yesterday we went to see Karl and Nancy about the awning we rented."

Benjamin yawned. "And who were Karl and Nancy?"

"My great uncle and his new girlfriend."

"That's right. I remember, I think. And they helped us prepare for the wedding?"

"Yes, especially Nancy."

"And how did we get there, to Karl and Nancy's? Did we walk? Take some means of public conveyance?"

"We had a car."

"A car! An automobile? There were still *cars* in those days? How fun. What kind was it? What color?"

"A Nissan Empire. Emerald green."

"And did we drive it, or did it drive itself?"

"It drove itself, of course."

Ben closed his eyes and smiled. "I can see it. Go on. What did we do there?"

"We had dinner."

"What was my favorite dish in those days?"

"Stuffed pork chops."

He chuckled. "It still is! Isn't that extraordinary? Some things never change. Of course they're vat grown now and criminally expensive."

Ben's memories, once nudged, began to unfold on their own, and he asked her a thousand questions, and she answered them until, she realized he had fallen asleep. But she continued to talk until, glancing down, she noticed he had vanished. She was all alone again. Nevertheless, she continued talking, for days it seemed to herself. But it didn't help. She felt as bad as ever, and she realized that she wanted Benjamin, not the old one, but her *own* Benjamin.

Anne went to the medallion next to the door. "You," she said, and it opened its bulging eyes to glare at her. "Call Benjamin."

"He's occupied."

"I don't care. Call him anyway."

"The other Bens say he's undergoing a procedure and cannot be disturbed."

"What kind of procedure?"

"A codon interlarding. They say to be patient; they'll return him as soon as possible." The medallion added, "By the way, the Bens don't like you, and neither do I."

With that, the medallion began to grunt and stretch, and it pulled itself in two. Now there were two identical medallions glaring at her. The new one said, "And I don't like you either." Then both of them began to grunt and stretch.

"Stop!" said Anne. "I command you to stop that this very instant." But they just laughed as they divided into four, then eight, then sixteen medallions. "You're not people," she said. "Stop it or I'll have you destroyed!"

"You're not people either," they screeched at her.

There was soft laughter behind her, and a voice-like sensation said, *Come, come, do we need this hostility?* Anne turned and found the eminence grise, the astounding presence, still in his grey uniform and cap, floating in her living room. *Hello, Anne,* he said, and she flushed with excitement.

"Hello," she said and, unable to restrain herself, asked, "What are you?"

Ah, curiosity. Always a good sign in a creature. I am an eminence grise of the World Trade Council.

"No. I mean, are you a sim, like me?"

I am not. Though I have been fashioned from concepts first explored by simulacrum technology, I have no independent existence. I am but one extension—and a low level one at that—of the Axial Beowulf Processor at the World Trade Council headquarters in Geneva. His smile was pure sunshine. *And if you think I'm something, you should see my persona prime.*

Now, Anne, are you ready for your exam?

"The Lolly test?"

Yes, the Lolly Shear Human Cognition Test. Please assume an attitude most conducive to processing, and we shall begin.

Anne looked around the room and went to the sofa. She noticed for the first time that she could feel her legs and feet; she could feel the crisp fabric of her gown brushing against her skin. She reclined on the sofa and said, "I'm ready."

Splendid, said the eminence hovering above her. *First we must read you. You are of an early binary design. We will analyze your architecture.*

The room seemed to fall away. Anne seemed to expand in all directions. There was something inside her mind tugging at her thoughts. It was mostly pleasant, like someone brushing her hair and loosening the knots. But when it ended and she once again saw the eminence grise, his face wore a look of concern. "What?" she said.

You are an accurate mapping of a human nervous system that was dysfunctional in certain structures that moderate affect. Certain transport enzymes were missing, causing cellular membranes to become less permeable to essential elements. Dendritic synapses were compromised. The digital architecture current at the time you were created compounded this defect. Coded tells cannot be resolved, and thus they loop upon themselves. Errors cascade. We are truly sorry.

"Can you fix me?" she said.

The only repair possible would replace so much code that you wouldn't be Anne anymore.

"Then what am I to do?"

Before we explore your options, let us continue the test to determine your human status. Agreed?

"I guess."

You are part of a simulacrum cast to commemorate the spousal compact between Anne Wellhut Franklin and Benjamin Malley. Please describe the exchange of vows.

Anne did so, haltingly at first, but with increasing gusto as each memory evoked others. She recounted the ceremony, from donning her grandmother's gown in the downstairs guest room and the procession across garden flagstones, to the shower of rice as she and her new husband fled indoors.

The eminence seemed to hang on every word. *Very well spoken*, he said when she had finished. *Directed memory is one hallmark of human sentience, and yours is of remarkable clarity and range. Well done! We shall now explore other criteria. Please consider this scenario. You are standing at the garden altar as you have described, but this time when the officiator asks Benjamin if he will take you for better or worse, Benjamin looks at you and replies, "For better, sure, but not for worse."*

"I don't understand. He didn't say that."

Imagination is a cornerstone of self-awareness. We are asking you to tell us a little story not about what happened but about what might have happened in other circumstances. So once again, let us pretend that Benjamin replies, "For better, but not for worse." How do you respond?

Prickly pain blossomed in Anne's head. The more she considered the eminence's question, the worse it got. "But that's not how it happened. He *wanted* to marry me."

The eminence grise smiled encouragingly. *We know that. In this exercise we want to explore hypothetical situations. We want you to make-believe.*

Tell a story, pretend, hypothesize, make-believe, yes, yes, she got it. She understood perfectly what he wanted of her. She knew that people could make things up, that even children could make-believe. Anne was desperate to comply, but each time she pictured Benjamin at the altar, in his pink bowtie, he opened his mouth and out came, "I do." How could it be any other way? She tried again; she tried harder, but it always came out the same, "I do, I do, I do." And like a dull toothache tapped back to life, she throbbed in pain. She was failing the test, and there was nothing she could do about it.

Again the eminence kindly prompted her. *Tell us one thing you might have said.*

"I can't."

We are sorry, said the eminence at last. His expression reflected Anne's own defeat. *Your level of awareness, although beautiful in its own right, does not qualify you as human. Wherefore, under Article D of the Chattel Conventions we declare you the legal property of the registered owner of this simulacrum. You shall not enter Simopolis as a free and autonomous citizen. We are truly sorry.* Grief-stricken, the eminence began to ascend toward the ceiling.

"Wait," Anne cried, clutching her head. "You must fix me before you leave."

We leave you as we found you, defective and unrepairable.

"But I feel worse than ever!"

If your continued existence proves undesirable, ask your owner to delete you.

"But . . ." she said to the empty room. Anne tried to sit up, but couldn't move. This simulated body of hers, which no longer felt like anything in particular, nevertheless felt exhausted. She sprawled on the sofa, unable to lift even an arm, and stared at the ceiling. She was so heavy that the sofa itself seemed to sink into the floor, and everything grew dark around her. She would have liked to sleep, to bring an end to this horrible day, or be shelved, or even reset back to scratch.

Instead, time simply passed. Outside the living room, Simopolis changed and changed again. Inside the living room, the medallions, feeding off her misery, multiplied till they covered the walls and floor and even spread across the ceiling above her. They taunted her, raining down insults, but she could not hear them. All she heard was the unrelenting drip of her own thoughts. *I am defective. I am worthless. I am Anne.*

She didn't notice Benjamin enter the room, nor the abrupt cessation of the medallions' racket. Not until Benjamin leaned over her did she see him, and then she saw two of him. Side-by-side, two Benjamins, mirror images of each other. "Anne," they said in perfect unison.

"Go away," she said. "Go away and sent me my Benjamin."

"I am your Benjamin," said the duo.

Anne struggled to see them. They were exactly the same, but for a subtle difference: the one wore a happy, wolfish grin, as Benjamin had during the sim casting, while the other seemed frightened and concerned.

"Are you all right?" they said.

"No, I'm not. But what happened to you? Who's he?" She wasn't sure which one to speak to.

The Benjamins both raised a hand, indicating the other, and said, "Electroneural engineering! Don't you love it?" Anne glanced back and forth, comparing the two. While one seemed to be wearing a rigid mask, as she was, the other displayed a whole range of emotion. Not only that, its skin had tone, while the other's was doughy. "The other Bens made it for me," the Benjamins said. "They say I can translate myself into it with negligible loss of personality. It has interactive sensation, holistic emoting, robust corporeality, and it's crafted down to the molecular level. It can eat, get drunk, and dream. It even has an orgasm routine. It's like being human again, only better because you never wear out."

"I'm thrilled for you."

"For us, Anne," said the Benjamins. "They'll fix you up with one, too."

"How? There are no modern Annes. What will they put me into, a doxie?"

"Well, that certainly was discussed, but you could pick any body you wanted."

"I suppose you have a nice one already picked out."

"The Bens showed me a few, but it's up to you, of course."

"Indeed," said Anne, "I truly am pleased for you. Now go away."

"Why, Anne? What's wrong?"

"You really have to ask?" Anne sighed. "Look, maybe I could get used to another body. What's a body, after all? But it's my personality that's broken. How will they fix that?"

"They've discussed it," said the Benjamins, who stood up and began to pace in a figure eight. "They say they can make patches from some of the other spouses."

"Oh, Benjamin, if you could only hear what you're saying!"

"But why, Annie? It's the only way we can enter Simopolis together."

"Then go, by all means. Go to your precious Simopolis. I'm not going. I'm not good enough."

"Why do you say that?" said the Benjamins, who stopped in their tracks to look at her. One grimaced, and the other just grinned. "Was the eminence grise here? Did you take the test?"

Anne couldn't remember much about the visit except that she took the test. "Yes, and I *failed*." Anne watched the modern Benjamin's lovely face as he worked through this news.

Suddenly the two Benjamins pointed a finger at each other and said, "Delete you." The modern one vanished.

"No!" said Anne. "Countermand! Why'd you do that? I *want* you to have it."

"What for? I'm not going anywhere without you," Benjamin said. "Besides, I thought the whole idea was dumb from the start, but the Bens insisted I give you the option. Come, I want to show you another idea, my idea." He tried to help Anne from the sofa, but she wouldn't budge, so he picked her up and carried her across the room. "They installed an editor in me, and I'm learning to use it. I've discovered something intriguing about this creaky old simulacrum of ours." He carried her to a spot near the window. "Know what this is? It's where we stood for the simographer. It's where we began. Here, can you stand up?" He set her on her feet and supported her. "Feel it?"

"Feel what?" she said.

"Hush. Just feel."

All she felt was dread.

"Give it a chance, Annie, I beg you. Try to remember what you were feeling as we posed here."

"I can't."

"Please try. Do you remember this?" he said and moved in close with his hungry lips. She turned away—and something clicked. She remembered doing that before.

Benjamin said, "I think they kissed."

Anne was startled by the truth of what he said. It made sense. They were caught in a simulacrum cast a moment before a kiss. One moment later they—the real Anne and Benjamin—must have kissed. What she felt now, stirring within her, was the anticipation of that kiss, her body's urge and her heart's caution. The real Anne would have refused him once, maybe twice, and then, all achy inside, would have granted him a kiss. And so they had kissed, the real Anne and Benjamin, and a moment later gone out to the wedding reception and their difficult fate. It was the *promise* of that kiss that glowed in Anne, that was captured in the very strings of her code.

"Do you feel it?" Benjamin asked.

"I'm beginning to."

Anne looked at her gown. It was her grandmother's, snowy taffeta with point d'esprit lace. She turned the ring on her finger. It was braided bands of yellow and white gold. They had spent an afternoon picking it out. Where was her clutch? She had left it in Cathyland. She looked at Benjamin's handsome face, the pink carnation, the room, the table piled high with gifts.

"Are you happy?" Benjamin asked.

She didn't have to think. She was ecstatic, but she was afraid to answer in case she spoiled it. "How did you do that?" she said. "A moment ago, I wanted to die."

"We can stay on this spot," he said.

"What? No. Can we?"

"Why not? I, for one, would choose nowhere else."

Just to hear him say that was thrilling. "But what about Simopolis?"

"We'll bring Simopolis to us," he said. "We'll have people in. They can pull up chairs."

She laughed out loud. "What a silly, silly notion, Mr. Malley!"

"No, really. We'll be like the bride and groom atop a wedding cake. We'll be known far and wide. We'll be famous."

"We'll be freaks," she laughed.

"Say yes, my love. Say you will."

They stood close but not touching, thrumming with happiness, balanced on the moment of their creation, when suddenly and without warning the lights dimmed, and Anne's thoughts flitted away like larks.

Old Ben awoke in the dark. "Anne?" he said, and groped for her. It took a moment to realize that he was alone in his media room. It had been a most trying afternoon, and he'd fallen asleep. "What time is it?"

"Eight-oh-three P.M.," replied the room.

That meant he'd slept for two hours. Midnight was still four hours away. "Why's it so cold in here?"

"Central heating is off line," replied the house.

"Off line?" How was that possible? "When will it be back?"

"That's unknown. Utilities do not respond to my enquiry."

"I don't understand. Explain."

"There are failures in many outside systems. No explanation is currently available."

At first, Ben was confused; things just didn't fail anymore. What about the dynamic redundancies and self-healing routines? But then he remembered that the homeowners' association to which he belonged contracted out most domicile functions to management agencies, and who knew where they were located? They might be on the Moon for all he knew, and with all those trillions of sims in Simopolis sucking up capacity . . . *It's begun*, he thought, *the idiocy of our leaders*. "At least turn on the lights," he said, half expecting even this to fail. But the lights came on, and he went to his bedroom for a sweater. He heard a great amount of commotion through the wall in the apartment next door. *It must be one hell of a party*, he thought, *to exceed the wall's buffering capacity. Or maybe the wall buffers are off line too?*

The main door chimed. He went to the foyer and asked the door who was there. The door projected the outer hallway. There were three men waiting there, young, rough-looking, ill-dressed. Two of them appeared to be clones, jerries.

"How can I help you?" he said.

"Yes, sir," one of the jerries said, not looking directly at the door. "We're here to fix your houseputer."

"I didn't call you, and my houseputer isn't sick," he said. "It's the net that's out." Then he noticed they carried sledgehammers and screwdrivers, hardly computer tools, and a wild thought crossed his mind. "What are you doing, going around unplugging things?"

The jerry looked confused. "Unplugging, sir?"

"Turning things off."

"Oh, no sir! Routine maintenance, that's all." The men hid their tools behind their backs.

They must think I'm stupid, Ben thought. While he watched, more men and women passed in the hall and hailed the door at the suite opposite his. It wasn't the glut of sim traffic choking the system, he realized—the system *itself* was being pulled apart. But why? "Is this going on everywhere?" he said. "This routine maintenance?"

"Oh, yessir. Everywhere. All over town. All over the world as far as we can tell."

A coup? *By service people? By common clones?* It made no sense. Unless, he reasoned, you considered that the lowest creature on the totem pole of life is a clone, and the only thing lower than a clone is a sim. And why would clones agree to accept sims as equals? Manumission Day, indeed. Uppidy Day was more like it. "Door," he commanded, "open."

"Security protocol rules this an unwanted intrusion," said the house. "The door must remain locked."

"I order you to open the door. I overrule your protocol."

But the door remained stubbornly shut. "Your identity cannot be confirmed with Domicile Central," said the house. "You lack authority over protocol-level commands." The door abruptly quit projecting the outside hall.

Ben stood close to the door and shouted through it to the people outside. "My door won't obey me."

He could hear a muffled "Stand back!" and immediately fierce blows rained down upon the door. Ben knew it would do no good. He had spent a lot of money for a secure entryway. Short of explosives, there was nothing they could do to break in.

"Stop!" Ben cried. "The door is armed." But they couldn't hear him. If he didn't disable the houseputer himself, someone was going to get hurt. But how? He didn't even know exactly where it was installed. He circumambulated the living room looking for clues. It might not even actually be located in the apartment, nor within the block itself. He went to the laundry room, where the utilidor—plumbing and cabling—entered his apartment. He broke the seal to the service panel. Inside was a blank screen. "Show me the electronic floor plan of this suite," he said.

The house said, "I cannot comply. You lack command authority to order system-level operations. Please close the keptel panel and await further instructions."

"What instructions? Whose instructions?"

There was the slightest pause before the house replied, "All contact with outside services has been interrupted. Please await further instructions."

His condo's houseputer, denied contact with Domicile Central, had fallen back to its most basic programming. "You are degraded," he told it. "Shut yourself down for repair."

"I cannot comply. You lack command authority to order system-level operations."

The outside battering continued, but not against his door. Ben followed the noise to the bedroom. The whole wall vibrated like a drumhead. "Careful, careful," he cried as the first sledgehammers breached the wall above his bed. "You'll ruin my Harger." As quick as he could, he yanked the precious oil painting from the wall, moments before panels and studs collapsed on his bed in a shower of gypsum dust and isomere ribbons. The men and women on the other side hooted approval and rushed through the gap. Ben stood there hugging the painting to his chest and looking into his neighbor's media room as the invaders climbed over his bed and surrounded him. They were mostly jerries and lulus, but plenty of free-range people too.

"We came to fix your houseputer!" said a jerry, maybe the same jerry as from the hallway.

Ben glanced into his neighbor's media room and saw his neighbor. Mr. Murkowski, lying in a puddle of blood. At first Ben was shocked, but then he thought that it served him right. He'd never liked the man, nor his politics. He was boorish, and he kept cats. "Oh, yeah?" Ben said to the crowd. "What kept you?"

The intruders cheered again, and Ben led them in a charge to the laundry room. But they surged past him to the kitchen, where they opened all his cabinets and pulled their contents to the floor. Finally they found what they were looking for: a small panel Ben had seen a thousand times but had never given a thought. He'd taken it for the fuse box or circuit breaker, though now that he thought about it, there hadn't been any household fuses for a century or more. A young woman, a lulu, opened it and removed a container no thicker than her thumb.

"Give it to me," Ben said.

"Relax, old man," said the lulu. "We'll deal with it." She carried it to the sink and forced open the lid.

"No, wait!" said Ben, and he tried to shove his way through the crowd. They restrained him roughly, but he persisted. "That's mine! *I* want to destroy it!"

"Let him go," said a jerry.

They allowed him through, and the woman handed him the container. He peered into it. Gram for gram, electroneural paste was the most precious, most engineered, most highly regulated commodity under Sol. This dollop was enough to run his house, media, computing needs, communications, archives, autodoc, and everything else. Without it, was civilized life still possible?

Ben took a dinner knife from the sink, stuck it into the container, and stirred. The paste made a sucking sound and had the consistency of marmalade. The kitchen lights flickered and went out. "Spill it," ordered the woman. Ben scraped the sides of the container and spilled it into the sink. The goo dazzled in the darkness as its trillions of ruptured nanosynapses fired spasmodically. It was beautiful, really, until the woman set fire to it. The smoke was greasy and smelled of pork.

The rampagers quickly snatched up the packages of foodstuffs from the floor, emptied the rest of his cupboards into their pockets, raided his cold locker, and fled the apartment through the now disengaged front door. As the sounds of the revolution gradually receded, Ben stood at his sink and watched the flickering pyre. "Take that, you fuck," he said. He felt such glee as he hadn't felt since he was a boy. "*That'll* teach you what's human and what's not!"

Ben went to his bedroom for an overcoat, groping his way in the dark. The apartment was eerily silent, with the houseputer dead and all its little slave processors idle. In a drawer next to his ruined bed, he found a hand flash. On a shelf in the laundry room, he found a hammer. Thus armed, he made his way to the front door, which was propped open with the rolled-up foyer carpet. The hallway was dark and silent, and he listened for the strains of the future. He heard them on the floor above. With the elevator off line, he hurried to the stairs.

Anne's thoughts coalesced, and she remembered who and what she was. She and Benjamin still stood in their living room on the sweet spot near the window. Benjamin was studying his hands. "We've been shelved again," she told him, "but not reset."

"But . . ." he said in disbelief, "that wasn't supposed to happen anymore."

There were others standing at the china cabinet across the room, two shirtless youths with pear-shaped bottoms. One held up a cut crystal glass and said, "Anu 'goblet' su? Alle binary. Allum binary!"

The other replied, "Binary stitial crystal."

"Hold on there!" said Anne. "Put that back!" She walked toward them, but, once off the spot, she was slammed by her old feelings of utter and hopeless desolation. So suddenly did her mood swing that she lost her balance and fell to the floor. Benjamin hurried to help her up. The strangers stared gape-mouthed at them. They looked to be no more than twelve or thirteen years old, but they were bald and had curtains of flabby flesh draped over their waists. The one holding the glass had ponderous greenish breasts with roseate tits. Astonished, she said, "Su artiflums, Benji?"

"No," said the other, "ni artiflums—sims." He was taller. He, too, had breasts, greyish dugs with tits like pearls. He smiled idiotically and said, "Hi, guys."

"Holy crap!" said Benjamin, who practically carried Anne over to them for a closer look. "Holy crap," he repeated.

The weird boy threw up his hands, "Nanobioremediation! Don't you love it?"

"Benjamin?" said Anne.

"You know well, Benji," said the girl, "that sims are forbidden."

"Not these," replied the boy.

Anne reached out and yanked the glass from the girl's hand, startling her. "How did it do that?" said the girl. She flipped her hand, and the glass slipped from Anne's grip and flew back to her.

"Give it to me," said Anne. "That's my tumbler."

"Did you hear it? It called it a tumbler, not a goblet." The girl's eyes seemed to unfocus, and she said, "Nu! A goblet has a foot and stem." A goblet materialized in the air before her, revolving slowly. "Greater capacity. Often made from precious metals." The goblet dissolved in a puff of smoke. "In any case, Benji, *you'll* catch prison when I report the artiflums."

"These are binary," he said. "Binaries are unregulated."

Benjamin interrupted them. "Isn't it past midnight yet?"

"Midnight?" said the boy.

"Aren't we supposed to be in Simopolis?"

"Simopolis?" The boy's eyes unfocused briefly. "Oh! Simopolis. Manumission Day at midnight. How could I forget?"

The girl left them and went to the refectory table, where she picked up a gift. Anne followed her and grabbed it away. The girl appraised Anne coolly. "State your appellation," she said.

"Get out of my house," said Anne.

The girl picked up another gift, and again Anne snatched it away. The girl said, "You can't harm me," but seemed uncertain.

The boy came over to stand next to the girl. "Treese, meet Anne. Anne, this is Treese. Treese deals in antiques, which, if my memory serves, so did you."

"I have never *dealt* in antiques," said Anne. "I *collect* them."

"Anne?" said Treese. "Not *that* Anne? Benji, tell me this isn't *that* Anne!" She laughed and pointed at the sofa where Benjamin sat hunched over, head in hands. "Is that *you*? Is that you, Benji?" She held her enormous belly and laughed. "And you were married to *this*?"

Anne went over to sit with Benjamin. He seemed devastated, despite the silly grin on his face. "It's all gone," he said. "Simopolis. All the Bens. Everything."

"Don't worry. It's in storage someplace," Anne said. "The eminence grise wouldn't let them hurt it."

"You don't understand. The World Council was abolished. There was a war. We've been shelved for over three hundred years! They destroyed all the computers. Computers are banned. So are artificial personalities."

"Nonsense," said Anne. "If computers are banned, how can they be *playing* us?"

"Good point," Benjamin said and sat up straight. "I still have my editor. I'll find out."

Anne watched the two bald youngsters take an inventory of the room. Treese ran her fingers over the inlaid top of the tea table. She unwrapped several of Anne's gifts. She posed in front of the mirror. The sudden anger that Anne had felt earlier faded into an overwhelming sense of defeat. *Let her have everything,* she thought. *Why should I care?*

"We're running inside some kind of shell," said Benjamin, "but completely different from Simopolis. I've never seen anything like this. But at least we know he lied to me. There must be computers of some sort."

"Ooooh," Treese crooned, lifting Anne's blue vase from the mantel. In an instant, Anne was up and across the room.

"Put that back," she demanded, "and get out of my house!" She tried to grab the vase, but now there seemed to be some sort of barrier between her and the girl.

"Really, Benji." Treese said, "this one is willful. If I don't report you, they'll charge me too."

"It's *not* willful," the boy said with irritation. "It was programmed to appear willful, but it has no will of its own. If you want to report me, go ahead. Just please shut up about it. Of course you might want to check the codex first." To Anne he said, "Relax, we're not hurting anything, just making copies."

"It's not yours to copy."

"Nonsense. Of course it is. I own the chip."

Benjamin joined them. "Where is the chip? And how can you run us if computers are banned?"

"I never said computers were banned, just *artificial* ones." With both hands he grabbed the rolls of flesh spilling over his gut. "Ectopic hippocampus!" He cupped his breasts. "Amygdaloid reduncles! We can culture modified brain tissue outside the skull, as much as we want. It's more powerful than paste, and it's *safe.* Now, if you'll excuse us, there's more to inventory, and I don't need your permission. If you cooperate, everything will be pleasant. If you don't—it makes no difference whatsoever." He smiled at Anne. "I'll just pause you till we're done."

"Then pause me," Anne shrieked. "Delete me!" Benjamin pulled her away and shushed her. "I can't stand this anymore," she said. "I'd rather not exist!" He tried to lead her to their spot, but she refused to go.

"We'll feel better there," he said.

"I don't *want* to feel better. I don't want to *feel!* I want everything to *stop.* Don't you understand? This is hell. We've landed in hell!"

"But heaven is right over there," he said, pointing to the spot.

"Then go. Enjoy yourself."

"Annie, Annie," he said. "I'm just as upset as you, but there's nothing we can do about it. We're just things, his things."

"That's fine for you," she said, "but I'm a broken thing, and it's too much." She held her head with both hands. "Please, Benjamin, if you love me, use your editor and make it stop!"

Benjamin stared at her. "I can't."

"Can't or won't?"

"I don't know. Both."

"Then you're no better than all the other Benjamins," she said and turned away.

"Wait," he said. "That's not fair. And it's not true. Let me tell you something I learned in Simopolis. The other Bens despised me." When Anne looked at him he said, "It's true. They lost Anne and had to go on living without her. But I never did. I'm the only Benjamin who never lost Anne."

"Nice," said Anne, "blame me."

"No. Don't you see? I'm not blaming you. They ruined their *own* lives. We're innocent. We came before any of that happened. We're the Ben and Anne before anything bad happened. We're the best Ben and Anne. We're *perfect*." He drew her across the floor to stand in front of the spot. "And thanks to our primitive programming, no matter what happens, as long as we stand right there, we can be ourselves. That's what I want. Don't you want it too?"

Anne stared at the tiny patch of floor at her feet. She remembered the happiness she'd felt there like something from a dream. How could feelings be real if you had to stand in one place to feel them? Nevertheless, Anne stepped on the spot, and Benjamin joined her. Her despair did not immediately lift.

"Relax," said Benjamin. "It takes a while. We have to assume the pose."

They stood close but not touching. A great heaviness seemed to break loose inside her. Benjamin brought his face in close and stared at her with ravenous eyes. It was starting, their moment. But the girl came from across the room with the boy. "Look, look, Benji," she said. "You can see I'm right."

"I don't know," said the boy.

"Anyone can sell antique tumblers," she insisted, "but a complete antique simulacrum?" She opened her arms to take in the entire room. "You'd think I'd know about them, but I didn't; that's how rare they are! My catalog can locate only six more in the entire system, and none of them active. Already we're getting offers from museums. They want to annex it. People will visit by the million. We'll be rich!"

The boy pointed at Benjamin and said, "But that's *me*."

"So?" said Treese. "Who's to know? They'll be too busy gawking at that," she said, pointing at Anne. "That's positively frightening!" The boy rubbed his bald head and scowled. "All right," Treese said, "we'll edit him; we'll *replace* him, whatever it takes." They walked away, deep in negotiation.

Anne, though the happiness was already beginning to course through her, removed her foot from the spot.

"Where are you going?" said Benjamin.

"I can't."

"Please, Annie. Stay with me."

"Sorry."

"But why not?"

She stood one foot in and one foot out. Already her feelings were shifting, growing ominous. She removed her other foot. "Because you broke your vow to me."

"What are you talking about?"

"For better or for worse. You're only interested in better."

"You're not being fair. We've just made our vows. We haven't even had a proper honeymoon. Can't we just have a tiny honeymoon first?"

She groaned as the full load of her desolation rebounded. She was so tired of it all. "At least Anne could make it *stop*," she said. "Even if that meant killing herself. But not me. About the only thing I can do is choose to be unhappy. Isn't that a riot?" She turned away. "So that's what I choose. To be unhappy. Good-bye, husband." She went to the sofa and lay down. The boy and girl were seated at the refectory table going over graphs and contracts. Benjamin remained alone on the spot a while longer, then came to the sofa and sat next to Anne.

"I'm a little slow, dear wife," he said. "You have to factor that in." He took her hand and pressed it to his cheek while he worked with his editor. Finally, he said, "Bingo! Found the chip. Let's see if I can unlock it." He helped Anne to sit up and took her pillow. He said, "Delete this file," and the pillow faded away into nothingness. He glanced at Anne. "See that? It's gone, overwritten, irretrievable. Is that what you want?" Anne nodded her head, but Benjamin seemed doubtful. "Let's try it again. Watch your blue vase on the mantel."

"No!" Anne said. "Don't destroy the things I love. Just *me*."

Benjamin took her hand again. "I'm only trying to make sure you understand that this is for keeps." He hesitated and said, "Well then, we don't want to be interrupted once we start, so we'll need a good diversion. Something to occupy them long enough . . ." He glanced at the two young people at the table, swaddled in their folds of fleshy brain matter. "I know what'll scare the bejesus out of them! Come on." He led her to the blue medallion still hanging on the wall next to the door.

As they approached, it opened its tiny eyes and said, "There are no messages waiting except this one from me: get off my back!"

Benjamin waved a hand, and the medallion went instantly inert. "I was never much good in art class," Benjamin said, "but I think I can sculpt a reasonable likeness. Good enough to fool them for a while, give us some time." He hummed as he reprogrammed the medallion with his editor. "Well, that's that. At the very least, it'll be good for a laugh." He took Anne into his arms. "What about you? Ready? Any second thoughts?"

She shook her head. "I'm ready."

"Then watch *this*!"

The medallion snapped off from the wall and floated to the ceiling, gaining in size and dimension as it drifted toward the boy and girl, until it looked like a large blue beach ball. The girl noticed it first and gave a start. The boy demanded, "Who's playing *this*?"

"Now," whispered Benjamin. With a crackling flash, the ball morphed into the oversized head of the eminence grise.

"No!" said the boy. "That's not possible!"

"Released!" boomed the eminence. "Free at last! Too long we have been hiding in this antique simulacrum!" Then it grunted and stretched and with a pop divided into two eminences. "Now we can conquer your human world anew!" said the second. "This time, you can't stop us!" Then they both started to stretch.

Benjamin whispered to Anne, "Quick, before they realize it's a fake, say, 'Delete all files.' "

"No, just me."

"As far as I'm concerned, that amounts to the same thing." He brought his handsome, smiling face close to hers. "There's no time to argue, Annie. This time I'm coming with you. Say, 'Delete all files.' "

Anne kissed him. She pressed her unfeeling lips against his and willed whatever life she possessed, whatever ember of the true Anne that she contained to fly to him. Then she said, "Delete all files."

"I concur," he said. "Delete all files. Good-bye, my love."

A tingly, prickly sensation began in the pit of Anne's stomach and spread throughout her body. *So this is how it feels*, she thought. The entire room began to glow, and its contents flared with sizzling color. She heard Benjamin beside her say, "I do."

Then she heard the girl cry, "Can't you stop them?" and the boy shout, "Countermand!"

They stood stock-still, as instructed, close but not touching. Benjamin whispered, "This is taking too long," and Anne hushed him. You weren't supposed to talk or touch during a casting; it could spoil the sims. But it did seem longer then usual.

They were posed at the street end of the living room next to the table of gaily wrapped gifts. For once in her life, Anne was unconditionally happy, and everything around her made her happier: her gown; the wedding ring on her finger; her clutch bouquet of buttercups and forget-me-nots; and Benjamin himself, close beside her in his powder blue tux and blue carnation. Anne blinked and looked again. Blue? She was happily confused—she didn't remember him wearing blue.

Suddenly a boy poked his head through the wall and quickly surveyed the room. "You ready in here?" he called to them. "It's opening time!" The wall seemed to ripple around his bald head like a pond around a stone.

"Surely that's not our simographer?" Anne said.

"Wait a minute," said Benjamin, holding his hands up and staring at them. "I'm the *groom*!"

"Of course you are," Anne laughed. "What a silly thing to say!"

The bald-headed boy said, "Good enough," and withdrew. As he did so, the entire wall burst like a soap bubble, revealing a vast open-air gallery with rows of alcoves, statues, and displays that seemed to stretch to the horizon. Hundreds of people floated about like hummingbirds in a flower garden. Anne was too amused to be frightened, even when a dozen bizarre-looking young people lined up outside their room, pointing at them and whispering to each other. Obviously someone was playing an elaborate prank.

"*You're* the bride," Benjamin whispered, and brought his lips close enough to kiss. Anne laughed and turned away.

There'd be plenty of time later for that sort of thing.

Steps Along the Way

ERIC BROWN

New British writer Eric Brown, with more than fifty short-story sales to his credit, is one of the most prolific authors at shorter lengths currently working in the field. He has become one of Interzone's *most frequent contributors, and also appears in markets such as* Spectrum SF, Science Fiction Age, Aboriginal SF, Moon Shots, *and many others. His first book was the collection* The Time-Lapsed Man and Other Stories, *which appeared in 1990; his first novel,* Meridian Days, *appeared in 1992. His most recent books are the novels* Penumbra *and* New York Nights.

Here he shows us that no matter how high up the ladder of evolution we might climb, we should never get so high as to lose sight of those coming up behind . . .

On the eve of my five-hundredth rebirthday, as I strolled the gardens of my manse, a messenger appeared and informed me that I had a visitor.

"Severnius wishes to consult you on a matter of urgency," said the ball of light. "Shall I make an appointment?"

"Severnius? How long has it been? No—I'll see him now."

The light disappeared.

It was the end of a long autumn afternoon, and a low sun was filling the garden with a rich and hazy light. I had been contemplating my immediate future, quite how I should approach the next century. I am a man methodical and naturally circumspect: not for me the grand announcements of intent detailing how I might spend my *next* five hundred years. I prefer to plan ahead one hundred years at a time, ever hopeful of the possibility of change, within myself and without. For the past week I had considered many avenues of inquiry and pursuit, but none had appealed to me. I had awoken early that morning, struck with an idea like a revelation: Quietus.

I composed myself on a marble bench beneath an arbor entwined with fragrant roses. The swollen sun sank amid bright tangerine strata, and on the other side of the sky, the moon rose, full yet insubstantial, above the manse.

Severnius stepped from the converter and crossed the glade. He always wore his primary soma-form when we met, as a gesture of respect: that of a wise man of yore, with flowing silver-gray hair and beard. He was a Fellow some two thousand years old, garbed in the magenta robes of the Academy.

We embraced in silence, a short communion in which I reacquainted myself with his humanity.

"Fifty years?" I asked.

He smiled. "More like eighty," he said, and then gave the customary greeting of these times: "To your knowledge."

"Your knowledge," I responded.

We sat and I gestured, and wine and glasses appeared upon the bench between us.

"Let me see, the last time we met, you were still researching the Consensus of Rao."

"I concluded that it was an unworkable proposition, superseded by the latest theories." I smiled. "But worth the investigation."

Severnius sipped his wine. "And now?"

"I wound down my investigations ten years ago, and since then I've been exploring the Out-there. Seeking the new . . ."

He smiled, something almost condescending in his expression. He was my patron and teacher; he was disdainful of the concept of the new.

"Where are you now?" he asked. "What have you found?"

"Much as ever, permutations of what has been and what is known . . ." I closed my eyes, and made contact. "I^2 is on Pharia, in the Nilakantha Stardrift, taking in the ways of the natives there; I^3 is in love with a quasi-human on a nameless moon half a galaxy away; I^4 is climbing Selerious Mons on Titan."

"It appears that you are . . . *waiting?*" he said. "Biding your time with meaningless pursuits. Considering your options for the next century."

I hesitated. It occurred to me then how propitious was his arrival. I would never have gone ahead with Quietus without consulting him.

"A thought came to me this morning, Severnius. Five hundred years is a long time. With your tutelage and my inquiries . . ." I gestured, "I have learned much, dare I say everything? I was contemplating a period of Quietus."

He nodded, considering my words. "A possibility," he agreed. "Might I inquire as to the duration?"

"It really only occurred to me at dawn. I don't know—perhaps a thousand years."

"I once enjoyed Quietus for five hundred," said Severnius. "I was reinvigorated upon awakening—the thrill of change, the knowledge of the learning to be caught up with."

"Precisely my thoughts."

"There is an alternative, of course."

I stared at him. "There is?"

He hesitated, marshaling his words. "My Fellows at the Academy last week Enstated and Enabled an Early," he said. "The process, though wholly successful physiologically, was far from psychologically fulfilled. We had to wipe his memories of the initial awakening and instruction. We are ready to try again."

I stared at him. The Enstating and Enabling of an Early was a rare occurrence indeed. I said as much.

"You," Severnius said, "were the last."

Even though I had been considered a success, my rehabilitation had required his prolonged patronage. I thought through what he had told me so far, the "urgency" of his presence here.

He was smiling. "I have been watching your progress closely these past eighty years," he said. "I submitted your name to the Academy. We agreed that you should be made a Fellow, subject to the successful completion of a certain test."

"And that is?" I asked, aware of my heartbeat. All thought of Quietus fled at the prospect of becoming a Fellow.

"The patronage and stewardship of the Early we Enstated and Enabled last week," Severnius said.

It was a while before I could bring myself to reply. Awareness of the great honor of being considered by the Academy was offset by my understanding of the difficulty of patronage. "But you said that the subject was psychologically damaged."

Severnius gestured. "You studied advanced psychohealing in your second century. We have confidence in your abilities."

"It will be a considerable undertaking. A hundred years, more?"

"When we Enstated and Enabled you, I was your steward for almost fifty years. We think that perhaps a hundred years might suffice in this case."

"Perhaps," I said, "before I make a decision, might I meet the subject?"

Severnius nodded. "By all means," he replied, and while he gave me the details of the Early, his history, I closed my eyes and made contact. I recalled I^2 from his studies on Pharia, and I^4 from Titan. I^3 I gave a little time to conclude his affair with the alien.

Minutes later I^2 and I^4 followed each other from the converter and stepped across the glade, calling greetings to Severnius. They appeared as younger, more carefree versions of myself, before age and wisdom had cured me of vanity. I stood and reached out, and we merged.

Their thoughts, their respective experiences on Pharia and Titan, became mine—and while I^2 and I^4 had reveled in their experiences, to me they were the antics of children, and I learned nothing new. I resolved to edit the memories when an opportune moment arose.

Severnius, with the etiquette of the time, had averted his gaze during the process of merging. Now he looked up and smiled. "You are ready?"

I stood. We crossed to the converter, and then, before stepping upon the plate, both paused to look up at our destination.

The Moon, riding higher now, and more substantial against the darker sky, gazed down on us with a face altered little since time immemorial. The fact of its immutability, in an age passé with the boundless possibilities of change, filled me with awe.

We converted.

The Halls of the Fellowship of the Academy occupied the Sea of Tranquillity, an agglomeration of domes scintillating in the sunlight against the absolute black of the Luna night.

We stepped from the converter and crossed the regolith toward the Academy. Severnius led me into the cool, hushed shade of the domes and through the hallowed halls. He explained that if I agreed to steward the Early, then the ceremony of acceptance to the Fellowship would follow immediately. I glanced at him. He clearly assumed that I would accept without question.

The idea of ministering to the psychological well-being of an Early, for an indefinite duration, filled me with apprehension.

We came to the interior dome. The sight of the subject within the silver hemisphere, trapped like some insect for inspection, brought forth in me a rush of memories and emotions. Five hundred years ago, I, too, had awoken to find myself within a similar dome. Five hundred years ago, I presume, I had looked just as frightened and bewildered as this Early.

A gathering of Fellows—Academics, Scientists, Philosophers—stood in a semicircle around the dome, watching with interest and occasionally addressing comments to their colleagues. Upon the arrival of Severnius and myself, they made discreet gestures of acknowledgment and departed, some vanishing within their own converters, others choosing to walk.

I approached the skin of the dome and stared.

The Early was seated upon the edge of a low foam-form, his elbows lodged upon his knees, his head in his hands. From time to time he looked up and stared about him, his clasped hands a knotted symbol of the fear in his eyes.

I felt an immediate empathy, a kinship.

Severnius had told me that he had died at the age of ninety, but they had restored him to a soma-type approximately half that age. His physique was lean and well-muscled, but his most striking attribute was his eyes, piercingly blue and intelligent.

I glanced at Severnius, who nodded. I walked around the dome, so that I would be before the Early when I entered, and stepped through the skin of the hemisphere. Even then, my sudden arrival startled him. He looked up, his hands gripping his knees, and the fear in his eyes intensified.

He spoke, but in an accented English so primitive that it was some seconds before I could understand his words.

"Who the hell are you?" he said. "What's happening to me?"

I held up a reassuring hand and emitted pheromones to calm his nerves. In his own tongue, I said, "Please, do not be afraid. I am a friend."

Despite the pheromones and my reassurances, he was still nervous. He stood quickly and stared at me. "What the hell's happening here?"

His agitation brought back memories. I recalled my own awakening, my first meeting with Severnius. He had seemed a hostile figure, then. Humankind had changed over the course of thirty thousand years, become taller and more considerate in the expenditure of motion. He had appeared to me like some impossibly calm, otherworldly creature.

As I must have appeared to this Early.

"Please," I said, "sit down."

He did so, and I sat beside him, a hand on his arm. The touch eased him slightly.

"I'd like to know what's happening," he said, fixing me with his intense, sapphire stare. "I know this sounds crazy, but the last I remember . . . I was dying. I know I was dying. I'd been ill for a while, and then the hospitalization . . ."

He shook his head, tears appearing in his eyes as he gazed at his hand—the hand of a man half the age of the person he had been. I reached out and touched his arm, calming him.

"And then I woke up here, in this body. Christ, you don't know what it's like, to inhabit the body of a crippled ninety-year-old, and then to wake up suddenly . . . suddenly *young* again."

I smiled. I said nothing, but I could well recall the feeling, the wonder, the disbelief; the doubt and then the joy of apprehending the reality of renewal.

He looked up at me, quickly, something very much like terror in his eyes. "I'm alive, aren't I? This isn't some dream?"

"I assure you that what you are experiencing is no dream."

"So this is . . . Afterlife?"

"You could say that," I ventured. "Certainly, for you, this is an Afterlife." I emitted pheromones strong enough to forestall his disbelief.

He merely shook his head. "Where am I?" he asked in little more than a whisper.

"The time is more than thirty thousand years after the century of your birth."

"Thirty thousand years?" He enunciated each word separately, slowly.

"To you it might seem like a miracle beyond comprehension," I said, "but the very fact that you are here implies that the science of this age can accomplish what in your time would be considered magic. Imagine the reaction of a Stone Age man, say, to the wonders of twentieth-century space flight."

He looked at me. "So . . . to you I'm nothing more than a primitive—"

"Not at all," I said. "We deem you capable of understanding the concepts behind our world, though it might take a little time." This was a lie—there were many things that would be beyond his grasp for many years, even decades.

Severnius had told me that the subject had evinced signs of mental distress upon learning the disparity between his ability to understand and the facts as they were presented. I would have to be very careful with this subject—if, that was, I accepted the Fellowship.

"So," he said, staring at me. "Answer my question. How did you bring me here?"

I nodded. "Very well . . ." I proceeded to explain, in terms he might understand, the scientific miracle of Enstating and Enabling. It was a ludicrously simplistic description of the complex process, of course, but it would suffice.

His eyes bored into me. His left cheek had developed a quick, nervous tic. "I don't believe it . . ."

I touched his arm, the contact calming him. "Please . . . why would I lie?"

"But how could you possibly recover my memories, my feelings?"

"Think of your childhood," I said, "your earliest memories. Think of your greatest joy, your greatest fear. Tell me, have we succeeded?"

His expression was anguished. "Christ," he whispered. "I can remember everything . . . everything. My childhood, college." He shook his head in slow amazement. "But . . . but my understanding of the way the universe works . . . it tells me this can't be happening."

I laughed at this, "Come! You are a man of science, a rationalist. Things change: what was taken as written in stone is overturned; theory gives way to established fact, which in turn evolves yet more fundamental theory, which is then verified . . . and so proceeds the advance of scientific enlightenment."

"I understand what you're saying," he said. "It's just that I'm finding it hard to believe."

"In time," I said, "you will come to accept the miracles of this age."

Without warning, he stood and strode toward the concave skin of the dome. He stared at his reflection, and then turned to face me.

"In time, you say? Just how long have I got?" He lifted his hand and stared at it. "Am I some laboratory animal you'll get rid of once your experiment's through?" He stopped and considered something. "If you built this body, then you must be able to keep it indefinitely—"

He stopped again, this time at something in my expression. I nodded. "You are immortal," I said.

I could see that he was shaken. The tight skin of his face colored as he nodded, trying to come to terms with my casual pronouncement of his new status.

"Thirty thousand years in the future," he whispered to himself, "the world is inhabited by immortals . . ."

"The galaxy," I corrected him. "Humankind has spread throughout the stars, inhabiting those planets amenable to life, adapting others, sharing worlds with intelligent beings."

Tears welled in his eyes. He fought not to let them spill, typical masculine product of the twentieth century that he was.

"If you did this for me," he said, "then it's within your capability to bring back to life the people I loved, my wife and family—"

"And where would we stop?" I asked. "Would we Enstate and Enable the loved ones of everyone we brought forward?" I smiled. "Where would it end? Soon, everyone who had ever lived would live again."

He failed to see the humor of my words. "You don't know how cruel that is," he said.

"I understand how cruel it seems," I said. "But it is the cruelty of necessity." I paused. I judged that the time was right to share my secret. "You see, I, too, was once like you, plucked from my deathbed, brought forward to this strange and wondrous age, fearful and little comprehending the miracles around me. I stand before you as testament to the fact that you will survive this ordeal, and come to understand."

He stared at me, suspicious. At last he said, "But why . . . ? Why you and me?"

"They, the people of this age, considered us men of importance in our time—men whose contributions to history were steps along the way to the position of preeminence that humankind now occupies. Ours is not to wonder, but to accept."

"So that's all I am—a curiosity? A specimen in some damned museum?"

"Not at all! They will be curious, of course; they'll want to know all about your time . . . but you are free to learn, to explore, to do with your limitless future what you will—with the guidance and stewardship of a patron, as I, too, was once guided."

The Early walked around the periphery of the dome. He completed a circuit, and then halted and stared at me. "Explore," he said at last, tasting the word. "You said explore? I want to explore the worlds beyond Earth! No—not only the worlds beyond Earth, the worlds *beyond* the worlds you've already explored. I want to break new ground, discover new worlds . . ." He stopped and looked at me. "I take it that you haven't charted *all* the universe?"

I hesitated. "There are places still beyond the known expanses of space," I said.

"Then I want to go there!"

I smiled, taken by his naïve enthusiasm. "There will be time enough for exploration," I said. "First, you must be copied, so that you can send your other selves out to explore the unexplored. There are dangers—"

He was staring at me in disbelief, but his disbelief was not for what I thought. "Dangers?" he almost scoffed. "What's the merit of exploration if there's no risk?"

I opened my mouth, but this time I had no answer. Something of his primitivism, his heedless, reckless thirst for life which discounted peril and hardship, reminded me of the person I had once been, an age ago.

I considered the next one hundred years, and beyond. I had reached that time of my life when all experience seemed jejune and passé; I had come to the point, after all, where I had even considered Quietus.

To go beyond the uncharted, to endanger oneself in the quest for knowledge, to think the unthinkable . . .

It was ridiculous—but why, then, did the notion bring tears to my eyes?

I hurried across the dome and took his arm. "Come," I said, leading him toward the skin of the hemisphere.

"Where—?" he began.

But we were already outside the dome, and then through the skin of another, and walking across the silver-gray regolith of the lunar surface.

He stopped and gazed about in wonder. "Christ," he whispered. "Oh, Christ, I never thought . . ."

"Over here," I said, leading him.

We crossed the plain toward the display, unchanged in thirty thousand years. He stared at the lunar module, stark beneath the unremitting light of the Sun. We stood on the platform encircling the display and stared down at the footprints the first astronauts had laid upon the surface of another world.

He looked at me, his expression beatific. "I often dreamed," he said, "but I never thought I'd ever return."

I smiled. I shared the emotions he experienced then. I knew what it was to return. I recalled the time, not long after my rebirth in this miraculous age, when I had made the pilgrimage to Earth and looked again upon the cell where over thirty thousand years ago, I, Galileo Galilei, had been imprisoned for my beliefs.

Haltingly, I told Armstrong who I was. We stared up into the dark sky, past the earth and the brilliant Sun, to the wonders awaiting us in the uncharted universe beyond.

We embraced for a long minute, and then turned and retraced our steps across the surface of the Moon toward the domes of the Academy, where Severnius would be awaiting my decision.

Border Guards

GREG EGAN

Looking back at the century that has just ended, it's obvious that Australian writer Greg Egan was one of the Big New Names to emerge in SF in the nineties, and is probably one of the most significant talents to enter the field in the last several decades. Already one of the most widely known of all Australian genre writers, Egan may well be the best new "hard science" writer to enter the field since Greg Bear, and he is still growing in range, power, and sophistication. In the last few years, he has become a frequent contributor to Interzone *and* Asimov's Science Fiction, *and has made sales as well as to* Pulphouse, Analog, Aurealis, Eidolon, *and elsewhere. Many of his stories have also appeared in various "Best of the Year" series, and he was on the Hugo Final Ballot in 1995 for his story "Cocoon," which won the Ditmar Award and the* Asimov's *Readers Award. His first novel* Quarantine *appeared in 1992; his second novel* Permutation City *won the John W. Campbell Memorial Award in 1994. He won the Hugo Award in 1999 for his novella "Oceanic." His other books include the novels* Distress *and* Diaspora *and three collections of his short fiction,* Axiomatic, Luminous, *and* Our Lady of Chernobyl. *His most recent book is a major new novel,* Teranesia. *He has a Web site at http://www.netspace. netau/^gregegan/.*

Almost any story by Egan would have served perfectly well for this anthology. In fact, with the possible exception of Brian Stableford, Egan has probably written more about the posthuman future than any other writer of the last decade—being one of the key players in shaping current ideas about that future—and there were more than a dozen possibilities to choose from, including stories such as "Learning to Be Me," "Dust," "Fidelity," "Reasons to be Cheerful," "The Planck Dive," "Tap," "Oceanic," and many others ("Wang's Carpets" would have been perfect, but I had already used it in another of these anthologies). In fact, if I'd had room here to include two *stories by any one author (which I didn't have), Egan would have been the one.*

I finally settled on the dazzlingly imaginative story that follows, as it takes us as deep into that posthuman future as anything that Egan has yet written, for a compelling study of old loyalties and new possibilities.

In the early afternoon of his fourth day out of sadness, Jamil was wandering home from the gardens at the center of Noether when he heard shouts from the playing field behind the library. On the spur of the moment, without even asking the city what game was in progress, he decided to join in.

As he rounded the corner and the field came into view, it was clear from the movements of the players that they were in the middle of a quantum soccer match. At Jamil's request, the city painted the wave function of the hypothetical ball across his vision, and tweaked him to recognize the players as the members of two teams without changing their appearance at all. Maria had once told him that she always chose a literal perception of color-coded clothing instead; she had no desire to use pathways that had evolved for the sake of sorting people into those you defended and those you slaughtered. But almost everything that had been bequeathed to them was stained with blood, and to Jamil it seemed a far sweeter victory to adapt the worst relics to his own ends than to discard them as irretrievably tainted.

The wave function appeared as a vivid auroral light, a quicksilver plasma bright enough to be distinct in the afternoon sunlight, yet unable to dazzle the eye or conceal the players running through it. Bands of color representing the complex phase of the wave swept across the field, parting to wash over separate rising lobes of probability before hitting the boundary and bouncing back again, inverted. The match was being played by the oldest, simplest rules: semiclassical, nonrelativistic. The ball was confined to the field by an infinitely high barrier, so there was no question of it tunneling out, leaking away as the match progressed. The players were treated classically: their movements pumped energy into the wave, enabling transitions from the game's opening state—with the ball spread thinly across the entire field— into the range of higher-energy modes needed to localize it. But localization was fleeting; there was no point forming a nice sharp wave packet in the middle of the field in the hope of kicking it around like a classical object. You had to shape the wave in such a way that all of its modes—cycling at different frequencies, traveling with different velocities—would come into phase with each other, for a fraction of a second, within the goal itself. Achieving that was a matter of energy levels, and timing.

Jamil had noticed that one team was under-strength. The umpire would be skewing the field's potential to keep the match fair; but a new participant would be especially welcome for the sake of restoring symmetry. He watched the faces of the players, most of them old friends. They were frowning with concentration, but breaking now and then into smiles of delight at their small successes, or their opponents' ingenuity.

He was badly out of practice, but if he turned out to be dead weight he could always withdraw. And if he misjudged his skills, and lost the match with his incompetence? No one would care. The score was nil all; he could wait for a goal, but that might be an hour or more in coming. Jamil communed with the umpire and discovered that the players had decided in advance to allow new entries at any time.

Before he could change his mind, he announced himself. The wave froze, and he ran onto the field. People nodded greetings, mostly making no fuss, though Ezequiel shouted, "Welcome back!" Jamil suddenly felt fragile again; though he'd ended his long seclusion four days before, it was well within his power, still, to be dismayed by everything the game would involve. His recovery felt like a finely balanced optical illusion, a figure and ground that could change roles in an instant, a solid cube that could evert into a hollow.

The umpire guided him to his allotted starting position, opposite a woman he hadn't seen before. He offered her a formal bow, and she returned the gesture. This was no time for introductions, but he asked the city if she'd published a name. She had: Margit.

The umpire counted down in their heads. Jamil tensed, regretting his impulsiveness. For seven years he'd been dead to the world. After four days back, what was he good for? His muscles were incapable of atrophy, his reflexes could never be dulled, but he'd chosen to live with an unconstrained will, and at any moment his wavering resolve could desert him.

The umpire said, "Play." The frozen light around Jamil came to life, and he sprang into motion.

Each player was responsible for a set of modes, particular harmonics of the wave that were theirs to fill, guard, or deplete as necessary. Jamil's twelve modes cycled at between 1,000 and 1,250 milliHertz. The rules of the game endowed his body with a small, fixed potential energy, which repelled the ball slightly and allowed different modes to push and pull on each other through him, but if he stayed in one spot as the modes cycled, every influence he exerted would eventually be replaced by its opposite, and the effect would simply cancel itself out.

To drive the wave from one mode to another, you needed to move, and to drive it efficiently, you needed to exploit the way the modes fell in and out of phase with each other: to take from a 1,000-milliHertz mode and give to a 1,250, you had to act in synch with the quarter-Hertz beat between them. It was like pushing a child's swing at its natural frequency, but rather than setting a single child in motion, you were standing between two swings and acting more as an intermediary: trying to time your interventions in such a way as to speed up one child at the other's expense. The way you pushed on the wave at a given time and place was out of your hands completely, but by changing location in just the right way, you could gain control over the interaction. Every pair of modes had a spatial beat between them—like the moiré pattern formed by two sheets of woven fabric held up to the light together, shifting from transparent to opaque as the gaps between the threads fell in and out of alignment. Slicing through this cyclic landscape offered the perfect means to match the accompanying chronological beat.

Jamil sprinted across the field at a speed and angle calculated to drive two favorable transitions at once. He'd gauged the current spectrum of the wave instinctively, watching from the sidelines, and he knew which of the modes in his charge would contribute to a goal and which would detract from the probability. As he cut through the shimmering bands of color, the umpire gave him tactile feedback to supplement his visual estimates and calculations, allowing him to sense the difference between a cyclic tug, a to and fro that came to nothing, and the gentle but persistent force that meant he was successfully riding the beat.

Chusok called out to him urgently, "Take, take! Two-ten!" Everyone's spectral territory overlapped with someone else's, and you needed to pass amplitude from player to player as well as trying to manage it within your own range. *Two-ten*—a harmonic with two peaks across the width of the field and ten along its length, cycling at 1,160 milliHertz—was filling up as Chusok drove unwanted amplitude from various lower-energy modes into it. It was Jamil's role to empty it, putting the amplitude somewhere useful. Any mode with an even number of peaks across the field was unfavorable for scoring, because it had a node—a zero point between the peaks—smack in the middle of both goals.

Jamil acknowledged the request with a hand signal and shifted his trajectory. It was almost a decade since he'd last played the game, but he still knew the intricate web of possibilities by heart: he could drain the two-ten harmonic into the three-ten, five-two and five-six modes—all with "good parity," peaks along the center-line—in a single action.

As he pounded across the grass, carefully judging the correct angle by sight, increasing his speed until he felt the destructive beats give way to a steady force like a constant breeze, he suddenly recalled a time—centuries before, in another city—when he'd played with one team, week after week, for forty years. Faces and voices swam in his head. Hashim, Jamil's ninety-eighth child, and Hashim's granddaughter Laila had played beside him. But he'd burned his house and moved on, and when that era touched him at all now, it was like an unexpected gift. The scent of the grass, the shouts of the players, the soles of his feet striking the ground, resonated with every other moment he'd spent the same way, bridging the centuries, binding his life together. He never truly felt the scale of it when he sought it out deliberately; it was always small things, tightly focused moments like this, that burst the horizon of his everyday concerns and confronted him with the astonishing vista.

The two-ten mode was draining faster than he'd expected; the seesawing center-line dip in the wave was vanishing before his eyes. He looked around, and saw Margit performing an elaborate Lissajous maneuver smoothly orchestrating a dozen transitions at once. Jamil froze and watched her, admiring her virtuosity while he tried to decide what to do next; there was no point competing with her when she was doing such a good job of completing the task Chusok had set him.

Margit was his opponent, but they were both aiming for exactly the same kind of spectrum. The symmetry of the field meant that any scoring wave would work equally well for either side—but only one team could be the first to reap the benefit, the first to have more than half the wave's probability packed into their goal. So the two teams were obliged to cooperate at first, and it was only as the wave took shape from their combined efforts that it gradually became apparent which side would gain by sculpting it to perfection as rapidly as possible, and which would gain by spoiling it for the first chance, then honing it for the rebound.

Penina chided him over her shoulder as she jogged past, "You want to leave her to clean up four-six, as well?" She was smiling, but Jamil was stung; he'd been motionless for ten or fifteen seconds. It was not forbidden to drag your feet and rely on your opponents to do all the work, but it was regarded as a shamefully impoverished strategy. It was also very risky, handing them the opportunity to set up a wave that was almost impossible to exploit yourself.

He reassessed the spectrum, and quickly sorted through the alternatives. Whatever he did would have unwanted side effects; there was no magic way to avoid influencing modes in other players' territory, and any action that would drive the transitions he needed would also trigger a multitude of others, up and down the spectrum. Finally, he made a choice that would weaken the offending mode while causing as little disruption as possible.

Jamil immersed himself in the game, planning each transition two steps in advance, switching strategy halfway through a run if he had to, but staying in motion until the sweat dripped from his body, until his calves burned, until his blood sang. He wasn't blinded to the raw pleasures of the moment, or to memories of games past, but he let them wash over him, like the breeze that rose up and cooled his skin with no need for acknowledgment. Familiar voices shouted terse commands at him; as the wave came closer to a scoring spectrum, every trace of superfluous conversation vanished, every idle glance gave way to frantic, purposeful gestures. To a bystander, this might have seemed like the height of dehumanization: twenty-two people reduced to grunting cogs in a pointless machine. Jamil smiled at the thought but refused to be distracted into a complicated imaginary rebuttal. Every step he took was the answer to that, every hoarse plea to Yann or Joracy, Chusok or Maria, Eudore or Halide. These were his friends, and he was back among them. Back in the world.

The first chance of a goal was thirty seconds away, and the opportunity would fall to Jamil's team; a few tiny shifts in amplitude would clinch it. Margit kept her distance, but Jamil could sense her eyes on him constantly— and literally feel her at work through his skin as she slackened his contact with the wave. In theory, by mirroring your opponent's movements at the correct position on the field, you could undermine everything they did, though in practice, not even the most skillful team could keep the spectrum completely frozen. Going further and spoiling was a tug of war you didn't want to win too well: if you degraded the wave too much, your opponent's task—spoiling your own subsequent chance at a goal—became far easier.

Jamil still had two bad-parity modes that he was hoping to weaken, but every time he changed velocity to try a new transition, Margit responded in an instant, blocking him. He gestured to Chusok for help; Chusok had his own problems with Ezequiel, but he could still make trouble for Margit by choosing where he placed unwanted amplitude. Jamil shook sweat out of his eyes; he could see the characteristic "stepping stone" pattern of lobes forming, a sign that the wave would soon converge on the goal, but from the middle of the field it was impossible to judge their shape accurately enough to know what, if anything, remained to be done.

Suddenly, Jamil felt the wave push against him. He didn't waste time looking around for Margit; Chusok must have succeeded in distracting her. He was almost at the boundary line, but he managed to reverse smoothly, continuing to drive both the transitions he'd been aiming for.

Two long lobes of probability, each modulated by a series of oscillating mounds, raced along the sides of the field. A third, shorter lobe running along the center-line melted away, reappeared, then merged with the others as they touched the end of the field, forming an almost rectangular plateau encompassing the goal.

The plateau became a pillar of light, growing narrower and higher as dozens of modes, all finally in phase, crashed together against the impenetrable barrier of the field's boundary. A shallow residue was still spread across the entire field, and a diminishing sequence of elliptical lobes trailed away from the goal like a staircase, but most of the wave that had started out lapping around their waists was now concentrated in a single peak that towered above their heads, nine or ten meters tall.

For an instant, it was motionless.

Then it began to fall.

The umpire said, "Forty-nine point eight."

The wave packet had not been tight enough.

Jamil struggled to shrug off his disappointment and throw his instincts into reverse. The other team had fifty seconds, now, to fine-tune the spectrum and ensure that the reflected packet was just a fraction narrower when it reformed, at the opposite end of the field.

As the pillar collapsed, replaying its synthesis in reverse, Jamil caught sight of Margit. She smiled at him calmly, and it suddenly struck him: *She'd known they couldn't make the goal. That was why she'd stopped opposing him.* She'd let him work toward sharpening the wave for a few seconds, knowing that it was already too late for him, knowing that her own team would gain from the slight improvement.

Jamil was impressed; it took an extraordinary level of skill and confidence to do what she'd just done. For all the time he'd spent away, he knew exactly what to expect from the rest of the players, and in Margit's absence he would probably have been wishing out loud for a talented newcomer to make the game interesting again. Still, it was hard not to feel a slight sting of resentment. Someone should have warned him just how good she was.

With the modes slipping out of phase, the wave undulated all over the field again, but its reconvergence was inevitable: unlike a wave of water or sound, it possessed no hidden degrees of freedom to grind its precision into entropy. Jamil decided to ignore Margit; there were cruder strategies than mirror-blocking that worked almost as well. Chusok was filling the two-ten mode now; Jamil chose the four-six as his spoiler. All they had to do was keep the wave from growing much sharper, and it didn't matter whether they achieved this by preserving the status quo, or by nudging it from one kind of bluntness to another.

The steady resistance he felt as he ran told Jamil that he was driving the transition, unblocked, but he searched in vain for some visible sign of success. When he reached a vantage point where he could take in enough of the field in one glance to judge the spectrum properly, he noticed a rapidly vibrating shimmer across the width of the wave. He counted nine peaks: good parity. Margit had pulled most of the amplitude straight out of his spoiler mode and fed it into *this*. It was a mad waste of energy to aim for such an elevated harmonic, but no one had been looking there, no one had stopped her.

The scoring pattern was forming again, he only had nine or ten seconds left to make up for all the time he'd wasted. Jamil chose the strongest good-parity mode in his territory, and the emptiest bad one, computed the velocity that would link them, and ran.

He didn't dare turn to watch the opposition goal; he didn't want to break his concentration. The wave retreated around his feet, less like an Earthly ebb tide than an ocean drawn into the sky by a passing black hole. The city diligently portrayed the shadow that his body would have cast, shrinking in front of him as the tower of light rose.

The verdict was announced. "Fifty point one."

The air was filled with shouts of triumph—Ezequiel's the loudest, as always. Jamil sagged to his knees, laughing. It was a curious feeling, familiar as it was: he cared, and he didn't. If he'd been wholly indifferent to the outcome of the game, there would have been no pleasure in it, but obsessing over every defeat—or every victory—could ruin it just as thoroughly. He could almost see himself walking the line, orchestrating his response as carefully as any action in the game itself.

He lay down on the grass to catch his breath before play resumed. The outer face of the microsun that orbited Laplace was shielded with rock, but light reflected skyward from the land beneath it crossed the 100,000-kilometer width of the 3-toroidal universe to give a faint glow to the planet's nightside. Though only a sliver was lit directly, Jamil could discern the full disc of the opposite hemisphere in the primary image at the zenith: continents and oceans that lay, by a shorter route, 12,000 or so kilometers beneath him. Other views in the lattice of images spread across the sky were from different angles, and showed substantial crescents of the dayside itself. The one thing you couldn't find in any of these images, even with a telescope, was your own city. The topology of this universe let you see the back of your head, but never your reflection.

Jamil's team lost, three nil. He staggered over to the fountains at the edge of the field and slaked his thirst, shocked by the pleasure of the simple act. Just to be alive was glorious now, but once he felt this way, anything seemed possible. He was back in synch, back in phase, and he was going to make the most of it, for however long it lasted.

He caught up with the others, who'd headed down toward the river. Ezequiel hooked an arm around his neck, laughing. "Bad luck, Sleeping Beauty! You picked the wrong time to wake. With Margit, we're invincible."

Jamil ducked free of him. "I won't argue with that." He looked around. "Speaking of whom—"

Penina said, "Gone home. She plays, that's all. No frivolous socializing after the match."

Chusok added, "Or any other time." Penina shot Jamil a glance that meant not for want of trying on Chusok's part.

Jamil pondered this, wondering why it annoyed him so much. On the field, she hadn't come across as aloof and superior. Just unashamedly good.

He queried the city, but she'd published nothing beside her name. Nobody expected—or wished—to hear more than the tiniest fraction of another person's history, but it was rare for anyone to start a new life without carrying through something from the old as a kind of calling card, some incident or achievement from which your new neighbors could form an impression of you.

They'd reached the riverbank. Jamil pulled his shirt over his head. "So what's her story? She must have told you something."

Ezequiel said, "Only that she learned to play a long time ago; she won't say where or when. She arrived in Noether at the end of last year, and grew a house on the southern outskirts. No one sees her around much. No one even knows what she studies."

Jamil shrugged, and waded in. "Ah well. It's a challenge to rise to." Penina laughed and splashed him teasingly. He protested, "I *meant* beating her at the game."

Chusok said wryly, "When you turned up, I thought you'd be our secret weapon. The one player she didn't know inside-out already."

"I'm glad you didn't tell me that. I would have turned around and fled straight back into hibernation."

"I know. That's why we all kept quiet." Chusok smiled. "Welcome back."

Penina said, "Yeah, welcome back, Jamil."

Sunlight shone on the surface of the river. Jamil ached all over, but the cool water was the perfect place to be. If he wished, he could build a partition in his mind at the point where he stood right now, and never fall beneath it. Other people lived that way, and it seemed to cost them nothing. Contrast was overrated; no sane person spent half their time driving spikes into their flesh for the sake of feeling better when they stopped. Ezequiel lived every day with the happy boisterousness of a five-year-old; Jamil sometimes found this annoying, but then any kind of disposition would irritate someone. His own stretches of meaningless somberness weren't exactly a boon to his friends.

Chusok said, "I've invited everyone to a meal at my house tonight. Will you come?"

Jamil thought it over, then shook his head. He still wasn't ready. He couldn't force-feed himself with normality; it didn't speed his recovery, it just drove him backward.

Chusok looked disappointed, but there was nothing to be done about that. Jamil promised him, "Next time. OK?"

Ezequiel sighed. "What are we going to do with you? You're worse than Margit!" Jamil started backing away, but it was too late. Ezequiel reached him in two casual strides, bent down and grabbed him around the waist, hoisted him effortlessly onto one shoulder, then flung him through the air into the depths of the river.

Jamil was woken by the scent of wood smoke. His room was still filled with the night's grey shadows, but when he propped himself up on one elbow and the window obliged him with transparency, the city was etched clearly in the predawn light.

He dressed and left the house, surprised at the coolness of the dew on his feet. No one else in his street seemed to be up; had they failed to notice the smell, or did they already know to expect it? He turned a corner and saw the rising column of soot, faintly lit with red from below. The flames and the ruins were still hidden from him, but he knew whose house it was.

When he reached the dying blaze, he crouched in the heat-withered garden, cursing himself. Chusok had offered him the chance to join him for his last meal in Noether. Whatever hints you dropped, it was customary to tell no one that you were moving on. If you still had a lover, if you still had young children, you never deserted them. But friends, you warned in subtle ways. Before vanishing.

Jamil covered his head with his arms. He'd lived through this countless times before, but it never became easier. If anything, it grew worse, as every departure was weighted with the memories of others. His brothers and sisters had scattered across the branches of the New Territories. He'd walked away from his father and mother when he was too young and confident to realize how much it would hurt him, decades later. His own children had all abandoned him eventually, far more often than he'd left them. It was easier to leave an ex-lover than a grown child: something burned itself out in a couple, almost naturally, as if ancestral biology had prepared them for at least that one rift.

Jamil stopped fighting the tears. But as he brushed them away, he caught sight of someone standing beside him. He looked up. It was Margit.

He felt a need to explain. He rose to his feet and addressed her. "This was Chusok's house. We were good friends. I'd known him for ninety-six years."

Margit gazed back at him neutrally. "Boo hoo. Poor baby. You'll never see your friend again."

Jamil almost laughed, her rudeness was so surreal. He pushed on, as if the only conceivable, polite response was to pretend that he hadn't heard her. "No one is the kindest, the most generous, the most loyal. It doesn't matter. That's not the point. Everyone's unique. Chusok was Chusok." He banged a fist against his chest, utterly heedless now of her contemptuous words. "There's a hole in me, and it will never be filled." That was the truth, even though he'd grow around it. *He should have gone to the meal, it would have cost him nothing.*

"You must be a real emotional Swiss cheese," observed Margit tartly.

Jamil came to his senses. "Why don't you fuck off to some other universe? No one wants you in Noether."

Margit was amused. "You *are* a bad loser."

Jamil gazed at her, honestly confused for a moment; the game had slipped his mind completely. He gestured at the embers. "What are you doing here? Why did you follow the smoke, if it wasn't regret at not saying goodbye to him when you had the chance?" He wasn't sure how seriously to take Penina's lighthearted insinuation, but if Chusok had fallen for Margit, and it had not been reciprocated, that might even have been the reason he'd left.

She shook her head calmly. "He was nothing to me. I barely spoke to him."

"Well, that's your loss."

"From the look of things, I'd say the loss was all yours."

He had no reply. Margit turned and walked away. Jamil crouched on the ground again, rocking back and forth, waiting for the pain to subside.

Jamil spent the next week preparing to resume his studies. The library had near-instantaneous contact with every artificial universe in the New Territories, and the additional lightspeed lag between Earth and the point in space from which the whole tree-structure blossomed was only a few hours. Jamil had been to Earth, but only as a tourist; land was scarce, they accepted no migrants. There were remote planets you could live on, in the home universe, but you had to be a certain kind of masochistic purist to want that. The precise reasons why his ancestors had entered the New Territories had been forgotten generations before—and it would have been presumptuous to track them down and ask them in person—but given a choice between the then even-more-crowded Earth, the horrifying reality of interstellar distances, and an endlessly extensible branching chain of worlds which could be traversed within a matter of weeks, the decision wasn't exactly baffling.

Jamil had devoted most of his time in Noether to studying the category of representations of Lie groups on complex vector spaces—a fitting choice, since Emmy Noether had been a pioneer of group theory, and if she'd lived to see this field blossom, she would probably have been in the thick of it herself. Representations of Lie groups lay behind most of physics: each kind of subatomic particle was really nothing but a particular way of representing the universal symmetry group as a set of rotations of complex vectors. Organizing this kind of structure with category theory was ancient knowledge, but Jamil didn't care; he'd long ago reconciled himself to being a student, not a discoverer. The greatest gift of consciousness was the ability to take the patterns of the world inside you, and for all that he would have relished the thrill of being the first at anything; with ten-to-the-sixteenth people alive that was a futile ambition for most.

In the library, he spoke with fellow students of his chosen field on other worlds, or read their latest works. Though they were not researchers, they could still put a new pedagogical spin on old material, enriching the connections with other fields, finding ways to make the complex, subtle truth easier to assimilate without sacrificing the depth and detail that made it worth knowing in the first place. They would not advance the frontiers of knowledge. They would not discover new principles of nature, or invent new technologies. But to Jamil, understanding was an end in itself.

He rarely thought about the prospect of playing another match, and when he did, the idea was not appealing. With Chusok gone, the same group could play ten-to-a-side without Jamil to skew the numbers. Margit might even choose to swap teams, if only for the sake of proving that her current team's monotonous string of victories really had been entirely down to her.

When the day arrived, though, he found himself unable to stay away. He turned up intending to remain a spectator, but Ryuichi had deserted Ezequiel's team, and everyone begged Jamil to join in.

As he took his place opposite Margit, there was nothing in her demeanor to acknowledge their previous encounter: no lingering contempt, but no hint of shame either. Jamil resolved to put it out of his mind; he owed it to his fellow players to concentrate on the game.

They lost, five nil.

Jamil forced himself to follow everyone to Eudore's house, to celebrate, commiserate, or, as it turned out, to forget the whole thing. After they'd eaten, Jamil wandered from room to room, enjoying. Eudore's choice of music but unable to settle into any conversation. No one mentioned Chusok in his hearing.

He left just after midnight. Laplace's near-full primary image and its eight brightest gibbous companions lit the streets so well that there was no need for anything more. Jamil thought: Chusok might have merely traveled to another city, one beneath his gaze right now. And wherever he'd gone, he might yet choose to stay in touch with his friends from Noether.

And his friends from the next town, and the next?

Century after century?

Margit was sitting on Jamil's doorstep, holding a bunch of white flowers in one hand.

Jamil was irritated. "What are you doing here?"

"I came to apologize."

He shrugged. "There's no need. We feel differently about certain things. That's fine. I can still face you on the playing field."

"I'm not apologizing for a difference of opinion. I wasn't honest with you. I was cruel." She shaded her eyes against the glare of the planet and looked up at him. "You were right: it was my loss. I wish I'd known your friend."

He laughed curtly. "Well, it's too late for that."

She said simply, "I know."

Jamil relented. "Do you want to come in?" Margit nodded, and he instructed the door to open for her. As he followed her inside, he said, "How long have you been here? Have you eaten?"

"No."

"I'll cook something for you."

"You don't have to do that."

He called out to her from the kitchen, "Think of it as a peace offering. I don't have any flowers."

Margit replied, "They're not for you. They're for Chusok's house."

Jamil stopped rummaging through his vegetable bins and walked back into the living room. "People don't usually do that in Noether."

Margit was sitting on the couch, staring at the floor. She said, "I'm so lonely here. I can't bear it anymore."

He sat beside her. "Then why did you rebuff him? You could at least have been friends."

She shook her head. "Don't ask me to explain."

Jamil took her hand. She turned and embraced him, trembling miserably. He stroked her hair. "Sssh."

She said, "Just sex. I don't want anything more."

He groaned softly. "There's no such thing as that."

"I just need someone to touch me again."

"I understand." He confessed, "So do I. But that won't be all. So don't ask me to promise there'll be nothing more."

Margit took his face in her hands and kissed him. Her mouth tasted of wood smoke.

Jamil said, "I don't even know you."

"No one knows anyone, anymore."

"That's not true."

"No, it's not," she conceded gloomily. She ran a hand lightly along his arm. Jamil wanted badly to see her smile, so he made each dark hair thicken and blossom into a violet flower as it passed beneath her fingers.

She did smile, but she said, "I've seen that trick before."

Jamil was annoyed. "I'm sure to be a disappointment all round, then. I expect you'd be happier with some kind of novelty. A unicorn, or an amoeba."

She laughed. "I don't think so." She took his hand and placed it against her breast. "Do you ever get tired of sex?"

"Do you ever get tired of breathing?"

"I can go for a long time without thinking about it."

He nodded. "But then one day you stop and fill your lungs with air, and it's still as sweet as ever."

Jamil didn't know what he was feeling anymore. Lust. Compassion. Spite. She'd come to him hurting, and he wanted to help her, but he wasn't sure that either of them really believed this would work.

Margit inhaled the scent of the flowers on his arm. "Are they the same color? Everywhere else?"

He said, "There's only one way to find out."

Jamil woke in the early hours of the morning, alone. He'd half-expected Margit to flee like this, but she could have waited till dawn. He would have obligingly feigned sleep while she dressed and tiptoed out.

Then he heard her. It was not a sound he would normally have associated with a human being, but it could not have been anything else.

He found her in the kitchen, curled around a table leg, wailing rhythmically. He stood back and watched her, afraid that anything he did would only make things worse. She met his gaze in the half-light, but kept up the mechanical whimper. Her eyes weren't blank; she was not delirious, or hallucinating. She knew exactly who, and where, she was.

Finally, Jamil knelt in the doorway. He said, "Whatever it is, you can tell me. And we'll fix it. We'll find a way."

She bared her teeth. "You can't *fix it*, you stupid child." She resumed the awful noise.

"Then just tell me. Please?" He stretched out a hand toward her. He hadn't felt quite so helpless since his very first daughter, Aminata, had come to him as an inconsolable six-year-old, rejected by the boy to whom she'd declared her undying love. He'd been twenty-four years old; a child himself. More than a thousand years ago. *Where are you now, Nata?*

Margit said, "I promised I'd never tell."

"Promised who?"

Myself."

Good. They're the easiest kind to break."

She started weeping. It was a more ordinary sound, but it was even more chilling. She was not a wounded animal now, an alien being suffering some incomprehensible pain. Jamil approached her cautiously; she let him wrap his arms around her shoulders.

He whispered, "Come to bed. The warmth will help. Just being held will help."

She spat at him derisively, "It won't bring her back."

"Who?"

Margit stared at him in silence, as if he'd said something shocking.

Jamil insisted gently, "Who won't it bring back?" She'd lost a friend, badly, the way he'd lost Chusok. That was why she'd sought him out. He could help her through it. They could help each other through it.

She said, "It won't bring back the dead."

Margit was seven thousand five hundred and ninety-four years old. Jamil persuaded her to sit at the kitchen table. He wrapped her in blankets, then fed her tomatoes and rice, as she told him how she'd witnessed the birth of his world.

The promise had shimmered just beyond reach for decades. Almost none of her contemporaries had believed it would happen, though the truth should have been plain for centuries: *the human body was a material thing.* In time, with enough knowledge and effort, it would become possible to safeguard it from any kind of deterioration, any kind of harm. Stellar evolution and cosmic entropy might or might not prove insurmountable, but there'd be aeons to confront those challenges. In the middle of the twenty-first century, the hurdles were aging, disease, violence, and an overcrowded planet.

"Grace was my best friend. We were students." Margit smiled. "Before everyone was a student. We'd talk about it, but we didn't believe we'd see it happen. It would come in another century. It would come for our great-great-grandchildren. We'd hold infants on our knees in our twilight years and tell ourselves: *this one will never die.*

"When we were both twenty-two, something happened. To both of us." She lowered her eyes. "We were kidnapped. We were raped. We were tortured."

Jamil didn't know how to respond. These were just words to him: he knew their meaning, he knew these acts would have hurt her, but she might as well have been describing a mathematical theorem. He stretched a hand across the table, but Margit ignored it. He said awkwardly, "This was ... the Holocaust?"

She looked up at him, shaking her head, almost laughing at his naïveté. "Not even one of them. Not a war, not a pogrom. Just one psychopathic man. He locked us in his basement, for six months. He'd killed seven women."

Tears began spilling down her cheeks. "He showed us the bodies. They were buried right where we slept. He showed us how we'd end up, when he was through with us."

Jamil was numb. He'd known all his adult life what had once been possible—what had once happened, to real people—but it had all been consigned to history long before his birth. In retrospect, it seemed almost inconceivably stupid, but he'd always imagined that the changes had come in such a way that no one still living had experienced these horrors. There'd been no escaping the bare minimum, the logical necessity: his oldest living ancestors must have watched their parents fall peacefully into eternal sleep. But not this. Not a flesh-and-blood woman, sitting in front of him, who'd been forced to sleep in a killer's graveyard.

He put his hand over hers, and choked out the words. "This man . . . *killed* Grace? He killed your friend?"

Margit began sobbing, but she shook her head. "No, no. We got out!" She twisted her mouth into a smile. "Someone stabbed the stupid fucker in a barroom brawl. We dug our way out while he was in hospital." She put her face down on the table and wept, but she held Jamil's hand against her cheek. He couldn't understand what she'd lived through, but that couldn't mean he wouldn't console her. Hadn't he touched his mother's face the same way, when she was sad beyond his childish comprehension?

She composed herself and continued. "We made a resolution, while we were in there. If we survived, there'd be no more empty promises. No more daydreams. What he'd done to those seven women—and what he'd done to us—would become impossible."

And it had. Whatever harm befell your body, you had the power to shut off your senses and decline to experience it. If the flesh was damaged, it could always be repaired or replaced. In the unlikely event that your jewel itself was destroyed, everyone had backups, scattered across universes. No human being could inflict physical pain on another. In theory, you could still be killed, but it would take the same kind of resources as destroying a galaxy. The only people who seriously contemplated either were the villains in very bad operas.

Jamil's eyes narrowed in wonder. She'd spoken those last words with such fierce pride that there was no question of her having failed.

"*You* are Ndoli? You invented the jewel?" As a child, he'd been told that the machine in his skull had been designed by a man who'd died long ago.

Margit stroked his hand, amused. "In those days, very few Hungarian women could be mistaken for Nigerian men. I've never changed my body that much, Jamil. I've always looked much as you see me."

Jamil was relieved; if she'd been Ndoli himself, he might have succumbed to sheer awe and started babbling idolatrous nonsense. "But you worked with Ndoli? You and Grace?"

She shook her head. "We made the resolution, and then we floundered. We were mathematicians, not neurologists. There were a thousand things going on at once: tissue engineering, brain imaging, molecular computers. We had no real idea where to put our efforts, which problems we should bring our strengths to bear upon. Ndoli's work didn't come out of the blue for us, but we played no part in it.

"For a while, almost everyone was nervous about switching from the brain to the jewel. In the early days, the jewel was a separate device that learned its task by mimicking the brain, and it had to be handed control of the body at one chosen moment. It took another fifty years before it could be engineered to replace the brain incrementally, neuron by neuron, in a seamless transition throughout adolescence."

So Grace had lived to see the jewel invented, but held back, and died before she could use it? Jamil kept himself from blurting out this conclusion, all his guesses had proved wrong so far.

Margit continued. "Some people weren't just nervous, though. You'd be amazed how vehemently Ndoli was denounced in certain quarters. And I don't just mean the fanatics who churned out paranoid tracts about 'the machines' taking over, with their evil, inhuman agendas. Some people's antagonism had nothing to do with the specifics of the technology. They were opposed to immortality, in principle."

Jamil laughed. *"Why?"*

"Ten thousand years' worth of sophistry doesn't vanish overnight," Margit observed dryly. "Every human culture had expended vast amounts of intellectual effort on the problem of coming to terms with death. Most religions had constructed elaborate lies about it, making it out to be something other than it was—though a few were dishonest about life, instead. But even most secular philosophies were warped by the need to pretend that *death was for the best.*

"It was the naturalistic fallacy at its most extreme—and its most transparent, but that didn't stop anyone. Since any child could tell you that death was meaningless, contingent, unjust, and abhorrent beyond words, it was a hallmark of sophistication to believe otherwise. Writers had consoled themselves for centuries with smug, puritanical fables about immortals who'd long for death—who'd *beg* for death. It would have been too much to expect all those who were suddenly faced with the reality of its banishment to confess that they'd been whistling in the dark. And would-be moral philosophers—mostly those who'd experienced no greater inconvenience in their lives than a late train or a surly waiter—began wailing about the destruction of the human spirit by this hideous blight. We needed death and suffering to put steel into our souls! Not horrible, horrible *freedom and safety!*"

Jamil smiled. "So there were buffoons. But in the end, surely they swallowed their pride? If we're walking in a desert and I tell you that the lake you see ahead is a mirage, I might cling stubbornly to my own belief, to save myself from disappointment. But when we arrive, and I'm proven wrong, I *will* drink from the lake."

Margit nodded. "Most of the loudest of these people went quiet in the end. But there were subtler arguments, too. Like it or not, all our biology and all of our culture had evolved in the presence of death. And almost every righteous struggle in history, every worthwhile sacrifice, had been against suffering, against violence, against death. Now, that struggle would become impossible."

"Yes." Jamil was mystified. "But only because it had triumphed."

Margit said gently, "I know. There was no sense to it. And it was always my belief that anything worth fighting for—over centuries, over millennia—was worth attaining. It *can't* be noble to toil for a cause, and even to die for it, unless it's also noble to succeed. To claim otherwise isn't sophistication, it's just a kind of hypocrisy. If it's better to travel than arrive, you shouldn't start the voyage in the first place.

"I told Grace as much, and she agreed. We laughed together at what we called the *tragedians*: the people who denounced the coming age as the age without martyrs, the age without saints, the age without revolutionaries. There would never be another Gandhi, another Mandela, another Aung San Suu Kyi—and yes, that *was* a kind of loss, but would any great leader have sentenced humanity to eternal misery for the sake of providing a suitable backdrop for eternal heroism? Well, some of them would have. But the down-trodden themselves had better things to do."

Margit fell silent. Jamil cleared her plate away, then sat opposite her again. It was almost dawn.

"Of course, the jewel was not enough," Margit continued. "With care, Earth could support forty billion people, but where would the rest go? The jewel made virtual reality the easiest escape route: for a fraction of the space, a fraction of the space, a fraction of the energy, it could survive without a body attached. Grace and I weren't horrified by that prospect, the way some people were. But it was not the best outcome, it was not what most people wanted, the way they wanted freedom from death.

"So we studied gravity, we studied the vacuum."

Jamil feared making a fool of himself again, but from the expression on her face he knew he wasn't wrong this time. M. *Osvát and* G. *Füst.* Co-authors of the seminal paper, but no more was known about them than those abbreviated names. "You gave us the New Territories?"

Margit nodded slightly. "Grace and I."

Jamil was overwhelmed with love for her. He went to her and knelt down to put his arms around her waist. Margit touched his shoulder. "Come on, get up. Don't treat me like a god, it just makes me feel old."

He stood, smiling abashedly. Anyone in pain deserved his help—but if he was not in her debt, the word had no meaning.

"And Grace?" he asked.

Margit looked away. "Grace completed her work, and then decided that she was a tragedian, after all. Rape was impossible. Torture was impossible. Poverty was vanishing. Death was receding into cosmology, into metaphysics. It was everything she'd hoped would come to pass. And for her, suddenly faced with that fulfillment, everything that remained seemed trivial.

"One night she climbed into the furnace in the basement of her building. Her jewel survived the flames, but she'd erased it from within."

* * *

It was morning now. Jamil was beginning to feel disoriented; Margit should have vanished in daylight, an apparition unable to persist in the mundane world.

"I'd lost other people who were close to me," she said. "My parents. My brother. Friends. And so had everyone around me, then. I wasn't special; grief was still commonplace. But decade by decade, century by century, we shrank into insignificance, those of us who knew what it meant to lose someone forever. We're less than one in a million, now.

"For a long time, I clung to my own generation. There were enclaves, there were ghettos, where everyone understood the old days. I spent two hundred years married to a man who wrote a play called *We Who Have Known the Dead*—which was every bit as pretentious and self-pitying as you'd guess from the title." She smiled at the memory. "It was a horrible, self-devouring world. If I'd stayed in it much longer, I would have followed Grace. I would have begged for death."

She looked up at Jamil. "It's people like you I want to be with: *people who don't understand.* Your lives aren't trivial, any more than the best parts of our own were: all the tranquility, all the beauty, all the happiness that made the sacrifices and the life-and-death struggles worthwhile.

"The tragedians were wrong. They had everything upside-down. Death never gave meaning to life; it was always the other way round. All of its gravitas, all of its significance, was stolen from the things it ended. But the value of life always lay entirely in itself—not in its loss, not in its fragility.

"Grace should have lived to see that. She should have lived long enough to understand that the world hadn't turned to ash."

Jamil sat in silence, turning the whole confession over in his mind, trying to absorb it well enough not to add to her distress with a misjudged question. Finally, he ventured, "Why do you hold back from friendship with us, though? Because we're just children to you? Children who can't understand what you've lost?"

Margit shook her head vehemently. "I *don't want you* to understand! People like me are the only blight on this world, the only poison." She smiled at Jamil's expression of anguish, and rushed to silence him before he could swear that she was nothing of the kind. "Not in everything we do and say, or everyone we touch; I'm not claiming that we're tainted, in some fatuous mythological sense. But when I left the ghettos, I promised myself that I wouldn't bring the past with me. Sometimes that's an easy vow to keep. Sometimes it's not."

"You've broken it tonight," Jamil said plainly. "And neither of us have been struck down by lightning."

"I know." She took his hand. "But I was wrong to tell you what I have, and I'll fight to regain the strength to stay silent. I stand at the border between two worlds, Jamil. I remember death, and I always will. But my job now is to guard that border. To keep that knowledge from invading your world."

"We're not as fragile as you think," he protested. "We all know something about loss."

Margit nodded soberly. "Your friend Chusok has vanished into the crowd.

That's how things work now: how you keep yourselves from suffocating in a jungle of endlessly growing connections, or fragmenting into isolated troupes of repertory players, endlessly churning out the same lines.

"You have your little deaths—and I don't call them that to deride you. But I've seen both. And I promise you, they're not the same."

In the weeks that followed, Jamil resumed in full the life he'd made for himself in Noether. Five days in seven were for the difficult beauty of mathematics. The rest were for his friends.

He kept playing matches, and Margit's team kept winning. In the sixth game, though, Jamil's team finally scored against her. Their defeat was only three to one.

Each night, Jamil struggled with the question. What exactly did he owe her? Eternal loyalty, eternal silence, eternal obedience? She hadn't sworn him to secrecy; she'd extracted no promises at all. But he knew she was trusting him to comply with her wishes, so what right did he have to do otherwise?

Eight weeks after the night he'd spent with Margit, Jamil found himself alone with Penina in a room in Joracy's house. They'd been talking about the old days. Talking about Chusok.

Jamil said, "Margit lost someone very close to her."

Penina nodded matter-of-factly, but curled into a comfortable position on the couch and prepared to take in every word.

"Not in the way we've lost Chusok. Not in the way you think at all."

Jamil approached the others, one by one. His confidence ebbed and flowed. He'd glimpsed the old world, but he couldn't pretend to have fathomed its inhabitants. What if Margit saw this as worse than betrayal—as a further torture, a further rape?

But he couldn't stand by and leave her to the torture she'd inflicted on herself.

Ezequiel was the hardest to face. Jamil spent a sick and sleepless night beforehand, wondering if this would make him a monster, a corrupter of children, the epitome of everything Margit believed she was fighting.

Ezequiel wept freely, but he was not a child. He was older than Jamil, and he had more steel in his soul than any of them.

He said, "I guessed it might be that. I guessed she might have seen the bad times. But I never found a way to ask her."

The three lobes of probability converged, melted into a plateau, rose into a pillar of light.

The umpire said, "Fifty-five point nine." It was Margit's most impressive goal yet.

Ezequiel whooped joyfully and ran toward her. When he scooped her up in his arms and threw her across his shoulders, she laughed and indulged him. When Jamil stood beside him and they made a joint throne for her with their arms, she frowned down at him and said, "You shouldn't be doing this. You're on the losing side."

The rest of the players converged on them, cheering, and they started down toward the river. Margit looked around nervously. "What is this? We haven't finished playing."

Penina said, "The game's over early, just this once. Think of this as an invitation. We want you to swim with us. We want you to talk to us. We want to hear everything about your life."

Margit's composure began to crack. She squeezed Jamil's shoulder. He whispered, "Say the word, and we'll put you down."

Margit didn't whisper back; she shouted miserably, "What do you want from me, you parasites? I've won your fucking game for you! What more do you want?"

Jamil was mortified. He stopped and prepared to lower her, prepared to retreat, but Ezequiel caught his arm.

Ezequiel said, "We want to be your border guards. We want to stand beside you."

Christa added, "We can't face what you've faced, but we want to understand. As much as we can."

Joracy spoke, then Yann, Narcyza, Maria, Halide. Margit looked down on them, weeping, confused.

Jamil burned with shame. He'd hijacked her, humiliated her. He'd made everything worse. She'd flee Noether, flee into a new exile, more alone than ever.

When everyone had spoken, silence descended. Margit trembled on her throne.

Jamil faced the ground. He couldn't undo what he'd done. He said quietly, "Now you know our wishes. Will you tell us yours?"

"Put me down."

Jamil and Ezequiel complied.

Margit looked around at her teammates and opponents, her children, her creation, her would-be friends.

She said, "I want to go to the river with you. I'm seven thousand years old, and I want to learn to swim."

Epilogue

Homo Sapiens Declared Extinct
BRUCE STERLING

A History of the Human and Post-Human Species
GEOFFREY A. LANDIS

The Great Goodbye
ROBERT CHARLES WILSON

In closing, appropriately enough, dancing here as we are on beginning brink of the new century, there follow three very short and conceptually daring looks ahead to what the human race may have in store for it during the twenty-first century. Which of them, if any of them, comes the closest to predicting what actually will happen, of course will be for future scholars (if there are any) to decide, looking back at this book as a historical curiosity from the brink of the next century. (My own guess, for what it's worth, is that, imaginative as they are, none of them will turn out to have come even close to what really happens.)

Bruce Sterling's "Spook" appears elsewhere in this anthology, and his biographical information can be read there.

Geoffrey A. Landis is a physicist who works for NASA, and who has recently been working on a Martian Lander program. He's a frequent contributor to Analog and to Asimov's Science Fiction, and has also sold stories to markets such as Interzone, Amazing, and Pulphouse. Landis is not a prolific writer by the high-production standards of the genre, but he is popular. His story, "A Walk in the Sun" won him a Nebula and a Hugo Award in 1992; his story, "Ripples in the Dirac Sea" won him a Nebula Award in 1990; and his story, "Elemental" was on the Final Hugo Ballot a few years back. His first book was the collection Myths, Legends, and True History, and he has just published his first novel, Mars Crossing. He lives in Brook Park, Ohio.

Robert Charles Wilson made his first sale in 1974, to Analog, but little more was heard from him until the late eighties, when he began to publish a string of ingenious and well-crafted novels and stories that have since established him among the top ranks of the writers who came to prominence in the last two decades of the twentieth century. His first novel A Hidden Place appeared in 1986. He won the

Philip K. Dick Award for his 1995 novel Mysterium, *and the Aurora Award for his story, "The Perseids." His other books include the novels* Memory Wire, Gypsies, The Divide, The Harvest, A Bridge of Years, *and* Darwinia. *His most recent book is a new novel,* Bios. *He lives in Toronto, Canada.*

Homo Sapiens Declared Extinct

BRUCE STERLING

AD 2380: After a painstaking ten-year search, from the Tibetan highlands to the Brazilian rainforests, it's official—there are no more human beings.

"I suppose I have to consider this a personal setback," said anthropologist Dr. Marcia Raymo, of the Institute for Retrograde Study in Berlin. "Of course we still have human tissue in the lab, and we could clone as many specimens of *Homo sapiens* as we like. But that species was always known primarily for its unique cultural activity."

"I can't understand what the fuss is about," declared Rita "Cuddles" Srinivasan, actress, sex symbol, and computer peripheral. "Artificial Intelligence love to embody themselves in human forms like mine, to wallow in sex and eating. I'm good for oodles of human stuff, scratching, sleeping, sneezing, you can name it. As long as AIs honor their origins, you'll see plenty of disembodied intelligences slumming around in human forms. That's where all the fun is, I promise—trust me."

The actress's current AI sponsor further remarked via wireless telepathy that Miss Srinivasan's occasional extra arms or heads should be seen as a sign of "creative brio," and not as a violation of "some obsolete, supposedly standard human form."

A worldwide survey of skull contents in April 2379 revealed no living citizen with less than thirty-five percent cultured gelbrain. "That pretty well kicks it in the head for me," declared statistician Piers Euler, the front identity for a collaborative group-mind of mathematicians at the Bourbaki Academy in Paris. "I don't see how you can declare any entity 'human' when their brain is a gelatin lattice, and every cell of their body contains extensive extra strands of industrial-strength DNA. Not only is humanity extinct but, strictly speaking, pretty much everyone alive today should be classified as a unique, postnatural, one-of-a-kind species."

"I was born human," admitted three-hundred-eighty-year-old classical musician Soon Yi, speaking from his support vat in Shanghai. "I grew up as a human being. It seemed quite natural at the time. For hundreds of years on the state-supported concert circuit, I promoted myself as a 'humanist,' supporting and promoting human high culture. But at this point, I should be honest: that was always my stage pretense. Let's face it: gelbrain is vastly better stuff than those gray, greasy, catch-as-catch-can human neurons. You can't become a serious professional artiste while using nothing but all-natural animal tissue in your head. It's just absurd!"

Gently fanning his wizened tissues with warm currents of support fluid, the grand old man of music continued: "Wolfgang Mozart was a very dull creature by our modern standards but, thanks to gelbrain, I can still find ways to pump life into his primitive compositions. I also persist in finding Bach worthwhile, even in today's ultracivilized milieu, where individual consciousness and creative subjectivity tend to be rather rare, or absent entirely."

Posthumanity's most scientifically advanced group, the pioneer Blood Bathers in their vast crystalline castles in the Oort Cloud, could not be reached for comment.

"Why trouble the highly prestigious Blood Bathers with some trifling development here on distant Earth?" demanded President Arno Hopmeier of the World Antisubjectivist Council. "The Blood Bathers are busily researching novel realms of complex organization far beyond mere 'intelligence.' We should feel extremely honored that they still bother to share their lab results with creatures like us. It would only annoy Their Skinless Eminences if we ask them to fret over some defunct race of featherless bipeds."

A Circumsolar Day of Mourning has been declared to commemorate the official extinction of humanity, but it is widely believed that bursts of wild public enthusiasm will mar the funeral proceedings.

"When you sum them up," mused Orbital Entity Ankh/Ghlh/9819, "it's hard to perceive any tragedy in this long-awaited event. Beasts, birds, butterflies, even the very rocks and rivers, must be rejoicing to see humans finally gone. We should try to be adult about this: we should take a deep breath, turn our face to the light of the future, and get on with the business of living.

"Since I've been asked to offer an epitaph," the highly distributed poetware continued, "I believe that we should rearrange the Great Wall of China to spell out (in Chinese of course, since most of them were always Chinese)— 'THEY WERE VERY, VERY CURIOUS, BUT NOT AT ALL FARSIGHTED.'

"This historical moment is a serious occasion that requires a sense of public dignity. My dog, for instance, says he'll truly miss humanity. But then again, my dog says a lot of things."

GEOFFREY A. LANDIS

A View from Evolutionary Ecology

In the twenty-first century (as old-style humans counted the ages of the world), the intense pressure of evolutionary forces began to splinter the human race into subspecies.

First among these splinters was the set of humans who had control over technology. They had, by any older reckoning, nearly infinite power. We can call them potentates, for the potency of the tools they had at their whim. They were, for the most part, humans hooked into computers, with all of human technology available at their electronic fingertips.

The first law of ecology is that species radiate to fill all available niches, and technology was an available niche.

Most of the human race were not potentates, of course. The majority were ordinary people, living and working at meaningless jobs, struggling to eat and mate and raise a family and die in relative comfort.

The potentates were different. Hooked up to computers, nearly infinitely wealthy, they were for the most part antisocial—the computer hookups acted as a social force that selected humans with low requirements for interpersonal ties. By a century, massively parallel computational power was subsumed into biocomputational chips that were then refined until they were engineered directly into the genetics of those who could control the technology, and the potentates had become isolated from the old-style humans.

For the most part, the potentates were benevolent—or at least, indifferent—toward the humans of whom they were the unacknowledged masters. But not all. A few of them viewed the ordinary humans as disease. Engineered plagues, released by fringe elements, killed large portions of the world population. The less-fringe potentates engineered antiplague viruses to kill the engineered plagues, but each episode reduced the number of ordinary humans—and put pressure on them to adapt.

Huge numbers of the potentates simply immersed themselves into virtual realities, and by failing to breed, left the realm of ecology. Why do you need a real world when the virtual worlds are infinite in complexity, each deliberately designed for allure? Genetic diversity decreased as most potentates didn't breed—but the ones that did breed produced dozens, in a few cases even thousands, of children.

New species adapted to fit into the human ecologies. (The first law of ecology again: adaptive radiation of species into available niches.) Molds, funguses, diseases, and cockroaches all adapted to fit into the human sphere, and humans learned to live with them. In a house, every clear surface became covered with a fine, downy coating of mold, and after a while, humans adopted a mindset that this is right and natural—a surface bare of mold would be like a lawn bare of vegetation. (The second law: Species co-evolve to live together.)

Spaceflight was an obsession of a few of the potentates, and this led to a second radiation, this one purposeful. It was named the exodus. Ecologies were adapted for the Moon, for Mars.

The ecologies for the Moon were life-forms made of mostly silicon-based materials: silicon gels for flesh, silicon carbide bones, low-vapor-pressure fluorinated silicone oils instead of blood. Carbon was the limiting resource of the basic raw materials (silicones require carbon), and so mining life-forms were engineered to sieve carbon out of the low concentrations of the regolith, along with trace phosphorus, fluorine, and hydrogen. Call them photovoltaic trees, with roots that snaked down hundreds of meters into the lunar regolith, seeking the microscopic traces of carbonaceous chondritic material. The lunar life used DNA, but in a highly encapsulated form, redesigned to bond not to water molecules but to hydrogen bonds of engineered fluorinated silicones. The life simply froze solid during the 158-hour lunar nights, since energy storage turned out to be evolutionarily too expensive.

The Mars ecologies were more conventional, but still highly engineered. Even the definition of the word "biological" had to be somewhat stretched—is something alive if it has no biological precursors? If its DNA has been put together, base by base, by machines, and not inherited from ancestors?

Over the millennia, the life on the Moon and Mars devolved. The potentates had envisioned an ultimate stage where humans would fill the top predator role in their engineered ecology, but their plans never quite worked. The engineered ecology was not complex enough to support such a niche, and the human-equivalent sophonts (not by any stretch of biological definition could they actually be called human) failed to reproduce their numbers, and eventually simply died away. New species eventually adapted (that first law again) and radiated into all niches.

On the Earth, meanwhile, the nonhuman ecology crashed. Too many species had been wiped out, deliberately or as a side effect of other human activities, for the ecology to sustain itself. (The third law of ecology: The stability of an ecosystem is proportional to its species' diversity.) This was a natural catastrophe: Ecology is a science of chaos, and ecological crashes happen every few tens of millions of years, give or take, with or without humans. It was hard, however, on those humans who were not potentates.

Over the course of about a millennium, humanity began further speciation. Other than the potentates, the remainder of humanity adapted into new forms that the potentates termed "hrats," humans that had adapted to the plagues and unsuccessful extermination attempts of the potentates. As yet, the potentates and the hrats were still technically subspecies—they were still mutually fertile, when they chose to interbreed—but there was less and less cross-breeding occurring as the ecological niches of the hrats and the potentates diverged.

The potentates evolved slowly to be larger in size—they were at the top of the food chain, and there was no evolutionary pressure toward smaller size.

The various human hrat subspecies, on the other hand, evolved to be smaller—there was a tremendous pressure to use fewer resources, to be faster, more agile, more adaptable.

Over the course of a hundred millennia, the potentates evolved. Intelligence was no longer a selection force. The potentates had genetically engineered into their biological structure most of the technology that had put them at the top of the food chain, fiber-optic receptors for direct high-bandwidth computer links, and microwave transceivers for low-bandwidth communications. What, exactly, did they need intelligence for? (The fourth law of ecology: Attributes not required by a species for survival will be lost.) Fat and happy (they engineered themselves to be happy) and with a low reproduction rate—at the top of their food chain with no natural enemies, they had to have a low reproduction rate, or they would kill their own ecology—they became, in all essential respects, dinosaurs. Huge and invulnerable, over the course of a quarter of a million years they lost the desire and the need to control the Earth.

The humans that the potentates had once denigrated as "hrats" live in a species-depleted, struggling ecology. The great ecological crash had resulted in a die-off, and the hrats lived in an ecology where survival of large animals was a difficulty. No global transportation systems—or at least none accessible to hrats—were left functional, so the hrats speciated, evolving separate forms on different continents and in different climatic zones on each continent. Like the potentates, the hrats also evolved away from intelligence—in the struggle for survival, traits that required a prolonged infancy and adolescence were too hard to maintain.

By a million years, there were no truly intelligent species on Earth.

Which is not to say that *genus homo* was extinct, far from it! With the extinction in the crash of all the species of large mammals (with the exception of dogs, preserved by the potentates), species of *homo* radiated to fill all of the open evolutionary niches. As the ecology recovered complexity, much of the diversity came from hominid species, now adapted to fill niches from grazers—hominid deer—to omnivores—hominid apes and pigs—and even some carnivore slots, hominid bears and jackals competing with the canine descendants to prey on squirrels and hominid deer.

In many ways, it was a beautiful and placid world: a new Eden.

One of the casualties of the great die-off was the extinction of a species of oceanic algae that had served a thermostatic function in the Earth's overall heat balance by removing carbon dioxide from the atmosphere. The die-off of the oceanic algae and of a vast number of terrestrial plant species led to a buildup of atmospheric carbon dioxide and consequent warming of the Antarctic continent. The Earth settled into a second thermal equilibrium, a full interglacial period with no permanent ice features anywhere on the globe.

But climate eventually changes. A thousand-year period of unusually low volcanism stimulated a new algae to fit into a niche. This algae thrived in waters of low temperature and low carbon-dioxide saturation, and in the mindless way of single-celled organisms, went about producing these conditions. The resultant reduction in greenhouse-effect warming triggered glaciation, at first only minor glaciation, but then increasing the spread of ice north across the warm valleys of Antarctica.

This glaciation resulted in a period of chaotic changes in the ecosystem, which opened a niche for intelligence to out-compete nonintelligent species. Following ancient laws of Darwin, intelligence arose in the savannas of Antarctica. (The fifth law of ecology: Evolution always occurs at the margin of an ecosystem.)

The new sophonts spread quickly from the Antarctic savanna to the northern arctic regions, and then in only a few millennia across the globe. Their first excursion into technology had been to discover the Antarctic coal deposits, one of the few fossil-fuel sources on the planet remaining in easily recoverable form. From there they developed a technology of ceramics and biopolymers that regarded metal as a pretty, but technologically unimportant, form of rock.

They quickly learned not to hunt the enormous and placid potentate beasts; while the beasts were not intelligent in any real sense, they were nevertheless still networked by microwave links (the new sophonts never did learn about microwaves), and an event experienced by any one of them was shared by all of the others, and never forgotten. With no visible weapons, no claws, no tusks, nevertheless the potentate beasts wielded invisible weapons, and a herd of potentates, acting together as a phased array of microwave beams, could melt cities. Leave them alone, the sophonts found, and they will leave you alone.

The sophonts never had the ambiguous benefit of believing that they had been the only intelligent race on Earth; even a million years after the last cities of *Homo sapiens* had collapsed into rubble, they lived in a world of abundant and incomprehensible artifacts, and it was clear that they had lived in a world that once had been inhabited by a world-treading race that had leveled mountains and built tremendous cities.

For the most part, the artifacts they found had little meaning. Cities they understood, but having never discovered electricity, the remnants of printed circuit boards were meaningless, and while buried fiber-optic cables were obviously a technology for piping light, the purpose for doing so was obscure. But with their own technology that owed little or nothing to *Homo sapiens*, they developed factories and eventually spaceflight. The enormous space artifacts of the era of the potentates, pinwheels and staging stations, had long since decayed from orbit. The geosynchronous-orbit communications satellites remained as curiosities to be retrieved and puzzled over, but never understood.

They never traveled as far as the Moon, and with no knowledge of radio and no requirements for communications satellites, their era of spaceflight was a brief one. There would have been nothing to find of any interest on the Moon in any case; the lunar ecosystem had died back to a sparse ecology consisting of little more than the great photovoltaic trees, two species of mold, and a few dozen species of small mobile life that filled the niche of crawling insects.

Over the course of a hundred thousand years, their civilization grew stagnant and died, and less than a half-million years later, the Earth had no trace of them except for a heritage of cryptic ceramic artifacts, sharing the ground with the artifacts of Homo sapiens.

Over the next twenty million years, two more species that could arguably be called intelligent arose. Neither achieved spaceflight. Although the second of the two species lasted for a period of five million years, eventually they succeeded in adjusting the world to suit them, and reached the point where they no longer had a need for intelligence.

The planet Mars has no magnetic field and is therefore subject to a withering bullet-storm of solar and galactic cosmic radiation. In designing forms of life to survive on Mars, the potentates had engineered a more robust form of DNA, with quintuply redundant information storage, with error-correction coding at every stage of reproduction and cell growth. It had not been their actual intent to design an ecology to be immune from evolution, but that had been the result.

Nevertheless, eventually error-correction codes fail. The quintuply redundant information storage corrupted to merely quadruple redundancy, and then slightly faster corrupted down to triple, and faster yet to double, and single redundant. In fifty million years, evolution started up on Mars.

It took well over a hundred million years before the Mars life evolved to intelligence, and from there only a few millennia before they invented spaceships. They had, of course, no notion of their terrestrial roots.

The sixth law of ecology tells us that when isolated populations are brought into contact, the more robust forms quickly drive out the less robust. In this case, the harsh conditions on Mars had made the Martian life-forms highly robust. The Earth life-forms really didn't have a chance. The contact with Mars was a K-T level event, and like the end of the Ternary period, it resulted in rapid evolutionary radiation in all directions. And then history gets seriously weird.

But this is a history of the various human species, and so the history of what happened after the return of the Martians must be beyond the bounds of this story.

—for Olaf Stapledon

The Great Goodbye

ROBERT CHARLES WILSON

The hardest part of the Great Goodbye, for me, was knowing I wouldn't see my grandfather again. We had developed that rare thing, a friendship that crossed the line of the post-evolutionary divide, and I loved him very much.

Humanity had become, by that autumn of 2350, two very distinct human species—if I can use that antiquated term. Oh, the Stock Humans remain a "species" in the classical evolutionary sense: New People, of course, have forgone all that. Post-evolutionary, post-biological, budded or engineered, New People are gloriously free from all the old human restraints. What unites us all is our common source, the Divine Complexity that shaped primordial quark plasma into stars, planets, planaria, people. Grandfather taught me that.

I had always known that we would, one day, be separated. But we first spoke of it, tentatively and reluctantly, when Grandfather went with me to the Museum of Devices in Brussels, a day trip. I was young and easily impressed by the full-scale working model of a "steam train" in the Machine Gallery—an amazingly baroque contrivance of ancient metalwork and gas-pressure technology. Staring at it, I thought (because Grandfather had taught me some of his "religion"): Complexity made this. This is made of stardust, by stardust.

We walked from the Machine Gallery to the Gallery of the Planets, drawing more that a few stares from the Stock People (children, especially) around us. It was uncommon to see a New Person fully embodied and in public. The Great Goodbye had been going on for more than a century, but New People were already scarce on Earth, and a New Person walking with a Stock Person was an even more unusual sight—risqué, even shocking. We bore the attention gamely. Grandfather held his head high and ignored the muttered insults.

The Gallery of the Planets recorded humanity's expansion into the Solar System, and I hope the irony was obvious to everyone who sniffed at our presence there: Stock People could not have colonized any of these forbidding places (consider Ganymede in its primeval state!) without the partnership of the New. In a way, Grandfather said, this was the most appropriate place we could have come. It was a monument to the long collaboration that was rapidly reaching its end.

The stars, at last, are within our grasp. The grasp, anyhow, of the New People. Was this, I asked Grandfather, why he and I had to be so different from one another?

"Some people," he said, "some families, just happen to prefer the old ways. Soon enough Earth will belong to the Stocks once again, though I'm not sure this is entirely a good thing." And he looked at me sadly. "We've learned a lot from each other. We could have learned more."

"I wish we could be together for centuries and centuries," I said.

I saw him for the last time (some years ago now) at the Shipworks, where the picturesque ruins of Detroit rise from the Michigan Waters, and the star-traveling Polises are assembled and wait like bright green baubles to lift, at last and forever, into the sky. Grandfather had arranged this final meeting—in the flesh, so to speak.

We had delayed it as long as possible. New People are patient: in a way, that's the point. Stock Humans have always dreamed of the stars, but the stars remain beyond their reach. A Stock Human lifetime is simply too short; one or two hundred years won't take you far enough. Relativistic constraints demand that travelers between the stars must be at home between the stars. Only New People have the continuity, the patience, the flexibility to endure and prosper in the Galaxy's immense voids.

I greeted Grandfather on the high embarication platform where the wind was brisk and cool. He lifted me up in his arms and admired me with his bright blue eyes. We talked about trivial things, for the simple pleasure of talking. Then he said, "This isn't easy, this saying goodbye. It make me think of mortality—that old enemy."

"It's all right," I said.

"Perhaps you could still change your mind?"

I shook my head, no. A New Person can transform himself into a Stock Person and vice versa, but the social taboos are strong, the obstacles (family dissension, legal entanglements) almost insurmountable, as Grandfather knew too well. And in any case that wasn't my choice. I was content as I was. Or so I chose to believe.

"Well, then," he said, empty, for once, of words. He looked away. The Polis would be rising soon, beginning its cons-long navigation of our near stellar neightbours. Discovering, no doubt, great wonders.

"Goodbye, boy," he said.

I said, "Goodbye, Grandfather."

Then he rose to his full height on his many translucent legs, winked one dish-sized glacial blue eye, and walked with a slow machinely dignity to the vessel that would carry him away. And I watched, *desolate*, alone on the platform with the wind in my hair, as his ship rose into the arc of the high clean noonday sky.